D0544660

By the same author

THE TIME SHIPS
VOYAGE
TITAN
ANTI-ICE
TRACES
MOONSEED

Novels and stories in the Xeelee Sequence

RAFT
TIMELIKE INFINITY
FLUX
RING
VACUUM DIAGRAMS

Novels in the Manifold Sequence

TIME

With Arthur C Clarke

THE LIGHT OF OTHER DAYS

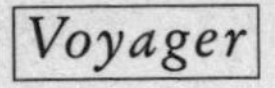

STEPHEN BAXTER

SPACE

MANIFOLD 2

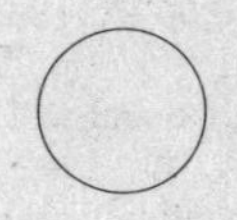

HarperCollins*Publishers*

Voyager
An Imprint of HarperCollins*Publishers*
77–85 Fulham Palace Road,
Hammersmith, London W6 8JB

www.voyager-books.com

This paperback edition 2001
5 7 9 8 6 4

First published in Great Britain by *Voyager* 2000

ISBN 0 00 651183 X

Set in Sabon and Gill Sans

Printed and bound in Great Britain by
Clays Ltd, St Ives plc

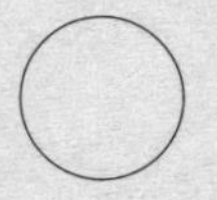

DEDICATION

To my nephew, Thomas Baxter and
Simon Bradshaw and Eric Brown

ACKNOWLEDGEMENTS

Sections of this novel appeared in substantially different versions in *Science Fiction Age* Magazine and in *Moonshots*, an anthology edited by Peter Crowther.

Innumerable suns exist; innumerable earths revolve around these suns in a manner similar to the way the seven planets revolve around our sun. Living beings inhabit these worlds . . .

GIORDANO BRUNO (1548–1600)

If they existed, they would be here.

ENRICO FERMI (1901–1954)

PROLOGUE

My name is Reid Malenfant.

You know me. And you know I'm an incorrigible space cadet.

You know I've campaigned for, among other things, private mining expeditions to the asteroids. In fact, in the past I've tried to get you to pay for such things. I've bored you with that often enough already, right?

So tonight I want to be a little more personal. Tonight I want to talk about why I gave over my life to a single, consuming project.

It started with a simple question:

Where is everybody?

As a kid I used to lie at night out on the lawn, soaking up dew and looking at the stars, trying to feel the Earth turning under me. It felt wonderful to be alive – hell, to be ten years old, anyhow.

But I knew that the Earth was just a ball of rock, on the fringe of a nondescript galaxy.

As I lay there staring at the stars – the thousands I could pick out with my naked eyes, the billions that make up the great wash of our Galaxy, the uncounted trillions in the galaxies beyond – I just couldn't believe, even then, that there was nobody out *there* looking back at me down *here*. Was it really possible that this was the *only* place where life had taken hold – that only *here* were there minds and eyes capable of looking out and wondering?

But if not, *where are they*? Why isn't there evidence of extraterrestrial civilization all around us?

Consider this. Life on Earth got started just about as soon as it could – as soon as the rocks cooled and the oceans gathered. Of course it took a good long time to evolve *us*. Nevertheless we have to believe that what applies on Earth ought to apply on all the other worlds out there, like or unlike Earth; life ought to be popping up everywhere. And, as there are *hundreds of billions* of stars out there in the Galaxy, there are presumably hundreds of billions of opportunities for life to come swarming up out of the ponds – and even more in the other galaxies that crowd our universe.

Furthermore, life spread over Earth as fast and as far as it could. And already we're starting to spread to other worlds. Again, this can't be a unique trait of Earth life.

So, if life sprouts everywhere, and spreads as fast and as far as it can, how come nobody has come spreading all over *us*?

Of course the universe is a big place. There are huge spaces between the stars. But it's not *that* big. Even crawling along with dinky ships that only reach a fraction of lightspeed – ships we could easily start building now – we could colonize the Galaxy in a few tens of millions of years. One hundred million, tops.

One hundred million years: it seems an immense time – after all, a hundred million years ago the dinosaurs ruled Earth. But the Galaxy is a hundred times older still. There has been time for Galactic colonization to have happened *many* times since the birth of the stars.

Remember, all it takes is for *one* race somewhere to have evolved the will and the means to colonize; and once the process has started it's hard to see what could stop it.

But, as a kid on that lawn, I didn't see them. I seemed to be surrounded by emptiness and silence.

Even *we* blare out on radio frequencies. Why, with our giant radio telescopes we could detect a civilization no more advanced than ours anywhere in the Galaxy. But we don't.

More advanced civilizations ought to be much more noticeable. We could spot somebody building a shell around their star, or throwing in nuclear waste. We could probably see evidence of such things even in other galaxies. But we don't. Those other galaxies, other reefs of stars, seem to be as barren as this one.

Maybe we're just unlucky. Maybe we're living at the wrong time. The Galaxy is an old place; maybe They have been, flourished, and gone already. But consider this: even if They are long gone, surely we should see Their mighty ruins, all around us. But we don't even see that. The stars show no signs of engineering. The solar system appears to be primordial, in the sense that it shows no signs of the great projects we can already envisage, like terraforming the planets, or tinkering with the sun, and so on.

We can think of lots of rationalizations for this absence.

Maybe there is something that kills off every civilization like ours before we get too far – for example, maybe we all destroy ourselves in nuclear wars or eco collapse. Or maybe there is something more sinister, plagues of killer robots sliding silently between the stars, which for their own antique purposes kill off fledgling cultures.

Or maybe the answer is more benevolent. Maybe we're in some kind of quarantine – or a zoo.

But none of these filtering mechanisms convinces me. You see, you have to believe that this magic suppression mechanism, whatever it is, works for *every* race in this huge Galaxy of ours. All it would take would be for *one* race to survive the wars, or evade the vacuum robots, or come sneaking through the quarantine to sell trinkets to the natives – or even just to start broadcasting some Eetie version of *The Simpsons*, anywhere in the Galaxy – and we'd surely see or hear them.

But we don't.

This paradox was first stated clearly by a twentieth-century physicist called Enrico Fermi. It strikes me as a genuine mystery. The contradictions are basic: life seems capable of emerging everywhere; just one starfaring race could easily have covered the Galaxy by now; the whole thing seems inevitable – but it hasn't happened.

Thinking about paradoxes is the way human understanding advances. I think the Fermi paradox is telling us something very profound about the universe, and our place in it. Or was.

Of course, everything is different now.

1

FOREIGNERS

AD 2020–2042

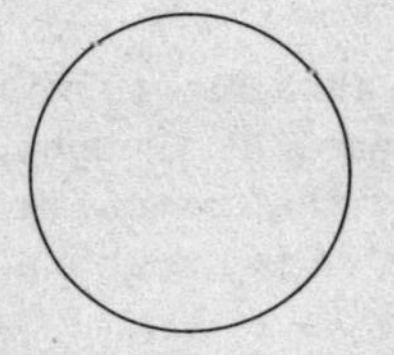

. . . And he felt as if he was drowning, struggling up from some thick, viscous fluid, up towards the light. He wanted to open his mouth, to scream – but he had no mouth – and no *words*. What would he scream?

I.

I am.

I am Reid Malenfant.

He could see the sail.

It was a gauzy sheet draped across the crowded stars of this place – where, Malenfant? why, the core of the Galaxy, he thought, wonder breaking through his agony – and within the sail, cupped, he could see the neutron star, an angry ball of red laced with eerie synchrotron blue, like a huge toy.

A star with a sail attached to it. Beautiful. Scary.

Triumph surged. I won, he thought. I resolved the *koan*, the great conundrum of the cosmos; Nemoto would be pleased. And now, together, we're fixing an unsatisfactory universe. Hell of a thing.

. . . But if you see all this, Malenfant, then what are *you*?

He looked down at himself.

Tried to.

A sense of body, briefly. Spread-eagled against the sail's gauzy netting. Clinging by fingers and toes, monkey digits, here at the centre of the Galaxy. A metaphor, of course, an illusion to comfort his poor human mind.

Welcome to reality.

The pain! Oh, God, the *pain*.

Terror flooded over him. And anger.

And, through it, he remembered the Moon, where it began . . .

Chapter 1

GAIJIN

A passenger in the HOPE-3 tug, Reid Malenfant descended towards the Moon.

The Farside base, called Edo, was a cluster of concrete components – habitation modules, power plants, stores, manufacturing facilities – half-buried in the cratered plain. Comms masts sprouted like angular flowers. The tug pad was just a splash of scorched Moon-dust concrete, a couple of kilometres further out. Around the station itself, the regolith was scarred by tractor traffic.

Robots were everywhere, rolling, digging, lifting; Edo was growing like a colony of bacilli in nutrient.

A *hi-no-maru*, a Japanese sun flag, was fixed to a pole at the centre of Edo.

'You are welcome to my home,' Nemoto said.

She met him in the pad's airlock, a large, roomy chamber blown into the regolith. Her face was broad, pale, her eyes black; her hair was elaborately shaved, showing the shape of her skull. She smiled, apparently habitually. She could have been no more than half Malenfant's age, perhaps thirty.

Nemoto helped Malenfant don the suit he'd been fitted with during the flight from Earth. The suit was a brilliant orange. It clung to him comfortably, the joints easy and loose, although the sewn-in plates of tungsten armour were heavy.

'It's a hell of a development from the old EMUs I wore when I was flying Shuttle,' he said, trying to make conversation.

Nemoto listened politely, after the manner of young people, to his fragments of reminiscence from a vanished age. She told him the suit had been manufactured on the Moon, and was made largely of spider silk. 'I will take you to the factory. A chamber in the lunar soil, full of immense spinnerets. A nightmare vision! . . .'

Malenfant felt disoriented, restless.

He was here to deliver a lecture, on colonizing the Galaxy, to senior executives of Nishizaki Heavy Industries. But here he was being met off the tug by Nemoto, the junior researcher who'd invited him out to the Moon, just a kid. He hoped he wasn't making some kind of fool of himself.

Reid Malenfant used to be an astronaut. He'd flown the last Shuttle mission – STS-194, on *Discovery* – when, ten years ago, the space transportation system had reached the end of its design life, and the International Space Station had finally been abandoned, incomplete. No American had flown into space since – save as the guest of the Japanese, or the Europeans, or the Chinese.

In this year 2020, Malenfant was sixty years old and feeling a lot older – increasingly stranded, a refugee in this strange new century, his dignity woefully fragile.

Well, he thought, whatever the dubious politics, whatever the threat to his dignity, he was *here*. It had been the dream of his long life to walk on another world. Even if it was as the guest of a Japanese.

And even if he was too damn old to enjoy it.

They stepped through a transit tunnel and directly into a small tractor, a lozenge of tinted glass. The tractor rolled away from the tug pad. The wheels were large and open, and absorbed the unevenness of the mare; Malenfant felt as if he were riding across the Moon in a soap bubble.

Every surface in the cabin was coated with fine, grey Moon dust. He could smell the dust; the scent was, as he knew it would be, like wood ash, or gunpowder.

Beyond the window, the Mare Ingenii – the Sea of Longing – stretched to the curved horizon, pebble-strewn. It was late in the lunar afternoon, and the sunlight was low, flat, the shadows of the surface rubble long and sharp. The lighting was a rich tan when he looked away from the sun, a more subtle grey elsewhere. Earth was hidden beneath the horizon, of course, but Malenfant could see a comsat crawl across the black sky.

He longed to step through the glass, to touch that ancient soil.

Nemoto locked in the autopilot and went to a little galley area. She emerged with green tea, rice crackers and dried *ika* cuttlefish. Malenfant wasn't hungry, but he accepted the food. Such items as the fish were genuine luxuries here, he knew; Nemoto was trying to honour him.

The motion of the tea, as she poured it in the one-sixth gravity, was complex, interesting.

'I am honoured you have accepted my invitation to travel here, to Edo,' Nemoto said. 'You will of course tour the town, as you wish. There is even a *Makudonarudo* here. A McDonald's. You may enjoy a *bifubaaga!* . . . soya, of course.'

He put down his plate and tried to meet her direct gaze. 'Tell me why I've been brought out here. I don't see how my work, on long-term space utilization, can be of real interest to your employers.'

She eyed him. 'You do have a lecture to deliver, I am afraid. But – no, your work is not of primary concern to Nishizaki.'

'Then I don't understand.'

'It is I who invited you, I who arranged the funding. You ask why. I wished to meet you. I am a researcher, like you.'

'Hardly a researcher,' he said. 'I call myself a consultant, nowadays. I am not attached to a university.'

'Nor I. Nishizaki Heavy Industries pay my wages; my research must be focused on serving corporate objectives.' She eyed him, and took some more fish. 'I am *salariman*. A good company worker, yes? But I am, at heart, a scientist. And I have made some observations which I am unable to reconcile with the accepted paradigm. I searched for recent scientific publications concerning the subject area of my – hypothesis. I found only yours.

'My subject is infrared astronomy. At our research station, away from Edo, the company maintains radiometers, photometers, photopolarimeters, cameras. I work at a range of wavelengths, from twenty to a hundred microns. Of course a space-borne platform is to be preferred: the activities of humankind are thickening the Moon's atmosphere with each passing day, blocking the invisible light I collect. But the lunar site is cheap to maintain, and is adequate for the company's purposes. We are considering the future exploitation of the asteroids, you see. Infrared astronomy is a powerful tool in the study of those distant rocks. With it we can deduce a great deal about surface textures, compositions, internal heat, rotation characteristics –'

'Tell me about your paradigm-busting hypothesis.'

'Yes.' She sipped her green tea. She said calmly, 'I believe I have observational evidence of the activity of extraterrestrial intelligences in the solar system.'

The silence stretched between them, electric. Her words were shocking, quite unexpected.

But now he saw why she'd brought him here.

Since his retirement from NASA, Malenfant had avoided following his colleagues into the usual ex-astronaut gravy ponds, lucrative aerospace executive posts and junior political positions. Instead, he'd thrown his weight behind research into what he regarded as long-term thinking: SETI, using gravitational lensing to hunt for planets and Eetie signals, advanced propulsion systems, schemes for colonizing the planets, terraforming, interstellar travel, exploration of the venerable Fermi paradox.

All the stuff that Emma had so disapproved of. *You're wasting your time, Malenfant. Where's the money to be made out of gravitational lensing? . . .*

But his wife was long gone, of course. Struck down by cancer: the result of a random cosmic accident, a heavy particle that had come whizzing out of an ancient supernova and flown across the universe to damage her *just* so . . . It could have been him; it could have been neither of them; it could have happened a few years later, when cancer had been reduced to a manageable disease. But it hadn't worked out like that, and Malenfant, burnt out, already grounded, had been left alone.

So he had thrown himself into his obsessions. What else was there to do?

Well, Emma had been right, and wrong. He was making a minor living on the lecture circuit. But few serious people were listening, just as she had predicted. He attracted more knee-jerk criticism than praise or thoughtful response; in the last few years, he'd become regarded as not much more than a reliable talk-show crank.

But now, *this*.

He tried to figure how to deal with this, what to say. Nemoto wasn't like the Japanese he had known before, on Earth, with their detailed observance of *reigi* – the proper manner.

She studied him, evidently amused. 'You are surprised. Startled. You think, perhaps, I am not quite sane to voice such speculations. You are trapped on the Moon with a mad Japanese woman. The American nightmare!'

He shook his head. 'It's not that.'

'But you must see that my speculations are not so far removed from your own published work. Like myself, you are cautious. Nobody listens. And when you do find an audience, they do not take you seriously.'

'I wouldn't be so blunt about it.'

'Your nation has turned inward,' Nemoto said. 'Shrunk back.'

'Maybe. We just have different priorities now.' In the US, flights into space had become a hobby of old men and women, dreams of an age of sublimated warfare which had left behind only images of charmingly antique rocket craft, endlessly copied around the data nets. Nothing to do with *now*.

She said, 'Then why do you continue, to argue, to talk, to expose yourself to ridicule?'

'Because –' Because if nobody thinks it, it definitely won't happen.

She was smiling at him; she seemed to understand. She said, 'The *kokuminsei*, the spirit of your people, is asleep. But in you, and perhaps others, curiosity burns strong. I think we two should defy the spirit of our age.'

'Why have you brought me here?'

'I am seeking to resolve a *koan*,' she said. 'A conundrum that defies logical analysis.' Her face lost its habitual smile, for the first time since they'd met. 'I need a fresh look – a perspective from a big thinker – someone like you. And –'

'Yes?'

'I am afraid, I think,' she said. 'Afraid for the future of the species.'

The tractor worked its way across the Moon, following a broad, churned-up path. Nemoto offered him more food.

The tractor drew up at an airlock at the outskirts of Edo. A big NASDA symbol was painted on the lock: NASDA for Japan's National Space Development Agency. With the minimum of fuss, Nemoto led Malenfant through the airlock and into Edo, into a colony on the Moon.

Here, at its periphery, Edo was functional. The walls were bare, of fused, glassy regolith. Ducts and cables were stapled to the roof. People wore plain, disposable paper coveralls. There was an air of bustle, of heavy industry.

Nemoto led him through Edo, a gentle guided tour. 'Of course the station is a great achievement,' she said. 'No less than ninety-five flights of our old H-2 rockets were required to ferry accommodation modules and power plants here. We build beneath the regolith, for shelter from solar radiation. We bake oxygen from the rocks, and mine water from the polar permafrost . . .'

At the centre of the complex, Edo was a genuine town. There were public places: bars, restaurants where the people could buy rice, soup, fried vegetables, *sushi, sake*. There was even a tiny park, with shrubs and bamboo grass; a spindly lunar-born child played there with his parents.

Nemoto smiled at Malenfant's reaction. 'At the heart of Edo, ten metres beneath lunar regolith, there are cherry trees. Our children study beneath their branches. You may stay long enough to see *ichi-buzaki*, the first state of blossoming.'

Malenfant saw no other Westerners. Most of the Japanese nodded politely. Many must have known Nemoto – Edo supported only a few hundred inhabitants – but none engaged her in conversation. His impression of Nemoto as a loner, rather eccentric, was reinforced.

As they passed one group he heard a man whisper, '*Wah! – gaijin-kusai.*'

Gaijin-kusai. The smell of foreigner. There was laughter.

Malenfant spent the night in what passed for a *ryokan*, an inn. His apartment was tiny, a single room. But, despite the bleak austerity of the fused-regolith walls, the room was decorated Japanese style. The floor was *tatami* – rice straw matting – polished and worn with use. A *tokonoma*, an alcove carved into the rock, contained an elaborate data net interface unit; but the owners had followed tradition and had hung a scroll painting there – of a dragonfly on a blade of grass – and some flowers, in an *ikebana* display. The flowers looked real.

There was a display of cherry blossom, fixed to the wall under clear plastic. The contrast of the pale living pink with the grey Moon rock was the most beautiful thing he had ever seen.

In this tiny room he was immersed in noise: the low, deep rumblings of the artificial lungs of the colony, of machines ploughing outward through the regolith. It was like being in the belly of a huge vessel, a submarine. Malenfant thought wistfully of his own study: bright Iowa sunlight, his desk, his equipment.

Edo kept Tokyo time, so Malenfant, here on the Moon, suffered jet lag. He slept badly.

Rows of faces.

'. . . How are we to populate the Galaxy? It's actually all a question of economics.' Over Malenfant's head a virtual image projected in the air of the little theatre, its light glimmering from the folded wooden walls.

Malenfant stared around at the rows of Japanese faces, like coins shining in this rich brown dark. They seemed remote, unreal. Many of these people were NASDA administrators; as far as he could tell there was nobody from Nishizaki senior management here, nominally his sponsors for the trip.

The virtual was a simple schematic of stars, randomly scattered. One star blinked, representing the sun.

Malenfant said, 'We will launch unmanned probes.' Ships, little dots of light, spread out from the toy sun. 'We might use ion rockets, solar sails, gravity assists – whatever. The first wave will be slow, no faster than we can afford. It doesn't matter. Not in the long term.

'The probes will be self-replicating: Von Neumann machines, essentially. Universal constructors. Humans may follow, by such means as generation starships. However it would be cheaper for the probes to manufacture humans in situ, using cell synthesis and artificial womb technology.' He glanced over the audience. 'You wish to know if we can build such devices. Not yet. Although your own Kashiwazaki Electric has a partial prototype.'

At that there was a stir of interest, self-satisfied.

As his virtual light-show continued to evolve, telling its own story, he glanced up at the walls around him, at the glimmer of highlights from wood. This was a remarkable place. It was the largest structure in Edo, serving as community centre and town hall and showpiece, the size of a ten-storey building.

But it was actually a *tree*, a variety of oak. The oaks were capable of growing to two hundred metres under the Moon's gentle gravity, but this one had been bred for width, and was full of intersecting hollowed-out chambers. The walls of this room were of smooth polished wood, broken only subtly by technology – lights, air vents, virtual display gear – and the canned air here was fresh and moist and alive.

In contrast to the older parts of Edo – all those clunky tunnels – this was the future of the Moon, the Japanese were implicitly saying. The living Moon. What the hell was an American doing here on the Moon, lecturing these patient Japanese about colonizing space? The Japanese were *doing* it, patiently and incrementally working.

But – yes, *incrementally*: that was the key word. Even these lunar colonists couldn't see beyond their current projects, the next few years, their own lifetimes. They couldn't see where this could all lead. To Malenfant, that ultimate destination was everything.

And, perhaps, Nemoto and her strange science would provide the first route map.

The little probe-images had reached their destination stars.

'Here is the heart of the strategy,' he said. 'A target system, we assume, is uninhabited. We can therefore program for massive and destructive exploitation of the system's resources, without restraint, by the probe. Such resources are useless for any other purpose, and are therefore economically free to us. And so we colonize, and build.'

More probes erupted from each of the first wave of target stars, at greatly increased speeds. The probes reached new targets; and again, more probes were spawned, and fired onwards. The volume covered by the probes grew rapidly; it was like watching the expansion of gas into a vacuum.

He said, 'Once started, the process is self-directing, self-financing. It would take, we think, ten to a hundred million years for the colonization of the Galaxy to be completed in this manner. But we must invest merely in the cost of the initial generation of probes. Thus the cost of colonizing the Galaxy will be less, in real terms, than that of our Apollo program of fifty years ago.'

His probes were now spreading out along the Galaxy's spiral arms, along lanes rich with stars. His Japanese audience watched politely.

But as he delivered his polished words he thought of Nemoto and her tantalizing hints of otherness – of a mystery which might render all his scripted invective obsolete – and he faltered.

Trying to focus, feeling impatient, he closed with his cosmic-destiny speech. '. . . This may be a watershed in the history of the cosmos. Think about it. *We know how to do this*. If we make the right decisions now, life may spread beyond Earth and Moon, far beyond the solar system, a wave of green transforming the Galaxy. We must not fail . . .' And so on.

Well, they applauded him kindly enough. But there were few questions.

He got out, feeling foolish.

The next day Nemoto said she would take him to the surface, to see her infrared spectroscopy results at first hand.

They walked through the base to a tractor airlock, and suited up once more. The infrared station was an hour's ride from Edo.

A kilometre out from Edo itself, the tractor passed one of the largest structures Malenfant had yet seen. It was a cylinder perhaps a hundred and fifty metres long, ten wide. It looked like a half-buried nuclear submarine. The lunar surface here was scarred by huge gullies, evidently the result of strip-mining. Around the central cylinder there was a cluster of what looked like furnaces, enclosed by semi-transparent domes.

'Our fusion plant,' Nemoto said. 'Edo is powered by the fusion of deuterium, the hydrogen isotope, with helium-3.'

Malenfant glared out with morbid interest. Here, as in most technological arenas, the Japanese were way out ahead of Americans. Twenty per cent of the US's power now came from the fusion of two hydrogen isotopes, deuterium and tritium. But hydrogen fusion processes, even with such relatively low-yield fuel, had turned out to be unstable and expensive: high-energy neutrons smashed through reactor walls, making them brittle and radioactive. The Japanese helium-3 fusion process, by contrast, produced charged protons, which could be kept away from reactor walls with magnetic fields.

However, the Earth had no natural supply of helium-3.

Nemoto waved a hand. 'The Moon contains vast stores of helium-3, locked away in deposits of titanium minerals, in the top three metres of the regolith. The helium came from the sun, borne on the solar wind; the titanium acted like a sponge, soaking up the helium particles. We plan to begin exporting the helium to Earth.'

'I know.' The export would make Edo self-sufficient.

She smiled brightly, young and confident in the future.

Out of sight of Edo, the tractor passed a cairn of piled-up maria rubble. On the top there was a *sake* bottle, a saucer bearing rice cakes, a porcelain figure. There were small paper flags around the figure, but the raw sunlight had faded them.

'It is a shrine,' Nemoto explained. 'To *Inari-samma*. The Fox God.' She grinned at him. 'If you close your eyes and clap your hands, perhaps the *kami* will come to you. The divinities.'

'Shrines? At a lunar industrial complex?'

'We are an old people,' she said. 'We have changed much, but we remain the same. *Yamato damashi* – our spirit – persists.'

At length the tractor drew up to a cluster of buildings set on the plain. This was the Nishizaki Heavy Industries infrared research station.

Nemoto checked Malenfant's suit, then popped the hatch.

Malenfant climbed stiffly down a short ladder. As he moved, clumsily, he heard the hiss of air, the soft whirr of exoskeletal multipliers. These robot muscles helped him overcome the suit's pressurization and the weight of his tungsten anti-radiation armour.

His helmet was a big gold-tinted bubble. His backpack, like Nemoto's, was a semi-transparent thing of tubes and sloshing water, six litres full of blue algae that fed off sunlight and his own waste products, producing enough oxygen to keep him going indefinitely. In theory.

Actually Malenfant missed his old suit: his Space Shuttle EMU, Extravehicular Mobility Unit, with its clunks and whirrs of fans and pumps. Maybe it was limited compared to this new technology. But he hated to wear a backpack that *sloshed,* for God's sake, its mass pulling him this way and that in the low gravity. And his robot muscles – amplifying every impulse, dragging his limbs and tilting his back for him – made him feel like a puppet.

He dropped down the last metre; his small impact sent up a little spray of dust, which fell back immediately.

And here he was, walking on the Moon.

He walked away from the tractor, suit whirring and lurching. He had to go perhaps a hundred metres to get away from tractor tracks and footsteps.

He reached unmarked soil. His boots left prints as crisp as if he had stepped out of Apollo 11.

There were craters upon craters, a fractal clustering, right down to little pits he could barely have put his fingertip into, and smaller yet. But they didn't look like craters – more like the stippling of raindrops, as if he stood in a recently ploughed and harrowed field, a place where rain had pummelled the loose ground. But there had been no rain here, of course, not for four billion years.

The sun cast brilliant, dazzling light. Otherwise the sky was empty, jet black. But he was a little surprised that he had no sense of openness, of immensity all around him, unlike a desert night sky at home. He felt as if he was on a darkened stage, under a brilliant spotlight, with the walls of the universe just a little way away, just out of view.

He looked back at the tractor, with the big red sun of Japan painted on its side. He thought of a terraformed Moon, of twin blue worlds. He felt tears, hot and unwelcome, prickle his eyes. Damn it. We were here first. We had all this. And we let it go.

Nemoto waited for him, a small figure on the Moon's folded plain, her face hidden behind her gold-tinted bubble of glass.

She led him into the cluster of buildings. There was a small fission power plant, tanks of gases and liquids. A living shelter was half-buried in the regolith.

The centre of the site was a crude cylindrical hut, open to the sky, containing a battery of infrared sensors and computer equipment. The infrared detectors themselves were immersed in huge vessels of liquid helium. Robots crawled between the detectors, monitoring constantly, their complex arms stained by Moon dust.

Nemoto walked up to a processor control desk. A virtual image appeared, hovering over the compacted regolith at the centre of the hut. The virtual was a ring of glistening crimson droplets, slowly orbiting.

Nemoto said, 'Here is a summary of my survey of the asteroid belt.

Or "belts", I should say, for there are gaps between the sub-belts – the Kirkwood gaps, swept clear by resonances with Jupiter's gravity field.' The Kirkwood gaps were dark bands, empty of crimson drops. 'Of course Nishizaki Heavy Industries is very interested in asteroids. There is a mine in Sudbury, Ontario, which for a long time was a rich source of nickel. The nickel seam is disc-shaped. It is almost certainly the scar of an ancient asteroid collision with the Earth.'

'Mineral extraction, then.'

'There is a scheme to retrieve a fragment of the asteroid Geographos, which crosses Earth's orbit. We may cleave it with controlled explosions. Perhaps we can deliver fragments to orbit, using lunar gravity assists and grazes against the Earth's atmosphere. Or we may initiate a controlled impact with the Moon. This exercise alone would yield more than nine hundred billion dollars' worth of nickel, rhenium, osmium, iridium, platinum, gold – so much, in fact, the planet's economy would be transformed, making estimates of wealth difficult.'

Malenfant walked around the instrument hut. The novelty of his Moonwalk was wearing off; his suit scratched, his helmet was hot, and his condom was itching. 'Nemoto, it's time you got to the point.'

'The *koan*,' she said. The virtual ring shone in her visor, making her face invisible. 'Let us look at the stars.'

She took his gloved hand in hers – through the thick layers of glove he could barely feel the pressure of her fingers – and she led him out of the building. The virtual asteroid ring, eerily, followed them out.

They stood in the deep shadow of the structure. With a motion, she indicated he should lift his visor.

He raised his head so he couldn't see the ground or the buildings, and he turned around and around, as he used to as a kid, on the darkest Moonless nights back home.

The stars, of course: thousands of them, peppering the sky all around him, crowding out the bright-star constellations seen from Earth. And now, at last, came that elusive feeling of immensity. From the Moon it was *much* easier to see that he was just a mote clinging to a round ball of rock, spinning endlessly in an infinite, three-dimensional starry sky.

'Look.' Nemoto, pointing, swept out an arc of the sky, where dusty light shone.

Despite the crowding stars, Malenfant recognized one or two constellations – Cygnus and Aquila, the swan and the eagle. And, where she pointed, a river of light ran through the constellations, a river of stars. It was the Milky Way: the Galaxy, the disc of stars in which Sol and all its planets were embedded, seen edge on and turned into a band of light that wrapped around the sky. But, as it passed through Cygnus and Aquila, that band of light seemed to split into two, twin streams separated by a dark gap. In fact the rift was a shadow, cast by dark clouds blocking the light from the star banks behind.

Nemoto pointed. 'See how the darkness starts out narrow in Cygnus, then broadens in Aquila, sweeping wider through Serpens and Opiuchus. This is the effect of perspective. We are seeing a band of dust as it comes from the distance in Cygnus, passing closest to the sun in Aquila and Opiuchus. Malenfant, we live in a spiral arm of this Galaxy – a small fragment, in fact, called the Orion Arm. And spiral arms typically have lanes of dust on their inside edges.'

'Like that one.'

'Yes. *That* is the inner edge of our spiral arm, hanging in the sky for all to see.' Her shadowed eyes glimmered, full of starlight. 'It is possible to make out the Galaxy's structure, you see: to witness that we are embedded in a giant spiral of stars – even with the naked eye. *This* is where we live.'

'Why are you showing me this?'

'Look at the Galaxy, Malenfant. It appears to be a giant machine – no, an ecology – evolved to make stars. And there are hundreds of millions of galaxies beyond our own. Is it really conceivable, given all of that immensity, all that structure, that we are truly alone? – that life emerged here, and nowhere else?'

Malenfant grunted. 'The old Fermi paradox. Troubled me as a kid, even before I heard of Fermi.'

'Me too.' He could see her smile. 'You see, Malenfant, we have much in common. And the logic behind the paradox troubles me still –'

'Even though you think you have found aliens.'

She let that hang, and he found he was holding his breath.

Cautiously, she said, 'How would it make you feel, Malenfant, if I was right?'

'If you had proof that another intelligence exists? It would be wonderful. I guess.'

'Would it?' She smiled again. 'How sentimental you are. Listen to me: humanity would be in extreme danger. Remember, by your own argument, the assumption on which such a colonizing expedition operates is that it is appropriating an empty system. Such a probe could destroy our worlds without even noticing us.'

He shivered; his spider-web suit felt thin and fragile.

'Think it through further,' she said. 'Think like an engineer. If an alien replicator probe were to approach the solar system, where would it seek to establish itself? What are its requirements?'

He thought about it. You'll need energy; plenty of it. So, stay close to the sun. Next: raw materials. The surface of a rocky planet? But you wouldn't want to dip into a gravity well if you didn't have to . . . Besides, your probe is designed for deep space –

'The asteroid belt,' he said, suddenly seeing where all this was leading. 'Plenty of resources, freely floating, away from the big gravity wells . . . Even the main belts aren't too crowded, but you'd probably settle in a Kirkwood gap, to minimize the chance of collision. Your orbit would be perturbed by Jupiter, just like the asteroids', but it wouldn't require much station-keeping to compensate for that. And some kind of ship or colony out there, even a few kilometres across, would be hard for us to spot.' He looked at her sharply. 'Is that what this is about? Have you found something in the belt?'

'The plain facts are these. I have surveyed the Kirkwood gaps with the sensors here. And, in the gap which corresponds to the one-to-three resonance with Jupiter, I have found –' She pointed to her virtual model, to a broad, precise gap.

At the centre of the gap, a string of rubies shone, enigmatic, brilliant in the shadows.

'These are sources of infrared,' she said. 'Sources I cannot explain.'

Malenfant bent to study the little beads of light. 'Could they be asteroids that have strayed into the gap after collisions?'

'No. The sources are too bright. In fact, they are each emitting more heat than they receive from the sun. I am, of course, seeking firmer evidence: for example, structure in the infrared signature; or perhaps there will be radio leakage.'

He stared at the ruby lights. My God. She's right. If these are *emitting* heat, this is unambiguous: it's evidence of industrial activity . . .

His heart thumped. Somehow he hadn't accepted what she had said to him, not in his gut, not up to now. But now he could see it, and his universe was transformed.

He made out her face in the dim light reflected from the regolith, the smooth sweep of human flesh here in this dusty wilderness. Though it must have been a big moment for her to show him this evidence – a moment of triumph – she seemed troubled. 'Nemoto, why did you ask me here? Your work is a fine piece of science, as far as I can see.

The interpretation is unambiguous. You should publish. Why do you need reassurance from me?'

'I know this is good science. But the answer is *wrong*. Very wrong. The *koan* is not resolved at all. Don't you see that?' She glared up at the sky, as if trying to make out the signature of aliens with her own eyes. '*Why now?*'

He glimpsed her meaning.

They must have just arrived, or we'd surely see their works, the transformed asteroids swarming . . . But why should they arrive *now*, just as we ourselves are ready to move beyond the Earth – just as we are able to comprehend them? A simple coincidence? Why shouldn't they have come here long ago?

He grinned. Old Fermi wasn't beaten yet; there were deeper layers of the paradox here, much to unravel, new questions to ask.

But it wasn't a moment for philosophy.

His mind was racing. '*We aren't alone.* Whatever the implications, the unanswered questions – my God, what a thought. We'll need the resources of the race, of all of us, to respond to this.'

She smiled thinly. 'Yes. The stars have intervened, it seems. Your *kokuminsei*, your people's spirit, must revive. It will be *satori* – a reawakening. Come.' She held out her hand. 'We should go back to Edo. We have much to do.'

He squinted, trying to make out the constellations against the glare of the regolith. There was *gaijin-kusai* there, the smell of foreigner, he thought. He felt exhilarated, awakened, as if a hiatus was coming to an end. *This changes everything.*

He took Nemoto's hand, and they walked back across the regolith to the tractor.

Chapter 2

BAIKONUR

The priest was not what Xenia Makarova had expected.

Xenia herself wasn't religious. And Xenia's family, emigrant to the United States four generations ago, had been Orthodox. What did she know about Catholic priests? So she had expected the cliché: some gaunt old man, Italian or Irish, shrivelled up by a lifetime of celibacy, dressed in a flapping black cassock that would soak up the toxic dust and prove utterly unsuitable for the conditions here at the launch site.

Her first surprise had come when the priest had expressed no special accommodation requirements, but had been happy to stay in the town of Baikonur, along with the technicians who worked for Bootstrap here at the old Soviet-era launch station. Baikonur – once called Leninsk, at the heart of Kazakhstan – was a place of burned-out offices and abandoned, windowless apartments, of roads and roofs coated with strata of gritty brown powder, blown from the pesticide-laden salt flats of the long-dead Aral Sea a few hundred kilometres away. Baikonur was a relic of Soviet dreams, plagued by crime and ill-health. Not a good place to stay.

So Xenia wasn't sure what to expect by the time the bus drew up to the security gate, and she went out to greet her holy guest.

The priest must have been sixty, small, compact: fit-looking, though she showed some stiffness climbing down from the bus. Camera drones, glittering toys the size of beetles, whirred out in a cloud around her head.

Her, yes: of course it would be a female, one of the Vatican's first cadre of women priests, that would be assigned to this most PR-friendly of operations.

And no black cassock. The priest, dressed in loose, comfortable-looking therm-aware shirt and slacks, could have held any one of a number of white collar professions: an accountant, maybe, or a space scientist of the kind Frank Paulis had recruited in droves, or even a lawyer like Xenia herself. It was only the dog collar, a thin band of white at the throat, that marked out a different vocation.

From the shadows of her broad, sensible sun-hat the priest smiled out at Xenia. 'You must be Ms Makarova.'

'Call me Xenia. And you –'

'Dorothy Chaum.' The smile grew a little weary. 'I'm neither Mother, nor Father, thankfully. You must call me Dorothy.'

'It's a pleasure to have you here, Ms – Dorothy.'

Dorothy flapped at the drones buzzing around her head like flies. 'You're a good liar. I'll try to trouble you as little as I can.' And she looked beyond Xenia, into the rocket compound, with questing, curious eyes.

Maybe this won't be so bad after all, Xenia thought.

Xenia, in fact, had been against the visit on principle, and she had told her boss so. 'For God's sake, Frank. This is a space launcher development site. It's a place for hard hats, not haloes.'

Frank Paulis – forty-five years old, squat, brisk, bustling, sleek with sweat even in his air-conditioned offices – had just tapped his softscreen. 'Just like it says in the mail here. This character is here on behalf of the Pope, to gather information on the mission –'

'And bless it. Frank, the *Bruno* is a mission to the asteroids. We're going out to find Eeties, for God's sake. To have some quack waving incense and throwing holy water over our ship is – ridiculous. Mediaeval.'

Frank had got a look in his eyes she'd come to recognize. *You have to be realistic, Xenia. Live in the real world.* 'The Vatican are one of our principal sponsors. They've a right to access.'

'The Church is using us as part of its repositioning,' she'd protested sourly. It was true; the Church had spent much of the new millennium rebuilding, after the multiple crises that had assailed it after the turn of the century: sexual scandals, financial irregularities, a renewed awareness of the horrors of Christian history – the Crusades and the Inquisition chief amongst them. 'Not to mention,' Xenia said bitterly, 'the Church's refusal to acknowledge female reproductive rights and to address the issue of population growth, a position not abandoned until 2013, a historic wrong which must be on a par with –'

'Nobody's arguing,' Frank said gently. 'But – who are you suggesting is cynical? Us or them? Look, I don't care about the Church. All I care about is its money, and there's still a hell of a lot of *that*.

And, just like any other corporate sponsor, the Church is entitled to its slice of the PR pie.'

'Sometimes I think you'd take money from the Devil himself if it got your Big Dumb Booster a little closer to the launch pad.'

'Since we have a bunch of those apocalyptic cultists here – the ones who think the Gaijin are demons sent to punish us, or whatever – I suppose I *am* taking money from the other guy. Well, at least it shows balance.' Frank put his arm around her – he had to reach up to do it – and guided her out of his office. 'Xenia, this witch doctor isn't going to be with us for long. And, believe me, a priest is going to be a lot easier for you to entertain than some of the fat cats we have to put up with.'

'*Me* . . . Frank, if you knew how much I resent the implication that my time isn't valuable –'

'Bring her to the lecture. That will eat up a couple of hours.'

'What lecture?'

He frowned. 'I thought you knew. Reid Malenfant, on the philosophy of extraterrestrial life.'

She had to retrieve the name from deep memory. 'The dried-up old coot from the talk shows?'

'Reid Malenfant, the ex-astronaut. Reid Malenfant, the co-discoverer of alien life five years back. Reid Malenfant, modern icon, come to give our grease monkeys a pep talk.' He grinned. 'Lighten up, Xenia. Maybe it will be interesting.'

'Are *you* going?'

'Of course I am.' And, gently, he had closed the door.

Xenia and Dorothy were SmartDriven around Baikonur, the standard-issue corporate tour.

Baikonur, the Soviet Union's long-hidden space centre, had been pretty much a derelict by the time Frank Paulis took it over and began renovation. Stranded at the heart of a chill, treeless steppe, connected to the Russian border by a single antique rail line, it was like a run-down military base, dotted with hangars and launch pads and fuel tanks. Even after years of work by Bootstrap here, there were still piles of rusty junk strewn over the more remote corners of the base – some of it said to be the last relics of Russia's never-successful Moon rockets.

But Dorothy's attention was diverted, away from Xenia's sound bites on the history and the engineering and the mission of Bootstrap, by the folks Frank Paulis referred to as the Sports Fans: adherents of one view or another about the Gaijin, seemingly attracted here irresistibly.

The Sports Fans lived at the fringe of the launch complex in semi-permanent camps, contained by tough link fences. They spent their time chanting, costume-wearing, leafleting, performing protests of one baffling kind or another, right up against the fences, carefully watched over by Bootstrap security staff and drone robots. They were funded, presumably, by savings, or sponsors, or by whatever they could sell of their experiences and their witness on the data nets, and they were a fat, easy revenue source for the local Kazakhs – which was why they were tolerated here.

Xenia tried to guide Dorothy away from all this, but Dorothy demurred. And so they began a slow drive around the fences, as Dorothy peered out, and Xenia struggled to contain her impatience.

Public reaction to the Gaijin – as it had developed over the five years since the announcement of the discovery by Nemoto and Malenfant – had bifurcated. There were two broad schools of thought. The technical terms among psychologists and sociologists, Xenia had learned, were 'millennialists' and 'catastrophists'.

The millennialists, taking their lead from thinkers like Carl Sagan – not to mention Gene Roddenberry – believed that no star-spanning culture could possibly be hostile to a more primitive species like humanity, and the Gaijin must therefore be on their way to educate us or uplift us or save us from ourselves. The more intellectual millennialists had at least produced some useful, if slanted, material: careful studies of parallels with intercultural contact in Earth's past, ranging from the dreadful fall-out of western colonialism through to the essentially benevolent impact of the transmission of learning from Arabian and ancient Greek cultures to the medieval west.

But some millennialists were more direct. Various giant, elaborate structures had been cut or burned or painted on Earth's surface – featuring the peace sigil, the yin and yang, the Christian cross, a human hand – giant graffiti, Dorothy thought, painted in the deserts of America and Africa and Asia and Australia and even, illegally, on the Antarctic ice cap, its creators wistfully hoping to catch the eye of the anonymous, toiling strangers out in the belt.

Others were even less subtle. Right here before her now there was a circle of people, hands open and faces raised to the desert sky, all steadily praying. She knew there had been similar gatherings, some in continuous session, at many of the world's key religious and mystic sites: Jerusalem, Mecca, the pyramids, the European stone circles. *Take me! Take me!*

Meanwhile, the catastrophists believed that the aliens represented terrible danger.

Much of their fear and anger was directed at the aliens themselves, of course, and there were elaborate schemes for military assaults on their supposed asteroid bases – justified, in some cases, by appeal to the evident malice of most of the aliens reported in UFO abduction cases of the past. There was even one impressive presentation – complete with animation and sound effects, emanating from softscreen posters draped over Bootstrap's link fence – from a major aerospace cartel. The military-industrial-complex types were as always seeking to turn the new situation into lucrative new contracts, and how better than to be asked to build giant asteroid-belt battle cruisers?

But the catastrophists had plenty of rage left over to be directed at other targets, healthily fuelled by conspiracy theorists. There were still some who held that the US government had been collaborating with the aliens since Roswell, 1947 – 'I wish they had been,' Frank once said tiredly; 'it would make life a lot easier' – and there were protests aimed at government agencies at all levels, the United Nations, scientific bodies, and anybody thought to be involved in the general cover-up. The most spectacular of the related assaults had been the grenade attack which had caused the destruction of the decrepit, never-flown Saturn V Moon rocket which had lain for decades as a monument outside NASA's Johnson Space Center.

It kept the Bootstrap guards watchful.

'Intriguing,' Dorothy murmured. 'Disturbing.'

Xenia said gently, 'But places like this always concentrate the noise. The vast majority of people out there in the real world are simply indifferent to the whole thing. When the news about the Gaijin first broke it was an immediate sensation, taking over every media outlet – for a day or two, perhaps a week. I was already working with Frank at the time. He was electrified – well, we both were; we thought the news the most significant of our lifetimes. And the business opportunities it might open up sent Frank running around in circles.'

Dorothy smiled. 'That sounds like the Frank Paulis I've read about.'

'But then there was no more fresh news . . .'

After a couple of weeks, the Gaijin had been crowded off the front pages. Politics had assumed its usual course, and all the funds hastily promised in that first startling morning after the Nemoto–Malenfant discovery – for deeper investigations and robot probes and manned missions and the rest – had soon evaporated.

'But the news was too – lofty,' Dorothy murmured. 'Inhuman. It changed everything. Suddenly the universe swivelled around us; suddenly we knew we weren't alone, and how we felt about ourselves, about the universe and our place in it, could never be the same again.

'And yet, *nothing* changed. After all the Gaijin didn't *do* anything but crawl around their asteroids. They didn't respond to any of the signals they were sent, whether by governments or churches or ham-radio crackpots.'

Frank had gotten involved in some of that, in fact; the early messages had been framed using a universal-language methodology that dated back to the 1960s, called Lincos: lots of redundancy and framing to make the message patterns clear, a simple primer which worked up from basic mathematical concepts through physics, chemistry, astronomy . . . A lot of beautiful, fascinating work, none of which had raised so much as a peep from the Gaijin.

'And meanwhile,' Dorothy went on, 'there were still babies to deliver, crops to grow, politicking to pursue and wars to fight. As my father used to say, the next morning you still had to put your pants on one leg at a time.

'You know,' she said thoughtfully, 'I'm generally in favour of all this activity. Your Sports Fans, I mean. The only way we have to absorb such changes in our view of the world, and ourselves, is like this: by talking, talking, talking. At least the people here care enough to express an opinion. Look at that.' It was a softscreen poster showing a download from the net: a live image returned by some powerful telescope, perhaps in orbit or on the Moon, of the asteroid belt anomalies: a dark, grainy background, a line of red stars, twinkling, blurred. 'Alien industry, live from space. The most popular Internet site, I'm told. People use it as wallpaper in their bedrooms. They seem to find it comforting.'

Xenia snorted. 'Sure. And you know who makes most use of that image? The astrologers. Now you can have your fortune told by the lights of Gaijin factories. I mean, Jesus . . . Sorry. But it says it all.'

Dorothy laughed good-naturedly.

They drove away from the Sports Fans' pens, and approached the pad itself: the true centre of attention, bearing Bootstrap's first interplanetary ship, Frank Paulis's pride and joy.

Xenia could see the lines of a rust-brown external tank, the slim pillars of solid rocket boosters. The stack was topped by a tubular cover that gleamed white in the sun. Somewhere inside that fairing rested the *Giordano Bruno,* a complex robot spacecraft that would some day ride out to the asteroids, and seek out the Gaijin that lurked there – if Frank could drive the test program to completion, if Xenia could guide the corporation through the maze of legislation that still impeded them.

As Xenia studied the ship, Dorothy studied her.

Dorothy said, 'Frank Paulis relies on you a lot, doesn't he? I know that formally you are head of Bootstrap's legal department . . .'

'I'm the first name on Frank's call list. He relies on me to get things done.'

'And you're happy with your role.'

'We do share the same goals, you know.'

'Umm. Your ship looks something like the old Space Shuttle.'

'So it should,' said Xenia, and she launched into a standard line. 'This is what we here at Bootstrap call our Big Dumb Booster. It's actually comprised largely of superannuated Space Shuttle components. You'll immediately see one benefit over the standard Shuttle design, which is in-line propulsion; we have a much more robust stack –'

Dorothy said with smooth humour, 'I'm no more an engineer than you are, Xenia.'

Xenia allowed herself a grin. 'Sorry. It's hard to change the script after doing this so many times . . . This is primarily a launcher to the planets. Or the asteroids.'

Dorothy smiled. 'You have built a rocket ship for America.'

Xenia bristled. 'It does seem rather a scandal that America, first nation to land a human being on another planet, has let its competence degrade to the point that it has no heavy-lift space launch capability at all.'

'But the Chinese are in Earth orbit, and the Japanese are on the Moon. There's even a rumour that the Chinese are preparing a flight of their own out to the asteroids.'

Xenia squinted at the washed-out, dusty sky. 'Dorothy, it's five years since the Gaijin showed up in the solar system. But you can't call it contact. Not yet. As you said, they haven't responded to any of our signals. All they do is build, build, build. Maybe if we do manage to send a probe there, we'll achieve real contact, the kind of contact we've always dreamed of.'

'And you think America should be first.'

'If not us, who? The Chinese? . . .'

A siren sounded: an engine test was due. With smooth efficiency, the car's SmartDrive cut in and swept them far from danger.

* * *

'. . . We used to think that life was pretty unlikely – maybe even unique to Earth,' Malenfant was saying. 'An astronomer called Fred Hoyle once said that the idea that you could shuffle organic molecules in some primeval soup and, purely by chance, come up with a DNA molecule is about like a whirlwind passing through an aircraft factory and assembling scattered parts into a 747.' Laughter. 'But now we think those notions are wrong. Now we think that the complexity that defines and underlies life is somehow hardwired into the laws of physics. Life is *emergent*.

'Imagine boiling a pan of water. As the liquid starts to convect, you'll see a regular pattern of cells form, kind of like a honeycomb – just before the proper boiling cuts in and the motion becomes chaotic. Now, all there is in the pan is water molecules, billions of them. Nobody is *telling* those molecules how to organize themselves into those striking patterns. And yet they do it.

'That's an example of how order and complexity can emerge from an initial uniform and featureless state. And maybe life is just the end product of a long series of self-organizing steps like that . . .'

Malenfant was giving his lecture in Bootstrap's roomy, air-conditioned public affairs auditorium: the one place Frank had been prepared to spend some serious money, aside from on the engineering itself. Xenia and Dorothy arrived a little late. To Xenia's surprise, the auditorium was pretty nearly full, and she had to squeeze them into two seats at the back.

The stage was bare save for a lectern and a plastic mock-up, three metres tall, of the Big Dumb Booster – that, and Malenfant.

To Xenia, Reid Malenfant – a lithe but sun-wrinkled sixty-something, his polished-bald head shining under the overhead lights – was an unprepossessing sight. Even as he spoke he seemed oddly out of place, blinking at his audience as if he wasn't sure what he was doing here.

But the audience, mostly of young engineers, seemed spellbound. She spotted Frank himself in the front row, a dark, hulking figure before the grounded astronaut, gazing raptly with the rest. That old space dust still carried some magic, she supposed; there was something primal here, about wanting to be close to the wizard, the sage who had been involved in that first wondrous discovery – as if, just by being close, it was possible to soak up a little of that marvellous light.

Malenfant went on, 'We'd come to believe, even before the Gaijin showed up, that life must be common. We believe nature is uniform, so the laws and processes that work here work everywhere else. And now we hold to the Copernican principle: we believe that we aren't in any unique place in space or time. So if life is here, on Earth, it must be everywhere – in one form or another.

'So the fact that living things have come sailing into the asteroid belt from the stars (if they *are* living, that is) isn't much of a surprise. But what is a surprise is that they should be *just* arriving, here, now. If they exist, why weren't they here before?

'It is good scientific practice, when you're facing the unknown, to assume a condition of *equilibrium*: a stable state, not a state of change. Because change is unusual, special.

'Now, maybe you see the problem. What we seem to face with the Gaijin is the arrival – the very first arrival we can detect – of alien colonists in the solar system. And so we find ourselves – not in a time of equilibrium – but at a time of *transition*, in fact of possibly the most fundamental change of all. It's so unlikely it isn't true.

'To put it another way, this is the question that was avoided by all those terrible alien-invasion sci-fi movies I grew up with as a kid.' Laughter, a little baffled, from the younger guys. *What's a 'movie'?* 'Why should these bug-eyed guys arrive *now*, just when we have tanks and nukes to fight them with?'

Malenfant gazed around at his audience, his eyes deep-sunken, tired-looking, wary. 'I'm telling you this because you people are the ones who have taken up the challenge, where governments and others have shamefully failed, to get out there and figure out what's going on. There are obvious mysteries about the Gaijin – some of which might be resolved as soon as we get our first good look at them. But there are other, deeper questions which their very presence here poses, questions which go right to the heart of the nature of the universe itself, and our place in it. And right now, only *you* are doing anything which might help us tackle those questions.

'You have my support. Do your work well. Godspeed. Thank you.'

The applause began, politely at first.

It was a polished performance, Xenia supposed. She imagined this man thirty years ago giving pep talks at Space Shuttle component factories. *Do good work!*

But, to her surprise, the applause was continuing, even growing thunderous. And to her deeper surprise, she found herself joining in.

Xenia and Dorothy had some trouble reaching Frank Paulis and Malenfant, so walled off was the astronaut by a crowd of eager young engineer types.

Dorothy studied Xenia's expression. 'You don't quite go for all this hero worship, do you, Xenia?'

'Do you think I'm cynical?'

'No.'

Xenia grimaced. 'But it – frustrates me. We're living through first contact, an era unique in the human story, whatever the future holds. At least Bootstrap is trying to respond. Away from here, aside from what we're doing, all I see is irrationalism. That, and positioning. Various bodies trying to use this discovery for their own purposes.'

'Like the Church?'

'Well, isn't it?'

'We all must pursue our own goals, Xenia. At least the Church's involvement in this project of yours represents a tangible demonstration that we are working our way through the crisis of faith the Gaijin have caused us.'

'What crisis?'

'The Vatican began its first modern evaluation of the implication of extraterrestrial life for Christianity back in the '90s. But the debate has been going on much longer than that. We seem to have believed there were other minds out there long before we even had any clear notion of what *out there* actually was . . . This intuition seems to be an expression of our deep embedding in the universe; if the cosmos created us, it could surely create others. Did you know that Saint Augustine, back in the sixth century, speculated about Eeties?'

'He did?'

'Augustine decided they couldn't exist. If they did, you see, they would require salvation – a Christ of their own. But that would remove the uniqueness of Christ, which is impossible. Such theological conundrums plague us to this day . . . You can laugh if you like.'

Xenia shook her head. 'The idea that we might go out there and try to convert the Gaijin does seem a little odd.'

'But we don't know *why* they are here,' Dorothy pointed out. 'Would seeking truth be such an invalid reason?'

'And now you're here to bless the BDB,' Xenia said.

'Not exactly. Perhaps you've already done that, by naming it after Giordano Bruno. I take it you know who he was.'

'Of course.' The first thinker to have expressed something like the modern notion of a plurality of worlds – planets orbiting suns, many of them inhabited by beings more or less like humans. Earlier thinkers on other worlds had imagined parallel versions of a Dante's-*Inferno* pocket universe, centred on a stationary Earth. 'You have to imagine other worlds before you can conceive of travelling there.'

'But Bruno was anticipated,' Dorothy said gently. 'A cardinal we know as Nicolas of Cusa, who lived in the fifteenth century . . .'

Dorothy's lecturing tone seemed quite inappropriate to Xenia, making her impatient. 'Whatever his antecedents, Bruno was killed by the Church for his heresy.'

Dorothy said, 'He was burned, in 1600, for a mystical attack on Christianity, not for his argument about aliens, or even his defence of Copernicus.'

'That makes it okay?'

Dorothy continued to study her quietly.

At last the crowd of techie acolytes was breaking up.

'. . . You can't know how much I admire you, Colonel Malenfant,' Frank was saying. 'I'm twenty years younger than you. But I modelled myself on you.'

Malenfant eyed him dubiously. 'Then I'm in hell.'

'No, I mean it. You started a company called Bootstrap. You had plans to exploit the asteroids.'

'It failed. I was a lousy businessman. And when I lost my wife –'

'Sure, but you had the right idea. If not for that –'

Malenfant was looking longingly at the BDB mock-up. 'If not for that, if the universe was a different shape – yes; maybe *I'd* have done all this. And who knows what I'd have found?'

The silence stretched. Dorothy Chaum was frowning, Xenia noticed, as she studied Malenfant's cloudy, troubled expression.

Chapter 3

DEBATES

It was four more years before Malenfant encountered Frank J Paulis again.

In 2029, Malenfant was invited to the Smithsonian at Washington, DC as a guest at the annual meeting of the American Association of the Advancement of Science – or at least, a stream of it supported by the SETI Institute, a privately funded outfit based in Colorado and devoted to the study of the Gaijin, the search for extraterrestrial intelligence, and other good stuff.

Despite the subject matter of the conference, Malenfant had come here with some reluctance.

He had grown wary of appearing in public. As Paulis's robot probe swung relentlessly out from Earth, the unwelcome notoriety he had attracted nine years back was picking up again. He thought of it as the Buzz Aldrin syndrome: *But you were there . . .* When people looked at him, he thought, they saw a symbol, not a human being; they saw somebody who was incapable of doing original work ever again. It was a regard that was embarrassing, paralysing, and it made him feel very old. Not only that, Malenfant had found himself the target of unwelcome attention of the most extreme factions from either side of the spectrum, both the xenophobes and xenophiles.

But he had been invited here by Maura Della, a now-retired Congresswoman he'd encountered in the course of the unravelling of that initial discovery.

Maura Della was about Malenfant's age, small, neat and spry. She had served as part of the President's science advisory support at the time of the Gaijin announcement, when Malenfant and Nemoto had been dragged before the President himself, the Secretary of Defense, the Industrial Relations Council, and various Presidential task forces, as the Administration sought an official posture concerning the Gaijin. Unlike some of the Beltway apparatchiks Malenfant had encountered in those days, Della had proved to be tough but straightforward in her dealings with Malenfant, and he had grown to respect her sense of responsibility about SETI and other issues. It would be good to see her again.

And, he hoped, maybe she was still close enough to the centre of power to give him a genuine insight into anything *new*.

In that, as it turned out, he would not be disappointed.

At first, though, the conference – summing up what was known about the Gaijin, nine long years after discovery – proved to be meagre stuff. In the absence of new fact the proceedings were dominated by presentations on the impact of the Gaijin's existence on philosophical principles.

Thus, the first talk Maura Della escorted him to was on the brief and unrewarding history of SETI, the search for extraterrestrial intelligence.

Since the 1950s appropriately tuned radio telescopes had been turned on promising nearby stars, like Tau Ceti and Epsilon Eradini. Over the years the search was taken up by NASA and upgraded and automated, until it was possible to search thousands of likely radio frequencies at very high speed.

But decades of patient, longing search had turned up nothing but a few evanescent, tantalizing whispers of pattern.

As Malenfant listened to the stream of detail and acronyms, of project after project – Ozma, Cyclops, Phoenix – he became consumed with pity for these patient, hungry listeners, hoping to hear the faintest of whispers from beyond the stars. For, of course, it had always been futile, wrong-headed. *Equilibrium*, he thought: either the sky is silent because it is empty, or else the aliens should be everywhere. There should have been no need to seek out whispers; if we weren't alone, the sky should, metaphorically, have been blazing with light.

The next speaker impressed Malenfant rather more. She was a geologist from Caltech called Carole Lerner – no older than thirty, spiky, argumentative. She had tried to come up with a new answer to the conundrum of the arrival of the Gaijin. Maybe there had been no sign of the Gaijin before, said Lerner, because they had only recently evolved – and not among the stars, but where they had been found, in the asteroid belt itself.

There had been suggestions for some decades that life could get a foothold in comets – perhaps in pockets of liquid water, drenched with the organic compounds that laced cometary interiors – and, of course, some asteroids were believed to be burned-out comets, or at least to have a comparable composition to comets. The coincidence of the emergence of a spacefaring alien race in the asteroids *now*, just as we reached a similar state, might be explained by a convergence of timescales. Perhaps it simply took this long, a few billion years, for life to crawl its way from the ponds to the stars, no matter where it originated.

It was a nice hypothesis, Malenfant reflected, but he judged that the coincidence of timescales was surely too neat to be convincing. Still, this was the first speaker Malenfant had heard at the conference who had attempted to address the deeper issues which obsessed the likes of Nemoto. He glanced at his softscreen, seeking presenters' bio details.

Lerner's general specialism was the volcanic history of the planet Venus. Malenfant wasn't surprised to learn she was having trouble finding funding to continue her work. One side-effect of the arrival of the Gaijin had been a decline of interest in the sciences. It seemed to be generally assumed that the Gaijin would eventually hand over the answers to any questions humans could possibly pose; so why spend time – and, more significantly, money – seeking out answers now? No genuine scientist Malenfant had ever met would have been satisfied with such passivity, of course; it seemed to him this Carole Lerner might be consumed with exactly that impatience.

The next paper, given by a heavy-set academic from the SETI Institute, turned out to have his own name in the title: 'The Nemoto–Malenfant Contact – An Example of How Not to Do It'.

Maura Della sat back to listen with an expression of intense enjoyment.

The presentation was based on a bureaucratic protocol devised to cover the event of alien contact. The protocol was first worked out by NASA in the 1990s, and then, after the cancellation of government funding for SETI and the NASA project's take-over by private institutions, developed further by the UN and national governments.

Malenfant – as one of only two people in all history to have been placed in the situation covered by the protocol – had never bothered to read it. He wasn't surprised to learn now that it was top-down, officious and almost comically foolish in its optimism that central control could be maintained:

> 'After concluding that the discovery appears to be credible evidence of extraterrestrial intelligence, and after informing other parties to this declaration, the discoverer should inform

observers throughout the world through the Central Bureau for Astronomical Telegrams of the International Astronomical Union, and should inform the Secretary General of the United Nations in accordance with Article XI of the Treaty on Principles Governing the Activities of States in the Exploration and Use of Outer Space, Including the Moon and Other Bodies. Because of their demonstrated interest in and expertise concerning the question of the existence of extraterrestrial intelligence, the discoverer should simultaneously inform the following international institutions of the discovery and should provide them with all pertinent data and recorded information concerning the evidence: the International Telecommunication Union, the Committee on Space Research, of the International Council of Scientific Unions, the International Astronautical Federation, the International Academy of Astronautics, the International Institute of Space Law, Commission 51 of the International Astronomical Union and Commission J of the International Radio Science Union . . .'

Malenfant and Nemoto, by comparison, had gone straight on the talk shows.

Playfully, Maura slapped Malenfant's wrist. 'Naughty, naughty. All those Commissions you skipped. You made a lot of enemies there.'

'But,' he said, 'I did get to sleep in the Lincoln Bedroom at the White House. You know, this guy makes it sound as if he'd rather we hadn't made the discovery at all, rather than making it the wrong way.'

'Human nature, Malenfant. You took away his toy.'

Now the speaker opened the floor for comments.

The discussion soon turned to how the situation should be managed from here. There were plenty of calls for behavioural scientists to study ways in which the public response to the news could be somehow anticipated and controlled, for research into popular public images of Eeties, discussion of analogies with the response to missions like Apollo to the Moon and Viking to Mars, and suggestions that SETI proponents should make use of media like webcasts, games and music to present SETI and Eetic themes 'responsibly'.

Maura pulled an elaborate face. 'Don't these people realize the cat is already out of the bag? You can't control the public's access to information any more – and you certainly can't control their response. Nor should you try, in my opinion.'

At last the speaker cleared off the stage, and Malenfant's spirits lifted a little. As an engineer, he knew that a bucket-load of philosophical principles wasn't worth a grain of good hard fact. And that was why the next item, by Frank Paulis, was a breath of fresh air. After all, it was Paulis, with his money and his initiative, who was actually going out there to look.

Paulis's images of his en-route spacecraft, the *Bruno*, showed a gangly, glittering dragonfly of solar-cell panels and gauzy antennae and sensors mounted on long booms, surrounded by a swarm of microsats devoted to fly-around inspections and repairs.

The launch had been uneventful, the first years of the long flight enlivened only by the usual hardware glitches and nail-biting techie dramas. It struck Malenfant as remarkable how little space technology seemed to have progressed in seventy years since the first Sputnik; the design of the *Bruno* would probably have been recognizable, give or take a few sapphire-based quantum chips, to Wernher von Braun. But flying in space had always been a conservative business; if you had only one shot, you wanted your ship to work, not to serve as the test bed for new gadgets and ideas.

Anyhow, the *Bruno* had survived its man-made crises. The ship was still a year away from its rendezvous with what appeared to be the primary construction site – or colony, or nest – of the Gaijin. The asteroid belt was a broad lane of rubble; already the probe had encountered a number of those dusty wanderers, never visited before or seen in close-up. But – Paulis promised, standing before slide after slide of coal-dark, anonymous rocks – the best was yet to come. For, in the darkness, the Gaijin awaited.

After a morning of such thin gruel, Malenfant retreated to his hotel room.

He travelled light these days: just bathroom stuff, a couple of self-cleaning suits and sets of underwear, a softscreen that was all he needed to connect him to the rest of the species – and a single ornament, a piece of unbelievably ancient rock from the far side of the Moon, carved into an exquisite fox god. He had become minimal. The time he spent on the Japanese Moon, he supposed, had changed him, no doubt for the better.

He spent a half hour watching heavily filtered and interpreted news on his softscreen. He needed to know what was going on, but he was too old to have any patience with the evanescent buzz of instant commentaries.

A corner of his softscreen rippled with light: an incoming message.

It was Nemoto. It was the first time she'd contacted Malenfant in years.

'Nemoto! Where are you?'

There was a delay of a few seconds before her reply came back, her face creasing into a thin smile. That could place her on the Moon. But the delay could be a fake . . .

'You should know better than to ask me that, Malenfant.'

'Yeah. Sorry.'

She was still under forty, but she wasn't ageing well, he thought. Her hair remained thick and jet black, but her oval face had shed its prettiness: grown angular, the bones showing, her eyes dark and sunken with suspicion. Her voice, from the softscreen's tiny speakers, was an insect whisper. 'You are enjoying the conference?'

'Not much.' He shared with her his gripe over too many philosophers.

'But there are worse fools. Here is some more philosophy for you. "This is the way I think the world will end – with general giggling by all the witty heads, who think it is a joke." Kierkegaard.'

'He got it right.' Whoever he was.

'And philosophy can sometimes guide us, Malenfant.'

'For instance –'

'For instance, the notion of equilibrium . . .'

It was like resuming a conversation they had pursued, on and off, for nine years; a slow teasing-out of the *koan*.

After their notoriety following the announcement of the aliens in the belt, Nemoto had recoiled completely. She'd refused all offers of public appearances, had quit her job, had turned down offers of research positions from a dozen of the world's most prestigious universities and corporations, and had effectively disappeared. All this while Malenfant had slogged around the public circuit with diminishing enthusiasm, enduring the brickbats and bouquets that came from his sliver of fame. She had been an Armstrong, he sometimes thought wryly, to his own Aldrin.

But she was continuing her researches – though what her purpose was, and where her money was coming from, he couldn't have said.

She didn't like the Gaijin, though. That much was obvious.

She said softly, 'We imagined only two possible equilibrium states: no aliens, or aliens everywhere. We have diagnosed this moment, the moment of first contact, as a transition between equilibriums, brief and therefore unlikely for us to be living through. But what if that's wrong? What if *this* is the true state of equilibrium?'

Malenfant frowned. 'I don't get it. Contact changes everything. How can a *change* be described as an equilibrium?'

'If it happens more than once. Over and over and over. In that case it's no coincidence that I happen to be alive, here and now, to witness this. It's no coincidence that we happen to have a technical culture capable of detecting the signals, even initiating contact, of a sort, just at this moment. *Because this isn't unique.*'

'You're saying this happened before? That others have been here? Then where did they go?'

'I can't think of any answers that don't scare me, Malenfant.'

He studied her. Her eyes were almost invisible, her face an expressionless mask. The background was dark, anonymous, no doubt scrambled beyond the reach of image enhancement routines.

He considered what to say. *You're spending too much time alone. You need to get out more.* But he was scarcely a friend to this strange, obsessive woman. 'You've spent a lot of time thinking about this, haven't you?'

She seemed offended. 'This is the destiny of the species.'

He sighed. 'What is it you called me about, Nemoto?'

'To warn you,' she said. 'It isn't quite true that we are waiting on Frank Paulis and his space probe for new data. There are two items of interest. First, a fresh interpretation. I've been able to deduce patterns from the infrared signature of the Gaijin's activity in the belt. I believe I have determined their pattern of propagation.'

Her face disappeared, to be replaced by the virtual display of the type she'd first shown him in the silence of the Moon. It was a ring of glistening crimson droplets, slowly orbiting: the asteroid belt, complete with dark Kirkwood gaps. And there was the gap with the one-to-three resonance with Jupiter, with its string of rubies, enigmatic, brilliant.

'Watch, Malenfant . . .'

Malenfant bent close to the screen and studied the little beads of light. The images cycled with small vector arrows, which showed velocity and acceleration. The rubies weren't in simple orbits about the sun, he saw; they seemed to be spreading around the belt, some of them actually moving retrograde, against the motion of the rest of the belt.

The motion was intriguing.

Nemoto said, 'Imagine the arrows projected backwards.'

'Ah,' Malenfant said. 'Yes. They might converge.'

Nemoto cut in a routine to extrapolate back from the Gaijin sites' velocity vectors. 'This is rough and ready,' she admitted. 'I had to make a lot of assumptions about how the objects' trajectories had deviated from simple orbits through the sun's gravitational field. But it did not take long before I found an answer.'

The projected paths arced out of the asteroid belt – out, away from the sun, into the deeper darkness, before converging.

Malenfant tapped the screen. 'You found it. The prime radiant. Where these probes, or factories, or whatever the hell they are, are emanating from.'

Nemoto said, 'It is one point four times ten to power fourteen metres from the sun. That is –'

'About a thousand astronomical units out.' A thousand times as far as Earth from the sun. 'Somewhere in the direction of Virgo . . . But why there?'

'I do not know. I need more data, more work.'

'And your second item?'

She eyed him. 'You are meeting Maura Della. Ask her about Rigil Kent.'

Rigil Kent. Also known as Alpha Centauri, nearest star system to the sun, four light years away.

'Nemoto –'

But the softscreen had already filled up with the everyday froth of the online news channels; Nemoto had receded into darkness.

He was taken to lunch by former Congresswoman Della.

After lunch they strolled around the conference hall, glancing at poster presentations and the fringe sessions. Malenfant felt uncomfortable being out in public like this.

'I wouldn't be too concerned,' Maura said. 'Not here; you have to be afraid of the ones who stay at home polishing the telescope sights on their rifles.'

'Not funny, Maura.'

'Perhaps not. Sorry.'

She hadn't said a significant word during lunch; now he couldn't contain himself any more. '*Rigil Kent*,' he said.

She slowed to a halt. Her voice low, she said, 'You spoiled my surprise. I should have known you'd find out.'

'What's going on, Maura?'

For answer she took him to a small, over-priced coffee bar. On a handheld softscreen she showed him images of the great radio telescope at Arecibo, various microwave satellites, activity in the Main Bay at

JPL: arcs of consoles, young, excited engineers on roller chairs, information flickering over screens before them.

'Malenfant, we've picked up a signal. From Alpha Centauri.'

'What – how –'

She pressed a finger to his lips.

As it turned out – though this bit of news had been Maura's true motive for inviting him here – there was little more to tell. Maura had gotten the news from her contacts in the government. The signal was faint, first picked up by an orbital microwave satellite. But it was nothing like the neatly structured Lincos signals humans had been sending to the asteroid belt. It was heavily compressed, a mush of apparently incoherent noise, with only evanescent hints of structure – much what Earth might have sounded like, from four light years away.

'Or it may be an efficient signal,' Malenfant said hoarsely. 'It can't be cheap to signal between the stars. You'd take out as much redundancy – repetitive structure – as possible. If you don't know how to decode it, such a signal must look like noise . . .' Either way the implication was clear. This wasn't a signal meant for humans.

But whoever was there, at Alpha Centauri, had only just started to broadcast – or rather, only four years in the past, given the time it took for signals to crawl to Earth.

In fact the signal's existence and nature were still being verified. '*This* time we're following the protocols, Malenfant . . .'

'Is it the Gaijin? Or somebody else?'

'We don't know.'

'Keep me informed.'

'Oh, yes,' she said. 'But keep it to yourself.'

Malenfant stayed in his hotel room the rest of the night, unable to relax, pacing back and forth until Nemoto called again.

He was furious Nemoto had known all about Centauri. But he controlled his irritation.

'At least,' he said, 'this discovery demolishes theories that the Gaijin might be native to our solar system. If they came from Centauri –'

'Of course they don't come from Centauri,' Nemoto said. 'Why would they suddenly start making such a radio clatter if that was so? No, Malenfant. They only just arrived in the Centauri system. Just as they only just arrived *here*. Apparently we are watching the vanguard of a wave of colonization, Malenfant, extending far from our system.'

'But –'

Nemoto waved a delicate hand before her face. 'But that isn't important, Malenfant. None of this is. Not even the activity in the asteroids.'

'Then what is?'

'I have determined the nature of the Gaijin's prime radiant, here in the solar system.'

'The nature? You said it is a thousand AU out. What's out there to have a nature at all?'

'A solar focus,' Nemoto said.

'The what?'

'That far out is where you will find the focal points of the sun's gravitational field. Images of remote stars, magnified by gravitational lensing. And the star that is focussed at the Gaijin prime radiant is –'

'Alpha Centauri?' The stubbly hairs on the back of his neck stood on end.

She said grimly, 'You see, Malenfant? Any number of probes to the belt won't answer the fundamental questions.'

'No.' Malenfant shook his head, mind racing. 'We've got to send somebody out there. Through a thousand AU; out to the solar focus . . . But that's impossible.'

'Nevertheless that is the challenge, Malenfant. *There* – at the solar focus – is where the answers will be found. *That* is where we must go.'

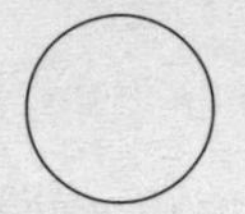

Chapter 4

ELLIS ISLAND

Maura was flying around an asteroid.

The asteroid – whimsically christened Ellis Island by the Bootstrap flight controllers at JPL – was three kilometres wide, twelve long. The compound body looked like two lumpy barbecue potatoes stuck end-to-end, dark and dusty. Maura could see extensions of the *Bruno*'s equipment ahead of her: elaborate claws and grapples, lines that coiled out across space to where rocket-driven pitons had already dug themselves into the asteroid's soft, friable surface.

With an effort she turned her head. Her viewpoint swivelled. The asteroid shifted out to the left; the image, heavily enhanced and extrapolated from the feed returned by *Bruno*, blurred slightly as the processors struggled to keep up with her wilfulness.

She was suspended in a darkness that was broken only by pinpoints of light. There were stars all around her: above, below, behind. Here she was in the middle of the asteroid belt, but there was not a single body, save for Ellis itself, large enough to show a disc. Even the sun had shrunk to a yellow dot, casting long shadows, and she knew that it shed on this lonely rock only a few per cent of the heat and light it vouchsafed Earth.

The asteroid belt had turned out to be surprisingly empty, a cold, excessively roomy place. And yet it was here the Gaijin had chosen to come.

Xenia Makarova, Bootstrap's VIP host for the day, whispered in her ear. 'Ms Della, are you enjoying the show?'

She suppressed a sigh. 'Yes, dear. Of course I am. Very impressive.'

And so it was. In her time as part of the President's science advisory team, she'd put in a lot of hours on spaceflight stunts like this, manned and unmanned. She had to admit that being able to share the experience vicariously – to be able to sit in her own apartment wearing her VR headband, and yet to ride down to the asteroid with the probe itself

– was a vast improvement on what had been on offer before: those cramped visitors' booths behind Mission Control at the Johnson Space Center, that noisy auditorium at JPL.

And yet she felt restless, here in the dark and cold. She longed to cut her VR link to the *Bruno* feed, to drink in the sunlight that washed over the Baltimore harbour area, visible from her apartment window just a metre away.

She said to Xenia, 'It's just that space operations are always so darn slow.'

'But we have to take it slow,' Xenia said. 'Encountering an asteroid is more like docking with another spacecraft than landing; the gravity here is so feeble the main challenge is not to bounce off and fly away.

'We're coming down at the asteroid's north pole. The main Gaijin site appears to be at the other rotation pole, the south pole. What we intend is to land out of sight of the Gaijin – assuming we haven't been spotted already – and work our way around the surface to the alien. That way we may be able to keep a measure of control over events . . .'

'This is a terribly dark and dusty place, isn't it?'

'That's because this is a C-type asteroid, Ms Della. Ice, volatiles and organic compounds: just the kind of rock we might have chosen to mine for ourselves, for life support, propellant.'

Yes, Maura thought with a flicker of dark anger. This is our belt, *our* asteroid. Our treasure, a legacy of the solar system's violent origins for our future. And yet there are Gaijin here – strangers, taking our birthright.

Her anger surprised her; she hadn't suspected she was so territorial. It's not as if they landed in Antarctica, she told herself. The asteroids aren't yet ours; we have no claim here, and therefore shouldn't feel threatened by the Gaijin's appropriation.

And yet I do.

The Alpha Centauri signal – though the first, picked up a year ago – was no longer unique. Whispers in the radio wavebands had been detected across the sky: from Barnard's Star, Wolf 359, Sirius, Luyten 726–8 – the nearby stars, the sun's close neighbours, the first destinations planned in a hundred interstellar-colonization studies, homes of civilizations dreamed of in a thousand science fiction novels.

One by one, the stars were coming out.

There were patterns to the distribution. No star further than around nine light years away had yet lit up with radio signals. But the signals weren't uniform. They weren't of the same type, or even on the same frequencies; such differences were just as confusing as the very existence of the signals. And meanwhile the Gaijin, the solar system's new residents, remained quiet: they seemed to be producing no electromagnetic output but the infrared of their waste heat.

It was as if a wave of colonization had abruptly reached this part of the Galaxy, this remote corner of a ragged spiral arm, and diverse creatures – or machines – were busily digging in, building, perhaps breeding, perhaps dying. Nobody knew how the colonists had gotten here. Nobody could even guess why they had come *now*.

But it seemed to Maura that already one fact was clear about the presumed Galactic community: it was messy and diverse, just as much as the human communities of Earth, if not more. In a way, she supposed, that was even healthy. If communities separated by light years had turned out to be identical, it would be an oppressive sky indeed. But it was sure going to make figuring out the meaning of it all a lot more difficult.

And, for Maura, that was a matter to regret.

She was never short of work, of invitations like this. She knew that as part of the amorphous community of pols and workers who never really got the stink of the Beltway out of their nostrils, she was prized by corporations like Bootstrap as an opinion-former, perhaps a conduit to power. But she was, officially, retired. Perhaps she should sit back and stop thinking so hard, and just let the pretty light shows from the sky wash over her.

But that wasn't in her nature. And, after all, Reid Malenfant was older than she was, and she knew he continued to agitate for a deeper engagement with the mystery of these Gaijin, for more probes, other missions. If *he* was still active, then perhaps she should be.

But, in this complicated universe, she was too damn *old*. The more complicated it was, the more likely it was that she would never live to see this puzzle – perhaps the greatest mystery ever to confront humanity – unravelled.

Now a technical feed faded up in Maura's other ear. 'Closing with the target at two metres per second, range just under a klick, one metre per second cross-range. Hydrazine thruster tests in progress: +X, –X, +Y, –Y, +Z, –Z, all check out. Counting down to the thruster burn to null our approach and cross-range velocities a klick above the ground. Then we're on gyro-lock to touchdown . . .'

With an effort of will, Maura tuned out the irrelevant voices.

The asteroid became a wall that approached her in slow, dusty silence; the tether lines twisted before her, retaining their coils in the absence of gravity. She made out surface features, limned by sunlight:

craters, scarps, ridges, valleys, striations where it looked as if the asteroid's surface had been crumpled or stretched. Some of the craters were evidently new, relatively anyhow, with neat bowl shapes and sharp rims. Others were much older, little more than circular scars overlaid by younger basins and worn down, presumably by a billion years of micrometeorite rain.

And there were colours on Ellis's folded-over landscape, spectral shades that emerged from the dominant grey-blackness. The sharper-edged craters and ridges seemed to be slightly bluish, while the older, low-lying areas were more subtly red. Perhaps this was some deep space weathering effect, she thought; perhaps aeons of sunlight had wrought these gentle hues.

She sighed. It really was lovely, in a quite unexpected way – like so much of the universe she found herself in. By God, I love it all, she thought. How can I retire? If I did, I would miss *this*.

And now, with a kiss of dust, the *Bruno* reached its destination.

The techs began cheering tinnily.

A year before the *Bruno*'s arrival – after the AAAS meeting – Malenfant had returned to the Johnson Space Center, for the first time in two decades.

The campus looked pretty much unchanged: the same blocky black and white buildings, with those big nursery-style numbers on their sides, scattered over square kilometres of grassy plain here at the south-east suburban edge of Houston, all contained by a mesh fence from NASA Road One. (But it wasn't called the NASA Road any more.) In the surrounding streets there were still run-down strip malls and fast food places and Seven-Elevens.

But inside the campus itself, there was no sign of the tourists who used to ride between the buildings in their long tram trains. And though there were plenty of historic-marker plaques, nobody was making history here any more.

The cherry trees were still here, though, and the green grass still seemed to glow.

He wasn't here to sight-see. He had come to meet Sally Brind, who ran a NASA department called the Solar System Exploration Division. He made his way to Building 31.

Inside, the air conditioning was ferocious, a hell of a contrast to the flat moist Houston heat outside. Malenfant welcomed the plummeting temperature; it was like old times.

* * *

Reid Malenfant had loomed over Sally Brind. He was leaning on her desk, resting his weight on big, bony knuckles. He was around twice Brind's age and he was a legend out of the past. And, to her, he was as intimidating as hell.

'We got to get out to the solar focus,' he began.

'Hello, good morning, nice to meet you, thanks for giving up your time,' she said dryly.

He backed off a little, and stood up straight. 'I'm sorry,' he said.

'Don't tell me. At your time of life, you don't have time to waste.'

'No, I'm just a rude asshole. Always was. Mind if I sit down?'

She said, 'Tell me about the solar focus.'

He moved a pile of glossies from a chair; they were digitized artist's impressions of a proposed, never-to-be-funded, unmanned mission to Io, Jupiter's moon. 'What I'm talking about, specifically, is a mission to the solar focus of Alpha Centauri – the nearest star system.'

'I know about Alpha Centauri.'

'Yes . . . The sun's gravitational field acts as a spherical lens, which magnifies the intensity of the light of a distant star. At the point of focus, out on the rim of the system, the gain can be hundreds of millions; at the right point, it would be possible to communicate across stellar distances with equipment no more powerful than you'd need to talk between planets. The Gaijin may be using the Centauri solar focus as a communication node. The theorists are calling it a Saddle Point. Actually there is a separate Saddle Point for each star. All roughly at the same radius, because of –'

'All right. And why do we need to go to Alpha Centauri's focus?'

'Because Alpha was the first source of extrasolar signals. And because the Gaijin are *there*. We have evidence that the Gaijin entered the system at the Alpha solar focus. From there, they sent a fleet of some kind of construction or mining craft into the asteroid belt. Sally, we now have infrared signatures, showing the activity in the asteroid belt, going back ten years.'

'There is an unmanned probe en route to the asteroid belt. Maybe we should wait for its results.'

Malenfant flared. 'A private initiative. Not relevant, anyhow. The solar focus – *that* is where the action is.'

'You don't actually have any direct evidence of anything out at the solar focus, do you?'

'No. Only what we've inferred from the asteroid belt data.'

'But there's no signature of any huge interstellar mother ship out there, at the rim. As there would have to be, if you're right.'

'I don't have all the answers. That's why we have to get out there and see. And to tell the damn Gaijin we're here.'

'I don't see how I can help you.'

'This is NASA's Solar System Exploration Division. Right? So, now we need to go do some exploring.'

'NASA doesn't exist any more,' she said. 'Not as you knew it, when you were flying Shuttle. The JSC is run by the Department of Agriculture –'

'Don't patronize me, kid.'

She sighed. 'I apologize. But I think you have to be realistic about this, sir. This isn't the 1960s. I'm really just a kind of curator, of the grey literature.'

'Grey?'

'Studies and proposals that generally never made it to the light of day. The stuff is badly archived; a lot of it isn't yet digitized, or even on fiche . . . Even this building is seventy years old. I bet it would be closed for good if it wasn't for the Moon rocks.'

That was true; elsewhere in this building, fifty per cent of the old Apollo samples still lay sealed in their sample boxes, still awaiting analysis, after six decades. Now that there were Japanese living on the Moon, Brind suspected the boxes would stay sealed forever, if only so they could serve as samples of the Moon as it used to be in its pristine, prehuman condition. An ironic fate for those billion-dollar nuggets.

'I know all that,' he said. 'But I used to work for NASA. Where else am I supposed to go? Look – I want you to figure out how it could be done. *How can we send a human to the solar focus?* It will all come together, once we have a viable scheme to fix on. I can get the hardware, the funding.'

She arched an eyebrow. 'Really?'

'Sure. And the science will be good. After all, we still haven't sent a human out beyond the orbit of the Moon. We can drop probes on Jupiter, Pluto en route. We'll get sponsorship from the Europeans and Japanese for that. The US government ought to contribute, too.'

You make it sound so easy, Colonel Malenfant . . . 'Why should these organizations back you? We haven't sent a human into orbit, other than as a passenger of NASDA or ESA, in twenty years.'

'Otherwise,' said Malenfant, 'we'll have to let the Japanese do this alone.'

'True.'

'Also there'll be a lot of media interest. It will be a hell of a stunt.'

'A stunt is right,' she said. 'It would be a spectacular one-shot. Just like Apollo. And look where that got us.'

'To the Moon,' he said severely, 'forty years before the Japanese.'

She chose her next words carefully. 'Colonel Malenfant, you must be aware that it will be difficult for me to support you.'

He eyed her. 'I know I'm thought of as an obsessive. Twenty years after Shuttle was grounded, I'm still working out a kind of long, lingering disappointment about the shape of my career. I want to pursue this Gaijin hypothesis because I'm obsessed with them, because I want America to get back into space. I have an agenda. Right?'

'I – yes. I guess so. I'm sorry.'

'Hell, don't be. It's true. I was never too good at the politics here. Not even in the Astronaut Office. I never got into any of the cliques: the spacewalkers, the sports fans, the commanders, the bubbas who hung out at Molly's Pub. I was never *interested* enough. Even the Russians mistrusted me because I wasn't enough of a team player.' He slapped his leathery hand on her desk. 'But the Gaijin are *here*. Sally, I've waited ten years for our government, *any* government, to act on that lunar infrared evidence. Only Frank Paulis responded – a private individual, with that one damn probe. Now, I've decided to do something about it, before I drop dead.'

'How far away is the solar focus?'

'A thousand astronomical units.' A thousand times as far as the distance between Earth and sun.

She whistled. 'You're crazy.'

'Sure.' He grinned, showing even, rebuilt teeth. 'Now tell me how to do it. Treat it as an exercise, if you like. A thought experiment.'

She said dryly, 'Do you have an astronaut in mind?'

His grin widened. 'Me.'

Dark, crumpled ground, a horizon that was pin-sharp and looked close enough to touch, a sky full of stars dominated by a single bright spark . . .

Maura felt herself lurch as the probe began to make its way across the folded-over asteroid earth. She saw pitons and tethers lance out ahead of her field of view, extruding and hauling back, tugging the robot this way and that. Her viewpoint swivelled up and down, and some augmentation routine in the virtual generators was tickling her hind brain, making her feel as if she was riding right along with the robot over this choppy, rocky sea. With a sub-vocalized command, she told the software to cut it out; some special effects she could live without.

Xenia whispered to her audience of VIPs. 'As we move we're being extremely cautious. The surface gravity is even weaker than you might expect for a body this size. Remember this "dumbbell asteroid" is a contact binary, a compound body; imagine two pool balls snuggled up against each other, spinning around their point of contact. We're a fly crawling over the far side of one of those pool balls. The dumbbell is spinning pretty rapidly, and here, at the pole, centrifugal force almost cancels out the gravity. But we modelled all these situations; *Bruno* knows what he's doing. Just sit tight and enjoy the ride.'

And now something was looming beyond that close horizon. It was like the rise of a moon – but this moon was small and dark and battered, a twin of the world over which she crawled. It was the other lobe of the dumbbell.

Xenia said, 'We're studying the ground as we travel. As we don't know what to look for, we've carried broad-spectrum surveying equipment. For instance, if the Gaijin came here to extract light metals such as aluminium, magnesium or titanium, they would most likely have used processes like magma electrolysis or pyrolysis. The same processes could be used for oxygen production. In the case of magma electrolysis the main slag component would be ferrosilicon. From a pyrolysis process we would expect to find traces of elemental iron and silicon, or perhaps slightly oxidized forms . . .'

We are crawling across a slag heap, Maura thought, trying to figure out what was made here. But are we being too anthropomorphic? Would a Neandertal conclude that *we* must be unintelligent because, searching our nuclear reactors, she could find no chippings from flint cores?

But what else can we do? How can we test for the unknowable?

The asteroid's second lobe had all but 'risen' above the horizon now. It was a ball of rock, black and battered, that hung suspended over the land, as if in some Magritte painting. She could even see a broad band of crushed, flattened rock ahead, where one flying mountain rested against the other.

The second lobe was so close it seemed Maura could see every fold in its surface, every crater, even the grains of dust there. How remarkable, she thought.

The probe's mode of travel had changed now, she noticed; the pitons were applying small sideways or braking tweaks to an accelerating motion towards the system's centre of gravity, that contact zone. Gravity must be decreasing in strength the tug of the rock below her balanced by the equal mass of rock above, so that the net force was becoming more and more horizontal, and the probe was simply pulled across the surface.

Now the second lobe was so close, in this virtual diorama, it was over her head. Its crumpled inverted landscape formed a rocky roof. It was dark here, with the sun occluded, and the slices of starlight in the gap between the worlds were growing narrower.

Lamps lit up on the probe, and they played on the land beneath, the folded roof above. She longed to reach up and touch those inverted craters, as if a toy Moon had been hung over her head, a souvenir from some Aristotelian pocket universe.

'. . . I think we have something,' Xenia said quietly.

Maura looked down. Her field of view blurred as the interpolation routines struggled to keep up.

There was something on the ground before her. It looked like a blanket of foil, aluminium or silver, ragged-edged, laid over the dark regolith. Aside from a fringe a metre or two wide, it appeared to be buried in the loose dirt. Its crumpled edges glinted in the low sunlight.

It was obviously artificial.

Brind had next met Malenfant a few months later, at Kennedy Space Center.

Malenfant found KSC depressing; most of the launch gantries had been demolished or turned into rusting museum pieces. But the visitors' centre was still open. The Shuttle exhibit – artefacts, photographs and virtuals – was contained within a small geodesic dome, yellowing with age.

And there, next to the dome, was *Columbia*, a genuine orbiter, the first to be flown in space. A handful of people were sheltering from the Florida sun in the shade of her wing; others were desultorily queuing on a ramp to get on board. *Columbia*'s main engines had been replaced by plastic mock-ups, and her landing gear was fixed in concrete. *Columbia* was forever trapped on Earth, he thought.

He found Brind standing before the astronaut memorial. This was a big slab of polished granite, with names of dead astronauts etched into it. It rotated to follow the sun, so that the names glowed bright against a backdrop of sky.

'At least it's sunny,' he said. 'Damn thing doesn't work when it's cloudy.'

'No.' The granite surface, towering over them, was mostly empty. The space program had shut down leaving plenty of room for more names.

Sally Brind was short, thin, intense, with spiky, prematurely grey hair; she was no older than forty. She affected small round black glasses, which looked like turn-of-the-century antiques. She seemed bright, alert, engaged. Interested, he thought, encouraged.

He smiled at her. 'You got any answers for me?'

She handed him a folder; he leafed through it.

'Actually it was a lot of fun, Malenfant.'

'I'll bet. Gave you something real to do.'

'For the first time in too long. First we looked at a continuous nuclear fusion drive. Specific impulse in the millions of seconds. But we can't sustain a fusion reaction for long enough. Not even the Japanese have managed that yet.'

'All right. What else?'

'Maybe photon propulsion. The speed of light – the ultimate exhaust velocity, right? But the power plant weight and energy you'd need to get a practical thrust are staggering. Next we thought about a Bussard ramjet. But it's beyond us. You're looking at an electromagnetic scoop that would have to be a hundred kilometres across –'

'Cut to the chase, Sally,' he said gently.

She paused for effect, like a kid doing a magic trick. Then she said: 'Nuclear pulse propulsion. We think that's the answer, Malenfant. A series of micro-explosions – fusion of deuterium and helium-3 probably – set off behind a pusher plate.'

He nodded. 'I've heard of this. Project Orion, back in the 1960s. Like putting a firecracker under a tin can.'

She shaded her eyes from the sun's glare. 'Well, they proved the concept, back then. The Air Force actually ran a couple of test flights, in 1959 and 1960, with conventional explosives. And it's got the great advantage that we could put it together quickly.'

'Let's do it.'

'Of course we'd need access to helium-3.'

'NASDA will supply that. I have some contacts . . . Maybe we should look at assembly in lunar orbit. How are you going to keep me alive?'

She smiled. 'The ISS is still up there. I figure we can cannibalize a module for you. Have you decided what you want to call your ship?'

'The *Commodore Perry*,' he said without hesitation.

'Uh huh. Who – ?'

'Perry was the guy who, in 1853, took the US Navy to Japan and demanded they open up to international trade. Appropriate given the nature of my mission, don't you think?'

'It's your ship.' She glanced about. 'Anyhow, what are you doing out here?'

He nodded at the Shuttle exhibit. 'They've got my old EMU in there, on display. I'm negotiating to get it back.'

'EMU?'

'My EVA Mobility Unit. My old pressure suit.' He patted his gut, which was trim. 'I figure I can still get inside it. I can't live with those modern Jap designs full of pond scum. And I want a manoeuvring unit . . .'

She was looking at him oddly, as if still unable to believe he was serious.

'Not ours,' whispered Xenia. 'Nothing to do with *Bruno*.'

Suddenly Maura found it difficult to breathe. This is it, she thought. This unprepossessing blanket: the first indubitably alien artefact, here in our solar system. Who put the blanket there? What was its purpose? Why was it so crudely buried?

A robot arm reached forward from the probe, laden with sensors and a sample-grabbing claw. She wished that was her hand, that she could reach out too, and stroke that shining, unfamiliar material.

But the claw was driven by science, not curiosity; it passed over the blanket itself and dug a shallow groove into the regolith that lay over it, sampling the material.

Within a few minutes the results of the probe's analysis were coming in, and she could hear the speculation begin in Bootstrap's back rooms.

'These are fines, and they are ilmenite-rich. About forty per cent, compared to twenty per cent in the raw regolith.' 'And the agglutinate has been crushed.' 'It's as if it has been beneficiated. It's just what we'd do.' 'Not like *this*. So energy-intensive . . .'

She understood some of this. Ilmenite was a mineral – a compound of iron, titanium, and oxygen – that was common in long-exposed regolith on airless bodies like the Moon and the asteroids. Its importance was that it was a key source of volatiles: light and exotic compounds implanted there over billions of years by the solar wind, the thin, endless stream of particles that fled from the sun. But ilmenite was difficult to concentrate, extract and process; the best mining techniques the lunar Japanese had thought up were energy-intensive and relied on a lot of heavy-duty, unreliable equipment.

'I knew it!' somebody cried. 'There's no helium-3 in the processed stuff! None at all!' 'None to the limits of the sensors, you mean.' 'Sure, but –' 'You mean they're processing the asteroids for helium-3? Is that *all*?'

Maura felt oddly disappointed. If the Gaijin were after helium-3, did that mean they used fusion processes similar to – perhaps no more advanced than – those already known to humans? And if so, they can't be so smart – can they?

In her ears, the speculation raged on.

'. . . I mean, how dumb can these guys be? Helium-3 is *scarce* in asteroid regolith because you're so far from the sun, which implants it. The Moon is a *lot* richer. If they came in a couple of astronomical units –' 'They could just buy all they want from the Japanese.'

Laughter.

'But maybe they can't come in any closer. Maybe they need, I don't know, the cold and the dark.' 'Maybe they are scared of *us*. You thought about that?'

'They aren't so dumb. You see any rock-crushers and solar furnaces here? That's what *we'd* have to use to get as efficient an extraction process. Think about that blanket, man. It *has* to be nanotech.'

She understood what that meant too: there was no brute force here, no great ugly machines for grinding and crushing and baking as humans might have deployed, nothing but a simple and subtle reworking of the regolith at a molecular, or even atomic, level.

'That blanket must be digging its way into the asteroid grain by grain, picking out the ilmenite and bleeding the helium-3. Incredible.' 'Hey, you're right. Maybe it's extending itself as it goes. The ragged edge –' 'It might eat its way right through that damn asteroid.' 'Or else wrap the whole thing up like a Thanksgiving turkey . . .' 'We got to get a sample.' '*Bruno* knows that . . .'

Nanotechnology: something, at last, beyond the human. Something *other*. She shivered.

But now there was something new, at the corner of her vision, something that shouldered its way over the horizon. It was glittering, very bright against the dark sky. Huge.

It was as if a second sun had risen above the grimy shoulder of Ellis. But this was no sun.

The prattling, remote voices fell silent.

It was perhaps a kilometre long, and wrought in silver. There was a bulky main section, a smoothly curved cylinder, with a mess of silvery ropes trailing behind. Dodecahedral forms – perhaps two or three metres across, silvered and anonymous – clung to the tentacles. There were hundreds of them, Maura saw. Thousands. Like insects, beetles.

A ship. Suddenly she remembered why they were here: not to inspect samples of regolith, not to pick at cute nanotechnological toys. They were here to make contact.

And this was it. She imagined history's view swivelling, legions of scholars in the halls of an unknown future inspecting this key moment in human destiny.

She found she had to force herself to take a breath.

The ship was immense, panning out of her view, cutting the sky in half. Its lower rim brushed the asteroid's surface, and plasma sparkled.

The Bootstrap voices in her ear buzzed. 'My God, it's beautiful.' 'It looks like a flower.' 'It must be a Bussard ramjet. That's an electromagnetic scoop –' 'It's so beautiful, a flower-ship . . .' 'Yeah. But you couldn't travel between the stars in a piece of junk like that!'

Now those shining beetles drifted away from the ropes. They skimmed across space towards the *Bruno*. Were these dodecahedra individual Gaijin? What was their intention?

Silver ropes descended like a net across her point of view now, tangling up the *Bruno*, until the view was criss-crossed with silver threads. The threads seemed to tauten. To cries of alarm from the insect voices at Bootstrap's mission control, the probe was hauled backwards, and its gentle grip on the asteroid was loosened, tethers and pitons flying free in a slow flurry of sparkling dust.

The brief glimpse of the Gaijin ship was lost. Stars and diamond-sharp sun wheeled, occluded by dust specks and silver ropes.

Maura felt her heart beat fast, as if she was herself in danger. She longed for the *Bruno* to burst free of its restraints and flee from these grasping Gaijin, running all the way back to Earth. But that was impossible. In fact, she knew, the *Bruno* was designed to be captured, even dissected; it contained cultural artefacts, samples of technology, attempts to communicate based on simple diagrams and prime number codes. *Hello. We are your new neighbours. Come over for a drink, let's get to know each other . . .*

But this did not feel like a welcoming embrace, a contact of equals. It felt like capture. Maura made a stern effort to sit still, not to struggle against silver ropes that were hundreds of millions of kilometres away.

Chapter 5

SADDLE POINT

The *Commodore Perry* was assembled in lunar orbit.

The fuel pellets were constructed at Edo, on the Moon, by Nishizaki Heavy Industries, and hauled up to orbit by a fleet of tugs. Major components like the pusher plate and the fuel magazine frame were manufactured on Earth, by Boeing. The components were lifted off Earth by European and Japanese boosters, Ariane 12s and H-VIIIs.

After decades in orbit the old International Space Station module had a scuffed, lived-in look. When the salvage crew had moved in the air had been foul and the walls covered with a scummy algae, and it had taken a lot of renovation to render it habitable again.

The various components of the *Perry* were plastered with sponsors' logos. That didn't matter a damn to Malenfant; he knew most of his paintwork would be scoured off in a few months anyhow. But he made sure that the Stars and Stripes was large, and visible.

Malenfant prepared himself for the trip.

In her cramped office at JSC, Brind challenged him, one last time. She felt, obscurely, that it was her duty.

'Malenfant, this is ridiculous. We know a lot more about the Gaijin now. We have the results returned by the probe –'

'The *Bruno*.'

'Yes. The glimpses of the beautiful flower-ship. Fascinating.'

'But that was two years ago,' Malenfant growled. 'Two years! The Gaijin still won't respond to our signals. And we aren't even going back. The government shut down Frank Paulis's operation after that one shot. National security, international protocols . . .'

She shrugged.

'Exactly,' he snapped. 'You shrug. People have lost interest. We've got the attention span of mayflies. Just because the Gaijin haven't come storming into the inner system in flying saucers –'

'Don't you think that's a good point? The Gaijin aren't doing us any harm. We're over the shock of learning that we aren't alone. What's the big deal? We can deal with them in the future, when we're ready. When *they* are ready.'

'No. Colonizing the solar system is going to take centuries, minimum. The Gaijin are playing a long game. And we have to get into the game before it's too late. Before we're cut out, forever.'

'What do you think their ultimate intentions are?'

'I don't know. Maybe they want to dismantle the rocky planets. Maybe take apart the sun. What would you do?'

Oddly, in her mundane, cluttered office, her security badge dangling at her neck, she found herself shivering.

The *Perry* looped through an elliptical two-hour orbit around the Moon. On the lunar surface, the lights of the spreading Japanese colonies and helium-3 mines glittered.

The completed ship was a stack of components fifty metres long. At its base was a massive, reinforced pusher plate, mounted on a shock-absorbing mechanism of springs and crushable aluminium posts. The main body of the craft was a cluster of fuel magazines. Big superconducting hoops encircled the whole stack.

Now pellets of helium-3 and deuterium were fired out of the back of the craft, behind the pusher plate. They formed a target the size of a full stop. A bank of carbon dioxide lasers fired converging beams at the target.

There was a fusion pulse, lasting two hundred and fifty nanoseconds. And then another, and another.

Three hundred micro-explosions each second hurled energy against the pusher plate. Slowly, ponderously, the craft was driven forward.

From Earth, the new Moon was made brilliant by fusion fire.

The acceleration of the craft was low, just a few per cent of G. But it was able to sustain that thrust for a long time – years, in fact – and once the *Perry* had escaped lunar orbit, its velocity mounted inexorably.

Within, Reid Malenfant settled down to the routines of long-duration spaceflight.

His hab module was a shoebox, big enough for him to stand up straight. He drenched it with light from metal halide lamps, hot white light like sunlight, to keep the blues away. The walls were racks which held recovery units, designed for easy replacement. There were wires and cables and ducts, running along the corners of the hab module and across the walls. A robot spider called Charlotte ran along the wires, cleaning and sucking dust out of the air. Despite his best efforts, the whole place was soon messy and cluttered, like an overused utility room. Gear was scattered everywhere, stuck to the floor and walls and ceiling with straps and Velcro. If he brushed against a wall he could cause an eruption of gear, of pens and softscreens and clipboards and data discs and equipment components, and food cans and toothpaste and socks.

Much of the key equipment was of Russian design – the recycling systems, for instance. He had big generators called Elektrons which could produce oxygen from water distilled from his urine. Drinking water was recovered from humidity in the air. There was a system of scrubbers called Vozdukh that removed carbon dioxide from the air. He had a backup oxygen generator system based on the use of 'candles', big cylinders containing a chemical called lithium perchlorate which, when heated, gave off oxygen. He had emergency oxygen masks that worked on the same principle. And so on.

It was all crude and clunky, but – unlike the fancier systems American engineers had developed for the Space Station – it had been proven, over decades, actually to work in space, and to be capable of being repaired when it broke down. Still, Malenfant had brought along two of most things, and an extensive tool kit.

Malenfant's first task, every day, was to swab down the walls of his hab module with disinfected wipes. In zero gravity micro-organisms tended to flourish, surviving on free-floating water droplets in the air. It took long, dull hours.

When he was done with his swabbing, it was exercise time. Malenfant pounded at a treadmill bolted to a bracket in the middle of the habitation module. After an hour Malenfant would find pools of sweat clinging to his chest. Malenfant had to put in at least two hours of hard physical exercise every day.

On it went. *Boring a hole in the sky,* the old astronauts had called it, the dogged cosmonauts on *Salyut* and *Mir*. *Looking at stars, pissing in jars.* To hell with that. At least he was going someplace, unlike those guys.

He communicated with his controllers on Earth and Moon using a ten-watt optical laser, which gave him a data rate of twenty kilobits a second. He followed the newscasts that were sent up to him, which he picked up with his big, semi-transparent main antenna.

As the months wore on, interest in his mission faded. Something else he'd expected. Nobody followed his progress but a few Gaijin obsessives – including Nemoto, he hoped, who had, deploying her shadowy, vast resources, helped assemble the funding for this one-shot mission – not that she ever made her interest known.

Sometimes, even during his routine comms passes, there was nobody to man the other end of the link.

He didn't care. After all they couldn't call him back, however bored they were.

While he worked his treadmill, his only distraction was a small round observation port, set in the pressure hull near him, and so he stared into that. To Malenfant's naked eye, the *Perry* was alone in space. Earth and Moon were reduced to star-like points of light. Only the diminishing sun still showed a disc.

The sense of isolation was extraordinary. Exhilarating.

He had a sleeping nook called a *kayutka*, a Russian word. It contained a sleeping bag strapped to the wall. When he slept he kept the *kayutka* curtained off, for an illusory sense of privacy and safety. He kept his most personal gear here, particularly a small animated image of Emma, a few seconds of her laughing on a private NASA beach close to the Cape.

He woke up to a smell of sweat, or sometimes antifreeze if the coolant pipes were leaking, or sometimes just mustiness – like a library, or a wine cellar.

Brind had tried another tack. 'You're seventy-two years old, Malenfant.'

'Yeah, but seventy-two isn't so exceptional nowadays. And I'm a damn fit seventy-two.'

'It's pretty old to be enduring a many-year spaceflight.'

'Maybe. But I've been following lifespan-extending practices for decades. I eat a low fat, low calorie diet. I'm being treated with a protein called co-enzyme Q10, which inhibits ageing at the cellular level. I'm taking other enzymes to maintain the functionality of my nervous system. I've already had many of my bones and joints rebuilt with biocomposite enhancements. Before the mission I'm going to have extensive heart bypass surgery. I'm taking drugs targeted at preventing the build-up of deposits of amyloid fibrils, proteins which could cause Alzheimer's –'

'Jesus, Malenfant. You're a kind of grey cyborg, aren't you? You're really determined.'

'Look, microgravity is actually a pretty forgiving environment for an old man.'

'Until you want to return to a full Earth gravity.'

'Well, maybe I don't.'

After two hundred and sixty days, half-way into the mission, the fusion-pulse engine shut down. The tiny acceleration faded, and Malenfant's residual sense of up and down disappeared. Oddly, he felt queasy; a new bout of space adaptation syndrome floored him for four hours.

Meanwhile, the *Perry* fired its nitrogen tet and hydrazine reaction control thrusters, and turned head over heels. It was time to begin the long deceleration to the solar focus.

The *Perry*, at peak velocity now, was travelling at around seven million metres per second. That amounted to two per cent of the speed of light. At such speeds, the big superconducting hoops came into their own. They set up a plasma shield forward of the craft, which sheltered it from the thin interstellar hydrogen it ran into. This turnaround manoeuvre was actually the most dangerous part of the trajectory, when the plasma field needed some smart handling to keep it facing ahead at all times.

The *Perry* was by far the fastest man-made object ever launched, and so – Malenfant figured, logically – he had become the fastest human. Not that anyone back home gave a damn.

That suited him. It clarified the mind.

Beyond the windows now there was only blackness, between Malenfant and the stars. At five hundred astronomical units from the sun, he was far beyond the last of the planets; even Pluto reached only some forty astronomical units. His only companions out here were the enigmatic ice moons of the Kuiper Belt, fragments of rock and ice left undisturbed since the birth of the sun, each of them surrounded by an emptiness wider than all the inner solar system. Further beyond lay the Oort cloud, the shadowy shell of deep space comets; but the Oort's inner border, at some thirty thousand astronomical units, was beyond even the reach of this attenuated mission.

When the turnaround manoeuvre was done, he turned his big telescopes and instrument platforms forward, looking ahead to the solar focus.

'You must want to come home. You must have family.'

'No.'

'And now –'

'Look, Sally, all we've done since finding the Gaijin is talk, for twelve years. Somebody ought to *do* something. Who better than me?

And so I'm going to the edge of the system, where I expect to encounter Gaijin.' He grinned. 'I figure I'll cross all subsequent bridges when I come to them.'

'Godspeed, Malenfant,' she said, chilled. She sensed she would never see him again.

The *Perry* slowed to a relative halt. From a thousand AU, the sun was an overbright star in the constellation Cetus, and the inner system – planets, humans, Gaijin and all – was just a puddle of light.

Malenfant, cooped up in his hab module, spent a week scanning his environment. He knew he was in the right area, roughly; the precision was uncertain. Of course, if some huge interstellar mother craft was out here, it should be hard to miss.

There wasn't a damn thing.

He went in search of Alpha Centauri's solar focus. He nudged the *Perry* forward, using his reaction thrusters and occasional fusion-pulse blips.

The focusing of gravitational lensing was surprisingly tight. Alpha Centauri's focal point spot was only a few kilometres across, in comparison with the hundred *billion* kilometres Malenfant had crossed to get here.

He took his time, shepherding his fuel.

At last he had it. In his big optical telescope there was an image of Alpha Centauri A, the largest component of the multiple Alpha system. The star's image was distorted into an annulus, a faintly orange ring of light.

He recorded as much data as he could and fired it down his laser link to Earth. The processors there would be able to deconvolve the image and turn it into an image of the multiple-star Alpha Centauri system, perhaps even of any planets hugging the two main stars.

This data alone, he thought, ought to justify the mission to its sponsors.

But he still didn't turn up any evidence of Gaijin activity.

A new fear started to gnaw at him. For the first time he considered seriously the possibility that he might be wrong about this. What if there was nothing here, after all? If so, his life, his reputation, would be wasted.

And then his big supercooled infrared sensors picked up a powerful new signature.

The object passed within a million kilometres of him.

His telescopes returned images, tantalizingly blurred. The thing was tumbling, sending back glimmering reflections from the remote sun; the reflections helped the processors figure out its shape.

The craft was maybe fifty metres across. It was shaped something like a spider. A dodecahedral central unit sprouted arms, eight or ten of them, which articulated as it moved. It seemed to be assembling itself as it travelled.

It wasn't possible to identify its purpose, or composition, or propulsion method, before it passed out of sight. But, he was prepared to bet, it was heading for the asteroid belt.

It was possible to work out where the drone had come from. It was a point along the sun's focal line, further out, no more distant from the *Perry* than the Moon from Earth.

Malenfant turned his telescopes that way, but he couldn't see a thing.

Still, he felt affirmed. Contact, by damn. I was right. I can't figure out how or what, but there sure is something out here.

He powered up his fusion-pulse engine, one more time. It would take him twenty hours to get there.

It was just a hoop, some kind of metal perhaps, facing the sun. It was around thirty metres across, and it was sky blue, the colour dazzling out here in the void. It was silent, not transmitting on any frequency, barely visible at all in the light of the point-source sun.

There was no huge mother-ship emitting asteroid-factory drones. Just this enigmatic artefact.

He described all this to Sally Brind, back in Houston. He would have to wait for a reply; he was six light-days from home.

After a time, he decided he didn't want to wait that long.

The *Perry* drifted beside the Gaijin hoop, with only occasional station-keeping bursts of its thrusters.

Malenfant shut himself up inside the *Perry*'s cramped airlock. He'd have to spend two hours in here, purging the nitrogen from his body. His antique Shuttle-class EVA Mobility Unit would contain oxygen only, at just a quarter of sea level pressure, to keep it flexible.

Malenfant pulled on his thermal underwear, and then his Cooling and Ventilation Garment, a corrugated layering of water coolant pipes. He fitted his urine collection device, a huge, unlikely condom.

He lifted up his Lower Torso Assembly; this was the bottom half of his EMU, trousers with boots built on, and he squirmed into it. He fitted a tube over his condom attachment; there was a bag sewn into his Lower Torso Assembly garment big enough to store a couple of pints of urine. The LTA unit was heavy, the layered material awkward and stiff. Maybe I'm not quite the same shape as I used to be, forty years ago.

Now it was time for the HUT, the Hard Upper Torso piece. His HUT was fixed to the wall of the airlock, like the top half of a suit of armour. He crouched underneath, reached up his arms, and wriggled upwards. Inside the HUT there was a smell of plastic and metal. He guided the metal rings at his waist to mate and click together. He fixed on his Snoopy flight helmet, and over the top of that he lifted his hard helmet with its visor, and twisted it into place against the seal at his neck.

The ritual of suit assembly was familiar, comforting. As if he was in control of the situation.

He studied himself in the mirror. The EMU was gleaming white, with the Stars and Stripes still proudly emblazoned on his sleeve. He still had his final mission patch stitched to the fabric, for STS-194. Looking pretty good for an old bastard, Malenfant.

Just before he depressurized, he tucked his snap of Emma into an inside pocket.

He opened the airlock's outer hatch.

For twenty months he'd been confined within a chamber a few metres across; now his world opened out to infinity.

He didn't want to look up, down or around, and certainly not at the Gaijin artefact. Not yet.

Resolutely he turned to face the *Perry*. The paintwork and finishing over the hull's powder-grey meteorite blanket had pretty much worn away and yellowed; but the dim sunlight made it look as if the whole craft had been dipped in gold.

His MMU, the Manned Manoeuvring Unit, was stowed in a service station against the *Perry*'s outer hull, under a layer of meteorite fabric. He uncovered the MMU and backed into it; it was like fitting himself into the back and arms of a chair. Latches clasped his pressure suit. He powered up the control systems, and checked the nitrogen-filled fuel tanks in the backpack. He pulled his two hand controllers round to their flight positions, and released the service station's captive latches.

He tried out the manoeuvring unit. The left hand controller pushed him forward, gently; the right hand enabled him to rotate, dip and roll. Every time a thruster fired a gentle tone sounded in his headset.

He moved in short straight lines around the *Perry*. After years in a glass case at KSC, not all of the pack's reaction control thrusters were working. But there seemed to be enough left for him to control his flight. And the automatic gyro stabilization was locked in.

It was just like working around Shuttle, if he focused on his immediate environment. But the light was odd. He missed the huge, comforting presence of the Earth; from low Earth orbit, the daylit planet was a constant overwhelming presence, as bright as a tropical sky. Here there was only the sun, a remote point source that cast long, sharp shadows; and all around he could see the stars, the immensity which surrounded him.

Now, suddenly – and for the first time in the whole damn mission – fear flooded him. Adrenaline pumped into his system, making him feel fluttery as a bird, and his poor old heart started to pound.

Time to get with it, Malenfant.

Resolutely, he worked his right hand controller, and he turned to face the Gaijin artefact.

The artefact was a blank circle, mysterious, framing only stars. He could see nothing that he hadn't seen through the *Perry*'s cameras, truthfully; it was just a ring of some shining blue material, its faces polished and barely visible in the wan light of the sun.

But that interior looked jet black, not reflecting a single photon cast by his helmet lamp.

He glared into the disc of darkness. What are you for? Why are you here?

There was, of course, no reply.

First things first. Let's do a little science here.

He pulsed his thrusters and drifted towards the hoop itself. It was electric blue, glowing as if from within, a wafer-thin band the width of his palm. He could see no seams, no granularity.

He reached out a gloved hand, fabric encasing monkey fingers, and tried to touch the hoop. Something invisible made his hand slide away, sideways.

No matter how hard he pushed, how he braced himself with the thrusters, he could get his glove no closer than a millimetre or so from the material. And always that insidious, soapy feeling of being pushed sideways.

He tried running his hand up and down, along the hoop. There were – ripples, invisible but tangible.

He drifted back to the centre of the hoop. That sheet of silent darkness faced him, challenging. He cast a shadow on the structure from the distant pinpoint sun. But where the light struck the hoop's dark interior, it returned nothing: not a highlight, not a speckle of reflection.

Malenfant rummaged in a sleeve pocket with stiff gloved fingers. He held up his hand to see what he had retrieved. It was his Swiss Army knife. He threw the knife, underarm, into the hoop.

The knife sailed away in a straight line.

When it reached the black sheet it dimmed, and it seemed to Malenfant that it became reddish, as if illuminated by a light that was burning out.

The knife disappeared.

Awkwardly, pulsing his thrusters, he worked his way around the artefact. The MMU was designed to move him in a straight line, not a tight curve; it took some time.

On the far side of the artefact, there was no sign of the knife.

A gateway, then. A gateway, here at the rim of the solar system. How appropriate, he thought. How iconic.

Time to make a leap of faith, Malenfant. He fired his RCS, and began to glide forward.

The gate grew, in his vision, until it was all around him. He was going to pass through it – if he kept going – somewhere near the centre.

He looked back at the *Perry*. Its huge, misty main antenna was pointed back towards Earth, catching the light of the sun like spiderweb. He could see instrument pallets held away from the hab module's yellowed, cloth-clad bulk, like rear-view mirrors. The pallets were arrays of lenses, their black gazes uniformly fixed on him.

Just one press of his controller and he could stop right here, go back.

He reached the centre of the disc. An electric blue light bathed him. He leaned forward inside his stiff HUT unit, so he could look up.

The artefact had come to life. The electric blue light was glowing from the substance of the circle itself. He could see speckles in the light. Coherent, then. And when he looked down at his suit, he saw how the white fabric was criss-crossed by the passage of dozens of points of electric blue glow.

Lasers. Was he being scanned?

He said, 'This changes everything.'

The blue light increased in intensity, until it blinded him. There was a single instant of pain –

Chapter 6

TRANSMISSION

'We think a Gaijin flower-ship is a variant of the old Bussard ramjet design,' Sally Brind said. She had spread a fold-up softscreen over one time-smoothed wall of Nemoto's lunar cave. Now – Maura squinted to see – the 'screen filled up with antique design concepts: line images of gauzy, unlikely craft, obsessively labelled with captions and arrows. 'It is a notion that goes back to the 1960s . . .'

Nemoto's home – here on the Japanese Moon, deep in Farside – had turned out to be a crude, outmoded subsurface shack close to the infrared observatory where she'd made her first discovery of Gaijin activity in the belt. Here, it seemed, Nemoto had lived for the best part of two decades. Maura thought *she* couldn't stand it for more than a couple of hours.

There wasn't even anywhere to sit, aside from Nemoto's low pallet, Maura had immediately noticed, and both Sally and Maura had carefully avoided *that*. Fortunately the Moon's low gravity made the bare rock floor relatively forgiving, even for the thin flesh that now stretched over Maura's fragile bones. There were some concessions to humanity – an ancient and worn scrap of *tatami*, a *tokonoma* alcove containing a *jinja*, a small, lightweight Shinto shrine. But most of the floor and wall space, even here in Nemoto's living area, was taken up with science equipment: anonymous white boxes that might have been power sources or sensors or sample boxes, cables draped over the floor, a couple of small, old-fashioned softscreens.

As Sally spoke, Nemoto – thin, gaunt, eyes invisible within dark hollows – pottered about her own projects. Walking with tiny, cautious steps, she minutely adjusted her equipment – or, bizarrely, watered the small plants that flourished on brackets on the walls, bathed by light from bright halide lamps.

Still, the languid flow of the water from Nemoto's can – great fat droplets oscillating as they descended towards the tiny green leaves – was oddly soothing.

Sally continued her analysis of the Gaijin's putative technology. 'The ramjet was always seen as one way to meet the challenge of interstellar journeys. The enormous distances even to the nearest stars would require an immense amount of fuel. With a ramjet, you don't need to carry any fuel at all.

'Space, you see, isn't empty. Even between the stars there are tenuous clouds of gas, mostly hydrogen. Bussard, the concept originator, proposed drawing in this gas, concentrating it, and pushing it into a fusion reaction – just as hydrogen is burned into helium at the heart of the sun.

'The trouble is, those gas clouds are *so* thin your inlet scoop has to be gigantic. So Bussard suggested using magnetic fields to pull in gas from an immense volume, hundreds of thousands of kilometres around.'

She brought up another picture: an imaginary starship startlingly like a marine creature – a squid, perhaps, Maura thought – a cylindrical body with giant outreaching magnetic arms, preceded by darting shafts of light.

'The interstellar gas would first have to be electrically charged, to be deflected by the magnetic scoops. So you would pepper it with laser beams, as you see here, to heat it to a plasma, as hot as the surface of the sun. It's an exotic, difficult concept, but it's still easier than hauling along all your fuel.'

'Except,' Nemoto murmured, labouring at her gadgets, 'that it could never work.'

'Correct . . .'

Maura had been privy to similar breakdowns and extrapolations emanating from the Department of Defense and the US Air & Space Force, and – given that Sally's summary was based on no more than piecework by various space buff special-interest groups and NASA refugees in various corners of the Department of Agriculture – Maura thought it hung together pretty well.

The problem with Bussard's design was that only a hundredth of all that incoming gas could actually be used as fuel. The rest would pile up before the accelerating craft, clogging its magnetic intakes; Bussard's beautiful ship would expend so much energy pushing through this logjam it could never achieve the kind of speeds essential for interstellar flight.

Sally presented various developments of the basic proposal to get around this fundamental limitation. The most promising was called RAIR – pronounced 'rare' – for Ram-Augmented Interstellar Rocket. Here, the intake of interstellar hydrogen would be greatly reduced, and used only to top up a store of hydrogen fuel the starship was already carrying. It was thought that the RAIR design could perform two or three times better than the Bussard system, and achieve perhaps ten or twenty per cent of the speed of light.

'And, as far as we can tell from the *Bruno* data,' said Sally, 'that Gaijin flower-ship was pretty much a RAIR design: exotic-looking, but nothing we can't comprehend. *Bruno* actually passed through what seemed to be a stream of exhaust, before it ceased to broadcast.' A nice euphemism, thought Maura, for *trapped and dismantled.* 'The exhaust was typical of products of a straightforward deuterium–helium-3 fusion reaction, of the type we've been able to achieve on Earth for some decades.'

Sally hesitated. She was a small woman, neat, earnest, troubled. 'There are puzzles here. *We* can think of a dozen ways the Gaijin design could be improved – nothing that's in our engineering grasp right now, but certainly nothing that's beyond our physics. For instance the deuterium–helium fusion reaction is about as low-energy and clunky as you can get. There are *much* more productive alternatives, like reactions involving boron or lithium. I think I always imagined that when Eetie finally showed up, she would have technology beyond our wildest dreams – beyond our imagining. Well, the flower-ships are pretty, but they aren't the way *we'd* choose to travel to the stars –'

'Especially not in this region,' Nemoto said evenly.

Maura said, 'What do you mean?'

Nemoto smiled thinly, the bones of her face showing through papery skin. 'Now that we are, like it or not, part of an interstellar community, it pays to understand the geography of our new terrain. The interstellar medium, the gases that would power a ramjet, is not uniform. The sun happens not to be in a very, umm, cloudy corner of the Orion Spiral Arm. We are moving, in fact, through what is called the ICM – the intercloud medium. Not a good resource for a ramjet. But of course the flower-ships are not interstellar craft.' She eyed Maura. 'You seem surprised. Isn't that obvious? These ships, with their small fraction of lightspeed, would take many decades even to reach Alpha Centauri.'

Maura said, 'But time dilation – clocks slowing down as you speed up –'

Nemoto shook her head. 'Ten per cent of lightspeed is much too slow for such effects to become significant. The flower-ships are interplanetary cruisers, designed for travel at speeds well below that of light, within the relatively dense medium close to a star. The Gaijin are interplanetary voyagers; only accidentally did they become interstellar pioneers.'

'Then,' asked Maura reasonably, 'how did they get here?'

Nemoto smiled. 'The same way Malenfant has departed the system.'

'Just tell me.'

'Teleportation.'

Maura had brought Sally Brind here because she'd grown frustrated, even worried, by the passage of a full year since Malenfant's disappearance: a year in which nothing had happened.

Nothing obvious had changed about the Gaijin's behaviour. The whole thing had long vanished from the mental maps of most of the public and commentators, who had dismissed Malenfant's remarkable jaunt as just another odd subplot in a slow, rather dull saga that already spanned decades. The philosophers continued to debate and agonize over the meaning of the reality of the Gaijin for human existence. The military were, as always, wargaming their way through various lurid scenarios, mostly involving the Gaijin invasion of Earth and Moon, huge armed flower-ships hurling lumps of asteroid rock at the helpless worlds.

Meanwhile, the various governments and other responsible authorities were consumed by indecision.

Truthfully, the facts were still too sparse, questions still proliferating faster than answers were being obtained, mankind's image of these alien intruders still informed more by old fictional images than any hard science. The picture was not converging, Maura realized with dismay, and history was drifting away from meaningful engagement with the Gaijin.

Which was why she had set up this meeting. Nemoto had, after all, been the first to detect the Gaijin – she had quickly understood the implications of her discovery – and she had immediately selected the one person, Reid Malenfant, who had, in retrospect, been best placed to help articulate her discovery to the world, and even to do something about it.

If anybody could help Maura think through the jungle of possibilities of the future, it was surely Nemoto.

But still – teleportation?

* * *

Maura closed her eyes. So I have to imagine these Gaijin e-mailing themselves from star to star. She suppressed a foolish laugh.

Nemoto continued to tinker with her apparatus, her plants.

Sally Brind said slowly, 'Let's be clear. You think the hoop Malenfant found was some kind of teleportation node. Then why not locate this – gateway – in the asteroid belt? Why place it all the way out on the rim of the system, with all the trouble and effort that causes? . . .'

Nemoto kept her counsel, letting the younger woman think it through.

Sally snapped her fingers. 'But if you teleport from another star you must basically fire a stream of complex information by conventional signal channels – that is, light or radio waves – at the solar system, the target. And the place to pick that up with greatest fidelity is the star's solar focus, where the signal gain is in the hundreds of millions . . . But Malenfant can't have known this. He can't have deduced the mechanism of teleportation.'

'But his intuition is strong,' Nemoto said, smiling. 'He recognized a gateway, and he stepped through it. Contact had been his purpose, after all.'

'I thought,' Maura said doggedly, 'teleportation was impossible. Because you'd need to map the position and velocity of every particle making up the artefact you want to transmit. And that violates the Uncertainty Principle.' The notion that, because of quantum fuzziness, it was impossible to map precisely the position and momentum of a particle. And if you couldn't make such a map, how could you encode, transmit and reconstruct such a complex object as a human being?

'If you did it so crudely as that, yes,' Nemoto said. 'In a quantum universe, no such classical process could possibly work. Even in principle we know only one way to do this, to teleport. An unknown quantum state can be disassembled into, then later reconstructed from, purely classical information and purely non-classical correlations . . .'

Maura said tightly, 'Nemoto, please.'

'*This* is a teleport machine,' Nemoto said, waving her hand at her strung-out junk. 'Sadly I can only teleport one photon, one grain of light, at a time. For the moment.'

'Sally, do you understand any of this?'

'I think so,' Sally said. 'Look, quantum mechanics allows for the long-range correlation of particles. Once two objects have been in contact, they're never truly separated. There is a kind of spooky entanglement, called EPR correlation.'

'EPR?'

'For Einstein–Podolsky–Rosen, the physicists who came up with the notion.'

'I do not transport the photon,' Nemoto said. 'I transmit a *description* of the photon. The quantum description.' She tapped two boxes. 'Transmitter and receiver. These contain a store of EPR-correlated states – that is, they were once in contact, and so are forever entangled, as Sally puts it.

'I allow my photon to, umm, interact with ancillary particles in the receiver. The photon is absorbed, its description destroyed. But the information I extract about the interaction can then be transmitted over to the receiver. There I can use the other half of my entangled pair to reconstruct the original quantum state.'

Sally said, still figuring it out, 'The receiver has to be entangled with the transmitter. What the builders must have done is send over the receiver gate – the hoop Malenfant found – by some conventional means, a slower-than-light craft like a flower-ship. The gate is EPR-correlated with another object back home, a transmitter. The transmitter makes a joint measurement on itself and the unknown quantum system of the object to be teleported. The transmitter then sends the receiver gate the classical result of the measurement. Knowing this, the receiver can convert the state of its EPR twin into an exact replica of the unknown quantum state at the transmitter . . .'

'So now you have two photons,' Maura said slowly to Nemoto. 'The original and the version you've reconstructed.'

'No,' said Nemoto, with strained patience. 'I explained this. The original photon is destroyed when it yields up its information.'

Sally said, 'Maura, quantum information isn't like classical information, the stuff you're used to. Quantum information can be transformed, but not duplicated.' She studied Maura, seeking understanding. 'But, even if we're right about the principle here, there is a lot here that is far beyond us. Think about it. Nemoto can teleport a single photon; the Gaijin gateway can teleport something with the mass of a human being. Malenfant's body contained –'

'Some ten to power twenty-eight atoms,' Nemoto said. 'That is ten billion billion *billion*. And therefore it must take the same number of kilobytes, to order of magnitude, to store the data. If not more.'

'Yes,' Sally said. 'By comparison, Maura, all the books ever written probably amount to a mere thousand billion kilobytes. The data compression involved must be spectacular. If we could get hold of that technology alone, our computing and telecoms industries would be transformed.'

'And there is more,' Nemoto said. 'Malenfant's body was effectively destroyed. That would require the extraction and storage of an energy equivalent of some one thousand megaton bombs . . .'

His body was destroyed. Nemoto said it so casually.

'So,' Sally said slowly, 'the signal that encodes Malenfant is currently being transmitted between a transmitter-receiver link –'

'Or links,' said Nemoto.

'Links?'

'Do you imagine that such a technology would be limited to a single route?'

Sally frowned. 'You're talking about a whole network of gateways.'

'Perhaps placed in the gravitational foci of every star system. Yes.'

And now, all at once, Maura saw it: a teleport network spanning the huge gaps between the stars, grand data highways along which one could travel – and without being aware even of the passing of time. 'My God,' she murmured. 'The roads of empire.'

'And so,' Sally said, working her way through Nemoto's thinking, 'the Gaijin built the gateways. Right?'

'Oh, no,' said Nemoto gently. 'The Gaijin are much too – *primitive*. They were limited to their system, as we are to ours. In their crude ramjet flower-ships, exploring the rim of the system, they stumbled on a gateway – or perhaps they were guided to look there by others, as we have been by the Gaijin in turn.'

Maura said, 'If not the Gaijin, then who?'

'For now, that is unknowable.' Nemoto gazed at her clumsy apparatus, as if studying the possibilities it implied.

Sally Brind got to her feet and moved slowly around the cramped apartment, drifting dreamily in the low lunar gravity. 'It takes years for a signal, even a teleport signal, to travel between the stars. This must mean that nobody out there has developed faster-than-light technology. No warp drives, no wormholes. Kind of low tech, don't you think?'

Nemoto said, 'In such a Galaxy, processes – cultural contacts, conflicts – will take decades, at least, to unfold. If Malenfant is heading to a star, it will take years for his signal to get there, more years before we could ever know what became of him.'

'And so,' Maura said dryly, 'what must we do in the meantime?'

Nemoto smiled, her cheekbones sharp. 'Why, nothing. Only wait. And try not to die.'

* * *

In the silent years that followed, Maura Della often thought of Malenfant.

Where *was* Malenfant?

Even if Nemoto was right, with his body destroyed – as the detailed information about the contents and processes of his body and brain shot towards the stars – *where was his soul*? Did it ride the putative Gaijin laser beam with him? Was it already dispersed?

And would the thing that would be reconstructed from that signal actually *be* Malenfant, or just some subtle copy?

Still, in all this obscure physics there was a distinct human triumph. Malenfant had found this mysterious gateway. And passed through. She remembered the resentment she had felt while watching the Gaijin's calm appropriation of solar system resources in the asteroid belt, their easy taking of the *Bruno*. Now Malenfant had fired himself back through the transport system the Gaijin themselves had used, back to the nest of the Gaijin, and Maura felt a stab of savage satisfaction.

Hey, Gaijin. You have mail . . .

But these issues weren't for Maura.

She had done her best to use Nemoto's insights and other inputs to rouse minds, to shape policy. But the time had come for her to retire, to drive out of the Beltway at last. She went home, to a small town called Blue Lake, in northern Iowa, her old state, the heart of the Midwest.

Her influence was ended. Too damn old.

I don't have decades left; I don't have the strength to stay alive, waiting, like Nemoto, while the universe ponderously unfolds; for me, the story ends here. You'll just have to get along by yourself, Malenfant.

Godspeed, Godspeed.

Chapter 7

RECEPTION

The blue light faded.

He realized he'd been holding his breath. He let it out, gasping; his chest ached. He was grasping the MMU hand controllers compulsively. He flexed his hands; the gloves were stiff.

The blue artefact was all around him, inert once more. He couldn't see any difference; the sun's light glimmered from its polished surface, casting double shadows –

Double?

He looked up, to the sun, and flipped up his gold visor.

The sun seemed a little brighter, a strong yellow-white. And it was a double pinprick now, two jewels on a setting of velvet. The light was actually so bright it hurt his eyes, and when he looked away there were tiny double spots on his retina, bright yellow against red mist.

It wasn't the sun, of course. It was a binary star system. There was a misty lens-shaped disc around the twin stars: a cloud of planetary material, asteroids, comets – a complex inner system, illuminated by double starlight. Even from here, just from that smudge of diffuse light, he could see this was a busy, crowded place.

He worked his controller and swivelled. Beyond the gate, the *Perry* was gone.

No. Not gone. Just parked a few light years away, is all.

He had no idea how the artefact had worked its simple miracle. Nor, frankly, did he care. It was a gateway – and it had worked, and taken him to the stars.

Yes, but where the hell, Malenfant?

He looked around the sky. The stars were a rich carpet, overwhelming the familiar constellations.

After some searching he found Orion's belt, and the rest of that great constellation. The hunter looked unchanged, as far as he could see. Orion's stars were scattered through a volume of space a thousand light years deep, and the nearest of them – Betelgeuse, or maybe Bellatrix, he couldn't recall – was no closer than five hundred light years from the sun.

That told him something. If you moved across interstellar distances your viewpoint would shift so much that the constellation patterns would distort, the lamps scattered through the sky swimming past each other like the lights of an approaching harbour. He couldn't have come far, then, not on the scale of the distances to Orion's giant suns: a handful of light years, no more.

And, given that, he knew where he was. There was only one system like this – two Sol-like stars, bound close together – in the sun's immediate neighbourhood. This was indeed Alpha Centauri, no more remote from Sol than a mere four light years plus change. Just as he had expected.

Alpha Centauri: the dream of centuries, the first port of call beyond Pluto's realm – a name that had resonated through a hundred starship studies, a thousand dreams. And here he was, by God. He felt his mouth stretch wide in a grin of triumph.

He blipped his thrusters and swivelled, searching the sky until he found another constellation, a neat, unmistakable W-shape picked out by five bright stars. It was Cassiopeia, familiar from his boyhood astronomy jags. But now there was an extra star to the left of the pattern, turning the constellation into a crude zigzag. He knew what that new star must be, too.

Suspended in immensity, here at the rim of the Alpha Centauri system, Malenfant looked back at the sun.

The sun is a star – just a star. Giordano Bruno was right after all, he thought.

But if it took light four years to get here, it had surely taken him at least as long, however the portal worked. Suddenly I am four years into the future. And, even if I was to step home now – assuming that was possible – it would be another four years before I could feel the heat of the sun again.

How strange, he thought, and he felt subtly cold.

Movement, just ahead of him. He rotated again.

It was a spider robot, like a scaled-down copy of the one he had seen on the other side of the portal. There was a puff of what looked like reaction control engines, little sprays of crystals that glittered in the remote double light. Crude technology, he thought, making assessments automatically. It was heading towards the gate, its limbs writhing stiffly.

It seemed to spot him.

It stopped dead, in another flurry of crystals, a good distance away, perhaps a kilometre. But distances in space were notoriously hard to estimate, and he had no true idea of the robot's size.

Those articulated limbs were still writhing. Its form was complex, shifting – obviously functional, adaptable to a range of tasks in zero gravity. But overall he saw that the limbs picked out something like a W shape, like the Cassiopeia constellation, centred on a dodecahedral core. He had no idea what it was doing. Perhaps it was studying him. He could barely see it, actually; the device was just an outline in Alpha Centauri light.

Malenfant calculated.

He hadn't expected a reception committee. This was just a workaday gateway, a portal for unmanned robot worker drones. Maybe the Gaijin themselves were off in the warmth of that complex, crowded inner system.

He reckoned he had around five hours life support left. If he went back – assuming the portal was two-way – he might even make it back to the *Perry*.

Or he could stay here.

It would be one hell of a message to send on first contact, though, when the inhabitants of the Centauri system came out to see what was going on, and found nothing but his desiccated corpse.

But you've come a long way for this, Malenfant. And if you stay, dead or alive, they'll sure know we are here.

He grinned. Whatever happened, he had achieved his goal. Not a bad deal for an old bastard.

He worked his left hand controller; with a gentle shove, the MMU thrust him forward, towards the drone.

He took his time. He had five hours to reach the drone. And he needed to keep some fuel for manoeuvring at the close, if he was still conscious to do it.

But the drone kept working its complex limbs, pursuing its incomprehensible tasks. It made no effort to come out to meet him.

And, as it turned out, his consumables ran out a lot more quickly than he had anticipated.

By the time he reached the drone, his oxygen alarm was chiming, softly, continually, inside his helmet. He stayed conscious long enough to reach out a gloved hand, and stroke the drone's metallic hide.

When he woke again, it was as if from a deep and dreamless sleep.

The first thing he was aware of was an arm laid over his face. It was his own, of course. It must have wriggled free of the loose restraints around his sleeping bag.

Except that his hand was contained in a heavy spacesuit glove, which was not the way he was accustomed to sleeping.

And his sleeping bag was light years away.

He snapped fully awake. He was floating in golden light. He was rotating, slowly.

He was still in his EMU – but, Christ, his helmet was gone, the suit compromised. For a couple of seconds he fumbled, flailing, and his heart hammered.

He forced himself to relax. You're still breathing, Malenfant. Wherever you are, there is air here. If it's going to poison you, it would have done it already.

He exhaled, then took a deep lungful – filtered through his nose, with his mouth clamped closed. The air was neutral temperature, transparent. He could smell nothing but a faint sourness, and that probably emanated from himself, the cramped confines of a suit he'd worn for too long.

He was stranded in golden light, beyond which he could make out the stars, slightly dimmed, as if by smoke. There was the dazzling-bright pairing of Alpha Centauri. He hadn't come far, then.

Were there walls around him? He could see no edges, no seams, no corners. He stretched out his feet and gloved fingers. His questing fingers hit a soft membrane. Suddenly the wall snapped into focus, just centimetres from his face: a smooth surface, overlaid by what felt like cables the width of his thumb, but welded somehow to the wall. The cables were a little hard to grip, but he clamped his fingers around them.

Anchored, he felt a lot more comfortable.

The wall itself was soft, neither warm nor cold, smooth beyond the discrimination of his touch. It curved tightly around him. Perhaps he was in some kind of inflated bubble; it could be no more than a few metres across. And it wasn't inflated to maximum tension. When he pushed at the wall it rippled in great languid waves, pulses of golden light that briefly occluded the stars.

He picked at the membrane with one fingernail. It felt like some kind of plastic. He had no reason to believe it was anything more advanced; the Gaijin had not shown themselves to be technological super-beings. He could have easily taken a scraping of this stuff, analysed it with a small portable lab. Except he didn't have a portable lab.

Something bumped against his leg. 'Shit,' he said. He whirled, scrabbling at the embedded ropes, until he was backed up against the wall.

It was the helmet from his Shuttle EMU.

He picked it up and turned it over in his gloved hands. The helmet had a snap-on metal ring, to fit it to the rest of the suit – or rather, it used to. The attachment had been cut, as if by a laser.

The Gaijin – or their robot drones, here on the edge of the Alpha system – had found him in a shell of gases: air that roughly matched what they must have known, from some equivalent of spectrograph studies, of the composition of Earth's atmosphere. So they had provided more of the gases in this containment, and broken open his suit – and then, presumably, hoped for the best.

He took off his gloves. He found he was still wearing his lightweight comms headset. He pulled it off and tucked it inside the helmet. There was no sign of his manoeuvring unit.

. . . And now a kind of after-shock cut in. He rested against the slowly rippling wall, lit up by gold-filtered Centauri light, four light years from home. The robots had been smart, he realized with a shiver. After all the robots, if not the Gaijin themselves, shared nothing like human anatomy. What if they'd decided to see if his whole head was detachable? He felt very old, fragile, and unexpectedly lonely – as he hadn't during the long months of his *Perry* flight to the Saddle Point.

What now?

First things first. You need a bio break, Malenfant.

He forced himself to take a leak into the condom he still wore. He felt the warm piss gather in the sac inside his suit. Piss that had been magically transported across four light years. He probably ought to bottle it; if he ever got back home he could probably sell it, a memento of man's first journey to the stars.

There was movement, a wash of light beyond the bubble wall. Something immense, bright, cruising by silently.

He swivelled, still pinching hold of the embedded ropes, until he faced outwards. He pressed his face against the bubble wall, much as he used to as a kid, staring out of his bedroom window, hoping for snow.

The moving light was a flower-ship.

The Gaijin craft sailed across the darkness, heading for the warm glow at the heart of the Centauri system. The cables and filaments that shaped the maw of its electromagnetic scoops were half-furled, and they waved with slow grace as the ship slowly swivelled on its long axis, perhaps intent on some complex course correction. Dodecahedral shapes swarmed over its flanks, reduced by distance to toy-like specks, fast-moving, intent, purposeful. They almost looked as if they were rebuilding the ship as it travelled – as perhaps they were; Malenfant imagined a flexible geometry, a ship that could adjust its form to the competing needs of the cold stillness here at the rim of this binary system, and the crowded warmth at its heart.

But still, despite its strangeness, he felt a tug at his heart as the flower-ship receded. Don't leave me here, drifting in space.

But he wasn't adrift, he saw now. There were ropes embedded in the outer surface of his shell, ropes which gathered in a loosely plaited tether, as if this bubble of air had been trapped by spider-web. The tether, loosely coiled, led across space – not to the flower-ship – but to something hidden by the curve of the bubble.

He pushed himself across the interior of the bubble to look out the other side.

In the dim light of the distant Alpha suns, he made out only an outline: a rough ball that must have been kilometres across, the glimmer of what looked like frost from crater dimples and low mountains.

From one spacesuit pocket he dug out a fold-up softscreen, unpacked it and plastered it against the wall of the bubble. This 'screen had been designed as a low-light and telescopic viewer. Soon its enhancement routines were cutting in, and it became a window through which he peered, angling his head to change his view.

The object seemed to be a ball of ice. It might have been an asteroid, but he was a long way from those double suns. This was more likely the Alpha equivalent of a Kuiper object, an ice moon – or maybe he was even in this system's Oort cloud, and this was the head of some long-period comet.

And now he made out movement on that icy surface: continual, complex, almost rippling. He tapped at the softscreen, instructing it to magnify and enhance some more.

He saw drone robots, swarming everywhere, their complex limbs working like cockroach legs. The drones moved back and forth in files and streams, endless traffic. Here and there in the flow there were islands of stillness, nodes where the swirl gathered in knots and eddies. And in a few places he saw the gleam of silvery blankets, perhaps like the nano-blankets Frank Paulis's probe had found on that belt asteroid back home. Maybe they were making more flower-ships. Or perhaps these were von Neumann machines, he thought, replicators engaged primarily on making more copies of themselves, and they would continue until every gram of this remote ball of ice and rock had been converted into purposeful machinery.

But everywhere he looked, as he scanned his 'screen, he could see endless, purposeful movement – perhaps millions of drones, the toiling community making up a glinting, robotic sea. His overwhelming impression was of cooperation, of blind, unquestioning, smoothly efficient obedience to a higher communal goal. These robots had more in common with hive insects, he thought, ants or termites, than with humans.

. . . But perhaps I should have expected this, he thought. Humans were competitive. But there was no reason to suppose that everybody else had to be that way. Maybe a competitive technological community could only reach a certain point before it became unstable and destroyed itself. Arms races could only take you so far. Perhaps only the cooperative could survive. In which case, he thought, what we are going to find as we move further out is, inevitably, more of *this*. Termite colonies. And, perhaps, nobody like us.

Damn, he thought. I might be the only true individual in this whole star system. What a bleak and terrifying notion.

But if the robots were replicators they weren't very good ones.

They all seemed to be based on the design of the type he had first met, with that chunky dodecahedral body, limbs sprouting in a variety of configurations, apparently specialized. But otherwise these toiling drones appeared somewhat diverse. The differences weren't great: a few extra limbs here, a touch of asymmetry there, each dodecahedron slightly diverging from the geometric ideal – but they were there.

Perhaps the authentic von Neumann vision – of identical replicators spawning each other – was impossible without true nanotech, a command of materials and manufacturing right down to the atomic level. He imagined a fleet of these limited, imperfect robots being unleashed on the Galaxy, ordered to travel from star to star, to build others of their kind . . . and, with each generation, getting it subtly wrong.

But for there to be such a wide variety of 'mutations' as he saw here, there surely had to have been an awful lot of generations.

Or, he thought, what if these *are* the Gaijin?

He had been assuming that behind these 'mere' machines there had to be something bigger, something smarter, something more complex. Lack of imagination, Malenfant. Anthropomorphic. Deal with what you see, not what you imagine might be waiting for you.

He tired of watching the incomprehensible swarming of the robots, and he turned his enhancement softscreen on Alpha Centauri.

Each of the near-twins looked hauntingly like the sun – but if the brighter star, Alpha A, were set in place of the sun, its companion, Alpha B, would be within the solar system: closer than planet Neptune, in fact.

And there were planets here. The interpretative software built into his softscreen began to trace out orbits – one, two, three of them, tight around bright Alpha A – of small rocky worlds, perhaps twins of Earth or Venus or Mars. A couple of minutes later, similar orbits had been sketched out around the companion, B.

Alpha Centauri wasn't just a twin star; it was a twin solar system. If Earth had been transplanted here the second sun would be a brilliant star. There would be double sunrises, double sunsets, strange eclipses of one star by the other; the sky would be a bright and complex place. And there would have been a whole other planetary system a few light-hours away: so close humans would have been able to complete interstellar journeys maybe as early as the 1970s. He felt an odd ache of possibilities lost, nostalgia for a reality that had never come to be.

The double system contained only one gas giant – and that was small compared to mighty Jupiter, or even Saturn. It was looping, it seemed, on a strange metastable orbit that caused it to fly, on decades-long trajectories, back and forth between the two stars. And as the stars followed their own elliptical orbits around each other, it seemed highly likely that within a few million years the rogue planet would be flung out into the dark, from whence, perhaps, it had come.

If there were few giants, the Alpha sky was full of minor planets, asteroids, comet nuclei. Unlike the orderly lanes of Earth, these asteroid clouds extended right across the space between the stars, and into the surrounding volume. As the 'screen's software began to plot density contours within the glittering asteroid clouds, Malenfant made out knots and bands and figure-of-eight loops, even what looked like spokes radiating from each star's central system: clouds of density marked out by the sweeping paths of flocks of asteroids, shepherded by the competing pulls of the stars and their retinues of planets. From an Earth orbiting Alpha A or B, there would be a line across the sky, marking out the plane of the ecliptic: dazzling, alluring, the sparkle of trillions of asteroids, the promise of unimaginable wealth.

The pattern seemed clear. The mutual influence of A and B had prevented the formation of giant planets. All the volatile material that had been absorbed into Sol's great gas giants had here been left unconsolidated. Malenfant, who had spent half his life arguing for the mining of space resources, felt his fingers itch as he looked at those immense clouds of floating treasures. Here it would have been easy, he thought with some bitterness.

But this was not a place for humanity, and perhaps it never would be. For now the software posted tiny blue flags, all around the rim of the system. These were points of gravitational-lensing focus, Saddle Points, far more of them than in Sol's simple unipolar gravity field. And there was movement within those dusty lanes of light: bright yellow sparks, Gaijin flower-ships, everywhere.

The solar system is impoverished by comparison, he thought. *This* is where the action is in this part of space: Alpha Centauri, riddled with so many Saddle Points it's like Grand Central Station, and with a sky full of flying mines to boot. He felt humbled, embarrassed, like a country cousin come to the big city.

There was a blur of motion, washing across his magnified vision.

He rocked back, peering out of his bubble with naked eyes.

It was a robot, skittering this way and that on its attitude thrusters, crystals of reaction gas sparkling in Alpha light. It came to rest and hovered, limbs splayed, no more than ten metres from the bubble.

Malenfant pushed himself to the wall nearest the robot, pressed his face against the membrane, and stared back.

Its attitude suggested watchfulness. But he was probably anthropomorphizing again.

That dodecahedral core, fat and compact, must have been a couple of metres across. It glistened with panels of complex texture, and there were apertures in the silvery skin within which more machinery gleamed, unrecognizable. The robot had various appendages. A whole forest of them no more than centimetres long bristled from every surface of the core, wiry, almost like a layer of fur. But two of the limbs were longer – ten metres each, perhaps – and articulated like the robot arms carried by the old Space Shuttle, each ending in a knot of machinery. He noticed small attitude thruster nozzles spread along the arms. The whole thing reminded him of one of the old space probes – Voyager, perhaps, or Pioneer – that dense solid core, the flimsy booms, a spacecraft built like a dragonfly.

The robot showed signs of wear and age: crumpled panels on the dodecahedral core; an antenna-like protrusion that was pitted and scarred, as if by micrometeorite rain; one arm that appeared to have been broken and patched by a sheath of newer material. This is an old machine, he thought, and it might have been travelling a long, long time; he wondered how many suns had baked its fragile skin, how many dusty comet trails clouds had worn away at those filmy structures.

Right now the two arms were held upwards, as if in an air of supplication, giving the robot an overall W-shape – like the first robot he'd seen.

Could this be the same machine I met when I came through the hoop? Or, he wondered, am I anthropomorphizing again, longing for individuality where none exists? After all, this thing could never be mistaken for something alive – could it? If nothing else its lack of symmetry – one arm was a good two metres longer than the others – was, on some profound level, deeply disturbing.

He gave in to his sentimentality.

'Cassiopeia,' he said. 'That's what I'll call you.'

Female, Malenfant? But the thing did have a certain delicacy and grace. Cassiopeia, then. He raised a hand and waved.

He half-expected a wave back from those complex robot arms, but they did not move.

. . . But now there was a change. An object that looked for all the world like a telephoto lens came pushing out of an aperture in the front of Cassiopeia's dodecahedral torso, and trained on him.

He wondered if Cassiopeia had just manufactured the system, in response to its – her – perceived need, in some nano factory in her interior. More likely the technology was simpler, and this 'camera' had been assembled from a stock of parts carried within. Maybe Cassiopeia was like a Swiss Army knife, he thought: not infinitely flexible, but with a stock of tools that could be deployed and adapted to a variety of purposes.

And then, once again, he was startled – this time by a noise from within his bubble.

It was a radio screech. It had come from the comms headset tucked inside his helmet.

He grabbed the helmet, pulled out the headset and held one speaker against his ear. The screech was so loud it was painful, and, though he thought he detected traces of structure in the signal, there was nothing resembling human speech.

He glanced out at the robot, Cassiopeia, still patiently holding her station alongside his membrane.

She's trying to communicate, he thought. After years of ignoring the radio and other signals we beamed at her colleagues in the asteroid belt, she's decided I'm interesting enough to talk to.

He grinned. Objective achieved, Malenfant. You made them notice us, at least.

. . . Yes, but right now it wasn't doing him much good. The signal he was being sent might contain whole libraries of interstellar wisdom. But he couldn't decode it; not without banks of supercomputers.

They still have no real idea what they're dealing with here, he thought, how limited I am. Maybe I'm fortunate they didn't try hitting me with signal lasers.

If we're going to talk, it will have to be in English. Maybe they can figure that out; we've been bombarding them with dictionaries and encyclopaedias for long enough. And it will have to be slow enough for me to understand.

He dug in a pocket on the leg of his suit until he found a thick block of paper and a propelling pencil.

Another moment of contact, then: the first words exchanged between human being and alien. Words that would presumably be remembered, if anybody ever found out about this, long after Shakespeare was forgotten.

What should he say? Poetry? A territorial challenge? A speech of welcome?

At last, he grunted, licked the pencil lead, and wrote out two words in blocky capitals. Then he pressed the pad up against the clear membrane.

THANK YOU

With its – her – telescopic eye, Cassiopeia peered at the paper block for long minutes.

From her angular body Cassiopeia extruded a new pseudopod. It carried a small metal block the size and shape of his note pad.

The block bore a message. In English. The text was in a neat, unadorned font.

COMMUNICATION DYSFUNCTION. REPAIRS MANDATED. REPAIRS PERFORMED. DECISION CONSTRAINED.

He frowned, trying to figure out the meaning. *We don't understand. Why are you thanking us? You would have died. We had no choice but to help you.*

He thought, then wrote out: IT SHOWED GOODWILL BETWEEN OUR SPECIES. Not the right word, that *species*; but he couldn't think of anything better. MAYBE WE WILL UNDERSTAND EACH OTHER IN THE FUTURE. MAYBE WE WILL LIVE IN PEACE.

The reply: DECISION CONSTRAINED BUT NOT SINGLE-VALUED. INFORMATION REQUIRED CONCERNING OBJECTIVE: REPLICATION; RESOURCE APPROPRIATION; ACTIVITY PROHIBITION; EXOTIC. WHICH.

We didn't have to keep you alive, asshole. We didn't know what the hell you were doing here, and we needed to find out. Maybe you wanted to make lots of little Malenfants from Centauri asteroids. Maybe you wanted to take away our resources for some other purposes. Maybe you wanted to stop us doing what we're doing. Or maybe something else we can't even guess. What are you doing here?

Take care with your answer, Malenfant. Most of those options, from a Gaijin point of view, aren't too healthy; you mustn't let them think you're some kind of von Neumann rapacious terminator robot yourself, or they'll slit open this air sac, and then your belly.

I'M HERE OUT OF CURIOSITY.

A pause. COMMUNICATION DYSFUNCTION.

What??

He wrote, WHERE DID YOU COME FROM? WHO MADE YOU? ARE THEY NEARBY?

Another, longer pause. SEVERAL THOUSAND ITERATIONS SINCE INITIALIZATION. *We are thousands of generations removed from those who began the migration.*

Then these *are* the Gaijin, he thought. They don't know who made them. They've forgotten. Or maybe *nobody* made them. After all, you believe *you* evolved, Malenfant; why not them?

He wrote out, WHAT IS YOUR PURPOSE HERE?

REPLICATION. CONSTRUCTION. SEARCH.

So they did come here from somewhere else . . . and that last word, finally, gave him hope he was dealing with something more than a fixed machine here, more than simple mechanical goals.

SEARCH, he wrote. SEARCH FOR WHAT?

The answer chilled him. SEARCH OBJECT: OPTION TO AVOID COMING STERILIZATION EVENT. EXISTENCE OF OPTION QUERY.

My God, he thought. We always thought the aliens would come and teach us. Wrong. These guys are coming to *us* for answers.

Answers to whatever it is they are fleeing. The 'sterilization event'.

For long minutes he gazed at Cassiopeia's crumpled, complex hide. Then he wrote carefully, WE MUST TALK. BUT I NEED FOOD.

OPTION: RETURN BEFORE EXPIRATION. *We can take you home before you die.*

WHAT ELSE?

OPTION: MANUFACTURE FOOD. ITERATIVE PROCESS, SUCCESS ANTICIPATED.

Reassuring, he thought dryly.

COROLLARY: CONTINUE.

He wrote, CONTINUE? YOU MEAN I CAN GO ON?

OPTION: ORIGIN NODE. OPTION: OTHER NODES. *We can take you home. Or we can take you further. Other places. Even further than this.*

Even deeper in time, too. My God.

He thought about it for sixty seconds.

I WANT TO GO ON, he said. MAKE ME FOOD.

Then he added, PLEASE.

Maura Della died eight years after Malenfant's disappearance into the Gaijin portal, a few months before a signal at lightspeed could have completed the journey to Alpha Centauri and back.

But when those months had passed – when the new signals arrived, bearing news from Alpha Centauri – the great asteroid belt flower-ships at last opened up their electromagnetic wings, and a thousand of them began to sail in towards the crowded heart of the solar system, and Earth.

II

TRAVELLERS

AD 2061–2186

He told himself: All this – the neutron star sail, the toiling community – is a triumph of life over blind cosmic cruelty. We ain't taking it any more.

But when he thought of Cassiopeia, anger flooded him. Why?

It had been just minutes since she had embraced him on that grassy simulated plain . . . hadn't it?

How do you *know*, Malenfant? How do you know you haven't been frozen in some deep data store for ten thousand years?

And . . . how do you know this isn't the first time you surfaced like this?

How *could* he know? If his identity assembled, disintegrated again, what trace would it leave on his memory? What *was* his memory? What if he was simply restarted each time, wiped clean like a reinitialized computer? How would he *know*?

But it didn't matter. I did this to myself, he thought. I wanted to be here. I laboured to get myself here. Because of what we learned, as the years unravelled. That the Gaijin would be followed by a great wave of visitors. And that the Gaijin were *not even the first* – just as Nemoto had intuited from the start. And nothing we learned about those earlier visitors, and what had become of them, gave us comfort.

Slowly, as they began to travel the stars, humans learned to fear the universe, and the creatures who lived in it. Lived and died.

Chapter 8

AMBASSADORS

Madeleine Meacher barely got out of N'Djamena alive.

Nigerian and Cameroon troops were pushing into the airstrip just as the Sänger's undercarriage trolley jets kicked in. She heard the distant crackle of automatic fire, saw vehicles converging on the runway. Somewhere behind her was a clatter, distant and small; it sounded as if a stray round had hit the Sänger.

Then the spaceplane threw itself down the runway, pressing her back into her seat, its leap forward sudden, gazelle-like. The Sänger tipped up on its trolley, and the big RB545 engines kicked in, burning liquid hydrogen. The plane rose almost vertically. The gunfire rattle faded immediately.

She shot into cloud and was through in a second, emerging into bright, clear sunshine.

She glanced down: the land was already lost, remote, a curving dome of dull desert-brown, punctuated with the sprawling grey of urban development. Fighters – probably Nigerian, or maybe Israeli – were little points of silver light in the huge sky around her, with contrails looping through the air. They couldn't get close to Madeleine unless she was seriously unlucky.

She lit up the scramjets, and was kicked in the back, hard, and the fighters disappeared.

The sky faded down to a deep purple. The turbulence smoothed out as she went supersonic. At thirty thousand metres, still climbing, she pushed the RB545 throttle to maximum thrust. Her acceleration was a Mach a minute; on this sub-orbital hop to Senegal she'd reach Mach 15, before falling back to Earth.

She was already so high she could see stars. Soon the reaction control thrusters would kick in, and she'd be flying like a spacecraft.

It was the nearest she'd ever get to space, anyhow.

For the first time since arriving in Chad with her cargo of light artillery shells, she had time to relax. The Sänger was showing no evidence of harm from the gunfire.

The Sänger was a good, solid German design, built by Messerschmitt–Boelkow–Blohm. It was designed to operate in war zones. But Madeleine was not; safe now in her high-tech cocoon, she gave way to the tension for a couple of minutes.

While she was still shaking, the Sänger logged into the nets and downloaded her mail. Life went on.

That was when she found the message from Sally Brind.

Brind didn't tell Madeleine who she represented, or what she wanted. Madeleine was to meet her at Kennedy Space Center. Just like that; she was given no choice.

Over the years Madeleine had received a lot of blunt messages like this. They were usually either from lucrative would-be employers, or some variant of cop or taxman. Either way it was wise to turn up.

She acknowledged the message, and instructed her data miners to find out who Brind was.

She pressed a switch, and the RB545s shut down with a bang. As the acceleration cut out she was thrust forward against the straps. Now she had gone ballistic, like a hurled stone. Coasting over the roof of her trajectory in near-silence, she lost all sensation of speed, of motion.

And, at her highest point, she saw a distant glimmer of light, complex and serene: it was a Gaijin flower-ship, complacently orbiting Earth.

When she got back to the States, Madeleine flew out to Orlando. To get to KSC she drove north along US 3, the length of Merritt Island. There used to be security gates; now there was nothing but a rusting fence, with a new smart-concrete road surface cut right through it.

She parked at the Vehicle Assembly Building. It was early morning. The place was deserted. Sand drifted across the empty car park, gathering in miniature dunes.

She walked out to the old press stand, a wooden frame like a baseball bleacher. She sat down, looking east. The sun was in her eyes, and already hot; she could feel it draw her face tight as a drum. To the right, stretching off to the south, there were rocket gantries. In the mist they were two-dimensional, colourless. Most of them were disused, part-dismantled, museum pieces. The sense of desolation, abandonment, was heavy in the air.

Sally Brind had turned out to work for Bootstrap, the rump of the corporation which had sent a spacecraft to the Gaijin base in the asteroid belt, three decades earlier.

Madeleine was not especially interested in the Gaijin. She had been born a few years after their arrival in the solar system; they were just a part of her life, and not a very exciting part. But she knew that four decades after the first detection of the Gaijin – and a full nineteen years after they had first come sailing in from the belt, apparently prompted by Reid Malenfant's quixotic journey – the Gaijin had established something resembling a system of trade with humanity.

They had provided some technological advances: robotics, vacuum industries, a few nanotech tricks like their asteroid mining blankets, enough to revolutionize a dozen industries and make a hundred fortunes. They had also flown human scientists on exploratory missions to other planets: Mars, Mercury, even the moons of Jupiter. (Not Venus, though, oddly, despite repeated requests.) And the Gaijin had started to provide a significant proportion of Earth's resources from space: raw materials from the asteroids, including precious metals, and even energy, beamed down as microwaves from great collectors in the sky.

Humans – or rather, the governments and corporations who dealt with the Gaijin – had to 'pay' for all this with resources common on Earth but scarce elsewhere, notably heavy metals and some complex organics. The Gaijin had also been allowed to land on Earth, and had been offered cultural contact. The Gaijin had, strangely, shown interest in some human ideas, and a succession of writers, philosophers, theologians, and even a few discreditable science fiction authors had been summoned to converse with the alien 'ambassadors'.

The government authorities, and the corporations who were profiting, seemed to regard the whole arrangement as a good deal. With the removal of the great dirt-making industries from the surface of the Earth – power, mining – there was a good chance that eco recovery could, belatedly, become a serious proposition.

Not everybody agreed. All those shut-down mines and decommissioning power plants were creating economic and environmental refugees. And there were plenty of literal refugees too, for instance, all the poor souls who had been moved out of the great swathes of equatorial land that had been given over to the microwave receiving stations.

Thus the Gaijin upheaval had, predictably, caused poverty, even famine and war.

It was thanks to that last Madeleine made her living, of course. But everybody had to survive.

'. . . I wonder if you know what you're looking at, here.' The voice had come from behind her.

A woman sat in the stand, in the row behind Madeleine. Her bony wrists stuck out of an environment-screening biocomp bodysuit. She must have been sixty. There was a man with her, at least as old, short, dark and heavy-set.

'You're Brind.'

'And you're Madeleine Meacher. So we meet. This is Frank Paulis. He's the head of Bootstrap.'

'I remember your name.'

He grinned, his eyes hard.

'What am I doing here, Brind?'

For answer, Brind pointed east, to the tree line beyond the Banana River. 'I used to work for NASA. Back when there was a NASA. Over there used to be the site of the two great launch complexes: 39-B to the left, 39-A to the right. 39-A was the old Apollo gantry. Later they adapted it for Shuttle.' The sunlight blasted into her face, making it look flat, younger. 'Well, the pads are gone now, pulled down for scrap. The base of 39-A is still there, if you want to see it. There's a sign the pad rats stuck there for the last launch. *Go, Discovery!* Kind of faded now, of course.'

'What do you *want*?'

'Do you know what a burster is?'

Madeleine frowned. 'No kind of weapon I've ever heard of.'

'It's not a weapon, Meacher. It's a *star*.'

Madeleine was, briefly, electrified.

'Look, Meacher, we have a proposal for you.'

'What makes you think I'll be interested?'

Brind's voice was gravelly and full of menace. 'I know a great deal about you.'

'How come?'

'If you must know, through the tax bureau. You have operated your –' she waved a hand dismissively '– *enterprises* in over a dozen countries over the years. But you've paid tax on barely ten per cent of the income we can trace.'

'Never broken a law.'

Brind eyed Madeleine, as if she had said something utterly naive. 'The law is a weapon of government, not a protection for the likes of you. Surely you understand that.'

Madeleine tried to figure out Brind. Her biocomposite suit looked efficient, not expensive. Brind was a wage slave, not an entrepreneur. She guessed, 'You're from the government?'

Brind's face hardened. 'When I was young, we used to call what you do gun-running. Although I don't suppose that's how you think of it yourself.'

The remark caught Madeleine off guard. 'No,' she said. 'I'm a pilot. All I ever wanted to do is fly; this is the best job I could get. In a different universe, I'd be –'

'An astronaut,' said Frank Paulis.

The foolish, archaic word got to Madeleine. *Here,* of all places.

'We know about you, you see,' Sally Brind said, almost regretfully. 'All about you.'

'There are no astronauts any more.'

'That isn't true, Meacher,' Paulis said. 'Come with us. Let us show you what we're planning.'

Brind and Paulis took her out to Launch Complex 41, the old USASF Titan pad at the northern end of ICBM Row. Here, Brind's people had refurbished an antique Soviet-era Proton launcher.

The booster was a slim black cylinder, fifty-three metres tall. Six flaring strap-on boosters clustered around the first stage, and Madeleine could pick out the smaller stages above. A passenger capsule and hab module would be fixed to the top, shrouded by a cone of metal.

'Our capsule isn't much more sophisticated than an Apollo,' Brind said. 'It only has to get you to orbit and keep you alive for a couple of hours, until the Gaijin come to pick you up.'

'Me?'

'Would you like to see your hab module? It's being prepared in the old Orbiter Processing Facility . . .'

'Get to the point,' Madeleine said. 'Where are you planning to send me? And what exactly is a burster?'

'A type of neutron star. A very interesting type. The Gaijin are sending a ship there. They've invited us – that is, the UN – to send a representative. An observer. It's the first time they've offered this, to carry an observer beyond the solar system. We think it's important to respond. We can send our own science platform; we'll train you up to use it. We can even establish our own Saddle Point gateway in the neutron star system. It's all part of a wider trade and cultural deal, which –'

'So you represent the UN?'

'Not exactly.'

Paulis said, 'We need somebody with the qualifications and experience to handle a journey like this. You're about the right age, under forty. You've no dependants that we can trace.' He sighed. 'A hundred years ago, we'd have sent John Glenn. Today, the best fit is the likes of you. You'll be well paid.' He eyed Madeleine. 'Believe me, very well paid.'

Madeleine thought it over, trying to figure the angles. 'That Proton is sixty years old, the design even older. You don't have much of a budget, do you?'

Paulis shrugged. 'My pockets aren't as deep as they used to be.'

Brind prickled. 'What does the budget matter? For Christ's sake, Meacher, don't you have any wonder in your soul? I'm offering you, here, the chance to *travel to the stars*. My God – if I had your qualifications, I'd jump at the chance.'

'And you aren't truly the first,' Paulis said. 'Reid Malenfant –'

'– is lost. Anyhow it's not exactly being an astronaut,' Madeleine said sourly. 'Is it? Being live cargo on a Gaijin flower-ship doesn't count.'

'Actually a lot of people agree with you,' Paulis said. 'That's why we've struggled to assemble the funding. Noone is interested in human spaceflight in these circumstances. Most people are happy just to wait for the Gaijin to parachute down more interstellar goodies from the sky . . .'

'Why don't you just send along an automated instrument pallet? Why send a human at all?'

'No.' Brind shook her head firmly. 'We're deliberately designing for a human operator.'

'Why?'

'Because we want a human there. A human like you, God help us. We think it's important to try to meet them on equal terms.'

Madeleine laughed. 'Equal terms? We limp into orbit, and rendezvous with a giant alien ramjet capable of flying to the outer solar system?'

'Symbolism, Meacher,' Paulis said darkly. 'Symbols are everything.'

'How do you know the Gaijin respond to symbols?'

'Maybe they don't. But *people* do. And it's people I'm interested in. Frankly, Meacher, we're seeking advantage. Not everybody thinks we should become so completely reliant on the Gaijin. You'll have a lot of discretion out there. We need someone with – acumen. There may be opportunities.'

'What kind of opportunities?'

'To get humanity out from under the yoke of the Gaijin,' Paulis said. For the first time there was a trace of anger in his voice, passion.

Madeleine began to understand.

There were various shadowy groups who weren't happy with the deals the governments and corporations had been striking with the Gaijin. This trading relationship was *not* between two equals. And besides the Gaijin must be following their own undeclared goals. What about the stuff they were keeping back? What would happen when the human economy was utterly dependent on the trickle of good stuff from the sky? And suppose the Gaijin suddenly decided to turn off the faucets – or, worse, decided to start dropping rocks?

Beyond that, the broader situation continued to evolve, year on year. More and more of the neighbouring stars were lighting up with radio and other signals, out to a distance of some thirty light years. It was evident that a ferocious wave of emigration was coming humanity's way, scouring along the Orion-Cygnus spiral arm. Presumably those colonists were propagating via Saddle Point gateways, and they were finding their target systems empty – or undeveloped, like the solar system. And as soon as they arrived they started to build, and broadcast.

Humans knew precisely nothing about those other new arrivals, at Sirius and Epsilon Eridani and Procyon and Tau Ceti and Altair. Maybe humans were lucky it was the Gaijin who found them first, the first to intervene in the course of human history. Or maybe not. Either way, facing this volatile and fast-changing future, it seemed unwise – to some people – to rely entirely on the goodwill of the first new arrivals to show up. Evidently those groups were now trying, quietly, to do something about it.

But Madeleine's first priority was the integrity of her own skin.

'How far is it to this burster?'

'Eighteen light years.'

Madeleine knew the relativistic implications. She would come back stranded in a future thirty-six years remote. 'I won't do it.'

'It's that or the Gulf,' Brind said evenly.

The Gulf. *Shit.* After twenty years of escalating warfare over the last oil reserves the Gulf was like the surface of Io: glassy nuke craters punctuated by oil wells which would burn for decades. Even with biocomp armour, her life expectancy would be down to a few months.

She turned, and lifted her face to the Florida sun. It looked like she didn't have a choice.

But, she suspected, she was kind of *glad* about that. Something inside her began to stir at the thought of this improbable journey.

And crossing the Galaxy with the Gaijin might be marginally safer than flying Sängers into N'Djamena, anyhow.

Paulis seemed to sense she was wavering. 'Spend some time,' he said. 'We'll introduce you to our people. And –'

'And you'll tell me how you're going to make me rich.'

'Exactly.' He grinned. He had very even, capped teeth.

She was flown to Kefallinia, the Ionian island which the Gaijin had been granted as a base on planet Earth. From the air the island looked as if it had been painted on the blue skin of the sea, a ragged splash of blue-grey land, everywhere indented with bays and inlets, like a fractal demonstration. Off the coast she spotted naval ships, grey slabs of metal, principally a US Navy battle group.

On the ground the sun was high, the air hot and still and very bright, like congealed light, and the rocks tumbled from a spine of mountains down to the tideless sea.

People had lived here, it was thought, for six thousand years. Not any more, of course: not the natives anyhow. When the UN deal with the Gaijin had been done, the Kefallinians were evacuated by the Greek government, most to sites in mainland Greece, others abroad. Those who came to America had been vocal. They regarded themselves as refugees, their land stolen, their culture destroyed by this alien invasion. Rightly so, Madeleine thought.

But the Kefallinians weren't the only dispossessed on planet Earth, and their plight, though newsworthy, wasn't attention-grabbing for long.

At the tiny airport she saw her first piece of close-up genuine Gaijin technology: a surface-to-orbit shuttle, a squat cone of some shimmering metallic substance. It looked too fragile to withstand the rigours of atmospheric entry. And yet there it was, large as life, sitting right next to the Lear jets and antiquated island-hoppers.

From the airport she was whisked to the central UN facility, close to the old capital of Argostoli. The facility was just a series of hastily prefabricated buildings and bunkers, linked by walkways and tunnels. The central building, containing the Gaijin themselves, was a crude aluminium box.

Surrounding the Gaijin shelter there were chapels and temples and mosques, embassies from various governments and inter-governmental bodies, a science park, representatives of most of the world's major corporations. All of these groups, she supposed, were here trying to get a piece of the action, one way or another.

The senior US government official here, she learned, was called the Planetary Protection Officer. The PPO post had been devised in the 1990s to coordinate quarantine measures to handle samples of Mars rock returned to Earth, and such-like. With the arrival of the Gaijin, the joke post had become somewhat more significant.

The military presence was heavy, dug in all over the complex. There were round-the-clock patrols by foot soldiers and armoured vehicles. Copters hovered overhead continually, filling the languid air with their crude rattle, and fighter planes soared over the blue dome of the sky, flight after flight of them.

To some extent this show of military power, as if the Gaijin were being contained here by human mil technology, was a sop for public opinion. Look: we are dealing with these guys as equals. We are in control. We have *not* surrendered . . . Madeleine had even heard senior military officers describing the Gaijin as 'bogeys' and 'tin men', and seeking approval to continue their wargaming of hypothetical Gaijin assaults. But she'd seen enough warfare herself to believe that there was no way humans could prevail in an all-out conflict with the Gaijin. The hoary tactic of dropping space rocks on the major cities would probably suffice for them to win. So the smarter military minds must know that mankind had no choice but to accommodate.

But there was a splash of darkness on the concrete, close to the Gaijin facility: apparently a remnant of a near-successful protest assault on the Gaijin, an incident never widely publicized. Happily the Gaijin had shown none of the likely human reaction to such an incident, no desire to retaliate. It made Madeleine realize that the military here were looking two ways: protecting mankind from its alien visitors, and vice versa.

She stood on heat-soaked concrete and looked up at the sky. Even now, in the brightness of a Mediterranean day, she could see the ghostly shapes of flower-ships, their scoops hundreds of kilometres wide, cruising above the skies of Earth. At that moment, the idea that humans could contain the Gaijin, engage them in dialogue, control this situation, seemed laughable.

They had to put on paper coveralls and overboots and hats, and they were walked through an airlock. The Gaijin hostel worked to about the cleanliness standard of an operating theatre, Madeleine was told.

Inside the big boxy buildings, it was like a church, of a peculiarly stripped-down, minimalist kind: there was a quiet calm, subdued light, and people in uniform padded quietly to and fro in an atmosphere of reverence.

In fact, Madeleine found, that church analogy was apt. For the Gaijin had asked to meet the Pope.

'And other religious leaders, of course,' said Dorothy Chaum, as she shook Madeleine's hand. 'Strange, isn't it? We always imagined the aliens would make straight for the Carl Sagan SETI-scientist types, and immediately start "curing" us of religion and other diseases of our primitive minds. But it isn't working out that way at all. They seem to have more questions than answers . . .'

Chaum turned out to be an American, a Catholic priest who had been assigned by the Vatican to the case of the Gaijin from their first detection. She was a stocky, sensible-looking woman who might have been fifty, her hair frizzed with a modest grey. Madeleine was shocked to find out she was over one hundred years old. Evidently the Vatican could buy its people the best life-extending treatments.

They walked towards big curtained-off bays. The separating curtain was a nearly translucent sheet stretched across the building, from ceiling to floor, wall to wall.

And there – beyond the curtain, bathed in light – was a Gaijin.

Machinery, not life: that was her first impression. She recognized the famous dodecahedral core. It was reinforced at its edges – presumably to counter Earth's gravity – and it was resting, incongruously, on a crude Y-frame trailer. A variety of instruments, cameras and other sensors, protruded from the dodecahedron's skin, and the skin itself was covered with fine bristly wires. Three big robot arms stuck out of that torso, each articulated in two or three places. Two of the arms were resting on the ground, but the third was waving around in the air, fine manipulators at the terminus working.

She looked in vain for symmetry.

Humans had evolved to recognize symmetry in living things – left-to-right, anyhow, because of gravity. Living things were symmetrical; non-living things weren't – a basic human prejudice hard-wired in from the days when it paid to be able to pick out the predator lurking against a confusing background. In its movements this Gaijin had the appearance of life, but it was angular, almost clumsy-looking – and defiantly not symmetrical. It didn't fit.

Human researchers were lined up with their noses pressed against the curtain. A huge bank of cameras and other apparatus was trained on the Gaijin's every move. She knew a continuous image of the Gaijin was being sent out to the net, twenty-four hours a day. There were bars which showed nothing but Gaijin images on huge wall-covering softscreens, all day and all night.

The Gaijin was reading a book, turning its pages with cold efficiency. Good grief, Madeleine thought, disturbed.

'The Gaijin are deep space machines,' said Brind. 'Or life forms, whatever. But they're hardy; they can survive in our atmosphere and gravity. There are three of them, here in this facility: the only three on the surface of the planet. We've no way of knowing how many are up there in orbit, or further out, of course . . .'

Dorothy Chaum said to her, 'We think we're used to machinery. But it's eerie, isn't it?'

'If it's a machine,' Madeleine said, 'it was made by no human. And it's operated by none of us. Eerie. Yes, you're right.' She found herself shuddering, oddly, as that crude mechanical limb clanked. She'd lived her life with machinery, but this Gaijin was spooking her, on some primitive level.

Dorothy Chaum murmured, 'We speak to them in Latin, you know.' She grinned, dimpling, looking younger. 'It's the most logical human language we could find; the Gaijin have trouble with all the irregular structures and idioms of modern languages like English. We have software translation suites to back us up. But of course it's a boon to me. I always knew those long hours of study in the seminary would pay off.'

'What do you talk about?'

'A lot of things,' Brind said. 'They ask more questions than they volunteer answers. Mostly, we figure out a lot from clues gleaned from inadvertent slips.'

'Oh, I doubt that anything about the Gaijin is inadvertent,' Chaum said. 'Certainly their speech is not like ours. It is dull, dry, factual, highly structured, utterly unmemorable. There seems to be no rhythm, no poetry – no sense of *story*. Simply a dull list of facts and queries and dry logic. Like the listing of a computer program.'

'That's because they are machines,' Paulis growled. 'They aren't conscious, like we are.'

Chaum smiled gently. 'I wish I felt so sure. The Gaijin are clearly intelligent. But are they conscious? We know of examples of intelligence without consciousness, right here on Earth: social insects like ant colonies, the termites. And you could argue there can be consciousness without much intelligence, as in a mouse. But is *advanced* intelligence possible without consciousness of some sort?'

'Jesus,' said Paulis with disgust. 'You gave these clanking tin men a whole island, they've been down here for five whole years, and you can't even answer questions like that?'

Chaum stared at him. 'If I could be sure *you* are conscious, if I even knew for sure what it meant, I'd concede your point.'

'Conscious or not they are different from us,' Brind said. 'For example, the Gaijin can turn their brains off.'

That startled Madeleine.

'It's true,' Chaum said. 'When they are at repose, as far as we can tell, they are deactivated. Madeleine, if you had an off-switch on the side of your head – even if you could be sure it would be turned back on again – would you use it?'

Madeleine hesitated. 'I don't think so.'

'Why not?'

'Because I don't see how I could tell if I was still me, when I rebooted.'

Chaum sighed. 'But that doesn't seem to trouble the Gaijin. Indeed, the Gaijin seem to be rather baffled by our big brains. Madeleine, your mind is constantly working. Your brain doesn't rest, even in sleep; it consumes the energy of a light bulb – a big drain on your body's resources – all the time; that's why we've had to eat meat all the way back to *Homo Erectus*.'

Madeleine protested, 'But without our brains we wouldn't be us.'

'Sure,' said Chaum. 'But to be *us*, to the Gaijin, seems to be something of a luxury.'

'Ms Chaum, what do *you* want from them?'

Frank Paulis laughed out loud. 'She wants to know if there was a Gaijin Jesus. Right?'

Chaum smiled without resentment. 'The Gaijin do seem fascinated by our religions.'

Madeleine was intrigued. 'And do *they* have religion?'

'It's impossible to tell. They don't give away a great deal.'

'That's no surprise,' Paulis said sourly.

'They are very analytical,' Chaum said. 'They seem to regard our kind of thinking as pathological. *We* spread ideas to each other – right or wrong, useful or harmful – like an unpleasant mental disease.'

Brind nodded. 'This is the old idea of the meme.'

'Yes,' said Chaum. 'A very cynical view of human culture.'

'And,' Paulis asked dryly, 'have your good Catholic memes crossed the species barrier to the Gaijin?'

'Not as far as I can tell,' Dorothy Chaum said. 'They think in an orderly way. They build up their knowledge bit by bit, testing each new element – much as our scientists are trained to do. Perhaps their minds are too organized to allow our memes to flourish. Or perhaps they have their own memes, powerful enough to beat off our feeble intruder notions. Frankly I'm not sure what the Gaijin make of our answers to the great questions of existence. What seems to interest them is that we *have* answers at all. I suspect they don't . . .'

Madeleine said, 'You sound disappointed with what you've found here.'

'Perhaps I am,' Chaum said slowly. 'As a child I used to dream of meeting the aliens: who could guess what scientific and philosophical insights they might bring? Well, these Gaijin do appear to be a life form millions of years old, at least. But, culturally and scientifically, they are really little evolved over us.'

Madeleine felt herself warming to this earnest, thoughtful woman. 'Perhaps we'll find the really smart ones out there among the stars. Maybe they are on their way now.'

Chaum smiled. 'I certainly envy you your chance to go see for yourself. But even if we did find such marvellous beings, the result may be crushing for us.'

'How so?'

'God shows His purposes through us, and our progress,' she said. 'At least, this is one strand of Christian thinking. But what, then, if our spiritual development is far behind that of the aliens? Somewhere else He may have reached a splendour to which we can add nothing.'

'And we wouldn't matter any more.'

'Not to God. And, perhaps, not to ourselves.'

They turned away from the disappointing aliens, and walked out into the flat light of Kefallinian noon.

Later, Frank Paulis took Madeleine to one side.

'Enough bullshit,' he said. 'Let's you and me talk business. You're fast-forwarding through thirty-six years. If you're smart, you'll take advantage of that fact.'

'How?'

'Compound interest,' he said.

Madeleine laughed. After her encounter with such strangeness, Paulis's blunt commercial calculation seemed ludicrous. 'You aren't serious.'

'Sure. Think about it. Invest what you can of your fee. After all you won't be touching it while you're gone. At a conservative five per cent you're looking at a five-fold payout over your thirty-six years. If you can make ten per cent that goes up to *thirty-one* times.'

'Really.'

'Sure. What else are you going to do with it? You'll come back a few months older, subjectively, to find your money has grown like Topsy. And think about this. Suppose you make *another* journey of the same length. You could multiply up that factor of thirty-fold to nearer a thousand. You could shuttle back and forth between here and Sirius, let's say, getting richer on every leg, just by staying alive over the centuries.'

'Yeah. If everything stays the same back home. If the bank doesn't fail, the laws don't change, the currency doesn't depreciate, there's no war or rebellion or plague, or a take-over of mankind by alien robots.'

He grinned. 'That's a long way off. A lifetime pumped by relativity is a whole new way of making money. *You'd be the first*, Meacher. Think about it.'

She studied him. 'You really want me to take this trip, don't you?'

His face hardened. 'Hell, yes, I want you to make this trip. Or, if you can't get your head sufficiently out of your ass, somebody. We have to find our own way forward, a way to deal with the Gaijin and those other metal-chewing cyborgs and giant interplanetary bugs and whatever else is heading our way from the Galactic core.'

'Is that really the truth, Paulis?'

'Oh, you don't think so?'

'Maybe you're just *disappointed*,' she goaded him. 'A lot of people were disappointed because the Gaijin didn't turn out to be a bunch of father figures from the sky. They didn't immediately start beaming down high technology and wisdom and rules so we can all live together in peace, love and understanding. The Gaijin are just *there*. Is that what's really bugging you, Paulis? That infantile wish to just give up responsibility for yourself – '

He eyed her. 'You really are full of shit, Meacher. Come on. You still have to see the star of this freak show.' He led her back into the facility. They reached another corner, another curtained-off Gaijin enclosure. 'We call *this* guy Gypsy Rose Lee,' he said.

Beyond the curtain was another Gaijin. But it was in pieces. The central dodecahedron was intact, save for a few panels, but most of those beautiful articulated arms lay half-disassembled on the floor. The last attached arm was steadily plucking wiry protrusions off the surface of the dodecahedron, one by one. Lenses of various sizes lay scattered over the floor, like gouged-out eyeballs.

Human researchers in white all-over isolation gear were crawling over the floor, inspecting the alien gadgetry.

'My God,' Madeleine said. 'It's taking itself apart.'

'Cultural exchange in action,' Paulis said sourly. 'We gave them a human cadaver to take apart – a volunteer, incidentally. In return we get this. A Gaijin is a complicated critter; this has been going on six months already.'

A couple of the researchers – two earnest young women – overheard Paulis, and turned their way.

'But we're learning a lot,' one of the researchers said. 'The most basic question we have to answer is: *are the Gaijin alive*? From the point of view of their complexity, you'd say they are; but they seem to have no mechanism for heredity, which we think is a prerequisite for any definition of a living thing –'

'Or so we thought at first. But seeing the way this thing is put together has made us think again –'

'We believed the Gaijin might be von Neumann machines, perfect replicators –'

'But it may be that *perfect* replication is impossible in principle. Uncertainty, chaos –'

'There will be drift in each generation. Like genetic drift. And where there is variation, there can be selection, and so evolution –'

'But we still don't know what the *units* of replication are here. It may be a lower level than the individual Gaijin –'

'The subcomponents that comprise them, perhaps. Maybe the Gaijin are a kind of vehicle for replication of their components, just as you could say we humans are a vehicle to enable our genes to reproduce themselves . . .'

Breeding, evolving *machines*? Madeleine found herself shuddering.

Paulis said, 'Do you see now? We are dealing with the truly alien here, Madeleine. These guys might spout Latin in their synthesized voices, but they are *not* like us. They come from a place we can't even imagine, and we don't know where they are going, and we sure as hell don't know what they are looking for here on Earth. And that's why we have to find a way to deal with them. Go ahead. Take a good long look.'

The Gaijin plucked a delicate panel of an aluminium-like soft metal off its own hide; it came loose with a soft sucking tear, exposing jewel-like innards. Perhaps it would keep on going until there was only that grasping robot hand left, Madeleine thought, and then the hand would take itself apart too, finger by gleaming finger, until there was nothing left that could move.

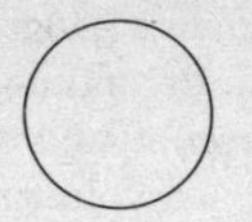

Chapter 9

FUSION SUMMER

Brind drew up contracts. Madeleine tidied up her affairs; preparing for a gap of thirty-six years, at minimum, had a feeling of finality. She said goodbye to her tearful mother, rented out her apartment, sold her car. She took the salary up front and invested it as best she could, with Paulis's help.

She decided to give her little capsule a call-sign: *Friendship-7*.

And, before she knew it, before she felt remotely ready for this little relativistic death, it was launch day.

Friendship-7's protective shroud cracked open. The blue light of Earth flooded the cabin. Madeleine could see fragments of ice, shaken free of the hull of the booster; they glittered around the craft like snow. And she could see the skin of Earth, spread out beneath her like a glowing carpet, as bright as a tropical sky. On the antique Proton, it had been one mother of a ride. But here she was – at last – in orbit, and her spirits soared. To hell with the Gaijin, to hell with Brind and Paulis. Whatever else happened from here on in, they couldn't take this memory away from her.

She travelled through a single orbit of the Earth. There were clouds piled thickly around the equator. The continents on the night side were outlined by chains of city lights.

She could see the big eco-repair initiatives, even from here, from orbit. Reforestation projects were swathes of virulent green on the continents of the northern hemisphere. The southern continents were filled with hot brown desert, their coasts lined grey with urban encrustation. Patches of grey in the seas, bordering the land, marked the sites of disastrous attempts to pump carbon dioxide into the deep oceans. Over Antarctica, laser arrays glowed red, labouring to destroy tropospheric chlorofluorocarbons. The Gulf was just a sooty smudge, drowning in petrochemical smog. And so on.

From here she could see the disturbing truth: that space was doing Earth no damn good at all. Even though this was a time of off-world colonies and trade with interstellar travellers, most of mankind's efforts were directed towards fixing up a limited, broken-down ecology, or dissipated on closed-economy problems: battles over diminishing resources in the oceans, on the fringes of the expanding deserts.

She wondered, uneasily, what she would find when she returned home, thirty-six years from now.

Madeleine would live in an old Shuttle Spacelab – a tiny reusable space station, seventy years old and flown in orbit twice – dug out of storage at KSC, gutted and refurbished. At the front was her small pressurized hab compartment, and there were two pallets at the rear fitted with a bunch of instruments which would be deployed at the neutron star: coronagraphs, spectroheliographs, spectrographic telescopes.

Brind gave her a powerful processor to enable her to communicate, to some extent, with her Gaijin hosts. It was a bioprocessor, a little cubical unit. The biopro was high technology, and it was the one place they had spent serious amounts of Paulis's money. And it was human technology, not Gaijin. Madeleine was fascinated. She spent a long time going over the biopro's specs. It was based on ampiphiles, long molecules with watery heads and greasy tails, that swam about in layers called Langmuir–Blodgett films. The active molecules used weak interactions – hydrogen bonding, van der Waals forces and hydrophobic recognition – to assemble themselves into a three-dimensional structure, supramolecular arrays thousands of molecules long.

Playing with the biopro was better than thinking about what was happening to her, where she was headed.

She wasn't so happy to find, though, when she first booted up the biopro, that its human interface design metaphor was a two-dimensional virtual representation of Frank Paulis's leathery face.

'Paulis, you egotistical bastard.'

'Just want to make you feel at home.' The image flickered a little, and his skin was blocky – obviously digitally generated. It – he – turned out to be backed up by a complex program, interactive and heuristic. He could respond to what Madeleine said to him, learn, and grow.

He would be company, of a sort.

'Are you in contact with the Gaijin?'

He hesitated. 'Yes. In a way. Anyhow I'll keep you informed. In the meantime, the best thing you can do is follow your study program.'

He started downloading some kind of checklist; it chattered out of an antique teletype.

'You have got to be kidding.'

'You've a lot of training on the equipment still to complete,' virtual Paulis said.

'Terrific. And should I study neutron stars, bursters, whatever the hell they are?'

'I'd rather not. I want your raw reactions. If I coach you too much it will narrow your perception. Remember, you'll be observing on behalf of all mankind. *We may never get another chance.* Now. Maybe we can start with the spectroheliograph deployment procedure . . .'

When she flew once more over the glittering east coast of North America, the Gaijin ship was waiting to meet her.

In Earth orbit, the Gaijin flower-ship didn't look so spectacular. It was laid out something like a squid, a kilometre long and wrought in silver, with a bulky main section as the 'head' and a mess of 'tentacles' trailing behind.

Dodecahedral forms, silvered and anonymous, drifted from the cables, and clustered around Madeleine's antique craft. Her ship was hauled into the silvery rope stuff. Strands adhered to her hull, until her view was criss-crossed with shining threads, and she had become part of the structure of the Gaijin ship. She felt a mounting claustrophobia as she was knit into the alien craft. How did Malenfant stand all this?

Then the flower-ship unfolded its petals. They made up an electromagnetic scoop, a thousand kilometres wide. The lower edge of the scoop brushed the fringe of Earth's atmosphere, and plasma sparkled.

Madeleine felt her breath shortening. This is real, she thought. These crazy aliens are really going to do this. And I'm really *here*.

She fought panic.

After a couple of widening loops around the planet Madeleine sailed out of Earth's orbit, and she was projected into strangeness.

Eating interplanetary hydrogen, it took the flower-ship one hundred and ninety-eight days to travel out to the burster's Saddle Point, eight hundred AU from the sun.

Saddle Point gateways must destroy the objects they transport.

For eighteen years a signal crossed space, towards a receiver gateway which had been hauled to the system of the burster neutron star. For eighteen years Madeleine did not exist. She was essentially dead (though not legally).

Thus, Madeleine Meacher crossed interstellar space.

There was no sense of waking – *is it over?* – she was just *there*, with the Spacelab's systems whirring and clicking around her as usual, like a busy little kitchen. Her heart was pounding, just as it had been a second before – eighteen years before.

Everything was the same. And yet –

'Meacher.' It was virtual Paulis's voice. 'Are you all right?'

No. She felt extraordinary: renewed, revived. She remembered every instant of it, that burst of exquisite pain, the feeling of reassembling, of *sparkling*. Was it possible she had somehow retained some consciousness during the transition?

My God, she thought. This could become addictive.

A new, complex light was sliding over the back of her hand. She suddenly remembered where she was. She made for her periscope.

From the dimly-lit, barren fringe of the solar system, she had been projected immediately into a crowded space. She was, in fact, sailing over the surface of a star.

The photosphere, barely ten thousand kilometres below, was a flat-infinite landscape, encrusted by granules each large enough to swallow the Earth, and with the chromosphere – the thousand-kilometre-thick outer atmosphere – a thin haze above it all. Polarizing filters in the viewport periscope dimmed its light to an orange glow. As she watched, one granule exploded, its material bursting across the star's surface; neighbouring granules were pushed aside, so that a glowing, unstructured scar was left on the photosphere, a scar which was slowly healed by the eruption of new granules.

From the tangled hull of the flower-ship, an instrument pod of some kind uncoiled on a graceful pseudopod. Gaijin instruments peered into the umbra of a star-spot below her. 'This is an F-type white dwarf star, Meacher,' Paulis said. 'A close cousin of the sun, the dominant partner of the binary pair in this system.'

I mightn't have come here, she thought. She felt an odd, retrospective panic. Brind might have picked on somebody else. I might have turned them down. I might have died, without ever imagining this was possible.

. . . But I just lost eighteen years, she thought. Nearly half my life. Just like that. She tried to imagine what was happening on Earth, right now. Tried and failed.

Virtual Paulis had issues of his own. 'Remarkable,' he said.

'What?'

Paulis sounded wistful. 'Meacher, we didn't want to emphasize the point overmuch before you left, but you're the first human to have passed through a Saddle Point teleport – except for Malenfant, and he never reported back. We didn't know what would happen.'

'Maybe I would have arrived here as warm meat. All the lights on but nobody at home. Is that what you expected?'

'It was a possibility. Philosophically.'

'The Gaijin pass back and forth all the time.'

'Ah, but perhaps they don't have souls, as we do.'

'*Souls,* Frank?' She was growing suspicious. 'It isn't just you in there, is it? I can't imagine Frank Paulis discussing theology.'

'I'm a composite.' He grinned. 'But I – that is, Paulis – won the fight to be front man.'

'Now *that* sounds like Frank.'

'For thousands of years we've wondered about the existence of a soul. Does the mind emerge from the body, or does the soul have some separate existence, somehow coupled to the physical body? Consider a thought experiment. If I made an exact duplicate of you, down to the last proton and electron and quantum state, but a couple of metres to the left – would that copy be *you*? Would it have a mind? Would it be conscious?'

'But that's pretty much what we've done. Isn't it? But rather than a couple of metres . . .'

'Eighteen light years. Yes. But still, as far as I can tell you – I mean the inner you – have emerged unscathed. The teleport mechanism is a purely physical device. It has transported the machinery of your body – and yet your soul appears to have arrived intact as well. All this seems to prove that we are after all no more than machines – no more than the sum of our parts. A whole slew of religious beliefs are going to be challenged by this one simple fact.'

She looked inward. 'I'm still Madeleine. I'm still conscious.' But then, she reflected, I would think so, wouldn't I? Maybe I'm not truly conscious. Maybe I just think I am.

The ship surged as the flower scoop thumped into pockets of richly ionized gas; the universe was, rudely, intruding into philosophy.

'I don't understand how come the Saddle Point wasn't out on some remote rim, like in the solar system.'

'Meacher, the gravitational map of this binary system is complex, a lot more than Sol's. There is a solar focus point close to each of the system's points of gravitational equilibrium. We emerged from L4, the stable Lagrange point which precedes the neutron star in its orbit, and that's where we'll return.'

'There must be other foci, on the rim of the system. Other Saddle Points which would be a lot safer to use.'

'Sure.' Virtual Frank grinned. 'But the Gaijin aren't human, remember. They seem to have utter confidence in their technology, their shielding, the reliability and control of their ramjets. We have to assume that the Gaijin know what they're doing . . .'

Madeleine turned to the consoles. Soon her monitors showed that data was starting to come in on hydrogen alpha emission, ultraviolet line spectra, ultraviolet and X-ray imaging, spectrography of the active regions, zodiacal light, spectroheliographs. Training and practice took over as she went into the routine tasks, and as she worked, some of her awe went away.

'Meacher. Look ahead.'

She reached for the periscope again. She looked at the approaching horizon – over which dawn was breaking. Dawn, on a star?

A great pulse of torn gas fled towards her over the horizon. It subsided in great arcs to the star's surface, the battered atoms flailing in the star's magnetic field – and again, a few seconds later – and once again, at deadly regular intervals. And the breaths of plasma grew more violent.

'My God, Frank.'

'Neutron star rise,' Paulis said gently. 'Just watch. Watch and learn. And *remember*, for all of us.'

The neutron star came over the horizon now, stalking disdainfully over its companion's surface, their separation only a third that between the Earth and its Moon. The primary rose in a yearning tide as the neutron star passed, glowing gas forming a column that snaked up, no more than a few hundred metres across at its neck. Great lumps of glowing material tore free and swirled inwards to a central point, a tiny object of such unbearable brightness that the periscope covered it with a patch of protective darkness.

And then the explosion came.

Blackness.

Madeleine flinched. 'What the hell –'

The smart periscope had blanked over. The darkness cleared slowly, revealing a cloud of scattered debris through which the neutron star sailed serenely.

'*That's* a burster,' said Paulis dryly.

The cloak of matter around the neutron star was building up again.

Flash.

The periscope blacked out once more.

'You'll get used to it,' Paulis said. 'It comes every fourteen seconds, regular as your heartbeat. An X-ray flash bright enough to be seen from Earth.'

She studied her instruments. The data was flowing in, raw, uninterpreted. 'Paulis, I'm no double-dome. Tell me what's happening. The primary's star-stuff –'

Flash.

'– fuses when it hits the neutron star, right?'

'Yes. Hydrogen from the primary fuses to helium as it trickles to the neutron star's surface. In seconds, the helium collects over the crust into a kind of atmosphere, metres thick. But it is a transient atmosphere which abruptly fuses further, into carbon and oxygen and other complex molecules –'

Flash.

'– blasting away residual hydrogen as it does so.'

The neutron star roared towards the flower-ship, dragging its great hump of star-stuff beneath it, and –

Flash.

– bellowing out its fusion yells. The Gaijin pulled the flower-ship's petals in further; the mouth of the ram closed to a tight circle.

A circle which dipped towards the neutron star.

'What are they doing?'

'Try not to be afraid, Meacher.'

The flower-ship swooped closer to the primary; red vacuoles fled beneath Madeleine like crowding fish. She sailed *beneath* the neutron star, skirting the mouth of fire it tore open in the flesh of the primary.

Her body decided it was time for a fresh bout of space adaptation syndrome.

The Waste Management Station was another Shuttle-era veteran, and it took some operating. When she came out, she opened her medical kit and took a scopalomine/Dexidrene.

'Meacher, you're entitled to a little nausea. You're earning us a first-hand view of a neutron star. I'm proud of you.'

'Frank, I've been flying for twenty years, fifteen professionally. I've flown to the edge of space. I have *never* had a ride like this.'

'Of course not. No human has, in all of history.'

'No human except Reid Malenfant.'

'Yes. Except him.'

She looked inside herself, and found, despite the queasiness, she was hooked.

Maybe it didn't matter what she would find, back home. Maybe she would choose to go on, like Reid Malenfant. Submit herself to the beautiful blue pain, over and over. And travel on to places like this . . .

'Listen, Meacher. You'll have to prepare yourself for the next encounter with the burster. The neutron star's orbit around its parent is only eleven minutes.' His image seemed to be breaking up.

'Frank, I think I'm losing you.'

'No. I'm just diverting a lot of processing resources right now . . . I have something odd, from that neutron star flyby. I need some input from you.'

'What kind of input?'

'Interpretation. Look at this.'

He brought up an image of the neutron star, at X-ray wavelengths. He picked out a section of the surface, and expanded it. Bands of pixels swept over the image, enhancing and augmenting.

'Do you know anything about neutron stars, Meacher? A neutron star is the by-product of a supernova, the violent, final collapse of a massive star at the end of its life. This specimen is as heavy as the sun, but only around twenty kilometres wide. The matter in the interior is degenerate, the electron shells of its atoms collapsed by the pressure. The surface gravity is billions of G, although normal matter – bound by atomic bonds – can exist there. The surface is actually rigid, a metallic crust.'

She looked more closely at the image. 'Looks like there are patterns on the surface of the neutron star.' There were hexagons, faintly visible.

'Yeah,' Paulis said. 'Now look at this.'

He flicked to other wavelengths. The things showed up at optical frequencies, even: patterns of tidy hexagons each a metre or so across. In a series of shots shown in chronological order, she could see how the patterns were actually spreading, their six-fold symmetry growing over the crystalline surface of the neutron star.

Growing, to her unscientific mind, like a virus. Or a bacterial colony.

Life, she thought, and she dissolved into wonder.

'The Gaijin don't seem surprised,' virtual Frank said.

'Really?'

'*Life emerges everywhere it can.* So they say . . . The star creatures' metabolism is based on atomic bonds. Just as is ours – *yours*. Their growth paths follow the flux lines of the neutron star's magnetic field, which is enormously powerful. Evidently the complex heavy atoms deposited by the fusion processes assist and stimulate their development. But eventually –'

'I think I can guess.'

On multiple softscreens, hexagons split and multiplied into patterns of bewildering complexity, ever-changing. The images grew more blurred as the star's rudimentary, and transient, atmosphere built up.

'Think of it, Meacher,' Paulis said. His image was grainy, swarms of blocky pixels crossing his face like insects; nearly all the biopro's immense processing power was devoted to interpreting the neutron star data. 'The very air they move through betrays them; it grows too thick and explodes – wiping the creatures clean from the surface of their world.'

'Well, not quite,' Madeleine said. 'They survive somehow, for the next cycle.'

'Yes. I guess the equivalent of spores must be deposited on or below the surface of the star. To survive these global conflagrations, every fourteen seconds, they must be pretty rudimentary, however – probably no more advanced than lichen. I wonder how much these frenetic little creatures might achieve if the fusion cycle was removed from their world . . .'

She watched the surges of the doomed neutron star lichen, the hypnotic rhythm of disaster on a world like a trap.

She stirred. Did it *have* to be this way?

Paulis said, 'Meacher –'

'Shut up, Frank.'

Maybe she wasn't going to turn out to be just a passive observer on this mission after all. But she doubted if John Glenn would have approved of the scheme she was planning.

The Gaijin told Paulis, by whatever indirect channels they were operating, that they planned two more days in orbit.

Madeleine called up Paulis. 'We have a decision to make,' she said.

'A decision?'

'On the siting of our UN-controlled teleport gateway.'

'Yes. Obviously the recommendation is to place the gateway at L5, the trailing Lagrange stable point –'

'No. Listen, Frank. This system must have a Saddle Point on the line between the neutron star and its parent – somewhere in the middle of that column of hydrogen attracted from the primary.'

'Of course.' He looked at her suspiciously. 'There's a gravitational equilibrium there, the L1 Lagrange point.'

'That's where I want the gateway.'

He looked thoughtful – or rather his face emptied of expression, and she imagined mips being diverted to the data channel connecting him to the Gaijin. 'But L1 is unstable. It would be difficult to maintain the gateway's position. Anyway, there would be a net flow of hot hydrogen through the gateway, into the transmitter at the solar system end. We won't be able to use the gateway for two-way travel.'

'Frank, for Christ's sake, that's hardly important. We can't get out to the solar system Saddle Points anyhow without the Gaijin hauling us there. Listen – you sent me on this mission to seek advantage. I think I found a way to do that. Trust me.'

He studied her. 'Okay.' He went blank again. 'The Gaijin want more justification.'

'All right. We'll be disrupting the flow of hydrogen from the primary to its neutron-star companion. What will be the effect on the neutron star?'

Paulis said slowly, 'Without the steady drizzle of fusing hydrogen onto the surface, the helium layer will cease its cycle of growth and explosion. The burster will die.'

'*But the lichen life forms will live.* Won't they? No more fusion blow-outs every fourteen seconds.'

He thought it over. 'You may be right, Meacher. And, free of the periodic extinction pulse, they may advance. My God. What an achievement. It will be as if we'll have fathered a whole new race . . . But what's the benefit to the Gaijin?'

She said briskly, 'They say they've come to us seeking answers. Maybe this is a place they will find some. A new race, new minds.'

There was motion beyond her windows. She looked out, pressing her nose to the cool glass. The Gaijin were swarming over the hull of their flower-ship like metallic beetles, limbs flailing angularly. They were *merging*, she saw, becoming a gruesome metallic sea that writhed and rippled.

'The Gaijin seem . . . intrigued,' Paulis said carefully.

She waited while he worked his data stream to the Gaijin.

'They agree, Meacher. I hope you know what you're doing,' he said.

'Me too, Frank. Me too.'

The Gaijin opened up the flower-ship's petals, and once more Madeleine swooped around the thin column of star-stuff.

As soon as the UN Saddle Point gateway was established and operational, the result was extraordinary.

The gateway was set at the thinnest point of the column of hot hydrogen torn from the primary. The gateway flared lurid blue, continually teleporting. At least fifty per cent of the primary's hydrogen – according to Paulis – was disappearing into the maw of the teleport gate. It looked as if the column of material had been neatly pruned by some cosmic gardener, capped with an almost flat surface.

'Good,' Madeleine said. 'It's worked . . . We're moving again.' She returned to her periscopes.

The ship approached the neutron star. The star's ruddy surface sparkled softly as residual material fell into its gravity well. Once more the elaborate hexagonal patterns flowed vigorously across the surface of the star – but the lichen seemed, oddly, to pause after a dozen seconds or so, as if expectant of the destruction to come.

But the fusion fire did not erupt, and the creatures surged, as if with relief, to new parts of their world.

A fourteen-second cycle to their growth remained, but that was soon submerged in the exuberant complexity of their existence. Flowing along magnetic flux lines, the lichen quickly transformed their star-world; major sections of its surface changed colour and texture.

It was stunning to watch.

She felt a surge of excitement. The data she would take back on this would keep the scientists busy for decades. Maybe, she thought, this is how the double-domes feel, at some moment of discovery.

Or an intervening god.

. . . Then, suddenly, the growth failed.

It started first at the extremes; the lichen colonies began shrivelling back to their heart lands. And then the colour of the patterns, in a variety of wavelengths, began to fade, and the neat hexagonal structure became chaotic.

The meaning was obvious. Death was spreading over the star.

'Frank. What's happening?'

'I expected this,' the interface metaphor said.

'You did?'

'Some of my projections predicted it, with varying probability.

Meacher, the lichen can't survive without their fusion cycle. Our intervention from orbit was somewhat crude. Kind of anthropocentric. Maybe the needs of the little creatures down there are not as simple as we imagined. What if the fusion cycle is *necessary* to their growth and existence, in some way we don't understand?'

The fusion cycle had delivered layers of complex molecules to the surface. Maybe the crystalline soil down there needed its fusion summer, to wipe it clean and invigorate it, regularly. After all, extinction events on Earth led to increased biodiversity in the communities that derived from their survivors.

And Madeleine had destroyed all that. Guilt stabbed at her stomach.

'Don't take it hard, Madeleine,' Paulis said.

'Bullshit,' she said. 'I'm a meddler.'

'Your impulse was honourable. It was worth a try.' He gave her a virtual smile. '*I* understand why you did it. Even if the real Frank won't . . . I think we're heading for home, Meacher. We'll be at the Lagrange point gateway in a couple of minutes. Prepare yourself.'

'Thanks.' Thank God. Get me out of here.

A couple of minutes, and eighteen years into the future . . .

'And, you know,' Paulis said, 'maybe there are deeper questions we haven't asked here.' *That* didn't sound like Frank Paulis, but one of his more reflective companions. A little touch of Dorothy Chaum, perhaps. 'The Gaijin could have brought you – the first human passenger, after Malenfant – anywhere. Why *here*? Why did they choose to show you this? Nothing the Gaijin do is without meaning. They have layers of purpose.'

She thought of that grisly, slow dismantling in Kefallinia, and shuddered.

The Paulis composite said, 'Perhaps we are here because *this is the truth*. The truth about the universe.'

'*This*? This dismal cycle of disaster, helpless life forms crushed back into the slime, over and over?'

'On some symbolic level, perhaps, this is the truth for us all.'

'I don't understand, Frank.'

'Maybe it's better that you don't.'

The truth? No, she thought. Maybe for these wretched creatures, here on this bizarre star relic. Not for us; not for humans, the solar system. Even if this is the cosmos's cruel logic, why do we have to submit to it? Maybe we ought to find a way to fix it.

Maybe Reid Malenfant would know the answer to such questions by now – wherever he was, if he was still alive. She wondered if it would ever be possible to find him.

. . . But none of that mattered now, for electric blue light enveloped her, like fusion summer.

Chapter 10

TRAVELS

And, far from home, here was Malenfant, all alone save for a sky full of Gaijin, orbiting a planet that might have been Earth, circling a star that might have been the sun.

He peered down at the planet, using the telescopic features of his softscreen, for long hours. It might have been Earth, yes: a little heavier, a little warmer, but nevertheless compellingly familiar, with a jigsaw arrangement of grey-brown continents and blue oceans and streaky white clouds and even ice caps, all of it shining unbearably brightly. Was that textured greenery really forest? Did those equatorial plains breed some analogy of grass? And were those sweeping shadows great herds of herbivores, the buffalo or reindeer of this exotic place?

But, try as he might, he found no sign of intelligent life: no city geometries, no glowing artificial light, not even the thread of smoke or the sprinkling of firelight.

This wasn't a true copy of Earth. Of course not, how could it be? He knew there was no Africa here, no America, no Australia; these strange alien continents had followed their own long tectonic waltz. But those oceans really were made of liquid water – predominantly anyhow – and the air was mainly a nitrogen–oxygen mix, a bit thicker than Earth's.

Oxygen was unstable; left to itself it should soon combine with the rocks of the planet. So something had to be injecting oxygen into the atmosphere: free oxygen was a sure sign of life – life that couldn't be so terribly dissimilar to his own.

But that atmosphere looked deeper, mistier than Earth's; the blue of the oceans, the grey of the land, had a greenish tinge. And if he looked through the atmosphere towards the edge of the planet, he could see a pale yellow-green staining, a sickly, uncomfortable colour. The green was the mark of chlorine.

He tried to explain to his Gaijin companion, Cassiopeia, what it was that kept him staring down at this new world, long after he had exhausted the analytic possibilities of his eyeball scrutiny. 'Look down there.' He pointed, and he imagined interpretative software aligning his finger with the set of his eyes.

IT IS A PENINSULA.

'True . . .' Pendant from a greater continent, set in a blue equatorial sea, and surrounded by blue-white echoes of its outline, echoes that must be some equivalent of a coral reef. 'It reminds me of Florida. Which is a region of America –'

I KNOW OF FLORIDA. THIS PENINSULA IS NOT FLORIDA. Over the months (subjective) they'd been together, Cassiopeia's English had got a *lot* better, and now she spoke to him using a synthesized human voice relayed over his old Shuttle EMU headset.

'But it's *like* Florida. At least, enough to make me feel . . .'

WHAT?

He sighed.

It had taken him forty years to get here from Alpha Centauri – including around six months of subjective time, as he had coasted between various inner systems and Saddle Point gateways. System after system, world after world. Six months as he had tried to get to know the Gaijin, and they to know him.

It seemed very important to them that they understood how he saw the universe, what motivated him. As for himself, he knew that understanding was going to be the only way humans were ever going to deal with these strangers from the sky.

But it was hard.

Cassiopeia would *never* have picked out that peninsula's chance resemblance to Florida. Even if some mapping routine had done it for her, he supposed, it would have meant nothing, save as an example of convergent processes in geology. The Gaijin sought patterns, of course – it was hard to imagine a science which did not include elements of pattern recognition, of correlation and trend analysis – but they were not *distracted* by them, like humans.

No doubt this was simply a product of differing evolutionary origins. The Gaijin had evolved in the stately stillness of deep space, where there was, in general, time to think things through; humans had evolved in fast-moving, crowded environments where it paid to be able to gaze into the shadows of a tree, a complex visual environment of dapples and stripes, and pick out the tiger *fast*.

But the end-result was that he simply could not communicate to

Cassiopeia why it pleased him to pick out an analogue of Florida off the shore of some unnamed continent, on a planet light years from Earth.

Cassiopeia was still waiting for a reply.

'Never mind,' he said. He opaqued the membrane and began his routine for sleep.

Talking to aliens:

It didn't help that he didn't really have any idea who, or what, he was talking *to*.

He had no idea how complex an individual Gaijin was. Was Cassiopeia equivalent to a car, a bacterium, a person, something more?

And the question might have no meaning, of course. Just because he communicated with a discrete entity *he* called Cassiopeia, it didn't mean there had to be anything like a corresponding person behind his projection. Maybe he was talking to a limb, or a hand, or a digit, of some greater organism – a super-being, or some looser Internet of minds.

Still, he had found places to start. His first point of contact had been navigation.

Both he and Cassiopeia were finite, discrete creatures embedded in a wider universe. And that universe split into obvious categories – space, stars, worlds, you, me. It had been straightforward to agree on a set of labels for Sol, Earth and the nearby stars – even if that wasn't the custom of the Gaijin. They thought of each star as a point on a dynamic four-dimensional map, defined not by a *name* but by its orientation compared to some local origin of coordinates. So their label for Sol was something like get-to-Alpha-Centauri-and-hang-a-left-for-four-light-years . . . except that Alpha Centauri, the local centre of Gaijin operations, was itself defined by an orientation compared to another, more remote origin of coordinates – and so on, recursively back, until you reached the ultimate origin: the starting point, the home world of the Gaijin.

And this recursive web of directions and labelling was, of course, subject to constant change, as the stars slid through the sky, changing their orientations to each other.

It was a system of thinking that was logical, and obviously useful for a species who had evolved to navigate among the stars – a lot more so than the Earthbound human habit of seeking patterns in the random lamps of the sky, patterns called constellations, which shifted because of perspective if you moved more than a couple of light years from

Earth. But it was a system that was far beyond the capacity of any human mind to absorb.

Another point of contact: *You. Me. One. Two.* In this universe, it seemed, it was impossible not to learn to count.

Malenfant's math extended (shakily) as far as differential calculus, the basic tool mathematicians used to model reality. It did appear that Cassiopeia thought of the world in similar terms. Of course, Cassiopeia's mathematical models were smarter than any human's. The key to such modelling was to pick out the right abstractions from a complex background: close enough to reality to give meaningful answers, not so detailed they overwhelmed the calculations. For the Gaijin, the boundaries of abstraction and simplification were *much* further back than any human's, her models much richer.

And there were more fundamental differences. Cassiopeia seemed much smarter at *solving* the equations than Malenfant, or any human. He managed to set out for her the equations of fluid mechanics, one of his specialities at college, and she seemed to understand them qualitatively: she could immediately *see* how these equations, which in themselves merely described how scraps of flowing water interacted with each other, implied phenomena like turbulence and laminar flow, implications it had taken humans years – using sophisticated mathematical and computational tools – to tease out.

Could Cassiopeia look at the equations of relativity and *see* an implied universe of stars and planets and black holes? Could she look at the equations of quantum mechanics and *see* the intricate chemistry of living things?

Of course, that increased smartness must lead to a qualitative jump in understanding. A chimp didn't think about things more simply than Malenfant did; it couldn't grasp some of his concepts at all. There were clearly areas where Cassiopeia was simply working above Malenfant's wretched head.

Cassiopeia had spent time trying to teach him about a phenomenon just a little beyond his own horizon – as chaos theory might have been to an engineer of, say, the 1950s. It was something to do with the emergence of complexity. The Gaijin seemed able to *see* how complexity, even life, naturally emerged from the simplest of beginnings: not fundamental physical laws, but something even deeper than that – as far as he could make out, the essential mathematical logic which underlaid all things. Human scientists had a glimmering of this. His own DNA somehow contained, in its few billion bases, enough information to generate a brain of three *trillion* connections . . .

But for the Gaijin this principle went further. It was like being given a table of prime numbers and being able to deduce atoms and stars and people, as a *necessary* consequence of the existence of the primes. And since prime numbers, of course, existed everywhere, it followed there was life and people, humans and Gaijin, everywhere there could be.

Life sprouting everywhere, like weeds in the cracks of a pavement. It was a remarkable, chilling thought.

'Take me to your home,' he'd said one day.

Cassiopeia's choice of a human label for her remote home was Zero-Zero-Zero-Zero, the great sky map's origin of coordinates.

I AM THE SUCCESSOR OF A REPLICANT CHAIN WHICH EMERGED THERE. *I am descended from emigrants?* Not exactly, because she went on: I RETAIN RECORDS OF ZERO-ZERO-ZERO-ZERO. Memories? Did each Gaijin come to awareness with copies of the memories of those who bore her – or constructed her? Were they, then, *her* memories, or a mere copy? IT IS POSSIBLE TO TRANSLATE TO ZERO-ZERO-ZERO-ZERO. THERE IS NO PURPOSE.

'I'd like to see it.'

THERE ARE RECORDS WHICH –

'Your records only show me your world through your eyes. If we're ever going to understand each other, you have to let me see for myself.'

There was a long hesitation after that.

FINALLY.

'What?'

THERE ARE MANY PLACES TO SEE. MANY WORLDS. BEFORE ZERO-ZERO-ZERO-ZERO.

'I understand. One day . . .'

ONE DAY.

But not today, Malenfant thought, as he opened his eyes to the light of a foreign sun. Not today. Today, we are both far from home.

Cassiopeia provided him with an environment suit, a loosely cut coverall of what felt like a high-grade plastic. It had no zippers; he learned to seal it up by passing his thumb along the open seams. He lifted a hood-like helmet over his head. There was a clear faceplate, a slightly opaque filter near his mouth.

There was no independent air supply, just one layer of fabric. The whole thing jarred with Malenfant's intuition of the protection he would need to walk on an alien world. But Cassiopeia assured him it would be enough. And besides, the only alternative was his battered

Shuttle EMU suit, still with him, crammed into a corner of the lander, his only possession, long past its operational lifetime.

'Open the door. Please.'

The lander door dilated away. The world beyond was green and black.

The lander's cabin floor was almost flush with the ground, and he stepped out, pace by pace, testing his suit. Gravity was a little more than Earth normal, comfortingly familiar, and the air pressure just a little higher than Earth's sea level.

First impressions:

He was in an open forest, like park land. There were objects that were recognizably trees, about the size of Earth trees, and what appeared to be grass under his feet. Above his head a sun sailed through a sky littered with high, wispy cirrus clouds.

He closed his eyes. He could hear the soft hiss of wind over the grass, and a distant piping, for all the world like a bird's song, and when he breathed in he filled his lungs with cool, crisp air.

It might have been Earth.

But, when he opened his eyes, he saw a sky that was a lurid yellow-green. It was like a haze of industrial smog. The vegetation was a *very* deep green, almost black.

And he could smell chlorine.

His filter removed all but a trace of the chlorine compounds that polluted the atmosphere – including phosgene, toxic stuff humans had once used to slaughter each other. If not for his suit, this friendly-looking world would soon kill him.

Chlorine: *that* was the big difference here. Most of Earth's chlorine was locked up in the oceans, in the form of a stable chloride ion. This world seemed to have started out as roughly Earth-like. But something, one small detail, had been different: here, something had pumped all that chlorine into the air.

He walked forward, over grass that crushed softly under his feet.

He reached a narrow valley, a rushing brook. There was a stand of trees nearby. The bed of the little stream was just a soft muddy clay, no sign of any rocks. The water was colourless, clear. He knelt down, stiffly, and dipped his fingers into the water. It was cold, its pressure gentle against his gloved hands.

WARNING. SOLUTION OF HYDROGEN CHLORIDE. HYPOCHOLOROUS ACID.

He snatched back his fingers. Like a swimming pool, he thought: chlorine plus water gave a solution of acid and bleach. The weathering of any rocks here must be ferocious; no wonder only clays survived.

He straightened up to inspect a tree. He touched branches, leaves, a trunk, even blossom. But to his gloved fingers the leaves felt slippery, soapy.

From a hollow in the tree trunk, at about his eye level, a small face peered out: the size and shape of a mouse's, perhaps, but with a central mouth, three eyes arranged symmetrically around it. The mouth opened, showing flat grinding surfaces, and the little creature hissed, emitting a cloud of greenish gas. Then it ducked back into the hole, out of his sight.

The trunk didn't feel like wood. He reached up and broke off a twig; it snapped reluctantly. The interior was springy, fibrous. The leaves, the tree trunk, were made of some kind of natural plastic – perhaps a form of polyvinyl chloride, PVC. If he could smell the blossom, it would surely stink like toxic waste.

It was like a grotesque model of a tree, a thing of plastic and industrial waste. And yet the breeze ruffled it convincingly, and sunlight dappled the green-black grass beneath.

In his ear, Cassiopeia, from orbit, began to lecture him about biochemistry. THE LIVING THINGS HERE ARE CONSTRUCTED OF CELLS – ANALOGOUS TO LIVING THINGS ON EARTH, TO YOU. THEIR METABOLISM IS NOT TOLERANT OF THE CHLORINE. BUT THEY HAVE EVOLVED SHIELDING AT THE CELLULAR LEVEL . . .

He interrupted. 'There are trees here,' he said. 'Grass. Flowers. Animals.' *You see biochemistry. I see a flower.*

There was a long silence.

It was the Gaijin way of seeing reality: from the equations of quantum mechanics, working up to a world. But that wasn't the way Malenfant thought. Humans, it seemed, were better at broad comprehension than the Gaijin, quicker at abstracting simplicity from complexity. This object before Malenfant *wasn't* a tree, because trees only grew on Earth. But it helped Malenfant to think in those terms, to seek patterns and map them back to what he knew.

The Gaijin, slowly, were learning to ape his thinking.

YES, came the reply. THERE ARE TREES.

'Cassiopeia. Why did you bring me here, to this chlorine-drenched waste dump?'

TO GATHER MORE DATA, MALENFANT.

Malenfant scowled at the sky.

The Gaijin seemed to be trying to educate him, for purposes of their own. They had shown him worlds, all of them very different, all of them bearing life. All of them scarred, in some way.

The Gaijin saw the universe as some immense computer program, he was coming to believe, an algorithm for generating life and, presumably, mind wherever and whenever it could.

The trouble was, the program had bugs.

He grunted. 'All right. Where? How?'

WALK A KILOMETRE, TOWARDS THE SUN.

Muttering complaints, sipping cool water from a pipe inside his hood to dispel the swimming-pool taste of chlorine, he stalked on.

And, long before the kilometre was covered, he found people.

There was a crowd of them, a hundred or more, gathered around what appeared to be a pit in the ground. They moved in a kind of dance, chains of people weaving in and out to a murmur of noise, soft as a wind blowing.

Most of the dancers appeared to be somewhere near his own height. Few were taller, but several were a lot smaller – children? The elderly, withered by age?

Not humans, of course. But people, yes.

He glanced around, seeking cover. But Cassiopeia reassured him.

THERE IS A PERCEPTUAL DYSFUNCTION, MALENFANT. *They can't see you.*

'Why not? . . . Oh. Captain Cook.'

COMMUNICATION DYSFUNCTION.

There was a story – probably apocryphal – that on one of the islands visited by Cook, the natives had been unable even to *see* his great exploratory ships. They had never encountered such large floating artefacts before. It was only when Cook's crew put out in landing boats that the natives were able to comprehend.

Thus, Malenfant was simply too strange an element in the dancers' world for them to perceive.

'. . . Never mind. Humans have limits like that too.'

Feeling a little bolder, he stepped forward, looked more closely.

He picked out one of the dancers. She (he decided arbitrarily) stood upright. She had a clearly defined torso and head, sets of upper and lower limbs. But she had three of everything – three arms, three legs – and her limbs articulated back and forth in a complex, graceful way he found unnerving. She didn't walk, exactly, shifting her weight from foot to stomping foot as he did. Rather, she spun around, whirling, letting one foot after another press lightly on the ground. It was high speed and difficult to follow, like trying to figure out how a horse ran; but after he'd watched for a few seconds it seemed easy and natural.

Her head, positioned up at the top of her trunk, was about where his was. He saw three eyes, what appeared to be a mouth, other orifices that might be ears, nostrils. She seemed to be naked, save for a belt slung over one of her three shoulders, like a sash. He could see tools dangling there: a lump of quartz-like rock that could have been a hand-held hammer, what looked like a bow of the natural-plastic wood. Stone Age technology, he thought.

. . . Of course Stone Age. Most metals would just corrode here. Gold would survive, but try making a workable axe out of *that*. Even fire would be problematic; all that chlorine would inhibit flame. There could be no ceramics, for instance.

Because of an accident of biochemistry these people were stuck forever in the Stone Age. And since most rock would be corroded away, there wasn't even much of *that*.

Maybe these people had a rich culture, an oral tradition, dance. But that was all they could ever have. He watched the woman-thing whirl, with admiration, with pity.

WHAT IS THE PURPOSE OF THE PATTERNLESS SOUNDS THEY MAKE?

'Patternless –' Malenfant smiled. 'Perceptual incongruence, Cassiopeia. Transform your data. Look at the frequency content, the ratios between the tones . . . We've discussed this before.' The Gaijin analysed sound digitally, not with analogue microphone-like systems like the human ear. And so the patterns they judged as agreeable – valuable, anyhow – were complex numeric constructs, not the harmonies that pleased human ears.

A long silence. IT IS A FORM OF MUSIC.

'Yes. They're singing, Cassiopeia. Singing, that's all.'

Now the dancing reached a climax, the howl of voices more intense. One of the dancers spun out of the group, whirling in a decaying orbit towards that pit around which they all gyrated.

Then, with a fast, shimmying movement, she got to her belly and slid gracefully into the hole.

The dancers continued, for thirty seconds, a minute, two, three, four. Malenfant just watched.

At last the potholer returned. Malenfant saw that trio of upper arms come flopping over the rim of the pit. She seemed to be in trouble. Dancers broke away, four or five of them hurrying to haul their partner out of the hole.

She lay on her back, shuddering, obviously distressed. But she held up something to the light. It was long, dark brown, pitted and heavily corroded. It was a bone – bigger than any human bone, half Malenfant's height, and with a strange protrusion at one end – but unmistakably a bone even so.

'Cassiopeia – what's hurting her?'

CHLORINE POISONING. CHLORINE IS A HEAVY GAS. IT POOLS IN LOW PLACES.

'Like that hole in the ground.'

YES.

'And so, when she went down there to retrieve that bone –'

The dancer had been asphyxiated. She was tolerant of chlorine, but couldn't breathe it.

The potholer passed the bone on to another. Malenfant saw that where her long, flipper-like hand had wrapped around the bone, it had been corroded. And when the dancer took hold of it, the bone surface sizzled and smoked to her touch. Carbonate, burning in the air.

That's what would happen to *my* bones here, slowly but surely. That bone can't have belonged to any creature now extant, here on this chlorine-drenched planet.

SHE SACRIFICED HER LIFE.

'Why? What's the point?'

Cassiopeia seemed to hesitate. WE WERE HOPING YOU COULD TELL US.

He turned his back on the whirling, singing dancers, and trudged back to his lander.

He felt exhausted, depressed.

'This wasn't always a chlorine dump. Was it, Cassiopeia?'

NO, she replied.

That bone pit was the key. That, and the sparse biosphere.

Once this had been a world very much like Earth, with the chlorine locked in the ocean. Then it had been – seeded. All it had taken was a single strain of chlorine-fixing microbes. The bugs found themselves in a friendly, bland atmosphere, with lots of chloride just floating around in the ocean, waiting to be used. And so it began.

It had happened a *long* time ago, a hundred million years or more. Time enough for life forms to adapt. Some of them had evolved defences against the spreading stain of chlorine. Others had learned to incorporate chlorine into their cells to make themselves unpalatable to anyone wanting to eat them. Some even used the chlorine as a gas attack against predators or prey, like the tree mouse that had spat in his face. And so on. Thus, a chlorine-resistant biosphere had arisen.

But the bone pit contained relics of the original native life, sent to extinction by the chlorine. The relics must have been trapped for megayears under a layer of limestone; but at last the limestone just dissolved, under rain like battery acid, exposing the bones.

The Gaijin believed the seeding of the planet with chlorine-fixers had probably been deliberate.

WE HAVE FOUND MANY WAYS TO KILL A WORLD, MALENFANT. THIS IS ONE OF THE MORE SUBTLE.

Subtle and disguised; the chlorine-fixers *might* have evolved naturally, and after such a length of time it would be hard to prove otherwise. But the Gaijin had come across this *modus operandi* before.

The thought shocked him more deeply than he had thought possible. This world wasn't natural; it was like a corpse, strangled.

WE UNDERSTAND HOW TO KILL A WORLD, Cassiopeia said. WE EVEN UNDERSTAND WHY.

'Competition for resources?'

BUT WE DON'T UNDERSTAND WHY THAT DANCER KILLED HERSELF.

'It was ritual, Cassiopeia. As far as I could see. Religion, maybe.' The dancers couldn't possibly understand the story of their world, the meaning of the ancient fossils. Maybe they thought they were the bones of the giants who had created their world.

But this was the most alien thing of all to the Gaijin.

MALENFANT, WHAT IS IT THAT MAKES A SENTIENT BEING SACRIFICE THE POSSIBILITY OF A TRILLION YEARS OF CONSCIOUSNESS FOR AN IDEA?

'Hell, I can't tell you that.'

BUT YOU DID THE SAME, WHEN YOU CAME THROUGH THE SOL GATEWAY. YOU COULD NOT KNOW WHAT LAY ON THE OTHER SIDE. YOU MUST HAVE EXPECTED TO DIE.

'What is this, Anthropology 101? Is this so important to you?'

The answer startled him.

MALENFANT, IT MAY BE THE MOST IMPORTANT THING OF ALL.

The planet was folding over, dwindling into a watery-blue dot, achingly familiar.

But it was the scene of a huge crime, a biocide on a scale he could barely comprehend – and committed so impossibly long ago.

'So strange,' he murmured. 'Earth, the solar system, contains nothing like this.'

The Gaijin would not reply to that, and he felt a deep, abiding unease.

But the solar system was primordial. You could see that was true.

Wasn't it?

Chapter 11

ANOMALIES

Carole Lerner drifted out of the airlock.

She was tethered by a series of metal clips to a guide line, along which she pulled herself hand over hand. The line connected her ship to a moonlet. The line seemed flimsy and fragile, strung as it was between spaceship and moonlet, two objects that floated, resting on no support, in empty three-dimensional space.

But it was a space dominated by an immense, dazzling sphere, for Carole Lerner was in orbit around planet Venus.

Before Carole had come here – the first human to visit Venus, Earth's twin planet – nobody even knew Venus had a moon. Her mother had spent a life studying Venus, and never knew about the moon, probably never even dreamed of being here, like *this*.

With no sensation of motion, floating in space, she and her ship swept around the planet, moving into its shadow so that it narrowed to a fine-drawn crescent. Close to the terminator, the blurred sweep that divided day from night, she saw shadowy forms: alternating bands of faint light and dark, hazy arcs. And near the equator there seemed to be yellowish spots, a little darker than the background. But these details were nothing to do with any ground features. All of these wisps and ghosts were artefacts of the strange, complex structure of Venus's great cloud decks – or perhaps they were manufactured by her imagination, as she sought to peer through that thick blanket of air.

Now, at the apex of her looping trajectory, she moved deep into the shadow of the planet, and the crescent narrowed further, becoming a brilliant line drawn against the darkness. As the sun touched the cloud decks there was a brief, startling moment of sunset, and layers in the clouds showed as overlaid, smoothly curving sheets, fading from white down to yellow-orange. And then a faint, ghostly ring lit up all around the planet: sunlight refracted through the dense air.

As her eyes adjusted to the darkness she saw the stars coming out one by one, framing that ringed circle of darkness. But one star, as if a rogue, moved balefully across the equator of that black disc, glowing orange-yellow. It was a Gaijin flower-ship, one of the small fleet that had followed her all the way here from the Moon.

'The cloud tops of Venus,' Nemoto whispered, her voice turned to a dry autumn-leaf rustle by the low quality radio link. 'I envy you, Carole.'

Carole grunted. 'Another triumph for Man in Space.' She waited the long minutes as her words, encoded into laser light, crossed the inner solar system to Earth's Moon.

'You are facetious,' Nemoto eventually replied. 'It is not appropriate. You know, I grew up close to a railway line, a great transport artery. I lay in my parents' small apartment and I could hear the horns of the night freight trains. My parents were city dwellers; their lives had been static, unchanging. But the night trains reminded me every night that there were vehicles that could take me far away, to mountains, forest, or sea.

'The Gaijin frighten me. But when I see their great ships sailing across the night, I am stirred by a ghost of the wanderlust I enjoyed, or suffered, as a girl. I envy you your adventure, child . . .'

Incredible, Carole thought. I've travelled a hundred million kilometres with barely a word from that wizened old relic, and *now* she wants to open up her soul.

She twisted in space and looked back at her ship.

It was a complex collection of parts – a cylinder, bulging tanks, a cone, a giant umbrella shape, a rocky shield – all fixed to an open, loose framework of struts, made from lunar aluminium. The shield was made of blown lunar rock: grey, imposing, now heavily scorched and ablated, the shield had protected her on arrival at Venus, when her craft had dived straight into the upper atmosphere, giving up its interplanetary velocity to air friction. The big central cylinder was her hab module, the cramped box within which she had endured the long flight out here. The hab trailed a rocket engine unit – gleaming pipes and tanks surrounding a gaping, charred nozzle – and big soft-walled tanks of hydrogen and oxygen, the fuel that would bring her out of Venusian orbit and back home to Earth's Moon. A wide, filmy umbrella was positioned on long struts before the complex of components. The umbrella, glistening with jewel-like photovoltaic cells, doubled as sunshade, solar energy collector and long-range antenna.

Stuck to the side of the hab module was her lander, a small, squat, silvery cone with a fat, heavy heatshield. The lander was the size and shape of an old Apollo Command Module. This tiny, complex craft would carry her down through Venus's clouds to the hidden surface, keep her alive for a few days, and then – after extracting much of its fuel from Venus's atmosphere – bring her back to orbit once more.

The craft looked clunky, crude, and compared to the grace of Gaijin technology very obviously human. But, after such a long journey in its womb-like interior, Carole felt an illogical fondness for the ship. After all, the trip hadn't been easy for it either. The thick meteorite-shield blankets swathed over its surface were yellowed and pocked by tiny impact scars. The paintwork had been yellowed by sunlight and blistered by the burns of reaction control thrusters. The big umbrella had failed to open properly – one strut had snapped in unfurling – causing the ship to undergo ingenious manoeuvres to keep in its limited shade.

Fondness, yes. Before she left the Moon, Carole had failed to name her ship. She'd thought it sentimental, a habit from a past to which she didn't belong. She regretted it now.

'. . . No wonder we missed the moon,' Nemoto was saying. 'It's small, very light, and following an orbit that's even wider and more elliptical than yours, Carole. Retrograde, too. And it's loosely bound; energetically it's close to escaping from Venus altogether –'

She turned to face the moonlet. It swam in darkness. It was a rough sphere, just a hundred metres across, its dark and dusty surface pocked by a smattering of craters.

Carole knew she wasn't in control of this mission, even nominally. But she was the one who was *here*, looping extravagantly around Venus. 'Are you sure this is necessary, Nemoto? I came here for Venus, not for *this*.'

But Nemoto, of course, had not yet heard her question. '. . . A captured asteroid, perhaps? That would explain the orbit. But its shape appears too regular. And the cratering is limited. How old? Less than a billion years, more than five hundred million. And there is an anomaly with the density. Therefore – Ah. But what is *necessity*? You have a fat reserve of fuel, Carole, even now, more than enough to bring you home. And we are here, not for pure science, but to investigate anomalies. *Look* at this thing, Carole. This object is too small, too symmetrical to be natural. And its density is so low it must be hollow.

'Carole, this is an artefact. And it has been here, orbiting Venus, for hundreds of millions of years. *That* is its significance.'

* * *

She held her hands out before the approaching moonlet.

There was no discernible gravity. It was not like jumping down to the surface of a world, but more like drifting towards a dark, dusty wall.

When her gloves impacted, a thin layer of dust compressed under her fingertips. The gentle pressure was sufficient to slow her, and then she found a layer of hard rock beneath.

Grains billowed up around her hands, sparkling. Some of them clung to her gloves, immediately streaking their silvery cleanliness, and some drifted away, unrestrained by this odd moonlet's tenuous gravity.

It was an oddly moving moment. I've come a hundred million kilometres, she thought. All that emptiness. And now I've arrived. I'm *touching* this lump of debris. Perhaps all travellers feel like this, she mused.

Time to get to work, Carole.

She took a piton from her belt. She had hastily improvised it from framing bolts on the ship. With a geology hammer intended for Venus, she pounded at the spike. Then she clipped a tether line to the piton.

'It looks like Moon dust,' she reported to distant Nemoto. She scooped up a dust sample and passed it through a portable lab unit for a quick analysis. Then she held the lab over the bare exposed rock and let its glinting laser beam vaporize a small patch, to see if the colours of the resulting rock mist might betray its nature.

Then, spike by spike, she began to lay a line from her anchor point, working across the folds and ridges of this battered, tightly curved miniature landscape, towards the pole of the moonlet. There, Nemoto said, she had detected what appeared to be a dimple, a crater too deep for its width: it was an anomaly, here on this anomalous moon.

Nemoto, reacting to her first observations and images, began to whisper in her ear, a remote insect. 'Lunar regolith, yes. And that rock is very much like lunar highlands material: basically plagioclase feldspar, a calcium–aluminium silicate. Carole, this appears to be a bubble of lunar-type rock – a piece of a larger body, a true Venusian moon, perhaps? – presumably dug out, melted, shaped, thrown into orbit . . . but why? And why such a wide, looping trajectory? . . .'

She kept talking, speculating, theorizing. Carole tuned her out. After all, in a few more minutes, she would *know*.

She had reached the dimple. It was a crater perhaps two metres across – but whereas most of the craters here, gouged out by impacts, were neat, shallow saucers, this one was much deeper than its width – four, five metres perhaps.

Almost cylindrical.

She found her heart hammering as she clambered into this pit of ancient darkness; a superstitious fear engulfed her.

With brisk motions, she fixed a small radio relay box to the lip of the dimple. Then she stretched a thin layer of gas-trapping translucent plastic over the dimple. Of course by doing this she was walling herself up inside this hole in the ground. It was illogical, but she made sure she could punch out through that plastic sheet before she finished fixing it in place.

She saw something move in the sky above. She gasped and stumbled, throwing up a spray of dust.

A flower-ship cruised by, its electromagnetic petals folded, jewel-like Gaijin patrolling its ropy flanks.

She scowled up. 'I want company,' she said. 'But you don't count.'

She turned away, and let herself drift down to the bottom of the pit.

She landed feet-first. The floor of the pit felt solid, a layer of rock. But the dust was thicker here, presumably trapped by the pit. When she looked up she saw a circle of stars framed by black, occluded by a little spectral distortion from the plastic.

Nothing happened. If she'd expected this 'door' to open on contact, she was disappointed.

But Nemoto wasn't surprised. 'This artefact – if that's what it is – may predate the first mammals, Carole. You wouldn't expect complex equipment to keep functioning so long, would you? But there must be a backup mechanism. And I'll wager *that* is still working.'

So Carole got to her hands and knees, trying to keep from pushing herself away from the ground, and she scrabbled in the dirt, her gloved hands soon filthy.

She found a dent.

It was maybe a half-metre across. There was a bar across the middle of it. The bar was held away from the lower surface, and was fixed by a kind of hinge mechanism at one end.

Once more her heart hammered, and she felt a pulse in her forehead. Up to now, there had been nothing that could have *proven*, unambiguously, Nemoto's assertion that the moonlet was an artefact. But there was surely no imaginable natural process by which a moon could *grow* a lever, complete with hinge.

She wrapped both hands around the lever and pulled.

Nothing happened. The lever felt immovable, as if it was welded tight to the rocky moon – as, of course, it might be, after all this time.

She braced herself with a piton hammered into the 'door', and pushed. Nothing. She twisted the lever clockwise, without success.

Then she twisted it anticlockwise.

The lever turned smoothly. She felt the click of buried, heavy machinery – bolts withdrawing, perhaps. The floor fell away beneath her.

Quickly she let go of the lever. She was left floating, surrounded by dust, suspended over a pit of darkness. Some kind of vapour sparkled out around her.

Making sure her pitons were secure, she slid past walls of rock, and through the open door.

Nemoto's recruitment pitch had been simple. 'The flight will make you rich,' she'd promised.

Carole had been sceptical. After all, she was only going as far as Venus, a walk around the block compared to the light-years-long journeys undergone by the handful of interstellar travellers who had followed Reid Malenfant through the great Saddle Point gateways – even if, twenty years after the departure of Madeleine Meacher, the first, none of them had yet returned.

But still, Nemoto turned out to be right. Nemoto's subtle defiance of the Gaijin's unstated embargo on Venus had evidently struck a chord, and Carole's shallow fame had indeed led to lucrative opportunities she hadn't been ashamed to exploit.

But it wasn't the money that had persuaded Carole to commit three years of her life to this unlikely jaunt.

'Think of your mother,' Nemoto had whispered, her mask-like face twisted in a smile. 'You know that I met her once, at a seminar in Washington. Reid Malenfant himself introduced us. She was fascinated by Venus. She would have loved to go there, to a new world.'

Guilt, of course, the great motivator.

But, of course, Nemoto was right. Her mother had grown to love Venus, this complex, flawed sister world of Earth. She used to tell her daughter fantastic bedtime tales of how it would be to sink to the base of those towering acid clouds, to stand on Venus itself, immersed in an ocean of air.

But her mother's studies had been based on scratchy data returned by a handful of automated probes, sent by human governments in the lost pre-Gaijin days of the last century. When the Gaijin had showed up, all of that had stopped, of course.

Now humans rode Gaijin flower-ships to Mars, Mercury, even the moons of Jupiter. Where the Gaijin granted access, an explosion of data resulted, and human understanding advanced quickly. But the Gaijin were very obviously in control, and that caused a lot of frustration among the scientific community. The scientists wanted to see it *all*, not just what the Gaijin chose to present.

And there were major gaps in the Gaijin's gift. Notably, Venus. There hadn't been a single Gaijin-hosted human visit to Venus – although it was obvious, from telescopic sightings of flower-ship activity, that this was a major observation site for the Gaijin.

Not too many people cared about such things. To spend one's entire life labouring in some obscure corner of science – when it was obvious that the Gaijin already had so much more knowledge – was dispiriting. Carole herself hadn't followed her mother's footsteps. She had gone instead into theology, one of the many broadly philosophical boom areas of academic discipline. And her mother had gone to her grave unfulfilled, leaving Carole with a burden of obscure guilt.

The truth was, to Carole, these issues – the decline of science, the obscure activities and ambitions of the Gaijin – were dusty, the concerns of another century, of vanished generations. This was 2081: sixty years after Nemoto's discovery of the Gaijin. To Carole, as she had grown up, the Gaijin were *here*, they had always been here, they always would be here. And so she had put aside her guilt, as much as any child can about her mother.

Until Nemoto had come along.

Nemoto: herself a weird historic relic, riven by barely comprehensible obsessions, huddled on the Moon, nursing her fragile body with a suite of ever more exotic anti-ageing technologies. Nemoto continually railed against the complacency of governments and other bodies regarding the Gaijin and their activities. 'We have no sense of history,' she would say. 'We have outlived our shock at the discovery of the Gaijin. We do not see trends. Perhaps the Gaijin rely on our mayfly lifespan to wear away our scepticism. But those of us who remember a time before the Gaijin know that this is *not right* . . .'

And Nemoto was worried about Venus.

One thing that was well known about the Gaijin was that their favoured theatre of operations was out in the dark, among the asteroids, or the stately orbits of the giant planets, or in the deeper cold of the comet clouds even further out. They didn't appear to relish the solar system inward of Earth's orbit, crammed with dust and looping rogue asteroids, drenched by the heat and light of a too-close sun, a place where the gravity well was so deep that a ship had to expend huge amounts of energy on even the simplest manoeuvre.

So *why* were the Gaijin so drawn to Venus?

Nemoto had begun to acquire funding, from a range of shadowy sources, to initiate a variety of projects: all more or less anti-Gaijin – including this one.

And that was why the first human astronaut to Venus was under Nemoto's control: not attached to a Gaijin flower-ship, but riding in a clunky and crude human-built spacecraft, little advanced from Apollo 13 as far as Carole could tell, a ship that had been fired into space from a great electromagnetic cargo launcher on the Moon.

The Gaijin could have stopped her, Carole supposed. But, though they had shadowed her all the way here, they had shown no inclination to oppose her directly. Perhaps that would come later.

Or perhaps, to the Gaijin, Carole and her fragile ship simply didn't matter.

She was surrounded by blackness, the only lights the telltales in her helmet and on her chest panel. The aperture above her was a star field framed by the open doorway.

Nemoto, time-delayed, began to speculate about the vapours that had been trapped by the translucent sheet. 'A good deal of sulphuric acid,' she said. 'Other compounds . . . some clay particles . . . a little free oxygen! How strange . . .'

On her belt Carole carried a couple of miniaturized floods. She lit them now. Elliptical patches of light splashed on the walls of the chamber, which curved around her. She glimpsed an uneven, smoothly textured inner surface, some kind of structure spanning the interior.

She reported to Nemoto. 'The moonlet is hollowed out. The chamber is roughly spherical, though the walls are not smooth. This single chamber must take up most of the volume of the moonlet. The walls can't be much more than a few metres thick anywhere . . .' She aimed her beams at the centre of the cavern. There was a dark mass there, about the size of a small car. It was fixed in place by a series of poles that jutted out radially, like the spokes of a wheel, to the wall of the chamber, fixing themselves to the moonlet's equator. The spokes looked as if they were made from rock too. Perhaps they had just been left in place when the chamber had been carved out.

She described all this, without speculating about the purpose of the structures. Then she blipped her thruster pack and drifted to the wall.

The wall looked carved. She saw basins, valleys, little mountains and ridges, all on the scale of metres. It was like flying over a miniaturized landscape at some theme park.

'. . . The central structure is obviously a power source,' Nemoto was saying. 'There is deuterium in there. Fusion, perhaps. A miniature sun, suspended at the centre of this hollow world. And from the topography of that inner surface it seems that the moonlet's basins and valleys have been carved to take a liquid. Water? A miniature sun, model rivers and seas – or at least, lakes. Perhaps the moonlet was spun up to provide artificial gravity . . . This is a bubble world, Carole, designed to support some form of life, independent of the outside universe.'

'But that makes no sense,' Carole replied. 'We're orbiting Venus. There's a gigantic sun just the other side of that wall, pumping out all the energy anybody could require. Why would anybody hide away in this – cave?'

But Nemoto, time-delayed, kept talking, of course, oblivious of her questions.

Carole stopped a metre or so short of the wall. She deployed her portable lab, letting its laser shine on the wall.

She stroked the wall's surface. The texture was nothing like the lunar-surface rock and regolith of the moonlet's exterior. Instead there seemed to be an underlay of crystalline substances that glinted and sparkled – quartz perhaps. Here and there, clinging to the crystalline substrate, she found a muddy clay. Though the 'mud' was dried out in the vacuum, she saw swirls of colour, complex compounds mixed in with the basic material. It reminded her of the gloopy mud of a volcanic hot spring.

The first results of her lab's analysis began to chatter across its surface. Quartz, yes, and corundum – aluminium oxide. And everywhere, especially in those clay traces, she found traces of sulphuric acid.

Nemoto understood immediately.

'. . . Sulphuric acid. Of course. That is the key. What if these artificial lakes and rivers were once filled with acid? An acid biosphere is not as unlikely as it sounds. Sulphuric acid stays liquid over a temperature range three times that of water. Of course the acids dissolve most organic compounds – have you ever seen a sugar cube dropped in acid? But alkanes – simple straight-chain hydrocarbons – can survive. Or perhaps there is a biochemistry based on silicones, long-chain molecules based on silicon-oxygen pairs . . . Only a few common minerals can resist an acidic environment: quartz, corundum, a few sulphates. These walls have been weathered. Your mother would have understood

... Venus is full of acid, you see. The clouds are filled with floating droplets of it. This is a good place to be, if what you *need* is acid ...'

Carole gazed into the empty lake basins, and tried to imagine creatures whose veins ran with acid. But this toy world, Nemoto had said, was hundreds of millions of years old. If any of their descendants survived they must be utterly transformed by time, she thought, as different from those who built this moonlet as I am from my mindless Mesozoic ancestors.

And if we found them – if we ever touched – we would destroy each other.

'... This bubble world is surely not meant to stay here, drifting around Venus, forever. We may presume that this was merely the construction site, Venus a resource mine. The bubble is already on a near-escape orbit; a little more energy and it could have escaped Venus altogether – perhaps even departed the sun's gravity field. You see?'

'I think so –'

'This rogue moonlet could travel to the nearer stars in a few centuries, perhaps, with its occupants warmed against the interstellar chill by their miniature interior sun ...'

They had been migrants to the solar system, born in some remote, acidic sea. Perhaps they had come in a single, ancient moonlet, a single spore landing here as part of a wider migration. They had found raw materials in Venus's orbit – perhaps a moon or captured asteroids – to be dismantled and worked. They had made more bubble worlds, filled them with oceans of sulphuric acid mined from Venus's clouds, and sent them on their way – thousands, even millions of moon-ships, the next wave of colonization, continuing the steady diffusion of their kind.

'It's a neat method,' Nemoto said. 'Efficient, reliable. A low-technology way to conquer the stars ...'

'Could it have been the Gaijin?' Carole asked.

'... But how convenient,' Nemoto was saying, 'that these sulphur-eaters should arrive in the solar system and find *precisely* what they needed: a planet like Venus whose clouds they could mine for their acid oceans, a convenient moon to dismantle. And where did the energy come from for all this? ... Oh, no, Carole, these weren't Gaijin. Whatever the secrets of this sulphuric-acid biology, it is nothing like the nature of the Gaijin. And this is all so much *older* than the Gaijin.'

Not the Gaijin, Carole thought, chilled. An earlier wave of immigrants, hundreds of millions of years in the past. The Gaijin weren't even the first.

'We can't know why they stopped before they had completed their project,' Nemoto said softly. 'War. Cataclysm. Who knows? Perhaps we will find out on Venus. Perhaps that is what the Gaijin are here to discover.'

My mother's generation grew up thinking the solar system was primordial – basically unmodified by intelligence, before we crawled out of the pond. And now, though we barely started looking, we found this: the ruin of a gigantic colonization and emigration project, ancient long, long before there were humans on Earth.

'You expected to find this,' she said slowly. 'Didn't you, Nemoto?'

'. . . Of course,' Nemoto said at last. 'It was logically inevitable that we would find something like this – not the details, but the essence of it, somewhere in the solar system. The violation. And the secretive activities of the Gaijin drew me here, to find it.

'One more thing,' Nemoto whispered. 'Your data has enabled me to make a better estimate of the artefact's age. It is eight hundred million years old.' Nemoto laughed softly. 'Yes. Of course it is.'

Carole frowned. 'I don't understand. What's the significance of that?'

'Your mother would have known,' said Nemoto.

Chapter 12

SISTER PLANET

Four hundred kilometres high, Carole was falling towards Venus. The lander had no windows; the conditions it had to survive were much too ferocious for that. But the inner walls were plastered with soft-screens, to show Carole what lay beyond the honeycombed metal that cushioned her. Thus, the capsule was a fragile windowed cage, full of light and her universe was divided into two: stars above, glowing planet below.

Her descent would be a thing of skips and hops and long glides as she shed her orbital energy. The sensation was so gentle, the panorama so elemental, that it was almost like a virtual simulation back on Earth. But this was no game, no simulation; she was really here, alone in this flimsy capsule, like a stone thrown into the immense air ocean of Venus, a hundred million kilometres from any helping hand.

Still she fell. The cloud decks below her remained featureless, but they were flattening to a perfect plain, like some geometric demonstration. Looking up, she could see a great cone of shining plasma trailing after her lander as it cut into the high air. She imagined seeing herself from space, a fake meteorite shining against the smooth face of Venus.

As her altitude unravelled the air thickened, and the bites of deceleration came hard and heavy, the buffeting more severe. Now the noise began, a thin screaming of tortured air, molecules broken apart by the heat of her descent, and there were flashes of plasma light at her virtual windows, like flashbulb pops. The temperature of the thin air outside rose to Earth-like levels, twenty or thirty centigrade.

But the air was not Earth-like. Sulphuric acid was already congealing around her, tiny droplets of it, acid formed by the action of sunlight on sulphur products and traces of oxygen that leaked up from the pool of air below.

At seventy kilometres she fell into the first clouds.

The stars winked out, and thick yellow mist closed around her. Soon even the sun was perceptibly dimming, becoming washed-out, as if seen through high winter clouds on Earth. Still the bulk of Venus's air ocean lay beneath her. But she was already in the main cloud deck, twenty kilometres thick, the opaque blanket which had, until the age of space probes, hidden Venus's surface from human eyes.

The buffeting became still more severe. But her capsule punched its way through this thin, angry air, and soon the battering of the high superstorms ceased.

Her main parachute blossomed open; she was briefly pushed back hard in her seat, and her descent slowed further. There was a rattle as small unmanned probes burst from the skin of her craft and arced away, seeking their own destiny.

The visibility was better than she had expected: perhaps she could see as far as one, even two kilometres. And she could make out layers in the cloud, sheets of stratum-like mist through which she fell, one by one.

Now came a patter against the hull: gentle, almost like hail, just audible under the moaning wind noise. She glimpsed particles slapping against the window: long crystals, like splinters of quartz. Were they crystals of solid sulphuric acid? Was that possible?

The hail soon disappeared. And, still fifty kilometres high, she dropped out of the cloud layer into clear air.

She looked up at rigging, giant orange parachutes. The capsule was swaying, very slowly, suspended from the big parachute system. The clouds above were thick and solid, dense, with complex cumulus structures bulging below like misty chandeliers, almost like the clouds of Earth. The sun was invisible, and the light was deeply tinged with yellow, fading to orange at the blurred horizon, as if she was falling into night. But there was still no sign of land below, only a dense, glowing haze.

With a clatter of explosive bolts her parachutes cut away, rippling like jellyfish, lost. She dropped further, descending into thickening haze. The lower air here was so dense it was more like falling into an ocean: Venus was not a place for parachutes.

The light was dimming, becoming increasingly more red.

Telltales lit up as her capsule's protective systems came online. The temperature outside was rising ferociously, already far higher than the boiling point of water – though she was still twice as high as Earth's highest cirrus clouds. The lander's walls were a honeycomb, strong enough to withstand external pressures that could approach a hundred atmospheres. And the lander contained sinks, stores of chemicals like hydrates of lithium nitrate, which, evaporating, could absorb much of the ferocious incoming heat energy. But the real heat dump was a refrigeration laser; every few minutes it fired horizontally, creating temperatures far higher even than those of Venus's air.

I'm floating in a sea of acid, she thought, in a mobile refrigerator. It all seemed absurd, a system of clunky gadgetry. It was hard to believe the Gaijin would do it this way.

And yet it was all somehow wonderful.

Now there was a fresh pattering against the hull of the ship. More hail? No, rain – immense drops slamming against her virtual walls, streaking and quickly evaporating. This was true acid rain, she supposed, sulphuric acid droplets formed kilometres above. The rain grew ferocious, a sudden storm rattling against her walls, and the drops streaked and ran together, blurring her vision. For a brief moment she felt frightened, adrift in this stormy sky.

But, as quickly as it had begun, the rain tailed off. It was so hot now the rain was evaporating. A little deeper the intense heat would destroy the acid molecules themselves, leaving a mist of sulphur oxides and water.

Abruptly the haze cleared below her. As if she was peering down towards the bed of some orange sea, she made out structure below: looming forms, shadows, what looked like a river valley.

Land.

Suspended from a balloon, she drifted over a continent.

'This is Aphrodite,' Nemoto murmured from the distant Moon. 'The size of Africa. Shaped like a scorpion – look at the map, Carole; see the claws in the west, the stinging tail to the east? But this is a scorpion fourteen thousand kilometres long, and stretching nearly halfway around the planet's equator . . .'

Carole – in her refrigerated balloon-lifted lander, still very high – was drifting from the west, past the claws of the scorpion. She saw a monstrous plateau: nearly three thousand kilometres across, she learned, its surface some three kilometres above the surrounding plains, to which it descended sharply. But the surface of the plateau was far from smooth. She saw ridges, troughs and domes, a bewildering variety of features, all crowded within a landscape that was blocky, jumbled, cut by intersecting ridges and gouges.

'The land looks as if it's been cracked open,' she said. 'And then reassembled. Like a parquet floor.'

'. . . Yes,' Nemoto whispered at last. 'This is the oldest landscape on Venus. It shows a history of great heat, of cataclysm. We will see much geological violence here.'

Everywhere she looked the world was murky red, both sky and land, still, windless. The sky above was like an overcast Earth sky, the light a sombre red, like a deep sunset – brighter than she had expected, but more Mars-like, she thought, than Earthly. The sun itself was invisible, save for an ill-defined glare, low on the horizon. The 'day' here would last more than a hundred Earth days, a stately combination of Venus's orbit around the sun and its slow rotation – the 'day' here was longer than Venus's year, in fact.

Beyond the great plateau, she crossed a highland region that was riven by immense valleys – spectacular, stunning, and yet forever hidden by the kilometres of cloud above, hidden away on this blasted planet where no eyes could see it. The easternmost part of Aphrodite was a broad, elongated dome, obviously volcanic, with rifts, domes, lava flows and great shield volcanoes. But the most spectacular feature was a huge volcanic formation called Maat Mons: the largest volcano on Venus, three hundred kilometres wide and eight kilometres high. It was a twin to Mauna Loa, Earth's largest volcano, stripped of concealing ocean.

This was a world of volcanism. The vast plains were covered by flood basalts – frozen lakes of lava, like the maria of the Moon – and punctured by thousands of small volcanoes, shield-shaped, built up by repeated outpourings of lava. But there were some shield structures – like the Hawaiian volcanoes, like Maat Mons – that towered five or eight kilometres above the plains, covered in repeated lava flows.

As she drifted further east, away from Aphrodite and over a smooth basalt lowland, Carole learned to pick out features which had no counterparts on Earth. There were steep-sided, flat-topped domes formed by sticky lava welling up through flaws in the crust. There were volcanoes with their flanks gouged away by huge landslides that left ridges like protruding insect legs. There were domes surrounded by spiderweb patterns of fractures and ridges. There were volcanoes with flows that looked like petals, pushing out across the plains.

And, most spectacular, there were coronae: utterly unearthly, rings of ridges and fractures. Some of these were thousands of kilometres across, giant features each big enough to straddle much of the continental United States. Perhaps they were formed by blobs of upwelling magma that pushed up the crust and then spread out, allowing the centre to implode, like a failed cake. To Carole the rings of swollen, distorted and broken crust, looked like the outbreak of some immense chthonic mould from Venus's deep interior.

There were even rivers here.

Her balloon ship drifted over valleys kilometres wide and thousands of kilometres in length, unlikely Amazons complete with flood plains, deltas, meanders and bars, here on a world where no liquid water could have flowed for billions of years – if ever. One of these, called Baltis Vallis, was longer than the Nile, and so it was the longest river valley in the solar system. Perhaps the rivers had been cut by an exotic form of lava – for example, formed by a salty carbon-rich rock called carbonatite, that might have flowed in Venus's still hotter past.

Suspended from a balloon, Carole would drift over this naked world for a week, while her eyes and the lander's sensors probed at the strange landscapes below. And then, perhaps, she would land.

She was, despite herself, enchanted. Venus had no water, no life; and yet it was a garden, she saw, a garden of volcanism and sculptured rock. My mother would have understood all this, Carole thought with an echo of her old, lingering guilt. But my mother isn't here. *I'm* here.

But Nemoto, coldly, told her to look for patterns. 'You are not a tourist. Look beyond the spectacle, Carole. What do you see?'

What Carole saw was wrinkles and craters.

Wrinkles: the ground was covered with ridges and cracks, some of them running hundreds of kilometres, as if the whole planet was an apricot left too long in the sun.

And *craters*: they were everywhere, hundreds of them, spread evenly over the whole of the planet's surface. There were few very large craters – and few very small ones too; hardly any less than five or ten kilometres across.

'. . . Violence, you see,' Nemoto said. 'Global violence. Those wrinkles in the lowlands, like the tesserae cracks of the highlands, are proof that the whole of the lithosphere, the outer crust of this planet, was stretched or compressed – *all at the same time*. What could do such a thing?

'And as for the craters, there is little wind erosion here, Carole; the air at the bottom of this turgid ocean of gas is very still, and so the craters have remained as fresh as when they were formed. Few are small, for that thick air screens out the smaller impactors, destroying them before they reach the ground. But, conversely, few of the craters are *large*. Certainly none of them compare with the giant basins of the Moon. But those immense lunar basins date back to the earliest days of the solar system, when the sky was still full of giant rogue planetesimals. And so we can tell, you see –'

'– that these craters are all young,' Carole said.

'– that no crater is much older than eight hundred million years,' Nemoto said, not yet hearing her. 'In fact, no feature on the surface of this planet appears older than that. *Eight hundred million years*: it might seem an immense age to you, but the planets are *five times* older still. Carole, eight hundred million years ago, something happened to Venus – something that distorted the entire surface, wiping it clean of older features, destroying four billion years of geologic heritage. We can never know what was lost, what traces of continents and seas were brutally melted . . .'

Eight hundred million years, Carole thought. *The same age as the moonlet artefacts.* That was the significance Nemoto saw. Her skin prickled.

What had been done to Venus, eight hundred million years ago?

She drifted into the planet's long night. But there was no relief from the searing warmth, so effectively did the great blanket of air redistribute the heat; at midnight the air was only a few degrees cooler than at noon.

Nemoto's automated probes, she learned, had found life on Venus, here on this baked, still planet.

Or rather, traces of life.

Like the heat-loving microbes of Earth's deep ocean vents, these had been creatures that had once swum in a hot, salty ocean of water. Carole learned that human scientists had long expected to find such organisms here: organisms that must now be extinct everywhere, their potential lost forever, destroyed by the planet's catastrophic heating. Nothing left but microscopic fossils in the oldest rocks . . .

The sky wound down through degrees of deepening crimson. As her eyes adapted to the dark, she saw that there was still light here – but no starlight could penetrate the immense column of air above. *The ground itself* was shining: she saw wrinkles and ridges and volcanic cones looming eerily from the dark.

On Venus, even at night, the rock was so hot it glowed.

But this faint illumination did not seem hellish. It was as if she was drifting over a fairyland, a land halfway to unreality; and the inversion of her perspective – darkness above, light below – seemed very strange.

When she reached the dawn terminator, there was a slow and subtle change, of ground glow to sky shine, and the world became normal once more.

Nemoto told her to prepare for landing. Nemoto's agitated excitement was obvious. She directed Carole to head for the mountains. Through her automated probes, Nemoto had found something, a worthy target for their one-and-only attempt at landing.

Ishtar Terra was a continent the size of Australia, rising high above the global plains. Carole drifted in from the west, over a plateau called Lakshmi Planum: twice the size of Tibet, a place of huge volcanic outflows. The perimeter of the Planum was composed of rough mountain ranges – long, curved ridges with deep troughs between, terrain that reminded her of the Appalachians seen from the air. And its southern perimeter was a huge cliff-like feature: three kilometres high, sloping at more than twenty degrees, its great flanks littered by landslides.

To the east the ground began to rise up towards the immense, towering mountain range called Maxwell Montes. She drifted south over one great summit. It was eleven kilometres tall, one and a half times as tall as Everest, and with a giant impact crater punched into its flank. She descended towards the south-western corner of the massif.

The landing was gentle, flawless.

The first human on Venus. Mom, you should see me now.

Carole stepped forward, picking her way between loose plates of rock. There was no wind noise. But when her metal-booted feet crunched on loose rock, the noise was very sharp and piercing; sound, it seemed, would carry a long way in this dense, springy air.

The world was red.

The sky was tall above her, a vast diffuse dome of dull, oppressive red. The air was thick – it resisted her motions, like a fluid, as if she was immersed in some sea – but it was clear, and still. The rocks were crimson plates. There seemed to be some kind of frost on them; here and there they sparkled, dully. Now, how could that be?

She walked forward. She tried to describe the ground, to be a geologist.

'The plain has many fine features: honeycombs, small ridges, fissures. It is littered with flat plates of rock, one or two metres wide. It is like a flat, rocky desert on Earth.' She knelt to inspect a rock more closely; exoskeletal multipliers prodded her limbs, helping her position her heavy suit. 'I can see strata in this rock. It looks like a terrestrial volcanic rock, perhaps a gabbro, but it seems to have been formed by multiple lava flows, over time. The rock is speckled by dark spots. They seem to be erosion pits. They are filled with soil. There is something like frost glittering, a very fine shimmer, clusters of crystals.' She had a lab unit. She pressed it against the surface of a rock, being sure she caught a little of that strange layer of frost.

Cautiously, with a hand encased in an articulated tungsten glove like a claw, she reached out to touch the rock. That frosty layer scraped away. It was clearly very thin. Of course it couldn't be water-ice frost. What, then?

At her gentle prod, a section of the rock the size of her hand broke away along a plane, and crumbled to dust and fragments that sank slowly to the ground.

She straightened up. Experimentally she raised one foot and stepped up onto a rock. It crumbled like a meringue, breaking along cracks that ran deep into the rock's fabric.

This was chemical weathering. There was no water here to wash away the rocks, no rain to drench them, no frost to crack them, no strong winds to batter them with sand. But the dense, corrosive atmosphere worked its way into the fine structure of the rocks, eating them away from the inside. All over Venus, she thought, the rocks must simply be rotting in place, waiting for a nudge to crumble and fall.

She looked around.

She was standing on a plateau, here in the Maxwell Montes. To the south, no more than a kilometre away, a steep cliff led down to the deeper plains. To the north – beyond the squat lander on its sturdy legs – she could see the great shadowy bulks of the mountains, cones of a deeper crimson painted against the red sky.

She had landed some five kilometres above the mean level (no sea level on Venus; no seas). Here, in the balmy heights of Ishtar Terra, it was some forty degrees cooler than on the great volcanic plains – though, at more than four hundred degrees centigrade, that was little help to her equipment – but the air pressure was only a third of its peak value, on the lowest plains. But this was nearly as deep into Venus's air ocean as she could go.

Still, her suit was a monstrous shell of tungsten, more like a deep sea diver's suit than a spacesuit. On her back and chest she wore packs laden with consumables and heat exchangers, sufficient to keep her alive for a few hours. But, like her ship, her key piece of refrigeration technology was a set of lasers which periodically dumped her excess heat into the Venusian rock. The suit was ingenious, but hardly comfortable; Venus's gravity was ninety per cent of Earth's, and the suit was heavy and confining.

She tilted back and looked up into the sky.

She couldn't see the sun; the dim crimson light was uniform, thoroughly scattered, apparently without a source. But the sky was not featureless. She could see through the lower air and the haze to those great cloud decks, all of fifty kilometres above. There were holes in the clouds, patches of brighter sky, making it a great uneven sheet of light. And the patches were moving. The sky was full of giant shifting shapes of light and darkness, slowly forming and dissolving, like fragments of a nightmare. The flow was stately, silent, a sign of huge stratospheric violence far removed from the still, windless pool of air in which she stood.

Astonishing, beautiful. And nobody in all human history had seen this before her.

'. . . I've analysed your frost,' Nemoto said evenly. 'It's tellurium. Almost pure metal. On Venus, tellurium would vaporize at lower altitudes. So it has snowed out here, just as water snows out at the peaks of our own mountains.'

A snow of metal. How remarkable, Carole thought.

'Now,' said Nemoto slyly, 'tellurium is rare. It makes up only one-billionth of one per cent of our surface rocks, and we've no reason to believe the rocks of Venus differ so significantly. But tellurium, for a technological society, is useful stuff. We use it to improve stainless steel, and in electrolysis, and in electronics, and as a catalyst in refining petroleum. How did so much tellurium, such an exotic high-tech material, get deposited on Venus? . . .'

Not by the natives, Carole thought, those wretched long-extinct bacteria. *Visitors*. Those who came here before us, before the Gaijin, long before. Perhaps they were the acid-breathers who built the moonlets. Perhaps they crashed here, and the tellurium was a relic of their ship: all that remains of them after eight hundred million years, a thin metallic frost on the mountains of Venus.

There was a sudden flash, far above. Many minutes later, she heard what sounded like thunder. Giant electrical storms raged in those high clouds. But there was no rain, of course.

She watched the clouds, entranced.

She walked steadily forward, heading south-west, away from the lander. Soon she was approaching the lip of the plateau. She could see no land beyond; evidently the fall-off was steep.

'. . . Let me tell you what I believe,' Nemoto whispered. 'When Venus formed, it was indeed a twin of Earth. I believe Venus rotated quickly, much as Earth does, as Mars does, taking no more than a few

Earth days to spin on its axis; why should Venus have been different? I believe Venus was formed with a moon, like Earth's. And I believe it had oceans, of liquid water. There is no reason why Venus should not have formed with as much water as Earth. There were oceans, and tides . . .'

With surprising suddenness, she came to the edge.

A cliff face fell away before her, marked here and there by the lobed flow of landslides. This great ridge ran for kilometres to either side, all the way to the horizon and beyond. And the slope continued down – on and on, down and down, as if she was looking over the edge of a continental shelf into some deeper ocean – until it merged with a plateau, far below, and then the planet-circling volcanic plain beyond that.

This was the edge of the Maxwell mountains region. This cliff descended six kilometres in just eight kilometres' distance, an average slope of thirty-five degrees. There was nothing like it on Earth, anywhere.

She had to descend to the level of the Lakshmi Planum, six kilometres below, to study Nemoto's puzzle. They hadn't anticipated any surface journey of such length and difficulty; she hadn't brought a surface vehicle, and the lander had neither the fuel nor the capability to fly her deeper into the ocean of air. And so she had to walk.

Nemoto had said she owed it to the human race to accept the risk, to complete her mission. Carole just thought she owed it to her mother, who would surely not have hesitated.

'Of course Venus is closer to the sun; even wet Venus was not an identical twin of Earth. The air was dominated by carbon dioxide. The oceans were hot – perhaps as hot as two hundred degrees – and the atmosphere humid, laden with clouds. But, thanks to the water, plate tectonics operated, and much of the carbon dioxide was kept locked up in the carbonate rocks, which were periodically subducted into the mantle, just as on Earth.

'Venus was a moist greenhouse, where life flourished . . .'

She found talus slopes, rubble left by crumbled rocks. It would require care, but this type of climb wasn't so unfamiliar to Carole. She had hiked in places in the Rocky Mountains that were rather like this, places where chemical weathering seemed to dominate, even on Earth. But the depth would push the envelope of her suit's design. And, of course, there was nobody here to help her up. So she took care not to fall.

After a couple of kilometres she paused for breath. She looked down, across kilometres of steeply sloping rock, to the Planum below.

She thought she could see something new, emerging from the murk: a long dark line, oddly straight, that disappeared here and there among folds in the rock, only to emerge once more further along. As if somebody had reached down with a straight-edge and scoured a deep dark cut into these hot rocks.

There was something beside the line, squat and dark, like a beetle. It seemed to her to be moving along the line. But perhaps that was her imagination.

She continued her careful climb downwards.

'... But then the visitors came in their drifting interstellar moonlets,' Nemoto had said. 'And they cared nothing for Venus or its life forms. They just wanted to steal the moon, to propagate their rocky spore. So they stopped Venus spinning.'

At the base of the cliffs she paused for a few minutes, letting her heartbeat subside to something like normal, sipping water.

The black line was a cable. It was maybe two metres thick, featureless and black, and it was held a metre from the ground by crude, sturdy pylons of rock.

'How do you despin a planet?' Nemoto whispered. 'We can think of a number of ways. You could bombard it with asteroids, for instance. But I think Venus was turned into a giant Dyson engine. Carole, I have observed cables like this all over the planet, wrapped east to west. They are fragmentary, broken – after all they are eight hundred million years old – but they still exist in stretches hundreds of kilometres long. Once, I would wager, the surface of Venus was wrapped in a cage of cables that followed the lines of latitude, like geographical markings on a schoolroom globe ...'

She pressed her lab box against the cable. She even ran her hand along it, cautiously, but could feel nothing through the layers of her suit.

She began to walk alongside the cable. Some of the pylons were missing, others badly eroded. It was remarkable any of this stuff had lasted so long, she thought; it must be strongly resistant to Venus's corrosive air.

'Electric currents would be passed through the cables,' Nemoto whispered. 'The circulating currents would generate an intense magnetic field. This field would be used to couple the planet to its moon – perhaps the moon was dragged within its Roche limit, deliberately broken apart by tides.

'Thus they used the planet's spin energy to break up its moon.

'They rebuilt the fragments into their habitats, their rocky bubbles. The moonlets would be hurled out of the system, each of them robbing Venus of a little more of its spin. I wonder how long it took – thousands, millions of years? . . . And, as they worked, they waited for Venus to bake itself to death.

'The climate of Venus was destabilized by the spin-down, you see,' Nemoto said. 'It got hotter. There must have been a paucity of rain, a terrible drought, at last no rain at all . . . And finally, the oceans themselves started to evaporate.

'When all the oceans were gone – life must already have been extinguished – the water in the air started to drift to the top of the atmosphere. There, it was broken up by sunlight. The hydrogen escaped to space, and the oxygen and remnant water made sulphuric acid in the clouds.

'And that was what the moonlet builders wanted, you see. *The acid.* They mined the acid out of the ruined air, perhaps with ships like our profac crawlers.

'It's an efficient scheme, if you think it over. All you need is a fat, fast-spinning planet with a moon, and you get a source of moonlet ships, a way to launch them, and even a sulphuric acid mine. Venus, despun, was ruined. But *they* didn't care. They had what they wanted.

'We are lucky they did not select Earth. Perhaps our Moon was too large, too distant; perhaps the sun was too far away . . .'

But they didn't finish the job, Carole thought. What great catastrophe, eight hundred million years ago, stopped them? Were some of Venus's great impact craters the wounds left by remnants of that vanished moon falling from the sky, uncontrolled – or even the scars of some disastrous war? . . . For Venus, Nemoto said, things got worse still. When all its water was lost, plate tectonics halted. The shifting continents seized up, like an engine run out of oil. The planet's interior heat was trapped, built up – until it was released catastrophically. 'Mass volcanism erupted. There were immense lava floods, giant new volcanoes. Much of the surface fractured, crumpled, melted – and the carbon dioxide locked up in the rocks began to pump into the atmosphere, thickening it further . . .'

Something was moving, directly ahead of her.

It was the beetle-like thing that she had observed from the cliff. And it was working its way along the cable, gouging at it with complex tools she couldn't make out, scoring it deeply.

It was a grey-black form, the size of a small car. It was as tall as she was, its surface featureless, returning glinted highlights of Venus's complex sky. And it was based on a dodecahedral core.

'Hello,' she said. '*You* haven't been here for eight hundred million years.'

'Gaijin technology,' Nemoto whispered when she saw the image. 'It is here to scavenge. Carole, this ancient cable is a superconductor, working at Venusian temperatures. Remarkable. Even the Gaijin have nothing like this. And what,' she hissed, 'do they intend to do with it? Which of our planets or moons will *they* wrap up, like a Christmas parcel?'

An alarm chimed softly in Carole's helmet. She must soon turn back, if she was to complete her long climb back to the lander in safety.

From here she could see the lower plains, the true floor of Venus, the great basalt ocean that covered the planet, still kilometres below her altitude. She longed to go further, to climb down and explore. But she knew she must not. My mission is over, she realized. Here, at this moment; I have come as far as I can, and must turn back.

She was surprised how disappointed she felt. Earth would seem very confining after this, despite the wealth she expected to claw in from her celebrity. She glanced up at the twisting, pulsing clouds, fifty kilometres up. But no matter how far I travel, she thought, I will always remember this: Venus, where I was first to set foot.

This, and the immense crime I have witnessed here.

'. . . If this happened once, it must have happened again and again,' whispered Nemoto. 'A wave of colonists come to a solar system like ours. They take what they want, ruinously mining out the resources, trashing what remains. And then they move on . . . or are somehow stopped. And then, later, when the planets have begun to heal, others follow, and the process begins again. Over and over.

'I predict we will find this everywhere. We can't assume that *anything* in the solar system is truly primordial. We don't yet know how to look, and the scars will be buried deep in time. But *here*, it is unmistakable, the mark of their wasteful carelessness . . .'

Carole stepped carefully behind the blindly toiling Gaijin beetle machine, and, peering patiently through the ruddy murk, sought scraps of superconductor.

Chapter 13

THE ROADS OF EMPIRE

Different suns, a sheaf of worlds: Malenfant drifted among the stars, between flashes of blue teleport light.

It was a strange thought that because the Saddle Point links were so long – in some cases spanning hundreds of light years, with transit times measured in centuries – there could be whole populations in transit at any moment, stored in Saddle Point transmissions: whole populations existing as frozen patterns of data arrowing between the stars, without thought or feeling, hope or fear.

And he was slowly learning something of the nature of the Saddle Point system itself.

A teleport interstellar transportation system made economic sense – of course, or else it wouldn't have been built. Saddle Point signals were minimum strength. They seemed to be precisely directed, as if lased, and operated just above the background noise level, worked at frequencies designed to avoid photon quantization noise. And the gateways, of course, were placed at points of gravitational focussing, in order to exploit the billion-fold gain available there. He figured, with back-of-the-envelope calculations, that with such savings the cost of information transfer was at least a billion times less than the cost of equivalent physical transfer, by means of ships crawling between the stars.

It was an interstellar transport system designed for creatures like the Gaijin, who relished the cold and dark at the rim of star systems, working at low temperatures and low energies and with virtually no leaked noise. No wonder we had such trouble detecting them, he thought.

But the physics of the system imposed a number of constraints.

Each receiver had to be quantum-entangled with a transmitter. What the Builders must have done was to haul receiver gates to the stars by some conventional means, slower-than-light craft like flower-ships. But it was a system with a limited life. Each gate's stock of entangled states would be depleted every time a teleportation was completed – and so each link could only be used a finite number of times.

Perhaps the Builders still existed, and had sustained the motivations that led them to build the gates in the first place, and so were maintaining the gates. If not, the system must be fragmenting, as the key, much-used links ceased to operate. Perhaps the oldest sections had already failed.

It might be that the hubs, the oldest parts of the system, would be inaccessible to humans and Gaijin, the Builders isolated, forever unknowable.

He wondered if that was important. It depended on how smart the Builders had been, he supposed, how much they understood about what the hell was going on in this cruel universe. He was getting the impression that the Gaijin knew little more than humanity did: that they too were picking their way through this Galaxy of ruins and battle scars, trying to figure out *why* this kept happening.

Confined for most of his time to the habitats the Gaijin provided, Malenfant was a virtual prisoner. After a time – after *years* – he knew he was becoming institutionalized, a little stir crazy, too dependent on the small rituals that got him through the day.

He became devoted, obsessively so, to his suit, his Shuttle EMU, his one possession. He spent hours repairing it and maintaining it and cleaning it. As much as possible he tried to leave his animated photo of Emma in the spacesuit pocket where it had lain for years. He already knew every grain of it, every scrap of motion and sound; he couldn't bear the thought of wearing it out, of it fading to white blankness; it would be like losing his own existence.

After a time it seemed to him he was getting ill. He sensed he was growing weaker. If he pinched his cheek – or even cut himself – it didn't seem to hurt the way it should.

It didn't trouble him, cocooned as he was in the tight confines of his habitats.

He did find out that the Gaijin didn't suffer such problems.

The very basis of their minds was different. *His* consciousness was based on quantum-mechanical processes going on in his brain, which was why his whole brain – and his body, his brain's support system – had to be transported, and was therefore somewhat corrupted by every Saddle Point transition.

Cassiopeia's 'mind' was more like a computer program. It was composed purely of classical information, stuff you could copy and store at will, stuff that didn't have to be destroyed to be transmitted by the Saddle Points. When she went 'through' a gateway, Cassiopeia's program was simply halted. That way she used up fewer of the Saddle Point link's stock of entangled states.

He wasn't enough of a philosopher to say if all this disqualified her from being conscious, from having a soul.

There were other differences.

Periodically he would watch the Gaijin swarming like locusts over the hull of a flower-ship, thousands of them. They would *merge*, in clattering, glistening sheets, as if melting into each other, and then separate, Gaijin coalescing one by one as if dripping out of a solute.

The purpose of these great dissolved parliaments seemed to be a transfer of information, perhaps the making of decisions. If so it was an efficient system. The Gaijin did not need to talk to each other, as humans did, imperfectly striving to interpret for each other the contents of their minds. They certainly did not need to argue, or persuade; the shared data and interpretations of the merged state were either valid and valuable, or they were not.

But how was it possible to say that *this* Gaijin, who came out of the cluster, was the *same* individual as had entered such a merge? Was it meaningful even to pose the question?

To the Gaijin, mind and even identity were fluid, malleable things. To them, identity was something to be copied, broken up, shared, merged; it didn't matter that the *self* was lost, it seemed to him, as long as continuity was maintained, so that each of the Gaijin, as currently manifested, could trace their memories back along a complex path to the remote place that had birthed the first of them.

And, likewise, he supposed, they could anticipate an unbounded future, of sentience, if not identity. A cold mechanical immortality.

He was less and less interested in the blizzard of worlds the Gaijin showed him. Even though, as it turned out, everywhere you looked there was life. Life and war and death. He strove to understand what the Gaijin were telling him – what they wanted him to do.

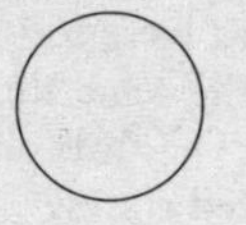

Chapter 14

DREAMS OF ANCESTRAL FISH

Madeleine Meacher flew into Kourou from Florida.

The plane door slid open, and hot, humid air washed over her. This was East Guiana, a chunk of the north-eastern coast of South America. All Madeleine could see, to the horizon, was greenery: an equatorial rainforest, thick, crowding trees, clouds of insects shimmering above mangrove swamps.

Already she felt oppressed by this crowding layer of life, the dense, moist air. In fact she felt a stab of panic at the thought that this big, heavy biosphere was unmanaged. *Nobody at the controls.* Madeleine guessed she'd spent too long in spacecraft.

Some kind of truck – good grief, it looked like it was running on *gasoline* – had dragged up a flight of steps to the plane. Madeleine was going to have to walk down herself, she realized. It was the year 2131, and, through the Saddle Points, Madeleine had travelled as far as twenty-seven light years from Sol. And here, seventy years out of her time, she was walking down airline steps, as if it was 1931.

Not a good start to my new career, Madeleine thought bleakly.

A man was waiting at the bottom of the steps. He looked about thirty, and he was a head shorter than Madeleine, with crisp black hair and a round face, the skin brown and leathery. He was wearing some kind of toga, white and cool.

She wanted to touch that face, feel its texture.

'Madeleine Meacher?'

'Yes.'

He stuck out his hand. 'Ben Roach. I'm on the Triton project here. Welcome to South America's spaceport.' His accent was complex – multinational – but with an Australian root.

She took his hand. It was broader than hers, the palm pink-pale; his flesh was warm, dry.

They walked towards a beat-up terminal building. There was vegetation here: scrubby, yellowed grass, drooping palms. It was a contrast to the lush blanket she'd glimpsed from the air.

'What happened to the jungle here?'

He grinned. 'Too many fizzers.' He glanced down, then took her hand again. 'Oh. You are hurt.'

There was a deep cut on the index finger; a wound she'd somehow suffered on that creaky old staircase, probably. Madeleine studied the damaged finger, pulling it this way and that as if it were a piece of meat. 'It's my own fault; the plane was so hot I left off my biocomp gloves.' The gloves, like the rest of the body suit Madeleine wore, were made of a semi-sentient mesh of sensors which warned her when she was damaging herself.

'This is the Discontinuity,' said Ben, curious.

'Yeah. Too much teleportation is bad for you.' Eventually, as she played with the finger, she reopened the drying cut.

Ben stared curiously as fresh blood oozed.

Madeleine's employer had set up an office in the spaceport Technical Centre. This housed a run-down mission control centre, a press office, a hospitality area and a dusty, shut-down space museum: tinfoil models of forgotten satellites.

The office itself was cool, light, airy. Too neat. There was rice straw matting on the floor, and scroll paintings on the wall, and flowers. It was all traditional Japanese, though Madeleine could see the 'paintings' were on some kind of softscreen, so configurable.

The office had a view of the full-scale Ariane 5 mock-up that stood outside the entrance to the Technical Centre. Sitting on its mobile launch table, the Ariane looked a little like the old American Shuttles, with a fat liquid-propelled core booster (called the EPC, for *Etage Principal Cryotechnique*), flanked by two shorter strap-on solid boosters. The launch table itself was a lot more elegant than the Shuttle's Apollo-era gantries, though; it was a slim curved tower of concrete and steel, like a piece of modern sculpture, dwarfed by the booster. This mock-up had to be a hundred and fifty years old, Madeleine figured; its paintwork was eroded away, the old ESA markings barely visible. Mould and creepers clawed at the sides of the rocket, a slow, irreversible vegetable onslaught; the booster was drowned in green, as ancient and meaningless as the ruins of a Mayan temple.

Madeleine's employer was sitting on the floor, cross-legged, before a small *butsudan*, a Buddha shelf, under the window. She was a

Japanese, a small, wizened woman, her face imploded, criss-crossed by Vallis Marineris grooves. Her remnant of hair was a handful of grey wisps, clinging to a liver-spotted scalp. She had been born in 1990. That made her more than a hundred and forty years old, close to the record. Nobody knew how she was keeping herself alive.

She was, of course, Nemoto.

Nemoto touched a carved statue. 'A Buddha,' she said, 'of fused regolith from the Mare Ingenii. Once such an artefact would have seemed very exotic.' She got up stiffly and went to a coffee pot. 'You want some? I also have green tea.'

'No. I burn my mouth too easily.'

'That's a loss.'

'Tell me about it.' An inability to drink hot black coffee was the Discontinuity handicap which Madeleine felt most severely.

She studied Nemoto, this legendary figure from the deep past, and sought awe, even curiosity. She felt only numbness, impatience. 'When do you want me to start work?'

Nemoto smiled thinly. 'Straight to business, Meacher? As soon as you can. The first launches start in a month.'

Madeleine had been hired to prepare two hundred rookie astronauts for spaceflight.

'Not astronauts,' Nemoto corrected her. 'Emigrants.'

'Emigrants to Triton.'

'Yes. Two hundred Aborigines, from the heart of the Australian outback, establishing a new nation on a moon of Neptune. Inspiring thought, don't you think?'

Or absurd, Madeleine reflected.

'All you have to do is familiarize them with microgravity. We've established a hydro training facility here, and so forth. Just stop them throwing up or going crazy before we can get them transferred to the transport. I assigned Ben Roach to shepherd you for your first couple of days. He's a smart-ass kid, but he has his uses.'

Madeleine tried to focus on what Nemoto was saying, the details of her outlandish scheme. Triton? Why, for God's sake? Surrounded by strangeness, numbed by the Discontinuity, it was hard to care.

Nemoto eyed Madeleine. 'You feel – disoriented. Here we sit: mirror images, relics of the twenty-first century, both stranded in an unanticipated future. The only difference is in how we got here. You by your relativistic hop, skip and jump across light years and decades – the scenic route.' She grinned. 'And I came the hard way.' Her teeth were black, Madeleine noticed.

She said, 'But we're both damaged by the experience, in our different ways.'

Nemoto shrugged. 'I ended up with all the power.'

'Power over me, anyhow.'

'Meacher, I still need crew for the transport.'

'You're offering me a flight to Triton?'

'If you're interested. Your Discontinuity won't be a serious liability if –'

'Forget it.'

Madeleine stood up. Her left leg buckled and she nearly fell; she had to cling to the desk top. It was as if Madeleine was the old woman. She found she'd been applying too much weight to the leg and the blood supply had been cut off. She hadn't noticed, of course; and that kind of damage was too subtle for the biocomp suit to pick up.

Nemoto watched her, calculating, without sympathy. 'The Triton colony is crucial,' she said. 'Strategic.'

This was the Nemoto Madeleine had heard of. 'You're still working for the future of the species, Nemoto.'

'Yes, if you want to know.'

Madeleine's heart sank. Nemoto would be hard to deal with rationally. People with missions always were.

But only Nemoto would give her a job.

Aside perhaps from Reid Malenfant – and even after all this time nobody knew what had become of *him* – Madeleine had been the first human to leave the solar system. Her experiences in the light of other stars had been astonishing.

Her first return to the solar system had been something of a triumph – although even then she'd been aware of a historical dislocation, as if the world had had a layer of strangeness thrown over it. And she had been shocked by the sudden – to her – deaths of her mother, and of poor Sally Brind, and many others she had known.

At least Frank Paulis's get-rich-slow compound interest scheme had worked out that first time. And she had earned herself a little fame. She was the first star traveller – aside from Malenfant – and that earned her some profile.

But she hadn't been sorry to leave again, to escape into the clean blue light of the Saddle Points, replacing the baffling human world with the cold external mysteries of the stars.

Her later returns had been less enjoyable.

The truth was that as the decades peeled away on Earth, and the novelty wore off, nobody much cared about the star travellers – and few were prepared to protect the interests of these historical curiosities. So, the last time she came back, Madeleine had returned to find that a devaluation of the UN dollar, the new global currency, had wiped out a lot of the value of her savings. And then had come the banks' decision to close the swelling accounts of the star travellers, a step that had been backed by inter-government agencies up to and including the UN.

Meanwhile no insurance company would touch her, or anyone else who had been through the Saddle Point gateways, after the Discontinuity condition had been diagnosed.

Which was why Madeleine needed money.

Nemoto was attached to no organization. Madeleine couldn't have defined her role. But her source of power was clear enough: she had stayed alive.

Thanks to longevity treatments, Nemoto, and a handful of privileged others, had gotten so old that they formed a new breed of power-player, their influence coming from contacts, webs of alliances, ancient debts and favours granted. Nemoto was a gerontocrat, modelling herself on the antique Communist officials who still ran China.

Madeleine wouldn't have been surprised to find it was Nemoto herself, or the other gerontocrats, who lay behind the whole scam. The closure of the star travellers' accounts had given Nemoto a good deal of leverage over Madeleine, and those who had followed in her path. And the strategy had put a block on any ambitions the star travellers might have had to use *their* effective longevity to accrue power back home.

She wondered if the gerontocrats – conservative, selfish, reclusive, obsessive – were responsible for a more general malaise that seemed to her to have afflicted this fast-forwarded world. There had been change – new fashions, gadgetry, terminology – but, it seemed to her, no progress. In science and art she could see no signs of meaningful innovation. The world's nations evolved, but the various supranational structures had not changed for decades: the political institutions that wielded the power had ossified.

And meanwhile, the world still laboured under the old burdens of a fast-changing ecology and resource shortages, and minor wars continued to be an irritant at every fractured joint between peoples.

Nobody was solving these ancient problems. Worse, it seemed to her, nobody was even trying any more. You could no longer, for example, get reliable statistics on population numbers, or disease occurrences, or poverty. It was as if history had stopped when the Gaijin had arrived.

. . . But it didn't *matter*. She wouldn't have changed a thing. The travelling itself was the thing, the point of it all. The rest was ancient history, even to Madeleine herself.

Ben showed her to her apartment. He had to show her how to open the door. In 2131, God help her, you had to work door locks with foot studs.

The East Guiana spaceport, built up by the Europeans in the 1980s, extended maybe twenty kilometres along the coast of the Atlantic, from Sinnamary to Kourou, which was actually an old fishing village. There were control buildings, booster integration buildings, solid booster test stands and launch complexes, all identified by baffling French acronyms: BAF, BIL, BEAP – and connected by roads and rail tracks that looked, from her window, like gashes in the foliage.

Ariane had been nice-looking technology, for its time, a hundred and fifty years earlier. It had been superseded by new generations of spaceplanes, even before the Gaijin had taken over most of Earth's ground-to-orbit traffic with their clean, flawless landers. But when the French released political control of East Guiana, the new government decided to refurbish what was left at Kourou.

So East Guiana, one of the smallest and poorest nations on Earth, suddenly had a space program.

Ariane had kept flying even as history moved on, and nations and corporations and alliances had formed and dissolved, leaving new configurations whose very names were baffling to Madeleine. But Ariane remained, an antique, disreputable, dirty, unreliable launcher, used by agencies without the funds to afford something better.

Like Nemoto.

Maybe, Madeleine thought, it wasn't a surprise that Nemoto, another relic of the first Space Age, had gravitated here.

The residential quarters had been set up in an abandoned solid-propellant factory, a building that dated back to before Madeleine's birth. The cluster of buildings was still called UPG, for *Usine de Propergol de Guyane*. It was a jumble of white cubes spilling over a hill-side, like a Mediterranean village. It was sparsely set up, but comfortable enough. About four hundred people lived here: the Aborigine emigrants, and permanent technical and managerial staff to operate the automated facilities. Once twenty thousand had been housed in Kourou, a fifth of the country's population. The feeling of emptiness, of age and abandonment, was startling.

She slept for a few hours. Then she drifted about her apartment, tinkering.

It was startling how often and how much everyday gadgets changed. The toilet, for instance, was just a hole in the ground, and it took her an age to figure out how to make it flush. The shower was just as bad; it took a call to Ben to establish that to set the heat, you had to put your finger in a little test sink, and let the thing read your body temperature.

And so on. All stuff everybody else here had grown up with. It was like being in a foreign country, wherever she went, even in her home town; she'd long grown tired of people not taking her requests for basic information seriously. And every time she came back from another Einsteinian fast-forward it got worse.

Anyhow, a few minutes after stepping out of the shower, her skin was prickling with sweat again.

She felt no discomfort, of course. The Discontinuity left her with numbness where pain or discomfort should sit. Like a fading-down of reality. She towelled herself dry again, trying not to scrape her skin.

Perhaps it should have been expected. Before the reality of Saddle Point teleportation had been demonstrated, there had been those who had doubted whether human minds could ever, even in principle, be downloaded, stored or transmitted. The way data was stored in a brain was not simple. A human mind appeared to be a process, dynamic, and no static 'snapshot', no matter how sophisticated the technology, could possibly capture its richness. So it was argued.

The fact that the first travellers, including Madeleine, had survived Saddle Point transitions seemed to belie this pessimistic point of view. But perhaps, in the longer term, those doubts had been borne out.

She knew there was talk of treatment for Discontinuity sufferers. Madeleine wasn't holding her breath: nobody was putting serious money into the problem. There were only a handful of star travellers, and nobody cared much about them anyhow. And so Madeleine had to wear a constricting biocomp sensor suit, which warned her when she'd sat still for too long, or when her skin was burned or frozen, and woke her up in the night to turn her over.

Maybe the Gaijin weren't affected the same way. Nobody knew.

She stood, naked, at an open window, trying to get cool. It was evening. She looked across kilometres of hilly country, all of it coated by burgeoning life. There was a breeze, lifting loose leaves high enough to cross the balcony. But the breeze served only to push more water-laden air into her face.

The blanket of foliage coating the hills around the launch areas looked etiolated: the leaves yellowed, stunted, the trees sickly and small by comparison with their neighbours further away. And the leaves at her feet were yellow and black, others holed, as if burned.

She pulled on a loose dress and walked a kilometre to the block containing Ben's apartment.

She glimpsed Aborigines: her trainees, men, women and children, passing back and forth in little groups, engaged in their own errands and concerns. They showed no interest in her. They were loose-limbed people, many of them going barefoot, some of the women overweight; they wore loose togas like Ben's, the cloth worn, dirty, well-used. Their faces were round, a paler brown than she had expected, with blunt noses, prominent brows. Many of them wore breathing filters or sun screen, and their skin was marked by cancer scars.

They were alien to Madeleine, but no more so than most of the people of the year 2131.

Ben welcomed her. He served her a meal: couscous rice with saffron, chunks of soya, a light local wine.

He told her about his wife. She was called Lena; she was only twenty, a decade younger than Ben. She was in orbit, working on the big emigrant transports Nemoto was assembling. Ben hadn't seen her for months.

Madeleine felt easy with Ben. He even took care with the words he used. Language drift seemed remarkably rapid; less than a century out of her time, even if she was familiar with a word, she couldn't always recognize its pronunciation, and had learned it wasn't safe to assume she knew its modern usage. But Ben made sure that she understood.

'It's strange finding Aborigines here,' Madeleine said. 'So far from home.'

'Not so strange. After all East Guiana is another colonial relic. The French wanted to follow the example of the British in Australia, by peopling East Guiana with convicts.' He grinned, his teeth white and young, a contrast in Madeleine's mind to the ruined mouth of Nemoto. He said, 'Anyhow, now we can escape on the fizzers.' He mimed a rocket launch with two hands clasped as in prayer. 'Whoosh.'

'Ben – why Triton? I know Nemoto has her own objectives. But for you . . .'

'Nemoto's offer was the only one we had. We have nowhere else to go. But perhaps we would follow her anyway. Nemoto is marginalized, her ideas ridiculed – most vigorously by friends of the Gaijin. *But she is right*, on the deepest of levels. We used to think we were alone in a primordial universe. Suddenly we find ourselves in a dangerous, crowded universe littered with ruins. There was fear, and deep anger at the discovery of the violation of Venus. It might have been a sister world to Earth – or Earth might have been the victim. With time, the outrage faded – but we remembered; we, a people who have been dispossessed already.'

More leaves blew in from a darkening sky, broken, damaged by rocket exhaust.

Ben told her he came from central Australia, born into a group called the Yolgnu. 'When I was a boy my family lived by a river bank, living in the old way. But the authorities, the white people, came and moved us to a place called Framlingham. Just a row of shacks and tin houses. Then, when I was eight years old, more white men took me away to an orphanage. The men were from the Aboriginal Protection Board. When they thought I was civilized enough, they sent me to foster parents in Melbourne. White people, called Nash. They were rich and kind. You see, it was the policy of the Government to solve their Aboriginal problem once and for all, by making me white.'

All of this stunned her, embarrassed her. She said, 'You must hate them.'

He smiled. 'It had been tried before. They were always frightened, first of the Japanese, then of Indonesians and Chinese, flowing down from the north, with their eyes on Australia's empty spaces, its huge mineral deposits. Now perhaps they fear the Gaijin, come to take their land. And each time they exorcise their fears using us. I do not hate them. I understand them.'

To her surprise, he turned out to hold a doctorate in black hole physics. But he had been drawn back to Framlingham, as had others of his generation. Slowly they had constructed a dream of a new life. Almost all of the people escaping to Triton were from Framlingham, he said. 'It was a wrench to leave the old lands. But we will find new lands, make our own world.'

Ben served her *sambuca*, an Italian liqueur: a new craze, it seemed. *Sambuca* was clear, aniseed flavoured. Ben floated Brazilian coffee beans in her glass, and set it alight. The alcohol burned blue in the fading light, cupped in the open space above the liquid, and the coffee beans hissed and popped. The flames were to release the oils from the beans, Ben said, and infuse the drink with the flavour of the coffee.

He doused the flames and took careful sips from her glass, testing its temperature for her so that Madeleine would not burn her lips. The flavour of the hot liquid was strong, sharp enough to push at the boundary of her Discontinuity.

They sat under the darkling sky, and the stars came out.

Ben pointed out constellations for her, and he traced out other features of the celestial sphere for her, the geography of the sky.

There was the celestial equator, an invisible line that was a projection of Earth's equator on the sky. From here, of course, the equator passed right over their heads. Lights moved along that line, silent, smoothly traversing, like strangely orderly fireflies. They were orbital structures: factories, dwellings, even hotels. Many of them were Chinese, Ben told her; Chinese corporations had built up a close working relationship with the Gaijin. Then he distracted her with another invisible line called the ecliptic. The ecliptic was the equator of the solar system, the line the planets traced out. It was different from the Earth's equator, because Earth's axis was tipped over through twenty-three degrees or so.

. . . Rather, the ecliptic *used* to be invisible. Now, Madeleine found, it was marked out by a fine row of new stars, medium bright, some glowing white but others a deeper yellow to orange. It was like a row of street lamps.

Those lights were cities, Madeleine learned: the new Gaijin communities, hollowed out of the giant rocks that littered the asteroid belt, burning with fusion light. No human had gotten within an astronomical unit of those new lamps in space.

It was beautiful, chilling, remarkable. The people of this time had grown up with all this. But, nevertheless, she thought, the sky is full of cities, and huge incomprehensible ruins. New toilets and telephones she could accept. But even the *solar system* had changed while she had been away, and who would have anticipated that?

She felt too hot, dizzy.

She considered making a pass at Ben. It would be comforting.

He seemed receptive.

'What about Lena?'

He smiled. 'She is not here. I am not there. We are human beings. We have ties of *gurrutu,* of kinship, which will forever bind us.'

She took that as assent. She reached out in the dark, and he responded.

* * *

They made love in the equatorial heat, a slick of perspiration lubricating their bodies. Ben's skin was a sculpture of firm planes, and his hands were confident and warm. She felt remote, as if her body was a piece of equipment she had to control and monitor.

Ben sensed this. He was tender, and held her for comfort. He was fascinated by her skin, he said. The skin of a woman tanned by the light of different stars.

She couldn't feel his touch.

She slept badly. In her dreams Madeleine spun through rings of powder-blue metal, confronted visions of geometric forms. Triangles, dodecahedra, icosahedra. When Madeleine cried out, Ben held her.

At one point she saw that Ben, sleeping, was about to knock the coffee pot, and still-hot liquid would pour over his chest. She grabbed the spout, taking a few splashes, and pushed it away. She felt nothing, of course. She wiped her hand dry on a tissue, and waited for sleep.

When they woke they found that the coffee had burned her hand severely.

Ben treated her. 'The absence of pain,' he said, 'is evidently a mixed blessing.'

She'd heard this before, and had grown impatient. 'Pain is an evolutionary relic. Sure, it serves as an early warning system. But we can replace that, right? Get rid of sharp edges. Soak the world with software implants, like my biocomp, to warn and protect us.'

Ben studied her. He said, 'Do you know what the central reticular formation is?'

'Why don't you tell me?'

'It's a small section of the brain. And if you excite this formation – in the brain of a normal human – the perception of pain disappears. This is the locus of the Discontinuity damage. I am talking of *qualia*, the inner sensations, aspects of consciousness. Your pain, objectively, still exists, in terms of the response of your body; what has been removed is the corresponding qualia, your perception of it. Put an end to discomfort, and there is an end to the emotions linked with pain. Fear. Grief. Pleasure.'

'So my inner life is diminished.'

'Yes. Consciousness is not well understood, nor the link between mind and body. Perhaps other qualia, too, are being distorted or destroyed by the Saddle Point transitions.'

But, Madeleine thought, my dreams are of alien artefacts. Perhaps my qualia are not simply being destroyed. Perhaps they are being –

replaced. It was a thought that hadn't struck her before. Resolutely she pushed it away.

'How do you know so much about this?'

'I have ambitions myself to travel to the stars. To see a black hole, before I build my farm on Triton. It is worth my studying what would happen to me . . . Madeleine,' he said slowly, 'there is something I should tell you. Even though Nemoto has forbidden it.'

'What?'

'The Chinese discovered it first, in their dealings with the Gaijin. Some say it is a Gaijin gift, in fact. Nemoto has worked to suppress knowledge of it. But I –'

'Tell me, damn it.'

'There is a cure for the Discontinuity.'

She was electrified. Terrified.

He said, 'You know, the remarkable thing is that the reticular formation is in the oldest part of the brain. We share it with our most ancient ancestors. Madeleine, you have returned from the stars, changed. There are those who think we are forging a new breed of humans, out there beyond the Saddle Points. But, perhaps, we are merely swimming through the dreams of ancestral fish.'

He smiled and held her again.

She stormed into Nemoto's office.

Nemoto was busy; an Ariane launch was imminent. She took a look at the bandaging swathing Madeleine's hand. 'You ought to be careful.'

'There's a way to reverse the Discontinuity. Isn't there?'

'. . . Oh.' Nemoto stood and faced the window, the Ariane mock-up framed there. She held her hands behind her back, and her posture was stiff. 'That smart-ass kid. Sit down, Madeleine.'

'*Isn't there?*'

'I said sit down.'

Madeleine complied. She had trouble arranging herself on Nemoto's office furniture.

'Yes, there's a way,' Nemoto said. 'If you're treated correctly before you go through a gateway, the translation can be used to *reverse* the Discontinuity damage.'

'Then why are you hiding this?' Madeleine asked, and then, 'Send me to a Saddle Point.'

Nemoto looked at Madeleine from her mask of a face. 'You're sure you want *this* back? The pain, the anguish of being human –'

'Yes.'

Nemoto turned and sat down; she nested her hands on the table top, the fingers like intertwined twigs. 'You have to understand the situation we face,' she said. 'Most of us are sleeping. But some of us believe we're at war.' She meant the Gaijin, of course, and their great belt cities, their swooping forays through the inner solar system – and the other migrants who were following, still decades or centuries away but nevertheless on the way, noisily building along the spiral arm. 'You must see it – *you*, when you return from your jaunts to the stars. Everybody's busy, too busy with the short term, unable to see the trends. Only us, Madeleine; only us, stranded out of time.'

Something connected for Madeleine. '. . . Oh. That's why you have kept the cure so quiet.'

'Do you see why we must do this, Meacher? We need to explore every option. To have soldiers – warriors – who are free of pain –'

'Free of consciousness itself.'

'Perhaps. If that's necessary.'

Madeleine felt disgusted, sullied. Discontinuity was, after all, nothing less than the restructuring of her consciousness by Saddle Point transitions. How typical of humanity to turn this remarkable experience into a weapon. How monstrous.

She sat back. 'Send me through a Saddle Point.'

'Or?'

'Or I expose what you've been doing. Concealing a cure for the Discontinuity.'

Nemoto considered. 'This is too big an issue to horse-trade with the likes of you. But,' she said, 'I will make you an exchange.'

'An exchange?'

'I'll send you to a Saddle Point. But afterwards you go to Triton with the Aborigines. We have to make sure that colony succeeds.'

Madeleine shook her head. 'It will take decades for me to complete a round-trip through a gateway.'

Nemoto smiled thinly. 'It doesn't matter. It will take the Yolgnu years to reach Neptune, more years to establish any kind of viable colony. And we're playing a long game here. Some day the Gaijin will confront us directly. Some of us don't understand why that hasn't already happened. We need to be prepared, when it does.'

'And Triton is a part of this scheme?'

Nemoto didn't answer.

But of course it was, Madeleine thought. Everything is a part of Nemoto's grand design. Everything, and everyone: my need for money and healing, Ben's people's need for refuge – all just levers for Nemoto to press.

Nemoto said, 'Where?'

'Where what?'

'Where do you want to go, on your health cruise?'

'I don't care. What does it matter?'

'. . . There might be something suitable,' Nemoto said at length. 'There is another alien species, here in the Earth-Moon system. Did you know that? They are called the Chaera. *Their* star system is exotic. It includes a miniature black hole, which . . . well.' She eyed Madeleine. 'Your friend Ben is a black hole specialist. Perhaps he will go with you. How amusing.'

Amusing. Another little relativistic death.

There was a rumble of noise. They turned to the window. Kilometres away, beyond the mangrove swamps, Madeleine could see the booster's slim nose lift above the trees, the first glow of the engines. The light of the solid boosters seemed to spill over the tree line – startlingly bright rocket light glimmering from the flat swamps – as Ariane rolled on its axis.

'There,' Nemoto said. 'You made me miss the launch.'

Chapter 15

COLONISTS

Six months:

Once Nemoto had given her the date of her Saddle Point mission it was all she could think about. The rest of her life – her work in Kourou and elsewhere, her legal struggles to get back some of the money that had been impounded from her accounts, even her developing, low-key relationship with Ben – all of that faded to a background glow compared to the diamond-bright prospect of encountering another Saddle Point gateway, at that specified, slowly approaching date in the future.

She'd met other star travellers, returned from one or two hops into the sky with the Gaijin. All of them were determined to go on. She imagined a cloud of human travellers, journeying deeper and deeper into the strange cosmos, their ties to a blurred, fast-forwarding Earth stretching and loosening.

It wasn't just the Discontinuity. She didn't *belong* here. After all, she couldn't even work the toilets.

She longed to leave.

The Japanese-built lander touched the Moon, its rockets throwing up a cloud of fast-settling dust. There were various artefacts here, sitting on the surface of the Moon, and Nemoto, the spider at the heart of this operation, was waiting for them, anonymous in a black suit.

Ben and Madeleine suited up carefully. Madeleine made sure Ben followed her lead; she was, after all, the experienced astronaut.

She climbed down a short ladder to the surface. She dropped from step to step, in the gentle gravity. She stepped off the last rung onto regolith, which crunched like snow under her weight.

She walked away from the lander.

The colours of the Moon weren't strong: in fact the most colourful thing here was their Nishizaki Heavy Industries aluminium-frame lander, which, from a distance, looked like a small, fragile insect, done out in brilliant black, silver, orange and yellow. The Sea of Tranquillity was close to the Moon's equator, so Earth was directly above her head, and it was difficult to tip back in her pressure suit to see it. But when Ben goes to live on Triton, she thought, the sun will be a bright point source. And Earth will be no more than a pale blue point of light, only made visible by blocking out the sun itself. How strange that will be.

Nemoto was showing Ben the various artefacts she had assembled here. Madeleine saw a set of blocky metal boxes, trailing cables. These were, it turned out, a pair of high-power X-ray lasers. 'A small fission bomb is the power source. When the bomb is detonated, a burst of X-ray photons is emitted. The photons travel down long metal rods. This generates an intense beam. In effect, the power of the bomb has been focused . . .'

These were experimental weapons, it emerged, dating from the late twentieth century. They had been designed as satellite weapons, intended to shoot down intercontinental ballistic missiles.

Madeleine asked, 'And what have the Gaijin paid us for this obscene old gadgetry?'

'That's not your concern.'

The habitat which would keep them alive was another masterpiece of improvisation and low cost, Madeleine thought, like her fondly-remembered *Friendship-7*. It was based on two modules – called FGB, Russian-built, and the Service Module, American-built – scavenged from the old NASA International Space Station. The Service Module had been enhanced with an astrophysics instrument pallet.

Madeleine slipped her gloved hand into Ben's. 'We ought to name our magnificent ship,' she said.

Ben thought it over. '*Dreamtime Ancestor*.'

Nemoto said, 'Come meet the Chaera.'

The last artefact, sitting on the regolith, was a tank, a glass cube. It contained a translucent disc about a metre across, swimming slowly through oxygen-blue fluid.

It was an Eetie: a Chaera, an inhabitant of the black hole system that was the destination of this mission. The Chaera had, after the Gaijin, been the second variant of Eetie to come to the solar system.

Aside from all the dead ones in the past, of course.

Ben stepped forward. He touched the glass walls of the tank with his gloved hand. The Chaera rippled; it looked something like a sting-ray. She wondered if it was trying to talk to Ben.

. . . *The Chaera had eyes*, she saw: four of them spaced evenly around the rim of the stingray shape, dilating lids alternately opening. Human-like eyes, gazing out at her, eyes on a creature from another star. She shivered with recognition.

Through a hairline crack in the Chaera's tank, fluid bubbled and boiled into vacuum.

'You need to understand that the nature of this mission is a little different,' Nemoto said. 'You are going to a populated system. The Chaera have technology, it seems, but they lack spaceflight. The Gaijin made contact with them and initiated a trading relationship. The Chaera requested specific artefacts, which we've been able to supply.' She grunted. 'Interesting. The Gaijin actually seem to be learning to run rudimentary trading relationships, from *us*. Before, perhaps they simply appropriated, or killed.'

Ben said, '*Killed*? Your view of the Gaijin is harsh indeed, Nemoto.'

Madeleine asked, 'What are the Gaijin getting from the Chaera in return for this?'

'We don't know. The Chaera spend their days quietly in the service of their God. And their requirement, it seems, is simple. You will help them talk to God.'

Ben said dryly, 'With an X-ray laser?'

'Just focus on the science,' Nemoto said, sounding weary. 'Learn about black holes, and about the Gaijin. That's what you're being sent for. Don't worry about the rest.'

The Chaera swam like melting glass, glimmering in Earthlight.

Ben Roach seemed to sense her urgency, her longing for time to pass.

He offered to take her to Australia, to show her places where he'd grown up. 'You ought to reconnect a little. No matter how far you travel, you're still made of Earth atoms, rock and water.'

'Aborigine philosophy?' she asked, a little dismissive.

'If you like. The Earth gave you life, gave you food and language and intelligence, and will take you back when you die. There are stories that humans have already died, out there among the stars. *Their* atoms can't return to the Earth. And, conversely, there are Gaijin here.'

'None of the Gaijin have died here.' That was true; the three ambassadors she had encountered on Kefallinia were still there, still functioning decades later. 'Perhaps they can't die.'

'But if they do, then their atoms, not of the Earth, will be absorbed by the Earth's rocks.'

'Perhaps that is a fair trade,' she said. 'We should extend your philosophy. The universe is the greater Earth; the universe births us, takes us back when we die. All of us, humans, Gaijin, everybody.'

'Yes. Besides, there are lessons to learn.'

'Are you trying to educate me, Ben? What is there to see in Australia?'

'Will you come?'

It would eat up time. 'Yes,' she said.

From the air Australia looked flat, rust-red, and littered with rippling, continent-spanning sand dunes and shining salt flats, the relics of dead seas. It was eroded, very dry, very ancient; even the sand dunes, she learned, were thirty thousand years old. Human occupancy seemed limited to the coastal strip, and a few scattered settlements in the interior.

They flew into Alice Springs, in the dry heart of the island continent.

As they approached the airport she saw a modern facility: a huge white globe, other installations. In among the structures she saw the characteristic gleaming cones of Gaijin landers. New silvery fencing had been flung out across the desert for kilometres around the central structures.

The extent of the Gaijin holding, here in central Australia, startled her. The days when the Gaijin had been restricted to a heavily-guarded compound on a Greek island were long past, it seemed.

Ben grimaced. 'This is an old American space tracking facility called Pine Gap. There used to be a lot of local hostility to it. It was said that even the Prime Minister of Australia didn't know what went on in there. And the local Aboriginal communities were outraged when their land was taken away.'

'But now,' she said dryly, 'the Americans have gone. We don't do any space tracking, because we don't have a space program that requires it any more.'

'No,' he murmured. 'And so they gave Pine Gap to the Gaijin.'

'When?'

He shrugged. 'Forty years ago, I think.' Before he was born.

It was the same all over the planet, Madeleine knew. Everywhere they touched the Earth, the Gaijin were moving out: slowly, almost imperceptibly, but it was all one way. And every year there were more weary human refugees, forced to flee their homes.

Few people protested strongly, because few saw the trends. Nemoto is right, she thought. The Gaijin are exploiting our short lives. Nemoto is right to try to survive, to stretch out her life, to *see* what is being done to us.

But Ben surprised her. Being here, seeing this, he lost his detachment; he became unhappy, angry. 'The Gaijin care even less about our feelings than the Europeans. But we were here before the Gaijin, long before the Europeans. They are all Gaijin to us. Some of us are fleeing. But maybe one day they will all have gone, all the foreigners, and we will slip off our manufactured clothes and walk into the desert once more. What do you think? . . .'

The plane landed heavily, in a cloud of billowing red dust.

Alice Springs – Ben called it *the Alice* – turned out to be a dull, scrubby town, a grid of baking-hot streets. Its main strip was called Todd Street, a dreary stretch of asphalt that dated back to the days of horses and hitching posts. Now it might have been transplanted from small-town America, a jumble of bars, soda fountains and souvenir stores.

Madeleine studied the store windows desultorily. There were Australian mementoes – stuffed kangaroos and wallabies, animated T-shirts and books and data discs – but there was also, to cash in on the nearness of the Pine Gap reserve, a range of Gaijin souvenirs, models of landers and flower-ships, and animated spider-like Gaijin toys that clacked eerily back and forth across the display front. But there were few tourists now, it seemed; that industry, already dwindling before Madeleine's first Saddle Point jaunt, was now all but vanished.

They stayed in an anonymous hotel a little way away from Todd Street. There was an ugly old eucalyptus outside, pushing its way through the asphalt. The tree had small, tough-looking dark green leaves, and it was shedding its bark in great ash-grey strips that dangled from its trunk. 'A sacred monument,' Ben said gently. 'It's on the Caterpillar Dreaming.' She didn't know what that meant. SmartDrive cars wrenched their way around the tree's stubborn, ancient presence; once, in the days when people drove cars, it must have been a traffic hazard.

A couple of children ambled by – slim, lithe, a deep black, plastered with sunblock. They stared at Ben and Madeleine as they stared at the tree. Ben seemed oddly uncomfortable under their scrutiny.

It's because he's a foreigner too, she thought. He's been away too long, like me. This place isn't his any more, not quite. She found that saddening, but oddly comforting. Always somebody worse off than yourself.

They rested for a night.

At her window the Moon was bright. Fat bugs swarmed around the hotel's lamps, sparking, sizzling. It was so hot it was hard to sleep.

She longed for the simple, controllable enclosure of a spacecraft.

The next morning they prepared to see the country – to go *out bush*, as Ben called it. Ben wore desert boots, a loose singlet, a yellow hard hat and tight green shorts he called 'stubbies'. Meacher wore a loose poncho and a broad reflective hat and liberal layers of sunblock on her face and hands. After all, she wouldn't even be able to tell when this ferocious sun burned her.

They had rented a car, a chunky four-wheel-drive with immense broad tyres, already stained deep red with dust. Ben loaded up some food – tucker, he called it, his accent deepening as he spoke to the locals – and a *lot* of water, far more than she imagined they would need, in big chilled clear-walled tanks called Eskis, after Eskimo. In fact the car wouldn't allow itself to be started unless its internal sensors told it there was plenty of water on board.

The road was a straight black strip of tarmac – probably smart concrete, she thought, self-repairing, designed to last centuries without maintenance. It was empty of traffic, save for themselves.

At first she glimpsed fences, wind-pumps with cattle clustered around them, even a few camels.

They passed an Aboriginal settlement, surrounded by a link fence. It was a place of tin-roof shacks, and a few central buildings that were just brown airless boxes – a clinic, a church perhaps. Children seemed to be running everywhere, limbs flashing. Rubbish blew across the ground, where bits of glass sparkled.

They didn't stop; Ben barely glanced aside. Madeleine was shocked by the squalor.

Soon they moved beyond human habitation, and the ground was crimson and treeless. Nothing moved but the wispy shadows of high clouds. It was too arid here to farm or even graze.

'A harsh place,' she said unnecessarily.

'You bet,' Ben said, his eyes masked by mirrored glasses. 'And getting harsher. It's becoming depopulated, in fact. But it was enough for *us*. We touched the land lightly, I suppose.'

It was true. After tens of millennia of trial and error and carefully accumulated lore, the Aborigines had learned to survive here, in a land starved of nutrient and water. But there was no room for excess: there had been no fixed social structure, no prophets or chiefs, no leisured classes, and their myths were dreams of migration. And, before the coming of the Europeans, the weak, infirm and elderly had been dealt with harshly.

In a land the size of the continental United States, there had been only three hundred thousand of them. But the Aborigines had survived, where it might seem impossible.

As the ground began to rise, Ben stopped the car and got out. Madeleine emerged into hot, skin-sucking dust, flat dense light, stillness.

She found herself walking over a plateau of sand hills and crumbled, weathered orange-red rock, red as Mars, she thought, broken by deep, dry gulches. But there was grass here, tufts of it, yellow and spiky; even trees and bushes, such as low, spiky-leaved mulgas. Some of the bushes had been recently burned, and green shoots prickled the blackened stumps. To her eyes, there was the look of park land about these widely separated trees and scattered grass; but this land had been shaped by aridity and fire, not western aesthetics.

Ben seemed exhilarated to be walking, stretching his legs, thumbs hooked in the straps of a backpack. 'Australia is a place for creatures who walk,' he said. 'That's what we humans are adapted for. Look at your body some time. Every detail of it, from your long legs to your upright spine, is built for long, long walks through unforgiving lands, of desert and scrub. Australia is the kind of land we've been evolved for.'

'So we've been evolved to be refugees,' Madeleine said sourly.

'If you like. Looking at the crowd that seems to be on the way along the spiral arm, maybe that's a good thing. What do you think?'

Walking, he said, was the basis of the Dreamtime, the Aboriginal Genesis.

'In the beginning there was only the clay. And the Ancestors created themselves from the clay – thousands of them, one for each totemic species . . .' Each totemic Ancestor travelled the country, leaving a trail of words and musical notes along the lines of his footprints. And these tracks served as ways of communication between the most far-flung tribes.

Madeleine had heard of this. 'The song lines.'

'We call them something like "The Footprints of the Ancestors". And the system of knowledge and law is called the *Tjukurpa* . . . But, yes. The whole country is like a musical score. There is hardly a rock or a creek that has been left unsung. My "clan" isn't my tribe, but all the people of my Dreaming, whether on this side of the continent or the other; my "land" isn't some fixed patch of ground, but a trade route, a means of communication.

'The main song lines seem to enter Australia from the north or north-west, perhaps from across the Torres Strait, and then weave their way southwards across the continent. Perhaps they represent the routes of the first Australians of all, when they ventured over the narrow Ice Age strait from Asia. That would make the lines remnants of trails that stretch much further back, over a hundred thousand years, across Asia and back to Africa.'

'From Africa,' she said, 'to Triton.'

'Where the land is unsung. Yes.'

They climbed a little further, through clumps of the wiry yellow-white grass, which was called spinifex. She reached out to touch a clump, feeling nothing; Ben snatched her hand back. He turned it over. She saw spines sticking out of her palm.

Patiently he plucked out the spines. 'Everything here has spines. Everything is trying to survive, to hold onto its hoard of water. Just remember that . . . *Look*.'

There was a crackle of noise. A female kangaroo, with a cluster of young, had broken cover from a stand of bushes.

The kangaroos looked oddly like giant mice, clumsy but powerful, with rodent-like faces and thick fur. Their haunches were white against the red of the dirt. When the big female moved, she used a swivelling gait Madeleine had never seen before, using her tail and forelegs as props while levering herself forward on her great lower legs. There was a cub in her pouch – no, Ben said it was called a *joey* – a small head that protruded, curious, and even browsed on the spinifex as the mother moved.

The creatures, seen close up, seemed extraordinarily alien to Madeleine: a piece of different biological engineering, as if she had wandered into some alternate world. The Chaera, she thought, are hardly less exotic.

Something startled the kangaroos. They leapt away with great efficient bounds.

Madeleine grinned. 'My first kangaroo.'

'You don't understand,' Ben said tightly. 'I think that was a *Procoptodon*. A giant kangaroo. They grow as high as three metres . . .'

Madeleine knew nothing about kangaroos. 'And that's unusual?'

'Madeleine, *Procoptodon* has been extinct for ten thousand years. *That's* what makes it unusual.'

They walked on, further from the car, sipping water from flasks.

'It's the Gaijin,' he said. 'Of course it's the Gaijin. They are restoring megafauna that have long been extinct here. There have been sightings of *wanabe*, a snake a metre in diameter and seven long, a flightless bird twice the mass of an emu called *genyornis*. The Gaijin seem to be tinkering with the genetic structure of existing species, exploring these archaic, lost forms.'

They came upon an area of bare rock that was littered with bones. The bones were broken up and scattered, and had apparently been gnawed. Few of the fragments were large enough for her to recognize – was this an eye socket, that a piece of jaw?

'We think they use parsimony analysis,' Ben was saying. 'DNA erodes with time. But you can deconstruct evolution if you have access to the evolutionary products. You track backwards to find the common gene from which all the products descended; the principle is to seek the smallest number of branch points from which the present family could have evolved. When you have the structure you can recreate the ancient gene by splicing synthesized sequences into modern genes. You see?' He stopped, panting lightly. 'And, Madeleine, here's a thought. Australia has been an island, save for intervals of bridging during the Ice Ages, for a hundred million years. The genetic divergence between modern humans is widest between Australian natives and the rest of the population.'

'So if you wanted to think about picking apart the human genome –'

'– here would be a good place to start.'

She thought of the Gaijin she had seen undoing itself, decades back, in Kefallinia. 'Perhaps they are dismantling us. Taking apart the biosphere, to see how it works.'

'Perhaps. You know, humans always believed that when the aliens arrived, they would bring wisdom from the stars. Instead they seem to have arrived with nothing but questions. Now, they have grown dissatisfied with *our* answers, and are seeking their own . . . Of course it might help if they told us what it is they are looking for. But we are starting to guess.'

'We are?'

They walked on, slowly, conserving their energy.

He eyed her. 'For somebody who has travelled so far, you sometimes seem to understand little. Let me tell you another theory. Can you see any cactus, here in our desert?'

No, as it happened. In fact, now she thought about it, there were none of the desert plants she was accustomed to from the States.

Ben told her now that this was because of Australia's long history. Once it had been part of a giant super-Africa continent called Gondwanaland. When Australia had split off and sailed away, it had carried a freight of rainforest plants and animals which had responded to the growing aridity by evolving into the forms she saw here.

He rubbed his fingers in the red dirt. 'The continents are rafts of granite that ride on currents of magma in the mantle. We think the continents merge and break up, moving this way and that, under the influence of changes in those currents.'

'All right.'

'But we don't know *what* causes those magma currents to change. We used to think it must be some dynamic internal to the Earth.'

'But now –'

'Now we aren't so sure.' He smiled thinly. 'Imagine a huge war. A bombardment from space. Imagine a major strike, an asteroid or comet, hitting the ocean. It would punch through the water like a puddle, not even noticing it was there, and then crack the ocean floor.' His lips pursed. 'Think of a scum on water. Now throw in a few rocks. Imagine the islands of dirt shattering, convulsing, whirling around and uniting again. *That* was what it was like. If it happened, it shaped the whole destiny of life on Earth. The impact structures wouldn't be easy to spot, because the ocean floor gets dragged under the continents and melted. After two hundred million years, the ocean floor is wiped clean. Nevertheless there are techniques . . .'

A huge war. Rocks hurled from the sky, battering the Earth. Tens of millions of years ago. The hot dusty land seemed to swivel around her.

It sounded like an insane conspiracy theory. To attribute the evolution of Venus to the activities of aliens was one thing. But this . . . Could it possibly be true that everything she had seen today – the animals, the ancient land – all of it was shaped by intelligence, by careless war?

'Is this why you brought me to Australia? To tell me this?'

He grinned. 'On Earth, as it is in Heaven, Madeleine. We seem to find it easy to discuss the remaking of remote rocky worlds by waves of invaders – even Venus, our twin. *But why should Earth have been spared?*'

'And this is why you follow Nemoto?'

'If the Gaijin understand this – that we live in a universe of such dreadful violence – don't you think they should, at the very least, *tell us*? . . .' Ben found what looked like a piece of thigh bone. 'I'm not an expert,' he said. 'But I think this was a *diprotodon*. A wombat-like creature the size of a rhino.'

'Another Gaijin experiment.'

'Yes.' He seemed angry again, in his controlled, internalized way. 'Who knows how it died? From hunger, perhaps, or thirst, or just simple sunburn. These are archaic forms; this isn't the ecology they evolved in.'

'And so they die.'

'And so they die.'

They walked on, and found more bones of animals that should have been dead for ten thousand years, huge failed experiments, bleached in the unrelenting sun.

The Saddle Point gateway was a simple hoop of some powder-blue material, facing the sun, perhaps thirty metres across. Madeleine thought it was classically beautiful. Elegant, perfect.

As the flower-ship approached, Madeleine's fear grew. Ben told her Dreamtime stories, and she clung to him. 'Tell me . . .'

There was no deceleration. At the last minute the flower-ship folded up its electromagnetic petals, and the silvery ropes coiled back against the ship's flanks, turning it into a spear that lanced through the disc of darkness.

Blue light bathed Madeleine's face. The light increased in intensity, until it blinded them.

With every transition, there is a single instant of pain, unbearable, agonizing.

. . . But this time, for Madeleine, the pain didn't go away.

Ben held her, as the cool light of different suns broke over the flower-ship, as she wept.

Chapter 16

ICOSAHEDRAL GOD

The Saddle Point for the Chaera's home system turned out to be within the accretion disc of the black hole itself. Ben and Madeleine clung to the windows as smoky light washed over the scuffed metal and plastic surfaces of the habitat.

The accretion disc swirled below the flower-ship, like scum on the surface of a huge milk churn. The black hole was massive for its type, Madeleine learned – metres across. Matter from the accretion disc tumbled into the hole continually; X-rays sizzled into space.

The flower-ship passed through the accretion disc. The view was astonishing.

The disc foreshortened. They fell into shadows a million kilometres long.

A crimson band swept upwards past the flower-ship. Madeleine caught a glimpse of detail, a sea of gritty rubble. The disc collapsed to a grainy streak across the stars; pea-sized pellets spanged off *Ancestor*'s hull plates. Then the ship soared below the plane of the disc.

A brilliant star gleamed beneath the ceiling of rubble. This was a stable G2 star, like the sun, some five astronomical units away – about as far as Jupiter was from Sol. The black hole was orbiting that star, a wizened, spitting planet.

Soon, the monitors mounted on the *Ancestor*'s science platform started to collect data on hydrogen alpha emission, ultraviolet line spectra, ultraviolet and X-ray imaging, spectrography of the active regions. Ben took charge now, and training and practice took over as the two of them went into the routine tasks of studying the hole and its disc.

Nemoto had hooked up to the Chaera's tank a powerful bioprocessor, a little cubical unit, which would enable the humans to communicate, to some extent, with the Chaera, and with their Gaijin hosts. When they booted it up, a small screen displayed the biopro's human interface design metaphor. It was a blocky, badly synched, two-dimensional virtual representation of Nemoto's leathery face.

'The vanity of megalomaniacs,' Madeleine murmured. 'It's a pattern.'

Ben didn't understand. The Nemoto virtual grinned.

Ben and Madeleine hovered before a window into the Chaera's tank.

If Madeleine had encountered this creature in some deep sea aquarium – and given she was no biologist – she mightn't have thought it outlandishly strange. After all it had those remarkable eyes.

The eyes were, of course, a stunning example of convergent evolution. On Earth, eyes conveyed such a powerful evolutionary advantage that they had been developed independently perhaps forty times – while wings seemed to have been invented only three or four times, and the wheel not at all. Although details differed – the eyes of fish, insects and people were very different – nevertheless all eyes showed a commonality of design, for they were evolved for the same purpose, and were constrained by physical law.

You might have expected Eeties to show up with eyes.

The Chaera communicated by movement, their rippling surfaces sending low-frequency acoustic signals through the fluid in which they swam. In the tank, lasers scanned the Chaera's surface constantly, picking up the movements and affording translations.

Inter-species translation was actually getting easier, after the first experience with the Gaijin. A kind of meta-language had been evolved, an interface which served as a translation buffer between Eetie 'languages' and every human tongue. The meta-language was founded on concepts – space, time, number – which had to be common to any sentient species embedded in three-dimensional space and subject to physical law, and it had verbal, mathematical and diagrammatic components; to Madeleine's lay understanding it seemed to be a fusion of Latin and Lincos.

Madeleine felt an odd kinship with the spinning, curious creature, a creature that might have come from Earth, much more sympathetic than any Gaijin. And if we have found *you* so quickly, perhaps we will find less strangeness out there than we expect.

Ben asked, 'What is it saying?'

Virtual Nemoto translated. 'The Chaera saw the disc unfolding. "What a spectacle. I am the envy of generations . . ."'

Mini black holes, Madeleine learned, were typically the mass of

Jupiter. Too small to have been formed by processes of stellar collapse, they were created a millionth of a second after the Big Bang, baked in the fireball at the birth of the universe.

Mini black holes, then, seemed to be well understood. The oddity here was to find such a hole in a neat circular orbit around this sun-like star.

'And the real surprise,' said virtual Nemoto, 'was the discovery, by the Gaijin, of life, infesting the accretion disc of a mini black hole. The Chaera. It seems that this black hole is God for the Chaera.'

'They *worship* a black hole?' Madeleine asked.

'Evidently,' said Nemoto impatiently. 'If the translation programs are working. If it's possible to correlate concepts like "God" and "worship" across species barriers.'

Ben murmured wordlessly. Madeleine looked over his shoulder.

In the central glare of the accretion disc, there was something surrounding the black hole, embedding it.

The black hole was set into a net-like structure that started just outside the Schwarzschild radius, and extended kilometres. The structure was a regular solid of twenty triangular faces.

'It's an icosahedron,' Ben said. 'My God, it is so obviously artificial. The largest possible Platonic solid. Triumphantly three-dimensional.'

Madeleine couldn't make out any framework within the icosahedron, or any reinforcement for its edges; it was a structure of sheets of almost transparent film, each triangle hundreds of metres wide. The glow of the flower-ship's hungry ramscoop shone and sparkled from the multiple facets.

'It must be mighty strong to maintain its structure against the hole's gravity, the tides,' Ben said. 'It seems to be directing the flow of matter from the accretion disc into the event horizon . . .'

It was a jewel-box setting for a black hole. A comparative veteran of interstellar exploration, Madeleine felt stunned.

The Chaera thrashed in its tank.

Nemoto said, 'Time to pay the fare. Are we ready to speak to God?'

Madeleine turned to Ben. 'We didn't know about *this*. Maybe we should think about what we're doing here.'

He shrugged. 'Nemoto is right. It is not our mission.' He began the operations they'd rehearsed.

Reluctantly, Madeleine worked a console to unship the first of the old X-ray lasers; the monitors showed it unfolding from its mount like a shabby flower.

The self-directed laser dove into the heart of the system, heading for its closest approach to the hole.

Ben murmured, 'Three, two, one.'

There was a flash of light, pure white, which shone through the Service Module's ports.

Various instruments showed surges, of particles and electromagnetic radiation. The laser's fission-bomb power source had worked. The shielding of *Ancestor* seemed adequate.

The X-ray beam washed over the surface of 'God'. The net structure stirred, like a sleeping snake.

The Chaera quivered.

Ben was watching the false-colour images. 'Madeleine. Look.'

The surface of 'God' was alive with motion; the icosahedral netting was bunching itself around a single, brooding point, like skin crinkling round an eye.

'I can give you a rough translation from the Chaera,' said Nemoto. '"She heard us."'

Madeleine asked, '"She"?'

'God, of course. "If I have succeeded . . . Then I will be the most honoured of my race. Fame – wealth – my choice of mates –"'

Madeleine laughed sourly. 'And, of course, religious fulfilment.'

Ben monitored a surge, of X-ray photons and high-energy particles, coming from the hole – and the core at the centre of the crinkled net exploded. A pillar of radiation punched through the accretion disc like a fist.

The Chaera wobbled around its tank.

'"God is shouting,"' Nemoto said. She peered out of her biopro monitor tank, her wizened virtual face creased with doubt.

The beam blinked out, leaving a trail of churning junk.

The flower-ship entered a long powered orbit which would take it, for a time, away from the black hole, and in towards the primary star and its inner system. Madeleine and Ben watched the black hole and its enigmatic artefact recede to a toy-like glimmer.

The Chaera inhabited the accretion disc's larger fragments.

In the *Ancestor*'s recorded images, Chaera were everywhere, spinning like frisbees over the surface of their worldlets – or whipping through the accretion mush to a neighbouring fragment – or basking like lizards, their undersides turned up to the black hole.

The beam from 'God' had left a track of glowing debris through the accretion disc, like flesh scorched by hot iron. The track ended in a knot of larger fragments.

In the optical imager, jellyfish bodies drifted like soot flakes.

'Let me get this straight,' Madeleine said. 'The Chaera have evolved to feed off the X-radiation from the black hole . . . from "God". Is that right?'

'Evolved or adapted. So it seems,' Nemoto said dryly. '"God provides us in all things."'

Ben said, 'So the Chaera try to – *shout* – to "God". Some of them pray. Some of them build great artefacts to sparkle at Her. Like worshipping the sun, praying for dawn. Basically they're trying to stimulate X-radiation bursts. All the Gaijin have done is to sell them a more effective communication mechanism.'

'A better prayer wheel,' Madeleine murmured. 'But what are the Gaijin interested in here? The black hole artefact?'

'Possibly,' Nemoto said. 'Or perhaps the Chaera's religion. The Gaijin seem unhealthily obsessed with such illogical belief systems.'

'But,' Madeleine said, 'that X-ray laser delivers orders of magnitude more energy into the artefact than anything the Chaera could manage. It looks as if the energy of the pulse they get in return is magnified in proportion. Perhaps the Chaera don't understand what they're dealing with, here.'

Nemoto translated: '"God's holy shout shatters worlds."'

The main star was very sun-like. Madeleine, filled with complex doubts about her mission, pressed her hand to the window, trying to feel its warmth, hungering for simple physical pleasure.

There was just one planet here. It was a little larger than the Earth, and it followed a neat circular path through the star's habitable zone, the region within which an Earth-like planet could orbit.

But they could see, even from a distance, that this was no Earth. It was silent on all wavelengths. And it gleamed, almost as bright as a star itself; it must have cloud decks like Venus.

On a sleep break, Ben and Madeleine, clinging to each other, floated before the nearest thing they had to a picture window. Madeleine peered around, seeking constellations she might recognize, even so far from home, and she wondered if she could find Sol.

'Something's wrong,' Ben whispered.

'There always is.'

'I'm serious.' He let his fingers trace out a line across the black sky. 'What do you see?'

With the sun eclipsed by the shadow of the FGB Module, she gazed out at the subtle light. There was that bright planet, and the dim red disc of rubble surrounding the Chaera black hole, from here just visible as more than a point source of light.

Ben said, 'There's a *glow*, around the star itself, covering the orbit of that single planet. Can you see?' It was a diffuse shine, Madeleine saw, cloudy, ragged-edged. Ben said, 'That's an oddity in itself. But –'

Then she got it. 'Oh. No zodiacal light.'

The zodiacal light, in the solar system, was a faint glow along the plane of the ecliptic. Sometimes it was visible from Earth. It was sunlight, scattered by dust that orbited the sun in the plane of the planets. Most of the dust was in or near the asteroid belt, created by asteroid collisions. And in the modern solar system, of course, the zodiacal light was enhanced by the glow of Gaijin colonies.

'So if there's no zodiacal light –'

'There are no asteroids here,' said Ben.

'Nemoto. What happened to the asteroids?'

'You already know, I think,' virtual Nemoto hissed.

Ben nodded. 'They were mined out. Probably long ago. This place is *old*, Madeleine.'

The electromagnetic petals of the flower-ship sparkled hungrily as it chewed through the rich gas pocket at the heart of the system, and the shadows cast by the sun – now nearby, full and fat, brimming with light – turned like clock hands on the ship's complex surface. But that diffuse gas cloud was now dense enough that it dimmed the further stars.

Data slid silently into the FGB Module.

Ben said, 'It's like a fragment of a GMC – a giant molecular cloud. Mostly hydrogen, some dust. It's thick – comparatively. A hundred thousand molecules per cubic centimetre . . . The sun was born out of such a cloud, Madeleine.'

'But the heat of the sun dispersed the remnants of *our* cloud . . . didn't it? So why hasn't the same thing happened here?'

'Or,' virtual Nemoto said sourly, 'maybe the question should be: *how come the gas cloud got put back around this star?*'

They flew around the back of the sun. Despite elaborate shielding, light seemed to fill every crevice of the FGB module. Madeleine was relieved when they started to pull away, and headed for the cool of the outer system, and that single mysterious planet.

It took a day to get there.

They came at the planet with the sun behind them, so it showed a nearly full disc. It glared, brilliant white, just a solid mass of cloud from pole to pole, blinding and featureless. And it was surrounded by a pearly glow of interstellar hydrogen, like an immense, misshapen outer atmosphere.

The flower-ship's petals opened wide, the lasers working vigorously, and decelerated smoothly into orbit.

They could see nothing of the surface. Their instruments revealed a world that was indeed like Venus: an atmosphere of carbon dioxide, kilometres thick, scarcely any water.

There was, of course, no life of any kind.

The Chaera spun in its tank, volunteering nothing.

Ben was troubled. 'There's no reason for a Venus to form this far from the sun. This world should be temperate. An Earth.'

'But,' Nemoto hissed, 'think what this world has that Earth doesn't share.'

'The gas cloud,' Madeleine said.

Ben nodded. 'All that interstellar hydrogen. Madeleine, we're so far from the sun now, and the gas is so thick, that the hydrogen is neutral – not ionized by sunlight.'

'And so –'

'And so the planet down there has no defence against the gas; its magnetic field could only keep it out if it was charged. Hydrogen has been raining down from the sky, into the upper air.'

'Once there, it will mix with any oxygen present,' Nemoto said. 'Hydrogen plus oxygen gives –'

'Water,' Madeleine said.

'*Lots* of it,' Ben told her. 'It must have rained like hell, for a million years. The atmosphere was drained of oxygen, and filled up with water vapour. A greenhouse effect took off –'

'All that from a wisp of gas?'

'That wisp of gas was a planet-killer,' Nemoto whispered.

'But why would anyone kill a planet?'

Nemoto said, 'It is the logic of growth. This has all the characteristics of an *old* system, Meacher. Caught behind a wave of colonization – all its usable resources dug out and exploited . . .'

Madeleine frowned. 'I don't believe it. It would take a hell of a long time to eat up a solar system.'

'How long do you think?'

'I don't know. Millions of years, perhaps.'

Nemoto grunted. 'Listen to me. The growth rate of the human population on Earth, historically, was two per cent a year. Doesn't sound much, does it? But it's compound interest, remember. At that rate your population doubles every thirty-five years, an increase by tenfold every century or so. Of course after the twentieth century *our* growth rates collapsed; we ran out of resources.'

'Ah,' Ben said. 'What if we'd kept on growing?'

'How many people could Earth hold?' Nemoto whispered. 'Ten, twenty billion? Meacher, the whole of the inner solar system out to Mars could supply only enough water for maybe fifty billion people. It might have taken us a century to reach those numbers. Of course there is much more water in the asteroids and the outer system than in Earth's oceans, perhaps enough to support ten thousand *trillion* human beings.'

'A huge number.'

'But not infinite – and only six tenfold jumps away from ten billion.'

'Just six or seven centuries,' Ben said.

'And then what?' Nemoto whispered. 'Suppose we start colonizing, like the Gaijin. Earth is suddenly the centre of a growing sphere of colonization, whose volume must keep increasing at two per cent a year, to keep up with the population growth. And that means that the leading edge, the colonizing wave, has to sweep on faster and faster, eating up worlds and stars and moving on to the next, because of the pressure from behind . . .'

Ben was doing sums in his head. 'That leading edge would have to be moving at lightspeed within a few centuries, no more.'

'Imagine how it would be,' Nemoto said grimly, 'to inhabit a world in the path of such a wave. The exploitation would be rapid, ruthless, merciless, burning up worlds and stars like the front of a forest fire, leaving only ruins and lifelessness. And then, as resources are exhausted throughout the lightspeed cage, the crash comes, inevitably. Remember Venus. Remember Polynesia.'

'Polynesia? . . .'

'The nearest analogue in our own history to interstellar colonization,' Ben said. 'The Polynesians spread out among their Pacific islands for over a thousand years, across three thousand kilometres. But by about AD 1000 their colonization wavefront had reached as far as it could go, and they had inhabited every scrap of land. Isolated, each island surrounded by others already full of people, they had nowhere to go.

'On Easter Island they destroyed the native ecosystem in a few generations, let the soil erode away, cut down the forests. In the end they didn't even have enough wood to build more canoes. Then they went to war over whatever was left. By the time the Europeans arrived the Polynesians had just about wiped themselves out.'

Nemoto said, 'Think about it, Meacher. *The lightspeed cage.* Imagine this system fully populated, a long way behind the local colonization wavefront, and surrounded by systems just as heavily populated – and armed – as they were. And they were running out of resources. There surely were a lot more space dwellers than planet dwellers, but they'd already used up the asteroids and the comets. So the space dwellers turned on the planet. The inhabitants were choked, drowned, baked.'

'I don't believe it,' Madeleine said. 'Any intelligent society would figure out the dangers long before breeding itself to extinction.'

'The Polynesians didn't,' said Ben dryly.

The petals of the flower-ship opened once more, and they receded from the corpse-like planet into the calm of the outer darkness.

It was time to talk to the icosahedral God again. The second X-ray punch laser was launched.

After studying the records of the last encounter, Ben had learned how the configuration of the icosahedral artefact anticipated the direction of the resulting beam. Now Madeleine watched the core squint into focus. The killer beam would again lance through the accretion disc – and, this time, right into one of the largest of the Chaera worldlets.

Millions of Chaera were going to die. Madeleine could *see* them, infesting their accretion disc, swarming and living and loving.

In its tank, their Chaera passenger drifted like a Dali watch.

Madeleine said, 'Nemoto, we can't go ahead with the second firing.'

'But they understand the consequences,' virtual Nemoto said blandly. 'The Chaera have disturbed the artefact a few times in the past, with their mirrors and smoke signals. Every time it's killed some of them. But they need the X-ray nourishment . . . Meacher,' she warned, 'don't meddle as you did at the burster. If you meddle, the Gaijin may not allow human passengers on future missions. And we won't learn about systems like *this*. We'll have no information; we won't be able to plan . . . Besides, the laser is already deployed. There's nothing you can do about it.'

'It *is* the Chaera's choice, Madeleine,' Ben said gently. 'Their culture. It seems they're prepared to die to attain what they believe is perfection.'

Nemoto quoted the Chaera. 'It knows we're arguing here. "Where there are prophecies, they will cease. Where there are tongues, they will be stilled; where there is knowledge, it will pass away. For we know in part and we prophesy in part, but when perfection comes, the imperfect disappears."'

'Who's the philosopher?' Madeleine asked sourly. 'Some great Chaera mind of the past?'

Ben smiled. 'Actually, it was quoting Saint Paul.'

Nemoto looked startled, as Madeleine felt.

'But there remain mysteries,' Ben said. 'The Chaera look too primitive to have constructed that artefact. After all, it manipulates a black hole's gravity well. Perhaps their ancestors built this thing. Or some previous wave of colonists, who passed through this system.'

'You aren't thinking it through,' virtual Nemoto whispered. 'The Chaera have eyes filled with salty water. They must have evolved on a world with oceans. They can't have evolved *here*.'

'Then,' Madeleine snapped, 'why are they here?'

'Because they had no place else to go,' Nemoto said. 'They fled here – even modified themselves, perhaps. They huddled around an artefact left by an earlier wave of colonization. They knew that nobody would follow them to such a dangerous, unstable slum area as this.'

'They are refugees.'

'Yes. As, perhaps, we will become in the future.'

'Refugees from what?'

'From the resource wars,' Nemoto said. 'From the hydrogen suffocation of their world. Like Polynesia.'

The core artefact trembled.

And Nemoto kept talking, talking. 'This universe of ours is a place of limits, of cruel equations. The Galaxy must be full of lightspeed cages like this, at most a few hundred light years wide, traps for their exponentially growing populations. And then, after the ripped-up worlds have lain fallow, after recovery through the slow processes of geology and biology, it all begins again, a cycle of slash and burn, slash and burn . . . *This is our future*, Meacher. Our future and our past. It is after all a peculiar kind of equilibrium: the contact, the ruinous exploitation, the crash, the multiple extinctions – over and over. And it is happening again, to us. The Gaijin are already eating their way through *our* asteroid belt. Now do you see what I'm fighting against? . . .'

Madeleine remembered the burster, the slaughter of the star lichen fourteen times a second. She remembered Venus and Australia, the evidence of ancient wars even in the solar system – the relics of a previous, long-burned-out colonization bubble.

Must it be like this?

Something in her rebelled. To hell with theories. The Chaera were real, and millions of them were about to die.

And there was – she realized, thinking quickly – something she could do about it.

'Oh, damn it . . . Ben. Help me. Go down to the FGB Module. Get everything out of there you think we have to save.'

For long seconds, Ben thought it over. Then he nodded. 'I'll trust your instincts, Madeleine.'

'Good,' she said. 'Now I have a little figuring to do.' She rushed to the instrument consoles.

Ben gathered their research materials: the biological and medical samples they'd taken from their bodies, data cassettes and diskettes, film cartridges, notebooks, results of the astrophysical experiments they had run in the neighbourhood of the black hole. There was little personal gear in here, as their sleeping compartments were in the Service Module. He pulled everything together in a spare sleeping bag, and hauled it all up into the Service Module.

Madeleine glanced down for the last time through the FGB Module's picture window, at smoky accretion-disc light. The flower-ship skimmed past the flank of 'God'; the netting structure swarmed around the pulsing core.

The Chaera thrashed in its tank.

Ben pulled down the heavy hatch between the modules – it hadn't been closed since the flower-ship had swept them up from the surface of Earth's Moon – and dogged it tight. Madeleine was running a hasty computer program. She called, 'Remember the drill for a pressure hull breach?'

'Of course. But –'

'Three, two, one.'

There was a clatter of pyrotechnic bolts, an abrupt jolt.

'I just severed the FGB,' she said. 'The explosive decompression should fire it in the right direction. I hope. I didn't have time to check my figures, or verify my aim –'

Bits of radiation spat out like javelins as the core began to open.

Nemoto thundered, 'What have you done, Meacher?'

She saw the FGB Module for one last instant, its battered, patched-up form silhouetted against the gigantic cheek of 'God'. In its way it was a magnificent sight, she thought: a stubby twentieth-century human artefact orbiting a black hole, fifty-four light years from Earth.

And then the core opened.

The FGB Module got the X-ray pulse right in the rear end. Droplets of metal splashed across space . . . But the massive Russian construction lasted, long enough to shield the Chaera worldlets.

Just as Madeleine had intended.

The core closed; the surface of the net smoothed over. The slowly-cooling stump of the FGB Module drifted around the curve of the hole. Madeleine saluted it silently.

'The journey back is going to be cramped,' Ben said dryly.

The Saddle Point gateway hung before them, anonymous, eternal, indistinguishable from its copies in the solar system, visible only by the reflected light of the accretion disc.

'You saved a world, Madeleine,' Ben said.

'But nobody asked you to,' virtual Nemoto said, her voice tinny. 'You're a meddler. Sentimental. You always were. The Chaera are still protesting. "Why did you hide God from us?" . . .'

Ben shrugged. 'God is still there. I think all Madeleine has done is provide the Chaera with a little more time to consider how much perfection they really want to achieve.'

'Meacher, you're such a fool,' Nemoto said.

Perhaps she was. But she knew that what she was learning, the dismal, stupid secret of the universe, would not leave her. And she wondered what she would find when she reached home this time.

The blue glow of transition flooded over them, and there was an instant of searing, welcoming pain.

Chapter 17
LESSONS

World after world after world.

He saw worlds something like Earth, but with oceans of ammonia or sulphuric acid or hydrocarbons, airs of neon or nitrogen or carbon monoxide. All of them alive, of course, one way or another.

But such relatively Earth-like planets turned out to be the exception.

He was shown a giant world closely orbiting a star called 70 Virginis. This world was a cloudy ball six times the mass of Jupiter. The Gaijin believed there were creatures living in those clouds, immense, tenuous whales feeding off the organics created in the air by the central star's radiation. But colonists had visited here, long ago. At one pole of the planet there was what appeared to be an immense mining installation, perhaps there to extract organics or some other valuable volatile like helium-3. The installation was desolate, apparently scarred by battle.

Close to a star called Upsilon Andromedae, forty-nine light years from Earth, he found a planet with Jupiter's mass orbiting closer than Mercury to its sun. It had been stripped of its cloud decks by the sun's heat, leaving an immense rocky ball, with canyons deep enough to swallow Earth's Moon. Malenfant saw creatures crawling through those deep shadows, immense beetle-like beings. They were protected from the sun's heat by tough carapaces, and had legs like tree trunks strong enough to lift them against the ferocious gravity. Perhaps they fed off volatiles trapped in the eternal shadows, or seeping from the planet's deep interior. Here the battles seemed to have been fought out over the higher ground; Malenfant saw a plain littered with the wreckage of starships.

Not far from the star Procyon there was a nomadic world, a world without a sun, hurled by some random gravitational accident away from its parent star. It was in utter darkness, of course, a black ball swimming alone through space. But it was a big planet with a hydrogen-rich atmosphere; it warmed itself with the dwindling heat of the radioactive elements in its core, with volcanoes and earthquakes and tectonic shifts. Thus, under a lightless sky, there were oceans of liquid water – and in their depths life swarmed, feeding off minerals from the deeper hot rocks, not unlike the deep-sea animals which clustered around volcanic vents in Earth's seas. Here, though, life was doomed, for the world's core was inexorably cooling, as the heat of its formation was lost.

But even this lonely planet had been subject to destructive exploitation by colonists; there were signs, Malenfant learned, of giant strip-mine gouges in the ocean floors, huge machines now abandoned, perhaps deliberately wrecked.

Everywhere, he had learned, life had emerged. But every world, every system, had been overrun by waves of colonization, followed by collapse or destructive wars – not once, but many times. Everywhere the sky was full of engineering, of ruins.

And the bad news continued. The universe itself could prove a deadly place. He was taken through a region a hundred light years wide where world after world was dead, land and oceans littered with the diverse remains of separately-evolved life.

There had been a gamma ray burster explosion here, the Gaijin told him: the collision of two neutron stars, causing a three-dimensional shower of high-energy electromagnetic radiation and heavy particles that had wiped clean the worlds for light years around. It had been a random cosmic accident that had cared nothing for culture and ambition, hope and love and dreams. Some life survived – on Earth, the deep-ocean forms, perhaps pond life, some insects would have endured the lethal showers. But nothing advanced made it through, and certainly nothing approaching sentience; after the accident, its effects over in weeks or months, it would require a hundred million years of patient evolution to fix the rent in life's fabric suffered in this place.

But nothing was without cost, he learned; nothing without benefit. The intense energy pulse of nearby gamma ray bursts could shape the evolution of young star systems; primordial dust was melted into dense iron-rich droplets, which settled quickly to the central plain of a dust cloud and so accelerated the formation of planets. Without a close-by gamma ray burst, it was possible that star systems like the solar system could never have formed. Birth, amid death; the way of the universe.

Maybe. But such cold logic was no comfort for Malenfant.

The Gaijin seemed determined to show him as much as possible of this vast star-spanning graveyard, to drive home its significance. After a time it became unbearable, the lesson blinding in its cruelty: that if the universe didn't get you, other sentient beings would.

Sometimes a spark within him rebelled. *Does it have to be like this? Can't we find another way?*

But he was very weak now, very lonely, very old.

He huddled in his shelter, eyes closed, while the years, of the universe and of his life, wore away, drenched in blue Saddle Point light.

There is only so much, all things considered, that a man can take.

III

TRENCHWORKS

AD 2190–2340

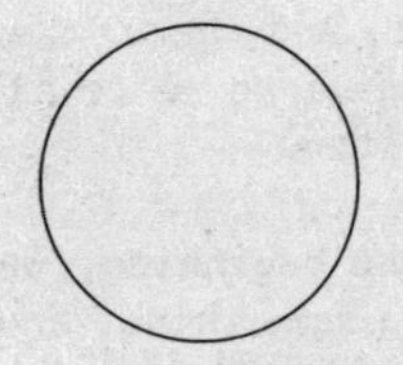

The Gaijin had a somewhat mathematical philosophy. Malenfant thought it sounded suspiciously like a religion.

The Gaijin believed that the universe was fundamentally comprehensible by creatures like themselves – like humans, like Malenfant. That is, they believed it possible that an entity could exist that could comprehend the entire universe, arbitrarily well.

And they had a further principle which mandated that if such a being could exist, it must exist.

The catch was that they believed there was a manifold of possible universes, of which this was only one. So She may not exist in this universe.

It – She – was the final goal of the Gaijin's quest.

But until the God of the Manifold shows up, there's only us, Malenfant thought. And there is work to do. We have to fix the bugs in this universe we're all stuck in. Hence, we throw a net around a star.

Hence, my sacrifice.

But, almost from the beginning, we humans fought back. We barely understood a damn thing, and nothing we did alone was going to make a difference, and the whole time we were swept along by historical forces that we could barely understand, let alone control, much as it had always been. We didn't even know who the bad guys were. But, by God, we tried.

At whatever cost to ourselves.

Chapter 18

MOON RAIN

There were only minutes left before the comet hit the Moon.

'You got to beat the future! – or it will beat you. Believe me, I've been there. Look around you, pal. You guys have lasted a hundred and fifty years up here, in your greenhouses and your mole holes. A hell of an achievement. *But the Moon can't support you . . .*'

Xenia Makarova had a window seat, and she gazed out of the fat, round portholes. Below the shuttle's hull she could see the landing pad, a plain of glass microwaved into lunar soil, here on the edge of the green domes of the Copernicus Triangle. And beyond that lay the native soil of the Moon, just subtle shades of grey, softly moulded by a billion years of meteorite rain.

And bathed, for today, in comet light.

Xenia knew that Frank J Paulis thought this day, this year 2190, was the most significant in the history of the inhabited Moon, let alone his own career. And here he was now, a pile of softscreens on his lap, hectoring the bemused-looking Lunar Japanese in the seat alongside him, even as the pilot of this cramped, dusty evacuation shuttle went through her countdown check.

Xenia had listened to Frank talk before. She'd been listening to him, in fact, for fifteen years, or a hundred and fifty, depending on what account you took of Albert Einstein.

'. . . You know what the most common mineral is on the Moon? Feldspar. And you know what you can make out of that? Scouring powder. Big fucking deal. On the Moon, you have to bake the air out of the rock. Sure, you can make other stuff, rocket fuel and glass. But there's no water, or nitrogen, or carbon –'

The Japanese, a businessman type, said, 'There are traces in the regolith.'

'Yeah, traces, put there by the sun, and it's being sold off anyhow, by Nishizaki Heavy Industries, to the Gaijin. Bleeding the Moon even drier . . .'

A child was crying. The shuttle was just a cylinder-shaped cargo scow, hastily adapted to support this temporary evacuation. It was crammed with people, last-minute refugees, men and women and tall, skinny children, subdued and serious, in rows of canvas bucket seats like factory chickens.

And all of them were Lunar Japanese, save for Frank and Xenia, who were American; for, while Frank and Xenia had taken a time-dilated hundred-and-fifty-year jaunt to the stars – and while America had disintegrated – the Lunar Japanese had been quietly colonizing the Moon.

'You need volatiles,' Frank said now. 'That's the key to the future. But now that Earth has fallen apart nobody is resupplying. You're just pumping around the same old shit.' He laughed. 'Literally, in fact. I give you another hundred years, tops. *Look around*. You've already got rationing, strict birth control laws.'

'There is no argument with the fact of –'

'How *much* do you need? I'll tell you. Enough to future-proof the Moon.'

'And you believe the comets can supply the volatiles we need for this.'

'Believe? That's what Project Prometheus is for. The random impact today, which alone will deliver a trillion tonnes of water, is a piece of luck. It's going to make my case for me, pal. And when we start purposefully harvesting the comets, those big fat babies out in the Oort cloud –'

'Ah.' The Lunar Japanese was smiling. 'And the person who has control of those comet volatiles –'

'That person could buy the Moon.' Frank reached for a cigar, a twentieth-century habit long frustrated. 'But that's incidental . . .'

But Xenia knew that Frank was lying about the comets, and their role in the Moon's future. Even before this comet had hit the Moon, Project Prometheus was already dead.

A month ago, Frank had called her into his office.

He had his feet up on his desk. He was reading, on a softscreen, some long, text-heavy academic paper about deep-implanted volatiles on the Earth. She tried to talk to him about work in progress, but he patently wasn't interested. Nor was he progressing Prometheus, his main project.

He had gotten straight to the point. 'The comet is history, babe.'

At first she hadn't understood. 'I thought it was going to supply us all with volatiles. I thought it was going to be the demonstration we needed that Prometheus was a sound investment.'

'Yeah. But it doesn't pan out.' Frank tapped the surface of his desk, and it lit up with numbers, graphics. 'Look at the analysis. We'll get some volatiles, but most of the nucleus's mass will be blasted back to space. Comets are spectacular fireworks, but they are inefficient cargo trucks. However you steer the damn things down, most of the incoming material is lost. I figure now you'd need around a *thousand* impactors to future-proof the Moon fully, to give it a stable atmosphere, thick enough to persist over significant periods before leaking away. And we aren't going to get a thousand impactors, not with the fucking Gaijin everywhere.' He looked thoughtful, briefly. 'One thing, though. Did you know the Moon *is* going to get an atmosphere out of this? It will last a thousand years –'

'*Iroonda.*'

'No, it's true. Thin, but an atmosphere, of comet mist. Happens every time a comet hits. Carbon dioxide and water and stuff. How about that.' He shook his head. 'Anyhow it's no use to us.'

'Frank, how come nobody figured this out before? How come nobody questioned your projections?'

'Well, they did.' He grinned. 'You know I'm never too sympathetic when people tell me something is impossible. I figured there would be time to fix it, to find a way.'

This was, on the face of it, a disaster, Xenia knew. Project Prometheus had got as far as designs for methane rockets, which could have pushed Oort comets out of their long, slow, distant orbits and brought them in to the Moon. The project had consumed all Frank's energies for years, and cost a fortune. He needed investors, and had hoped this chance comet impact, a proof of concept, would bring them in.

And now, it appeared, it had all been for nothing.

'Frank, I'm sorry.'

He seemed puzzled. 'Huh? Why?'

'If comets are the only source of volatiles –'

'Yesterday I thought they were. But look at this.' He tapped his softscreen. He was talking fast, excited, enthusiastic, his mind evidently racing. 'There's a woman here who thinks there are all the volatiles you could want, a hundred times over – *right here on the Moon.* Can you believe that?'

'That's impossible. Everyone knows the Moon is dry as a bone.'

He smiled. 'That's what everyone *thinks*. I want you to find this woman for me. The author of the paper.'

'Frank –'

'And find out about mining.'

'Mining?'

'The deeper the better.' His grin widened. 'How would you like a journey to the centre of the Moon, baby?'

And that was how she first learned about Frank's new project, his new obsession, his latest way to fix the future.

Ten seconds. Five. Three, two, one.

Stillness, for a fraction of a second. Then there was a clatter of explosive bolts, a muffled bang.

Xenia was ascending as if in some crowded elevator, pressed back in her bucket seat by maybe a full G. Beyond her window, stray dust streaked away across the pad glass, heaping up against fuel trucks and pipelines.

But then the shuttle swivelled sharply, twisting her around through a brisk ninety degrees. She heard people gasp, children laugh. The shuttle twisted again, and again, its attitude thrusters banging. This lunar shuttle was small, light, crude. Like the old Apollo landers, it had a single fixed rocket engine that was driving the ascent, and it was fitted with attitude control jets at every corner to turn it and control its trajectory. Just point, twist, squirt, as if she was a cartoon character carried into the air by hanging onto an out-of-control water hose.

Three hundred metres high the shuttle swivelled again, and she found she was pitched forward, looking down at the lunar surface, over which she skimmed. They were rising out of lunar night, and the shadowed land was dark, lit here and there by the lights of human installations, captured stars on dark rock. She felt as if she was falling, as if the ascent engine was going to drive her straight down into the unforgiving rocks. Sunrise. *Wham.*

It was not like Earth's slow-fade dawn; the limb of the sun just pushed above the Moon's rocky horizon, instantly banishing the stars into the darkness of a black sky. Light spilled on the unfolding landscape below, fingers of light interspersed with inky-black shadows hundreds of kilometres long, the deeper craters still pools of darkness. The Moon could never be called beautiful – it was too damaged for that – but it had a compelling wildness.

But everywhere she could see the work of humans: the unmistakable tracks of tractors, smooth lines snaking over the regolith, and occasional orange tents that marked the position of emergency supply dumps, all of it overlaid by the glittering silver wires of mass driver rails.

The shuttle climbed further. The Lunar Japanese around her applauded the smooth launch.

Now Earth rose. It looked as blue and beautiful as when she and Frank had left for the stars. But it had changed, of course. Even from here, she could see Gaijin flower-ships circling the planet, the giant ramscoops of the alien craft visible as tiny discs. She felt a stab of antique resentment at those powerful, silent visitors, who had watched as humanity tore itself apart.

And now, as the shuttle tilted and settled into its two-hour orbit around the Moon, Xenia saw a sight she knew no human had ever seen before today:

Comet rise, over the Moon.

The coma, a diffuse mass of gas and fine particles, was a ball as big as the Earth, so close now it walled off half the sky, a glare of lacy, diffuse light. Massive clumps in the coma, backlit, cast shadows across the smoky gases, straight lines thousands of kilometres long radiating at her. The comet was coming out of the sun, straight toward the Moon at seventy thousand kilometres an hour. She looked for the nucleus, a billion-tonne ball of ice and rock. But it was too small and remote, even now, a few minutes from impact. And the tail was invisible from here, fleeing behind her, running ahead of the comet and stretching far beyond the Moon, reaching halfway to Mars in fact.

Suddenly there was light all around the shuttle. The little ship had plunged *inside* the coma. It was like being inside a diffuse, luminous fog.

'*Vileekee bokh.*'

Frank leaned across her, trying to see. He was seventy years old, physiological; his nose was a misshapen mass of flesh. He was a small, stocky man, with thick legs and big prize-fighter muscles built for Earth's gravity, so that he always looked like some restless, half-evolved ape alongside the tall, slim Lunar Japanese.

'*Eta prikrasna,*' Xenia murmured.

'Beautiful. Yeah. How about that: we're the last off the Moon.'

'Oh, no,' she said. 'There's a handful of old nuts who won't move, no matter what.'

'Even for a comet?'

'Takomi. He's still there, for one,' she said.

'Who?'

'He's notorious.'

'I don't read the funny papers,' Frank snapped.

'Takomi is the hermit out in the ruins of Edo, on Farside. Evidently he lives off the land. He won't even respond to radio calls.'

Frank frowned. 'This is the fucking Moon. How does he live off the land? By sucking oxygen out of the rock? . . .'

The light changed. There was a soft Fourth-of-July gasp from the people crammed into the shuttle.

The comet had struck the Moon.

A dome of blinding white light rose like a new sun from the surface of the Moon: comet material turned to plasma, mixed with shattered rock. Xenia thought she could see a wave passing *through* the Moon's rocky hide, a sluggish ripple in rock turned to powder, gathering and slowing.

Now, spreading out over the Moon's dusty grey surface, she saw a faint wash of light. It seemed to pool in the deeper maria and craters, flowing down the contours of the land like a morning mist on Earth. It was air: gases from the shattered comet, an evanescent atmosphere pooling on the Moon.

And, in a deep, shadowed crater, at the ghostly touch of the air, she saw light flare.

It was only a hint, a momentary splinter at the corner of her eye. She craned to see. Perhaps there was a denser knot of smoke or gas, there on the floor of the crater; perhaps there was a streak, a kind of contrail, reaching out through the temporary comet atmosphere.

It must be some by-product of the impact. But it looked as if somebody had launched a rocket from the surface of the Moon.

Already the contrail had dispersed in the thin, billowing comet air.

People were applauding again, at the beauty of the spectacle, with relief at being alive. Frank wasn't even watching.

It was only after they landed that it was announced that the comet nucleus had landed plumb on top of the Fracastorius Crater dome.

Fracastorius, on the rim of the Sea of Nectar, was one of the largest settlements away from the primary Copernicus–Landsberg–Kepler triangle. The Lunar Japanese grieved. The loss of life was small, but the economic and social damage huge – perhaps unrecoverable, in these straitened times, as the Moon's people tried to adapt to life without their centuries-old umbilical to Earth's rich resources.

Frank Paulis seemed unconcerned. He got back to work, even before the shuttle landed. And he expected Xenia to do the same.

Xenia and Frank had spent a year of their lives on a Gaijin flower-ship, submitted themselves to the unknown hazards of several Saddle Point gateway teleport transitions, and got themselves relativistically stranded in an unanticipated future. On their way home from the Saddle Point radius, Frank and Xenia had grown concerned when nobody in the inner system answered their hails. At last they tapped into some low-bit-rate news feeds.

The news seemed remarkably bad.

Earth had fallen into a state of civil war. There were battles raging around the equatorial region, the Sahara and Brazil and the far east. Frank and Xenia listened, bemused, to reports laced with names they'd never heard of, of campaigns and battles, of generals and presidents and even emperors. Even the nations involved seemed to have changed, split and coalesced. It was hard even to figure out what they were fighting over – save the generic, the diminishing resources of a declining planet.

One thing was for sure. All their money was gone, disappeared into electronic mist. They had landed on the Moon as paupers, figuratively naked.

It turned out to be a crowded Moon, owned by other people. But they had nowhere else to go. And, even on the Moon, nobody was interested in star travellers and their tales.

Frank had felt cheated. Going to the stars had been a big mistake for him. He'd gone looking for opportunity; he'd grown impatient with the slow collapse of Earth's economy and social structure, even before the wars began, long before people started dying in large numbers.

Not that he hadn't prospered here.

The Moon of the late twenty-second century, as it turned out, had a lot in common with early twenty-first century Earth. Deprived of its lifelines from the home world, the Moon was full: a stagnant, closed economy. But Frank had seen all this before, and he knew that economic truth was strange in such circumstances. For instance, Frank had quickly made a lot of money out of reengineering an old technology that made use of lunar sulphur and oxygen as a fuel source. As the scarcity of materials increased, industrial processes that had once been abandoned as unprofitable suddenly became worthwhile.

Within five years Frank J Paulis had become one of the hundred wealthiest individuals on the Moon, taking Xenia right along with him.

But it wasn't enough. Frank found it impossible to break into the long-lived, close-knit business alliances of the Lunar Japanese. And besides, Xenia suspected, he felt cooped up here, on the Moon.

Anyhow, that was why this comet had been so important for Frank. It would shake everything up, he said. Change the equation.

It was either admirable, she thought, or schizophrenic.

After all these years – during which time she had been his companion, lover, employee, amateur therapist – Xenia still didn't understand Frank; she freely admitted it. He was an out-and-out capitalist, no doubt about that. But every gram of his huge ambition was constantly turned on the most gigantic of projects. The future of a world! The destiny of mankind! What Xenia couldn't work out was whether Frank was a visionary who used capitalism to achieve his goals – or just a capitalist after all, sublimating his greed and ambition.

But, swept along by his energy and ambition, she found it hard to focus on such questions.

Bathed in blue-water light, pacing his stage, Frank J Paulis was a solid ball of terrestrial energy and aggression, out of place on the small, delicate Moon. 'You got to beat the future! – or it will beat you. I believed that before I went to the stars, and I believe it now. I'm here to tell you how . . .'

To launch his new project, Frank, feverish with enthusiasm, had hired the Grand Auditorium, the heart of Landsberg. The crater's dome was a blue ceiling above Xenia, a thick double sheet of quasiglass, cable-stayed by engineered spider-web, filled with water. The water shielded Landsberg's inhabitants from radiation, and served to scatter the raw sunlight. During the long lunar day, here in Landsberg, the sky was royal blue and full of fish, goldfish and carp. After five years, Xenia still couldn't get used to it.

Frank was standing before a huge three-dimensional cartoon, a Moon globe sliced open to reveal arid, uninteresting geological layers. Beside him sat Mariko Kashiwazaki, the young academic type whose paper had fired Frank off in this new direction. She looked slim and uncertain in the expensive new suit Frank had bought for her.

Xenia was sitting at the back of the audience, watching rows of cool faces: politicians, business types. They were impassive. Well, they were here, and they were listening, and that was all Frank cared about right now.

'Here on the Moon, we need volatiles,' Frank was saying. 'Not just to survive, but to expand. To grow, economically. Water. Hydrogen, helium. Carbon dioxide. Nitrogen. Maybe nitrates and phosphates to supplement the bio cycles.

'But the Moon is deficient in every essential of life. A molecule of water, out there on the surface, lasts a few hours before it's broken up by the sunlight and lost forever. The Moon's atmosphere is so thin some of the molecules are actually *in orbit*. Frankly, it's no damn use.'

It was true. All this had been well known from the moment the first Apollo astronaut had picked up the first lump of unprepossessing Moon rock, and found it dry as a bone – dryer, in fact.

For a time there had been hope that deep, shadowed craters near the Moon's poles might serve as stores for water ice, brought there by cometary impacts. But, to the intense disappointment of some dreamers, no more than a trace of such ice had been found. As the Fracastorius impact had demonstrated, such impacts deposited little volatile material anyhow. And even if any ice was trapped it wouldn't be there forever; the Moon's axis turned out to be unstable, and the Moon tipped this way and that over a period of hundreds of millions of years – a long time, but short enough that no crater remained in shadow forever.

Dry or not, Moon rock wasn't useless. In fact, it was about forty per cent oxygen by weight. There were other useful elements: silicon which could be used to make glass, fibreglass, polymers; aluminium, magnesium and titanium for machinery, cables, coatings; chromium and magnesium for metal alloys.

But Frank was essentially right. If a mine on Earth had turned up the highest-grade lunar ore, you'd throw it out as slag.

And that was why Frank had initiated Project Prometheus, his scheme for importing volatiles *and* spinning up the Moon by hitting it with a series of comets or asteroids. But it hadn't worked.

'So where do we turn next?' He eyed his audience, as always in command, even before these wary, slightly bemused Lunar Japanese. 'Believe me, we need to find something. The Moon, *your* Moon, is dying. We didn't come to the Moon so our children could live in a box. We came to live as humans, with freedom and dignity.' He threw back his arms and breathed the recycled air. 'Let me tell you my dream. One day, before I die, I want to throw open the damn doors and walk out of the dome. And I want to breathe the air of the Moon. The air we put there.' He began to pace back and forth, like a preacher – or a huckster. '*I want to see a terraformed Moon.* I want to see a Moon where breathable air blankets the planet, where there is so much water the deep maria will become the seas they were named for, where plants and trees grow out in the open, and every crater will glisten with a circular lake . . . It's a dream. Maybe I won't live to see it all. But I know it's the only way forward for us. Only a *world* – stable, with deep biological reservoirs of water and carbon and air – is going to be big enough to sustain human life, here on the Moon, over the coming centuries, the millennia. Hell, we're here for the long haul, people, and we got to learn to think that way. Because nobody is going to help us – not Earth, not the Gaijin. None of them care if we live or die. We're stuck in this trench, in the middle of the battleground, and we have to help ourselves.

'But to make the Moon a twin of Earth we'll need volatiles, principally water. The Moon has no volatiles, and so we must import them. Correct?'

Now he leaned forward, intimidating, a crude but effective trick, Xenia thought dryly.

'*Dead wrong*. I'm here today to offer you a new paradigm. I'm here to tell you that the Moon *itself* is rich in volatiles, almost unimaginably so, enough to sustain us and our families, hell, for millennia. And, incidentally, to make us rich as Croesus in the process . . .'

It was the climax, the punch-line, Frank's big shock. But there was barely a flicker of interest in the audience, Xenia saw. Three centuries and a planetary relocation hadn't changed the Japanese much, and cultural barriers hadn't dropped; they were still suspicious of the noisy foreigner who stood before them, breaking into the subtle alliances and protocols that ruled their lives.

Frank stood back. 'Tell 'em, Mariko.'

The slim Lunar Japanese scientist got up, evidently nervous, and bowed deeply to the audience.

Earth-Moon and the other planets – said Mariko, supported by smooth softscreen images – had condensed, almost five billion years ago, from a swirling cloud of dust and gases. That primordial cloud had been rich in volatiles: three per cent of it was water, for instance. You could tell that was so from the composition of asteroids, which were left-over fragments of the cloud.

But there was an anomaly. All the water on Earth, in the oceans and atmosphere and the ice sheets, added to less than a *tenth* of that three per cent fraction. Where did the rest of the water go?

Conventional wisdom held that it had been baked out by the intense heat of Earth's formation. But Mariko believed much of it was still there, that water and other volatiles were trapped deep within the Earth: perhaps four hundred kilometres down, deep in the mantle. The water wouldn't be present as a series of immense buried oceans. Rather it would be scattered as droplets, some as small as a single molecule, trapped inside crystal lattices of the minerals with names like wadsleyite and hydrous-D. These special forms could trap water within their structure, essentially exploiting the high pressure to overcome the tendency of the rising temperature to bake the water out.

Some estimates said there should be as much as *five times* as much water buried within the Earth as in all its oceans and atmosphere and ice caps.

And what was true of Earth might be true of the Moon.

According to Mariko, the Moon was mostly made of material like Earth's mantle. This was because the Moon was believed to have been budded off the Earth itself, ripped loose after a giant primordial collision, popularly called the 'big whack'. The Moon was smaller than the Earth, cooler and more rigid, so that the centre of the Moon was analogous to the Earth's mantle layers a few hundred kilometres deep. And it was precisely at such depths, on Earth, that you found such water-bearing minerals . . .

Frank watched his audience like a hawk.

His cartoon Moon globe suddenly lit up. The onion-skin geological layers were supplemented by a vivid blue ocean, lapping in unlikely fashion at the centre of the Moon. Xenia smiled. It was typical Frank: inaccurate, but compelling.

'Listen up,' he said. 'What if Mariko is right? What if even *one tenth of one per cent* of the Moon's mass by weight is water? That's the same order as five per cent of Earth's surface water. A hidden ocean indeed.

'And that's not all. Where there is water there will be other volatiles: carbon dioxide, ammonia, methane, even hydrocarbons. All we have to do is go down there and find it.

'And it's *ours*. We don't own the sky; with the Gaijin around, maybe humans never will. But we inhabitants of the Moon do own the rocks beneath our feet.

'Folks, I'm calling this new enterprise Roughneck. If you want to know why, go look up the word. I'm asking you to invest in me. Sure it's a risk. But if it works it's a way past the resource bottleneck we're facing, here on the Moon. *And* it will make you rich beyond your wildest dreams.' He grinned. 'There's a fucking ocean down there, folks, and it's time to go skinny-dipping.'

There was a frozen silence, which Frank milked expertly.

* * *

After the session, Xenia took a walk.

The Moon's surface, beneath the dome, was like a park. Grass covered the ground, much of it growing out of bare lunar regolith. There was even a stand of mature palms, thirty metres tall, and a scattering of cherries. People lived in the dome's support towers, thick central cores with platforms of lunar concrete slung from them. The lower levels were given over to factories, workshops, schools, shops and other public places.

Far above her head, Xenia could see a little flock of schoolchildren in their white and black uniforms, flapping back and forth on Leonardo wings, squabbling like so many chickens. It was beautiful. But it served to remind her there were no birds here, outside pressurized cages. Birds tired too quickly in the thin air; on the Moon, against intuition, birds couldn't fly.

Water flowed in streams and fountains and pools, moistening the air.

She passed Landsberg's famous water-sculpture park. Water tumbled slowly from a tall fountain-head, in great shimmering spheres held together by surface tension. The spheres were caught by flickering mechanical fingers, to be teased out like taffy and turned and spun into rope and transformed, briefly, into transient, beautiful sculptures, no two ever alike. It was entrancing, she admitted, a one-sixth gravity art form that would have been impossible on the Earth, and it had immediately captivated her on her arrival here. As she watched, a gaggle of children – eight or ten years old, Moon legs as long as giraffes' – ran *across* the surface of the pond in the park's basin, Jesus-like, their slapping footsteps sufficient to keep them from sinking as long as they ran fast enough.

Water was everywhere here; it did not *feel* dry, a shelter in a scorched desert. But overhead, huge fans turned continually, extracting every drop of moisture from the air to be cleansed, stored and reused. She was surrounded by subtle noises: the bangs and whirrs of fans and pumps, the bubbling of aerators. And, when the children had gone, she saw tiny shimmering robots whiz through the air, fielding scattered water droplets as if catching butterflies, not letting a drop go to waste.

Landsberg, a giant machine, had to be constantly run, managed, maintained. Landsberg was no long-term solution. The various recycling processes were extraordinarily efficient – they had got to the levels of counting molecules – but there were always losses; the laws of thermodynamics saw to that. And there was no way to make good those losses.

It didn't *feel* like a dying world. In fact it was beginning to feel like home to her, this small, delicate slow-motion world. But the human Moon was, slowly but surely, running down. Already some of the smaller habitations had been abandoned; smaller ecospheres had been too expensive. There was rationing. Fewer children were being born than a generation ago, as humanity huddled in the remaining, shrivelling lunar bubbles.

And there was nowhere else to go.

Xenia had an intuition about the rightness of Frank's vision, whatever his methods. At least he was fighting back: trying to find a way for humans to survive, here in the system that had birthed them. Somebody had to. It seemed clear that the aliens, the all-powerful Gaijin, weren't here to help; they were standing by in their silent ships, witnessing as human history unfolded, and Earth fell apart.

If humans couldn't figure out how to save themselves soon, they might not have another chance.

And if Frank could make a little profit along the way to achieving that goal, she wasn't about to begrudge him.

Well, Frank convinced enough people to get together his seedcorn investment; jubilantly, he went to work.

But getting the money turned out to be the easy part.

There never had been a true mining industry, here on the Moon. All anybody had ever done was strip-mine the regolith, the shattered and desiccated outer layers of the Moon, already pulverized by meteorites and so not requiring crushing and grinding. And nobody had attempted – save for occasional science surveys – to dig any deeper than a few tens of metres.

So Frank and Xenia were forced to start from scratch, inventing afresh not just an industrial process but the human roles that went with it. They were going to need a petrophysicist and a geological engineer to figure out the most likely places they would find their imagined reservoirs of volatiles; they needed reservoir engineers and drilling engineers and production engineers for the brute work of the borehole itself; they needed construction engineers for the surface operations and support. And so on. They had to figure out job descriptions, and recruit and train to fill them as best they could.

All the equipment had to be reinvented. There was no air to convect away heat, so their equipment needed huge radiator fins. Even beneficiation – concentrating ungraded material into higher-quality ore – was difficult, as they couldn't use traditional methods like froth flotation and gravity concentration; they had to experiment with methods based on electrostatic forces. There was of course no water – a paradox, for it turned out that most mining techniques refined over centuries on Earth depended highly on the use of water, for cooling, lubrication, the movement and separation of materials and the solution and precipitation of metals. It was circular, a cruel trap.

They hit more problems as soon as they started to trial heavy equipment in the ultra-hard vacuum that coated the Moon.

Friction was a killer. In an atmosphere every surface accreted a thin layer of water vapour and oxides that reduced drag. But that didn't apply here. They even suffered vacuum welds. Not only that, the ubiquitous dust – the glass-sharp remains of ancient, shattered rocks – stuck to everything it could, scouring and abrading. Stuff wore out *fast,* on the silent surface of the Moon.

But they persisted, and solved the problems, or found old references of how it had been done in the past, when the Lunar Japanese had worked more freely beyond their domed cities. They learned to build in a modular fashion, with parts that could be replaced easily by a guy in a spacesuit. They learned to cover all their working joints with sleeves of a flexible plastic, to keep out the dust. After much experimentation they settled on a lubricant approach, coating their working surfaces with a substance the Lunar Japanese engineers called quasi-glass, hard and dense and very smooth; conventional lubricants just boiled or froze off.

The work soon became all-absorbing, and Xenia found herself immersed.

The Lunar Japanese, after generations, had become used to their domes. It was hard for them even to imagine a Moon without roofs. But once committed to the project, they learned fast, and were endlessly, patiently inventive in resolving problems. And it seemed to Xenia a remarkably short time from inception to the day Frank told her he had chosen his bore site.

'The widest, deepest impact crater in the fucking solar system,' he boasted. 'Nine kilometres below the datum level, all of thirteen kilometres below the rim wall peaks. Hell, just by standing at the base of that thing we'd be half way to the core already. And the best of it is, we can buy it. Nobody has lived there since they cleaned out the last of the cold-trap ice . . .'

He was talking about the South Pole of the Moon.

Encased in a spider-web pressure suit, Xenia stepped out of the hopper.

The Moon's Pole was a place of shadows. The horn of crescent

Earth poked above one horizon, gaunt and ice-pale. Standing at the base of the crater called Amundsen, Xenia could actually see the sun, a sliver of light poking through a gap in the enclosing rim mountains, casting long, stark, shadows over the colourless, broken ground. She knew that if she stayed here for a month the Moon's glacial rotation would sweep that solar searchlight around the horizon. But the light was always flat and stark, like an endless dawn or sunset.

And, at the centre of Amundsen, Frank's complex sprawled in a splash of reflected light, ugly, busy, full of people.

Xenia had never walked on the Moon's surface before, not once. Very few people did. Nobody was importing tungsten, and it was too precious to use on suits for sight-seeing. The waste of water and air incurred in donning and doffing pressure suits was unacceptably high. And so on. On the Moon of 2190, people clung to their domed bubbles, riding sealed cars or crawling through tunnels, while the true Moon beyond their windows was as inaccessible as it had been before Apollo.

That thought – the closeness of the limits – chilled Xenia, somehow even more than the collapse of Earth. It reinforced her determination to stick with Frank, whatever her doubts about his objectives and methods.

Here came Frank in his spacesuit, Lunar Japanese spider-web painted with a gaudy Stars and Stripes. 'I wondered where you were,' he said.

'There was a lot of paperwork, last-minute permissions –'

'You might have missed the show.' He was edgy, nervous, restless; his gaze, inside his gold-tinted visor, swept over the desolate landscape. 'Come see the rig.'

Together they loped towards the centre of the complex, past Frank's perimeter of security guards.

New Dallas, Frank's roughneck boomtown, was a crude cluster of buildings put together adobe-style from lunar concrete blocks. It was actually bright here, the sunlight deflected into the crater by heliostats, giant mirrors perched on the rim mountains or on impossibly tall gantries. The 'stats worked like giant floodlights, giving the town, incongruously, the feel of a floodlit sports stadium. The primary power came from sunlight too, solar panels which Frank had had plastered over the peaks of the rim mountains.

She could recognize shops, warehouses, dormitories, mess halls; there was a motor pool, with hoppers and tractors and heavy machinery clustered around fuel tanks. The inhabited buildings had been covered over for radiation-proofing by a few metres of regolith. And there was Frank's geothermal plant, ready for operation, boxy buildings linked by fat, twisting conduits.

The ground for kilometres around was flattened and scored by footprints and vehicle tracks. It was hard to believe *none* of this had been here two months ago, that the only signs of human occupation then had been the shallow, abandoned strip mines in the cold traps.

And at the centre of it all was the derrick itself, rising so far above the surface it caught the low sunlight, high enough, in fact, to stack up three or four joints of magnesium alloy pipe at a time. There was a pile of the pipe nearby, kilometres of it spun out of native lunar ore, the cheapest component of the whole operation. Sheds and shops sprawled around the derrick's base, along with huge aluminium tanks and combustion engines. Mounds of rock, dug out in test bores, surrounded the derrick like a row of pyramids.

They reached the drilling floor. At its heart was the circular table through which the pipe would pass, and which would turn to force the drill into the ground. There were foundries and drums to produce and pay out cables and pipes: power conduits, fibre-optic light pipes, hollow tubes for air and water and sample retrieval.

The derrick above her was tall and silent, like the gantry for a Saturn V. Stars showed through its open, sunlit frame. And suspended there at the end of the first pipe lengths she could see the drill head itself, teeth of tungsten and diamond, gleaming in the lights of the heliostats.

Frank was describing technicalities that didn't interest her. 'You know, you can't turn a drill string more than a few kilometres long. So we have to use a downhole turbine . . .'

'Frank, *eta ochin kraseeva*. It is magnificent. Somehow, back in Landsberg, I never quite believed it was real.'

'Oh, it's real,' Frank said tensely. 'Just so long as it works.' He checked his chronometer, a softscreen patch sewn into the fabric of his suit. 'It's nearly time.'

They moved out into the public area.

Roughneck was the biggest public event on the Moon in a generation. There must have been a hundred people here, men, women and children walking in their brightly coloured surface suits and radiation ponchos, or riding in little short-duration bubble rovers – the richest Lunar Japanese, who could still afford such luxuries. Cameras hovered everywhere. She saw Virtual Observers, adults and children in softscreen suits, their every sensation being fed out to the rest of the Moon.

Frank had even set up a kind of miniature theme park, with toy derricks you could climb up, and a towering roller-coaster based on an old-fashioned pithead rail – towering because you needed height, here on the Moon, to generate anything like a respectable G-force. The main attraction was Frank's Fish Pond, a small crater he'd lined with ceramic and filled up with water. The water froze over and was steadily evaporating, of course, but water held a lot of heat, and the Pond would take a long time to freeze to the bottom. In the meantime Frank had fish swimming back and forth in there, goldfish and handsome koi carp, living Earth creatures protected from the severe lunar climate by nothing more than a few metres of water, a neat symbol of his ambition.

The openness scared Xenia to death. 'Are you sure it's wise to have so many people?'

'The guards will keep out those Grey assholes.'

The Greys were a pressure group who had started to campaign against Frank: arguing it was wrong to go digging holes to the heart of the Moon, to rip out the *uchujin* there, the cosmic dust. They were noisy but, as far as Xenia could see, ineffective.

'Not that,' she said. 'It's so public. It's like Disneyland.'

He grunted. 'Xenia, all that's left of Disneyland is a crater that glows in the dark. Don't you get it? This PR stunt is *essential*. We'll be lucky if we make hole at a couple of kilometres a day. It will take fifty days just to get through the crust. We're going to sink a hell of a lot of money into this hole in the ground before we see a red cent of profit. We need those investors on our side, for the long term. They have to be here, Xenia. They have to *see* this.'

'But if something goes wrong –'

'Then we're screwed anyhow. What have we lost?'

Everything, she thought, if somebody gets killed, one of these cute Lunar Japanese five-year-olds climbing over the derrick models. But she knew Frank would have thought of that, and discounted it already, and no doubt figured out some fallback plan.

She admired such calculation, and feared it.

Frank tipped back on his heels and peered up at the sky. 'Well, well,' he said. 'Looks like we have an audience.'

A Gaijin flower-ship was sailing high overhead, wings spread and sparkling, like some gaudy moth.

'This is ours,' Frank murmured, glaring up. 'You hear me, assholes? *Ours*. Eat your mechanical hearts out.'

A warning tone was sounding on their headsets' open loops now, and in silence the Lunar Japanese, adults and children alike, were lining up to watch the show. Xenia could see the drill bit descend towards the regolith, the pipe sweeping silently downwards inside the framework, like a muscle moving inside a sheath of flesh.

The bit cut into the Moon.

A gush of dust sprayed up immediately from the hole, ancient regolith layers undisturbed for a billion years, now thrown unceremoniously towards space. At the peak of the parabolic fountain, glassy fragments sparkled in the sunlight. But there was no air to suspend the debris, and it fell back immediately.

Within seconds the dust had coated the derrick, turning its bright paintwork grey, and was raining over the spectators like volcanic ash.

There was motion around her. People were applauding, she saw, in utter silence, joined in this moment. Maybe Frank was right to have them here, after all, right about the mythic potential of this huge challenge.

Frank was watching the drill intently. 'Twenty or thirty metres,' he said.

'What?'

'The thickness of the regolith here. The dust. Then you have the megaregolith, rock crushed and shattered and dug out and mixed by the impacts. Probably twenty, thirty kilometres of that. Easy to cut through. Below that the pressure's so high it heals any cracks. We should get to that anorthosite bedrock by the end of the first day, and then –'

She took his arm. Even through the layers of suit she could feel the tension in his muscles. 'Hey. Take it easy.'

'I'm the expectant father, right?'

'Yeah.'

He took little steps back and forth, stocky, frustrated. 'Well, there's nothing we can do here. Come on. Let's get out of these Buck Rogers outfits and hit the bar.'

'All right.'

Xenia could hear the dust spattering over her helmet. And children were running, holding out their hands in the grey Moon rain, witnesses to this new marvel.

Chapter 19

DREAMS OF ROCK AND STILLNESS

Her world was simple: the Land below, the Dark above, the Light that flowed from the Dark. Land, Light, Dark. That, and herself.

Alone save for the Giver.

For her, all things came from the Giver. All life, in fact.

Her first memories were of the Giver, at the interface between parched Land and hot Dark. He fed her, sank rich warm moist substance into the Land, and she ate greedily. She felt her roots dig into the dry depths of the Land, seeking the nourishment that was hidden there. And she drew the thin soil into herself, nursed it with hot Light, made it part of herself.

She knew the future. She knew what would become of herself and her children.

They would wait through the long hot-cold bleakness for the brief Rains. Then they would bud, and pepper this small hard world with life, in their glorious blossoming. And she would survive the long stillness to see the Merging itself, the wonder that lay at the end of time, she and her children.

. . .But she was the first, and the Giver birthed her. None of it would have come to be without the Giver.

She wished she could express her love for him. She knew that was impossible.

She sensed, though, that he knew anyhow.

Overwhelmed by work as she was, Xenia couldn't get the memory of the comet impact out of her head. For, in the moment of that gigantic collision she had glimpsed a contrail: for all the world as if someone, something, had launched a rocket from the surface of the Moon.

But who, and why?

She had no opportunity to consider the question as the Roughneck project gathered pace. At last, though, she freed up two or three days from Frank, pleading exhaustion. She determined to use the time to resolve the puzzle. She went home, for the first time after many nights of sleeping at the Roughneck project office.

She took a long, hot bath, to soak out the gritty lunar dust from the pores of her skin. In her small tub the water sloshed like mercury. Condensation gathered on the ceiling above her, and soon huge droplets hung there suspended, like watery chandeliers. When she stood up the water clung to her skin, like a sheath; she had to scrape it loose with her fingers, depositing it carefully back in the tub. Then she took a small vacuum cleaner and captured all the loose droplets she could find, returning every scrap to the drainage system, where it would be cleansed and fed back into Landsberg's great dome reservoirs.

Her apartment was a glass-walled cell in the great catacomb that was Landsberg. It had, in fact, once served as a *genkan*, a hallway, for a greater establishment in easier, less cramped times, long before she had returned from the stars; it was so small her living room doubled as a bedroom. The floor was covered with rice straw matting, though she kept a *zabuton* cushion for Frank Paulis. Miniature Japanese art filled the room with space and stillness.

She had been happy to accept the style of the inhabitants of this place – unlike Frank, who had turned *his* apartment into a shrine to Americana. It was remarkable, she thought, that the Japanese had turned out to be so well adapted to life on the Moon. It was as if thousands of years on their small, crowded islands had readied them for this greater experience, this increasing enclosure on the Moon.

She made herself some coffee – fake, of course, and not as hot as she would have liked. She tuned the walls to a favourite scene – a maple forest, carpeted with bright green moss – and padded, naked, to her workstation. She sat on a *tatami* mat, which was unreasonably comfortable in the low gravity, and sipped her drink.

There was no indexed record of that surface rocket launch, as she had expected. There was, however, a substantial database on the state of the whole Moon at the time of the impact; every sensor the Lunar Japanese could deploy had been turned on the Moon, the events of that momentous morning.

And, after a few minutes' search, in a spectrometer record from a low-flying satellite, she found what she wanted. There was the contrail, bright and hot, arcing through splashed cometary debris. Spectrometer results told her she was looking at the products of aluminium burning in oxygen.

So it had been real.

She widened her search further.

Yes, she learned, aluminium could serve as a rocket fuel. It had a specific impulse of nearly three hundred seconds, in fact, not as good as the best chemical propellant – that was hydrogen, which burned at four hundred – but serviceable. And aluminium-oxygen could even be manufactured from the lunar soil.

Yes, there were other traces of aluminium-oxygen rockets burning on the Moon that day, recorded by a variety of automated sensors. More contrails, snaking across the lunar surface, from all around the Moon. There were a dozen, all told, perhaps more in parts of the Moon not recorded in sufficient detail.

And each of these rocket burns, she found, had been initiated when the gushing comet gases reached its location.

She pulled up a virtual globe of the Moon, and mapped the launch sites. They were scattered over a variety of sites on the Moon: highlands and maria alike, Nearside and Farside. No apparent pattern.

Then she plotted the contrails forward, allowing them to curl around the rocky limbs of the Moon.

The tracks converged, on a single Farside site. Edo. The place the hermit, Takomi, lived.

It was the first Rain of all.

Suddenly there was air here, on this still world. At first there was the merest trace, a soft comet Rain which settled, tentatively, on her broad leaves, where they lay in shade. But she drank it in greedily, before it could evaporate in the returning Light, incorporating every molecule into her structure, without waste.

With gathering confidence she captured the Rain, and the Light, and continued the slow, patient work of building her seeds, and the fiery stuff that would birth them, drawn from the patient dust.

And then, suddenly, it was time.

In a single orgasmic spasm the seeds burst from her structure. She was flooded with a deep joy, even as she subsided, exhausted.

The Giver was still here with her, enjoying the Rain with her, watching her blossom. She was glad of that.

And then, so soon after, there was a gusting wind, a rush of the air molecules over her damaged surfaces, as the comet drew back its substance and leapt from the Land, whole and intact, its job done. The noise of that great escape into the Dark above came to her as a great shout.

Soon after, the Giver was gone too.

But it did not matter. For, soon, she could hear the first tentative scratching of her children, carried to her like whispers through the still, hard rock, as they dug beneath the Land, seeking nourishment. There was no Giver for them, nobody to help; they were beyond her aid now. But it did not matter, for she knew they were strong, self-sufficient, resourceful.

Some would die, of course. But most would survive, digging in, waiting for the next comet Rain.

She settled back into herself, relishing the geologic pace of her thoughts. Waiting for Rain, for more comets to gather from the dirt and leap into the sky.

Xenia took an automated hopper, alone, to the Sea of Longing, on Farside. The journey was seamless, the landing imperceptible.

She donned her spider-web suit, checked it, and stepped into the hopper's small, extensible airlock. She waited for the hiss of escaping air, and – her heart oddly thumping – she collapsed the airlock around her, and stepped onto the surface of the Moon.

A little spray of dust, ancient pulverized rock, lifted up around her feet. The sky was black – save, she saw, for the faintest wisp of white, glowing in the flat sunlight. They were ice crystals, suspended in the thin residual atmosphere of the comet impact. Cirrus clouds on the Moon: relics of the death of a comet. The mare surface was like a gentle sea, a complex of overlapping, slowly undulating curves.

And here were two cones, tall and slender, side by side, geometrically perfect. They cast long shadows in the flat sunlight. She couldn't tell how far away they were, or how big, so devoid was this landscape of visual cues. They simply stood there, stark and anomalous.

She shivered. She walked forward, loping easily.

She came to a place where the regolith had been *raked*. She stopped, standing on unworked soil.

The raking had made a series of parallel ridges, each maybe six or eight centimetres tall, a few centimetres apart, a precise combing. When she looked to left or right, the raking went off to infinity, the lines sharp, their geometry perfect. And when she looked ahead, the lines receded to the horizon, as far as she could see undisturbed in their precision.

Those two cones stood, side by side, almost like termite mounds. The shallow light fell on them gracefully. She saw that the lines on the ground curved to wash around the cones, like a stream diverting around islands of geometry.

'Thank you for respecting the garden.'

She jumped at the sudden voice. She turned.

A figure was standing there – man or woman? a man, she decided, shorter and slimmer than she was – in a shabby, much-patched suit.

He bowed. '*Sumimasen.* I did not mean to startle you.'

'Takomi?'

'And you are Xenia Makarova.'

'You know that? How?'

A gentle shrug. 'I am alone here, but not isolated. Only you sought and compiled information on the Moon flowers.'

'*What* flowers?'

He walked towards her. 'This is my garden,' he said.

'A zen garden.'

'You understand that? Good. This is a *karė sansui*, a waterless stream garden.'

'Are you a monk?'

'I am a gardener.'

She considered. 'Even before humans came here, the Moon was already like an immense zen garden, a garden of rock and soil.'

'You are wise.'

'Is that why you came here? Why you live alone like this?'

'Perhaps. I prefer the silence and solitude of the Moon to the bustle of the human world. You are Russian.'

'My forebears were.'

'Then you are alone here also. There are some of your people on Mars.'

'So I'm told. They won't respond to my signals.'

'No,' he said. 'They won't speak to anybody. In the face of the Gaijin onslaught, we humans have collapsed into scattered, sullen tribes.'

Onslaught. It seemed a strange word to use, stronger than she had expected. Briefly, she was reminded of somebody else, another reclusive Japanese.

She pointed. 'I understand the ridges represent flow. Are those mountains? Are they rising out of cloud, or sea? Or are they diminishing?'

'Does it matter? The cosmologists tell us that there are many time streams. Perhaps they are both falling and rising. You have travelled far to see me. I will give you food and drink.'

He turned and walked across the Moon. After a moment, she followed.

* * *

The abandoned lunar base, called Edo, was a cluster of concrete components – habitation modules, power plants, stores, manufacturing facilities – half-buried in the cratered plain. There were robots everywhere, but they were standing silent, obviously inert.

But a single lamp burned again at the centre of the old complex. Takomi lived at the heart of Edo, in what had once been, he said, a park, grown inside a cave dug in the ground. The buildings here were dark, gutted, abandoned. There was even, bizarrely, an ancient McDonald's, stripped out, its red and yellow plastic signs cracked and faded. A single cherry tree grew, its leaves bright green, a splash of colour against the drab grey of the fused regolith.

This had been the primary settlement established by the Japanese government, back in the twenty-first century. But Nishizaki Heavy Industries had set up in Landsberg, using the crater originally as a strip mine. Now, hollowed out, Landsberg was the capital of the Moon, and Edo, cramped and primitive, had been abandoned.

She clambered out of her suit. She had tracked in Moon dust. It clung to the oils of her hand and looked like pencil lead, shiny on her fingers, like graphite. It would be hard to wash out, she knew.

He brought her green tea and rice cake.

Out of his suit Takomi was a small, wizened man; he might have been sixty, but such was the state of life-extending technology it was hard to tell. His face was round, a mass of wrinkles, and his eyes lost in leathery folds; he spoke with a wheeze, as if slightly asthmatic.

'You cherish the tree,' she said.

He smiled. 'I need one friend. I regret you have missed the blossom. I am able to celebrate *ichi-buzaki* here. We Japanese like cherries; they represent the old Samurai view that the blossom symbolizes our lives. Beautiful, but fragile, and all too brief.'

'I don't understand how you can live here.'

'The Moon is a whole world,' he said gently. 'It can support one man.'

Takomi, she learned, used the lunar soil for simple radiation shielding. He baked it in crude microwave ovens to make ceramic and glass. He extracted oxygen from the lunar soil by magma electrolysis: melting the soil with focused sunlight, then passing an electric current through it to liberate the oh-two. The magma plant, lashed up from decades-old salvage, was slow and power-intensive, but the electrolysis process was efficient in its use of soil; Takomi said he wasn't short of sunlight, but the less haulage he had to do the better.

He operated what he called a grizzly, an automated vehicle already a century old, so caked with dust it was the same colour as the Moon. The grizzly toiled patiently across the surface of the Moon, powered by sunlight. It scraped up loose surface material and pumped out glass sheeting and solar cells, just a couple of square metres a day. Over time, the grizzly had built a solar farm covering square kilometres, and producing megawatts of electric power.

'It is astonishing, Takomi.'

He cackled. 'If one is modest in one's request, the Moon is generous.'

'But even so, you lack essentials. It's the eternal story of the Moon. Carbon, nitrogen, hydrogen –'

He smiled at her. 'I admit I cheat. The concrete of this abandoned town is replete with water.'

'You *mine concrete*?'

'It is better than paying water tax.'

'But how many humans could the Moon support this way?'

'Ah. Not many. But how many humans does the Moon need? Thus, I am entrenched.'

It struck her as another strange choice of word. There was much about this hermit she did not understand, she realized.

She asked him about the contrails she had seen, their convergence on this place. He evaded her questions, and began to talk about something else.

'I conduct research, you know. Of a sort. There is a science station, not far from here, which was once equipped by Nishizaki Heavy Industries. Now abandoned, of course. It is – was – an infrared study station. It was there that a Japanese researcher called Nemoto first discovered evidence of Gaijin activity in the solar system, and so changed history.'

She wasn't interested in Takomi's hobby work in some old observatory. But there was something in his voice that made her keep listening.

'So you use the equipment,' she prompted.

'I watched the approach of the comet. From here, some aspects of it were apparent which were not visible from Nearside stations. The geometry of the approach orbit, for example. And something else.'

'What?'

'I saw evidence of methane burning,' he said. 'Close to the nucleus.'

'Methane?'

'A jet of combustion products.'

A rocket. She saw the implications immediately. Somebody had stuck a methane rocket on the side of the comet nucleus, burned the comet's own chemicals, to divert its course.

Away from the Moon? Or – towards it?

And in either case, who?

'. . . Why are you telling me this?'

But he would not reply, and a cold, hard lump of suspicion began to gather in her gut.

Takomi provided a bed for her, a thin mattress in an abandoned schoolhouse. Children's paintings adorned the walls, preserved under a layer of glass. The pictures showed flowers and rocks and people, all floating in a black sky.

In the middle of the night, Frank called her. He was excited.

'It's going better than we expected. We're just sinking in. Anyhow the pictures are great. Smartest thing I ever did was to insist we dump the magnesium alloy piping, make the walls transparent so you can see the rocks. We have the best geologists on the Moon down that fucking well, Xenia. Seismic surveys, geochemistry, geophysics, the works. The sooner we find some ore lode to generate payback, the better . . .'

The Roughneck bore had passed the crust's lower layers, and was in the mantle. *The mantle of the Moon*: sixty kilometres deep, a place unlike any other reached by humans before.

The Moon was turning out to be *much* easier to deep-mine than the Earth, for it was old and silent and still. There was a temperature rise of maybe ten degrees per kilometre of depth, compared to four times as much as on Earth. The pressure scaled similarly; even now Frank's equipment was subject only to a few thousand atmospheres, less than could be replicated in the laboratory. Strangely, the density of the Moon hardly varied across its whole interior.

But Xenia knew the project had barely begun. If Frank was to find the water and other volatiles he sought, if he was to reach the conditions of temperature and pressure that would allow the water-trapping minerals to form, it could only be at enormous depths – probably beneath the rigid mantle, a thousand kilometres deep, just a few hundred kilometres from the centre of the Moon itself.

She tried to ask him technical questions, about how they were planning to cope with the more extreme pressures and temperatures they would soon encounter. She knew that at first, in the impact-shattered upper regolith, he had been able to deploy comparatively primitive mechanical drilling techniques like percussion and rotary. But faced by the stubborn, hard, fine-grained rocks of the mantle, he had had to try out more advanced techniques – lasers, electric arcs, magnetic induction techniques. Stretching the bounds of possibility.

But he wouldn't discuss such issues.

'Xenia, it doesn't matter. You know me. I can't figure any machine more complicated than a screwdriver. And neither can our investors. I don't *need* to know. I just have to find the right technical guys, give them a challenge they can't resist, and point them downwards.'

'Paying them peanuts the while.'

He grinned. 'That's the beauty of those vocational types. Christ, we could even get those guys to pay to work here. No, the technical stuff is piss-easy. It's the other stuff that's the challenge. We have to make the project appeal to more than just the fat financiers and the big corporations. Xenia, this is the greatest lunar adventure since Neil and Buzz. That party when we first made hole was just the start. I want everybody involved, and everybody paying. Now we're in the mantle we can market the TV rights –'

'Frank, they don't have TV any more.'

'Whatever. I want the kids involved, all those little dark-eyed kids I see flapping around the palm trees the whole time with nothing to do. I want games. Educational stuff. Clubs to join, where you pay a couple of l-yen for a badge and get some kind of share certificate. I want little toy derricks in cereal packets.'

'They don't have cereal packets any more.'

He eyed her. 'Work with me here, Xenia. And I want their parents paying too. Tours down the well, at least the upper levels. Xenia, for the first time the folks on this damn Moon are going to see some hint of an expansive future. A frontier, beneath their feet. They have to *want* it. Including the kids.' He nodded. 'Especially the kids.'

'But the Greys –'

'Screw the Greys. All they have is rocks. We have the kids.'

And so on, on and on, his insect voice buzzing with plans, in the ancient stillness of Farside.

The next day Takomi walked her back to her tractor, by the zen garden.

She had been here twenty-four hours. The sun had dipped closer to the horizon, and the shadows were long, the land starker, more inhospitable. Comet-ice clouds glimmered high above.

'I have something for you,' Takomi said. And he handed her what looked like a sheet of glass. It was oval-shaped, maybe a half-metre long. Its edges were blunt, as if melted, and it was covered with bristles. Some kind of lunar geologic formation, she thought, a relic of some impact event. A cute souvenir; Frank might like it for the office.

She said, 'I have nothing to give you in return.'

'Oh, you have made your *okurimono* already.'

'I have?'

He cackled. 'Your shit and your piss. Safely in my reclamation tanks. On the Moon, shit is more precious than gold . . .'

He bowed, once, then turned to walk away, along the rim of his rock garden.

She was left looking at the oval of Moon glass in her hands. It looked, she thought now, rather like a flower petal.

Back at Landsberg, she gave the petal-like object to the only scientist she knew, Mariko Kashiwazaki. Mariko was exasperated; as Frank's chief scientist she was already under immense pressure, as Roughneck picked up momentum. But she agreed to pass on the puzzling fragment to a colleague, better qualified. Xenia agreed, provided she used only people in the employ of one of Frank's companies.

Meanwhile – discreetly, from home – Xenia repeated Takomi's work on the comet. She searched for evidence of the anomalous signature of methane burning at the nucleus. It had been picked up, but not recognized, by many sensors.

Takomi was right.

Clearly, someone had planted a rocket on the side of the comet nucleus, and deflected it from its path. It was also clear that most of the burn had been on the far side of the sun, where it would be undetected. The burn had been long enough, she estimated, to have deflected the comet, to *cause* its lunar crash. Undeflected, the comet would surely have sailed by the Moon, spectacular but harmless.

She then did some checks of the tangled accounts of Frank's companies. She found places where funds had been diverted, resources secreted. A surprisingly large amount, reasonably well concealed.

She'd been cradling a suspicion since Edo. Now it was confirmed, and she felt only disappointment at the shabbiness of the truth.

She felt that Takomi wouldn't reveal the existence of the rocket on the comet. He simply wasn't engaged enough in the human world to consider it. But, such was the continuing focus of attention on Fracastorius, Takomi wouldn't be the only observer who would notice the trace of that comet-pushing rocket, follow the evidence trail.

The truth would come out.

Without making a decision on how to act on this, she went back to work with Frank.

* * *

The pressure on Xenia, on both of them, was immense and unrelenting.

After one gruelling twenty-hour day, she slept with Frank. She thought it would relieve the tension, for both of them. Well, it did, for a brief oceanic moment. But then, as they rolled apart, it all came down on them again.

Frank lay on his back, eyes fixed on the ceiling, jaw muscles working, restless, tense.

Later Mariko Kashiwazaki called Xenia. Xenia took the call in her *tokonoma,* masking it from Frank.

Mariko had preliminary results about the glass object from Edo. 'The object is constructed almost entirely of lunar surface material.'

'Almost?'

'There are also complex organics in there. We don't know where they came from, or what they are for. There is water, too, sealed into cells within the glass. The structure itself acts as a series of lenses, which focus sunlight. Remarkably efficient. There seems to be a series of valves on the underside which draw in particles of regolith. The grains are melted, evaporated, in intense focused sunlight. It's a pyrolysis process similar to –'

'What happens to the vaporized material?'

'There is a series of traps, leading off from each light-focusing cell. The traps are maintained at different temperatures by spicules – the fine needles protruding from the upper surface – which also, we suspect, act to deflect daytime sunlight, and conversely work as insulators during the long lunar night. In the traps, at different temperatures, various metal species condense out. The structure seems to be oriented towards collecting aluminium. There is also an oxygen trap further back.'

Aluminium and oxygen. *Rocket fuel*, trapped inside the glass structure, melted out of the lunar rock by the light of the sun.

Mariko consulted notes in a softscreen. 'Within this structure the organic chemicals serve many uses. A complex chemical factory appears to be at work here. There is a species of photosynthesis, for instance. There is evidence of some kind of root system, which perhaps provides the organics in the first place . . . But there is no source we know of. This is the *Moon.*' She looked confused. 'You must remember I am a geologist. My contact works with biochemists and biologists, and they are extremely excited.'

Biologists? 'You'd better tell me.'

'Xenia, this is essentially a vapour-phase reduction machine of staggering elegance of execution, mediated by organic chemistry. It must be an artefact. And yet it looks –'

'What?'

'As if it *grew*, out of the Moon ground. There are many further puzzles,' Mariko said. 'For instance, the evidence of a neural network.'

'Are you saying this has some kind of a nervous system?'

Mariko shrugged. 'Even if this *is* some simple lunar plant, why would it need a nervous system? Even, perhaps, a rudimentary awareness?' She studied Xenia. 'What is this thing?'

'I can't tell you that.'

'There has been much speculation about the form life would take, here on the Moon. It could be seeded by some meteorite-impact transfer from Earth. But volatile depletion seemed an unbeatable obstacle. Where does it get its organic material? Was it from the root structure, from deep within the Moon? If so, you realize that this is confirmation of my hypotheses about the volatiles in –'

Xenia stopped her. '*Mariko*. This isn't to go further. News of this – discovery. Not yet. Tell your colleagues that too.'

Mariko looked shocked, as Xenia, with weary certainty, had expected. 'You want to *suppress* this?'

That caused Xenia to hesitate. She had never thought of herself as a person who would *suppress* anything. But she knew, as all the star travellers had learned, that the universe was full of life: that life emerged everywhere it could – though usually, sadly, with little hope of prospering. Was it really so strange that such a stable, ancient world as the Moon should be found to harbour its own, quiet, still form of life?

Life was trivial, compared to the needs of the project.

'This isn't science, Mariko. I don't want anything perturbing Roughneck.'

Mariko made to protest again.

'Read your contract,' Xenia snapped. 'You must do what I say.' And she cut the connection.

She returned to bed. Frank seemed to be asleep.

She had a choice to make. Not about the comet deflection issue; others would unravel that, in time. About Frank, and herself.

He fascinated her. He was a man of her own time, with a crude vigour she didn't find among the Japanese-descended colonists of the Moon. He was the only link she had with home. The only human on the Moon who didn't speak Japanese to her.

That, as far as she could tell, was all she felt.

In the meantime, she must consider her own morality.

Lying beside him, she made her decision. She wouldn't betray him. As long as he needed her, she would stand with him.

But she would not save him.

Life was long, slow, unchanging.

Even her thoughts were slow.

In the timeless intervals between the comets, her growth was chthonic, her patience matching that of the rocks themselves. Slowly, slowly, she rebuilt her strength: Light traps to start the long process of drawing out fire for the next seeds, leaves to catch the comet Rain that would come again.

She spoke to her children, their subtle scratching carrying to her through the still, cold rock. It was important that she taught them: how to grow, of the comet Rains to come, of the Giver at the beginning of things, the Merging at the end.

Their conversations lasted a million years.

The Rains were spectacular, but infrequent. But when they came, once or twice in every billion years, her pulse accelerated, her metabolism exploding, as she drank in the thin, temporary air, and dragged the fire she needed from the rock.

And, with each Rain, she birthed again, the seeds exploding from her body and scattering around the Land.

But, after that first time, she was never alone. She could feel, through the rock, the joyous pulsing of her children as they hurled their own seed through the gathering comet air.

Soon there were so many of them that it was as if all of the Land was alive with their birthing, its rocky heart echoing to their joyous shouts.

And still, in the distant future, the Merging awaited them.

As the comets leapt one by one back into the sky, sucking away the air with them, she held that thought to her exhausted body, cradling it.

Eighty days in and Frank was still making hole at his couple-of-kilometres-a-day target pace. But things had started to get a lot harder.

This was *mantle*, after all. They were suffering rock bursts. The rock was like stretched wire, under so much pressure it exploded when it was exposed. It was a new regime. New techniques were needed.

Costs escalated. The pressure on Frank to shut down was intense.

Many of the investors had already become extremely rich from the potential of the ore lodes discovered in the lower crust and upper mantle. There was talk of opening up new, shallow bores elsewhere on the Moon to seek out further lodes. Frank had proved his point. Why go further, when the Roughneck was already a commercial success?

But metal ore wasn't Frank's goal, and he wasn't about to stop now.

. . . That was when the first death occurred, all of a hundred kilometres below the surface of the Moon.

She found him in his office at New Dallas, pacing back and forth, an Earthman caged on the Moon, his muscles lifting him off the glass floor.

'Omelettes and eggs,' he said. 'Omelettes and eggs.'

'That's a cliché, Frank.'

'It was probably the fucking Greys.'

'There's no evidence of sabotage.'

He paced. 'Look, we're in the *mantle of the Moon* –'

'You don't have to justify it to me,' she said, but he wasn't listening.

'The mantle,' he said. 'You know, I hate it. A thousand kilometres of worthless shit.'

'It was the changeover to the subterrene that caused the disaster. Right?'

He ran a hand over his greasy hair. 'If you were a prosecutor, and this was a court, I'd challenge you on "caused". The accident happened when we switched over to the subterrene, yes.'

They had already gone too deep for the simple alloy casing or the cooled lunar glass Frank had used in the upper levels. To get through the mantle they would use a subterrene, a development of obsolete deep-mining technology, a probe that melted its way through the rock and built its own casing behind it, a tube of hard, high-melting-point quasiglass.

Frank started talking, rapidly, about quasiglass. 'It's the stuff the Lunar Japanese use for rocket nozzles. Very high melting point. It's based on diamond, but it's a quasicrystal, so the lab boys tell me, halfway between a crystal and a glass. Harder than ordinary crystal because there are no neat planes for cracks and defects to propagate. And it's a good heat insulator similarly. Besides that we support the hole against collapse and shear stress. Rock bolts, fired through the casing and into the rock beyond. We do everything we can to ensure the integrity of our structure . . .'

This was, she realized, a first draft of the testimony he would have to give to the investigating commissions.

When the first subterrene started up, it built a casing with a flaw, undetected for a hundred metres. There had been an implosion. They lost the subterrene itself, a kilometre of bore, and a single life, of a senior toolpusher.

'We've already restarted,' Frank said. 'A couple of days and we'll have recovered.'

'Frank, this isn't a question of schedule loss,' she said. 'It's the wider impact. Public perception. Come on; you know how important this is. If we don't handle this right we'll be shut down.'

He seemed reluctant to absorb that. He was silent, for maybe half a minute.

Then his mood switched. He started pacing. 'You know, we can leverage this to our advantage.'

'What do you mean?'

'We need to turn this guy we lost – what was his name? – into a hero.' He snapped his fingers. 'Did he have any family? A ten-year-old daughter would be perfect, but we'll work with whatever we have. Get his kids to drop cherry blossom down the hole. You know the deal. The message has to be right. *The kids want the bore to be finished, as a memorial to the brave hero.*'

'Frank, the dead engineer was a she.'

'And we ought to think about the Grey angle. Get one of them to call our hero toolpusher a criminal.'

'Frank –'

He faced her. 'You think this is immoral. Bullshit. It would be immoral to stop; otherwise, believe me, *everyone* on this Moon is going to die in the long run. Why do you think I asked you to set up the kids' clubs?'

'For *this*?'

'Hell, yes. Already I've had some of those chicken-livered investors try to bail out. Now we use the kids, to put so much fucking pressure on it's impossible to turn back. If that toolpusher had a kid in one of our clubs, in fact, that's perfect.' He hesitated, then pointed a stubby finger at her face. 'This is the bottleneck. Every project goes through it. I need to know you're with me, Xenia.'

She held his gaze for a couple of seconds, then sighed. 'You know I am.'

He softened, and dropped his hands. 'Yeah. I know.' But there was something in his voice, she thought, that didn't match his words. An uncertainty that hadn't been there before. 'Omelettes and eggs,' he muttered. 'Whatever.' He clapped his hands. 'So. What's next?'

* * *

This time, Xenia didn't fly directly to Edo. Instead she programmed the hopper to make a series of slow orbits of the abandoned base.

It took her an hour to find the glimmer of glass, reflected sunlight sparkling from a broad expanse of it, at the centre of an ancient, eroded crater. She landed a kilometre away, to avoid disturbing the flower structures. She suited up quickly, clambered out of the hopper, and set off on foot.

She made ground quickly, over this battered, ancient landscape, restrained only by the Moon's gentle gravity. Soon the land ahead grew bright, glimmering like a pool. She slowed, approaching cautiously.

The flower was larger than she had expected. It must have covered a quarter, even a third of a hectare, delicate glass leaves resting easily against the regolith from which they had been constructed, spiky needles protruding. There was, too, another type of structure: short, stubby cylinders, pointing at the sky, projecting in all directions.

Miniature cannon muzzles. Launch gantries for seed-carrying aluminium-burning rockets, perhaps.

'. . . I must startle you again.'

She turned. It was Takomi, of course: in his worn, patched suit, his hands folded behind his back. He was looking at the flower.

'Life on the Moon,' she said.

'Its lifecycle is simple, you know. It grows during periods of transient comet atmospheres – like the present – and lies dormant between such events. The flower is exposed to sunlight, through the long Moon day. Each of its leaves is a collector of sunlight. The flower focuses the light on regolith, and breaks down the soil for the components it needs to manufacture its own structure, its seeds, and the simple rocket fuel used to propel them across the surface.

'Then, during the night, the leaves act as cold traps. They absorb the comet frost which falls on them, water and methane and carbon dioxide, incorporating that, too, into the flowers' substance.'

'And the roots?'

'The roots are kilometres long. They tap deep wells of nutrient, water and organic substances. Deep inside the Moon.'

So Frank, of course, was right about the existence of the volatiles, as she had known he would be.

'I suppose you despise Frank Paulis.'

He said mildly, 'Why should I?'

'Because he is trying to dig out the sustenance for these plants. Rip it out of the heart of the Moon. Are you a Grey, Takomi?'

He shrugged. 'We have different ways. Your ancestors have a word. *Mechta.*'

'Dream.' It was the first Russian word she had heard spoken in many months.

'It was the name your engineers wished to give to the first probe they sent to the Moon. *Mechta.* But it was not allowed, by those who decide such things. Well, I am living a dream, here on the Moon, a dream of rock and stillness, here with my Moon flower. That is how you should think of me.'

He smiled, and walked away.

The Land was rich with life now: her children, her descendants, drinking in air and Light. Their songs echoed through the core of the Land, strong and powerful.

But it would not last, for it was time for the Merging.

First there was a sudden explosion of Rains, too many of them to count, the comets leaping out of the ground, one after the other.

Then the Land itself became active. Great sheets of rock heated, becoming liquid, and withdrawing into the interior of the Land.

Many died, of course. But those that remained bred frantically. It was a glorious time, a time of death and life.

Changes accelerated. She clung to the thin crust which contained the world. She could feel huge masses rising and falling far beneath her. The Land grew hot, dissolving into a deep ocean of liquid rock.

And then the Land itself began to break up, great masses of it hurling themselves into the sky.

More died.

But she was not afraid. It was glorious! – as if the Land itself was birthing comets, as if the Land was like herself, hurling its children far away.

The end came swiftly, more swiftly than she had expected, in an explosion of heat and light that burst from the heart of the Land itself. The last, thin crust was broken open, and suddenly there was no more Land, nowhere for her roots to grip.

It was the Merging, the end of all things, and it was glorious.

Chapter 20

THE TUNNEL IN THE MOON

Frank and Xenia, wrapped in their spider-web spacesuits, stood on a narrow aluminium bridge. They were under the South Pole derrick, suspended over the tunnel Frank had dug into the heart of the Moon.

The area around the derrick had long lost its pristine theme-park look. There were piles of spill and waste and ore, dug out of the deepening hole in the ground. LHDs, automated load-haul-dump vehicles, crawled continually around the site. The LHDs, baroque aluminium beetles, sported giant fins to radiate off their excess heat – no conduction or convection here – and most of their working parts were two metres or more off the ground, where sprays of the abrasive lunar dust wouldn't reach. The LHDs, Xenia realized, were machines made for the Moon.

The shaft below Xenia was a cylinder of sparkling lunar glass. The tunnel receded to the centre of the Moon, to infinity. Lights had been buried in the walls every few metres, so the shaft was brilliantly lit, like a passageway in a shopping mall, the multiple reflections glimmering from the glass walls. Refrigeration and other conduits snaked along the tunnel. It was vertical, perfectly symmetrical, and there was no mist or dust, nothing to obscure her view.

Momentarily dizzy, she stepped back, anchored herself again on the surface of the Moon.

Frank rubbed his hands. 'It's wonderful. Like the old days. Engineers overcoming obstacles, building things.' He seemed oddly nervous; he wouldn't meet her eyes.

'And,' she said, 'thanks to all this problem-solving, we got through the mantle.'

'Hell, yes, we got through it. You've been away from the project too long, babe.' He took her hands. Squat in his suit, his face invisible, he was still, unmistakably, Frank J Paulis. 'And now, it's our time.'

Without hesitation – he never hesitated – he stepped to the lip of the delicate metal bridge.

She walked with him, a single step. A stitched safety harness, suspended from pulleys above, impeded her.

He said, 'Will you follow me?'

She took a breath. 'I've always followed you.'

'Then come.'

Hand in hand, they jumped off the bridge.

Slow as a snowflake, tugged by gravity, Xenia fell towards the heart of the Moon. The loose harness dragged gently at her shoulders and crotch, slowing her fall. She was guided by a couple of spider-web cables, tautly threaded down the axis of the shaft; through her suit's fabric she could hear the hiss of the pulleys.

There was nothing beneath her feet save a diminishing tunnel of light. Xenia could hear her heart pound. Frank was laughing.

The depth markers on the wall were already rising up past her, mapping her acceleration. But she was suspended here, in the vacuum, as if she was in orbit; she had no sense of speed, no vertigo from the depths beneath her.

Their speed picked up quickly. In seconds, it seemed, they had already passed through the fine regolith layers, the Moon's pulverized outer skin, and they were sailing down through the megaregolith. Giant chunks of deeply shattered rock crowded against the glassy, transparent tunnel walls like the corpses of buried animals.

The material beyond the walls turned smooth and grey now. This was lunar bedrock, anorthosite, buried beyond even the probings and pulverizing of the great impactors. Unlike Earth, there would be no fossils here, she knew, no remnants of life in these deep levels; only a smooth gradation of minerals, processed by the slow workings of geology. In some places there were side shafts dug away from the main exploratory bore. They led to stopes, lodes of magnesium-rich rocks extruded from the Moon's frozen interior, which were now being mined out by Frank's industry partners. She saw the workings as complex blurs, hurrying upwards as she fell, gone like dream visions.

Despite the gathering warmth of the tunnel, despite her own acceleration, she had a sense of cold, of age and stillness.

They dropped through a surprisingly sharp transition into a new realm, where the rock on the other side of the walls glowed of its own internal light. It was a dull grey-red, like a cooling lava on Earth.

'The mantle of the Moon,' Frank whispered, gripping her hands. 'Basalt. Up here it ain't so bad. But further down the rock is so soft it pulls like taffy when you try to drill it. A thousand kilometres of mush, a pain in the ass.'

They passed a place where the glass walls were marked with an engraving, stylized flowers with huge lunar petals. This was where a technician had been killed in an implosion. The little memorial shot upwards and was lost in the light. Frank didn't comment.

The rock was now glowing a bright cherry-pink, rushing upwards past them. It was like dropping through some immense glass tube full of fluorescing gas. Xenia sensed the heat, despite her suit's insulation and the refrigeration of the tunnel.

Falling, falling.

Thick conduits surrounded them now, crowding the tunnel, flipping from bracket to bracket. The conduits carried water, bearing the Moon's deep heat to hydrothermal plants on the surface. She was becoming dazzled by the pink-white glare of the rocks.

The harness tugged at her sharply, slowing her. Looking down along the forest of conduits, she could see that they were approaching a terminus, a platform of some dull, opaque ceramic that plugged the tunnel.

'End of the line,' Frank said. 'Down below there's only the downhole tools and the casing machine and other junk . . . Do you know where you are? Xenia, we're more than a thousand kilometres deep, two-thirds of the way to the centre of the Moon.'

The pulleys gripped harder and they slowed, drifting to a halt a metre above the platform. With Frank's help she loosened her harness and spilled easily to the platform itself, landing on her feet, as if after a sky-dive.

She glanced at her chronometer patch. The fall had taken twenty minutes.

She got her balance, and looked around. They were alone here.

The platform was crowded with science equipment, anonymous grey boxes linked by cables to softscreens and batteries. Sensors and probes, wrapped in water-cooling jackets, were plugged into ports in the walls. She could see data collected from the lunar material flickering over the softscreens, measurements of porosity and permeability, data from gas meters and pressure gauges and dynamometers and gravimeters. There was evidence of work here, small inflatable shelters, spare backpacks, notepads – even, incongruously, a coffee cup. Human traces, here at the heart of the Moon.

She walked to the walls. Her steps were light; she was almost floating. There was rock, pure and unmarked, all around her, beyond the window-like walls, glowing pink.

'The deep interior of the Moon,' Frank said, joining her. He ran his gloved hands over the glass. 'What the rock hounds call primitive material, left over from the solar system's formation. Never melted and differentiated like the mantle, never bombarded like the surface. Untouched since the Moon budded off of Earth itself.'

'I feel light as a feather,' she said. And so she did; she felt as if she was going to float back up the borehole like a soap bubble.

Frank glared up into the tunnel above them, and concentric light rings glimmered in his face plate. 'All that rock up there doesn't pull at us. It might as well be cloud, rocky cloud, hundreds of kilometres of it.'

'I suppose, at the centre itself, you would be weightless.'

'I guess.'

On one low bench stood a glass beaker, covered by clear plastic film. She picked it up; she could barely feel it, dwarfed within her thick, inflexible gloves. It held a liquid that sloshed in the gentle gravity. The liquid was murky brown, not quite transparent.

Frank was grinning. Immediately she understood.

'I wish you could drink it,' he said. 'I wish we could drink a toast. You know what that is? *It's water*. Moon water, water from the lunar rocks.' He took the beaker and turned around, in a slow, ponderous dance. 'It's all around us. Just as Mariko predicted, a fucking ocean of it. Wadsleyite and majorite with three per cent water by weight . . . Incredible. We did it, babe.'

'Frank. You were right. I had no idea.'

'I sat on the results. I wanted you to be the first to see this. To see my – ' He couldn't find the word.

'Affirmation,' she said gently. 'This is your affirmation.'

'Yeah. I'm a hero.'

It was true, she knew.

It was going to work out just as Frank had projected. As soon as the implications of the find became apparent – that there really were oceans down here, buried inside the Moon – the imaginations of the Lunar Japanese would be fast to follow Frank's vision. *This*, after all, wasn't a simple matter of plugging holes in the environment support system loops. There was surely enough resource here, just as Frank said, to future-proof the Moon. And, perhaps, this would be a pivot of human history, a moment when humanity's long decline was halted, and mankind found a place to live in a system that was no longer theirs.

Not for the first time Xenia recognized Frank's brutal wisdom in his dealings with people: to bulldoze them as far as he had to, until they couldn't help but agree with him.

Frank would become the most famous man on the Moon.

That wasn't going to help him, though, she thought sadly.

'So,' she said. 'You proved your point. Will you stop now?'

'Stop the borehole?' He sounded shocked. 'Hell, no. We go on, all the way to the core.'

'Frank, the investors are already pulling out.'

'Chicken-livered assholes. I'll go on if I have to pay for it myself.' He put the beaker down. 'Xenia, the water isn't enough; it's just a first step. We have to go on. *We still have to find the other volatiles.* Methane. Organics. We go on. Damn it, Roughneck is my project.'

'No, it isn't. We sold so much stock to get through the mantle that you don't have a majority any more.'

'But we're rich again.' He laughed. 'We'll buy it all back.'

'Nobody's selling. They certainly won't after you publish this finding. You're too successful. I'm sorry, Frank.'

'So the bad guys are closing in, huh. Well, the hell with it. I'll find a way to beat them. I always do.' He grabbed her gloved hands. 'Never mind that now. Listen, I'll tell you why I brought you down here. *I'm winning.* I'm going to get everything I ever wanted. Except one thing.'

She was bewildered. 'What?'

'I want us to get married. I want us to have kids. We came here together, from out of the past, and we should have a life of our own, on this Japanese Moon, in this future.' His voice was heavy, laden with emotion, almost cracking. In the glare of rock light, she couldn't see his face.

She hadn't expected this. She couldn't think of a response.

Now his voice was almost shrill. 'You've gone quiet.'

'The comet,' she said softly.

He was silent for a moment, still gripping her hands.

'The methane rocket,' she said. 'On the comet. It was detected.'

She could tell he was thinking of denying all knowledge. Then he said: 'Who found it?'

'Takomi.'

'The piss-drinking old bastard out at Edo?'

'Yes.'

'That still doesn't prove –'

'I checked the accounts. I found where you diverted the funds, how you built the rocket, how you launched it, how you rendezvoused it with the comet. Everything.' She sighed. 'You never were smart at that kind of stuff, Frank. You should have asked me.'

'Would you have helped?'

'No.'

He released her hands. 'I never meant it to hit there. On Fracastorius.'

'I know that. Nevertheless, that's what happened.'

He picked up the glass of lunar water. 'But you know what, I'd have gone ahead even if I had known. I needed that fucking comet to kick-start *this*. It was the only way. You can't stagnate. That way lies extinction. If I gave the Lunar Japanese a choice, they'd be sucking water out of old concrete for the rest of time.'

'But it would be their choice.'

'And that's more important than not dying?'

She shrugged. 'It's inevitable they'll know soon.'

He turned to her, and she sensed he was grinning again, irrepressible. 'At least I finished my project. At least I got to be a hero . . . Marry me,' he said again.

'No.'

'Why not? Because I'm going to be a con?'

'Not that.'

'Then why?'

'Because I wouldn't last, in your heart. You move on, Frank.'

'You're wrong,' he said. But there was no conviction in his voice. 'So,' he said. 'No wedding bells. No little Lunar Americans, to teach these Japanese how to play football.'

'I guess not.'

He walked away. 'Makes you think, though,' he said, his back to her.

'What?'

He waved a hand at the glowing walls. 'This technology isn't so advanced. Neil and Buzz couldn't have done it, but maybe we could have opened up some kind of deep mine on the Moon by the end of the twentieth century, say. Started to dig out the water, live off the land. If only we'd known it was here, all this wealth, even NASA might have done it. And then you'd have an American Moon, and who knows how history might have turned out?'

'None of us can change things,' she said.

He looked at her, his face masked by rock light. 'However much we might want to.'

'No.'

'How long do you think I have, before they shut me down?'

'I don't know. Weeks. No more.'

'Then I'll have to make those weeks count.'

He showed her how to hook her suit harness to a fresh pulley set, and they began the long, slow ride to the surface of the Moon.

Abandoned on its bench top at the bottom of the shaft, she could see the covered beaker, the Moon water within.

After her descent into the Moon, she returned to Edo, seeking stillness.

The world of the Moon, here on Farside, was simple: the regolith below, the sunlight that flowed from the black sky above. Land, light, dark. That, and herself, alone. When she looked downsun, at her own shadow, the light bounced from the dust back towards her, making a halo around her head.

The Moon flower had, she saw, significantly diminished since her last visit; many of the outlying petals were broken off or shattered.

After a time, Takomi joined her.

He said: 'Evidence of the flowers has been found before.'

'It has?'

'I have, discreetly, studied old records of the lunar surface. Another legacy of richer days past, when much of the Moon was studied in some detail. But those explorers, long dead now, did not know what they had found, of course. The remains were buried under regolith layers. Some of them were billions of years old.' He sighed. 'The evidence is fragmentary. Nevertheless I have been able to establish a pattern.'

'What kind of pattern?'

'It is true that the final seeding event drew the pods, with unerring accuracy, *back* to this site. As you observed. The pods were absorbed into the structure of the primary plant, here, which has since withered. The seeding was evidently triggered by the arrival of the comet, the enveloping of the Moon by its new, temporary atmosphere. But I have studied the patterns of earlier seedings –'

'Triggered by earlier comet impacts.'

'Yes. All of them long before human occupancy began here. Just one or two impacts per billion years. Brief comet rains, spurts of air, before the long winter closed again. And each impact triggered a seeding event.'

'. . . Ah. I understand. These are like desert flowers, which bloom in the brief rain. Poppies, rockroses, grasses, chenopods.'

'Exactly. They complete their lifecycles quickly, propagate as vigorously as possible, while the comet air lasts. And then their seeds lie dormant, for as long as necessary, waiting for the next chance event, perhaps as long as a billion years.'

'I imagine they spread out, trying to cover the Moon. Propagate as fast and as far as possible.'

'No,' he said quietly.

'Then what?'

'At every comet event, the seedings *converge*. Just as they did here. These plants work backwards, Xenia.

'A billion years ago there were a thousand sites like this. In a great seeding, these diminished to a mere hundred: those fortunate few were bombarded with seeds, while the originators withered. And later, another seeding reduced that hundred to twelve or so. And finally, the twelve are reduced to one. This one.'

She tried to think that through; she pictured the little seed pods converging, diminishing in number. 'It doesn't make sense.'

'Not for us, who are ambassadors from Earth,' he said. 'Earth life spreads, colonizes, whenever and wherever it can. But this is lunar life, Xenia. And the Moon is an old, cooling, dying world. Its richest days were brief moments, far in the past. And so life has adjusted to the situation. Do you understand?'

'. . . I think so. But now, this is truly the last of them? The end?'

'Yes. The flower is already dying.'

'But why here? Why now?'

He shrugged. 'Xenia, your colleague Frank Paulis is determined to rebuild the Moon, inside and out. Even if he fails, others will follow where he showed the way. The stillness of the Moon is lost.' He sniffed. 'My own garden might survive, but in a park, like your old Apollo landers, to be gawked at by tourists. It is a – diminishing. And so with the flowers. There is nowhere for them to survive, on the new Moon, in our future.'

'But how do they *know* they can't survive? – oh, that's the wrong question. Of course the flowers don't know anything.'

He paused, regarding her. 'Arc you sure?'

'What do you mean?'

'We are smart, and aggressive. We think smartness is derived from aggression. Perhaps that is true. But perhaps it takes a greater imagination to comprehend stillness than to react to the noise and clamour of our shallow human world.'

She frowned, remembering Mariko's evidence about neural

structures in the flowers. 'You're saying these things are *conscious?*'

'I believe so. It would be hard to prove. I have spent much time in contemplation here, however. And I have developed an intuition. A sympathy, perhaps.'

'But that seems *cruel*. What kind of God would plan such a thing? Think about it. You have a conscious creature, trapped on the surface of the Moon, in this desolate, barren environment. And its way of living, stretching back billions of years maybe, has had the sole purpose of diminishing itself, to prepare for this final extinction, this death, this *smyert*. What is the purpose of consciousness, confronted by such desolation?'

'But perhaps it is not so,' he said gently. 'The cosmologists tell us that there are many time streams. The future of the Moon, in the direction *we* face, may be desolate. But not the past. So why not face *that* way?'

She barely followed him. But she remembered the *kare sansui*, the waterless stream traced in the regolith. It was impossible to tell if the stream was flowing from past to future, or future to past; if the hills of heaped regolith were rising or sinking.

He said, 'Perhaps to the flowers – to *this* flower, the last, or perhaps the first – this may be a beginning, not an end.'

'*Vileekee bokh*. You are telling me that these plants are living backwards in time? Propagating – not into the future – but *into the past?*'

'In the present there is but one of them. In the past there are many – billions, perhaps. In our future lies death for them; in our past lies glory. So why not look that way?' He touched her gloved hand. 'The important thing is that you must not grieve for the flowers. They have their dream, their *mechta*, of a better Moon, in the deep past, or deep future. The universe is not always cruel, Xenia Makarova. And you must not hate Frank, for what he has done.'

'I don't hate him.'

'There is a point of view from which he is not *taking* nutrients from the heart of the Moon, but *giving*. He is pumping the core of the Moon full of water and volatiles, and when he is done he will even fill in the hole . . .You see?'

'Takomi.'

He was still.

'That isn't your real name, is it? This isn't your identity.'

He said nothing, face averted from hers.

'I don't think you are even a man. I think your name is Nemoto. And you are hiding here on the Moon, whiling away the centuries.'

Takomi stood silently for long seconds. 'My Moon plants recede into a better past. That, for me, isn't an option. I must make my way into the unwelcome future. But at least, here, I am rarely disturbed. I hope you will respect that.

'Now come,' said Takomi, or Nemoto. 'I have green tea, and rice cake, and we will sit under the cherry tree, and talk further.'

Xenia nodded, dumbly, and let him – her? – take her by the hand. Together they walked across the yielding antiquity of the Moon.

It was another celebration, here at the South Pole of the Moon. It was the day Project Roughneck promised to fulfil its potential, by bringing the first commercially useful loads of water to the surface.

Once again the crowds were out: investors with their guests, families with children, huge softscreens draped over drilling gear, Virtual Observers everywhere so everyone on the Moon could share everything that happened here today. Even the Greys were here, to celebrate the project's end, dancing in elaborate formations.

Earth hovered like a ghost on one horizon, ignored, its sparking wars meaningless.

This time, Xenia didn't find Frank strutting about the lunar surface in his Stars and Stripes spacesuit, giving out orders. Frank said he knew which way the wind blew, a blunt Earthbound metaphor no Moon-born Japanese understood. So he had confined himself to a voluntary house arrest, in the new *ryokan* that had opened up on the summit of one of the tallest rim mountains here.

When she arrived, he waved her in and handed her a drink, a fine sake. The suite was a penthouse, magnificent, decorated in a mix of western-style and traditional Japanese. One wall, facing the borehole, was just a single huge pane of tough, anhydrous lunar glass. She saw a tumbler of murky water, covered over, on a table top. Moon water, his only trophy of Roughneck.

'This is one hell of a cage,' he said. 'If you've got to be in a cage.' He laughed darkly. 'Civilized, these Lunar Japanese. Well, we'll see.' He eyed her. 'What about you? Will you go back to the stars?'

She looked at the oily ripple of the drink in her glass. 'I don't think so. I – like it here. I think I'd enjoy building a world.'

He grunted. 'You'll marry. Have kids. Grandkids.'

'Perhaps.'

He glared at her. 'When you do, remember me, who made it possible, and got his ass busted for his trouble. Remember *this*.'

He walked her to the window.

She gazed out, goddess-like, surveying the activity. The drilling site was an array of blocky machinery, now stained deep grey by dust, all of it bathed in artificial light. The stars hung above the plain, stark and still, and people and their vehicles swarmed over the ancient, broken plain like so many spacesuited ants.

'You know, it's a great day,' she said. 'They're making your dream come true.'

'*My* dream, hell.' He fetched himself another slug of sake, which he drank like beer. 'They stole it from me. And they're going inward. That's what Nishizaki and the rest are considering now. I've seen their plans. Huge underground cities in the crust, big enough for thousands, even hundreds of thousands, all powered by thermal energy from the rocks. In fifty years you could have multiples of the Moon's present population, burrowing away busily.' He glanced at his wristwatch, restless.

'What's wrong with that?'

'It wasn't the fucking *point*.' He glared up at Earth's scarred face. 'If we dig ourselves into the ground, we won't be able to see *that*. We'll forget. Don't you get it? . . .'

But now there was activity around the drilling site. She stepped to the window, cupped her hands to exclude the room lights.

People were running, away from the centre of the site.

There was a tremor. The building shuddered under her, languidly. A quake, on the still and silent Moon?

Frank was checking his watch. He punched the air and strode to the window. 'Right on time. Hot damn.'

'Frank, what have you done?'

There was another tremor, more violent. A small Buddha statue was dislodged from its pedestal, and fell gently to the carpeted floor. Xenia tried to keep her feet. It was like riding a rush hour train.

'Simple enough,' Frank said. 'Just shaped charges, embedded in the casing. They punched holes straight through the bore wall into the surrounding rock, to let the water and sticky stuff flow right into the pipe and up –'

'A blow-out. You arranged a blow-out.'

'If I figured this right the interior of the whole fucking Moon is going to come gushing out of that hole. Like puncturing a balloon.' He took her arms. 'Listen to me. We will be safe here. I figured it.'

'And the people down there, in the crater? Your managers and technicians? The *children*?'

'It's a day they'll tell their grandchildren about.' He shrugged, grinning, his forehead slick with sweat. 'They're going to lock me up anyhow. At least this way –'

But now there was an eruption from the centre of the rig, a tower of liquid, rapidly freezing, that punched its way up through the rig itself, shattering the flimsy buildings covering the head. When the fountain reached high enough to catch the flat sunlight washing over the mountains, it seemed to burst into fire, crystals of ice shining in complex parabolic sheaves, before falling back to the ground.

Frank punched the air. 'You know what that is? Kerogen. A tarry stuff you find in oil shales. It contains carbon, oxygen, hydrogen, sulphur, potassium, chlorine, other elements . . . I couldn't believe it when the lab boys told me what they found down there. Mariko says kerogen is so useful we might as well have found chicken soup in the rocks.' He cackled. 'Chicken soup, from the primordial cloud. *I won*, Xenia. With this blow-out I stopped them from building Bedrock City. I'm famous.'

'What about the Moon flowers?'

His face was hard. 'Who the fuck cares? I'm a human, Xenia. I'm interested in human destiny, not a bunch of worthless plants we couldn't even *eat*.' He waved a hand at the ice fountain. 'Look out there, Xenia. I beat the future. I've no regrets. I'm a great man. I achieve great things.'

The ground around the demolished drill head began to crack, venting gas and ice crystals; and the deep, ancient richness of the Moon rained down on the people.

Frank Paulis whispered, 'And what could be greater than this?'

. . . She was in the Dark, flying, like one of her own seeds. She was surrounded by fragments of the shattered Land, and by her children.

But she could not speak to them, of course; unlike the Land, the Dark was empty of rock, and would not carry her thoughts.

It was a time of stabbing loneliness.

But it did not last long.

Already the cloud was being drawn together, collapsing into a new and greater Land that glowed beneath her, a glowing ocean of rock, a hundred times bigger than the small place she had come from.

And at the last, she saw the greatest comet of all tear itself from the heart of this Land, a ball of fire that lunged into the sky, receding rapidly into the unyielding Dark.

She fell towards that glowing ocean, her heart full of joy at the Merging of the Lands . . .

In the last moment of her life, she recalled the Giver.

She was the first, and the Giver birthed her. None of it would have come to be without the Giver, who fed the Land.

She wished she could express her love for him. She knew that was impossible.

She sensed, though, that he knew anyhow.

Chapter 21

HOMECOMING

After their journey to the stars, Madeleine and Ben returned to a silent solar system.

Over a century had elapsed. They themselves had aged less than a year. It was now, astonishingly, the year 2240, an unimaginable, futuristic date. Madeleine had been braced for more historic drift, more cultural isolation.

Not for silence.

As the long weeks of their flight inward from the Saddle Point radius wore away, and the puddle of crowded light that was the inner system grew brighter ahead, they both grew increasingly apprehensive. At length, they were close enough to resolve images of Earth in the *Ancestor*'s telescopes. They huddled together by their monitors.

What they saw was an Earth that was brilliant white.

Ice swept down from both poles, encroaching towards the equator. The shapes of the northern continents were barely visible under the huge frozen sheets. The colours of life, brown and green and blue, had been crowded into a narrow strip around the equator. Here and there, easily visible on the night side of the planet, Madeleine made out the spark of fires, of explosions. Gaijin ships orbited Earth, tracking from pole to pole, their ramscoops casting golden light that glimmered from the ice and the oceans, mapping and studying, still following their own immense, patient projects.

Madeleine and Ben were both stunned by this. They studied Earth for hours, barely speaking, skipping meals and sleep periods.

Ben, fearful for his wife, his people on Triton, grew silent, morbid, withdrawing from Madeleine. Madeleine found the loneliness hard to bear. When she slept her dreams were intense, populated by drifting alien artefacts.

* * *

The Gaijin flower-ship dropped them into orbit around Earth's Moon.

Nemoto came to them, at last. She appeared as a third figure in the cramped, scuffed environment of *Dreamtime Ancestor*'s Service Module, a digital ghost coalescing from a cloud of cubical pixels.

Her gaze lit on Madeleine. 'Meacher. You're back. You were expected. I have an assignment for you.' She smiled.

Madeleine said, 'I don't believe you're still alive. You must be some kind of virtual simulation.'

'I don't care what you think. Anyhow, you'll never know.' Nemoto was small, shrunken, her face a leathery mask, as if with age she was devolving to some earlier proto-human form. She glanced around. 'Where's the FGB Module? . . . *Oh*.' Evidently she had just downloaded a summary of their mission from the virtual counterpart who had travelled with them. She glared. 'You have to meddle, don't you, Meacher?'

Madeleine passed a hand through Nemoto's body; pixels clustered like butterflies. To Madeleine, ten more decades out of her time, the projection was impressive new technology. There was no sign of time-delay; Nemoto – or the projector – must be *here*, on the Moon or in lunar orbit, or else her responses would be delayed by seconds.

Ben asked tightly, 'What about Triton?'

Nemoto's face was empty. 'Triton is silent. It's wise to be silent. But your wife is still alive.'

Madeleine sensed a shift in Ben's posture, a softening.

'But,' Nemoto said now, 'the colony is under threat. A fleet of Gaijin flower-ships and factories is moving out from the asteroids. They're already in orbit around Jupiter, Saturn, even Uranus. They have projects out there, for instance on Jupiter's moon Io, which we don't understand.' Her face worked, her anger visible, even after all this time, her territoriality powerful. 'The Earth has collapsed, of course. And though the fools down there don't know it, the Moon faces long-term resource crises, particularly in metals. And so on. *The Gaijin are winning*, Meacher. Triton is the only foothold we humans have in the outer system. The last trench. We can't let the Gaijin take it.'

And you have a plan, Madeleine realized, with a sinking heart. A plan that involves me. So she was immediately plunged back into Nemoto's manipulation and scheming.

Ben was frowning. He asked Nemoto some pointed questions about her presence, her influence, her resources. What was the political situation now? Who was backing her? What was her funding?

She'd answer none of his questions. She wouldn't even tell them where, physically, she was, before she disappeared, promising – or threatening – to be back.

Madeleine spent long hours at the windows, watching the Moon.

The Moon was controlled by a tight federal-government structure which seemed to blend seamlessly with a series of corporate alliances, which had grown mainly from the Japanese companies that had funded the first waves of lunar colonization. The lunar authorities had let the *Ancestor* settle into a wide two-hour orbit, but they wouldn't let Madeleine and Ben land. It was clear to Madeleine that, to these busy lunar inhabitants, returned star travellers were an irrelevance.

Huge glowing Gaijin flower-ships looped around the Moon from pole to lunar pole.

This new Moon glowed green and blue, the colours of life and humanity. The Lunar Japanese had peppered the great craters – Copernicus, Eudoxus, Gassendi, Fracastorius, Tsiolkovsky, Verne, many others – with domes, enclosing a freight of water and air and life. Landsberg, the first large colony, remained the capital. The domes were huge now, the crests of some of them reaching two kilometres above the ancient regolith, hexagonal-cell spaceframe structures supported by giant, inhabited towers. Covered roads and linear townships connected some of the domes, glowing lines of light over the maria. The Japanese planned to extend their structures until the entire surface of the Moon was glassed over, in a worldhouse. It would be like an immense arboretum, a continuously managed biosphere.

All of this – Madeleine learned, tapping into the web of information which wrapped around the new planet – was fuelled by huge core-tapping bores called Paulis mines. Frank Paulis himself was still alive. Madeleine felt a spark of pride that one of her own antique generation had achieved such greatness. But, fifty years after his huge technical triumph, Paulis was disgraced, incommunicado.

Virtual Nemoto materialized once more.

Madeleine had found out that Nemoto was still alive, as best anybody knew. But she had dropped out of sight for a long period. It was rumoured she had lived as a recluse on Farside, still relatively uninhabited. It had been a breakdown, it seemed, that had lasted for decades. Nemoto would say nothing of any of this, nothing of herself, even of the history Madeleine and Ben had skipped over. Rather, she wanted to talk only of the future, her projects, just as she always had.

'Good news.' She smiled, her face skull-like. 'I have a ship.'

Ben said, 'What ship?'

'The *Gurrutu.* One of my colony ships. It's completed the Earth-Neptune round trip twice already. It's in high Earth orbit.' She looked wistful. 'It's actually safer there than orbiting the Moon. Here, it would be claimed and scavenged for its metals.' She studied them. 'You must go to Triton.'

Ben nodded. 'Of course.'

Nemoto eyed her. 'And you, Meacher.'

Of course Ben must, Madeleine thought. Those are his people, out there in the cold, struggling to survive. It's his wife, still conveniently alive, having traversed those hundred years the long way. But – regardless of Nemoto's ambitions – it's nothing to do with me.

But, as she gazed at Nemoto's frail virtual figure, doggedly surviving, doggedly battling, she felt torn. Maybe you aren't as disengaged from all this as you used to be, Madeleine.

She said, 'Even if we make it to Triton, what are we supposed to do when we get there? What are you planning, Nemoto?'

Nemoto said bleakly, 'We must stop the Gaijin – and whoever follows them. What else is there to do?'

They would have to spend a month in Earth orbit, working on the *Gurrutu*.

The colony craft was decades old, and showing its age. *Gurrutu* had been improvised from the liquid-propellant core booster of an Ariane 12 rocket. It was a simple cylinder, with the fuel tanks inside refurbished and made habitable. The main living area of *Gurrutu* was a big hydrogen tank, with a smaller oxygen tank used for storage. A fireman's pole ran the length of the hydrogen tank, up through a series of mesh floor-partitions to an instrument cluster.

Big, fragile-looking solar-cell wings had been fixed to the exterior. But reconditioned fission reactors provided power in the dimly lit outer reaches of the solar system. These were old technology: heavy Soviet-era antiques, of a design called Topaz. Each Topaz was a clutter of pipes and tubing and control rods set atop a big radiator cone of corrugated aluminium.

There was a docking mount and an instrument module at one end of the core booster, and a cluster of ion rockets at the other. The ion thrusters were suitable for missions of long duration, missions measured in years, to the outer planets and beyond. And they worked; they had ferried the Yolgnu to Triton. But the ion thrusters needed much refurbishment. And they, too, were old technology. The newest Lunar Japanese helium-3 fusion drives were, Madeleine learned, much more effective.

It wouldn't be a comfortable ride out to Neptune. The toilets never seemed to vent properly. There was a chorus of bangs, wheezes and rattles when they tried to sleep. The solar panels had steadily degraded, so that there was never enough power, even this close to the sun. Madeleine soon tired of half-heated meals, and lukewarm coffee, and tepid bathing water.

But forty people had lived in this windowless cavern-slum for the five years it had taken *Gurrutu* to reach Neptune: eating hydroponically grown plants, recycling their waste, trying not to drive each other crazy. The tank had been slung with hammocks and blankets, little nests of humans seeking privacy. Three children had been born here.

Madeleine found scratches on an aluminium bulkhead that recorded a child's growth, the image of a favourite uncle tucked into the back of a storage cupboard.

The ship could have been built in the twenty-first century – even the twentieth. Human research into spaceflight engineering had all but stopped when the Gaijin had arrived. Madeleine thought of the Gaijin flower-ships which had carried her to the Saddle Point radius and beyond: jewelled, perfect, faultless.

But *Gurrutu* was simply the best Nemoto could do. And so it was heroic. With such equipment, Nemoto had reached Neptune – thirty times Earth's distance from the sun, ten times further out than the asteroid belt. Only Malenfant himself, unaided by Gaijin, had gone further – and his mission had been a one-man stunt. Nemoto had sent two hundred colonists.

As she laboured over the lashed-up systems, improvising repairs, Madeleine's respect for Nemoto deepened.

. . . And, while Madeleine worked, the Earth slid liquidly past the windows of the *Gurrutu*.

Those old environmentalist Cassandras had been proven right, Madeleine learned. The climate really had been only metastable; in the end, after forty thousand years of digging and building and burning, humans managed to destabilize the world, tip over the whole damn bowl of cherries, until it settled with stunning rapidity into this new, lethal state.

Madeleine could see patterns in the ice: ripples, lines of debris, varying colours, where the ice had flowed from its fastnesses at the poles and the mountain peaks. There was little cloud over the great ice sheets – merely wisps of cirrus, streaked by winds which tore perpetually around immense low-pressure systems squatting over the frozen poles.

The ice covered most of Canada, and a great tongue of it extended far into the American Midwest, reaching further south than the Great Lakes – or where the Lakes used to be. Chicago, Detroit, Toronto and the other cities were all gone now, drowned. The familiar lobed shapes of the Lakes themselves had been overwhelmed by a new, glimmering ocean that stretched a thousand kilometres inland from the eastern seaboard. And to the west, a ribbon of water stretched up from Puget Sound towards Alaska. The land itself was crushed down under the weight of the ice, and sea water had flowed eagerly into the shallow depressions so formed.

Even to the south of the ice line, the land was grievously damaged. Desert stretched from Oregon through Idaho, Wyoming, Nebraska and Iowa, a belt of immense, rippled sand dunes. It was a place of violent winds, for heavy, cold air poured off the ice over the exposed land, and she saw giant dust storms that persisted for days. At night she saw lights glimmer in that vast expanse, flickering: just camp fires lit by descendants of mid-western Americans who must be reduced to living like Bedouins in that great cold desert.

South of the ice, Earth at first glance looked as temperate and habitable as it had always done. She could see green in the tropical areas, coral reefs, ships plying to and fro through warm, ice-free seas. But nowhere was unaffected. The great rain forests of equatorial Africa and the Amazon Basin had shrunk back into isolated pockets, surrounded by swathes of what looked like grass lands. Conversely, the Sahara seemed to be turning green. Even the shapes of the continents had changed, as glistening sheets of continental shelves were exposed by the falling sea level.

In the southern United States there were still cities: great misty-grey urban sprawls around the coasts and along the river valleys, from Baja California, along the Mexican border, the Gulf of Mexico, to Florida. But New Orleans seemed to be burning continually, great fires blocks wide sending up black smoke plumes that streaked out over hundreds of kilometres. Likewise, there appeared to be a small war raging around Orlando; she made out what looked like tank tracks, frequent explosions that lit up the night.

It was impossible to gather direct news. Presumably all communication was carried out by land lines or with point-to-point modulated lasers; belatedly, it seemed, the inhabitants of Earth had learned the wisdom of not broadcasting their business to the stars. It did appear, though, that some of these wars had been blazing since before the return of the ice.

The most savage conflict appeared to be occurring in north Africa, where the population of Eurasia – hundreds of millions – had tried to drain into the southern European countries and the new North African grasslands. But any orderly relocation had long broken down. Huge black craters scarred the Sahara, some of them glimmering as if with puddles of glass; and, once, she made out the tell-tale shape of a mushroom cloud, rising like a perfect toy from an ochre African horizon.

And – more sinister still – she could see new forms on Earth's long-suffering hide. They were great sprawling structures, spider-like, silvery: not like human cities, more centrally organized, the pieces interconnected, like single buildings spanning tens of kilometres. These were Gaijin colonies. There were several of them in the ice-free middle latitudes, with no sign of human occupancy nearby. There were even a handful on the ice sheets themselves, places no human could survive. Nobody knew what the Gaijin were doing in there.

She felt a cold fury. Couldn't the Gaijin have done something to stop this, to halt the collapse of her world? If not, why the hell were they here?

Ben said he wanted to go to Earth, to Australia, one last time, before he left forever. Madeleine quailed at the idea. *That's not my planet any more.* But she didn't want to oppose Ben's complex impulse.

An automated ground-to-orbit shuttle came climbing up to meet them. Nemoto had found someone who had agreed to host them, if briefly.

They skimmed through morning light towards Australia, approaching from the south. They received no calls for identification; there was no attempt at traffic control, nothing from the ground. It was like approaching an uninhabited planet.

They drifted over Sydney. The city was still populated, its suburbs scarred by conflict, but there was no harbour; Sydney had been left beached in the country's drying interior. The rust-red deserts of the centre appeared still more desiccated than before. But she saw no signs of humanity. Alice Springs, for example, was burned out, a husk; nothing moved there.

They skimmed low over the great geological features south of the Alice, Ayers Rock and the Olgas. These were uncompromising lumps of hard, ancient sandstone protruding from the flat desert, extensively carved by megayears of water flows. To the Aborigines, nomads on this unforgiving tabletop landscape, these formations must have been as striking as the medieval cathedrals that had loomed over Europe. And so the Aborigines had made them places of totemic and religious significance, spinning Dreamtime stories from cracks and folds, until the rocks became a kind of mythic cinema, frozen in geological time. It had been a triumph of the imagination, she supposed, in a land like a sensory deprivation tank.

This had briefly been a centre for tourism. The tourists were long gone now, the western influence vanished in an instant, a dream of fat and affluence. But the Aborigines had remained. From the air she saw slim figures moving slowly over the landscape, round faces turned up to her vehicle, all as it had been for twelve thousand years – just as Ben had once foreseen, she remembered.

Ben peered from his window, silent, withdrawn.

Perhaps a hundred kilometres south of the Alice, they saw a structure of bright blue, a dot in the desert. A tent.

The shuttle dipped, fell like a brick, and skidded to a halt half a kilometre distant from the tent.

Nobody came to meet them. After a few minutes they climbed down to the ground and walked towards the tent.

The land was an immense orange-red table, the sky a sheet of washed-out blue. There was utter silence here: no bird song, no insects. The sun was high, ferocious, the heat tremendous and dry. They walked cautiously, unused to Earth's heavy gravity.

Madeleine felt overwhelmed. Save for a few space walks, it was the first time she had been out of a cramped hab module, out in a landscape, for years.

Ben touched her arm. She stopped. Through the heat haze of the horizon, something moved, stately, silent.

'It looks like a lizard,' she whispered. 'A komodo dragon, maybe. But –'

'But it's immense.'

'Another Gaijin experiment, you think?'

He said, 'I think we ought to keep still.'

The lizard, a Mesozoic nightmare, paused for long seconds, perhaps a minute, a tongue the length of a whip lashing out at something unseen. Then it moved on, turning away from the humans.

They hurried on.

Their host was a woman: an American, small, compact, stern-faced, her thick black hair tied back severely behind her head. She was dressed in a silvery coverall. She was called Carole Lerner.

Lerner looked them up and down contemptuously. 'Nemoto told me to expect you. She didn't tell me you were two babes in the wood.' She eyed them with hard suspicion. 'I have a hoard.'

Ben frowned. 'What?'

Lerner said, 'I'm not about to tell you where. If I die my caches will self-destruct.'

Madeleine understood quickly. Medicine had collapsed, along with everything else, when the ice had come. So no more anti-ageing treatments. Such supplies had become the most precious items on the planet. She held up her hands. 'We're no threat to you, Carole.'

Lerner kept watching them.

At last, sternly, she brought them into the tent, which was blessedly cool, the air moist. She dug out a couple of coveralls, indicated they should put them on. 'These are priceless. Literally. Therm-aware clothing, all but indestructible. Nobody makes them any more. People hand them down like heirlooms, mother to child. Be careful with them.'

'We will,' Madeleine promised.

The tent had no partitions. Ben shrugged, stripped naked, and climbed into his coverall. Madeleine followed suit.

Lerner began to boil water for a drink, and she gave them food, a rehydrated soup, its flavour unidentifiable. She looked about sixty. She was in fact much older than that. She turned out to be *the* Carole Lerner, the woman who had – following another project of Nemoto's – descended into the clouds of Venus, and become the first, and only, human to set foot there.

Ben glanced around, at piles of rock samples, data discs, a few old-fashioned paper books, heavily thumbed, their pages dusty and yellowed.

'My work,' Lerner growled, watching him. 'I'm a geologist. No previous generation has lived through the onset of an Ice Age.'

Ben asked, 'Are there still journals, science institutes, universities?'

'Not on Earth,' Lerner said, scowling. 'I'm caching my samples and notes. Buried deep enough so the animals can't get 'em. And I post my results and interpretation to the Moon, Mars.' She eyed Madeleine, hostile. 'I know what you're thinking. I'm some old nut, an obsessive. Science doesn't matter any more. You star travellers make me sick. You hop and skip through history, and you don't see a damn thing. I'll tell you this. The Gaijin work on long timescales. We're mayflies to them. And that's why science matters now. More than ever. So we can stay in the game.'

Madeleine raised her hands. 'I didn't . . .'

But Lerner had turned her attention to her soup, her anger subsiding. Ben touched Madeleine's arm, and she fell silent.

This is a woman, she thought, who has spent a *long* time alone.

Lerner had a small car, just a bubble of plastic on a light frame, powered by batteries kept topped up by a big solar cell array, and with a gigantic tank of water strapped to its roof. The next day she piled them in and drove them west.

After a couple of hours they reached an area which seemed a little less arid. Madeleine saw green vegetation, trees, tufts of grass, birds wheeling. They came to a shallow creek, dry, which Lerner turned to follow. They passed what appeared to be an abandoned farm, burned out.

They climbed a shallow rise, and Lerner slowed the car, let it run forward almost noiselessly. Finally, as they neared the crest, she cut the engine, and let the car's momentum carry it forward in silence.

As they went over the rise, the land opened up before Madeleine.

There was water, a great calm blue pool of it, stretching halfway to the horizon, utterly unexpected in this dry old place. She could actually smell the water. Her soul felt immediately lifted, some primitive instinct responding.

And it took a full minute of looking, of letting her eyes become accustomed to the landscape, before she could see the animals.

There was a herd of what looked like rhinoceros, lumbering cylinders of flesh, jostling clumsily at the water's edge. But they had no horns. One of them raised a massive head in which small black eyes were embedded like studs. It was quite spectacularly ugly. She saw that it had small, oddly human feet; it trod delicately.

'*Diprotodons*,' Lerner murmured. 'Very common now.'

Madeleine made out kangaroo-like creatures of all sizes, bizarre, overblown animals, some so huge it seemed they could barely lift themselves off the ground – but jump they did, in clumsy lollops. There were creatures like ground sloth, which Lerner said were a variety of giant wombat.

And there were predators. Madeleine saw packs of wolf-like animals, warily circling the grazing, drinking herbivores. Some resembled dogs, some cats.

'It's the same elsewhere,' Lerner said. 'As the ice spreads, the grasslands and forests of the temperate climes are retreating, to be replaced by tundra, steppe, spruce forests.'

'Places these reconstructed creatures can survive,' Ben said.

'Yes. But the Gaijin aren't responsible for everything. In Asia there are reindeer, musk oxen, horses, bison. In North America, the wolves and bears and even the mountain lions are making a recovery.' She smiled again. 'And in the valley of the Thames, I've heard, there are woolly mammoths . . . Now *that* I'd like to see.'

They sat for long hours watching ancient herbivores feed.

They drove on. They drove for hours.

It was only after they had returned to Lerner's camp, with the shuttle parked patiently by, that Madeleine realized she hadn't seen a single human being, not one, nor any sign of recent human habitation, all day.

They stayed three days. Gradually Lerner seemed to learn to tolerate them.

At the end of the last day, Lerner made them a final meal. As the sun sank to the horizon, they sat sipping recycled water in the shade of Lerner's tent.

They swapped sea stories. Lerner told them about Venus. In return, they told her of the Chaera, huddling in the dismal glow of a black hole. And they talked of the changes that had come over humanity.

Lerner said sourly, 'There were a lot of *words:* refugee, relocate, discontinuity, famine, disease, war. Death on a scale we haven't seen since the twentieth century. And people keep right on being born. You know what the average age of humans is now?'

'What?'

'Fifteen years old. Just fifteen. To most people on the planet *this* is normal.' She waved a hand, indicating the depopulated town, the ice-transformed climate, the strange reconstructed animals, the wispy flower-ships that crossed the sky above. 'We're in the middle of a fucking epochal catastrophe here, and people have *forgotten.*' She spat in the dirt, and wiped her mouth with the back of her hand.

Ben leaned forward. 'Carole. Do you think Nemoto is right? That the Gaijin are trying to destroy us?'

Lerner squinted. 'I don't think so. But they don't want to save us either. They are – studying us.'

'What are they trying to find out?'

'Beats me. But then, they probably wouldn't understand what *I'm* trying to find out.'

After a time, Lerner went out to fetch more drink.

In Ben's arms, Madeleine murmured, 'We humans don't seem to age very well, do we?'

'No.'

But then, she thought, humans aren't meant to live so long. Maybe the Gaijin are used to this perspective. *We* aren't. And the feeling of helplessness is crushing. No wonder Lerner is an obsessive, Nemoto a recluse.

Ben was silent.

'You're thinking about Lena,' she said. 'Are you frightened?'

'Why should I be frightened?'

'A hundred years is a long time,' Madeleine said gently.

'But we are *yirritja* and *dhuwa*,' he said. 'We are matched.'

She hesitated. 'And us?'

He just smiled, absently.

Too hot, she peered up at the sky. There was a lot of dust suspended in the air, obscuring many of the stars, and the Moon was almost full, grey splashed with virulent green. Nevertheless, she could see flower-ships swooping easily across the sky. Alien ships, orbiting Earth, unremarked.

And beyond the ships, she saw flickers among the stars. In the direction of the great constellation of Orion, for instance. Sparks, bursts. As if the stars were flaring, exploding. She'd noticed this before, found no explanation. It was strange. Chilling. The sky wasn't supposed to *change*.

Clearly, something was headed this way. Something that spanned the stars, a wavefront of colonizing aliens, perhaps.

'I don't like it here,' she said.

'You mean Australia?'

'No. The planet. The sky. It isn't ours any more.'

'If it ever was.'

Madeleine thought, I'm frightened of the sky. But I can't run away again. I'm involved – just as Nemoto intended.

I have to go to Triton.

To do what? Blindly follow Nemoto's latest insane scheme?

She smiled inwardly. Maybe I'll think of something when we get there.

Lerner brought back a bottle of some kind of hooch; it tasted like fortified wine.

She smiled at them coldly. 'I heard that in Spain and France people have gone back to the caves, where the art still survives, from the *last*

Ice Age. And they are adding new layers of painting, of the animals they see around them. Maybe it was all a dream, do you think? The warm period, the inter-glacial, our civilization. Maybe all that matters is the ice, and the cave.'

As the light failed, and the inhabited Moon brightened, they drank a series of toasts: to Venus, to the Chaera, to Earth, to the ice.

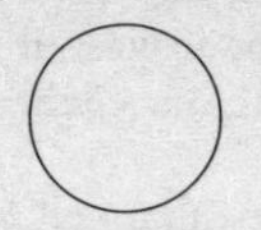

Chapter 22

TRITON DREAMTIME

Even before Neptune showed a disc, Madeleine could see that it was blue, and Triton white. Blue planet, white moon, swimming mistily out of the huge slow-moving dark like exotic deep sea fish.

Neptune swelled into a disc, made almost full by the pinpoint sun behind her. The looming planet was dim, at first just a faintly blue hole against the stars, gradually filling with misty detail as her eyes dark-adapted, becoming a ball of subtle blue and violet, visibly structured. Bands of darker blue girdled the planet, following lines of latitude. There were big storm systems, swirling knots like Jupiter's red spot. And there were thin stripes of white, higher clouds far above the blue, clouds that formed and dissipated within a few hours, surprisingly rapidly. Sometimes, when the angle of the sun was right, she could see those high clouds casting shadows on the deeper layers beneath.

She was a *long* way from home.

It was impossible even to grasp the immensities of scale here. The sun showed as no more than an intense star, bright enough to cast shadows, grey but razor-sharp. The sun's gravity grip was so loosened that Neptune took more than a hundred times as long as Earth to complete a single orbit. And Neptune was surrounded by emptiness more than ten times wider than Earth's orbit around the sun – an emptiness, indeed, that could have contained the whole of Jupiter's orbit.

Out here, in the stillness and cold and dark, the worlds that had spawned were not like Earth. Here the planets had grown immense, misty, stuffed with light elements like hydrogen and helium which had boiled away from the hot, busy inner worlds. So Neptune's rocky core was buried beneath thick layers of opaque gas; the blue was of methane, not water; there were no continents or ice caps here.

But she had not expected that Neptune would be so stunningly Earth-like. She felt tugs of nostalgic longing; for Earth itself, of course, was no longer blue, but a diseased white, the white of encroaching ice.

On the last day of its long flight, the *Gurrutu*, engines blazing, swept around the limb of Neptune. The manoeuvre occurred in complete silence, and as Madeleine watched the huge world swim past her, it was as if she was flying through some cold, dark, gigantic cathedral.

And there was Triton, already bright and growing brighter, a pink-white pearl floating in emptiness.

The final approach to Triton was a challenge for the navigation routines. Triton, uniquely among the solar system's larger moons, orbited Neptune in a retrograde manner, opposite to the spin of Neptune itself. And Triton's orbit was severely pitched up, some twenty degrees out of the plane of the ecliptic. It was thought these eccentricities of Triton were a relic of its peculiar origin: it had once been an independent body, like Pluto, but had been captured by Neptune, perhaps by impact with another moon or by grazing Neptune's atmosphere, a catastrophic event that had resulted in global melting before the moon had learned to endure its entrapment.

Gurrutu entered a looping elliptical orbit. Madeleine watched as a surface of crumpled, pink-streaked water ice rolled beneath the craft. Triton's misty twilight was marked by a single, yellow, man-made beacon: at the site of Kasyapa Township, home to Ben Roach's people. They were not alone in Triton orbit. Many emigrant transport ships, of the same design as *Gurrutu,* still circled here. Others had been driven into the surface, to be broken up for raw materials.

After a day, a small shuttle came up to meet them. Triton's atmosphere, a wisp of nitrogen laced with hydrocarbons, was too thin to support any kind of aircraft; so the shuttle would descend from orbit standing on its rockets, as Apollo astronauts had once landed on the Moon.

As the lander swivelled, the icy ground opened out before her. It was white, laced with pink and, here and there, darker streaks, like wind-blown dust. It was crowded with detail, she saw, with ridges and clefts and pits in the ice, as if the skin of the planet had shrivelled in some impossible heat.

The lander tipped up and fell sharply, entering the last phase of its descent routine. The horizon flattened out quickly, and detail exploded at her. She was descending into a region criss-crossed by shallow ridges, a parquetry of planes and pits in the ice. But there was evidence of human activity: two long straight furrows cut across the random geologic features, a pair of roadways as straight as any Roman road, neatly melted into the ice. And at their terminus, set at the centre of one of the walled ice pits, she saw a small octagonal pad of what looked like concrete, a cluster of silvery tanks and other buildings nearby.

The final landing was gentle. Madeleine and Ben suited up and climbed out of the lander.

The plain around them was still, the fuel tanks and crude surface buildings pale and silent. Under her boots there was a crunch of frost overlaying a harder, whiter rock.

. . . Not rock, she told herself. This was ice, water ice. She scraped at the ice with her boot. It was impenetrable, unyielding, and she failed to mark its surface; it was like a hard, compacted stone. Here, in the intense cold, ice played the part of silicate rocks on Earth. There was an elusive pink stain about the ice, almost too faint to see. Some kind of sunlight-processed organics, perhaps.

She took a step forward, two. She floated and hopped, Moonwalk-style. In fact, she knew, Triton's gravity was little more than half the strength of the Moon's. But she was a big clumsy human with a poor gravity sense; to her body, Triton and Moon were both lumped together in a catch-all category called 'weak gravity'.

She looked up, into a black sky. There was no sense of air above her, no scattering of the sunlight: only a deep starry sky, as if seen from the high desert – but with a dominant bright pinprick at the centre of it. The sun was bright enough to cast shadows, but it was not like authentic sunlight, she thought, more like illumination by a very bright planet, like Venus. The land was a plain of pale white, delicate, a land of midnight stillness, its planes and folds seeming gauzy in the thin light. It seemed a creation of smoke or mist, not of rock-solid ice.

Now she tipped back and peered overhead, where Neptune hung in the sky. The planet appeared as large as fifteen of Earth's full Moons, strung across the sky together. It was half-full, gaunt, almost spectral.

From the corner of her eye she saw movement: flakes of pure white, sparsely descending around her.

'Snow, on Triton?'

'I think it's nitrogen,' Ben said.

Madeleine tried to catch a flake of nitrogen snow on her glove. She wondered how the crystals would differ from the water-ice snow of Earth. But the flakes were too elusive, too sparse, and they were soon gone.

Ben tapped her shoulder and pointed to another corner of the sky, closer to the horizon. There was what looked like a star, perhaps surrounded by a diffuse disc of light.

It was a Gaijin engineering convoy: alien ships, built of asteroid rock and ice, en route to Triton.

The refugee Yolgnu had established their home in the rim wall of a shallow, circular depression called Kasyapa Cavus. This was on the eastern edge of Bubembe Regio, a region of so-called cantaloupe terrain, the complex, parquet-like landscape of the type Madeleine had noticed during the landing. The Cavus had a smooth, bowl-like floor, easy to traverse. There were tractors here, whose big, gauzy balloon tyres seemed to have made no impression on the icy ground. Kasyapa Township was a system of branching caverns. The colonists had burrowed far into the ice-rock, ensuring that a thick layer of ice and spacecraft hull-metal shielded them from the radiation flux of Neptune's magnetosphere, and from the relic cosmic radiation of deep space.

She was given a cabin, a crude cube dug into the ice. She moved her few personal belongings into the cabin – book chips, a few clothes, virtuals of an X-ray burster and a black hole accretion ring. Her things looked dowdy and old, out of place. The wall surface – Triton ice sealed and insulated by a clear plastic – was smooth and hard under Madeleine's hand. After the cool spaces of the Neptune system, she found Kasyapa immediately claustrophobic.

Ben Roach was swallowed up by the family he had left behind, two whole new generations of nephews and nieces and grand-nephews and grand-nieces.

And here, of course, was Lena Roach. She had become a small, precise woman whose silences suggested great depths. She hadn't seen her husband, Ben, for a hundred of her years, for most of her long life. But she had waited for him, built a home in the most unforgiving of environments.

It was immediately clear she still loved Ben, and he loved her, despite the gulfs of time that separated them. Madeleine watched their calm, deep reunion with awe and envy. It was like grandmother greeting grandson, like wife meeting husband, complex, multi-layered.

She explored fitfully, moodily.

It was obvious to her that the colony was failing.

The people were thin, their skins pale. Malnourished, they were spectres in the dim sunlight. People moved slowly, despite the welcoming gentleness of the gravity. Energy was something to be conserved.

There was an atmosphere of a prison here. These had once been people of openness, of the endless desert, she reminded herself. Now they were confined here, inside this icy warren. She thought that must be hurting them, perhaps on a level they didn't appreciate themselves.

There were few children.

The people of Kasyapa were welcoming, but she found they were locked into tight family groups. She would always be an outsider here.

Madeleine spent a lot of time alone, cooped up in her ice-walled box. She engaged in peculiar time-delayed conversations with Nemoto; with a minimum of ten hours between comment and reply, it was more like receiving mail. Still, they spoke. And gradually Nemoto revealed the deeper purpose she had concocted for Madeleine.

'These people are starving,' Nemoto whispered. 'And yet they are sitting on a frozen ocean . . .'

Triton was, Nemoto told her, probably the solar system's most remote significant and accessible cache of water, within the Kuiper Belt anyhow. She said that Robert Goddard, the American rocketry pioneer, had proposed – in a paper called 'The Last Migration' – that Triton could be used as an outfitting and launching post for interstellar expeditions. 'That was in 1927,' Nemoto said.

'Goddard was a far-sighted guy,' Madeleine murmured.

'. . . Even if he got it wrong,' Nemoto was saying – had said, five hours earlier. 'Even if, as it turns out, Triton will be used as a staging post for expeditions *from* the stars. And not used by us, but by Eeties. The Gaijin.'

But the ocean under Madeleine's feet, tens of kilometres thick, was useless to the colonists as long as it was frozen hard as rock.

'Imagine if we could melt that ocean,' Nemoto said, her face an expressionless mask.

But how? The sun was too remote. Of course the sunlight could be collected, by mirrors or lenses. But how big would such a mirror have to be? Thousands of kilometres wide, more? Such a project seemed absurd.

'It's not the way humans work,' Madeleine said gloomily. 'Look at the colonists here, burrowing like ants. We're small and weak. We have to take the worlds as they are given to us, not rebuild them.'

'. . . And yet,' came Nemoto's reply many hours later, 'that is exactly what we must do if we are to prevail. We are going to have to act more like Gaijin than humans.'

Nemoto had a plan. It involved diverting a moon called Nereid, slamming it into Triton.

Madeleine was immediately outraged. This was arrogance indeed. But she let Nemoto's data finish downloading.

It was a remarkable, bold scheme. The rocket engines which had brought the colonists here would now be used to divert a moon. The numbers added up. It could be done, Madeleine realized reluctantly. It would take a year, no more.

It was also, Madeleine thought, quite insane. She pictured Nemoto, stranded centuries out of her time, isolated, skulking in corners of the Moon, concocting mad schemes to hurl outer-planet moons back and forth, an old woman fighting the alien invasion, single-handed.

And yet, and yet . . .

She looked inward. What is it *I* want?

All her family, the people she had grown up with, were lost in the past, on a frozen world. She was rootless. And yet she had no pull to join this tight community, had felt no envy of Ben when Lena had *recaptured* him, on his arrival here. Her life had become a series of episodes, as she'd drifted through scenes of a more-or-less incomprehensible history. Was it even possible to sustain a consistent motivation – to find something to want?

Yes, she realized. It isn't necessary to be picaresque. Look at Nemoto. *She* still knows what she wants, the same as she always did, after all these years. Maybe the same applied to Reid Malenfant, wherever he was. And maybe that was why Madeleine was attracted to Nemoto's projects – not for the worth of the work, but for Nemoto's singular strength of mind.

She went to discuss it with Ben. His first reaction was like hers.

'What you're proposing is barbaric,' Ben said. 'You talk of smashing one moon into another. You will destroy both.'

'It's technically feasible. Nemoto's numbers prove that a deflection of Nereid by the thruster systems from the orbiting transports would –'

'I'm not talking about feasibility. Many things are feasible. That doesn't make them right. Once Triton is changed, it is changed forever. Who knows what future, wiser generations might have made of these resources we expend so carelessly?'

'*But the Gaijin are on their way now.*'

'We wreck this world, or they do. Is that the choice you offer?'

'Triton is ours to wreck, not theirs!'

He considered. He said at length, 'I will concede your plan has one positive outcome.'

'What?'

'We are barely surviving here. The Yolgnu. That much is obvious. Perhaps with what you intend –'

She nodded. 'It will work, Ben.'

'There will be a lot of opposition. People have been living here for generations. This is their home. As it is.'

'I know. It's going to be hard for all of us.'

'What will you do now?'

She considered. She hadn't thought it through that far. 'We can send probes to Nereid,' she said. 'Survey the emplacements of the thrust units, perhaps even initiate the work. Ben, those Gaijin are on their way, whatever we do. If we leave this too long we might not be able to do anything anyhow.' She squinted up at the ice roof, imagining the abandoned ships circling overhead. 'We could even begin the deflection, start the thrusters. It will take a year of steady burning to set up the collision. But I'll initiate nothing irrevocable until you get agreement from your people.'

He said sadly, 'You started out your career as a transporter of weapons. And you are still transporting weapons.'

That irritated her. 'Look, Triton is a lifeless planet. There is nothing here but humans, and what we brought.'

He eyed her. 'Are you sure?'

After a couple of months, to Madeleine's surprise, Lena Roach had invited her to 'go walkabout', as she called it, to go see something more of Triton.

Madeleine was a little suspicious. She remained the focus of the colony's intense debate about its future; few people were so open with her that such offers didn't come with strings.

She spoke to Ben.

He laughed. 'Well, you're right. Everybody's got a point of view. Lena has her opinion. But what harm can it do to go out and see some ice?'

Madeleine thought it over for a day.

The Nereid project had begun. Ben had loaned her Kasyapa engineers to detach the engine units from the transport hulks in orbit around Triton, reconfigure them for operation on Nereid, improvise systems to extract fuel from the substance of the moon. She had a small monitoring station set up in her ice cell, which showed her, by telemetry and a visual feed, that sparse array of engines burning, twenty-four hours a day, consuming Nereid's own material as fuel and reaction propellant, slowly, slowly pushing the battered moon out of its looping ellipse. It was good to have a project, to be able to immerse herself in engineering detail.

But she would have a year to wait, even if Kasyapa's great debate concluded in an acceptance of her program. Ben, torn between his lost family and the endless work of the colony, had little time to spend with her. There were few people here, nowhere to escape, little to do. She still spent much of her time alone, in her ice cell, immersed in virtuals, reading up on the dismal history she had skipped over.

Getting out of here would be a good thing. She agreed to go along with Lena.

So they climbed aboard a surface tractor, a big balloon-tyre bubble.

At first they drove in silence, the tractor bouncing gently. Madeleine felt as if she was floating, all but naked, above Triton's ice ground. The sky was a velvet dome crowded with stars, and with that subtle, misty hull of Neptune riding at the zenith above their heads.

Lena was a small, compact woman, her movements patient and precise. She had been just twenty when Ben had departed for the Saddle Point. Her age was over a hundred and twenty years old, but, thanks to rejuvenation treatments, she might have been forty. But she didn't act forty, Madeleine thought; she acted old.

The ground was complex. The tractor's lights showed how the ice was stained pink, as if by traces of blood, and there were streaks of darker material laid over the surface. But here and there the dirty water-ice rock was overlaid by splashes of white, brilliant in the lights; this was nitrogen snow, fresh-fallen.

The land became more uneven. The tractor climbed a shallow ridge, and Madeleine found herself tipped precariously back in her seat. From the summit of the ridge she caught a glimpse of a landscape pocked by huge craters, each some thirty kilometres wide or more. But they weren't like impact craters; many of them were oval in shape.

The tractor plunged into the nearest crater. The ground broke up into pits and flows, like frozen mud, and the tractor bounced and floated in great leaps.

Lena said, 'This is the oldest surface on Triton. It covers perhaps a third of the surface. From orbit, the land looks like the surface of a cantaloupe melon, and that gave it its name. But this is difficult and dangerous terrain.' Her accent was odd, shaped by time, sounding strangulated to Madeleine. 'These "craters" are actually collapsed bubbles in the ice. They formed when the world froze . . . You know that Triton was once liquid?'

'After its capture.'

'Yes.'

'Neptune raised great tides in Triton. There was an ocean hundreds of kilometres deep – crusted over by a thin ice layer at its contact with the vacuum – that stayed liquid and warm, for half a billion years, as the orbit became a circle.'

Madeleine eyed her suspiciously. '*Life*. That's what you're getting at. Native life, here in the tidal melt of Triton.' Just as Ben had hinted. She wasn't surprised, or much interested. Life emerged wherever it could; everybody knew that. Life was a commonplace.

Lena said, 'You know, when we first came here we spread out from Kasyapa, around this little world.'

'You sang Triton.'

'Yes.' Lena smiled. 'We made our roads with orbiting lasers, and we named the cantaloupe hollows and the snow fields and the craters. We were exhilarated, on this empty world. *We* were the Ancestors! But we grew – discouraged. Nothing moves here, save bits of ice and snow and gas. Nothing lives, save us. There aren't even bones in the ground. Soon we found we had to ration food, energy, air. We mapped from orbit, sent out robots.'

'Robots don't sing.'

'No. But there is nothing to sing here . . .'

Madeleine, with a sudden impulse, covered Lena's hand with her own. 'Perhaps one day. And perhaps there was life in the deep past.'

'You don't yet understand,' Lena said, frowning. She tapped a control pad and the motor gunned.

The tractor followed complex ridge pathways, heading steadily away from Kasyapa.

They talked desultorily, about planetary formation, Lena's long life on Triton, Madeleine's strange experiences among the stars. They were exploring each other, Madeleine thought; and perhaps that was the purpose of this jaunt.

Lena knew, of course, about Ben's relationship with Madeleine. At length they talked about that, tentatively.

Lena had known about it long before Ben had left for the stars. She knew such things were inevitable, even necessary, in a separation that crossed generations. She herself had taken lovers, even an informal second husband, with whom she'd raised children. The ties of *galay* and *dhuway* were, she said, too strong to be broken by mere time and space.

Madeleine found she liked Lena. She still wasn't sure if she envied Lena the ties she shared with Ben. To be bound by such powerful bonds, for a lifetime of indefinite duration, seemed claustrophobic to her. Perhaps I've been isolated too long, she thought.

After some hours they reached a polar cap. It turned out to be a region of cantaloupe terrain, where every depression was filled with nitrogen snow. They camped here, near the pole, on the fringe of interstellar space. Overhead, Madeleine saw cirrus clouds of nitrogen ice crystals.

The pole was a dangerous place to walk. She saw evidence of geysers: huge pits blasted clean of snow, and dark streaks across the land, tens of kilometres long, like the remnants of gigantic roads. All of this under Neptune's smoky light, and a rich dazzle of stars.

This was an enchanting world. Madeleine found herself, reluctantly, falling in love with Triton.

Reluctantly, because, she was coming to realize, she would have to destroy this place.

Lena brought her, on foot, to a small unmanned science station, painted bright yellow so it stood out from the pinkish snow.

'We are running a seismic survey,' she said. 'There are stations like this all over Triton. Every time we shake the surface, by so much as a footstep, waves travel through this world's frozen interior, and we can deduce what lies there.'

'. . . And?'

'You understand that Triton is a ball of rock, overlaid by an ocean – a frozen ocean. But ice is not simple.' Lena picked up a loose fragment of ice, and cupped it in her gloved hands. '*This* form is called ice I. It is the familiar form of ice, just as on Earth's surface.' She squeezed tighter. 'But if I were to crush it, eventually the crystal structure would collapse to an alternative, more closely packed, arrangement of molecules.'

'Ice II.'

'Yes. But that is not the end. There is a whole series of stable forms, reached with increasing pressure, the crystal structure more and more distorted from the pure tetrahedral form of ice I. And so, inside Triton, there are a series of layers: ice I at the surface, where we walk, all the way to a shell of ice VIII, which overlays the rocky core . . .'

Madeleine nodded, not very interested.

The snows seemed to be layered. The deeper she dug with her booted toe, the richer the purple-brown colours of the sediment strata she uncovered. This hemisphere was entering its forty-year spring, and the polar cap was evaporating; thin winds of nitrogen would eventually carry all this cap material to the other pole, where it would snow out.

And later, when it was autumn here, the flow was reversed. Triton's atmosphere was not permanent: it was only the polar caps in transit, from one axis to another.

But Lena was still talking. '. . . large scale rebuilding of the planet is the same as –'

Madeleine held up her hands. 'You left me behind. What are you telling me, Lena?'

'That there is evidence of tampering, planetary tampering, from the deepest past, here on Triton.'

Madeleine felt chilled. 'Even here?'

'Just like Venus. Just like Earth. Nothing is primordial. Everything has been shaped.'

That inner layer of ice VIII was no crude seam of compressed mush. It was very pure. And it seemed to have been sculpted.

When they got back to the tractor Lena showed Madeleine diagrams, seismic maps. The core had facets – triangles, hexagons – each kilometres wide. 'It's as if somebody encased the core in a huge jewel,' she said. 'And it must have been done before the general freezing.'

'Somebody came here,' Madeleine said slowly, 'and – somehow, manipulating temperature and pressure in that deep ocean – froze out this cage around the sea bed.'

'Yes.'

'And the life forms there –'

'Immediately destroyed, of course, their nutrient supply blocked, their very cells broken open by the freezing. We can see them, their relics, in the deep samples we have taken.'

Madeleine felt a deep, unreasoning anger well up in her. 'Why would anybody do such a thing?'

Lena shrugged. 'Perhaps it was not malice. *They* may have had a mission – insane, but a mission. Perhaps *they* thought they were helping these primitive Triton bugs. Perhaps *they* wished to spare the bugs the pain of growth, change, evolution, death. This great crystal structure encodes very little information. You need only a few bits to characterize its composition – pure ice VIII – and its regular, repeating structure. It is static, perfect – even incorruptible. Life, on the other hand, requires a deep complexity. It is this complexity which gives us our potential, and our pain. Perhaps, you see, they felt pity.'

Madeleine frowned. 'Lena, did Ben encourage you to show me this? Are you trying to persuade me to back off the Nereid project?'

Lena said, 'Ben and I have different experiences. He travelled to the stars, and saw many things. I worked here. Helping to uncover this strange, ancient tragedy.'

Yes. There was no need to go to the stars, Madeleine saw now. It was *here*, all the time, on Venus and Triton and God-knows-where, and even Earth. The central paradoxical mystery of the universe. Everywhere, life emergent. Everywhere, life crushed. And no explanation *why* it had to be this way. Over and over.

She felt her anger burn brighter. She had made her own decision. This wasn't simply what Nemoto wanted. It had become what *she* wanted. And that burning desire felt good.

Lena smiled, gnomic, wise.

By the time they got back to Kasyapa, the flower-ships had grown in Triton's sky, until at last their delicate filigree structure was visible, just, with the naked eye. The same fucking Gaijin who had watched as Earth had gone to hell.

She sailed up to orbit, boarded *Gurrutu*, and headed for Nereid.

Madeleine first sighted Nereid ten days out. It grew rapidly, day by day, finally hour by hour, until its battered grey hide filled the viewing windows.

Rendezvous with the hurtling rock was difficult. The *Gurrutu* couldn't muster the velocity change required to match Nereid's crashing orbit. So Madeleine had to burn her engines and use tethers, harpooning this great rock whale as it hurtled past, letting her ship be dragged along with it. *Gurrutu* suffered considerable damage, but nothing significant enough to make Madeleine abort.

She entered a loose, slow orbit, inspecting the moon's surface. Nereid was uninteresting: just a misshapen ball of dirty ice, pocked by craters; it was so small it had never melted, never differentiated into layers of rock and ice like Triton, never had any genuine geology. Nereid was a relic of the past, a ruin of the more orderly moon system that had been wrecked when Triton was captured.

But, despite its small size, it massed as much of five per cent of Triton's own bulk. And where Triton's orbit, though retrograde, was neatly circular, Nereid followed a wide, swooping ellipse, taking almost an Earth year to complete a single one of its 'months' around Neptune.

Nereid could be driven head-on into Triton. It would be a useful bullet.

She navigated with automatic star trackers, with radio Doppler fixes on Kasyapa, and by eye, using a sextant. Her purpose was to check the trajectory of the little moon, backing up the automated systems with this on-the-spot eyeballing, which, even now, was one of the most precise navigation systems known.

Nereid was right on the button. But this game of interplanetary pool was played on a gigantic table, and Triton was a small target. Even now, even so close, Nereid could be deflected from its impact.

At times the cold magnitude of the project – sending one world to impact another – awed her. This is too big for us. This is a project for the arrogant ones: the Gaijin, the others who strangled Venus and Triton.

But, when she was close enough, she could see the glow of engines on Nereid's far side: engines built by humans, placed by humans. Placed by *her*. She clung to her anger, seeking confidence.

Even now Ben debated the ethics of the situation with his people. Most people here had been born long after the emigration: born in the caverns of Kasyapa, now with children of their own. To them, Madeleine and Ben Roach were intruders from the muddy pool at the heart of the solar system, invaders from another time who proposed to smash their world. The shortness of human lives, she thought; our curse. Every generation thinks it is immortal, that it has been born into a world that has never changed, and will never change.

She slept in her sleeping compartment, a box little larger than she was. Inside, however, tucked into her sleeping bag with the folding door drawn to, she felt comfortable and secure. She would track Nereid as long as she could, guiding it to its destination, unless she was ordered to stand down.

She got a number of direct calls from Nemoto which she did not accept. Nemoto was irrelevant now.

At the very last minute Ben came through.

Somewhat to her surprise, the colonists had agreed to let the project go ahead. Ben would arrange for the temporary evacuation of the colonists from Kasyapa, to the hulks of the old transport ships still in orbit, now drifting without their engines.

'Lena is pleased,' he told her.

'Pleased?'

'By your reaction to the crystal shell around the core. The ice VIII. She wanted to make you angry. If the project succeeds then the crystal shell will be destroyed. And the last trace of the native life will surely be destroyed with it.'

Madeleine growled, '*I know*, Ben. I always knew. The Triton bugs lost their war a long time ago, before they even had a chance to voice an opinion. Their memory should motivate us, not stop us. The crystal builders have gone, but the Gaijin are on their way, here, now. Well, the hell with them. This is the trench we've dug, and we aren't going to quit it.'

'If,' he said, 'the Gaijin are the true enemy.'

'They will do for now.'

He smiled sadly. 'You sound like Nemoto.'

'None of us age gracefully. Why didn't you tell me about the native life, Ben?'

His virtual image shrugged. 'Not everybody who's grown up here knows about it. Life is hard enough here without people learning that there is an alien artefact of unknown antiquity buried at the heart of the world.'

She nodded. And yet he hadn't answered her question. Despite all we've been through – even though we're both refugees from another age, and we travelled to the stars together – I'm not close enough for you to share your secrets.

At that moment, she felt the ties between them stretch, break. Now, she thought, I am truly alone; I have lost my only companion from the past. It was surprising how little it hurt.

'Here is another possibility,' Ben said. 'Beyond ethics, beyond this perceived conflict with the Gaijin. You like to meddle, to smash things, Madeleine. You are like Nereid yourself, a rogue retrograde body, come to smash our little community. Perhaps this is why the plan is so appealing to you.'

'Perhaps it is,' she said, irritated. 'You'll have to judge my psychology for yourself.'

And with an angry stab, she shut down the comms link.

Alone in *Gurrutu,* she assembled a complete virtual projection of Triton, a three-dimensional globe a metre across. She looked for the last time at the ice surface of Triton, the subtle shadings of pink and white and brown.

She switched to a viewpoint at Triton's evacuated equator. It was as if she was standing on Triton's surface.

Nereid was supposed to do two things: to spin up Triton, and to melt its ancient oceans. Therefore she had steered the moon to come in at a steep angle, to deliver a sideways slap along Triton's equator. And so, when she turned her virtual head, Nereid was looming low on the horizon: a lumpy, battered moon, visibly three-dimensional, rotating, growing minute by minute.

An icon in the corner of her view recorded a steady countdown. She deleted it. She'd always hated countdowns.

Her imaging systems picked out Gaijin flower-ships in low orbit around the moon, golden sparks arcing this way and that. She smiled. So the Gaijin were curious too. Let them watch. It would be, after all, the greatest impact in the solar system since the end of the primordial bombardment.

Quite a show. And for once it would be humans lighting up the sky.

The end, when it came, seemed brutally fast. Nereid grew from a spot of darkness, to a pebble, to a patch of rock the size of her hand, to, *Jesus*, a roof of rock over the world, and then –

Blinding light. She gasped.

The image snapped back to an overview of the moon. She felt as if she had died and come back to life.

A plume of fragments was rising vertically from Triton's surface, like one last mighty geyser: bits of red hot rock, steam, glittering ice, some larger fragments that soared like cannonballs.

Nereid was gone.

Much of the little moon's substance must already have been lost, rock and ice and rich organic volatiles blasted to vapour in that first second of impact: lost forever, lost to space. Perhaps it would form a new, temporary ring around Neptune; perhaps eventually, centuries from now, some of it would rain back on Triton, or some other moon.

This was an astoundingly inefficient process, she knew, and that had been a key objection of some of the Kasyapa factions. *To burn up a moon, a whole four-billion-year-old moon, for such a poor gain is a crime.* Madeleine couldn't argue with that.

Except to say that this was war.

And now something emerged from the base of the plume. It was a circular shock wave, a wall of shattering ice like the rim of a crater, ploughing its way across the ground. The terrain it left behind was shattered, chaotic, and she could see the glint of liquid water there, steaming furiously in the vacuum and cold. Ice formed quickly, in sheets and floes, struggling to plate over the exposed water. But echoes of that great shock still tore at this transient sea, and immense plates, diamond white, arced far above the water before falling back in a flurry of fragments.

Now, in that smashed region – from cryovolcanoes kilometres wide – volatiles began to boil out of Triton's interior: nitrogen, carbon dioxide, methane, ammonia, water vapour. Nereid's heat was doing its work; what was left of the sister moon must be settling towards Triton's core, burning, melting, flashing to vapour. Soon a mushroom of thickening cloud began to obscure the broken, churning surface. Some of the larger fragments thrown up by that initial plume began to hurtle back from their high orbits, and burned streaks through Triton's temporary atmosphere. And when they hit the churning water-ice beneath, they created new secondary plumes, new founts of destruction.

The shock wall, kilometres high, ploughed on, overwhelming the ancient lands of ice, places where nitrogen frost still lingered. It was not going to stop, she realized now. The shock would scorch its way around the world. It would destroy all Triton's subtlety, churning up the nitrogen snows of the north, the ancient organic deposits of the south, disrupting the slow nitrogen weather, destroying forever the ancient, poorly understood cantaloupe terrain. The shock wall would be a great eraser, she thought, eliminating all of Triton's unsolved puzzles, four billion years of icy geology, in a few hours.

But those billowing ice-volcano clouds were already spreading in a great loose veil around the moon, the vapour reaching altitudes where it could outrun the march of the shattered ice. Mercifully, after an hour, Triton was covered, the death of its surface hidden under a layer of roiling clouds, within which lightning flashed, almost continually.

She heard from Ben that the Yolgnu were celebrating. *This* was Triton Dreamtime, the true Dreamtime, when giants were shaping the world.

After three hours there was a new explosion, a new gout of fire and ice from the far side of the moon. That great shock wave had swept right around the curve of the moon, until it had converged in a fresh clap of shattered ice at the antipode of the impact. Madeleine supposed there would be secondary waves, great circular ripples washing back and forth around Triton like waves in a bathtub, as the new ocean, seething, sought equilibrium.

Nemoto materialized before her.

'You improvised well, Madeleine.'

'Don't patronize me, Nemoto. I was a good little soldier.'

But Nemoto, of course, five hours away, couldn't hear her. '. . . Triton is useless now to the Gaijin, who need solid ice and rock for their building programs. But it is far from useless to humans. This will still be a cold world; a thick crust of ice will form. But that ocean could, thanks to the residual heat of Nereid and Neptune's generous tides, remain liquid for a long time – for millions of years, perhaps. And Earth life could inhabit the new ocean. Lightly modified anyhow – deep sea creatures, able to live off the heat of Triton's churning core – plankton, fish, even whales. Triton, here on the edge of interstellar space, has become Earth-like. Imagine the future for these Aborigines,' Nemoto said, seductively. 'Triton was the son of Poseidon and Aphrodite. How apt . . .'

This was Nemoto's finest hour, Madeleine thought, this heroic effort to deflect – not just worlds – but the course of history itself. She tried to cling to her own feelings of triumph, but it was thin, lonely comfort.

'One more thing, Meacher.' Virtual Nemoto leaned towards her, intent, wizened. 'One more thing I must tell you . . .'

Later, she called Ben.

He asked, 'When are you coming home?'

'I'm not.'

Ben frowned at her. 'You are being foolish.'

'No. Kasyapa is your home, and Lena's. Not mine.'

'Then where? Earth? The Moon?'

'I am centuries out of my time,' she said. 'Not there, either.'

'You're going back to the Saddle Points. But you are the great Gaijin hater, like Nemoto.'

She shrugged. 'I oppose their projects. But I'll ride with them. Why not? Ben, they run the only ship out of port.'

'What do you hope to learn out there?'

She did not answer.

Ben was smiling. 'Madeleine, I always knew I would lose you to starlight.'

She found it hard to focus on his face, to listen to his words. He was irrelevant now, she saw. She cut the connection.

She thought over the last thing Nemoto had said to her. *Find Malenfant. He is dying . . .*

Chapter 23

CANNONBALL

It had to be the ugliest planet Madeleine had ever seen.

It was a ball the size of Earth, spinning slowly, lit up by an unremarkable yellow star. The land was a contorted, blackened mess of volcano calderas, rift and compression features, and impact craters that looked as if they had been punched into a metal block. Seas, lurid yellow, pooled at the shores of distorted continents. And the air was a thin, smoggy, yellowish wisp, littered with high mustard-coloured cirrus clouds.

On the planet there were no obvious signs of life or intelligence: no cities gleaming on the dark side, no ships sailing those ugly yellow oceans. But there were three Gaijin flower-ships in orbit here, Madeleine's and two others.

Her curiosity wasn't engaged.

All the Gaijin would tell her about the planet was the name they gave it – Zero-Zero-Zero-Zero – the name, and the reason they had brought her here, across a hundred light years via a hop-skip-jump flight between Saddle Point gateways in half a dozen systems, a whole extra century deeper into the future: that they needed her assistance.

Malenfant is dying.

Reluctantly – after a year in transit, she had gotten used to her lonely life in her antique *Gurrutu* hab module – she collected her gear and clambered into a Gaijin lander.

Madeleine stepped onto the land of a new world.

Ridges in the hard crumpled ground hurt her feet. The air was murky grey, but more or less transparent; she could see the sun, dimmed to an unremarkable disc as if by high winter cloud. Immediately she didn't like it here. The gravity was high – not crushing, but enough to make her heavy-footed, the bio pack on her back a real burden.

Numbers scrolling across her faceplate told her the gravity was some forty per cent higher than Earth's. And, since this world was about the same size as Earth, that meant that its density had to be around forty per cent higher too: closer to the density of pure iron.

Earth was a ball of nickel-iron overlaid by a thick mantle of less dense silicate rock. The high density of *this* world must mean it had no rocky mantle to speak of. It was nickel-iron, all the way from core to surface, as if a much larger world had been stripped of its mantle and crust, and she was walking around on the remnant iron core.

That wasn't so strange. There were ways that could happen, in the violent early days of a system's formation, when immense rogue planetesimals continue to bombard planets that were struggling to coalesce. Mercury, the solar system's innermost planet, had suffered an immense primordial impact that had left that little world with the thinnest of mantles over its giant core.

At least human scientists had presumed it was primordial. Nobody was sure about such things any more.

She glanced around the sky. She was a hundred light years from home, a hundred light years in towards the centre of the Galaxy, roughly along a line that would have joined Earth to Antares, in Scorpio. But the sky was dark, dismal.

There were no asteroid belts, only a handful of comets left orbiting further out, and two gas giants both stripped of their volatiles, reduced to smooth rocky balls. She was well inside the interstellar colonization wavefront that appeared to be sweeping out along the spiral arm and was nearing Earth, a hundred light years back. And this was a typical post-wavefront system: colonized, ferociously robbed of its resources by one short-sighted, low-tech predatory strategy or another, trashed, abandoned.

Even the stars had been obscured, their light stolen by Dyson masks: dense orbiting habitat clouds, even solid spheres, asteroids and planets dismantled and made into traps for every stray photon. It was a depressing sight: an engineered sky, a sky full of scaffolding and ruins.

Earth's sky was primeval, comparatively. This was a glimpse of the future, for Earth.

She walked further, away from the lander, which was a silvery cone behind her. She was only a few kilometres from the shore of one of those yellow seas; she figured it was on the far side of a low, crumpled ridge.

She reached the base of the ridge and began to climb. In the tough gravity she was given a good workout; she could feel her temperature rising, the suit's exoskeletal multipliers discreetly cutting in to give her a boost.

She topped the ridge, breathing hard. A plain opened up before her: shaded red and black, littered by sand dunes and what looked like a big, heavily eroded impact crater. And off towards the smoky horizon, yes, there was that peculiar yellow ocean, wraiths of greenish mist hanging over it. It was a bizarre, surrealist landscape, as if all Earth's colours had been exchanged for their spectral complements.

And, only a hundred metres from the base of the ridge, she saw two Gaijin landers, silver cones side by side, each surrounded by fine rays of dust thrown out by landing rockets. Beside one of the landers was a Gaijin, utterly still, a spidery statue. Next to the other stood a human, in an exo-suit that didn't look significantly different to Madeleine's.

The human saw her, waved.

Madeleine hesitated for long seconds.

Suddenly the world seemed crowded. She hadn't encountered people since she last embraced Ben, on Triton. She'd certainly never met another traveller like this, among the stars. But it must have taken decades, even centuries, for the Gaijin to organize this strange rendezvous.

She began to clamber down the ridge towards the landers, letting the suit do most of the work.

The waving human turned out to be a Catholic priest, called Dorothy Chaum. Madeleine had met her before, subjective years ago. And inside one of the landers was another human, somebody she knew only by reputation.

It was Reid Malenfant. And he was indeed dying.

Malenfant was wasted. His head was cadaverous, the skull showing through thin, papery flesh, and his bald scalp was covered in liver-spots.

Dorothy and Madeleine got Malenfant suited up, and hauled him to Dorothy's lander. In this gravity it was hard work, despite their suits' multipliers. But Dorothy's lander had a more comprehensive med facility than Madeleine's. Malenfant had nothing at all, save what the Gaijin had been able to provide.

Malenfant had grown old, and had sunk into himself, like a tide going out, an ocean receding. He had managed to keep himself alive a good few years. But his equipment wasn't sufficient any more – and the Gaijin he travelled with sure didn't know enough about human biology to tinker. Not only that, he was suffering from the Discontinuity.

When he had started to die, the Gaijin were confounded.

'So they sent for us,' Dorothy Chaum said, marvelling. 'They sent signals out through the gateway links.'

'How did they keep him alive so long?'

'They didn't. They just preserved him. They bounced his signal around the Saddle Point network, never making him corporeal for more than a few seconds at a time . . .'

Madeleine studied Malenfant. Had he been aware, as he passed through one blue-flash gateway transition after another, of the light years and decades passing in seconds? Malenfant woke up while they were bed-bathing him. Stripped, washed, and immersed in a med tank. He looked Madeleine in the eyes. 'Are you *qualified* to be scrubbing my balls?'

'I'm the best you're going to find, pal.'

But now he was staring at Chaum, the diagrammatic white collar around her neck. 'What is this, the last rites?' He tried to struggle upright, on arms as thin as toothpicks.

Madeleine shoved him back. 'It will be if you don't cooperate.'

He swivelled that gaunt head. 'Where's my suit?'

Dorothy frowned, and pointed to the Gaijin-manufactured envelope they'd bundled up in one corner. 'Over there.'

'No,' he whispered. 'My *suit*.'

It turned out he meant his old NASA-era Shuttle EMU, a disgusting old piece of kit almost as far beyond its design limits as Malenfant himself. He wouldn't relax until Madeleine got suited up, went across to the lander that had brought him here, and retrieved the EMU for him. Then again, it was the only possession he had in the world, or worlds. She could understand how he felt.

He scrabbled in its pockets until he found a faded, much folded photograph, of a smiling woman on a beach.

When they had him in the tank, Madeleine spent a little time working on that gruesome old suit. She could fix the wiring shorts and the cooling-garment tubing leaks, polish out the scratches on the bubble helmet, patch the fabric. But she couldn't make it clean again; the dust of many worlds was ingrained too deep into the fabric. And she couldn't wash out the stink of Malenfant.

All the time, visible through the lander's windows, that Gaijin sat on the surface, as unmoving as a statue, watching, watching, as if waiting for Dorothy or Madeleine to make a mistake.

* * *

While Malenfant was sleeping off twenty subjective years of travelling, Dorothy Chaum and Madeleine took a walk, across the battered iron plain, towards the yellow sea.

They were each used to solitude and they were awkward, restless with each other – and with the notion that they'd been summoned here, given an assignment by the Gaijin. It didn't make for good conversation.

Dorothy was a short, squat woman, who looked as if she might have been built for this tough overloaded gravity. She seemed older than Madeleine remembered; her journey here had absorbed more of her subjective lifetime than Madeleine's had.

They passed the solitary Gaijin sentinel.

'Malenfant calls it *Cassiopeia*,' Dorothy murmured. 'He says it's been his constant companion since the solar system.'

'A boy and his Gaijin. Cute.'

Dorothy Chaum's personal star quest seemed to be a sublimated search for God. That was how it seemed to Madeleine, anyhow.

'I studied the Gaijin on Earth,' Dorothy said. Madeleine could see her smile. 'You remember that, on Kefallinia. I got my initial assignment from the Pope . . . I don't even know if there is a Pope any more. The Gaijin have some things in common with us. Sure, they are robot-like creatures, but they are finite, built on about the same scale as we are, and they seem to have at least some individuality. But in spite of their similarity – or maybe because of it – I was immediately overwhelmed by their strangeness. So I was drawn to follow them to the stars, to work with them.'

'And have you discovered yet if a Gaijin has a soul?'

Dorothy didn't seem offended. 'I don't know if that question has any meaning. Conversely, you see, the Gaijin seem fascinated by *our* souls. Perhaps they are envious . . .'

Dorothy stopped dead, and held out one hand. Madeleine saw there was some kind of black snow, or a thin rain of dust, settling on the white of her glove palm. 'This is carbon,' Dorothy said. 'Soot. Just raining out of the air. Remarkable.'

Madeleine supposed it was.

They walked on through the strange exotic air.

Madeleine prompted, 'So you travelled with the Gaijin to try to understand.'

'Yes. As I believe Malenfant did.'

'And did you succeed?'

'I don't think so. What may be more serious,' she said, 'is that I don't think the Gaijin are any closer to finding whatever it is *they* were seeking.'

They reached the shore of the sea. It was a hard beach, loosely littered with rusty sand, and blackened with soot, as if worn away from some offshore seam of coal.

The ocean was very yellow. The liquid was thin and it seemed to bubble, as if carbonated. Further out, mist banks hung, dense and heavy. Seeing this garish sea recede to a sharp yellow horizon was eerie.

They stepped forward, letting the liquid lap over their boots. It left a fine gritty scum, and it felt cool, not cold. Vapour sizzled around Madeleine's feet.

Dorothy dipped a gloved finger into the sea, and data chattered over her visor. 'Iron carbonyl,' she murmured. 'A compound of iron with carbon monoxide.' She pointed at the vapour. 'And *that* is mostly nickel carbonyl. A lower boiling point than the iron stuff . . .' She sighed. 'Iron compounds, an iron world. On Earth, we used stuff like this in industrial processes, like purifying nickel. Here, you could go swimming in it.'

'I wonder if there is life here.'

'Oh, yes,' Dorothy said. 'Of course there is life here. Don't you know where you are?'

Madeleine didn't reply.

Dorothy said, 'That's where the soot and the carbon dioxide comes from. I think there must be some kind of photosynthesis going on, making carbon monoxide. And then the monoxide reacts with itself to make free carbon and carbon dioxide. That reaction releases energy –'

'Which animals can use.'

'Yes.'

'There is life everywhere we look,' Madeleine said.

'Yes. Life seems to be emergent from the very fabric of the universe which contains us, hard-wired into physical law. And so, I suppose, mind is emergent too. *Emergent monism:* a nice label. Though we can scarcely claim understanding . . .'

They stepped back on the shore, and walked further across the rusty dirt without enthusiasm.

Then they saw movement.

There was something crawling out of the sea. It was like a crab. It was low and squat, about the size of a coffee table, with a dozen or more spindly legs, and what must be sensors – eyes, ears? – complex little pods on the end of flimsy stalks that waved in the murky air. The whole thing was the colour of rust.

And it had a dodecahedral body.

Madeleine could hear it wheezing.

'Lungs,' Dorothy said. 'It has lungs. But – look at those slits in the carapace there. Gills, you think?'

'It's like a lungfish.'

The crab was clumsy, as if it couldn't see too well, and its limbs slid about over the bone-hard shore. One of those pencil-thin legs caught in a crack, and snapped off. That hissing breath became noisier, and it hesitated, waving a stump in the air.

Then the crab moved on, picking its way over the beach, as if searching for something.

Dorothy bent and, fumbling with her gloved fingers, picked up the snapped-off limb. It looked simple: just a hollow tube, a wand. But there was a honeycomb structure to the interior wall. 'Strength and lightness,' she said. 'And it's made of iron.' She smiled. 'Iron bones. Natural robots. We always thought the Gaijin must have been manufactured, by creatures more or less like us – the first generation of them anyway. It was hard to take seriously the idea of such mechanical beasts evolving naturally. But perhaps that's what happened . . .'

'What are you talking about?'

She eyed Madeleine. 'You really don't know where you are? Didn't the Gaijin tell you?'

Madeleine had an aversion to chatting to Gaijin. She kept her counsel.

Dorothy said, 'This iron world is Zero-Zero-Zero-Zero, Madeleine. The origin of the Gaijin's coordinates, the place their own colonization bubble started. *The place they came from.* No wonder they brought Malenfant here, if they thought he was going to die.'

Madeleine felt no surprise, no wonder, no curiosity. *So what*? 'But if that's so, where are they all?'

Dorothy sighed. 'I guess the Gaijin are no more immune to the resource wars, and the predatory expansion of others, than we are.'

'*Even the Gaijin*?' The notion of the powerful, enigmatic, star-spanning Gaijin as victims was deeply chilling.

Dorothy said, 'If this is a robotic lungfish, maybe life here got pushed back into the oceans by the last wave of visitors. Maybe this brave guy is trying to take back the land, at last.'

The crab thing seemed to have reached its highest point, attained the objective of its strange expedition. It stood there on the rusty beach for long minutes, waving those eye-stalks in the air. Madeleine wondered if it even knew they were here, if it recognized the Gaijin as its own remote descendant.

Then it turned and crawled back into the yellow ocean, step by step, descending into that fizzing, smoky liquid with a handful of bubbles.

'The Gaijin are not like us,' Malenfant whispered. He was sitting propped up by cushions in a chair, wrapped in a blanket. He was bird-thin. They had had to bring him back to his own lander; after so long alone he had gotten too used to it, missed it too much. 'Cassiopeia is constantly in flux,' he said. '"Cassiopeia" is just the name I gave her, after all. Her *own* name for herself is something like a list of catalogue numbers for her component parts – with a breakdown for subcomponents – *and* a paper trail showing their history. A manufacturing record, not really a name. She constantly replaces parts, panels, internal components, switching them back and forth. So her name changes. And so does her identity . . .'

'*Your* cells wear out, Malenfant,' Dorothy said gently. 'Every few years there is a new you.'

'But not as fast as *that*. It's the way they breed, too – if you can call it that. Two or more of them will donate parts, and start assembling them, until you got a whole new Gaijin, who goes off to the store room to get the pieces to finish herself off. A whole new person. Now, where does *she* come from?' He sighed. 'They have continuity of memory, consciousness, but identity is fluid for them: you can divide it forever, or even mix it up. You see it when they debate. There's no persuasion, no argument. They just – *merge* – and make a decision. But the Gaijin are cautious,' he said slowly. 'They are rational, they consider every side of every argument, they sometimes seem paralysed by indecision.'

'Like Balaam's Ass,' Dorothy said, smiling. 'Couldn't decide between two identical bales of hay.'

Madeleine asked, 'What happened?'

'Starved to death.'

Malenfant went on, as if talking to himself, 'They aren't like us. They don't glom onto a new idea so fast as we do – '

Dorothy said, 'Their minds are not receptive to memes. They have no sense of self – '

'But,' Malenfant said, 'the Gaijin are *interested* in us. Don't know why, but they are. And creatures *like* us. Religious types. Folks who mount crusades and kill each other and even sacrifice their lives, for an idea.'

Madeleine remembered the Chaera, orbiting their black hole God, futilely worshipping it. Maybe Nemoto had been right; maybe it hadn't been black hole technology the Gaijin were interested in, but the Chaera themselves. But – why?

Dorothy leaned forward. 'Have the Gaijin ever talked about creatures like us? What becomes of us?'

'I gather we mostly wipe ourselves out. Or think ourselves to extinction. Memes against genes. That's if the colonization wars don't get us first.' He opened his rheumy eyes. 'Earth, the solar system, might be swept aside by the incoming colonists. It's happened before, and will happen again. *But it isn't the whole story*. It can't be.'

Dorothy was nodding. 'Equilibrium. Uniformity. Nemoto's old arguments.'

Madeleine didn't understand.

Malenfant smiled toothlessly at her. '*Why* does it have to be this way? That's the question. Endless waves of exploitation and trashing, everybody getting driven back down to the level of pond life . . . You'd think somebody would learn better. What stops them all?

'If what stopped an expansion was war, you'd have to assume that there are *no* survivors of such a war – not a single race, not a single breeding population. Or, if intelligent species are trashed by eco collapse, you have to assume that *every* species inevitably destroys itself that way.

'You see the problem. We can think of a hundred ways a species might get itself into trouble. But whatever destructive process you come up with, it has to be *one hundred per cent* effective. If a single species escapes the net, wham, it covers the Galaxy at near-lightspeed.

'But we don't see that. What we see is a Galaxy that fills up with squabbling races – and then *blam*. Some mechanism drives them *all* back down to the pond. There has to be something else, some other mechanism. Something that destroys them *all*. A Reboot.'

'A Galaxy-wide sterilization,' Madeleine murmured.

'And,' Chaum said, 'that explains Nemoto's first-contact equilibrium.'

'Yeah,' Malenfant said. '*That's* why they come limping around the Galaxy in dumb-ass ramscoops and teleport gates and the rest, time after time; that's why nobody has figured out, for instance, how to bust lightspeed, or build a wormhole. Nobody lasted long enough. Nobody had the *chance* to get smart.'

Madeleine stood, stretching in the dense gravity of this Cannonball world. She looked out the window at the dismal, engineered sky.

Could it be true? Was there something out there even more ferocious than the world-shattering aliens whose traces humans had encountered over and over, even in their own solar system? – some dragon that woke up every few hundred megayears, and roared so loud it wiped the Galaxy clean of advanced life?

And – how long before the dragon woke up again?

Madeleine said, 'You think the Gaijin know what it is? Are they trying to do something about it?'

'I don't know,' Malenfant said. 'Maybe. Maybe not.'

Madeleine growled, 'If they are just as much victims as we are, why don't they just *tell* us what they are doing?'

Malenfant closed his eyes, as if disappointed by the question. 'We're dealing with the alien here, Madeleine. They don't see the universe the way we do – not at all. They have their own take on things, their own objectives. It's amazing we can communicate at all when you think about it.'

'But,' Madeleine said, 'they don't want to go through a Reboot.'

'No,' he conceded. 'I don't think they want that.'

Dorothy said, 'Perhaps this is the next step, in the emergence of life and mind. Species working together, to save themselves. We need the Gaijin's steely robotic patience, just as they need us, our humanity . . .'

'Our faith?' Madeleine asked gently.

'Perhaps.'

Malenfant laughed, cynically. 'If the Gaijin know, they aren't telling me. They came to *us* for answers, remember.'

Madeleine shook her head. 'That's not good enough, Malenfant. Not from you. You're special to the Gaijin, somehow. You were the first to come out and confront them, the human who's spent longest with them.'

'And they saved your life,' Dorothy reminded him. 'They brought us here, to save you. You were dying.'

'I'm still dying.'

Madeleine said, 'Somehow you're important, Malenfant. You're the key.' Right there, right then, she had a powerful intuition that must be true.

But the key to what?

He held up skeletal hands, mocking. 'You think they're appointing me to save the Galaxy? Bullshit, with all respect.' He rubbed his eyes, lay on his side, and turned to face the lander's silver wall. 'I'm just an old fucker who doesn't know when to quit.'

But maybe, Madeleine thought, that's what the Gaijin cherish. Maybe they've been looking for somebody too stupid to starve to death, like that damn ass.

Dorothy said slowly, 'What *do* you want, Malenfant?'

'Home,' he said abruptly. 'I want to go home.'

Madeleine and Dorothy exchanged a glance.

Malenfant had been a long time away. He could return to the solar system, to Earth, if he wished. But they both knew that for all of them, home no longer existed.

IV

BAD NEWS FROM THE STARS

AD 3265–3793

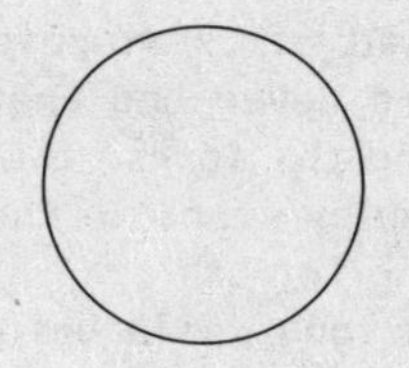

At the centre of the Galaxy there was a cavity, blown clear by the ferocious wind from a monstrous black hole. The cavity was laced by gas and dust, particles ionized and driven to high speeds by the ferocious gravitational and magnetic forces working here, so that streamers of glowing gas criss-crossed the cavity in a fine tracery. Stars had been born here, notably a cluster of blue-hot young stars just a fraction away from the black hole itself.

And here and there rogue stars fell through the cavity – and they dragged streaming trails behind them, glowing brilliantly, like comets a hundred light years long.

Stars like comets.

He exulted. I, Reid Malenfant, got to see *this*, the heart of the Galaxy itself, by God! He wished Cassiopeia were here, his companion during those endless Saddle Point jaunts to one star after another . . .

Again, at the thought of Cassiopeia, his anger flared.

But the Gaijin were never our enemy, not really. They learned patience among the stars. They were just trying to figure it all out, step by step, in their own way.

But it took too long for us.

It was after all a long while before we could even see the rest of them, the great wave of colonizers and miners that followed the Gaijin, heading our way along the Galaxy's spiral arm.

The wave of destruction.

Chapter 24

KINTU'S CHILDREN

Two hundred kilometres above the glowing Earth, a Gaijin flower-ship folded its electromagnetic wings. Drone robots pulled a scuffed hab module out of the ship's stringy structure, and launched it on a slow, precise trajectory towards the Tree.

Malenfant, inside the module, watched the Tree approach.

The bulk of the Tree, orbiting the Earth, was a glowing green ball of branches and leaves, photosynthesizing busily. It trailed a trunk, hollowed-out and sealed with resin, that housed most of the Tree's human population. Long roots trailed in the upper atmosphere: there were crude scoops to draw up raw material for continued growth, and cables of what Malenfant eventually learned was superconductor, generating power by being dragged through Earth's magnetosphere.

The Tree was a living thing twenty kilometres long, rooted in air, looping around Earth in its inclined circular orbit, maintaining its altitude with puffs of waste gas.

It was, Malenfant thought, ridiculous. He turned away, incurious.

He had been away from Earth for twelve hundred years, and had returned to the impossible date of AD 3265.

Malenfant was exhausted. Physically he was, after all, more than a hundred years old. And because of the depletion of the Saddle Point links between Zero-Zero-Zero-Zero and Earth, he had been forced to take a roundabout route on the way back here.

All he really wanted, if he was truthful, was to get away from strangeness: just settle down in his 1960s ranch house at Clear Lake, Houston, and pop a few beers, eat potato chips and watch *Twilight Zone* reruns. But here, looking out at all this orbiting foliage, he knew that wasn't possible, that it never would be. It was just as Dorothy Chaum had tried to counsel him, before they said their goodbyes back on the Cannonball. It was Earth down there, but it wasn't *his* Earth.

Malenfant was going to have to live with strangers, and strangeness, for whatever was left of his long and unlikely life.

At least the ice has gone, though, he thought.

His battered capsule slid to rest, lodging in branches, and Malenfant was decanted.

There was nobody to greet him. He found an empty room, with a window. There were *leaves,* growing around his window. On the *outside.*

Ridiculous. He fell asleep.

When Malenfant woke, he was in some kind of hospital gown.

He felt different. Comfortable, clean. He wasn't hungry or thirsty. He didn't even need a leak.

He lifted up his hand. The skin was comparatively smooth, the liver spots faded. When he flexed his fingers, the joints worked without a twinge.

Somebody had been here, done something to him. I didn't want this, he thought. I didn't ask for it. He cradled his resentment.

He propped himself up before his window, and looked out at Earth.

He could see its curve, a blue and white arc against black space. He made out a slice of pale blue seascape, with an island an irregular patch of grey and brown in the middle of it, and clouds scattered over the top, lightly, like icing sugar. He was so close to the skin of the planet that if he sat back the world filled his window, scrolling steadily past.

Earth was *bright:* brighter than he remembered. Malenfant used to be a Shuttle pilot; he knew Earth from orbit – how it used to be anyhow. Now he was amazed by the clarity of the atmosphere, even over the heart of continents. He didn't know if Earth itself had changed, or his memories of it. After all, his eyes were an old man's now: rheumy, filled with nostalgia.

One thing for sure, though. Earth looked empty.

When he passed over oceans he looked for ship wakes, feathering out like brush strokes. He couldn't see any. In the lower latitudes he could make out towns, a grey, angular patchwork, a tracery of roads. But no smog. No industries, then.

And in the higher latitudes, towards the poles, he could see no sign of human habitation at all. The land looked raw, fresh, scraped clean, the granite flanks of exposed mountains shining like burnished metal, and the plains were littered with boulders, like toys dropped by a child. His geography was always lousy, and now it was a thousand years out of date – but it seemed to him the coastlines had changed shape.

He wondered who, or what, had cleaned up the glaciation. Anyhow, it might have been AD 1000 down there, not 3265.

Two people came drifting into his room. Naked, all but identical, they were women, but so slim they were almost sexless. They had hair that floated around them, like Jane Fonda in *Barbarella*.

They were joined at the hip, like Siamese twins, by a tube of pink flesh.

They hadn't knocked, and he scowled at them. 'Who are you?'

They jabbered at him in a variety of languages, some of which he recognized, some not. Their arms and shoulders were big and well-developed, like tennis players, but their legs were wisps they kept tucked up beneath them. Microgravity adaptations. Their hair was blonde, but their eyes were almond-shaped, with folds of skin near the nose, like Chinese.

Finally they settled on heavily accented English.

'You must forgive stupidity.' 'We accommodate returning travellers –' '– from many time periods, spread across a millennium –' '– dating from Reid Malenfant himself.'

When they talked they swapped their speech between one and the other, like throwing a ball.

He said, 'In fact, I am Reid Malenfant.'

They looked at him, and then their two heads swivelled so that blank almond eyes stared into each other, their hair mingling. For these two, he thought, every day is a bad hair day.

'You must understand the treatment you have been given,' one said.

'I didn't want treatment,' he groused. 'I didn't sign any consent forms.'

'But your ageing was –' '– advanced.' 'We have no cure, of course.' 'But we can address the symptoms –' 'Brittle bones, loss of immunity, nervous degeneration.' 'In your case accelerated by –' 'Exposure to microgravity.' 'We reversed free radical damage with antioxidant vitamins.' 'We snipped out senescent cell clusters from your epidermis and dermis.' 'We reversed the intrusion of alien qualia into your sensorium, a side-effect of repeated Saddle Point transits.' 'We removed various dormant infectious agents which you might return to Earth.' 'We applied telomerase therapy to –'

'Enough. I believe you. I bet I don't look a day over seventy.'

'It was routine,' a Bad Hair Day twin said. They fell silent. Then: 'Are you truly Reid Malenfant?'

'Yes.'

* * *

The twins gave him food and drink. He didn't recognize any of the liquids they offered him, hot or cold; they were mostly like peculiar teas, of fruit or leaves. He settled on water, which was clean and cold and pure. The food was bland and amorphous, like baby food. The Bad Hair Day twins told him it was all processed algae, spiced with a little vacuum greenery from the Tree itself.

The twins pulled him gracefully through microgravity, along tunnels like wood-lined veins that twisted and turned, lit only by some kind of luminescence in the wood. It was like a fantasy spaceship rendered in carpentry, he thought.

There were a few dozen colonists here, living in bubbles of air inside the bulk of the Tree. They were all microgravity-adapted, as far as he could see, some of them even more evolved than the twins. There was one guy with a huge dome of a head over a shrivelled-up body, sticks of limbs, a penis like a walnut, no pubic hair. To Malenfant he looked like a real science fiction type of creation, like the boss alien in *Invaders from Mars*.

The people, however strange, looked young and healthy to Malenfant. Their skin was smooth, unwrinkled, unmarked save by tattoos; his own raisin-like face, the lines baked into it by years of exposure to Earth's weather and ultraviolet light and heavy gravity, was a curiosity here, a badge of exotica.

They all had almond eyes, folds of yellow skin.

As far as Malenfant could make out this was a kind of reverse colony from the near-Earth asteroids, which had been settled by descendants of Chinese. Out there, it seemed, there were great bubble habitats where everyone had lived in zero gravity for centuries.

Sometimes he thought he could hear a low humming, sniff a little ozone, feel hair-prickling static, as if he was surrounded by immense electrical or magnetic fields that tweaked at his body. Maybe it was so. Electromagnetic fields could be used to stimulate and stress muscles and bones, and even to counter bone wastage; NASA had experimented with such technologies. Maybe the Tree swaddled its human cargo in electricity, fixing their bones and muscles and flesh.

But maybe there was no need for such clunky gadgetry, a thousand years downstream. After all the Tree provided a pretty healthy environment, of clean air, pure water, toxin-free foods: no pollutants or poisons or pathogens here, and even natural hazards – like Earth's naturally-occurring radioactivity in soil and stone – could be designed out. Maybe if you gave people a good enough place to live, this was how they turned out, with health and longevity.

And as for adaptation to microgravity, maybe that came naturally too. After all, he recalled, the dolphins and other aquatic mammals had had no need of centrifuges or electro stimulation to maintain their muscles and bones in the no-gravity environment *they* inhabited. Maybe these space-dwelling humans had more in common with the dolphins than the bony dirt-treaders of his own kind.

The Tree itself had been gen-enged from giant ancestors on the Moon. Humans used the Tree for a variety of purposes: port, observation platform, resort. But the Tree's own purpose was simply to grow and survive, and there seemed no obstacle to its doing so until the sun itself flickered and died.

There was more than one Tree.

In 3265, Earth was encased in a spreading web of vegetation, space-going Trees and airborne spiders, reaching down from space to the surface. And, slowly, systems were evolving the other way. One day there might be some kind of unlikely biological ladder, reaching from Earth to space. It was a strategy to ensure long-term access from space via stable biological means. Nobody could tell Malenfant whose strategy this was, however.

The colonists in this Tree seemed to care for returning travellers like him with a breed of absent-minded charity. Beyond that, the twins' motive in speaking to him seemed to be a vague curiosity. Maybe even just politeness.

The Bad Hair Day twins' variant of English contained a fraction of words, a fifth or a quarter, that were unrecognizable to Malenfant. Linguistic drift, he figured. It had, after all, been a thousand years; he was Chaucer meeting Neil Armstrong.

They asked, 'Where did you travel?'

'I started at Alpha Centauri. After that I couldn't always tell. I kind of bounced around.'

'What did you find?'

He thought about that. 'I don't know. I couldn't understand much.'

It was true. But now – just as Madeleine Meacher and Dorothy Chaum had sought him out, saved his life on that remote Cannonball world without asking his by-your-leave – so the Bad Hair Day twins had thrust unwelcome youth on him. He felt *curious* again. Dissatisfied. Damn it, he'd gotten used to being old. It had been comfortable.

There were no other travellers here.

He soon got bored with the Tree, the incomprehensible artefacts and activities it contained. Lonely, disoriented, he tried to engage the Bad Hair Day twins, his enigmatic nurses. 'You know, I remember how Earth looked when I first went up in *Columbia*, back in '93. 1993, that is. In those days we had to ride these big solid rocket boosters up to orbit, you know, and then, and then ...'

The twins would listen politely for a while. But then they would lock on each other, mouths pressed into an airtight seal, small hands sliding over bare flesh, their hair drifting in clouds around them, that bridge of skin between them folded and compressed, and Malenfant was just a sad old fart boring them with war stories.

If he was going back to Earth, where was he supposed to land?

He asked the Bad Hair Day twins for encyclopaedias, history books. The twins all but laughed at him. The people of AD 3265, it seemed, had forgotten history. The Bad Hair Day twins seemed to know little beyond their speciality, which was a limited – if very advanced – medicine. It was – disappointing. On the other hand, how much knowledge or interest had he ever had in the year AD 1000?

He got frustrated. He railed at the twins. They just stared back at him.

He would have to find out for himself.

He still had the softscreen-like sensor pack Sally Brind had given him centuries ago, when he set off for the Saddle Point to the Alpha Centauri system. It would work as a multi-spectral sensor. He could configure it to overlay the images of Earth with representations in infrared, ultraviolet, radar imaging, whatever he wanted; he could select for the signatures of rock, soil, vegetation, water, and the products of industrialization like heavy metals, pollutants.

Alone, he found a window and studied the planet.

Earth was indeed depopulated.

There were humans down there, but no communities bigger than a few tens of thousands. There were no industrial products, save for a thin smear of relics from the past, clustered around the old cities and strung out along the disused roads. He couldn't even see signs of large-scale agriculture.

Malenfant studied what was left of the cities of his day, those that had somehow survived the ice. New York, for example.

In AD 3265, New York was green. It was a woodland of birch and oak, pushing out of a layer of elder thicket. He could still make out the shapes of roads, city blocks and parking lots, but they were green rectangles, covered with mosses, lichens and tough, destructive plants like buddleia. On Manhattan, some of the bigger concrete buildings still stood, like white bones poking above the trees, but they were bereft of windows, their walls stained by fires. Others had subsided, reduced to oddly shaped hummocks beneath the greenery. The bridges had collapsed, leaving shallow weirs along the river. He could see foxes, bats, wolves. There were more exotic creatures, maybe descended from zoo stock: deer, feral pigs.

Some of the roads looked in good condition, oddly. Maybe the smart-concrete that was being introduced just before his departure from Earth had kept working. But the big multi-lane freeway that ran up out of Manhattan looked a little crazy to Malenfant, a wild scribble over grassed-over concrete. Maybe it wasn't just repairing itself but actually growing, crawling like a huge worm across the abandoned suburbs, a semi-sentient highway over which no car had travelled for centuries.

Once Malenfant saw what looked like a hunting party, working its way along the coast of the widened Hudson, stalking a thing like an antelope. The people were tall, naked, golden-haired. One of the hunters looked up to the sky, as if directly at Malenfant. It was a woman, her blue eyes empty. She had a neck like a shot-putter. Her face was, he thought, somehow not even human.

When Malenfant left Earth, a thousand years ago, he had left behind no direct descendants. His wife, Emma, had died before they had a chance to have children together. But he'd had relatives: a nephew, two nieces.

Now there was hardly anybody left on Earth. Malenfant wondered if anybody down there still bore a trace of his genes. And if so, what they had become.

For sentimental reasons he looked for the Statue of Liberty. Maybe it was washed up on the beach, like in *Planet of the Apes*. There was no sign of the old lady.

But he did find a different monument: an artefact kilometres across, a monstrous ring, slap in the middle of downtown Manhattan. It looked like a particle accelerator. Maybe it had something to do with the city's battle against the ice. Whatever, it didn't look human. It was out of scale.

There was other evidence of high technology, scattered around the planet; but it didn't seem to have much to do with humans either. For example, when the Tree drifted over the Pyrenees, the mountains on the crease of land between France and Spain, he could see a threading of light, perfect straight lines of ruby light, joining the peaks like a spider-web. His screen told him this was coherent light: lased. There were similar systems in other mountainous regions, scattered around the planet. The laser arrays worked continuously. Maybe they were adjusting the atmosphere somehow: burning out CFCs, for instance.

And he observed flashes from sites around the equator, on Earth's water hemisphere. A few minutes after each flash the air would get a little mistier. He estimated they must be coming every minute or so, on a global scale. He remembered twenty-first century schemes to increase Earth's albedo – to increase the percentage of sunlight reflected back into space – by firing sub-micrometre dust up into the stratosphere: naval guns could have done the job. The point was to reduce global warming. But the dust would settle out: you would have needed to fire a shot every few seconds, maintained for years – decades, even centuries. Back then the idea was ridiculed. But such dust injections would account for the increase in global brightness he thought he'd observed.

This was planetary engineering. All he could see from here were the gross physical schemes. Maybe down on the planet there was more: nanotechnological adjustments, for instance.

Somebody was fixing the Earth. It didn't look to Malenfant like it was anybody human. It would, after all, take centuries, maybe millennia. No human civilization could handle projects of that duration, or ever would be able to. So, give the job to somebody else.

Not every change was constructive.

In southern Africa there was a dramatic new crater. It looked like a scar in the greenery of the planet. He didn't know if it was some kind of meteorite scar, or an open-cast mine, kilometres wide. Machines crawled over the walls and pit of the crater, visibly chewing up shattered rock, extracting piles of minerals, metals. From space, the machines looked like spiders: dodecahedral bodies maybe fifty metres wide, with eight or ten articulated limbs, working steadily at this open wound in the skin of Earth.

Malenfant had seen such machines before. They were Gaijin factory drones, designed to chew up ice and rock. But now they weren't off in the asteroid belt or stuck out on the cold rim of the solar system, billions of kilometres away. The Gaijin were *here*, on the surface of Earth itself. He wondered what they were doing.

He looked further afield, seeking people, civilization.

The most populous place on the planet, it appeared, was some kind of mountain-top community in the middle of Africa. It was, as far as he could remember his geography, in Uganda.

And there was something odd about its signature in his sensor pack. From a source at the centre of the community he plotted heavy particles, debris from what looked like short half-life fission products. And there were some much more energetic particles: almost like cosmic rays.

But they came from a source embedded deep within Earth itself.

The only other similar sources, scattered around the planet, looked like deep radioactive-waste dumps.

The Ugandan community wasn't civilization, but it was the most advanced-looking technological trace on the planet. Population, and an enigma. Maybe that was the place for him to go.

The Bad Hair Day twins showed him a wooden spaceship. It was, good God, his atmospheric entry capsule. It was like a seed pod, a flattened sphere of wood a couple of metres across. It was fitted with a basic canvas couch, and a life support system – just crude organic filters – that would last a couple of hours, long enough for the entry. The pod even had a window, actually grown into the wood, a blister of some clear stuff like amber. He would have to climb in through a dilating diaphragm that would seal up behind him, like being born in reverse.

He spent some time hunting for the pod's heatshield. The Bad Hair Day twins watched, puzzled.

They kept him on orbit for another month or so, giving him gravity preparation: exercise, a calcium booster, electromagnetic therapy. They gave him a coverall of some kind of biocomposite material, soft to the touch but impossible to rip, smart enough to keep him at the right temperature. He packed inside the sphere his sole personal possession: his old Shuttle pressure suit, with its faded Stars and Stripes and the NASA logo, that he'd worn when he flew through that first gateway, a thousand AU from home, a thousand years ago. It was junk, but it was all he had.

He enjoyed a last sleep in weightlessness.

When he awoke the Tree was passing over South America. Malenfant could see the fresh water of the Amazon, noticeably paler than the salt of the ocean, the current so strong the waters had still failed to mingle hundreds of kilometres off shore.

He climbed inside his capsule. The Bad Hair Day twins kissed him, one soft face to either cheek, and sealed him up in warm brown darkness.

He was whiplashed out of the Tree by a flexing branch. A sensation of weight briefly returned to Malenfant, and he was pressed into his seat. When the cast-off was done, the weight disappeared.

But now the pod was no longer in a free orbit, but falling rapidly towards the air.

At the fringe of the atmosphere, the pod shuddered around him. He felt very aware of the lightness and fragility of this wooden nut-shell within which he was going to have to fall ass-first into the atmosphere.

Within five minutes of separation from the Tree, frictional deceleration was building up: a tenth, two-tenths of a G. The deceleration piled up quickly, eyeballs-in, shoving him deeper against his couch.

The pod shuddered violently. Malenfant was cocooned in a dull roaring noise. He gripped his couch and tried not to worry about it.

As the heat shield rammed deeper into the air, a shell of plasma built up around the hull. Beyond the amber windows the blackness of space was masked by a deep brown, which quickly escalated through orange, a fiery yellow, and then a dazzling white. Particles of soot flew off the scorching outer hull of the pod and streaked over the window, masking his view; now all he could see were extreme surges of brightness, as if fireballs were flying past the craft.

From the surface of Earth, the ship would be a brilliant meteor, visible even in daylight. He wondered if there was anybody down there who would understand what they saw.

The oak-like wood of the hull made for a natural heatshield, the Bad Hair Day twins had told him. All that resin would ablate naturally. It was a neater solution than the crude, clanking mechanical gadgets of his own era. Maybe, but he was an old-fashioned guy; he'd have preferred to be surrounded by a few layers of honest-to-God metal and ceramic.

The glow started to fade, and the deceleration eased. Now the windows were completely blacked over by the soot, but a shield jettisoned with a bang, taking the soot away with it, and revealing a circle of clear blue sky.

There was another crack as the first parachute deployed. The chute snatched at the pod and made it swing violently from side to side. He was pressed against one side of his couch and then the other, with the cabin creaking around him; he felt fragile, helpless, trapped in the couch.

Two more drogue chutes snapped open, in quick succession, and then the main chute. He could see through his window a huge canopy of green leafy material, like a vegetable cloud against the blue sky. The chute looked reassuringly intact, despite its vegetable origins, and the swaying reduced.

Malenfant glimpsed the ground. He could even track his progress, with maps in his sensor pack. He'd come down over the island that used to be called Zanzibar, on the east coast of Africa. And now he was drifting inland, to the north-west, towards Lake Victoria. Forest lay like thick green cloth over mountains.

Malenfant felt his couch rise up beneath him. Collapsing sacs pumped compressed carbon dioxide into the base of his seat, preparing to act as a shock absorber on landing. He was pressed up against the curved roof of his pod, with only a small gap between his knees and the roof itself. He felt hemmed in, heavy, hot. Gravity pulled at him, tangibly.

The pod hit the ground.

The parachutes pulled the capsule forward, so Malenfant was tipped up onto his face, and then the pod started to careen across rocky ground, rocking backward and forward, spinning and rattling. His head rattled against his couch headrest.

Finally the pod slithered to a halt.

Malenfant found himself suspended on his side, with daylight pouring through the window behind him. The shock absorber was still pressing him against the roof, so he couldn't see outside. He lifted his hands to his face. There was blood in his mouth.

The pod wall dilated, releasing a flood of hot sunlit air into the capsule, so rich in oxygen and vegetable scents it made him gasp.

He began the painful process of climbing out.

His pod had come down on a low pebbly beach. The beach ran in a sinuous light-grey line between the darker grey face of a lake and the living green of a banana grove. From the margin of the lake to the highest hill-top, all he could see was contrasting shades of green, spreading like a carpet.

This was the northern coast of Lake Victoria. It was the closest place to that population centre, with its odd radioactivity signature, that the Bad Hair Day twins would deliver him.

Once he got his balance, he didn't have any trouble walking. He didn't feel dizzy, but oddly disoriented. He could feel his internal organs moving around, seeking a new equilibrium inside him. And he seemed to be immune to sunburn.

But it was odd to be walking around without his pressure suit. Disconcerting. And the sense of openness, of scale, was startling. After all his travels, Malenfant had become an alien, uncomfortable on the surface of his home world.

There was no sign of humanity.

Malenfant made camp in the inert, scorched shell of his pod. He used the bubble helmet of his old NASA pressure suit to collect water from a brook, a little way inland. He ate figs and bananas. He figured if he was stuck here for long he'd try to fish that lake.

The days were short and hot, although there was usually a scattering of cloud over the blue sky. He set up a stick in the sand, and watched its shadow shifting and lengthening with the hours. That way he figured out the time of local noon, and he reset his astronaut's watch. If he was stuck here long enough he might find the equinox, and start filling out a calendar.

The sunsets were spectacular. All that sub-micrometre dust.

The nights were cold, and he would wrap himself up inside the Beta-cloth outer layers of his pressure suit, there on the beach. But he stayed awake long hours, studying a changed sky.

The crescent Moon glowed blue.

The crescent's edge was softly blurred by a band of light, which stretched part way around the dark half of the satellite. There was a thick band of what looked like cloud, piled up over the Moon's equator. On the darkened surface itself there were lights, strung out in lines: towns, or cities, outlining hidden lunar continents. The Moon had a twin light, a giant mirror that orbited it slowly, shedding light on the Moon's shadowed hemisphere, which would otherwise languish in the dark for fourteen days at a time, probably long enough for the precious new air to start snowing out.

And in the centre of the darkened hemisphere which faced him was a dazzling point glow. The point source was Earthlight, reflecting from the oceans of the Moon.

Even a slim crescent Moon, now, drenched the sky with light, drowning out the stars and planets. The wildlife of Earth made use of the new light: he heard the croak of amphibians, the growl of some kind of cat. No doubt this changed Moon was working on the evolution of species, subtly.

The Moon was beautiful, wonderful, its terraforming one heck of an achievement. But to Malenfant it was as unreachable as before Apollo, a thousand years ago. And, even from here, Malenfant could see Gaijin craft orbiting over the lunar poles.

When the Moon set, taking its brilliant light with it, the full strangeness of the sky emerged.

Huge objects drifted against the blackness, green and gold: Trees, spectral patches of life green, and Gaijin flower-ships, their open ram-scoop mouths tangles of silvery threads, like dragonflies. There was a chain of lights clustered around the plain of the ecliptic, sparkles in knots and clusters, almost like streetlights seen from orbit. They were Gaijin asteroid-belt cities.

The shapes of the constellations were mostly unchanged, the stars' slow drift imperceptible in the mayfly beat he'd been away. A bright young star had come to life in Cassiopeia, turning that distinctive W shape into a zig-zag. But many more stars had dimmed, to redness or even lurid green – or they were missing altogether, masked by life. This was the mark of the colonization wave, pulsing along the Galaxy's star lanes, an engineered consumption of system after system, heading this way.

And in one part of the sky, loosely centred on the grand old constellation of Orion, stars were flickering, burning, sputtering to darkness. It was evidence of purposeful activity spread across many light years, and it made him shiver. Perhaps it was the war he had come to fear, breaking over the solar system.

In the deepest dark of the nights he made out a huge, beautiful comet, sprawled across the zenith. Even with his naked eye he could see the bright spark of its nucleus, a tail that swept, feathery, curved, across the dome of the sky.

Comets came from the Oort cloud. He wondered if there was any connection between this shining visitor, flying through the heart of the inner solar system, and the sparkling lights he saw around Orion, the remote disturbance there.

One morning he crawled out of his pod, bollix naked.

There was a man standing there, staring at him.

Malenfant yelped, and clamped his hands over his testicles.

The man – no more than a boy, probably – was tall, more than two metres high. His skin was copper brown, covered by a pale golden hair, so thick it was almost like fur, and his eyes were blue. He had muscles like an athlete's. He was wearing some kind of breech cloth made of a coarse white material. He was carrying a sack. There was a belt around his waist, of some kind of leather. It contained a variety of tools, all of them stone, bone or wood: round axes, cleavers, scrapers, a hammerstone.

His neck was thick, like a weightlifter's. He had a long low skull, with some kind of bony crest behind. And he had bony eyebrows, a sloping forehead under that blond hair. He had a big projecting jaw – no chin – strong-looking teeth, a heavy brow ridge shielding his eyes, a flat ape-like nose. He didn't, Malenfant thought, look quite human.

But he was beautiful for all that, his gaze on Malenfant direct and untroubled.

He grinned at Malenfant, and emptied out the sack over the sand. It contained bananas, sweet potatoes and eggs. 'Eat food hungry eat food,' he said. His voice was high and indistinct, the consonants blurred.

Malenfant, stunned, just stood and stared.

His visitor folded up his sack, turned and ran off over the sand, a blur of golden-brown, leaving a trail of Man Friday footsteps on the beach.

Malenfant grunted. 'First contact,' he said to himself. Curiouser and curiouser.

He went to the tree line to do his morning business, then came back to the food. It made a change from fruit and fish.

He settled down to waiting. Man Friday and his unseen compadres surely didn't mean him any harm. Even so, he found it impossible not to stay close to his pod, glaring out at the tree line.

He wondered what he could use for weapons. Discreetly, he got together a heap of the bigger stones he could gather from the beach.

When his next visitors came, it was from the lake. He heard the voices first.

Six canoes, crowded with men and women, came shimmering around the point of the bay. Malenfant squinted to focus his new, improved eyes.

The crew looked to be of all races, from Aryan to Negro. Malenfant spotted a few beautiful, golden-haired creatures like his Man Friday. He saw what looked like the commander, standing up in one of the canoes. He was dressed in a bead-worked head-dress, adorned with long white cock's feathers, and a snowy white and long-haired goat-skin, with a crimson robe hanging from his shoulders. To Malenfant he was a vision out of the Stone Age. But he was hunched over, as if ill.

Empty-handed, Malenfant went down the beach to meet them.

The canoes scraped onto the shore, and the commander jumped out and walked barefoot through shallow water to the dry sand. He stumbled, Malenfant saw, on legs swollen to the thickness of tree-trunks. His face was burned black, and patches of hair sprouted from his scalp like weeds. But his gaze was alert and searching.

He reached out. There was a stench of rotting skin, and it was all Malenfant could manage not to recoil in disgust. To Malenfant, it looked like an advanced case of radiation poisoning. Something, he thought, is going on here.

The commander opened his mouth to speak. His lips parted with a soft pop, and Malenfant saw how his mucous membranes were swollen up. He began talking to Malenfant in a language he couldn't recognize. Swahili or Kiganda, maybe.

Malenfant held up his hands. 'I'm sorry. I don't understand.'

The commander looked startled. 'Good God,' he said, 'a European . . . I never expected to see another European!' His English was heavily accented.

'Not European. American.'

'You're a deep traveller.'

'Deep?'

'Deep in time. Like me. I left Earth the first time in 2191. You?'

'Earlier,' said Malenfant.

'Listen, I'm a kind of ambassador from the Kabaka.'

'Kabaka?'

'The emperor. Among other duties, I meet travellers. Not that they come often.' He noticed Malenfant reacting to his condition. He smiled, his mouth a grisly gash that exposed black teeth. 'Don't worry about this. I fell out with the Kabaka for a while. Most people do. My name is Pierre de Bonneville. I used to be French. I went to Bellatrix with the Gaijin: Gamma Orionis, three hundred and sixty light years away. A remarkable trip.'

'Why?'

De Bonneville laughed. 'I was a writer. A poet, actually. My country believed in sending artists to the stars: eyes and ears to bring home the truth, the inner truth, you see, of what is out there. I rode one of the last Arianes, from Kourou. Vast, noisy affair! But when I got home everyone had left, or died. There was nowhere to publish what I observed, noone to listen to my accounts.'

'I know the feeling. My name's Malenfant.'

De Bonneville peered at him. He didn't seem to recognize the name, and that suited Malenfant.

The golden-haired crewmen poked curiously around the charred husk of Malenfant's reentry pod.

De Bonneville grinned. 'You're admiring my golden-haired crewmen. The Uprights. Kintu's children, I call them.'

'Kintu?'

'. . . But then, we are all children of Kintu now. What do you want here, Malenfant?'

Travellers and emperors, history and politics. Malenfant felt his new blood pump in his veins. He'd been among aliens too long. Now human affairs, with all their rich complexity, were embracing him again.

He grinned. He said, 'Take me to your leader.'

Chapter 25

WANPAMBA'S TOMB

Pierre de Bonneville, with his crew of humans and golden-haired hominids, spent a night on the beach where Malenfant had fallen from orbit. By firelight, the human crew ate dried fish and sweet potatoes. The Uprights served the humans, who didn't acknowledge or thank them in any way.

De Bonneville started drinking a frothy beer he called *pombe*, of fermented grain. Within an hour he was bleary-eyed, thick-tongued, husky-voiced.

When they were done with their chores the Uprights settled down away from the others. They built their own crude fire, and cooked something that sizzled and popped with fat; to Malenfant it smelled like pork.

The boy who Malenfant had dubbed 'Friday' turned out to be called Magassa.

De Bonneville told Malenfant how he had travelled here along the course of the Nile, from where Cairo used to be. Like Malenfant, he'd been drawn, on his return from the stars, to the nearest thing to a metropolis the old planet had to offer. The Nile journey sounded like quite a trip: in AD 3265, Africa was a savage place once more.

'Listen to me. The ruler here is called Mtesa. Mtesa is the Kabaka of Uganda, Usogo, Unyoro and Karagwe – an empire three hundred kilometres in length and fifty in breadth, the biggest political unit in all this pagan world. Things have – reverted – here on Earth, Malenfant, while we weren't looking. The people here have gone back to ways of life they enjoyed, or endured, centuries before your time or mine, before the Europeans expanded across the planet. You and I are true anachronisms. Do you understand? *These people aren't like us.* They have no real sense of history. No sense of change, of the possibility of a different future or past. The date, by your and my calendars, may be AD 3265. But Earth is now timeless.' He coughed, and hawked up a gob of blood-soaked phlegm.

'What happened to you, de Bonneville?'

The Frenchman grinned, and deflected the question. 'Let me tell you how this country is. We're like the first European explorers, coming here to darkest Africa, in the nineteenth century. And the Kabaka is a tough gentleman. When the traveller first enters this country, his path seems to be strewn with flowers. Gifts follow one another rapidly, pages and courtiers kneel before him, and the least wish is immediately gratified. So long as the stranger is a novelty, and his capacities or worth have not yet been sounded, it is like a holiday here. But there comes a time when he must make return. Do you follow me?'

Malenfant thought about it. De Bonneville's speech was more florid than Malenfant was used to. But then, he'd been born maybe two hundred years later than Malenfant; a lot could change in that time. Mostly, though, he thought de Bonneville had gotten a little too immersed in the local politics – who cared about this Kabaka? – not to mention becoming as bitter as hell.

'No,' he said. 'I don't know what you're talking about.'

De Bonneville seemed frustrated. 'Ultimately you must pay back the Kabaka for his hospitality. If you have weapons with you, you must give; if you have rings, or good clothes, you must give. And if you do not give liberally, there will be found other means to rid you of your superfluities. Your companions will desert, attracted by the rewards of Mtesa. And one day, you will find yourself utterly bereft of your entire stock – and be stranded here, a thousand kilometres from the nearest independent community.'

'And that's what happened to you.'

'When I stopped amusing him, the Kabaka dragged me before his court. And I – displeased him further. And, with a kiss from the Katekiro – Mtesa's lieutenant – I was sentenced to a month in the Engine of Kimera.'

'An Engine?'

'It is a yellow-cake mine. I was put in with the lowest of the low, Malenfant. The sentence left me reduced, as you see. When I was released, Mtesa – in the manner of the half-civilized ruler he is – found me work in the court. I am a book-keeper.

'Here's something to amuse you. From my memories of Inca culture I recognized the number recording system here, which is like the *quipu* – that is to say, numerical records made up of knotted strings. The Kabaka has embraced this technology. Every citizen in this kingdom is stored in numbers: the date of her birth, her kinship through birth and marriage, the contents of her granaries and warehouses. I was able to devise an accounting system to assist Mtesa with tax levies, for which he showed inordinate gratitude, and I became something of a favourite at the court again, though in a different capacity.

'But you see the irony, Malenfant. We travellers return from the stars to this dismal post-technological future – a world of illiterates – and yet I find myself a prisoner of an empire which lists the acts of every citizen as pure unadorned numbers. This may look like Eden to you; in fact it is a dread, soulless metropolis!'

The Uprights were laughing together. Malenfant could hear their voices, oddly monotonous, their jabbered speech.

'Their talk is simple,' Malenfant said.

'Yes. Direct and non-abstract. Sweet, isn't it? About the level of a six-year-old human child.'

'What are they, de Bonneville?'

'Can't you tell? They make me shudder. They are physically beautiful, of course. The women are sometimes compliant . . . Here. More *pombe*.'

'No.'

They sat in the cooling night, an old man and an invalid, stranded out of time, as in the distance the Uprights clustered around their fire, tall and elegant.

Malenfant agreed to travel with Pierre de Bonneville to Usavara, the hunting village of the Kabaka, and from there to the capital, Rubaga. Rubaga was the source of those radiation anomalies Malenfant had observed from orbit.

The next day they rowed out of the bay. De Bonneville's canoe was superb, and Magassa, the Upright, drummed an accompaniment to the droning chant of the oarsmen.

Malenfant, sitting astern, felt as if he had wandered into a theme park.

About two kilometres along the shore from Usavara, the hunting village, Malenfant saw what had to be thousands of Waganda – which was, de Bonneville said, this new race's name for themselves. They were standing to order on the shore in two dense lines, at the ends of which stood several finely-dressed men in crimson and black and snowy white. As the canoes neared the beach, arrows flew in the air. Kettle and bass drums sounded a noisy welcome, and flags and banners waved.

When they landed, de Bonneville led Malenfant up the beach. They were met by an old woman, short and bent. She was dressed in a crimson robe which covered a white dress of bleached cotton. De Bonneville kneeled before this figure, and told Malenfant she was the Katekiro: a kind of Prime Minister to the Kabaka.

The Katekiro's face was a wizened mask.

'Holy shit. *Nemoto.*' It was her; Malenfant had no doubt about it.

When she looked closely at Malenfant, her eyes widened, and she turned away. She would not meet his eyes again.

De Bonneville watched them curiously.

The Katekiro motioned with her head and, amid a clamour of beaten drums, Malenfant and de Bonneville walked into the village.

They reached a circle of grass-thatched huts surrounding a large house, which Malenfant was told would be his quarters. They were going to stay here a night, before moving inland. Nemoto left as soon as she could, and Malenfant didn't get to speak to her.

When Malenfant emerged from his hut he found gifts from the Kabaka: bunches of bananas, milk, sweet potatoes, green Indian corn, rice, fresh eggs, and ten pots of *maramba* wine.

Reid Malenfant, cradling his NASA pressure suit under his arm, felt utterly disoriented. And the presence of Nemoto, a human being he'd known a thousand years before, somehow only enhanced his sense of the bizarre.

He laughed, picked up a pot of wine, and went to bed.

The next day they walked inland, towards the capital.

Malenfant found himself trekking across a vast bowl of grass. The road was a level strip two metres wide, cutting through jungle and savannah. It had, it seemed, been built for the Kabaka's hunting excursions. Some distance away there was a lake, small and brackish, and beyond that a range of hills, climbing into mountains. The lower flanks of the mountains were cloaked in forest, their summits were wreathed in clouds. The dome-like huts of the Waganda were buried deep in dense bowers of plantains – flat leaves and green flowers – which filled the air with the cloying stink of over-ripe fruit.

Malenfant heard a remote bellowing.

He saw animals stalking across the plain, two or three kilometres away. They might have been elephants; they were huge and grey, and tusks gleamed white in the grey light of the pre-dawn sky. The tusks turned downwards, unlike the zoo animals Malenfant remembered.

He asked de Bonneville about the animals.

De Bonneville grunted. 'Those are *deinotherium.* The elephant things. Genetic archaeology.'

Malenfant tried to observe all this, to memorize the way back to the coast. But he found it hard to concentrate on what he was seeing.

Nemoto: God damn. She'd surely recognized him. But she'd barely acknowledged his existence, and during this long walk across Africa, he couldn't find a way to get close to her.

After three hours' march, they came into view of a flat-topped hill, which cast a long shadow across the countryside. The hill was crowned by a cluster of tall, conical grass huts, walled by a cane fence. This hill-top village, said de Bonneville, was the capital, Rubaga; the hill itself was known as Wanpamba's Tomb. Rubaga struck Malenfant as a sinister, brooding place, out of sympathy with the lush green countryside it ruled.

In the centre of the hill-top cluster of huts stood a bigger building. Evidently this was the Imperial Palace. To Malenfant it looked like a Kansas barn. Fountains thrust up into the air around the central building, like handfuls of diamonds catching the light. That struck Malenfant as odd. Fountains? Where did the power for fountains come from?

Broad avenues radiated down the hill's flanks. The big avenues blended into lower grade roads, which cut across the countryside. Along these radiating roads, Malenfant saw, much of the traffic – pedestrians and ox-carts – was directed, towards and away from the capital.

Two of the bigger roads, to east and west, seemed more rutted and damaged than the rest, as if they bore heavy traffic. The eastern road didn't ascend the hill itself but rather entered a tunnel cut into the hill-side. It looked like it was designed for delivering supplies of some sort to a mine or quarry inside the bulk of the hill, or maybe for hauling ore out of there. In fact he saw a caravan of several heavy, covered carts, drawn by labouring bullocks, dragging its way along the eastern road. It reminded Malenfant of a twenty-mule team hauling bauxite out of Death Valley.

They proceeded up the hill, along one of the big avenues. The ground was a reddish clay. The avenue was fenced with tall water-cane set together in uniform rows.

People crowded the avenues. The Waganda wore brown robes or white dresses, some with white goatskins over their brown robes, and others with cords folded like a turban around their heads. They didn't show much curiosity about de Bonneville's party. Evidently a traveller was a big deal out in Usavara, out in the sticks, but here in the capital everyone was much too cool to pay attention.

There wasn't so much as a TV aerial or a Coke machine in sight. But de Bonneville surprised Malenfant by telling him that people here could live as old as 150 years.

'We have been to the stars, and have returned. Rubaga might look primitive, but it is deceptive. We are living on the back of a thousand years' progress in science and technology. Plus what we bought from the Gaijin, and others. It is invisible – embedded in the fabric of the world – but it's *here*. For instance, many diseases have been eradicated. And, thanks to genetic engineering, ageing has been slowed down greatly.'

'What about the Uprights?'

'What?'

'What lifespan can they expect?'

De Bonneville looked irritated. 'Thirty or forty years, I suppose. What does it matter? I'm talking about *Homo Sapiens*, Malenfant.'

Despite de Bonneville's claims about progress, Malenfant soon noticed that mixed in with the clean and healthy and long-lived citizens there were a handful who looked a lot worse off. These unclean were dressed reasonably well. But each of them, man, woman or child, was afflicted by diseases and deformities. Malenfant counted symptoms: swollen lips, open sores, heads of men and women like billiard balls to which mere clumps of hair still clung. Many were mottled with blackness about the face and hands. Some of them had skin which appeared to be flaking away in handfuls, and there were others with swollen arms, legs and necks, so that their skin was stretched to a smooth glassiness.

All in all, the same symptoms as Pierre de Bonneville.

De Bonneville grimaced at his fellow sufferers. 'The Breath of Kimera,' he hissed. 'A terrible thing, Malenfant.' But he would say no more than that.

When these unfortunates moved through the crowds the other Waganda melted away from them, as if determined not even to glance at the unclean ones.

They reached the cane fence which surrounded the village at the top of the hill. They passed through a gate and into the central compound.

Malenfant was led to the house which had been allotted to him. It stood in the centre of a plantain garden and was shaped like a marquee, with a portico projecting over the doorway. It had two apartments.

Close by there were three dome-like huts for servants, and railed spaces for – he was told – his bullocks and goats.

Useful, he thought.

The prospect from up here was imperial. A landscape of early summer green, drenched in sunshine, fell away in waves. There was a fresh breeze coming off the huge inland sea. Here and there isolated cone-shaped hills thrust up from the flat landscape, like giant tables above a green carpet. Dark sinuous lines traced the winding courses of deep tree-filled ravines, separated by undulating pastures. In broader depressions Malenfant could see cultivated gardens and grain fields. Up towards the horizon all these details melted into the blues of the distance.

It was picture-postcard pretty, as if Europeans had never come here. But he wondered what this countryside had seen, how much blood and tears had had to soak into the earth, before the scars of colonialism had been healed.

Not that the land wasn't developed, pretty intensely: notably, with a network of irrigation channels and canals, clearly visible from up here. The engineering was impressive, in its way. Malenfant wondered how the Kabaka and his predecessors had managed it. The population wasn't so great, it seemed to him, that it could spare huge numbers of labourers from the fields for all these earthworks.

Maybe they used Uprights, whatever they were.

Anyhow, he thought sourly, so much for the pastoral idyll. It looked as if *Homo Sap* was on the move again, building, breeding, lording it over his fellows and the creatures around him, just like always.

In this unmanaged biosphere, immersed in air that was too dense and too hot and too humid, Malenfant had trouble sleeping; and when he did sleep, he woke to fuzzy senses and a sore head.

There was no way to get coffee, decaffeinated or otherwise.

The next afternoon Malenfant was invited to the Palace.

The Katekiro – Nemoto – came to escort him, evidently under orders. 'Come with me,' she said bluntly. It was the first time she'd spoken directly to Malenfant.

'Nemoto, I know it's you. And you know me, don't you?'

'The Kabaka is waiting.'

'How did you get here? How long have you been here? Are there any other travellers here?'

Nemoto wouldn't reply.

They approached the tall inner fence around the Palace itself. He wasn't the only visitor today, and a procession drew up. The ordinary Waganda weren't permitted beyond this point, but they crowded around the gates anyhow, gossiping and preening.

There was a rumbling roll of a kettle-drum, and the gate was drawn aside; and they proceeded, chiefs, soldiers, peasants, and three interstellar travellers, on into a complex of courtyards.

There was a wide avenue inside the fence, and at the fence's four corners those spectacular fountains thrust up into the air, rising fifteen metres or more. The water emerged from crude clay piping which snaked into the ground beneath the Palace. Maybe there were pumps buried in the hill-side.

Malenfant approached the nearest fountain. He reached out to touch the water – Christ, it was *hot,* so hot it almost scalded his fingers – and Nemoto pulled his arm back. Her hand on his was leathery and warm.

The drums sounded again. They passed through courtyard after courtyard, until finally they stood in front of the Palace itself.

It was only a grass hut. But it was tall and spacious, full of light and air. Malenfant, who had once visited the White House, had been in worse government buildings.

The heart of the Palace was a reception room. This was a narrow hall some twenty metres long, the ceiling of which was supported by two rows of pillars. The aisles were filled with dignitaries and officers. At each pillar stood one of the king's guards, wearing a long red mantle, a white turban ornamented with monkey skin, white trousers and black blouse. All were armed with spears. But there was no throne there, nor Mtesa himself. Instead there was only what Malenfant took to be a well, a rectangular pit in the floor.

Malenfant, Nemoto and the rest had to sit in rows before the open pit.

Drums clattered, and puffs of steam came venting up from the well-mouth, followed by a grinding, mechanical noise. A platform rose up out of the well, smoothly enough. Once again, Malenfant wondered where the energy for these stunts came from. The platform carried a throne – a seat like an office chair – on which sat the lean figure of Mtesa himself. Mtesa's head was clean-shaven and covered with a fez; his features were smooth, polished and without a wrinkle, and he might have been any age between twenty-five and thirty-five. His big, lustrous eyes gave him a strange beauty, and Malenfant wondered if there was Upright blood in there. Mtesa was sweating, his robes a little rumpled, but grinning hugely.

Nemoto, as Katekiro, and Mtesa's vizier and scribes all came forward to kneel at his feet. Some kissed the palms and backs of his hands; others prostrated themselves on the ground. Malenfant found it very strange to watch Nemoto do this.

Through all this, a girl stood at Mtesa's elbow. She was tall, dressed in white, her hair dark, but she had the broad neck and downy golden fur of an Upright. She couldn't have been more than fifteen. She moved like a cat, and – thought Reid Malenfant, dried-up hundred-year-old star voyager – she was sexy as all hell. But she looked troubled, like a child with a guilty conscience.

The main business of the afternoon was a bunch of petitioners and embassies, each of which Mtesa handled with efficiency – and, when he was displeased, brutality. In such cases the 'Lords of the Cord' were called forward: big beefy guards, whose job was to drag away the source of Mtesa's anger by ropes about the neck. It was, Malenfant thought, a striking management technique.

Nemoto, as the Katekiro, was heavily involved in all this: the presentation of cases and evidence, the delivery of the verdict. And each sentencing was preceded by Nemoto placing a dry kiss on the cheek of the terrified victim – a kiss of death, Malenfant thought with a shudder, planted by a thousand-year-old woman.

At last Mtesa turned to Malenfant. Through an interpreter, a dried-up little courtier, the Kabaka asked questions. He showed a child-like curiosity about Malenfant's story: where and when he had been born, the places he had seen in his travels.

After a while, Malenfant started to enjoy the occasion. For the first time in a thousand years, Reid Malenfant had found somebody who actually *wanted* to hear his anecdotes about the early days of the US space program.

Mtesa, it turned out, knew all about the Gaijin, and Saddle Point gateways, and, roughly speaking, the dispersal of humanity over the last thousand years. He wasn't uncomfortable with the idea of Malenfant having been born a millennium ago. But these were abstractions to him, since the Gaijin didn't intervene in affairs on Earth – not overtly anyhow – and Mtesa was more interested in what profit he could make out of this windfall.

Malenfant reminded himself that people were most preoccupied by their own slice of history; Mtesa was a man of his time, which had nothing to do with Malenfant's. Still, Malenfant wondered how many more generations would pass before only the kings and courtiers knew the true story of mankind, while everyone else subsided to flat-Earth ignorance, and started worshipping Gaijin flower-ships as gods in the sky.

Mtesa offered Malenfant various gifts, and an invitation to stay as long as he wished, and dismissed him.

The Katekiro, Nemoto, got away from Malenfant as soon as she could.

That evening, alone in his villa, Malenfant started to feel ill.

He couldn't keep down his food. He felt as if he was running up a temperature. And his hand hurt: there was a burning sensation, deep in the flesh, where the fountain water had splashed him.

In the bubble helmet of his EMU, he studied his reflection. He didn't look so bad. A little glassy about the eyes, perhaps. Maybe it was the food.

He went to bed early, and tried to forget about it.

He pursued the Katekiro, Nemoto. He tried everything he could think of to break through to her.

Eventually, with every evidence of reluctance, Nemoto agreed to spend a little time with Malenfant. She came to his hut, and they sat on the broad, wood-floored veranda, by the light of a small oil lamp and of the blue Moon.

She brought with her a buddha, a squat, ugly carving. It was made, she said, of fused regolith from the Mare Ingenii: Moon rock, worn smooth by time. The wizened little Japanese looked up at the blue-green Moon. 'And now the regolith is buried under metres of dirt, with fat lunar-gravity-evolved earthworms crawling through it. We have survived to see strange times, Malenfant.'

'Yeah.'

They talked, but Nemoto was no cicerone. The only way he could get any information out of her was to let her rehearse her obsession with the Gaijin – not to mention her former employers, Nishizaki Heavy Industries, who she thought had betrayed the human species.

He was astonished to find she'd travelled here, through a thousand years of history, the long way round: not by skipping from era to era as he and the other Saddle Point travellers had done, but simply by not dying. She gave him no indication of what technology she had used to exceed so greatly the usual human lifespan.

A thousand years of consciousness: no doubt this was dwarfed by Cassiopeia and her mechanical sisters, but such a span seemed unbearable on a human scale. He wondered how well Nemoto could retrieve the memories of her own deep past, of her first meeting with him on the Moon, for instance; perhaps she had been forced to resort to technology, to reorder and optimize her immense recollections. And, listening to Nemoto, he wondered how much of her sanity, her personality, had survived this long ordeal of life. She hinted at dark periods, slumps into poverty and powerlessness, even a period – centuries long – when she had lived as a recluse on the far side of the Moon.

However she had been damaged by time, though, she had retained one thing: her crystal-clear enmity of the Gaijin, and the Eeties who were following them.

'When I found the Gaijin I imagined we were destined for a thousand-year war. But now a thousand years have elapsed, and the war continues. Malenfant, when I still had influence, I struggled to restrict the Gaijin. I recruited the people called the Yolgnu. I established Kasyapa Township –'

'On Triton.'

'Yes. It was a beachhead, to keep the Gaijin from expanding their industrial activities in the outer system. I failed in that purpose. Now there are only a handful of human settlements beyond the Earth. There is a colony on Mercury, huddling close to the sun beyond the reach of the Gaijin . . . If it survives, perhaps *that* will be our final home. For *the Gaijin are here*.'

A moth was beating against the lamp. She reached up and grabbed the insect in one gnarled hand. She showed the crushed fragments to Malenfant.

Flakes of mica wing. The sparkle of plastic. A smear of what looked like fine engine oil.

'*Gaijin*,' Nemoto said. 'They are here, Malenfant. They are everywhere, meddling, building. And worse are following.' She pointed up to the stars, in a sky made muddy with light by the low Moon. He could pick out Orion, just. 'You must have seen the novae.'

'Is that what they are?'

'Yes. There has been a rash of novae, of minor stellar explosions, like an infection spreading along the spiral arm. It has been proceeding for centuries.'

'My God.'

She smiled grimly. 'I've missed you, Malenfant. You immediately see implications. This is deliberate, of course, a strategy of some intelligence. *Somebody is setting off the stars,* exploding them like fire-crackers. The stars selected are like the sun – more or less. We have seen the disruption of Castor and Pollux in Gemini. Castor is a binary of two A-class stars some forty-five light years away, Pollux a K-class thirty-five light years away. Then came Procyon, an F-class eleven light years away, and, more recently Sirius –'

'Just nine light years away.'

'Yes.'

'Why would anybody blow up stars?'

She shrugged. 'To mine them of raw materials. Perhaps to launch a fleet of solar-sail starships. Who knows?' She said darkly, 'I call them the Crackers. Appropriate, don't you think? The spread seems to have been patchy, diffuse.'

'But they are coming this way.'

'Yes. They are coming this way.'

'Perhaps the Gaijin will defend us.'

She snorted. 'The Gaijin pursue their own interest. *We* are incidental, just another victim species a few decades or centuries behind the general development, about to be burned up in an interstellar war between rapacious colonists.'

Just as Malenfant had seen among the stars. Over and over. And now it was happening here.

. . . But there was still much mystery, he thought. There was still the question of the Reboot, the greater cataclysm that seemed poised to sweep over the Galaxy, and all its squabbling species.

What were the Gaijin *really* up to, here in the solar system? Nemoto's blunt antagonism seemed simplistic to Malenfant, who had come to know the Gaijin better. They were hardly humanity's friends, but neither were they mortal enemies. They were just *Gaijin*, following their own star.

But Nemoto was still talking, resigned, fatalistic. 'I am an old woman. I was already an old woman a thousand years ago. All I can do now is survive, here, in this absurd little kingdom . . .'

Maybe. But, he reflected, if she'd chosen to retire, she could have done that anywhere. She didn't have to come *here*, to this dismal feudal empire, and serve its puffed-up ruler. The grassy metropolis – and the radiation signature, that trace of technology – had drawn her here, just like himself.

He said, testing her, 'I have a functioning pressure suit.'

She scarcely moved, as if trying to mask her reaction to that. She was like a statue, some greater Moon rock buddha herself.

There is, he realized, something she isn't telling me. Something significant.

He was woken before dawn.

De Bonneville's ruined face loomed over him like a black moon, the sweet stink of *pombe* on his breath. 'Malenfant. Come. They're hunting.'

'Who?'

'You'll see.'

A sticky, moist heat hit Malenfant as soon as he left his hut. He walked down the broad hill, after de Bonneville, working through a hierarchy of smaller and more sinuous paths, until there was savannah grass under his feet, long and damp with dew. Wagandans were following them, men and women alike, talking softly, some laughing.

The blue Moon had long set. There were still stars above. Malenfant saw a diffuse light, clearly green, tracking across the southern sky: it was a Tree, a living satellite populated by post-humans, floating above this primeval African landscape.

De Bonneville cast about and pointed. 'There's a track – see, where the grass has been beaten down? It leads towards the lake. Come. We will walk.' And, without waiting for acquiescence, he turned and led the way, limping and wheezing, his pains evidently forgotten in his eagerness for the spectacle.

Malenfant followed, tracking through the long damp grass. They passed a herd of the elephant analogues, the *deinotherium*. They seemed unaware of the humans. From a stand of trees, Malenfant saw the scowl of a cat – perhaps a lion – with long sabre teeth protruding over its lower jaw. De Bonneville said it was a *megantereon*. And he almost tripped over a lizard, hiding in the undergrowth at his feet; it was a half-metre long, with three sharp horns protruding from its crest. It scampered away from him and then sat in the grass, its huge eyes fixed on him.

They passed a skull, perhaps of an antelope, bleached of flesh. It had been cracked open by a stone flake – little more than a shaped pebble – embedded in a pit in the bone. Malenfant bent down and prised out the flake with his fingers. Was it made by the Uprights? It seemed too primitive.

De Bonneville grabbed his arm. 'There,' he whispered.

Perhaps a half-kilometre away, a group of what looked like big apes – muscular, hairy, big-brained – was gathered around a carcass. Malenfant could see curved horns; maybe it was another antelope. In the dawn light the hominids were working together with what looked like handheld stone tools, butchering the carcass. A number of them were keeping watch at the fringe of the group, throwing rocks at circling hyenas.

Malenfant said, 'Are these the hunters you brought me to see?'

De Bonneville snorted with contempt. 'These? No. They are not even hunters. They waited for the hyenas or jackals to kill that *sivatherium,* and now they steal it for themselves . . . Ah. Look, Malenfant.'

To Malenfant's left, crouching figures were moving forward through the grass. In the grey light, Malenfant could make out golden skin, flashes of white cloth. It was Magassa, and more of his people, moving towards the ape-like scavengers.

'*Now,*' de Bonneville hissed. 'Now the sport begins.'

'What are these creatures, de Bonneville?'

He grinned. 'When the ice was rolled back, the Earth was left empty. Various – experiments – were performed to repopulate it. But not as it had been before.'

'With older forms.'

'Of animals and even hominids, us. Yes.'

'So Magassa –'

'– is a once-extinct hominid, recreated here, in the year AD 3265. Magassa is *Homo Erectus.* And there are tigers once more in India, and mammoths in the north of Europe, and roaming the prairies of North America once more are many of the megafauna species destroyed by the Stone Age settlers there . . . Quite something, isn't it, Malenfant? I'm sure you didn't expect to find *this* on your return to Earth: the lost species of the past, restored to roam the empty planet, here at the end of time.'

It sounded, to Malenfant, like characteristic Gaijin tinkering. Just as they had poked around with Earth's climate and biosphere and geophysical cycles, so, it seemed, they were determined to explore the possibilities inherent in DNA, life's treasury of the past. Endless questing, as they sought answers to their unspoken questions. But still, here was a hunting party of *Homo Erectus,* by God, stalking easily across the plains of Africa in this year AD 3265. 'Is anyone studying this?'

De Bonneville looked at him curiously. 'Perhaps you don't understand. *Science is dead,* Malenfant. These are only Uprights. But . . .' He looked more thoughtful. 'I sometimes wonder if Magassa has a soul. Magassa can speak, you know, to some extent. His speech mechanism is closer to nonhuman primates. Still, he can make himself understood. Look into Magassa's eyes, Malenfant, and you will see a true consciousness – far more developed than any animal's – but a consciousness lacking much of the complexity, and darkness and confusion, of our own. Is there still a Pope or a mullah, somewhere on Earth or the Moon, concerned with such issues, perhaps declaring Magassa an abomination even now? But Magassa himself would not frame such questions; without our full inner awareness, he would lack the ability to impute consciousness in other beings, and so could not envisage consciousness in non-human animals and objects. That is to say, he would not be able to imagine God.'

'You envy him,' Malenfant said.

'Yes. Yes, I envy Magassa his calm sanity. Well. They make good labourers. And the women – Wait. Watch this.'

Magassa stood suddenly, whooped, and brandished a torch, which burst into flame. The other Uprights stood with him and hollered. Their high, clear voices carried across the grassy plain to Malenfant, like the cries of gulls.

At the noise, the primitive scavenging hominids jumped up, startled. With bleating cries they ran away from the Uprights and their fire, abandoning the antelope. One of the hominids – a female – was a little more courageous; she reached back and tore a final strip of flesh from the carcass before fleeing with the others, flat breasts flapping.

But now more Uprights burst out of the grass before the fleeing hominids. It was a simple trap, but obviously beyond the more primitive hominids' mental grasp.

At this new obstacle the scavengers hesitated for a second, like startled sheep. Then they bunched together and kept on running. They forced their way right through the cluster of Uprights, who hailed stones and bone spears at them. Some of the weapons struck home, with a crunching violence that startled Malenfant. But as far as he could see all the hominids got through.

All, that is, except one: the female who had hung back, and who was now a few dozen metres behind the rest.

The Uprights closed around her. She fought – she seemed to have a rock in her clenched fist – but she was overwhelmed. The Uprights fell on her, and she went down in a forest of flailing arms.

Her fleeing companions didn't look back.

De Bonneville stood up, his blackened face slick with sweat, breathing hard.

The Upright, Magassa, came stalking out of the pack, with a corpse slung over his shoulder. He had blood on his teeth and on the golden fur of his chest.

The body he carried was about the size of a twelve-year-old child's, Malenfant guessed, coated with fine dark hair. The arms were long, but the hands and feet were like a modern human's. The brain pan was crushed, a bloody mess, but the face was prominent: a brow ridge, a flat ape-like nose, the jaw protruding, big front teeth. That tool was still clutched in the female's hand; it was a lava pebble, crudely shaped.

The head, in life, had been held up. This was a creature that had walked upright.

Magassa dumped the corpse at de Bonneville's feet and howled his triumph.

'And what is *this*, de Bonneville?'

'Another reconstruction: Handy Man, some two million years vanished. Even less conscious, less self-aware, than our Upright friends.'

'*Homo Habilis*.'

'Malenfant, every species of extinct hominid is represented on this big roomy land of ours. I was pleased to see the prey were habilines, this morning – the Australopithecines can run, but are too stupid for good sport –'

'Get me out of here, de Bonneville.'

De Bonneville's ruined eyes narrowed. 'So squeamish. So hypocritical. Listen to me, Malenfant. *This is how we lived.* Sometimes they rape before the kill. Think of it, Malenfant! You and I have travelled to the stars. And yet, all the time, we carried the Old Men with us, asleep in our bones, waiting to be recalled . . .'

The Upright took a rock from his belt and started to hammer at the back of the dead habiline's skull. He dug his fingers into the hole he made, pulled out grey material, blood-soaked, and crammed it into his mouth.

Reid Malenfant knew, at last, that he had truly come home. He turned away from the habiline corpse.

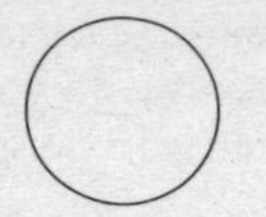

Chapter 26

KIMERA'S BREATH

Soon after the Upright hunt, de Bonneville disappeared. Nemoto warned Malenfant not to ask too many questions.

On his own, Malenfant wandered around the court, the streets outside, even out into the country. But he learned little.

He found it hard to make any human contact. The Waganda were incurious – even of his sleek biocomposite coverall, a gift from the Bad Hair Day space twins, an artefact centuries of technological advancement ahead of anything here.

Most definitely, he did not fit in here. Madeleine Meacher had warned him it would be like this.

Anyhow, he tired quickly, and his hand still ached. Maybe those Bad Hair Day twins hadn't done as good a job on him as they thought.

The days wore on, and his mind kept returning to de Bonneville. When he thought about it, Pierre de Bonneville – for all he was an asshole – was the only person in all this dead-end world who had tried to help him, to give him information. And besides, de Bonneville was a fellow star traveller who was maybe in trouble in this alien time.

So he started campaigning, with the Kabaka and Nemoto in her role as the Katekiro, to be allowed to see de Bonneville.

After a few days of this, Nemoto summoned Malenfant from his villa. Impatient and reluctant, she said she had been ordered to escort Malenfant to de Bonneville. It turned out he was being held in Kimera's Engine, the mysterious construct buried in the hill-side at the heart of this grass-hut capital.

'I do not advise this, Malenfant.'

'Why? Because it's dangerous? I've seen de Bonneville. I know how ill he is –'

'Not just that. What do you hope to achieve?' She looked at him out of eyes like splinters of lava; she seemed sunk in bitterness and despair. 'I survive, as best I can. That's what you must do. Find a place here, a niche you can defend. What else is there? Hasn't your hop-and-skip tour of a thousand years taught you that much?'

'If that's what you believe, why do you want my pressure suit?'

She coughed into a handkerchief; he saw the cloth was speckled by blood. 'Malenfant –'

'Take me to de Bonneville.'

Accompanied by a couple of guards, Nemoto led Malenfant from the Palace compound, and out into Rubaga. They followed streets, little more than tracks of dust, that wound between the grass huts.

After a while the huts became sparser, until they reached a place where there were no well-defined roads, no construction. The centre of the plateau – maybe a kilometre in diameter and fringed by huts – was deserted: just bare rock and lifeless soil, free of grass, bushes, insects or bird-song. Even the breeze from Lake Victoria seemed suppressed here.

It looked, he thought, as if a neutron bomb had gone off.

They marched on into this grim terrain. Nemoto was silent, her resentment apparent in every gesture and step.

Malenfant had been ill during the night, and hadn't got much sleep. He was feeling queasy, shivering. And the landscape didn't help. The ground here was like a little island of death, in the middle of this African ocean of life.

At last they reached the heart of the central plain. They came to a wide, deep well set in the ground. There were steps cut into the rock, spiralling into the ground around the cylindrical inner face of the well. In the low light of the morning Malenfant could see the steps for the first fifty metres or so, beyond that only darkness.

Nemoto began to clamber down the steps. She walked like the stiff old woman she had become, her gaudy court plumage incongruous in the shadows. Malenfant followed more slowly.

He wished he had a gun.

Within a few minutes they'd come down maybe thirty metres – the open mouth of the well was a disc of blue sky, laced with high clouds – and Nemoto rapped on a wooden door set in the wall.

The door opened. Beyond, Malenfant saw a lighted chamber, a rough cube dug out of the rock, lit up by rush torches. At the door stood one of the king's guards. He was a pillar of bone and muscle, overlaid by fat and leathery skin. Nemoto spoke briefly, and the guard, after a hostile inspection of Malenfant, let them through.

The room was surprisingly large. The heat was intense, and the smoke from wall-mounted torches was thick, despite air passages cut into the walls. But the smoke couldn't mask the sweet stenches of vomit, of corrupt and decaying flesh. Malenfant grabbed a handkerchief from his pocket and held it over his face.

Pallets of wood and straw, covered by grimy blankets, were arranged in rows across the floor, and Malenfant had to step between them to make his way. Maybe half of the pallets were occupied. The eyes that met Malenfant's flickered with only the dullest curiosity.

The invalids all seemed wasted by the disease which had afflicted de Bonneville, to a greater or lesser degree. Patches of skin were burned to blackness, and there were some people with barely any skin left at all. Malenfant saw heads free of hair – even eyelashes and eyebrows were missing as if burned off – and there were limbs swollen to circus-freak proportions, and broken and bleeding mouths and nostrils. There were attendants here, but as far as Malenfant could see they were all Uprights: *Homo Erectus,* reconstructed genetic fossils, tall and naked and golden-furred, moving between the sick and dying. There seemed to be no real medical care, but the Uprights were giving out water and food – some kind of thin soup – and they murmured comfort in their thin, consonant-free voices to the ill.

It was like a field hospital. But there had been no war: and besides there were women and children here.

At last Malenfant found de Bonneville. He lay sprawled on a pallet. He stared up, his face swollen and burned beyond expression. 'Malenfant – is it you? – have you any beer?' He reached up with a hand like a claw.

Malenfant tried to keep from backing away from him. 'I'll bring some. De Bonneville, you got worse. Is this a hospital?'

He made a grisly sound which might have been a laugh. 'Malenfant, this is – ah – a dormitory. For the workers, including myself, who service the yellow-cake.'

'Yellow-cake?'

'The substance which fuels the Engine of Kimera . . .' He coughed, grimacing from the pain of his broken mouth, and shifted his position on his pallet.

'What's wrong with you? Is it contagious?'

'No. You need not fear for yourself, Malenfant.'

'I don't,' Malenfant said.

De Bonneville laughed again. 'Of course you don't. Indeed, nor should you. The illness comes from contact with the yellow-cake itself. When new workers arrive here, they are as healthy as you. Like that child over there. But within weeks, or months – it varies by individual, it seems, and not even the strongest constitution is any protection – the symptoms appear.'

'De Bonneville, why did they send you back here?'

'I have a propensity for offending the Kabaka, Malenfant, most efficiently and with the minimum of delay. So here I am again.'

'You're a prisoner?'

'In a way. The guards ensure that the workers are kept here until such time as the Kimera sickness takes hold of their limbs and complexion. Then one is free to wander about the town without hindrance.' He touched his blackened cheeks; a square centimetre of skin came loose in his fingers, and he looked at this latest horror without shock. 'The stigmata of Kimera's punishment are all too obvious,' he said. 'None will approach a yellow-cake worker, and certainly none will feed or succour him. And so there is no alternative, you see, but to return to the Engine, where at least food and shelter is provided, there to serve out one's remaining fragment of life . . .'

'Who is Kimera?'

'Ah, Kimera!' he said, and he threw back his ravaged head. Kimera, it turned out, was a mythical figure: a giant of Uganda's past, so huge that his feet had left impressions in the rocks. 'He was the great-grandson of Kintu, the founder of Uganda, who came here from the north; and it was Wanpamba, the great-great-grandson of Kimera, who first hollowed out the hill of Rubaga and entombed the soul of Kimera here . . .' And so forth: a lot of poetical, mythical stuff, but little in the way of hard fact. 'You know, they had to reconstruct these old myths from the last encyclopaedias, for the people had forgotten them – but don't let the Kabaka hear you say it . . .' De Bonneville's eyes closed, and he sank back, sighing.

Nemoto, nervous, plucked at Malenfant's sleeve. Her mime was obvious. Time was up; they should go; this was an unhealthy place.

Malenfant didn't see what choice he had. All the way out, Malenfant was aware of de Bonneville's gaze, locked on his back.

Outside the grisly dormitory, Malenfant peered into the deeper blackness of the well. 'Nemoto, *what's down there*?'

'Danger. Death. Malenfant, we must leave.'

'It is the Engine of Kimera, whatever the hell that is. You know, don't you? Or you think you know. Rubaga has the only significant radiation-anomaly signature on Earth . . .'

Her face was as expressionless as her Moon rock buddha's. 'If you want to fry your sorry skin, Malenfant, you can do it by yourself.' She turned and walked off, leaving him with the guard.

The guard looked at him quizzically. Malenfant shrugged, and pointed downwards.

He walked to the ledge's rim – a sheer drop into darkness, no protective rail of any kind – and leaned over. There seemed to be a breeze blowing down from above, rustling over the back of his neck, into the pit itself, as if there was a leak in the world down there. Now, he couldn't figure that out at all. Where was the air going? Was there a tunnel, some kind of big extractor?

The only light came from the flames of rush torches, flickering in that downwards breeze, and Malenfant's impressions built up slowly.

He made out a large heap of ore, crushed to powder, contained within a rough open chamber hollowed out of the stone. Maybe that ore was the yellow-cake de Bonneville had talked about. Long spears of what appeared to be charcoal – like scorched tree-trunks – stuck out of the heap from all sides and above. Water was carried in channels in the walls and pipes of clay, and poured into the heart of the heap. He guessed the heap contained a hundred tonnes of yellow-cake; there were at least forty charred trunks protruding from it.

The chamber was full of people.

There were a lot of tall Uprights, many squat habilines, and some Waganda: men, women and children who limped doggedly through the darkness, intense heat and live steam, serving the heap as if it were some ugly god. They hauled at the charcoal trunks, drawing them from the yellow-cake, or thrusting them deeper inside. Or else they hauled simple wheelbarrows of the yellow-cake powder to and from the heap, continually replenishing it. Their illness was obvious, even from here. Peering down from far above, it was like looking over some grotesque ant-hill, alive with motion.

The heap was intensely hot – Malenfant could feel its heat burning his face – and the water emerged from the base of the heap as steam, which roared away through a further series of pipes. There was a lot of leakage, though, and live steam wreathed the heap's ugly contours.

The principle was obvious. The heap was an energy source. The steam produced by the heap must, by means of simple pumps and other hydraulic devices, power the various gadgets he'd witnessed: Mtesa's ascending throne, the fountains. Maybe the water which passed through the system was itself pumped up from some deeper water table by the motive power of the steam.

There had to be a lot of surplus energy, though.

And now he made out a different figure, emerging from some deeper chamber at the base of the pit. It was a woman. She looked like a cross between a habiline and an Upright: big frame, thick neck, head thrust forward. She was wearing a suit, of some translucent plastic, that enclosed her body, hands and head. She was familiar to him, from a hundred TV shows and school-book reconstructions. She was Neandertal: another of humanity's lost cousins.

Holy shit, he thought.

There was a flash of light from the hidden chamber, from some invisible source.

It was blue, a shade he recognized.

Neandertals, and pressure suits, and electric-blue light. Unreasoning fear stabbed him.

He got out of there as fast as he could.

The next day Malenfant visited de Bonneville again. Malenfant brought him a small bottle of *pombe*; de Bonneville fell on this avidly, jealously hiding it from the other inmates of the ward. Malenfant wanted to ask about the Engine, but de Bonneville had his own tale to tell.

'Listen, Malenfant. Let me tell you how I came to this pass. It started long before you arrived . . .'

De Bonneville told him that a gift had arrived for Mtesa, the emperor, from Lukongeh, king of the neighbouring Ukerewe. There had been five ivory tusks, fine iron wire, six white monkey-skins, a canoe large enough for fifty crew – and Mazuri, an Upright girl, a comely virgin of fourteen, a wife suitable for the Kabaka.

'Mtesa's harem numbers five hundred. Mtesa has the pick of many lands; and many of the harem are, as I can testify, of the most extraordinary beauty. But of them all, Mazuri was the comeliest.'

'I think I saw her in the Palace. Mtesa likes her.'

'She has –' de Bonneville waved his damaged hands in a decayed attempt at sensuality '– she has that *animal* quality of the Uprights. That intensity. When she looks you in the eyes, you see direct into her primeval soul. Do you know what I'm talking about, Malenfant?'

'Yes. But I'm a hundred years old,' Malenfant said wistfully.

'Mazuri was young, impetuous, impatient at her betrothal to Mtesa – a much older man, and lacking the vigour of her own kind . . .'

De Bonneville fell silent, in a diseased reverie.

'Tell me about the Engine.'

'The Waganda say the yellow-cake is suffused with the Breath of Kimera,' de Bonneville said, dismissive. 'It is the Breath which supplies the heat. But a given portion of yellow-cake is eventually exhausted of its Breath, and we must extract and replace the cake, continually.'

'What about the tree-trunks?'

'We must insert and extract the trunks, according to the instructions of –' He quoted a term Malenfant didn't know, evidently a sort of foreman. 'The Breath is invisible and too rapid to have much effect – except on the human body, apparently, which it ravages! The tree-trunks are inserted to slow down the Breath from the heart of the heap – do you see? Then it gets to work on the rest of the yellow-cake. And that is, in turn, encouraged to produce its own Breath in response. It's like a cascade, you see. But the Waganda can control this, by withdrawing their charred trunks; this has the effect of allowing the Breath to speed up, and escape the heap harmlessly . . .'

A cascade, yes, Malenfant thought. A chain reaction.

'And the water? What's that for?'

'The emission of the Breath is associated with great heat – which is the point of the Engine. Water flows through the hill-side, through the Engine. The water is a cooling agent, which carries off this heat before any damage is done to the Engine. And the heat, of course, turns the water to steam, which in turn is harnessed to drive Mtesa's various toy devices and fripperies . . .' Malenfant heard how de Bonneville's voice slowed as he said that, as if some new idea was coming to him.

To Malenfant, it all made sense.

Twentieth century nuclear fission piles had been simple devices. They were just heaps of a radioactive material, such as uranium, into which reaction-controlling moderators, for example carbon rods, were thrust. Technical complexity only came if you cared about human safety: shields, robot devices to control the moderators, a waste extraction process, and so forth. If you *didn't* care about wasting human life, a reactor could be made much more simply.

With a little instruction, a tribe of Neandertals could operate a nuclear reactor. A bunch of children could. *Especially* if you didn't care about safety.

'It's the Breath that makes you ill,' he said.

'Indeed.'

'Why not others? Why not Mtesa himself?'

'The Breath is contained by the hundreds of metres of rock within which the Engine is housed. But, though it is not spoken of, there is much illness among the general population; and there are elaborate taboos about associating too closely with products of the Engine – you shouldn't drink the water which has circulated through the yellow-cake, for instance.'

Malenfant remembered how Nemoto had warned him against inserting his hands in Mtesa's fountains. He felt, now, a renewed itching in his own damaged skin.

Shit, he thought. I must have taken a dose myself.

De Bonneville waved his gnarled hands. 'The Engine is clearly very ancient, Malenfant. The Waganda's legend says it was constructed by an old king, seventeen generations before our own glorious Mtesa. It seems to me the Waganda have learned how to control their crude device, not by proceeding from a body of established knowledge as *we* might have done, but by trial and error over generations – and expensive trial and error at that – expensive in human life, I mean!' But he was tiring, and losing interest. 'Let me tell you of Mazuri . . .'

'You screwed the king's favourite wife. You asshole, de Bonneville.'

'I tried to put her aside, when I left Rubaga to meet you. But when I returned, full of *pombe* and the excitement of the hunt, there she was . . . Ah, Malenfant, those eyes, that skin, that mouth . . .'

He was found out. Mtesa's fury had been incandescent. De Bonneville was expelled from his position in court – dragged, by a rope around his neck, by Mtesa's enthusiastic Lords of the Cord, and subjected to fifty blows with a stick, a punishment severe enough to lame him – and then banished to the lowliest position of Rubaga society: to work in the yellow-cake Engines, buried deep within the hill-side.

De Bonneville grasped Malenfant's arm with his ruined, claw-like hands. 'It was all a trap, Malenfant. One accumulates enemies so easily in such a place as this! And I – I was always impetuous rather than careful . . . I was led into a trap, and I have been destroyed! Seeing you now, a traveller, makes me understand anew how much has been robbed from me by these savages of the future. But –'

'Yes?'

His blue eyes gleamed in his blackened ruin of a face. 'But de Bonneville shall have his revenge, Malenfant. Oh, yes! His determination is sweet and pure . . .'

He confronted Nemoto.

'Nemoto, you know what the Engine is, don't you? It's a nuclear pile. A fucking nuclear pile.'

Nemoto shrugged. 'It's just a heap. Maybe a hundred tonnes of "yellow-cake" – which is a uranium ore – with burnt tree stumps used as graphite moderators. It was a geological accident: yellow-cake seams inside this hollow mountain, and some natural water stream running over the pile, cooling it . . .'

Natural nuclear reactors had formed in various places around the planet, where the geological conditions had been right. What was needed was a concentration of uranium ore, and then some kind of moderator. The function of the moderator was to slow down the neutrons, the heavy particles emitted by decaying uranium atoms. A slowed-down neutron would impact with another atomic nucleus and make *that* decay – and the neutron products of that event would initiate more decays – on and on, in the cascade of collapsing nuclei the physicists called a chain reaction.

Under Rubaga's mountain, the action of water, over billions of years, had washed uranium from the rock and caused it to collect in seams at the bottom of a shallow sea. The uranium had then been overlaid by inert sand, and the rocks compressed and uplifted by tectonic forces, the uranium further concentrated by the slow rusting of surrounding rocks in the air. Thus had been created seams of uranium, great lenticular deposits, two or three metres thick and perhaps ten times as wide, under their feet, right here.

At first there had been no chain reaction. But then water and organic matter, seeping into cracks in the uranium seams, had served as primitive moderators, slowing the neutrons down sufficiently for the reaction process to start.

Nemoto whispered, 'The reaction probably started as a series of scattered fires in concentrations of the uranium ore. Then it spread to less rich areas nearby. It was self-controlling; as the water was boiled by the reaction's heat it would be forced out of the rock – and the reaction would be dampened, until more water seeped back from the surface layers above, and the reaction could begin again.' She smiled thinly. 'And that is what the Neandertal community here discovered. It took them a couple of centuries, but they learned to tinker with the process, inserting burnt wood – graphite – as secondary moderators . . .'

The workers in the pile maintained it with their bare hands. At times the workers had to haul heaps of yellow-cake from one part of the pile to another, or they mixed the yellow-cake, by hand, with other moderator compounds, or they cleared out the coolant-water pipes – the small fingers of children were well adapted for that particular chore. And as well as the regular operation of the pile, they had to cope with accidents, types of which Nemoto listed in the local language: *leakages, spill-outs, crumbles, hot beds, slaps.*

'Why did the Neandertals need to do this?'

'Because of us. *Homo Sapiens*, Malenfant. For a while, after the ice, the Earth was empty. The Gaijin implanted their little pockets of reconstructed pre-humans. But then along *we* came, and it all unravelled as it had before, thirty or forty thousand years ago. You've seen how the locals treat the Uprights, the habilines.'

'Yes.'

'So it was with the Neandertals . . . except *here*. The Neandertals had their uranium, their radioactivity. They laced water supplies. They put tips on their spears . . . It helped keep back the humans, until a smart human leader – a predecessor of Mtesa – came along and struck a deal.'

'So Mtesa supplies human slaves to the Neandertals. To maintain the pile.'

'Essentially. Makes you think, doesn't it, Malenfant? If only the *true* Neandertals, of our own deep past, had discovered such a resource. Perhaps they could have kept us at bay, survived into modern times – I mean, *our* times.'

Malenfant frowned. 'It doesn't sound too stable. A nuclear pile isn't much of a weapon . . . You'd think that Mtesa's soldiers could overwhelm the Neandertals, take what they wanted, drive them out. And the radioactivity – we're all living on top of a raw nuke pile, here. Even those who don't have to go work in that hole in the ground are going to suffer contamination.'

Nemoto grimaced. 'You are not living in Clear Lake now, Malenfant. These people accept things we wouldn't have. The Waganda have built a stable social arrangement around their Engine. They keep their blood-lines reasonably pure by stigmatizing any individual showing signs of mutation or radiation sickness. It's a kind of symbiosis. The Waganda use the Engine's energy. But the Engine maintains itself by poisoning a proportion of the Waganda population. Mostly they use Uprights and habilines anyhow; among the humans, only Mtesa's victims finish up in the Engine.'

Malenfant said, 'Those toys of Mtesa's – the fountains and the Caesar's Palace trick throne – can't absorb more than a few per cent of the pile's energy . . . The rest of it runs that Saddle Point gateway. Doesn't it, Nemoto? And *that* is the true purpose of this place. *This is some huge Gaijin project*.'

'I am no tourist guide, Reid Malenfant. I don't know anything.' She looked away from him. 'Now leave me alone.'

* * *

Malenfant had trouble sleeping. He felt ill, and at times he felt overwhelmed by fear.

He'd glimpsed a Saddle Point gateway, buried deep in this African hill-side. That was where all the power went. And that downward breeze had been air passing through the gateway, a leak in the fabric of the world.

He felt drawn to the gateway, as if by some gravitational field.

I don't want this, he thought. I just wanted to run home. But I brought myself *here*. I chose to come to this place, kept digging until I found *this*, the centre of it all. A way back into the game. Just like Nemoto.

A way to fulfil whatever purpose the Gaijin seemed to have for him.

I can't do it. Not again. I just want to be left alone. I don't *have* to follow this path, to do anything.

But the logic of his life seemed to say otherwise.

Spare me, he thought; and he wished he believed in a god to receive his prayers.

Malenfant was woken, rudely, by a shuddering of his pallet. His eyes snapped open to darkness, and he sucked in hot African air. For a second he thought he was in orbit: *a blow-out in the Shuttle Orbiter, a micrometeorite that had smashed through Number Two Window . . .*

He was alone in his villa, and the grass roof was intact. He pushed off his cover and tried to stand.

The ground shook again, and there was a deep, subterranean groaning, a roar of stressed rock. A quake, then?

Through the glassless windows of the villa, a new light broke. He saw a glow, red-white and formless, which erupted in a gout of fire over the roof-tops of Rubaga. Grass huts ignited as tongues of glowing earth came licking back to ignite the flimsy constructions. He heard screaming, the patter of bare feet running.

That fount of flame came from the heart of the town, Malenfant saw immediately – from the well of Kimera – from the pit of that monstrous Engine.

De Bonneville. It had to be. In some way, he'd carried out his vague threat.

The shuddering subsided, and Malenfant was able to stand. He pulled on his biocomposite coverall and stepped out of the villa.

All of Rubaga's populace appeared to be out in the narrow streets: courtiers, peasants, courtesans and chiefs, all running in terror. The big gates of the capital's surrounding cane fence had been thrown open, and Malenfant could see how the great avenues were already thronged with people, running off into the countryside's green darkness.

Malenfant set off through the capital towards the centre of the plateau. He had to push his way through the panicking hordes of Waganda, who fled past him like wraiths of smoke.

By the time he'd reached the dead heart of the hill-top, even the great grass Palace of Mtesa was alight.

Malenfant hurried into the central plain, away from the scorching huts. He reached the blighted zone with relief; for the first time in many minutes, he could draw a full breath.

The fire of Kimera loomed out of the earth before Malenfant, huge and angry and deadly; and all around the rim of the plain he saw the glow of Rubaga's burning huts. Christ: he was in the middle of a miniature Chernobyl. And it scared the shit out of him to think that there was nobody here, *nobody,* who understood what was going on, nobody at the controls.

He walked on, his feet heavy, his chest and face scorching in the growing heat, his burned hands tingling, and the light of the fire was brilliant before him. He didn't see how he could get any closer. He began to circle the blaze. He stumbled frequently, and his eyes were sore and dry.

I am, he thought, too fucking old for this.

Then he saw what looked like a fallen animal, inert on the ground. Malenfant braved the fire, sheltering his head with his arms, and approached.

It was de Bonneville. He lay face-down in the barren earth of Rubaga. Malenfant could see, from scrabbles in the dirt, that he had walked away from the pit until he could walk no more, then crawled, and at last he had dragged himself by his broken fingertips across the ground.

Malenfant knelt down, and slid his arms beneath the deformed torso. De Bonneville was disconcertingly light, like a child, and Malenfant was able to turn him over, and lay that balloon-like head on his lap.

De Bonneville's blue eyes flickered open. 'Good God. Malenfant. Have you any beer?'

'No. I'm sorry, de Bonneville.'

'You must get away from here. Your life is forfeit, Malenfant, if you confront the Breath of Kimera . . .' His eyes slid closed. 'I did it. *I . . .*'

'The Engine?'

'It was the water,' he said dreamily. 'Once I made up my mind to act, it was simple, Malenfant . . . I just blocked the pipes, where they admit the water to the well . . .'

'You blocked the coolant?'

'All that heat, with nowhere for it to go . . . You know, it took just minutes. I could hear them crying and screaming, as the burning, popping yellow-cake scorched their bodies and feet, even as they thrust their tree-trunks into the heap. It took just minutes, Malenfant . . .'

De Bonneville, limping on his already damaged legs, had escaped the well minutes before the final ignition and explosion.

'And was it worth it?' Malenfant asked. 'You came back from the stars, to do this?'

'Oh, yes,' de Bonneville said, his eyes fluttering closed. 'For he had destroyed me. *Mtesa.* If I die, his empire dies with me . . . And more than that.' De Bonneville tried to lick his lips, but his mouth was a mass of popping sores. '*It was you,* Malenfant. You, a heroic figure returned from the deep past! From an age when humans, we Westerners, strove to do more than simply survive, in a world abandoned to the Gaijin. You and I come from an age where people *did* things, Malenfant. My God, we shaped whole worlds. You reminded me of that. And so I determined to shape mine . . .'

He subsided, and his body grew more limp.

Dawn light spread from the east, and Malenfant saw a cloud of smoke, a huge black thunderhead, lifting up into the sky.

It was you, de Bonneville had said. My fault, he thought. All my fault. I was probably meant to die, out there, among the stars. It should have been that way. Not *this.*

He cradled de Bonneville in the dawn light, until the shuddering breaths had ceased to rack him.

The morning after the explosion, Malenfant was arrested.

Malenfant was hauled by two silent guards to Mtesa's temporary court, in a spacious hut a couple of kilometres from Wanpamba's Tomb, and he was hurled to the dust before the Kabaka.

His trial was brief, efficient, punctuated with much shouting and stabbing of fingers. He wasn't granted a translator. But from the fragments of local language he'd picked up he learned he had been accused of causing the explosion, this great epochal crime.

Nemoto stood silently beside the Kabaka while the comic-opera charade ran its course. She did this, he realized. She framed me.

To his credit, Mtesa seemed sceptical of all this, irritated by the proceedings. He seemed to have taken a liking to Malenfant, and was shrewd enough to perceive this as an obscure dispute between Malenfant and the Katekiro. *Why are you involving me? Can't you sort it out yourself?*

But the verdict was never really in doubt to anyone.

When it was done, the Lords of the Cord came to Malenfant. Rope was looped around his neck, and he was dragged to his feet.

Nemoto walked forward, hunched over, and stood before him. In English, she said, 'You're to be treated leniently, Malenfant. You won't be working the Engine. You're to be cast –'

'Into the pit.' And then he saw it. 'The gateway. You're forcing me to the Saddle Point gateway. That's what this is all about, isn't it?'

'*You saw the light,* Malenfant. If I thought that pressure suit of yours would fit me, I would take it from you. I would walk into the Engine of Kimera and confront the enigma at its heart, following those mysterious others who come and go . . . But I cannot. It is my fate to remain here, amusing the Kabaka, until the ageing treatments fail, and I die.

'I had to do this, Malenfant. I could see your reluctance to go forward – *even though you brought yourself here*, to the centre of things. I could see you could not bring yourself to take the last step.'

'So you pushed me. *Why*, for God's sake? Why are you doing this?'

'Not for the sake of God. For history. Look around you, Malenfant. Look at the huge strangeness of this future Earth. Certainly the arrival of Eeties deflected our history – and those exploding stars in the sky tell of more deflections yet to come. But no human has ever been in control of the great forces that shaped a world, of history and climate and geology; only a handful of us have even witnessed such changes.'

'If none of us can deflect history, you're killing me for nothing.'

'Ah.' She smiled. 'But individual humans *have* changed history, Malenfant – not the way *I* tried to, with plots and schemes and projects – but by walking into the fire, by giving themselves. Do you see? And *that* is your destiny.'

'You're a monster, Nemoto. You play with lives. The right hand of this Stone Age despot is the right place for you.'

She raised a bony wrist and brushed blood-flecked spittle from her chin, seeming not to hear him.

He was overwhelmed with fear and anger. 'Nemoto. Spare me.'

She leaned forward and kissed his cheek; her lips were dry as autumn leaves, and he could smell blood on her breath. 'Goodbye, Malenfant.'

The cords around his neck tightened, and he was hauled away.

The rest of it unfolded with a pitiless logic. As a prisoner, condemned, Malenfant had no choice, no real volition; it was easy to submit to the process, to become detached, let his fear float away.

He was indeed treated with leniency. He was allowed to go back to his hut. He retrieved his EMU, his ancient pressure suit in its sack of rope.

He was taken to the rim of the central desolation.

There was a small party waiting: guards, with two other prisoners, both young women, naked save for loin-cloths, with their hands tied behind their backs. The prisoners returned his stare dully. Malenfant saw they'd both been beaten severely enough to lay open the skin over their spines.

I've come a long way, thought Malenfant, for this: a walk into hell, with two of the damned.

Once more he descended the crude spiral staircase.

Soon they were so deep that the circle of open sky at the top of the shaft was shrunk to a blue disc smaller than a dime, far above him. The only light came from irregularly-placed reed torches. The stairs themselves were crudely cut and too far apart to make the descent easy; soon Malenfant was hot, and his legs ached.

The prisoners' faces shone, taut with fear.

They passed two big exits gouged in the rock wall, one to either side of the cylindrical shaft. The air from these exits was marginally less stale than elsewhere. Perhaps they led to the great avenues from east and west which he'd noticed from outside, tunnels which led into the body of the hill-side itself.

A hundred metres down, water spouted from clay founts, elaborately shaped, mounted on the walls. The water, almost every drop of it, was captured by spiral canals which wound around the shaft, in parallel to the stairway. The founts gushed harder as they descended – water pressure, thought Malenfant – and soon the spiral canals were filled with bubbling, frothing liquid, which took away some of the staleness of the still air of the well. But the founts and channels were severely damaged by fire, cracked and crudely repaired; water leaked continually.

Already he was hot and dizzy; a mark of the dose he'd already taken, maybe. He reached towards a canal to get a handful of water.

But a dark, bony hand shot out of the darkness, pushing him away. It was one of the prisoners, her eyes wide in the gloom.

Malenfant watched the narrow, bleeding shoulders of the prisoner as she descended before him. Here she was, going down into hell, no more than a kid, and yet she'd reached out to keep a foreigner from harm.

Deeper and deeper. There was no trace of natural daylight left now.

They reached a point where the two prisoners were released to a dormitory, hollowed out of the rock, presumably to be put to work later. Before they were pushed inside, they peered down into the pit, with loathing and dread. For here, after all, was the Engine which was to be their executioner.

And Malenfant was going on, deeper. The guards prodded at his back, pushing him forward.

At last the descent became more shallow. Malenfant surmised they were approaching the heart of the hollowed-out mountain. They stopped maybe fifteen metres above the base of the well. From here, Malenfant had to go on alone.

By the light of a smoking torch, with a mime, he asked a favour of the guards. They shrugged, incurious, not unwilling to take a break.

Malenfant pulled his battered old NASA pressure suit from its sack.

He lifted up his Lower Torso Assembly, the bottom half of his EMU, trousers with boots built on, and he squirmed into it. Next he wriggled into the upper torso section. He fixed on his Snoopy flight helmet, and over the top of that he lifted his bubble helmet, starred and scratched with use. He twisted it into place against the seal at his neck.

The guards watched dully.

He looked down at himself. By the light of a different star, Madeleine Meacher had spent time repairing this suit for him. The EMU was still a respectable white, with the Stars and Stripes still proudly emblazoned on his sleeve.

. . . But then the little ritual of donning the suit was over, and events enfolded him in their logic once more.

Was this it? After all his travels, his long life, was he now to die, alone, here?

Somehow he couldn't believe it. He gathered his courage.

Leaving the staring guards behind, he walked further down the crude stairwell, deeper towards the fire. The starring of his battered old bubble helmet made the flames dance and sparkle; it was kind of pretty. His own breath was loud in the confines of the helmet, and he felt hot, oxygen-starved already, although that was probably just imagination. His backpack was inert – no hiss of oxygen, no whir of fans – and it was a heavy mass on his back. But maybe the suit would protect him a little longer.

He'd just keep walking, climbing down these steps in the dark, as long as he could. He didn't see what else he could do.

It didn't seem long, though, before the heat and airlessness got to him, and the world turned grey, and he pitched forward. He got his hands up to protect his helmet, and rolled on his back, like a turtle.

He couldn't get up. Maybe he ought to crawl, like de Bonneville, but he couldn't even seem to manage that.

He was, after all, a hundred years old.

He closed his eyes.

It seemed to him he slept a while. He was kind of surprised to wake up again.

He saw a face above him. A dark, heavy face. Was it de Bonneville? No, de Bonneville was dead.

Thick eye ridges. Deep eyes. An ape's brow, inside some kind of translucent helmet.

He was being carried. Down, down. Even deeper into the mountain of Kimera. There were strong arms under him.

Not human arms.

But then there was a new light. A blue glow.

He smiled. A glow he recognized.

Cradled in inhuman arms, lifted through the gateway, Reid Malenfant welcomed the pain of transition.

There was a flash of electric-blue light.

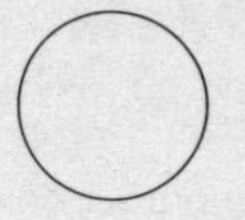

Chapter 27

THE FACE OF KINTU

Long ago, long long ago.

Kintu giant comes down from north.

Nothing.

No earths, no stars, no people. Kintu sad. Kintu lonely. Very lonely. Nothing nothing nothing.

Kintu breathes in. Breathes in what? Breathes in nothing.

Chest swells, big big big. Round. Mouth of Kintu here, Navel of Kintu there. Breathe in, big big big, blow in, all that nothing.

Skin pops, pop pop pop. Worlds. Stars. People. Popping out of skin, pop pop pop. Still breathes in, in in in, big big big.

Here. Now. The Face of Kintu. Here. See how skin pops, pop pop pop, new baby worlds, new life, things to eat. We live where, on Face of Kintu.

The Staff of Kintu. People die, people don't die. Inside the Staff of Kintu. Happy happy happy. Live how long, long time, long long time, forever.

In future, long long time. Kintu throw Staff, long long way. Throw Staff where, to Navel of Kintu. People live on belly of Kintu, long long time, long long way, how happy, happy happy happy.

Everyone else what? Dead.

The transition pain dissipated, like frost evaporating. He felt the hard bulge of the arms which carried him, the iron strength of biceps.

His head was tipped back. He saw the white fleshy underside of a tiny beardless chin. Beyond that, all he could see was black sky. Some kind of wispy high cloud, greenish. A rippling aurora.

His weight had changed. He was light as an infant, as a dried-up twig.

Not Earth, then.

He could be anywhere. Encoded as a stream of bits, he could have been sent a thousand light years from home. And because Saddle Point signals travelled at mere lightspeed, he could be a thousand years away from a return. Even the enigmatic Earth he'd returned to, the Earth of 3265, might be as remote as the Dark Ages from the year of his birth.

Or not.

Now a face loomed over him, as broad and smooth as the Moon, encased in a crude pressure-suit helmet that was not much more than a translucent sack. Obviously hominid. But the face had big heavy eye-ridges, and a huge flat nose that thrust forward, and a low hair-line. Thick black eyebrows, like a Slav, wide dark eyes. Those eye-ridges gave her a perpetually surprised look.

Her. It was a female. Young? The skin looked smooth, but he had no reference.

She smiled down at him. She was, of course, a Neandertal girl.

There was black around the edge of his vision.

He was running out of air. His suit was a non-functioning antique. It was all he had. But now it was going to kill him.

The girl's face creased with obvious concern. She lifted up her hand – now she was holding him with *one arm,* for God's sake – and she started waving her right hand up and down in front of her body. Those thick Russian eyebrows came down, so she looked quizzical.

She was miming, he thought. *Pain?*

'Yes, it hurts.' His radio wasn't working, and she didn't look to have any kind of receiver. She probably couldn't speak English, of course, which would be a problem for him. He was an American, and in his day, Americans hadn't needed to learn other languages. Maybe she could lip-read. 'Help me. I can't breathe.' He kept this up for a few seconds, until her expression dissolved into bafflement.

With big Moonwalk strides she began to carry him forward. Inside his bubble helmet his head rattled around, thumping against the glass.

Now, in swaying glimpses, he could see the landscape.

A plain, broken by fresh-looking craters. The ground was red, but overlaid by streaks of yellow, brown, orange, green, deep black. It looked muddy and crusted, like an old pizza. Much of it was frosted. From beyond the close horizon, he could see a plume of gas that turned blue as it rose, sparkling in the flat light of some distant sun. The plume fell straight back to the ground, like a garden sprinkler.

And there was something in the sky, big and bright. It was a dish of muddy light, down there close to the horizon, a big plateful of cloudy bands, pink and purple and brown. Where the bands met, he could see fine lines of turbulence, swoops and swirls, a crazy water-colour. Maybe it was a moon. But if so it was a hell of a size, thirty or forty times the size of the Moon in Earth's sky.

His lungs were straining at the fouling air. There was a hot stink, of fear and carbon dioxide and condensation. He tried to control himself, but he couldn't help but struggle, feebly.

. . . *Jupiter*. Think, Malenfant. That big 'moon' had to be Jupiter.

And if that was a volcanic plume he'd seen, he was on Io.

He felt a huge, illogical relief, despite the claustrophobic pain. He was still in the solar system, then. Maybe he was going to die here. But at least he wasn't so impossibly far from home. It was an obscure comfort.

But – *Io*, for God's sake. In the year AD 3265, it seemed, there were Neandertals, reconstructed from genetic residue in modern humans, living on Io. Why the hell, he still had to figure.

The blackness closed around his vision, like theatre curtains.

He drifted back to consciousness.

He was in a tent of some kind. It stretched above him, cone-shaped, like a teepee. He couldn't see through the walls. The light came from glow-lamps. Relics of the high-tech past, perhaps.

He was lying there naked. He didn't even have the simple coverall the Bad Hair Day twins had given him in Earth orbit. Feebly he put his hands over his crotch. He'd come a thousand years and travelled tens of light years, but he couldn't shake off that Presbyterian upbringing.

People moved around him. *Neandertals*. In the tent they shucked off their pressure suits, which they just piled up in a corner, and went naked.

He drifted to sleep.

Later, the girl who'd pulled him through the Saddle Point gateway, pulled him through to Io itself, nursed him. Or anyhow she gave him water and some kind of sludgy food, like hot yoghurt, and a thin broth, like very weak chicken soup.

He knew how ill he was.

He'd gotten radiation poisoning at the heart of that radioactive pile. He'd taken punishment in the mucous membranes of his mouth, oesophagus and stomach, where the membrane surfaces were coming off in layers; it was all he could do to eat the yoghurt stuff. He got the squits all the time, twenty-five or thirty times a day; his Neandertal nurse patiently cleaned him up, but he could see there was blood in the liquid mess. His right shin swelled up until it was rigid and painful; the skin was bluish-purple, swollen, shiny and smooth to the touch. He got soft blisters on his backside. He could feel that his body hair was falling out, his eyebrows, his groin, his chest.

He was sensitive to sounds, and if the Neandertals made much noise it set off his diarrhoea. Not that they often did; they made occasional high-pitched grunts, but they seemed to talk mostly with mime, pulling their faces and fluttering their fingers at each other.

He drifted through periods of uneasy sleep. Maybe he was delirious. He supposed he was going to die.

His Neandertal nurse's physique was not huge, but her body gave off an impression of density. Her midsection and chest were large – flat breasts – and the muscles of her forearm looked as thick as Malenfant's thigh muscles. Her aura of strength was palpable; she was much more physical than any human Malenfant had ever met.

But what immediately stood out was her face.

It was outsized, with her eyes too far apart, nose flattened, and features spread too wide, as if the whole face had been pulled wide. Her jaw was thick, but her chin was shallow and sliced back, as if it had been snipped off. Bulging out of her forehead was an immense brow, a bony swelling like a tumour. It pushed down the face beneath it and made the eyes sunken in their huge hard-boned sockets, giving her the effect of a distorted reflection, like an embryo in a jar. A swelling at the back of her head offset the weight of that huge brow, but it tilted her head downward, so that her chin almost rested on her chest, her massive neck snaking forward.

But those eyes were clear and human.

He christened his nurse Valentina, because of her Russian eyebrows: Valentina after Tereshkova, first woman in space, who he met once at an air show in Paris.

Valentina was more human than any ape, and yet she was not human. And it was that closeness-yet-difference which disturbed Malenfant.

He slept, he woke. Days passed, perhaps; he had no way to mark the passage of time.

He got depressed.

He got frightened. He cursed Nemoto for his renewed exile.

He clutched his ruined old spacesuit to his chest, running his aching hands over his mission patch and the Stars and Stripes, faded by harsh Alpha Centauri light. He stared at his fragment of Emma, the only human face here, and wept like a baby.

Valentina tolerated all this.

And, slowly, to his surprise, he started getting better. After a time he was even able to sit up, to feed himself.

Valentina, a dirt-caked bare-assed Neandertal, was curing him of radiation poisoning. He couldn't figure it, grateful as he was for the phenomenon. Maybe there was some kind of nanomachinery at work here, repairing the damage he had suffered at the cellular, even molecular level. He'd already seen evidence of how the Earth was suffused by ancient machinery from beyond the Saddle Points, from the stars.

Or maybe it was just the soup.

Soon Malenfant was able to walk, stiffly.

Most of the Neandertals ignored him. They stepped over and around him, as if they couldn't even see him.

For his part, he watched the Neandertals, amazed.

He counted around thirty people crammed into this teepee. There were adults, frail old people, children all the way down to babies in arms. But, he sensed, it would take a long time to get to know them so well that he could distinguish all the individuals. He was the archetype of the foreigner abroad, to whom everybody looked alike.

The women seemed as strong as the men. Even the children, muscled like Olympic shot-putters, joined in the chores. They used their teeth and powerful jaws, together with their stone tools, to cut meat and scrape hides – meat he presumed must have been hauled through from Earth, through the Saddle Point gateway he'd followed himself. They would bake some of the meat in hearths, if you could call them that: just shallow pits scraped in the ground, lined with fire-heated rocks and covered by soil. But the softer meat was given to the infants – and to Malenfant, incidentally, by Valentina. The adults took their meat mostly uncooked; those big jaws would chomp away at the tough flesh, grinding and tearing, muscles working, making it swallowable.

There was one old guy who showed some curiosity in Malenfant, a geezer who walked with a heavy limp, hunched over so that his belly drooped down over his shrivelled-up penis. Malenfant decided to call him Esau. The Book of Genesis, if he remembered right: *Behold, Esau my brother is a hairy man, and I am a smooth man.*

Malenfant looked into Esau's eyes, and wondered what he was thinking. He wondered *how* he was thinking.

This is my cousin, but far enough removed he represents an alien species, an alien consciousness. The first thing my remote ancestors did, stumbling out of Africa, was to close-encounter the alien, these

Eeties of the deep past: the true first contact. And when the last of the Neandertals lay dying, in some rocky fastness in France or Spain or China, there must have been a *last* contact: the last we'd have for thirty thousand years, until the Gaijin showed up in the asteroid belt.

Hell of a thing, to be alone all that time.

The Neandertals had a portable Saddle Point gateway. When they set it up and used it, Malenfant goggled.

It was a big blue hoop maybe three metres high. They were able to step through it, with the characteristic blue flash, thus disappearing from Io; later they would reappear with sacks of material, much of it rock and meat and metal canisters, maybe containing oxygen. This must be their link to Earth, to the Kimera mine – the way he had been brought here.

He toyed with the idea of going back through, trying to get back to Earth. Escape. But it would only lead him to the Kimera Engine, which would kill him; or if he evaded that, back into the clutches of Mtesa.

Maybe that was a last resort. For now he was stuck here.

What did Malenfant know about Neandertals? Diddley squat. But he did remember they weren't supposed to have speech. Their palates weren't formed correctly, or some such. He'd seen them miming, and they were clearly smart. But speech, so went the theories he remembered, had been the key advantage enjoyed by *Homo Sap*. So here he was, the speaking man in the country of the dumb.

Maybe Reid Malenfant could teach Neandertals to talk. Maybe he could civilize them. He was fired by sudden enthusiasm.

He pointed to Esau. 'You.' At himself. 'Me. You. Say it. You, you, you. Me. Malenfant. My name. Mal-en-fant. You try.'

Esau studied Malenfant for a while, then slapped him, hard. It knocked him back onto the floor.

Malenfant clambered upright. His cheek stung like hell; Esau was *strong*.

Esau rattled through gestures: pointing to him, two fingers to his own forehead, then a fist to Malenfant's forehead. He didn't seem angry: more like he was trying to teach Malenfant something. *Point. Fist to head. Point. Fist.*

'Oh.' Malenfant pointed to himself, then made the fist sign. 'I get it. This is the name you're giving me. A sign word.'

Esau slapped him again. There was no malice, but again he was knocked over.

When Malenfant got up this time, he made the signs, point, fist, without speaking.

So it went. If he spoke more than a couple of syllables, Esau would slap him.

His vocabulary of signs started to grow: ten words, a dozen, two dozen.

He observed mothers with children. They got the slaps too, if they made too much noise. He started to interpret the complex rattle of fingers and gestures as the adults communicated with each other, fluent and urgent. He'd pick up maybe one sign in a hundred.

So much for the speaking man in the country of the dumb. He was like a child to these people.

It was a long time before he found out that the fist-to-head sign, his name, meant *Stupid*.

One day, when he woke up, everyone was clambering into their translucent pressure suits: men, women, children, even infants in little sack-like papooses. A couple of the adults were working at the teepee, pulling at the poles which held it up, taking up the groundsheet.

It was, it seemed, time to move on.

Holding his bubble helmet in front of his genitals, Malenfant cowered against the wall of the collapsing teepee, naked, scared, as the smooth dismantling operation continued around him. Malenfant had no pressure suit: only the NASA antique he'd worn to come here in the first place. What if the Neandertals thought it was still functional? If he stepped out on the surface of Io, the suit would kill him, in fifteen minutes.

Valentina came up to him. She was in her suit already, with the soft helmet closed over. She was holding out another suit; it looked like a flayed skin.

He took it gratefully. She showed him how to step inside it, how to seal up the seams with a fingernail. It was too short and wide for him, but it seemed to stretch.

It *stank*: of urine, faeces, an ancient, milk-like smell. It smelled like Esau, like an old Neandertal geezer.

Somebody had died in this suit.

When he realized that he almost lost his breakfast, and tried to pull the suit off his flesh. But Valentina slapped him, harder than she'd done for a long time. There was no mistaking the commands in her peremptory signs. *Put it on. Now.*

This, he thought, is not the Manned Spaceflight Operations Building, Cape Canaveral. Things are different here. Accept it, if you want to keep breathing.

He pulled on the suit and sealed it up. Then he stood there trying not to throw up inside the suit's claustrophobic stink, as the Neandertals dismantled their camp, and the light of Jupiter was revealed.

Morning on Io:

Auroras flapped overhead, huge writhing sheets of light.

The sun was a shrunken disc, low down, brighter than any star in the sky. It cast long, point-source shadows over the burnt-pizza terrain. In the sky Jupiter hung above the horizon, just where it had before, a fat pink stripy-painted football. But now the phase was different; Jupiter was a crescent, the terminator blurred by layers of atmosphere, and the dark side was a chunk out of the starry background, a slab of night sparking with the crackles of electrical storms bigger than Earth, like giant flashbulbs exploding inside pink clouds.

In a red-green auroral glow, the Neandertals moved about, packing up their teepee and other gear, loading it all onto big sled-like vehicles, signing to each other busily. Malenfant picked up his only possession, the remnant of his NASA suit, and bundled it up on the back of a sled.

When they were loaded, the adult Neandertals started strapping themselves into traces at the front of the sled, simple harnesses made of the ubiquitous translucent plastic. Soon everybody was saddled up except the smallest children, who would ride on the top of the loaded sleds.

Nobody told Malenfant what to do. He looked for Valentina, and made sure he got into a slot alongside her. She helped him fit a harness around his body; it tightened with simple buckles.

And then they started hauling.

The Neandertals just leaned into the traces, like so many squat pack horses. And, by the light of Jupiter, they began to drag the sleds across the crusty Io surface. It turned out that Malenfant's sled was a little harder to move than the others, and his team had to strain harder, snapping signs at each other, until the runners came free of the clinging rock, with a jerk.

Valentina's gait, when walking, was – different. She seemed to lean forward as if her centre of gravity was somewhere over her hip joints, instead of further back like Malenfant's. And when she walked her whole weight seemed to pound down, with every stride, on her hips. It was clumsy, almost ape-like, the least human of her features, as far as Malenfant could see.

Valentina wasn't built for walking long distances, like Malenfant was. Maybe the Neandertals had evolved to be sedentary.

Malenfant did his best to pull with the rest. It wasn't clear to him why he was being kept alive, except as some vaguely altruistic impulse of Valentina's. But he sure wanted to be seen to be working for his supper. So he added his feeble *Homo Sap* strength to the Neandertals'.

Thus, hominids from Earth toiled across the face of Io.

The ground was mostly just rock: silicates, big lumps of it under his feet, peppered by bubbles. It was basalt, volcanic rock pumped out of Io's interior. Sulphur lay in great yellow sheets over the rock, crunching under his feet. Io was a rocky world, not an ice ball like most of the other outer-system moons; sized midway between Earth's Moon and Mars, Io was a terrestrial planet, lost out here in Jupiter orbit.

Jupiter changed constantly, a compelling, awesome sight.

Io was, he recalled, tidally locked to its giant parent; it kept the same face to Jupiter the whole time. But the moon skated around Jupiter's waist every forty-two hours, and so the gas giant went through its whole cycle of phases in less than two days. And Jupiter, meanwhile, rotated on its own axis every ten hours or so. He didn't have to watch that huge face for long to see the cloud decks turning, those turbulent bands and chains of little white globules chasing each other around the stripy bands. But there was no Big Red Spot, he was disappointed to find; evidently that centuries-long storm had blown itself out some time in the millennium he'd been away.

Jupiter had a powerful magnetosphere, a radiation belt of electrons and ions locked to the giant planet, within which Io circled. Jupiter's fast rotation made that magnetosphere whip over Io like an invisible storm. That was the cause of the huge auroras which flapped constantly over his head, energetic particles battering at the thin air of this forsaken moon, ripping away a tonne of atmospheric material every second. Malenfant shivered, naked inside his old man's suit, as he thought of that thin, fast sleet of energetic particles slamming down from the sky, pounding at his flesh.

But the Neandertals weren't concerned. They pulled for hours, and the tracks of the three sleds arrowed across the flat landscape, straight towards Jupiter. Malenfant – a hundred years old and still recovering from radiation exposure – could do little but lean into the traces and let the rest carry him along.

He'd built up an impression that the Neandertals worked hard. They used their big gorilla bodies where *Homo Sap* would have used tools. Their bodies were under intense physical stress, the whole time. Malenfant observed that Esau's body, for example, bore a lot of old injuries, scars and badly set bones. It was as if they climbed a mountain or ran a marathon every day of their lives.

But the Neandertals accepted this, an occupational hazard.

The compensation was the very physical nature of their lives. They lived immersed in their world. They were vigorous, intensely *alive*. By comparison Malenfant, as the only available sample of the species *Homo Sap*, felt weak, vague, as if he was blundering about in a mist. He found he envied them.

The Neandertals sang as they hauled – sign-sang, that is. It was a song about the Face of Kintu. Kintu was one of the few words they vocalized, and it was, Malenfant recalled, the name of a Ugandan god, the grandfather of Kimera. The song was about Kintu blowing himself up with breath until stars and worlds popped out over his body, like volcanoes on Io. Kintu was God and the universe for the Neandertals, and the Face of Kintu – it took him a while to realize – was their name for Io itself.

The signing was functional for the Neandertals, for their magic suits had no radios. But it was more than that. It was beautiful when you got to follow it a little, a mix of dance and speech.

He had to be shown how to use his magic suit's sanitary facilities. Basically the trick was just to let go. The suit's surface absorbed the waste, liquid and solid; it simply disappeared into that translucent wall, as if dissolving. Most of it anyhow. On the move, Malenfant had no chance to open his magic suit, this shell he had to share with the stink of a dead old man, and now of his own waste. The Neandertals clearly weren't hung up on personal hygiene. After a couple of days, however, Malenfant was longing for a shower.

After a time, snow fell around the Neandertals, fine little blue crystals that settled over Malenfant's head and shoulders, crisping the basaltic ground.

Valentina nudged him, and pointed. Over the horizon, a geyser was erupting. It was the source of the snow.

The sparkling plume was venting into space, tens of kilometres high. The plume was blue, sulphur dioxide. At the top of the plume the ice glittered brightly: ionized by Jupiter's magnetic winds, the charged molecular fragments shimmered with energy, a miniature aurora. At the base of the plume lava was flowing. Perhaps it was liquid sulphur. As it emerged it flowed stickily, slowly, like molasses, but as it cooled it became runnier, until it pooled down the shallow slopes of the vent, like machine oil.

A volcanic plume, glowing in the dark. It looked like a giant, twisted fluorescent tube: exotic, strange, spectacular. His heart lifted, the way it had when he first beheld Alpha Centauri. He might not understand everything he saw. But, he felt now, it was *worth* coming out here – worth exploring, worth suffering all the incomprehensible shit and endless culture shocks and even getting slapped around by Neandertals – worth it for sights like this.

The march was diverted to skirt the plume's caldera.

Soon the party started to stray into an area where a kind of frost lay over the ground, thick and green-blue, probably sulphur dioxide. The ground started to get significantly colder under Malenfant, and he was shivering.

The party moved away from the frost, seeking warmer ground.

They were walking over hot spots, he realized. But the hot spots must shift. Io, plagued by volcanism, squeezed like a rubber ball in a fist by Jupiter's tidal pumping, was resurfaced by lava flows all the time.

So the Neandertals had to move on, wandering over Io, in search of warmth from the ground.

It was one hell of a lifestyle. But they seemed to be happy.

About twice every Io day the caravan stopped.

The Neandertals didn't always set up camp. They would unload scuffed and scarred pieces of equipment, boxes the size of refrigerators or washing machines. They plugged their magic suits into these, at hip and mouth, for a couple of hours at a time. The mouth socket supplied food, edible mush that tasted of nothing.

Malenfant didn't know how his magic suit kept him supplied with oxygen; he wasn't carrying a tank. The suit must somehow break down the sulphur dioxide air, and scrub out carbon dioxide from his lungs. Maybe the hip socket extracted stored waste, carbon dioxide and urine and faecal matter, for recycling. Anyhow the boxes seemed to recharge the magic suits, making them good for another ten or twelve hours.

The suits just worked, without any fuss. But the Neandertals only had a finite number of magic suits, and seemed to have no way of manufacturing more. If some sad old geezer hadn't died, there would have been no magic suit for Malenfant. What then? Would they have abandoned him? Well, he hadn't been invited here.

He had no idea how old all this equipment was. It was clear to him somebody had set up this Neandertal community on Io. *Somebody.* The Gaijin, of course. Who else?

He had yet to figure out their purpose, however.

Every time the Neandertals stopped they checked over the Staff of Kintu.

This was a metallic rod, about the size of a relay baton. It seemed to be their most precious artefact. It was just a pipe a half-metre long, of a metal that looked like aluminium, and it seemed light. Sitting in Io frost, the adults would pass the Staff from hand to gloved hand, checking its weight, fondling it, signing over it. The songs they sang, about the breath of Kintu, concerned the Staff. Maybe it was some kind of religious totem. But it was too easy to assume that anything you didn't understand must have religious significance. Maybe there was more to it than that.

Malenfant envied them their community. Ignored even by the children, he felt shut out, lonely. He felt eager to learn to talk.

Malenfant observed signs, copied them, and repeated them to Valentina.

At first he had been able to grasp only simple concrete nouns, straightforward adjectives: a hand raised to the mouth for 'food', for instance, or a rubbed stomach for 'hungry'. But, more slowly, he learned to recognize representations of more abstract thoughts. Two forefingers brought together harmoniously seemed to mean 'same' or 'like'; two pointing fingers stabbing each other was 'argument' or 'fight'. There seemed to be a significance in the hand-shapes, their position relative to the body, and accompanying non-manual features like body language, posture and facial expression. And there was a grammar, it seemed, in the order of the signs. Get any one of the elements wrong and the sign made no sense, or the wrong sense.

It seemed to him that several signs could be transmitted at once, using fragments of multiple words. The Neandertals were not constrained to speak linearly, a word at a time, as he was. They could send across whole chunks of information simultaneously, at a much higher bit rate than humans. And, it occurred to him, these new reconstructed Neandertals must have devised their rich, complex language from scratch, in just a few generations. After all, there could be no way of retrieving the lost language of their genetic predecessors, the true Neandertals.

It was a wonderful, rich mode of communication.

He tried to avoid getting slapped. But he was punished if he got the signs too badly wrong.

'You don't know your own strength. I'm an old man, damn it!'

Slap.

When the Neandertals lay down to sleep, out in the open, they did it in their magic suits, out there on the bare surface of Io.

He picked out the constellations – and the pale stripe of another comet, a huge one, its double tail sprawled over the sky. And in the direction of Orion there was something new: bright flares, like distant explosions, scattered over a shield-shaped patch of sky. It was a silent, unending firework show: as if there was a battle going on, out there at the fringe of the solar system, a defensive fight against some besieging invader.

War in the Oort cloud, perhaps. Were the Gaijin battling Nemoto's star-cracking aliens out there, on the rim of the system, defending Sol? If so, why? Surely the Gaijin's motivation had little to do with humanity. If they fought, it was to protect their own interests, their projects.

And, of course, if there really was a comet-scrambling war going on in the Oort cloud, it had one dread implication: that the Crackers were no longer out there, at Procyon or Sirius – but *here*.

Sleep came with difficulty under such a crowded, dangerous sky. In the end he burrowed under his bulky NASA pressure suit, seeking darkness.

After maybe a week, to Malenfant's intense relief, they set up camp once more. It was at a site that had evidently been used before: a rough circle of kicked-up soil, scarred by hearths.

Inside the teepee the Neandertals immediately stripped off. After a week locked into the suits the stink of their bodies almost knocked Malenfant out.

There was a great spontaneous festival of the body. The kids wrestled, the adults coupled. Malenfant saw one girl pursuing an older man – literally pursuing him around the cave, her vulva visibly swollen and bright red, until she'd pinned him down and climbed on top of him. Then they slept together, in great heaps of stinking, hairy flesh. There was no lookout; presumably there were no predators on Io, no enemies.

Malenfant hunkered in a corner, generally ignored, though Valentina and Esau brought him food.

Sometimes – when the light was low, when he caught a woman or child out of the corner of his eye – he thought of them as like himself, like people. But they weren't people. No better or worse than humans. Just different. A different form of consciousness.

It seemed to him that the Neandertals lived closer to the world than he did. That intense physicality was the key. Their consciousness was dispersed at the periphery of their beings, in their bodies and the things and people that occupied their world. When two of them sat together – signing, or working, in peaceable silence – they seemed to move as one, in a slow clumsy choreography, as if their blurred identities had merged into one, in the ultimate intimacy. Malenfant felt he could see the flow of their consciousness like deep streams, untroubled by the turbulence and reflectiveness of his own nature.

Every day was like the first day of their lives, and a vivid delight.

Malenfant wondered how it was possible for such people as these – intelligent, complex, vibrant – to have become extinct.

Extinct: a brutal, uncompromising word. Extinction made death even more of a hard cold wall, because it was the death of the species. It no longer mattered, truthfully, how sophisticated the Neandertals' sign language had been, whether they had been capable of true human-like speech, how rich was their deep-embedded consciousness. Because it was all gone.

The Neandertals had been brought back for this short Indian summer to serve the Gaijin's purposes. But this had not cheated the extinction, because these Neandertals were *not* those who had gone before; they had no memory of their forebears, no continuity. The extinction of the Neandertals, in the deep past of Earth, had buried hope and memory, disconnected the past from the future.

And now, Malenfant feared, the time was drawing close for an extinction event on a still more massive scale, extinction across multiple star systems, so complete that not even bones and tools would be left behind for some future archaeologist to ponder.

Valentina woke him with a kick. She beckoned him, a universal gesture, and handed him his suit.

He got dressed groggily and followed her out of the teepee.

Out on the surface, he relieved himself, and looked around. Io was in eclipse right now, so that the pinpoint sun was hidden by Jupiter. The ground was darkened by the giant planet's shadow, illumined only by starlight, and by an auroral glow from Jupiter, which was otherwise a hole in the sky.

As the warm fluid trickled uncomfortably down his leg, he stumbled after Valentina, who had already set off across the crusty plain.

There were five Neandertals in the party, plus Malenfant. They were all carrying bags of tools. The Neandertals moved at a loping half-jog that Malenfant found almost impossible to match, despite the gravity.

They kept this up for an hour, maybe more. Then they stopped, abruptly. Malenfant leaned forward and propped himself up against his knees, wheezing.

There was something here. A line on the ground, shining silver in the starlight. It arrowed straight for the swollen face of Jupiter.

Malenfant recognized the texture. It was the same material he'd seen trailing from the roots of Trees, in orbit: material that had been found on the surface of Venus.

It was superconductor cable.

The Neandertals, signing busily, pressed a gadget to the cable. Malenfant couldn't see what they were doing. Maybe this was some kind of diagnostic tool. After a couple of minutes, they straightened up and moved on.

As they trotted, the eclipse was finishing. The sun started to poke out from behind Jupiter's limb, a shrunken disc that rose up through layers of cloud; orange-yellow light fled through the churning cloud decks, casting shadows longer than Earth's diameter.

The dawn light caught Io's flux tube. It was like a vast, wispy tornado reaching up over his head. The flux tube was a misty flow of charged particles hurled up from Io's endless volcanoes sweeping in elegant magnetic-field curves into the face of the giant planet. And where the tube hit Jupiter's upper atmosphere, hundreds of kilometres above the planet's cloud decks, there was a continuing explosion: gases made hotter than the surface of the sun, dragged across the face of the giant planet at orbital speed, patches of rippling aurora hundreds of kilometres across.

Io, a planet-sized body shoving its way through Jupiter's magnetosphere, was like a giant electrical generator. There was a potential difference of hundreds of thousands of volts across the moon's diameter, currents of millions of amps flowing through the ionosphere.

Standing here, peering up into the flux tube itself, the physical sense of energy was immense; Malenfant wanted to quail, to protect himself from the sleet of high-energy particles which must be gushing down from the sky. But he stood straight, facing this godlike play of energy. Not in front of the Neandertals, he told himself.

Soon they arrived at a place where the cable was buried by a flow of sulphurous lava, now frozen solid. After a flurry of signs, the Neandertals unpacked simple shovels and picks and began to hack away at the lava, exposing the cable.

Malenfant longed to rest. His legs seized up in agonizing cramps; the muscles felt like boulders. But, he felt, he had to earn his corn. He rubbed his legs and joined the others. He used a pick on the lava, and helped haul away the debris.

He couldn't believe this was the only length of superconductor on Io. He imagined the whole damn moon being swathed by a net of the stuff, wrapping the shifting surface like lines of longitude. Perhaps it had been mined from Venus, scavenged from that ancient, failed project, brought here for some new purpose of the Gaijin.

The Neandertals' job must be to maintain the superconductor network, to dig it out. Otherwise, such was the resurfacing rate on this ferocious little moon, the net would surely be buried in a couple of centuries or so. The work would be haphazard, as the Neandertals could travel only where the volcanic hot spots allowed them. But, given enough time, they could cover the whole moon.

It was a smart arrangement, he thought. It gave the Neandertals a world of their own, safe from the predations of *Homo Sap*. And it gave the builders of this net – presumably the Gaijin – a cheap and reliable source of maintenance labour.

Neandertals were patient, and dogged. On Earth, they had persisted with a technology that suited them, all but unchanged, for sixty thousand years. They might already have been here, on Io, for centuries. With Neandertals, the Gaijin had gotten a labour pool as smart as humans, not likely to breed themselves over their resource limits here, and lacking any of the angst and hassle that came with your typical *Homo Sap* workforce.

Smart deal, for the Gaijin.

All he had to do now was figure out the purpose of the net itself: this immense Gaijin project, evidently intent on tapping the huge natural energy flows of Io. What were they making here?

Without a word to Malenfant the Neandertals jogged off again, along the cable towards Jupiter.

Malenfant, wheezing, followed.

When they got back to the teepee, they found Esau had died.

Valentina was inordinately distressed. She hunkered down in a corner of the tent, her huge body heaving with sobs. Evidently she had had some close relation to Esau; perhaps he was her father, or brother.

Nobody seemed moved to comfort her.

Malenfant squatted down opposite her. He cupped her chinless jaw in his hand, and tried to raise up her huge head.

At first Valentina stayed hunched over. Then – hesitantly, clumsily, without looking at him – she lifted her huge hand, and stroked the back of his head.

She looked up in surprise. Her hard, strong fingers found a bony protrusion. It was called an occipital bun, Malenfant knew, a relic of his distant French ancestry. She grabbed his hand and pulled it to the back of her own scalp. There was a similar knotty bulge there, under her long black hair. Here was one place, anyhow, where they were similar. Maybe his own occipital bun was some relic of Neandertal ancestry, a ghost trace of some inter-species romance buried millennia in the past.

Valentina's human eyes, buried under that ridge of bone, stared out at him with renewed curiosity. Her breasts were flat, her waist solid, her build as bulky as a man's. And her face thrust forward with its great projecting nose, her puffed-up cheekbones, her long chinless jaw. But she wasn't ugly to him. She was even beautiful.

The moment stretched. This close to her, this still, Malenfant was uncomfortably aware of a tightness in his groin.

Damn those Bad Hair Day twins. He hadn't wanted any of this complication.

He tried to imagine Valentina behaving provocatively: those eyes coyly retreating, perhaps, tilting her chin, glancing over her shoulder, parting her mouth, signals common to women of his own species the world over, in his day.

But that wasn't the way Neandertal women behaved. They were *not* coy, he thought.

It may be humans and Neandertals couldn't interbreed anyhow. And for sure, a few hundred millennia of separate evolution had given them a different set of come-on signals. He began to understand how it might have been back in the deep past: how two equally gifted, resourceful, communicative, curious, emotionally rich human species could have been crammed together into one small space – and yet be as mindless of each other as two types of birds in his old back yard. It was chilling, epochally sad.

He thought of Valentina's massive hand grabbing his balls, and what was left of his erection drained away.

The Neandertals held a ceremony.

They pulled back the groundsheet of the teepee, to reveal a brick-red ground. The teepee filled up with a pungent, bleach-like stink: sulphur dioxide.

Briskly the Neandertals dug out a grave. They used their strong bare hands, working together efficiently and co-operatively. A metre or so down they started hauling out dirt that was stained a more vivid orange and blue.

Malenfant inspected it curiously: this was, after all, the soil of Io. The dirt looked just like crumbled-up rock, but it was laced with orange, yellow and green: sulphur compounds, he supposed, suffused through the rock. There were a few grains of native sulphur, crumbling yellow crystals.

The deeper dirt looked as if it was polluted by lichen.

Some of this was colourless, a dull grey, and some of it was green and purple. Malenfant had never been a biologist, but he knew there were types of bacteria on Earth that flourished in environments like this: acidic, sulphur-rich, oxygen free, like the volcanic vents on Earth. Maybe there was actually some photosynthesis going on here. Or maybe it was based on some more exotic kind of chemistry. There could be underground reservoirs where some kind of plants stored energy by binding up sulphur dioxide into a less stable compound, like sulphur trioxide; and maybe there were even simple animals which breathed that in, burning elemental sulphur, for energy . . .

Scientifically, he supposed, it was interesting. But he was never going to know. And he wasn't here for the science, any more than the Neandertals.

And anyhow, Malenfant, life in the universe is commonplace. And so, it seems, is death.

When the grave was dug, they lowered the body of Esau into it. Valentina got down there with him, and curled him up into a kind of foetus shape. The girl surrounded the old man with a handful of artefacts, maybe stuff that had been important to him: a flute, for instance, carved out of what looked like a femur.

And Valentina tucked the totem rod, the Staff of Kintu, into Esau's dead hand.

After that Valentina stayed in the grave with the corpse a long, long time. There was a lot of signing, back and forth; Malenfant couldn't follow many words, but he could see a rhythmic flow to the signs, as they washed around the grave. They were singing, he suspected.

When at last Valentina clambered out, Malenfant felt his own morbid mood start to lift. The Neandertals started to throw Io dirt back into the grave.

Then – just before the grave was closed over, Esau turned his shrunken head, lifted a stick-like arm.

Opened gummy eyes.

The Neandertals kept right on kicking in Io dirt.

... *But he was still alive.* Malenfant froze, with no idea what to say or do.

Stick to your own business, Malenfant. Be grateful they didn't do it to you.

After that, he found it difficult to sleep. He kept hearing scrabbling, scratching at the ground beneath him.

He was startled awake.

There was a bright electric-blue glow, coming from under the groundsheet, leaking into the teepee's conical space. A glow, coming from the old geezer's grave.

Malenfant had seen that glow before: a thousand astronomical units from Earth, and by the light of other suns, and in the heart of an African mountain, and even here, on Io. It was the glow of Saddle Point gateway technology.

He tried to ask Valentina, the others. But he didn't have the words, and they slapped him away.

A while after that – it might have been a couple of days – the Neandertals lifted the sheet and started to dig out the grave.

To Malenfant's relief, the stink wasn't too bad, and masked by the sulphur dioxide. Maybe the wrong bacteria in the soil, he wondered.

Valentina reached down into the grave and pulled out the metal Staff. She showed no signs of the distress she had exhibited before.

The Neandertals, with little fuss or ceremony, started to refill the grave.

Malenfant got close enough to look inside the grave. *It was empty.* He felt his skin prickle, a kid at Halloween.

He tried to get a look at the Staff. Maybe it was the cause of that electric-blue Saddle Point glow, the disappearance of the corpse. But the girl hid it away.

A party set out along the cables once more, Valentina and Malenfant included. Malenfant kept to himself, ignoring the fantastic scenery, even ignoring the aches of his own rebuilt body.

His head seemed to be starting to work again, if reluctantly. And slowly, step by step, he was figuring out the set-up here.

This arrangement with the Gaijin wasn't all one way. There was a reward for the Neandertals, it seemed, beyond the gift of this remote moon.

He thought about the electric-blue Saddle Point flash that came out of old Esau's grave. Saddle Point teleport gateways worked by destroying a body so as to record its quantum-mechanical structure. Every passage into a gateway was like a miniature death anyhow. Maybe the Staff of Kintu, that little metal artefact, stored some kind of recorded pattern, from the dying old geezer.

Maybe Esau – and perhaps all the Neandertals' ancestors, stretching back centuries – were still, in a sense, *alive*, their Saddle Point signals stored in the Staff. No wonder the Neandertals took such care of the artefact. Maybe that was their reward, to live on in the Staff, until –

Until what?

Until, he thought, they had gathered enough energy, with the huge engines which encased Io. Until Kintu was ready to throw his Staff, all the way to his Navel. Just like in the songs.

He grinned; he had it. That Staff, rattling around in some Neandertal backpack, was no totem. It was a fucking *spaceship*.

And *that* was why they were gathering all this energy, from the natural dynamo that was Io.

Malenfant, excited, grabbed Valentina's arm. 'Listen to me.'

She lifted a hand to slap him.

He backed off and tried to sign. *Wait. Tell me, you tell me. Staff of Kintu, Navel. You go Navel, in Staff. Navel what Navel, what what what.* 'Oh, damn it. What are the Gaijin making here? Antimatter? What is the Navel? Is that where the Gaijin are heading?' She slapped him, knocking him back, but he kept going. *Navel.* 'Kintu has belly, belly, Navel . . . I'm right, aren't I?' *Speak true know true.* 'I –'

She prepared to slap him again.

Beneath his feet the ground felt suddenly hot. It was like standing on a griddle. He backed away, instinctively, until he reached a place where the gritty dirt was cooler.

Valentina hadn't moved. She was looking down, as if baffled. The ground was starting to darken, its shade deepening down from the ubiquitous red. Blue gas erupted around Valentina's feet, like a stage effect.

It was a volcanic plume, opening up right under Valentina.

When the ground started to crumble, he didn't even think about it. He just lunged forwards, fists outstretched. It seemed to take an age to arc through Io's feeble gravity.

He hit her on her shoulders as hard as he could. Despite her greater mass and low centre of gravity, she toppled backwards, and fell away from the vent towards harder ground. She was safe.

Malenfant, on the other hand, was helpless.

He was falling in desperate low-gravity slow-motion, spread-eagled, right down into the centre of the vent, which had opened up into a bubbling pit of dark molten sulphur. He could feel the skin of his chest and face blistering, bubbling like the sulphurous ground. Evidently his magic suit wasn't going to protect him from this one.

He laughed. So it ends here. At least he'd gotten to know the answer. Some of it, anyhow.

There were worse deaths.

The sulphur bubbled up over him, and the pain was overwhelming.

But there was a strong hand at his neck –

After that, only fragments:

Lying flat. No feeling anywhere.

Stars overhead. Vision bouncing. One eye still working? Being carried?

Walls around him, lifting up, a circle of thick-browed faces.

. . . Oh. A grave. *He* was the old geezer now. He tried to laugh, but nothing seemed to be working.

A rain of blackness over him. Dirt. It spattered on his chest, his face. Pain stung where it hit exposed flesh. There were hands working above him, big powerful hands like spades, scooping up dirt to throw over him. Valentina's hands, others.

The dirt landed in his eyes, his mouth. It tasted of bleach.

I'm alive. They're burying me. I'm alive!

He tried to cry out, but his throat was clogged by dirt. He tried to rise, but his limbs had no strength, as if he was swaddled up in bandages.

The dirt rained on his face, a black sulphurous hail. He couldn't even move.

There was something in the corner of his vision. A metallic glint.

A flash of electric-blue light.

Chapter 28

PEOPLE CAME FROM EARTH

A little before Dawn, Xenia Makarova stepped out of her house into silvery light. The air frosted white from her nose, and the deep Moon chill cut through papery flesh to her spindly bones.

The silver-grey light came from Earth and Mirror in the sky: twin spheres, the one milky cloud, the other a hard image of the sun. But the light was still dim enough to allow her to see the changed, colonized stars, as well as the fainter stripes of the comets that hailed through the inner system, one after another, echoes of the titanic war being waged on the solar system's rim.

And beyond the comets the new supernova – the destructive blossoming of the star the astronomers had once labelled Phi Cassiopeiae – was still brilliant, as bright as Venus perhaps, though dimming. When Xenia had been born such a spectacle, a supernova a mere nine thousand light years away, would have been a source of great scientific and public interest. Not today, of course, not in the year AD 3480.

But now the sun itself was shouldering above the horizon, dimming even the supernova. Beads of light like trapped stars marked the summits of Tycho's rim mountains, and a deep bloody crimson was working its way high into the tall sky. Almost every scrap of the air in that sky had been drawn from the heart of the Moon by the great Paulis mines. But now the mines were shut down, the Moon's core exhausted, and she imagined she could see the lid of the sky, the millennial leaking of the Moon's air into space.

She walked down the path that led to the circular sea. There was frost everywhere, of course, but the path's lunar dirt, patiently raked in her youth, was friendly and gripped her sandals. The water at the sea's rim was black and oily, lapping softly. She could see the grey sheen of pack ice further out, though the close horizon hid the bulk of the sea from her. Fingers of sunlight stretched across the ice, and grey-gold smoke shimmered above open water.

There was a constant tumult of groans and cracks as the ice rose and fell on the sea's mighty shoulders. The water never froze at Tycho's rim; conversely, it never thawed at the centre, so that there was a fat torus of ice floating out there around the central mountains. It was as if the rim of this artificial ocean was striving to emulate the unfrozen seas of Earth which bore its makers.

She thought she heard a barking, out on the pack ice. Perhaps it was a seal. And a bell clanked: an early fishing boat leaving port, a fat, comforting sound that carried easily through the still, dense air. She sought the boat's lights, but her eyes, rheumy, stinging with cold, failed her.

She paid attention to her creaking body: the aches in her too-thin, too-long, calcium-depleted bones, the obscure spurts of pain in her urethral system, the strange itches that afflicted her liver-spotted flesh. She was already growing too cold. Mirror returned enough heat to the Moon's long Night to keep the seas from freezing, the air from snowing out. But she would have welcomed a little more comfort.

She turned and began to labour back up her regolith path to her house.

When she got there, Berge, her grandson, was waiting for her. She did not know then, of course, that he would not survive the new Day.

He was eager to talk about Leonardo da Vinci.

Berge had taken off his wings and stacked them up against the concrete wall of her house. She could see how the wings were thick with frost, so dense the paper feathers could surely have had little play. Even long minutes after landing he was still panting, and his smooth fashionably-shaven scalp, so bare it showed the great bubble profile of his lunar-born skull, was dotted with beads of grimy sweat.

She scolded him even as she brought him into the warmth, and prepared hot soup and tea for him in her pressure kettles. 'You're a fool as your father was,' she said. His father, of course, had been Xenia's son. 'I was with him when he fell from the sky, leaving you orphaned. You know how dangerous it is in the pre-Dawn turbulence.'

'Ah, but the power of those great thermals, Xenia,' he said, as he accepted the soup. 'I can fly kilometres high without the slightest effort . . .'

Only Berge called her Xenia.

She would have berated him further, which was the prerogative of old age. But she didn't have the heart. He stood before her, eager, heartbreakingly thin. Berge always had been slender, even compared to other skinny lunar folk; but now he was clearly frail.

And, most ominous of all, a waxy, golden sheen seemed to linger about his skin. She had no desire to comment on that – not here, not now, not until she was sure what it meant, that it wasn't some trickery of her own age-yellowed eyes.

So she kept her counsel.

They made their ritual obeisance – murmurs about dedicating their bones and flesh to the salvation of the world – and finished up their soup.

And then, with his youthful eagerness, Berge launched into the seminar he was evidently itching to deliver on Leonardo da Vinci, long-dead citizen of a long-dead planet. Brusquely displacing the empty soup bowls to the floor, he produced papers from his jacket and spread them out before her. The sheets, yellowed and stained with age, were covered in a crabby, indecipherable handwriting, broken with sketches of gadgets or flowing water or geometric figures.

She picked out a luminously beautiful sketch of the crescent Earth . . .

'No, Xenia,' said Berge patiently. 'Not Earth. Think about it. It must have been the crescent *Moon*.' Of course he was right; she'd lived on the Moon too long. 'You see, Leonardo understood the phenomenon he called the ashen Moon – like our ashen Earth, the old Earth visible in the arms of the new. He was a hundred years ahead of his time with *that* one.'

This document had been called many things in its long history, but most familiarly the Codex Leicester. Berge's copy had been printed off in haste during The Failing, those frantic hours when the Moon's dying libraries had disgorged great snowfalls of paper, a last desperate download of their stored electronic wisdom before the power failed. It was a treatise centring on what Leonardo called the 'body of the Earth', but with diversions to consider such matters as water engineering, the geometry of Earth and Moon, and the origins of fossils.

The issue of the fossils particularly excited Berge. Leonardo had been much agitated by the presence of the fossils of marine creatures, fishes and oysters and corals, high in the mountains of Italy. Lacking any knowledge of tectonic processes, he had struggled to explain how the fossils might have been deposited by a series of great global floods.

It made her remember how, when Berge was small, she once had to explain to him what a 'fossil' was. There were no fossils on the Moon: no bones in the ground, save those humans had put there. But now, of course, Berge was much more interested in the words of long-dead Leonardo than his grandmother's.

'You have to think about the world Leonardo inhabited,' he said. 'The ancient paradigms still persisted: the stationary Earth, a sky laden with spheres, crude Aristotelian proto-physics. But Leonardo's instinct was to proceed from observation to theory – and he observed many things in the world which didn't fit with the prevailing world view –'

'Like mountain-top fossils.'

'Yes. Working alone, he struggled to come up with explanations. And some of his reasoning was, well, eerie.'

'Eerie?'

'Prescient.' Gold-flecked eyes gleamed. The boy flicked back and forth through the Codex, pointing out spidery pictures of Earth and Moon and sun, neat circles connected by spidery light ray traces. 'Remember, the Moon was thought to be a crystal sphere. What intrigued Leonardo was why the Moon wasn't much brighter in Earth's sky. If the Moon *was* a crystal sphere, perfectly reflective, it should have been as bright as the sun.'

'Like Mirror.'

'Yes. So Leonardo argued the Moon must be covered in oceans.' He found a diagram showing a Moon coated with great out-of-scale choppy waves and bathed in spidery sunlight rays. 'Leonardo said waves on the Moon's oceans must deflect much of the reflected sunlight away from Earth. He thought the darker patches visible on the surface must mark great standing waves, or even storms, on the Moon.'

'He was wrong,' she said. 'In Leonardo's time, the Moon was a ball of rock. The dark areas were just lava sheets.'

'Yes, of course. But now,' Berge said eagerly, 'the Moon *is* mostly covered by water. You see? And there *are* great storms, wave crests hundreds of kilometres long, which are visible from Earth – or would be, if anybody was left to see . . .'

They talked for hours.

When he left, she went to the door to wave him goodbye.

The Day was little advanced, the rake of sunlight still sparse on the ice, and Mirror still rode bright in the sky. Here was another strange forward echo of Leonardo's, it struck her, though she preferred not to mention it to her already over-excited grandson: in these remote times, there *were* crystal spheres in orbit around the Earth. The difference was, people had put them there.

As she closed the door she heard the honking of geese, a great flock of them fleeing the excessive brightness of full Daylight.

* * *

Each Morning, as the sun laboured into the sky, there were storms. Thick fat clouds raced across the sky, and water gushed down, carving new rivulets and craters in the ancient soil, and turning the ice at the rim of the Tycho pack into a thin, fragile layer of grey slush.

The storms persisted as Noon approached on that last Day, and she travelled with Berge to the phytomine celebration to be held on the lower slopes of Maginus.

They made their way past sprawling fields tilled by human and animal muscle, thin crops straining towards the sky, frost shelters laid open to the muggy heat. And as they travelled they joined streams of battered carts, all heading for Maginus. Xenia felt depressed by the people around her: the spindly adults, their hollow-eyed children – even the cattle and horses and mules were skinny and wheezing. The Moon soil was thin, and the people and animals were all, of course, slowly being poisoned besides.

Most people chose to shelter from the rain. But to Xenia it was a pleasure. Raindrops here were fat glimmering spheres the size of her thumb. They floated from the sky, gently flattened by the resistance of the thick air, and they fell on her head and back with soft, almost caressing impacts, and water clung to her flesh in great sheets and globes she must scrape off with her fingers. So long and slow had been their fall from the high clouds that the drops were often warm, and the air thick and humid and muggy. She liked to think of herself standing in the band of storms that circled the whole of the slow-turning Moon.

It reminded her of the day of Frank Paulis's final triumph.

She remembered that first hour it was possible to step outside the domes – the first hour when unprotected people could survive on the Moon, swathed as it was by air drawn up by the great mines that bore Paulis's name – an hour that had come to pass thanks, of course, to Frank's ingenuity, courage, determination and downright unscrupulous dishonesty. Frank, doggedly, had lived to see it, and on that day the authorities let him out of house arrest, just briefly. They wouldn't permit him to be the first to walk out of a dome without a mask – they couldn't bring themselves to be as generous as *that*. But he was among the first. And that was, perhaps, enough. She remembered how he stalked in the fresh air, squat and defiant, sniffing up great lungfuls of the air he had made, and he laughed as the rain trickled into his toothless mouth, fat lunar drops of it.

And, soon after that, he died.

After that Xenia had left, with the Gaijin, for the stars.

When she returned home she found 1300 years of history had worn away, leaving the Earth a cloud-covered ruin, the solar system threatened by interstellar war, the last humans struggling to survive on Mercury and the Moon. Nobody remembered her, or much of the past: it was as if this attenuated, unstable present was all there ever had been, all that would ever be. So she had shed her old identity, settled into the community here.

Thanks to her engineered biology, a gift of the futures she had visited, she had remained young, physically. Young enough to bear children, even. But now, despite the invisible engineering in her flesh, she was slowly dying, of course, as was everybody, as was the Moon.

How strange that the inhabited Moon's life had been as brief as her own: that her birth and death would span this small world's, that *its* rocky bones would soon emerge through its skin of air and ocean, just as hers would push through her decaying flesh.

At last they approached Maginus.

Maginus was an old, eroded crater complex to the south-east of Tycho. Its ancient walls glimmered with crescent lakes and glaciers. Sheltered from the winds of Morning and Evening, Maginus was a centre of life, and long before they reached the foothills, as the fat rain cleared, she saw the tops of giant trees looming over the horizon. She thought she saw creatures leaping between the tree branches. They may have been lemurs, or even bats; or perhaps they were kites wielded by ambitious children.

Berge showed delight as they crossed the many water courses, pointing out engineering features which had been anticipated by Leonardo, dams and bridges and canal diversions and so forth, some of them even constructed since the Failing. But Xenia took little comfort, oppressed as she was by the evidence of the fall of mankind. For example, they journeyed along a road made of lunar glass, flat as ice and utterly impervious to erosion, carved long ago into the regolith by vast spaceborne engines. But they travelled this marvellously engineered highway in a cart that was wooden, and drawn by a spavined, thin-legged mule.

Such contrasts were unendingly startling, to a time-stranded traveller like Xenia. But, she thought with a grisly irony, all the technology around them would have been more than familiar to Berge's hero, Leonardo. There were gadgets of levers and pulleys and gears, their wooden teeth constantly stripped; there were turnbuckles, devices to help erect cathedrals of Moon concrete; there had even been pathetic lunar wars fought with catapults and crossbows, 'artillery' capable of throwing lumps of rock a few kilometres.

But once people had dug mines that reached the heart of the Moon. The people today knew this was so, else they could not exist here. *She* knew it was true, for she remembered it.

As they neared the phytomine, the streams of traffic converged to a great confluence of people and animals. There was a swarm of reunions of friends and family, and a rich human noise carried on the thick air.

When the crowds grew too dense Xenia and Berge abandoned their wagon and walked. Berge, with unconscious generosity, supported her with a hand clasped about her arm, guiding her through this human maelstrom.

Children darted around her feet, so fast she found it impossible to believe *she* could ever have been so young, so rapid, so compact, and she felt a mask of old-woman irritability settle on her. But many of the children were, at age seven or eight or nine, already taller than she was, girls with languid eyes and the delicate posture of giraffes. The one constant of human evolution on the Moon was how the children stretched out, ever more languorous, in the gentle gravity. But in later life they paid a heavy price in brittle, calcium-starved bones.

All Berge wanted to talk about was Leonardo da Vinci.

'Leonardo was trying to figure out the cycles of the Earth. For instance, how water could be restored to the mountaintops. Listen to this.' He fumbled, one-handed, with his dog-eared manuscript. '*We may say that the Earth has a spirit of growth, and that its flesh is the soil; its bones are the successive strata of the rocks which form the mountains; its cartilage is the tufa stone; its blood the veins of its waters . . . And the vital heat of the world is fire which is spread throughout the Earth; and the dwelling place of the spirit of growth is in the fires, which in divers parts of the Earth are breathed out in baths and sulphur mines* . . . You understand what he's saying? He was trying to explain the Earth's cycles by analogy with the systems of the human body.'

'He was wrong.'

'But he was more right than wrong, grandmother! Don't you see? This was centuries before geology was formalized, before matter and energy cycles would be understood. Leonardo had got the right idea, from somewhere. He just didn't have the intellectual infrastructure to express it . . .'

And so on. None of it was of much interest to Xenia. As they walked it seemed to her that *his* weight was the heavier, as if she, the foolish old woman, was constrained to support him, the young buck. It was evident his sickliness was advancing fast – and it seemed that others around them noticed it too, and separated around them, a sea of unwilling sympathy.

At last they reached the plantation itself. They had to join queues, more or less orderly. There was noise, chatter, a sense of excitement. For many people, such visits were the peak of each slow lunar Day.

Separated from the people by a row of wooden stakes and a few metres of bare soil was a sea of growing green. The vegetation was predominantly mustard plants. Chosen for their bulk and fast growth, all of these plants had grown from seed or shoots since the last lunar Dawn. The plants themselves grew thick, their feathery leaves bright. But many of the leaves were sickly, already yellowing.

The fence was supervised by an unsmiling attendant, who wore – to show the people their sacrifice had a genuine goal – artefacts of unimaginable value, ear rings and brooches and bracelets of pure copper and nickel and bronze.

The attendant told them, in a sullen prepared speech, that the Maginus mine was the most famous and exotic of all the phytomines: for here gold itself was mined, still the most compelling of all metals. These mustard plants grew in soil in which gold, dissolved out of the base rock by ammonium thiocyanate, could be found at a concentration of four parts per million. But when the plants were harvested and burned, their ash contained four *hundred* parts per million of gold, drawn out of the soil by the plants during their brief lives.

The phytomines, where metals were slowly concentrated by living things, were perhaps the Moon's most important remaining industry.

As Frank Paulis had understood centuries ago, lunar soil was sparse and ungenerous. And yet, now that Earth was wrecked, now that the spaceships no longer called, the Moon was all the people had.

The people of the Moon had neither the means nor the will to rip up the top hundred metres of their world to find the precious metals they needed. Drained of strength and tools, they must be more subtle.

Hence the phytomines.

The technology was old – older than the human Moon, older than spaceflight itself. The Vikings, marauders of Earth's dark age, would mine their iron from 'bog ore', iron-rich stony nodules deposited near the surface of bogs by bacteria which had flourished there: miniature miners, not even visible to the Vikings who burned their little corpses to make their nails and swords and pans and cauldrons.

And so it went, across this battered, parched little planet, a hierarchy of bacteria and plants and insects and animals and birds, collecting gold and silver and nickel and copper and bronze, their evanescent bodies comprising a slow merging trickle of scattered molecules stored in leaves and flesh and bones, all for the benefit of that future generation who must some day save the Moon.

Berge and Xenia, solemnly, took ritual scraps of mustard-plant leaf on their tongues, swallowed ceremonially. With her age-furred tongue she could barely taste the mustard's sharpness. There were no drawn-back frost covers here because these poor mustard plants would not survive to the sunset: they died within a lunar Day, from poisoning by the cyanide.

Berge met friends, and melted into the crowds.

Xenia returned home alone, brooding.

She found her family of seals had lumbered out of the ocean and onto the shore. These were constant visitors. During the warmth of Noon they would bask for hours, males and females and children draped over each other in casual abandon, so long that the patch of regolith they inhabited became sodden and stinking with their droppings. The seals, uniquely among the creatures from Earth, had not adapted in any apparent way to the lunar conditions. In the flimsy gravity they could surely perform somersaults with those flippers of theirs. But they chose not to; instead they basked, as their ancestors had on far-remote Arctic beaches.

Xenia didn't know why this was so. Perhaps the seals were, simply, wiser than struggling, dreaming humans.

The long Afternoon sank into its mellow warmth. The low sunlight diffused, yellow-red, to the very top of the tall sky.

Earth was clearly visible, wrapped in yellow clouds – they were clouds of dust and bits of rock and vaporized ocean, thrown up there by the great impact a hundred years back – clouds which, the scientists used to say, would take centuries to disperse. Now, nobody so much as looked at Earth, as if, now that it could no longer succour its blue satellite, the planet had become unmentionable, its huge wounds somehow impolite. But Xenia could make out a dim cloud of green, swathing the Earth: it was an orbiting forest, Trees that had survived the collision, still drawing their sustenance from the curdled air with superconductor roots.

The comet impact had been relatively minor, on the cosmic scale of such events. But it had been sufficient to silence Earth; nobody on the Moon knew who, or what, had survived on its surface. Xenia wondered if even those Trees could survive the greater and more frequent impacts which many had predicted were the inevitable outcome of the conflict in the Oort cloud, as the Crackers threatened to break through the Gaijin cordon, as warring Eeties hurled giant rogue objects into the system's crowded heart, century after century.

Such musing failed to distract her from thoughts of Berge's illness, which advanced without pity. She was touched when he chose to come stay with her, to 'see it out', as he put it.

Her fondness for Berge was not hard to understand. Her daughter had died in childbirth. This was not uncommon, as pelvises evolved in heavy Earth gravity struggled to release the great fragile skulls of Moon-born children – and Xenia's genes, of course, came direct from Earth, from the deep past.

So she had rejoiced when Berge was born, sired by her son of a lunar native; at least her genes, she consoled herself, which had emanated from primeval oceans now lost in the sky, would travel on to the furthest future. But now, it seemed, she would lose even that consolation.

But she was not important, nor the future, nor her complex past. All that mattered was Berge, here in the present, and on him she lavished all her strength, her love.

Berge spent his dwindling energies in feverish activities. Still his obsession with Leonardo clung about him. He showed her pictures of impossible machines, far beyond the technology of Leonardo's time: shafts and cogwheels for generating enormous heat, a diving apparatus, an 'easy-moving wagon' capable of independent locomotion. The famous helicopter intrigued Berge particularly. He built many spiral-shaped models of bamboo and paper; they soared into the thick air, easily defying the Moon's gravity, catching the reddening light.

She wasn't sure if he knew he was dying.

In her gloomier hours – when she sat with her grandson as he struggled to sleep, or as she lay listening to the ominous, mysterious rumbles of her own failing body, cumulatively poisoned, wracked by the strange distortions of lunar gravity – she wondered how much further humans must descend.

The heavy molecules of the thick atmosphere were too fast-moving to be contained by the Moon's gravity. The air would be thinned in a few thousand years: a long time, but not beyond comprehension. Long before then people would have to reconquer this world they had built, or they would die.

So they gathered metals, molecule by molecule.

And, besides that, they would need knowledge.

The Moon had become a world of patient monks, endlessly transcribing the great texts of the past, pounding the eroding wisdom of the millennia into the brains of the wretched young. It seemed essential to Xenia they did not lose their concentration as a people, their memory. But she feared it was impossible. Technologically they had already descended to the level of Neolithic farmers, and the young were broken by toil even as they learned.

She had lived long enough to realize that they were, fragment by fragment, losing what they once knew.

If she had one simple message to transmit to the future generations, one thing they should remember lest they descend into savagery, it would be this: *People came from Earth*. There: cosmology and the history of the species and the promise of the future, wrapped up in one baffling, enigmatic, heroic sentence. She repeated it to everyone she met. Perhaps those future thinkers would decode its meaning, and would understand what they must do.

Berge's decline quickened as the sun slid down the sky, the clockwork of the universe mirroring his condition with a clumsy, if mindless, irony. In the last hours she sat with him, quietly reading and talking, responding to his near-adolescent philosophizing with her customary brusqueness, which she was careful not to modify in this last hour.

'... But have you ever wondered why we are *here* and *now*?' He was whispering, the sickly gold of his face picked out by the dwindling sun. 'What are we, a few million, scattered in our towns and farms around the Moon? What do we compare to the *billions* who swarmed over Earth in the great years? Why do I find myself alive *now* rather than *then*? It is so unlikely ...' He turned his great lunar head. 'Do you ever feel you have been born out of your time, as if you are stranded in the wrong era, an *unconscious* time traveller?'

She would have confessed she often did, but he whispered on.

'Suppose a modern human – or someone of the great ages of Earth – was stranded in the sixteenth century, Leonardo's time. Suppose he forgot everything of his culture, all its science and learning –'

'Why? How?'

'*I* don't know ... But if it were true – and if his unconscious mind retained the slightest trace of the learning he had discarded – wouldn't he do exactly what Leonardo did? Study obsessively, try to fit awkward facts into the prevailing, unsatisfactory paradigms, grope for the deeper truths he had lost? Don't you see? Leonardo behaved *exactly* as a stranded time traveller would.'

'Ah.'

She thought she understood; of course, she didn't. And in her unthinking way she launched into a long and pompous discourse on feelings of dislocation: on how every adolescent felt stranded in a body, an adult culture, unprepared . . .

Berge wasn't listening. He turned away, to look again at the bloated sun.

'I think,' she said, 'you should drink more soup.'

But he had no more need of soup.

It seemed too soon when the Day was done, and the cold started to settle on the land once more, with great pancakes of new ice clustering around the rim of the Tycho sea.

Xenia summoned Berge's friends, teachers, those who had loved him.

She clung to the greater goal: that the atoms of gold and nickel and zinc which had coursed in Berge's blood and bones, killing him like the mustard plants of Maginus – killing them all, in fact, at one rate or another – would now gather in even greater concentrations in the bodies of those who would follow. Perhaps the pathetic scrap of gold or nickel which had cost poor Berge his life would at last, mined, close the circuit which would lift the first ceramic-hulled ships beyond the thick, deadening atmosphere of the Moon.

Perhaps. It was cold comfort.

But still they ate the soup, of Berge's dissolved bones and flesh, in solemn silence. They took his life's sole gift, further concentrating the metal traces to the far future, shortening their own lives as he had.

She had never been a skilful host. As soon as they could, the young people dispersed. She talked with Berge's teachers, but they had little to say to each other; she was merely his grandmother, after all. She wasn't sorry to be left alone.

Before she slept again, even before the sun's bloated hull had slid below the toothed horizon, the winds had turned. The warmer air was treacherously fleeing after the sinking sun. Soon the first flurries of snow came pattering on the black, swelling surface of the Tycho sea.

Her seals slid back into the water, to seek out whatever riches or dangers awaited them under Moon core ice.

Chapter 29

BAD NEWS FROM THE STARS

When Madeleine Meacher arrived back in the solar system – just moments after passing through the pain of her last Saddle Point transition – she was stunned to find Nemoto materializing in the middle of her small hab module.

'Nemoto. *You.* What – how –'

Nemoto was small, hunched over, her face a mask of sourness. This was a virtual, of course, and a low-quality one; Nemoto floated in the air, not quite lined up with the floor.

Nemoto glanced about, as if surprised to be here. 'Meacher. So it's you. What date is it?.'

Madeleine had to look it up. AD 3793.

Nemoto laughed hollowly. 'How absurd.'

There was no perceptible time delay. That meant the originating transmitter must be close. But, of course, there had been no way Nemoto could have known which Saddle Point gateway Madeleine would arrive from. 'Nemoto, what *are* you?'

Nemoto grunted impatiently. 'I am a limited-sentience projection. My function is to wait for the star travellers to return. I dusted the Saddle Point radius, all around the system. Dusted it with monitors, probes, transmitters. Technology has moved on, Meacher. Look it up. It scarcely matters . . . Listen to what I have to say.'

'Nemoto –'

'*Listen,* damn you. The Gaijin have been fighting the Crackers. Out on the rim of the system.'

'I know that –'

'The war has lasted five centuries, perhaps more. The Oort cloud is deep, Meacher, a deep trench. But now the war is lost.'

The simple, stunning brutality of the statement shocked Madeleine. 'Are you sure?'

Nemoto barked laughter. 'The Gaijin are withdrawing from the solar system. They don't bother to hide this from us. Just as most people don't bother to look up, into the sky, and *see* what is going on . . . Oh, many of the Gaijin remain. Scouts, observers, transit craft like *this* one. But the bulk of the Gaijin fleet – mostly constructed from stolen solar system resources, *our* asteroids – has begun to withdraw to the Saddle Points. The outer system war is over.'

'And the Crackers . . .'

'Are on the way into the inner system. They are already through the heliopause, the perimeter of the solar wind.' The virtual flickered, became blocky, all but transparent. 'The end game approaches.'

'Nemoto, what must I do?'

'Go to Mercury. Find *me*.' She looked down at herself, as if remembering. 'That is, find Nemoto.'

'And what of *you*? Nemoto, what is a *limited-sentience projection*?'

Nemoto raised a hand that was crumbling into bits of light. She seemed puzzled, as if she was finding out for herself as she spoke. 'I am autonomous, heuristic, sentient. I was born sixty seconds ago, to give you this message. But my function is fulfilled. I'm dying.' She looked at Madeleine, as if shocked by the realization, and reached out.

Madeleine extended a hand, but her fingers passed through a cloud of light.

With a thin wail, the Nemoto virtual broke up.

Sailing in from the rim of the solar system, Madeleine used Gaijin technology to study the strange new age into which she had been projected.

There was little Gaijin traffic, just as virtual Nemoto had said.

But she found signatures of unknown ships – solar sail craft, they appeared to be, great fleets of them, a gigantic shell that surrounded the system. They were still out among the remote orbits of the comets for now, but they were converging, like a fist closing on the fat warmth of the inner system.

Cracker fleets, come to disrupt the sun.

Earth seemed dead. The Moon was a fading blue, silent. There were knots of human activity in the asteroids, on Mars – and Triton. And she found signs of refugee fleets, humans fleeing inwards to the core of the system, to Mercury. But no ships arrived at or left remote Triton.

When she understood that, she knew where she must go first.

The Gaijin flower-ship sailed around Triton, its fusion light illuminating smooth plains of ice. It was a world covered by a chill ocean, like

Earth's Arctic, with not a scrap of solid land; but the thin ice crust was easily broken by the slow pulsing tides of this small moon, exposing great black leads of water that bubbled and steamed vigorously, trying to evaporate and fill up all of empty space.

There were six human settlements.

The settlements looked like clusters of bubbles on a pond, she thought. They were sprawling, irregular patches of modular construction – not rigid, clearly designed to float over the tides. Five settlements seemed abandoned – no lights, no power output, no sign of an internal temperature significantly above the background. Even the sixth looked largely shut down, with only a handful of lights at the centre of the bubble-cluster, the outskirts abandoned to the cold.

She radioed down requests for permission and instructions for landing. Only automated beacons responded. The answers came through in a human voice, but in a language she didn't recognize. The translation suite embedded in her equipment couldn't handle it either. She had the Gaijin put her down on what appeared to be a landing site, close to a system of airlocks.

Suited up, she stepped out of the conical Gaijin lander.

Frost covered every surface. But it was gritty, hard as sand. Remember, Madeleine, water ice is rock on Triton.

She walked carefully to the edge of the platform, and looked out beyond the bounds of the bubble city. A point source sun cast wan colourless light over smooth ice fields. Neptune was rising over the horizon, a faint, misty-blue ball, making the light on the ice deep, subtle, complex, the shadows softly glowing. Pointlessly beautiful, she thought. She turned away.

She found a door large enough for a suited human. She couldn't understand the elaborate script instructions beside the control panel. But there was one clear device, a big red button: *Press me.* She hit it with her fist.

Radio noise screeched. The door slid back, releasing a puff of air that crystallized immediately. She hurried into a small, brightly-lit airlock. The door slammed shut and the airlock immediately repressurized.

She twisted off her helmet. Air sighed out of her suit, and her ears popped. The air was biting cold. It smelled stale.

She palmed a panel that opened the inner door, and found herself looking into a long, unadorned corridor that twisted out of sight.

Wandering through the corridors, carrying her helmet, she was eventually met by a woman. She was evidently a cop: spindly, fragile-looking after fifteen hundred years of adaptation to low gravity, but she carried a mean-looking device that could only be a hand-gun.

The cop walked Madeleine, luggage pack and all, into the centre of town. The cop's skin was jet black. Madeleine's translator software couldn't interpret her language.

Madeleine caught glimpses of abandoned corridors, and some kind of complex, gigantic machinery at the heart of everything. In one area she passed over a clear floor, water rippling underneath, black and deep. She saw something swimming there, sleek and fast and white, quickly disappearing into the deeper darkness.

The cop delivered her to a cramped suite of offices. Madeleine sat in an anteroom, waiting for attention. Maybe this was the office of the Mayor, she thought, or the town council. There was no sign of the colony's Aboriginal origins, save for a piece of art on the wall: around a metre square, pointillist dots in shades of cobalt red. A Dreamtime representation, maybe.

Madeleine was starting to get the picture. Triton was a small town, at the fringe of interstellar space. They weren't used to visitors, and weren't much interested either.

Eventually a harassed-looking official – another woman, her frizzy hair tied back sharply from her forehead – came into the room. She studied Madeleine with dismay.

Madeleine forced a smile. 'Pleased to meet you. Who are you, the Mayor?'

The woman frowned, and jabbered back impatiently.

But Madeleine smiled and nodded, and tapped her helmet. 'That's it. Keep talking. My name is Madeleine Meacher. I've come from the stars . . .'

Her translator suite was essentially Gaijin. How ironic that seventeen centuries after the Gaijin came wandering unannounced into the asteroid belt, humans should need alien technology to talk to each other.

At last the translator began to whisper.

'At last. Thanks for your patience. I –'

'And I am very busy,' the translator whispered, ghosting the woman's speech. 'We should progress this issue, the issue of your arrival here.'

'My name is Meacher . . .' Madeleine summarized her CV.

The woman turned out to be called Sheela Dell-Cope. She was an administrative assistant in the office of the Headman here – although, as far as Madeleine could make out, the Headman was actually a woman.

'I have a mission,' Madeleine said. 'I bring bad news. Bad news from the stars.'

The woman silenced her with an upraised hand. 'There is the question of your residency, including the appropriate fee . . .'

Madeleine was forced to sit through a long and elaborate list of rules regarding temporary residency. To Dell-Cope, Madeleine Meacher was strange, incomprehensible, a visitor from another time, another place. Now *I* am the Gaijin, Madeleine thought.

She was going to have to apply for an equivalent of a visa. And she would have to pay for each day she stayed, or else work for her air. This was a closed, marginal world, where every breath had to be paid for.

'The work is not pleasant,' Dell-Cope said. 'Servicing the *otec*. Or working with the Flips, for instance.'

That meant nothing to Madeleine, but she got the idea. 'I'll pay.' She had a variety of Gaijin high-tech gadgets that she could use for a fee. Anyhow she wasn't going to be here long, come what may.

As it turned out, the painting on the wall was a representation of an ancient Aboriginal artwork: the Dreaming of a creature of the Australian Outback, the honey-ant. But it was a copy of a copy of a copy, done in seaweed dyes. And, she was prepared to bet, nobody on Triton knew what a honey-ant was anyhow.

She was given a room in a residential area. There seemed to be no hotels here.

The room was just a cube carved out of concrete. It had a bed, some scattered and unfamiliar furniture – spindly low-G chairs – a small galley, and a comms station with an utterly baffling human interface.

Not that the galley was so easy either. She shouted at it and poked it, her favoured way of dealing with new-fangled technology, until she found a way to make it decant a hot liquid, some kind of tea.

There were no windows. The room was just a concrete box, a sarcophagus, a cave. Here in the emptiness on the edge of interstellar space, humans were hiding from the sky.

What are you doing here, Meacher?

What was she *supposed* to do? Simply blurt out her news – that an alien invasion fleet had massed on the rim of the solar system, that it was almost certain to spill into the region of Neptune's orbit soon, that she was here, with her friendly Gaijin, to help these people evacuate to worlds their ancestors had left behind a thousand years earlier? It seemed absurd, melodramatic.

She worked at the comms equipment, striving to make it do what she wanted. It was a strange irony, she thought, that comms equipment, whose purpose was after all to join people together, always turned out to have the most baffling designs, presenting the worst challenges to the out-of-time traveller.

She tried to make an appointment to meet the Headman, but she was stalled. She tried further down the local hierarchy, as best she could figure it out, but got nowhere there either.

Nobody was interested in her.

Frustrated, on a whim, she decided to hunt for descendants of the colonists she had known. With the help of her translator she asked the comms station to find her people with 'Roach' in their surname.

Most of the surnames scrolling before her, phonetically rendered, were unfamiliar. But there were a few families with compound surnames which included the name 'Rush'.

Just around the corner, in fact, in the same floating bubble as this room, there was a man – apparently living alone – with the surname Rush-Bayley.

She spent a frustrating hour persuading the comms unit to leave him a message.

She took long walks through the city's emptiness. Lights turned themselves on, off again when she passed, so she walked in a moving puddle of illumination.

She walked from bubble to floating bubble over bridges of what seemed to be ceramic; when the bubbles shifted against each other, the interfaces creaked, ominously. She encountered few people. Her footsteps echoed, as if she was walking through immense hangars.

Madeleine imagined this place had been designed for ten, twenty times as many people as it held now. And she thought of those other colonies, abandoned on the waters of Triton.

It saddened her that nothing – save a few sentimental tokens like paintings – survived of the Aboriginal culture that Ben's generation had brought here. After all, even fifteen hundred years on Triton were dwarfed by maybe sixty *thousand* years of Australia. But the Dreamtime legends, it seemed, had not survived the translation from the ancient deserts of Australia to these enclosed, high-tech bubbles.

She reached the centre of the kilometres-wide colony. Here, a great structure loomed out of the ice-crusted sea, visible through picture windows. It was mounted on a stalk, and reared up to a great dome-shaped carapace, some hundreds of metres above the ice. It was a little like a water tower. She picked out engineering features: evaporators, demisters, generators, turbines, condenser tubing. Madeleine learned that this tower was based on a taproot that descended far into the ocean, kilometres deep, in fact.

This was the *otec*. The name turned out to be an acronym from old English, for Ocean Thermal Energy Converter. It was a device to extract energy from the heat difference between the deep ocean waters, at just four degrees below freezing, and the surface ice, at more than a hundred below. The *otec* turned out to be the main power source for the colony. It was fifteen hundred years old, as old as the colony itself, and maintained by the colonists with a diligent, monkish devotion. There were other power sources, like fusion plants. But the colonists were short of metal; the nearest body of rock, after all, was the silicate core of Triton, drowned under hundreds of kilometres of water. The colonists were able to fix the *otec*, clunky machinery though it was, with materials they could extract from the water around them.

After a couple of empty days, she found her comms unit glowing green. She poked at it, trying to figure out why.

It turned out there was a message on it, from Rush-Bayley.

Adamm Rush-Bayley was tall, thin, dark. He wore a loose smock-like affair, his skinny legs bare. The smock was painted with vibrant colours, red, blue, green, a contrast to the drab environment.

He turned out to be seventy years old, though he didn't look it.

He looked nothing like Ben, of course, or Lena. Had she been hoping that she could retrieve something of Ben, her own vanished past? How *could* he be like Ben, sixty generations removed?

His family had kept alive Ben's story, however, his name – and the story of the Nereid impact. And so he looked at her with mild curiosity. 'You're the *same* Madeleine Meacher who –'

'Yes.'

'How very strange. Of course we have records.' He smiled. 'There is a public archive, and my family kept its own mementoes. Perhaps you'd like to see them.'

'I was there for the live show, remember.'

'Yes. You must have fascinating stories.' He didn't sound all that fascinated, though, to Madeleine; it seemed clear he'd rather show her the records his family had cherished than hear her testimony from history. The past was a thing to own, to lock away in boxes and archives, not to explore.

It wasn't the first time she had encountered such a reaction.

He made her a meal in his home, which was a multi-chamber cave. The food was shellfish, with what appeared to be processed seaweed or algae as a side dish. They ate off plates made of a kind of paper. The paper wasn't based on cellulose, she learned, but on chitin extracted from the shells of lobsters.

Adamm's clothes were made from seaweed – or more precisely a seaweed extract called algin. Algin could be spun into silk-like threads, and was the basis of virtually all the colonists' clothing and other fabric, and products like films, gels, polishes, paints. There was even algin additive in her food.

They talked tentatively while they ate.

Adamm made a minor living making pearl artefacts. He showed her a pearl the size of her fist that had been sliced open and hollowed out to make a box for a mildly intoxicating snuff-like powder. The pearl was exquisite, the workmanship so-so.

Most of the work he did was for one engineering concern or another; luxury was at a premium here. He could only sell, after all, to his fellow citizens. It seemed to her that nobody was rich here, nobody terribly poor. But this was Adamm's home, and he was used to its conditions.

Most people, she learned, were probably older than they looked to her. Here in the low gravity environment of Triton, and with anti-ageing mechanisms wired centuries earlier into the human genome, life expectancy was around two centuries. And it would have been even higher if not for problems with the colony's life support. 'We have crashes and blooms, diseases, toxicity . . .'

The biosphere was just too small.

Right now Adamm lived alone. He had one child by a previous marriage. He was considering marrying again, trying for more children. But there was a quota.

He listened, without commenting, to her talk of interstellar war. Madeleine had the impression that Adamm was merely being polite to somebody who might have known his ancestors.

She felt herself losing concentration, overwhelmed by cultural inertia.

After the meal, they took a walk.

He guided her to an area like an atrium. It was walled, roofed and floored with transparent sheeting, and for once there was no sense of enclosure. Around her, stretching to a close, tightly curving horizon, was a sheet of ice; above her was Neptune's faint globe, slowly rising as Triton spun through its long artificial day; beneath her feet she could see the Triton ocean, through which pale white forms skimmed.

She said, 'I remember when Neptune hung in the sky, unmoving. Seeing it rise like that is – eerie. But I suppose it makes Triton more Earth-like.'

She glimpsed hostility on his face.

'Travellers like you have returned before,' he said, her translator filtering out any emotion from his voice. 'What does it matter if Triton is *Earth-like* or not? Madeleine, I've never seen Earth. Why would I want to?'

The little clash depressed her. Of course he's right, she thought; 'Earth-like' must sound as alien to Adamm as the accretion-disc home of the Chaera would have to me. Fifteen hundred years; fifty, sixty generations . . . We humans just can't maintain cultural concentration, even over such an insignificant span.

While the Gaijin sail on.

As if on cue, there was a flash in the sky, somewhere beyond the blue shoulder of Neptune.

She grabbed Adamm's hand; he recoiled from her touch. 'There. Did you see that?'

Ne. '. . . No.'

There was nothing to see now, no afterglow, no repeat show. She felt like a kid who had glimpsed a meteor in the desert sky, a flash nobody else had seen. She said defensively, 'It's not just a light in the sky. It might have been the destruction of an ice moon, or a comet nucleus –'

Adamm asked reluctantly, 'This is your war?'

'Adamm, the war isn't mine. But it is *real* . . .'

A sleek white shape broke the water beneath her feet. She stepped back, startled. She saw a smooth, streamlined head, closed eyes, a small mouth – something like a dolphin, she thought. The creature opened its mouth and uttered a cry, high-pitched, complex, like a door creaking.

Then it flipped backwards and disappeared from view, leaving Madeleine stunned, disturbed.

'*War*,' Adamm said sourly. Then he sighed. 'I suppose you mean well. But it seems so – remote.'

'Believe me, it isn't. Adamm, I'm going to need your help. The Headman won't see me. You have to help me convince people.'

He laughed, not unkindly. He pointed down to the black water. 'Start with them.'

'Who?'

'The Flips. Try convincing them. They're people too.'

She peered into the water, stunned.

He walked away. She had no choice but to follow.

The Headman's office loaned her a hard-shelled suit, full of smart stuff and heating elements. She descended into the water, from a bay on the outskirts of the bubble city, through a hole neatly cut in the ice.

She fell slowly, in deepening darkness. She moved around experimentally. She couldn't feel the cold, and the water pressure here on this low-G moon was pretty low, but the water resisted her movements. When the hole in the ice was just a pinpoint of blue light above her, she turned on her helmet lamps. The beams penetrated only a few metres into the murk. She ran a quick visual check of her systems, and glanced upwards to see her tether coiling reassuringly up through the water, her physical link to the world of air and light above.

Deep-sea diving on Triton. She'd never liked swimming, even on a real planet.

She was alone. The colonists didn't take to the water much. Their deep ocean was just a resource, a mine, not a place to explore, still less play.

Something wriggled past her faceplate.

She recoiled. Her chin jammed against her air inlet, and there was a sudden decrease in pressure; her ears popped alarmingly.

She calmed herself down. It had only been a fish. She didn't recognize the species – a native Earth type, or gen-enged for this peculiar environment?

She fell faster.

The murky dust grew thicker. It was probably organic debris, she had been warned: decomposed body parts, drifting down to the deep ocean floor. More critters and plants drifted up past her. There were strands of seaweed, what looked like tiny shrimps, more fish of a variety of shapes and sizes, even what appeared to be a sea horse.

There was a whole biosphere down here, gen-enged from Earth life. There was little photosynthesis: not enough sunlight for that. Most of the energy for life here came from the heat of Triton's interior. So the food chain was anchored in communities of exotic bugs clustered around smoking, mineral-laden vents, cracks in the ocean floor hundreds of kilometres from the light.

. . . She felt it before she could see it, a sudden and unexpected nuzzling at her legs, soft, warm, curious. She twisted around in the water, tether looping.

It was like a dolphin, yes: a small dolphin, sleek body a couple of metres long, streamlined fur pure white, powerful flukes and stubby fins. But it – no, *he*; there was a fully operational penis down there, beneath the sleek belly – *he* had a face that had little in common with a dolphin's: a blunt rounded shape, a wide, stretched mouth, a nose squashed flat and the nostrils extended into two slits. Bubbles streamed from a blowhole at the top of his head. And the eyes were closed; she could make out no brows, no lids.

No eyes, she realized. But what use were eyes, in this deep darkness?

This was a human, of course: or rather, a post-human, gen-enged for this environment, the true, deep heart of Triton, far beneath the cold, attenuated huddles of the surface.

He swum around her smoothly, brushing her legs, feet, arms, chest. She heard a pulsing click, perhaps some form of echo-sounding . . .

He rolled on his back.

Enough analysis, Madeleine.

Without thinking, she reached out with her gloved hand and scratched his corrugated, gun-metal-grey belly. She could feel nothing of the texture of his fur. But the clicks and pops he made deepened, seeming to denote satisfaction.

'Can you hear me? Can you understand? . . .' Are you a Roach too, she thought, some remote, metamorphosed child of Ben and Lena?

For reply he wriggled away and floated there, just out of her reach.

She had to let herself drift a little deeper to touch him again. He let her stroke him a couple more minutes, then wriggled away again. And she had to descend further, reach out again.

And again, and again.

He's testing me, she realized slowly. Playing some game with me. Psychology. Still human enough for that.

And, she saw by the swelling of his impressive penis, it was giving him a kick.

She rose up a little, folded her arms.

When he saw she wasn't playing any more, he rolled on his front and his fins beat at the water, as if in frustration. But then he quickly forgave her, and began rolling around her legs, nuzzling and butting.

More shadows in the water, she saw now: two, three, four Flips. They clustered around her curiously. She wondered if her first companion had called to them, in some manner she couldn't detect. She tried not to flinch as their powerful bodies brushed the equipment that kept her alive; they showed no malevolence, only a kind of affectionate curiosity, and her gear was surely designed to survive encounters like this.

Now one of them – her first friend maybe, impossible to say – began to emit a new kind of sound. It was a kind of whistle, much purer than the echo clicks or the squeaky-door groans she had heard before.

Another joined in, making a whistle that wavered a bit but soon settled on the same pitch as the first. And now she heard a pulsing, overlaid on their simple pure-tone singing. Beats, she thought, the interference of one tone with another.

The other Flips joined in, singing their own notes, producing more beats. As a piece of music it was simple, just a cluster of pure tones in straightforward harmony with each other. But the beats were more complex, an elusive pattern of pulses that shifted, hopping from one frequency to another, sometimes too rapidly for her to follow.

On a whim she activated a feed to her concrete cave room, up in the surface colony, and let the translator suite record the singing. Then she closed her eyes and let herself drift, immersed in song, oblivious even to the gentle touch of the Flips as they swam around her.

. . . The Flips scattered, suddenly, as if in panic, disappearing into the gloom, leaving her alone. She felt shocked, oddly bereft; without the song, the world seemed empty.

But now she heard a new noise: a deep regular thrumming. Something was approaching through the water ahead of her, something massive, a texture that spanned the ocean.

It was a net.

She paced back and forth in Adamm's lounge. 'What kind of people are you? Those Flips are your –'

'Children?' He smiled, languid, sipping a kind of wine whose principal ingredient was seaweed. 'Cousins? Brothers, sisters? Don't be absurd. They are a different species. They became that way by choice. When they first went into the sea, they took tools, ways of extracting metal. They discarded it all, bit by bit. They even discarded their hands, and their eyes, everything that makes us human. They *chose* to go back, you see, back to – mindlessness. It was ideological.'

She wondered how much, if any, of that was true. 'But to hunt them down –'

He studied her curiously. 'Do you imagine we *eat* them? You don't think much of us, do you? The Flips are just a pest. They disrupt the ecology. They interfere with the city's systems, the filter valves for instance . . .'

Perhaps, she thought.

The translator had analysed the Flips' singing.

With no referents, it was impossible to provide a one-to-one translation. But it was obvious the song was full of structure. The suite identified patterns in the choice of frequencies, the way the beats were manipulated, in their spacing and timing and intonation and pitch . . . The suite estimated that an hour of such singing could encode a million bits. Which was, for comparison, about the information content of Homer's *Odyssey*.

The Flips couldn't match the richness of whale song of Earth. Not yet. A few more centuries, she thought, and they'd have it.

So the Song went on after all, here in this watery desert, a place even more elemental than the Outback.

Adamm was still talking. '. . . And you needn't imagine they are some kind of cute pet. Some of them have turned predatory, you know. Ecological niches tend to be filled . . . *They* consume each other. Look, they're just Flips. They don't matter.'

'And nor did your ancestors, in white Australia.'

His face hardened. 'You created this world, I suppose, with your stunts, firing moons back and forth. And now you want to destroy it, evacuate thousands of people.' He smiled. 'History remembers you as a meddler. Grandiose. Ideas above your capabilities.' But even as he spoke he seemed distant, as if unable to believe he was challenging this historical figure – as if he was facing down Columbus, or Julius Caesar. He gazed out at interstellar darkness, the edge of the system. 'If these aliens are as powerful as you claim, maybe we should just accept what's going to happen. Like death. You can't fight that.'

She growled, 'No, but you can put it off.' She stood. 'I'm not interested in your opinion of me, or your analysis. I'm going to see the Headman, whether she likes it or not. I'll do what I can to arrange evacuation to the inner system for everybody who wants it. Even the Flips.'

He eyed her, saying nothing; somehow she sensed this remote grandson of long-dead Ben and Lena wasn't going anywhere, with or without her.

'Goodbye, Adamm.'

Goodbye, goodbye.

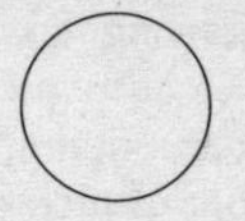

Chapter 30

REFUGE

The Gaijin flower-ship soared on a fast, efficient powered trajectory into the crowded heart of the solar system. The sun grew brighter, swamping the subtleties of the star-laden sky, its glaring light more and more the dominant presence in the universe.

Madeleine felt an unreasonable, illogical sense of claustrophobia. There were no walls here, and there was room for whole planets to swim through the dark; and yet this place felt oppressive, closed in, like the heart of a city. She spent much time with the lander's windows opaqued against the yellow-white glare, drifting beneath a cool, austere virtual Neptune.

The Gaijin refused to carry Madeleine any closer to the sun than the orbit of Earth. She was going to have to proceed on to Mercury in the cramped confines of a lander designed primarily for orbit-to-ground hops.

The few hundred refugees from Triton who had followed her back into the heart of the system would have to endure the same rigours. The transfer into the landers was ill-tempered, chaotic.

It had proved impossible to communicate to the deep-ocean aquatics the need to evacuate. So she had been forced to leave them behind, those dolphin-like post-humans, abandoning them to whatever mysterious fate awaited them, without ever even knowing if they understood what was happening to them.

Just as, perhaps, the retreating Gaijin wondered of her.

As she watched the flower-ship sail away back into the outer darkness, she felt an entirely unexpected pang of loneliness, of abandonment.

She'd always suspected that Malenfant's habit of giving his Gaijin companion a name – of treating Cassiopeia as some analogue of a human individual – was just anthropomorphism, sloppy sentimentality. But the fact was she actually *liked* these aloof, stately, rational

Gaijin a lot more than she liked some humans – notably the racist-type surface colonists she had encountered on Triton. The Gaijin were ancient, much-travelled, had endured experiences unimaginable to most humans; to them, a single, short-lived human and her concerns must seem as evanescent, as meaningless – and yet perhaps as beautiful – as the curl of a thread of smoke, the splash of a single raindrop.

At last, ten days after the Gaijin had left her, planet Mercury sailed into view. She was approaching at an angle from the night side, so to her it was a bony crescent against the black, slowly opening up, its cratering apparent even from a great distance.

She slid into orbit, and was held there while an electronic bureaucracy – run by a governing body called the Coalition – processed her requests to land, machines separated by centuries of technical and social development seeking a way to speak to each other.

Mercury, turning beneath her, was like the Moon's elder brother, just a ball of rock with a pale, thickly cratered surface. But there was no Mercury equivalent of the Moon's great maria; whatever process had formed those great lunar seas of frozen lava hadn't operated here. And there were features unlike anything on the Moon: zones of crumpling, ridges and folds and cracks, like the wrinkled skin of a dried tomato, as if the planet had shrunk after its formation.

The stand-out feature was one immense impact basin, maybe thirty degrees north of the equator. She sailed over a ragged ring of mountains – not a simple rim, but a structure, with the tallest mountains innermost, and lower foothills further out. Inside the ring there was a relatively smooth floor, scarred by ridges, folds and rifts that followed roughly concentric patterns, like the glaze on an old dinner plate. It was a fantastic sight, a basin that took her lander long minutes to skim over on its first approach pass, circles of mountains big enough neatly to encompass the Great Lakes.

And, in the deep shadows right at the huge crater's heart, she saw lights, a hint of order, buildings and tracks. It was a human settlement, here in the deepest scar on the most inhospitable planet in the solar system. She ought to have been uplifted by the spectacle. But that tiny spark in the midst of such ferocious desolation seemed merely absurd.

There was a lot of traffic in the sky.

They were human ships. Most of them were driven by solar sails, filmy and beautiful, wispy shapes that tacked against Mercury's impassive rocky face, the slow evolution of their forms betraying the intelligent control that guided them. The ships rode the hail of photons that came from the huge, nearby sun, a much more effective means of transportation here than at Earth's orbit and beyond.

It was immediately obvious that there were more ships arriving than leaving. But then there was no other place for humans to go, here in the solar system of the year AD 3793; Mercury was a sink of people, not a source.

On the far side of Mercury she saw a type of landscape she'd never seen before: broken up, chaotic, almost shattered. She worked out that it was at the exact antipode of that giant impact structure, the target of converging spherical shock waves that must have travelled around the world; rock-smashing energies had focused here and made the land flex and crumble and boil.

Once Madeleine had hurled moons around the outer solar system. Now she felt awed, humbled, by the evidence of such huge forces. Overwhelmed by a sense of impotence.

She was brought to land near the main human settlement. This was in a wide crater called Chao Meng-Fu, another giant impact structure, this one almost covering the south pole.

The gravity startled her with its strength, around twice that on the Moon. Strange for such a small planet, really little larger than the Moon; Mercury was very dense, another cannonball.

Madeleine suited up. It was straightforward; through the centuries, in contrast to comms units and coffee machines, she'd found that life-critical equipment like pressure suits and airlocks remained easy to operate, its operation obvious.

She stepped out of the tractor. Once again I set foot on a new world, she thought. Do I hold the record?

Within Chao Meng-Fu there were power plants and automated strip-mining robots. The surface structures cowered in rim mountain shadows, avoiding a sun which glared down for one hundred and seventy-six Earth days at a time – an unexpected number; Mercury's 'day' was fixed, by tidal effects, as two-thirds of the little planet's eighty-eight-day year, and so its calendar was a complex clockwork.

She looked up, towards the sun, which was low on the horizon. Filters in her helmet blocked out the disc of the sun itself, but that disc was three times as large as Earth's sun, a bloated monster.

She saw no humans above ground, none at all.

Her arrival at Chao City was processed by crude virtuals. These software robots had been designed to handle the arrival of speakers of incomprehensible languages, from all over the solar system. Their humanity smoothed out, they guided her wordlessly with simple mime and gesture. Chao City was a warren of corridors and tunnels, hastily cut out of the bedrock. It was crowded with a dozen diverse races, a place full of suspicion and territoriality.

She was assigned a poky room, another cave like the one she'd endured on Triton – though this time, at least, carved from familiar silicate rock rather than water ice. How strange it was that humans, on whatever world they settled from one end of the solar system to the other, were driven to burrow into the ground like moles.

The room contained a comms interface unit, inevitably of a very different design from those on Triton, with which, wearily, she battled. At last she found a way to instruct a contemporary analogue of a data miner to find Nemoto – if she was indeed here on Mercury.

The comms unit began to ping softly. After no more than thirty minutes' probing she found out that the sound meant the unit contained a message, waiting for her. *Come see me. Nowadays I live in a crater called Bernini. Not so far away from Chao. You'll enjoy the view.* It named a place and time.

It was from Dorothy Chaum.

She was kept waiting another twenty-four hours. Then she was taken to see somebody called an Immigration Officer. More bureaucracy, she thought with a sinking heart. Just like Triton; a universal human trait.

The Immigration Officer actually tried to speak to her in Latin. *Quo vadis? Quo animo?* – Where are you going? With what intention? She had brought her pressure suit helmet with its embedded translator suite, and the office had similar facilities, and she waited patiently for the equipment to work.

The Officer's name was Carl ap Przibram. He was a native of an asteroid: tall, spindly, with a great eggshell of a skull under thick hair, and long bony fingers, a cliché pianist's. His skin was pale, his features smoothed-out, as if his skin was stretched; perhaps there were folds at his eyes, traces of an Asian ancestry, but any ethnic antecedents from Earth were long mixed and blurred. He seemed profoundly uncomfortable – as well he might, Madeleine thought, as he was effectively operating in multiples of the gravity he was used to.

When they were able to communicate he took her name, requested various identification numbers she didn't have, then asked for a summary of her background. She listed her voyages beyond the stars. Using a workstation built into his desk, he brought up, from some deep database, a record on her, maintained over centuries. Ap Przibram seemed immersed in his job, all the documentation and procedure, utterly uninterested in the reality of the exotic fossil before him. It was a reaction she'd encountered on Triton, and many times before.

He requested that she make a donation of DNA samples. It was logical – a scheme to keep mankind's small, isolated gene pools refreshed – though she'd heard of travellers who had patronized a flourishing black market in traveller genetic samples, notably sperm; the latter-day legend, happily encouraged by some travellers, was that the good stuff from these crude near-barbarians from a thousand years ago was more vigorous, more potent than the etiolated modern vintage.

At last he handed her a piece of plastic embedded with temporary ident codes, preliminary to a full implant; she took it gravely. 'You are welcome here,' he told her.

'Thank you.' She raised the issue of her companions from Triton.

'Their application will be processed as speedily as possible.' He fell silent, his drawn face impassive.

She tapped the desk with a fingernail. She found it hard to read his posture, the language of his face. 'They've flown across the system, across thirty astronomical units, in landers designed for hundred-kilometre orbital hops. Those things are flying toilets. We have children, old people, disabled, ill . . .'

'We are processing their application. Until that is concluded there's nothing I can do.'

His eyes were hollow. The man is exhausted, she thought. He is overwhelmed, as Mercury is; and here I am with more refugees, boatloads of resentful ice dwellers from Triton. In such circumstances, bureaucracy is a medium of civilized discourse; at least he isn't throwing me out.

She resolved to be patient.

At the appointed time she set off to meet Dorothy. There was a monorail link from Chao City to Bernini – slow, bumpy, uncomfortable, real pioneer stuff – and then she had to take a ride in an automated tractor, a thing of giant wire-mesh wheels, over lightly occupied Mercury.

She arrived at what Dorothy had referred to as a solar sail farm.

Outside the tractor she studied the sky.

She could see few stars. Solar-sail ships swam, dimly visible, like sparks from a fire, swarming around Mercury's equator, bringing more refugees. But there was a haze across the sky, a mistiness surrounding that too-large sun disc, and a pale wash further out, like a starless Milky Way. She was seeing the sun's tenuous atmosphere, made visible by the artificial occulting of the central star. And the flat belt of light further out was the zodiacal light, the shining of dust particles and meteorites and asteroids in the plane of the ecliptic. Once Gaijin cities had shone there; now the asteroid belt was deserted once more.

When she cupped her hands around her faceplate she could see the tail of yet another giant comet, smeared milkily over the black dome of the sky. She couldn't see any Cracker ships, of course – not yet – even though, it was said, they had broken through the orbit of Neptune.

As the Oort war had turned sour, Mercury had been annexed by a coalition of nations from the asteroid colonies: the near-Earths, the main belt, even a few from the Trojans in Jupiter's orbit. It was hardly an occupation; nobody but a few hermit types had been living here anyhow. The set-up here was barely democratic – a situation which, to their credit, appeared to disturb the emergency government, the Coalition. But it was functioning.

The colonists had adapted technologies that had once been used in the initial colonization of the Moon: once more, humans were forced to bake their air out of unyielding rock. But there were plans for the longer term – such as a Paulis mine at Caloris Planitia, the giant impact crater she'd observed from orbit. But this was not the Moon. Mercury was all iron core, with a little rocky rind. A different world, different challenges.

Now she picked out a double star, a bright double pinpoint, one partner strikingly blue, the other a pale grey-white . . .

'Earth, of course.' Here was Dorothy standing close by her side, in a suit so coated with black Mercury dust it was all but invisible, despite the brightness of the sun. Her helmet was heavily shielded, just a golden bubble; Madeleine couldn't see her face.

They exchanged meaningless pleasantries, awkward; there were no obvious protocols for a relationship such as theirs.

Then Dorothy loped heavily across the dusty plain. Madeleine, reluctantly, followed.

The regolith crunched under her feet, the noise clearly audible, carried through her suit. In the virgin dust she left footprints, clear and sharp as on the Moon, and the dust she threw up clung to the fabric of her suit. But her footing was heavy here, in this double-Moon gravity. No bunny-hop Moonwalking here.

It was like the Moon, yes – the same undulating surface, heavily eroded, crater on crater, so the surface was like a sea of dusty waves.

But if anything the erosion was more complete here. There were hills – she was close to the rim wall of crater Bernini – but they were stoop-shouldered, coated in regolith. The smaller craters were little more than shadows of themselves, palimpsests, their features worn away.

She hadn't met Dorothy since they had been with Malenfant on the Gaijin's home world, and the three of them had set off to return to the solar system by their different routes. Dorothy seemed different to Madeleine: more closed-in, secretive, perhaps obsessive. Somehow older.

Dorothy paused, and pointed to a hole in the ground. 'Here's where I live. Subsurface shelter. It isn't so bad. Not if you already spent subjective years in spacecraft hab modules.'

At Madeleine's feet was a flattened boulder, its exposed top worn smooth, like a lens. She bent stiffly, scuffed at the soil, and prised the rock out of the dirt. Most of the rock had been hidden in the dirt, like an iceberg. Underneath it was sharp, a jagged boulder.

Dorothy said, 'It probably dropped here a billion years ago, thrown half-way around the planet by some impact. And since then any bits of it that stuck out have just been eroded flat, right here where it landed, layer by layer.'

Madeleine frowned. 'Micrometeorite impacts?'

'Not primarily. At noon it gets hot enough to melt lead. And in the night, which lasts nearly six months, it's cold enough to liquefy oxygen.'

'Thermal stress, then.'

'Yes. Shaped the landscape. Bane of the engineer's life, here on this hot little world. Come on. Let me show you what I do for a living . . .'

They walked briskly through a shallow crater littered with bits of glass.

That, anyhow, was how it seemed to Madeleine at first glance. She was surrounded by delicate glass leaves that rested against the regolith, spiky needles protruding. There was, too, another type of structure: short, stubby cylinders, pointing at the sky, projecting in all directions, like miniature cannon muzzles. It was like a sculpture park.

Dorothy stalked on without pausing. Some of the petal-shaped glass plates were crushed under Dorothy's careless feet; Madeleine walked more carefully. Dorothy said, 'We can just grow sail panels right out of the rock. These things are gen-enged descendants of vacuum flowers from the Moon. I've made myself something of an expert at this technology. Good to have a profession, on a world where you have to pay for the air you breathe, don't you think?' She tilted back her head, her face obscured. 'Next time you see a solar sailing ship, think of this place, how those gauzy ships are born, morphing right out of the rocks at your feet. Beautiful, isn't it?'

They walked on. Madeleine asked about Malenfant.

Dorothy shrugged. 'I got back twenty years before you did. If he came directly back to the system after we parted, as he said he would, he might have arrived here centuries earlier yet. I don't know what's become of him.'

Madeleine studied her. 'You're troubled. The time we had on the Cannonball –'

'Not troubled, exactly. Guilty, perhaps.' She laughed. '*Guilt*: the Catholic Church's first patent.'

'And that's why you work so hard here.'

Dorothy said dryly, 'Analysis now, Madeleine? I also work to live, as must we all . . . But still, yes, I failed Malenfant, there on the Cannonball. I used to be a priest. If ever there was a soul in torment, in his own silent, lonely way, it was Reid Malenfant. And I couldn't find a way to help him.'

Madeleine scowled, irritated. 'What happened on the Cannonball was about Malenfant, Dorothy; not you and your guilt. Malenfant was a victim. A tool of the Gaijin, dragged across the Galaxy, part of plans we still know nothing about. Why should he put up with that?'

'Because he knew, or suspected, that it was the right thing to do, if the Gaijin had any hope of changing –' she waved a gloved hand at the damaged sky '– *this*. The rapacious colonization waves, the wars, the trashing of worlds, the extinctions. Even if there was a chance of making a difference, it might have been right for Malenfant to sacrifice himself.'

'But he's just a man, a human. Why should he give himself up? Would you?'

Dorothy sighed. 'I'm not the right person to ask any more. Would *you*?'

'I don't know.' Madeleine was chilled. 'Poor Malenfant.'

'Wherever he is, whatever becomes of him, I hope he isn't alone. Even Christ had the comfort of His family, at the foot of the Cross. You brought refugees here, didn't you?'

Madeleine grunted. 'I'm told that everybody here is a refugee. But here we are as safe as anywhere.'

Dorothy barked laughter. 'You don't get it yet, do you? Obviously you haven't spoken to Nemoto . . . *She's* still alive. Did you know that? Centuries old . . . Of all the places to come – *this*, Mercury, as the last refuge of mankind? *Wrong.*'

'Mercury is deep in the inner system. So close to the sun the Gaijin don't want to come here.'

'But the Gaijin are not the enemy,' Dorothy hissed. 'You have to think things through, Madeleine. We think we know how the Crackers work. They manipulate the target star, causing it to nova . . .' A nova: a stellar explosion, releasing as much energy in a few days as a star would have expended in ten thousand years. 'The Crackers feed on the light pulse, you see,' Dorothy said. 'They ride their solar-sail craft out to more stars, scattering like seeds from a burst fungus, sailing past planets scorched and ruined. We used to think novae were natural. A question of a glitch in a star's fusion processes, perhaps caused by an infall of material from a binary companion. Now we wonder if *any* nova we have observed historically has been natural. Perhaps *all* of them, all over the sky, have been the responsibility of the Crackers – or foul species like them.'

And Madeleine started to see it. 'How do you make a star nova?'

'Simple. In principle. You set a chain of powerful particle accelerators in orbit around your target star. They create currents of charged particles, which set up a powerful magnetic field, caging the star – which can then be manipulated.'

'. . . Ah. But you need a resource base to manufacture those thousands, millions of machines. And a place to make your new generation of solar sailing boats.'

'Yes. Madeleine, here in the solar system, what would be the *ideal* location for such a mine?'

A rocky world orbiting conveniently close to the central star itself. A big fat core of iron and nickel just begging to be dug out and broken up and exploited, without even an awkward rocky shell to cut through . . .

'Mercury,' Madeleine whispered. 'What do we do? Do we have to evacuate?'

Dorothy said, comparatively gently, '*Where to*? Meacher, remember where you are. We've already lost the solar system. This is the last bolt hole. All we can do is dig deep, deep down, as deep as possible.'

Something about her emphasis on those words made Madeleine look hard at Dorothy, but her face remained obscured.

'What are you doing here, Dorothy? You're planning something, aren't you? . . .' Her mind raced. 'Some way of striking back at the Crackers – is that what this is about? *Are you working with Nemoto?*'

But Dorothy evaded the question. 'What can *we* do? The Crackers have already driven off the Gaijin, a species much older and wiser and more powerful than *us*. We're just vermin, infesting a piece of prime real estate.'

Madeleine said coldly, 'If you believe we're vermin, you really have lost your faith.'

Dorothy laughed. 'Compared to the Gaijin, even the Crackers, what other word would you use?' She peered up at the sky, her face obscured by scuffed glass. 'Remember, Madeleine. *Tell them to dig deep*. That's vital. As deep as they can . . .'

She went back to Carl ap Przibram to discuss the issue of the Aborigines. Interstellar war or not, *they* still had no other place to go.

'Please be straightforward with me. I appreciate you're trying to help. I don't want to offend you, or imply –'

'– that I'm some kind of immoral bastard,' he said tightly.

The archaic term surprised her. She wondered what thirty-eighth-century oath lay on the other side of the chattering translators.

He said, 'This isn't an easy job. People always find it hard to accept what I have to tell them.'

'I sympathize. But I need you to help me. I'm a long way from home – from my time. It's hard for me to understand what's happening here, to progress the issue.' She pointed to the ceiling. 'There are two hundred people up there. They've come all the way in from Triton, the edge of the solar system. They have absolutely no place to go. They are completely dependent, refugees.'

'*We are all refugees.*'

She grunted. 'That's the standard mantra here, isn't it?'

He frowned at her. 'But it's true. And I don't know if you understand how significant that is. I haven't met a traveller before, Madeleine Meacher. But I've read about your kind.'

'My *kind*?'

'You were born on Earth, weren't you? At a time when there were no colonies beyond the home planet.'

'Not quite true –'

'You are accustomed to think of us, the space dwellers, as exotic beings, somehow beyond the humanity you grew up with. But it isn't like that. *My* home society, on Vesta, was fifteen centuries old. My ancestors spent all that time making the asteroid habitable. Centuries living in tunnels and lava tubes and caves, cowering from radiation, knowing that a single mistake could kill everything they cared about

. . . We are a deeply conservative people, Madeleine Meacher. We are not used to travel. We are not world-builders. We, too, are a long way from home.'

'You got here first,' Madeleine said. 'And now you're driving everybody else off.'

He shook his head. 'It isn't like that. If not for us, *this* – a habitable corner of Mercury – wouldn't be here at all.'

She stood up. 'I know you'll do your job, Carl ap Przibram.'

He nodded. 'I appreciate your courtesy. But you understand that doesn't guarantee I will be able to let your party land here. If we cannot feed them . . .' He steepled his long fingers. 'In the long run,' he said, 'it may make no difference anyhow. Do you see that?'

If the Crackers win, if they come here. *That's* what he means.

He studied her face, as if pleading for help, for understanding.

Everybody does his best, she thought bleakly. How little it all means.

Chapter 31

END GAME

In the final months, events unfolded with shocking rapidity. The great spherical fleet of Cracker vessels sailed inwards, through the huge empty orbits of the outer planets, past abandoned asteroids, at last into the hot deep heart of the system.

One by one, all over the system, beacons were extinguished: on Triton, the asteroids, Mars, human stories concluded without witness, in the cold and dark.

The data miners found Nemoto – or, Madeleine thought, perhaps she consented to be found.

It turned out Nemoto had shunned the underground colonies. She was working on the surface, in an abandoned science base in a big, smooth-floored crater called Bach, some thousand kilometres north of Chao City.

Madeleine used the monorail to get to Bach. The 'rail was still functioning, for now; the encroaching Cracker ships had yet to interfere materially with Mercury in any way. Nevertheless there were no humans operating on the surface of Mercury, nobody amid the blindly toiling robots, diggers and scrapers. And everywhere, tended by the robots or not, Madeleine saw the gleam of solar sail flowers.

In the shade of an eroded-smooth crater wall, Nemoto was toiling at a plain of tilled regolith. Here, one of the glass-leafed arrays had spread out over the heat-shattered soil. Nemoto was hunched over, monk-like, a slow, patient figure, redolent of age, tending her plants of glass and light.

The sun was higher in the sky at this more northerly latitude, a ferocious ball, and Madeleine's suit, gleaming silver, warned her frequently of excessive temperatures.

'Nemoto –'

Nemoto straightened up stiffly. She silenced Madeleine with a gesture, beckoned for her to come deeper into the shade, and pointed upwards.

Madeleine lifted her visor. Gradually, as her eyes adapted, the stars came out. The sky's geography was swamped, in one corner, by the extensive glare of the sun's corona.

But the stars were just a backdrop to a crowd of ships.

They were all around Mercury now, spread out through three-dimensional space, like a great receding cloud of dragonflies, frozen in flight. Loose clusters of them already orbited the planet, looping east and west, north and south, cupping the light. And further out there was a ragged swarm still on the way, reaching back to the hidden sun, around which these misty invaders had sailed.

Their filmy, silvery wings were caught folded or twisted, in the act of shifting better to catch the sun's light. The spread of those gauzy wings was huge, some of them thousands of kilometres across. These were no trivial inner-system skimmers, as humans had built, made to sail in the dense light winds close to the sun; these were giant interstellar schooners, capable of travelling across light years, through spaces where the brightest, largest star was reduced to a point.

Not dragonflies, she thought. Locusts. For not one of those ships was human, Madeleine knew, or even Gaijin. Nothing but Crackers.

'It's remarkable to watch them,' Nemoto breathed. 'I mean, over hours or days. Simply to stand here and watch. You can see them deploying their sails, you know. The sunlight pushes outward from the sun, of course. But they sail in towards the sun by tacking into the light: they lose a little orbital velocity, and then simply fall inwards. But sailing ships that size are slow to manoeuvre. They must have been plotting their courses, here to Mercury, all the way in from the Oort cloud.'

'I wonder what the sails are made of,' Madeleine said.

Nemoto grunted. 'Nothing *we* have ever been capable of. Maybe the Gaijin would know. Only diamond fibre would be strong enough for the rigging. And as for the sails, the best *we* can do is aluminized spider-silk. Much too thick and heavy for ships of that size. Perhaps they grow the sails by some kind of vacuum deposition, molecule by molecule. Or perhaps they are masters of nanotech.'

'They really are coming, aren't they, Nemoto?'

Nemoto turned, face hidden. 'Of course they are. We are both too old for illusion, Meacher. They are wasps around a honey pot, which is Mercury's fat iron core.'

Together, they walked around the spreading array, glass flowers that sparkled with the light of stars and Eetie ships.

Madeleine tried to talk to Nemoto, to draw her out. After all, their acquaintance – never friendship – went back across *sixteen hundred years*, to that steamy office in Kourou, a tank of spinning Chaera on the pre-Paulis Moon. But Nemoto wouldn't talk of her life, her past: she would talk of nothing but the great issues of the day, Mercury and the Crackers and the great Eetie colonization pulse all around them, the huge and impersonal.

Madeleine wondered if that was normal.

But there was nothing *normal* about a woman who had lived through seventeen centuries, for God's sake. Nemoto was probably the oldest human being who had ever lived; to survive, Nemoto must have put herself through endless reengineering, of both body and mind. And, unlike the lonely star travellers, she had lived through all those years on worlds full of people: Earth, the Moon, Mercury. Her biography must run like an unbroken thread through the tangled tapestry of a millennium and a half of human history.

But Madeleine truthfully knew little of this ancient, enigmatic woman. Had she ever married, ever fallen in love? Had she ever had children? And if so, were *they* alive – or had she outlived generation after generation of descendants? Perhaps nobody knew, nobody but Nemoto herself. And Nemoto would talk of none of this, refused to be drawn as she tended her plants of glass.

But in her slow-moving, aged way, she seemed focused, Madeleine thought. Determined, vigorous. Almost happy. As if she had a mission.

Madeleine decided to challenge her.

She walked among the glassy leaves. She bent, awkwardly, and picked up a glimmering leaf; it broke away easily. It was very fine, fragile. When she crushed it carelessly, it crumbled.

Nemoto made a small move towards her, a silent admonition.

Madeleine dropped the leaf carefully. 'I've been reading up,' she said.

'You have?'

'On you. On your, umm, career.' She waved a hand at the leaves. 'I think I know what you're doing here.'

'Tell me.'

'Moon flowers. You brought them here, to Mercury. This isn't just about growing solar sails. There are Moon flowers all over this damn planet. You've been seeding them, haven't you?'

Nemoto hunkered down and studied the plant before her. 'They grow well here. The sunlight, you see. I gen-enged them – if you can call it that; the genetic material of these flowers is stored in a crystalline substrate which is quite different from our biochemistry. Well. I removed some unnecessary features.'

'Unnecessary?'

'The rudimentary nervous system. The traces of consciousness.'

'Nemoto – *why*? Will dying Mercury become a garden?'

'What do you *think*, Meacher?'

'That you're planning to fight back. Against the Crackers. You are remarkable, Nemoto. Even now, even here, you continue the struggle . . . And these flowers have something to do with it.'

Nemoto was as immobile as her flowers, the delicate glass petals reflected in her visor. She said, 'I wonder how they started. The Crackers. How they began this immense, destructive odyssey. Have you ever thought about that? Surely no species *intends* to become a breed of rapacious interstellar locusts. Perhaps they were colonists on some giant starship, a low-tech, multi-generation ark. But when they got to their destination they'd gotten too used to spaceflight. So they built more ships, and just kept going . . . Perhaps the gimmick – blowing up the target sun for an extra push – came later. And once they'd worked out how to do it, reaped the benefits, they couldn't resist using it. Over and over.'

'Not a strategy designed to make them popular.'

'But all that matters, in this Darwinian Galaxy of ours, is short term effectiveness. No matter how many suns you destroy, how many worlds you trash . . . There simply isn't the time to have qualms about such things. And so it goes, as the Galaxy turns, oblivious to the tiny beings warring and dying on its surface . . .'

She walked on, tending her garden, and Madeleine followed.

'You must help us,' said Carl ap Przibram.

Madeleine sat uncomfortably, wondering how to respond. She felt claustrophobic in this bureaucrat's office, crushed by the layers of Mercury rock over her head, the looming nearness of the sun: as if she could somehow sense its huge weight, its warp of space.

He leaned forward. 'For fifteen centuries my people lived like this.' He held up his hands, indicating the close rocky walls. 'In environments that were enclosed. Fragile. Shared.' His face clouded with anger, hostility. 'We didn't have the luxury for – aggression. Warfare.'

Now she understood. 'As *we* did, on "primitive Earth". Is that what you think? But my world was small too. *We* could have unleashed a war which might have made the planet uninhabitable.'

'That's true.' He jabbed a Chopin finger at her. 'But you didn't *think* that way, did you? *You*, Madeleine Meacher, used to ship weapons, from one war zone to another. That was your job, how you made a living.

'You come from a unique time. We remember it even now; we are taught about it. Uniquely wasteful. You were still fat on energy, from Earth's ancient reserves. You managed to get a toehold on other worlds, the Moon. But you squandered your legacy – turned it into poisons, in fact, that trashed your planet's climate.'

She stood up. 'I've heard this before.' It was true; the bitterness at the well-recorded profligacy of her own 'fat age' had scarcely faded in the centuries since, and the travellers, time-stranded refugees from that era, made easy targets for bile and prejudice. But it scarcely mattered *now*. 'Carl ap Przibram, tell me what you want of me.'

'I've been authorized to deal with you. To offer you what we can . . .'

It turned out to be simple, unexpected. Impossible. The Coalition wanted to put her in charge of Mercury's defences: assembling weapons and a fighting force of some kind, training them up, devising tactics. Waging war on the Crackers.

She laughed; ap Przibram looked offended. She said, 'You think I'm some kind of warrior barbarian, come from the past to save you with my primitive instincts.'

He glared. 'You're more of a warrior – and a barbarian – than I will ever be.'

'This is absurd. I know nothing of your resources, your technology, your culture. How could I lead you?' She eyed him, suspicious. 'Or is there another game being played here? Are you looking for a fall guy? Is that it?'

He puzzled over the translation of that. Then his frown deepened. 'You are facetious, or foolish. If we fail to defend ourselves, there will be no "fall guys". In the worst case there will be nobody left *at all*, blameworthy or otherwise. We are asking you because . . .'

Because they are desperate, she thought, these gentle, spindly asteroid-born people. Desperate, and terrified, in the face of this Darwinian onslaught from the stars.

'I'll help any way I can,' she said. 'But I can't be your general. I'm sorry,' she added.

He closed his eyes and steepled his fingers. 'Your friends, the refugees from Triton, are still in orbit.'

'I know that,' she snapped.

He said nothing.

'. . . Oh,' she said, understanding. 'You're trying to bargain with me.' She leaned on the desk. 'I'm calling your bluff. You haven't let them starve up there so far. You won't let them die. You'll bring them down when you can; you aren't serious in your threats.'

His thin face twisted with embarrassment. 'This wasn't my idea, Madeleine Meacher.'

More gently, she said, 'I know that.'

'In the end,' he said, 'none of this may matter. The Crackers have little interest in our history and our disputes and our intrigues with each other.'

'It's true. We're vermin to them.' Anger flared in her at that thought, the word Dorothy had used.

But it's true, she thought.

This, here on Mercury, may be the largest concentration of humans left anywhere. And if the Crackers succeed in their project, it will be the end of mankind. None of our art or history, our lives and hopes and loves, none of it will matter. We'll be just another forgotten, defeated race, just another layer of organic debris in the long, grisly history of a mined-out solar system.

I can't let that happen, she thought. And: I must see Nemoto again.

On the surface of Mercury, Nemoto sighed. 'You know, the Crackers' strategy – making suns nova – isn't really all that smart. When you're more than a few diameters away from your disrupted star it starts dwindling into a point source, and the light wind's intensity falls off rapidly. But if you have a *giant* star – say a red giant – you are sailing with a wall of light behind you, and you get a runaway effect; it takes *much* longer for the wind to dwindle. You see?'

'So –'

'So the best strategy for the Crackers would be to tamper with the sun's evolution. To make it old before its time, to balloon it to a red giant that would reach out to Earth's orbit, and ride out that fat crimson wind. But the Crackers aren't smart enough for that. None of the Eeties out there are *really* smart, you know.'

'Maybe the Crackers are working on an upgrade,' Madeleine suggested dryly.

'Oh, no doubt,' Nemoto said, matter-of-fact. 'The question is, will they have time to figure out how to do it, before *their* race is run?'

'Why haven't you told the refugees what you are up to, Nemoto?'

'Meacher, the people on this ball of iron are conservative. And split: there are many factions here. Some believe the Crackers may be placated. That these Eeties will just leave of their own accord.'

'That's ridiculous. The Crackers *can't* leave. They *must* dismantle the sun to continue their expansion.'

'Nevertheless, such views are held. And such factions would, if they knew of my project, seek to shut me down.'

'So what do we do?'

'The settlers here must go as deep as they can, deep into the interior.'

Just as Dorothy Chaum had said. 'When?'

'When the Cracker ships are here. When all the wasps have swarmed to the honey pot.'

'I'll try. But what of you, Nemoto?'

Nemoto just laughed.

Madeleine leaned forward. 'Tell me what happened to Malenfant.'

Nemoto would not meet her eyes.

She told Madeleine something of what sounded like a long and complicated story, embedded in Earth's tortured latter history, of a Saddle Point gateway in the heart of a mountain in Africa. Her account was cool, logical, without feeling.

'So he went back,' Madeleine said. 'Back through the Saddle Points, back to the Gaijin, after all.'

'You don't understand,' Nemoto said without emotion. 'He had no choice. *I* sent him back. I manipulated the situation to achieve that.'

Madeleine covered Nemoto's cold hand.

'. . . Just as I have manipulated half of mankind, it seems. I exiled Malenfant, against his will.' Nemoto said sharply, 'I believe I have sent him to his death, Meacher. But if it is a crime, it will be justified – if the Gaijin can make use of that death.'

'I guess you have to believe that,' Madeleine murmured.

'Yes. Yes, I have to.'

Her manner was odd – even for Nemoto – too cool, logical; too bright, Madeleine thought.

Madeleine knew that no human could survive more than a thousand years without emptying a clutter of memory from her overloaded head. Nemoto *must* have found a way to edit her memories, to reorder, even delete them – a process which, of course, meant the editing of her personality too.

Perhaps she has attempted to cleanse her memories of Malenfant, her guilt over her betrayal of him. That is how she has been able to achieve such distance from it.

But if so, she was only partially successful. For this action against the Crackers, whatever it is, will kill her, Madeleine realized.

And Nemoto is embracing the prospect.

Madeleine worked hard on Carl ap Przibram, trying to get him to take Nemoto's advice seriously. It wasn't easy, given her lack of any detailed understanding of what Nemoto might be trying to attempt. But at last he yielded, and got her a slot before the Coalition's top council.

It was an uneasy session. It took place in a steamy cave crammed with a hundred delegates from different factions, none of them natives, jammed in here against their will in the bowels of Mercury. There was a range of body types, she observed, mostly variants on the tall, stick-thin low-gravity template; but there were a number of delegates adapted for zero G, even exotic atmospheres, in environment tanks, wheel chairs and other supportive apparatus.

She faced rows of faces glaring with suspicion, fear, self-interest, even contempt. This wasn't going to be easy. But she recognized, here in the main governing council, one of the women from the Triton transports, which had at last been allowed to land. These people were prickly, awkward, superstitious, fearful. But, even in this dire strait, they welcomed refugees, and even gave them a place at the top table.

It made her obscurely proud. *This* is what the Gaijin should have studied, she thought. Not wrinkles in our genome. *This*: even in this last refuge, we refuse to give up, and we still welcome strangers.

She launched into her presentation. She stayed on her feet a good hour as speaker after speaker assailed her. She didn't always have answers, but she weathered the storm, trying to persuade by her steady faith, her unwavering determination.

Not everybody was convinced. That was never going to be possible. But in the end, factions representing a good sixty per cent of the planet's population agreed to concur with Nemoto's advice.

Immensely relieved, Madeleine went back to her room, and slept twelve hours.

The final evacuation was swift.

The remnants of humanity had fled inwards, to Mercury. And now they were converging even more tightly, flowing over the surface of Mercury in monorails or tractors or short-hop sub-orbit shuttles, gathering in the great basin of Caloris Planitia: the shattered ground where, under a high and unforgiving sun, humans had burrowed in search of water.

And, meanwhile, the last of the giant interstellar fleet of Cracker sailing craft were settling into dense, complex orbits around Mercury: wasps around honey, just as Nemoto had said. Data flowed between the Cracker craft, easily visible, even tapped by the cowering humans. These Eeties clearly had no fear of interference, now the Gaijin had withdrawn.

Maybe it would take the Crackers a thousand years to make ready for their great star-bursting project. Maybe it would take a thousand days, a thousand hours. Nobody knew.

Madeleine spent some time with Carl ap Przibram, the nearest thing to a friend she had here.

They had a very stiff dinner, in his apartment. The recycling loops were tight; illogical as it might be, she found it difficult to eat food that must have been through Carl's body several times at least. On the way, she'd decided to invite him to have sex. But it was an offer made more in politeness than lust; and his refusal was entirely polite, too, leaving them both – she suspected – secretly relieved.

Madeleine spent her last day on Mercury inside the Paulis mine in Caloris. This was a tube a half-kilometre wide, the walls clear, the rocks beyond glowing orange-hot. It was the big brother of Frank Paulis's first ancient well on the Moon. This mine had never been completed, and perhaps never would be; but now it served a new purpose as a deep shelter for the remnants of humanity.

Giant temporary floors of spider-silk and aluminium had been spun out over the shaft, cut through by supply ducts and cabling and a giant fireman's-pole of open elevators. Here – safe from radiation and the sun's heat and the shadow's cold – half Mercury's population, a million strong, was being housed in flimsy bubbles of spider-silk and aluminium. The Paulis tunnel wasn't pressurized, of course, and so big flexible walkways ran between the bubbles. The floors were misty and translucent, as were the hab bubbles; and, looking down into the glowing pit of humanity, Madeleine could see people scattered over floor after floor, moving around their habs like microbes in droplets of water, receding into a misty, light-filled infinity.

It was well known she was planning to leave today. In the upper levels many faces were turned up to her – she could see them, just pale dots. She had always been isolated, especially in this latest of her parachute-drops back into human history. Perhaps she was getting too old, too detached from the times. In fact she suspected the displaced Triton colonists rather resented her – as if she, who had guided them here, had somehow been responsible for the disaster that had befallen their home.

Anyhow, it was done. She turned her back on the glimmering interior of the Paulis mine, its cache of humans, and returned to the surface.

She flew up from Mercury, up through a cloud of Cracker ships.

Great sails were all around her. Even partly furled, they were huge, spanning tens of kilometres, like pieces of filmy landscapes torn loose and thrown into the sky. Some of them had been made transparent rather than furled, so that the bright light of the sun shone through skeletal structures of shining threads. And the wings had a complex morphology, each warping and twisting and curling, presumably in response to the density of the light falling on it, and the thin shadows cast by its neighbours.

The Cracker ships sailed close to each other: in great layers, one over the other, sometimes barely half a kilometre apart, a tiny separation compared to the huge expanse of the wings. Sometimes they were so close that a curl in one wing would cause a rippling response in others, great stacks of the wings turning like the pages of an immense book. But Madeleine never once saw those great wings touch; the coordination was stunning.

Madeleine rose up through all this, just bulling her way through in her squat little Gaijin lander. The wonderful wings just curled out of her way.

At ten Mercury diameters, she looked back.

Mercury was a ball of rock, maybe the size of her palm held at arm's length. It looked as if it was wrapped in silvery paper, shifting layers of it, as if it were some huge Christmas present – or perhaps as if immense silvery wasps were crawling all over it. Quite remarkably beautiful, she thought. But, she reflected bitterly, if there was one thing she had learned in her long and dubious career, it was that beauty clung as closely to objects of killing and pain and horror as to the good; and so it was here.

She stretched, weightless. She felt deeply – if shamefully – relieved to be alone once more, in control of her own destiny, without the complication of other people around her.

Nemoto called her from the surface.

'I'm surprised they let you through like that. The Crackers. You're in a Gaijin ship, after all.'

'But the Gaijin are gone. The Crackers clearly don't believe the Gaijin are a threat any more. And they don't even seem to have noticed us humans.' The Crackers are just kicking over the ant hill, she thought, without even looking to see what was there, what *we* were.

'Meacher, how far out are you?'

'Ten diameters.'

'That should be sufficient,' hissed Nemoto.

'Sufficient for what? . . . Never mind. Nemoto, how can you choose death? You've lived so long, seen so much.'

'I've seen enough.'

'And now you want to rest?'

'No. What rest is there in death? I only want to act.'

'To save the species one more time?'

'Perhaps. But the battle is never over, Meacher. The longer we live, the deeper we look, the more layers of deception and manipulation and destruction we will find . . . Consider Mercury, for example, which may be doomed to become a resource mine for the sun-breaking Crackers. Why, if I was a suspicious type, a conspiracy theorist, I might think it was a little *odd* that there should be a giant ball of crust-free nickel-iron placed so *conveniently* right here where the Crackers need it. What do you think? Could some predecessors of the Crackers – even their ancestors – have *arranged* the giant impact that stripped off Mercury's crust and mantle, left behind this rust ball?'

Madeleine was stunned by this deepening of the great violation of the solar system. But, deliberately, she shook her head. 'Even if that's true, what difference does it make?'

Nemoto barked laughter. 'None at all. You're right. One thing at a time. You always were practical, Meacher. And what next for you? Will you stay with the others, huddled in the caves of Mercury?'

Madeleine frowned. 'I'm not a good huddler, Nemoto. And besides, these are not my people.'

'The likes of us have no "people" –'

'Malenfant,' Madeleine said. 'Wherever he is, whatever he faces, he is alone. I'm going to try to find him.'

'Ah,' Nemoto whispered. 'Malenfant, yes. He may be the most important of us all. Goodbye, Meacher.'

'Nemoto? –'

Mercury exploded.

She had to go over it again, rerun the recordings, over and over, before she understood.

It had happened in an instant. It was as if the top couple of metres of Mercury's surface had just lifted off and hailed into the sky.

All over Mercury – from the depths of Caloris Planitia to the crumpled lands at the antipode, from Chao City at the south pole to the abandoned settlements of the north – miniature cannon snouts had poked their way out of the regolith, and fired into the sky. The bullets weren't smart: just bits of rock and dust, dug out of the deeper regolith. But they were moving fast, far faster than Mercury's escape velocity.

The Crackers didn't stand a chance. Mercury rocks tore through filmy wings, overwhelming self-repair facilities. The Cracker ships, like butterflies in a reverse hailstorm, were shredded. Ships collided, or plunged to Mercury's surface, or drifted into space, powerless, beyond the reach of help.

The Moon flowers, of course: they were the key, or rather their dumb, gen-enged descendants, transplanted to Mercury by Nemoto, a wizened, interplanetary Johnny Appleseed. The Moon flowers could make explosive, of aluminium and oxygen, extracted from Moon rock – or Mercury rock – a serviceable chemical-rocket propellant to propel their seed pores. Nemoto had engineered the flowers' descendants to make weapons.

The Crackers had nobody even to fire back at, no way to avoid the rising storm of rock and dust. Even one survivor might have been sufficient to resume the Crackers' mission, for all anybody knew. But there were no survivors. The Crackers had taken a thousand years to reach Mercury, to fly from Procyon and battle through a shell of Gaijin ships. It had taken humans – rock world vermin, contemptuously ignored – a thousand seconds to destroy them.

As she watched that cloud of peppery rock rise from the ground and rip through the gauzy ships – overwhelming them one by one, at last erupting into clear space – Madeleine whooped and howled.

The debris cloud continued to expand, now beginning to tail after Mercury in its slow orbit around the sun. It caught the brilliant light, like rain in sunshine. Maybe Mercury is going to have rings, she thought, rings that will shine like roadways in the sky. Nice memorial. The major features of the surface beneath had survived, of course; no backyard rocket was going to obliterate Caloris Planitia. But every square metre of the surface had been raked over.

She contacted the Coalition.

Every human on Mercury had survived – even those who hadn't taken Nemoto's advice about deep shelter. Already they were emerging, blinking, under a dusty, starry sky.

Every human but Nemoto, of course.

At least we have breathing space: time to rebuild, maybe breed a little, spread out, before the next bunch of Eetie assholes come chomping their way through the solar system. Good for you, Nemoto. You did the best you could. Good job.

As for me – story's over here, Madeleine. Time to face the universe again.

And so Madeleine fled before the hail of rubble from Mercury – still expanding, a dark and looming cloud that glittered with fragments of Cracker craft – fled in search of Gaijin, and Reid Malenfant.

V

THE CHILDREN'S CRUSADE

AD 8800, and Later

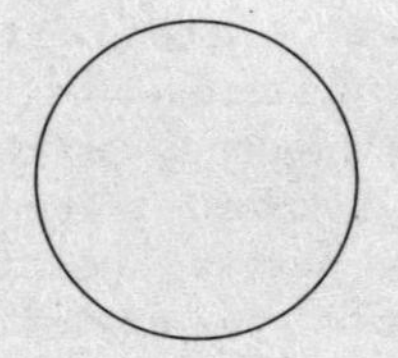

Near the neutron star there were multiple lobes of light. They looked like solar flares to Malenfant: giant, unending storms rising from the neutron star's surface. Further out still, the founts of gas lost their structure, becoming dim, diffuse. They merged into a wider cloud of debris which seemed to be fleeing from the neutron star, a vigorous solar wind. And beyond *that* there were only the Galaxy core stars, watchful, silent, still, peering down as if in disapproval at this noisy, spitting monster.

This was a pulsar. You could detect those radio beams from Earth.

Malenfant had grown up with the story of the first detection of a pulsar. Pre-Gaijin astronomers had detected an unusual radio signal: a regular, ticking pulse, accurate to within a millionth of a second. Staring at such traces, the scientists had at first toyed with the idea it might be the signature of intelligence, calling from the stars.

In fact, when envoys from the stars began to make their presence known, it was not as a gentle tick of radio noise but as a wave of destructive exploitation that scattered mankind and all but overwhelmed the entire solar system – and the same thing had occurred many times before.

We put up a hell of a fight, though, he thought. We even won some victories, in our tiny, scattershot way. But in the end it was going to count for nothing.

It was ironic, he thought grimly. Those old pre-Gaijin star gazers had thought that first pulsar was a signal from Little Green Men.

In fact it was a killer of Little Green Men.

Chapter 32

SAVANNAH

She woke to the movement of air: the rustle of wind in trees, perhaps the hiss of grass, a gentle breeze on her face, the scent of dew, of wood smoke. Eyes closed, she was lying on her back. She could feel something tickling at her neck, the slippery texture of leaves under the palms of her hand. Somewhere crickets were calling.

She opened her eyes. She was looking up at the branches of a tree, silhouetted against a blue-black sky.

And the sky was full of stars. A great river of light flowed from horizon to horizon. It was littered with pink-white glowing clouds, crowded, beautiful.

She remembered.

Io. She had been on Io.

Her Gaijin guides had taken her to a grave: Reid Malenfant's grave, they said, dug by strong Neandertal hands. She had, briefly, despaired; she had been too late in her self-appointed mission; he had died alone after all, a long way from home.

The Gaijin hadn't seemed to understand.

Then had come a blue flash, a moment of pain –

And now, *this*. Where the hell was she? She sat up, suddenly afraid.

She saw a flickering fire, a figure squatting beside it. A man. He was holding something on a stick, she saw, perhaps a fish. He stood straight now, and came walking easily towards her.

She felt herself tense up further.

His head was silhouetted against the crowded stars; he was bald, his skin smooth as leather. It was Reid Malenfant.

She whimpered, cowered back. '*You are dead.*'

He crouched before her, reached out and held her hand. He felt warm, real, calm. 'Take it easy, Madeleine.'

'They put you in a hole in the ground, on Io. Jesus Christ –'

'Don't ask questions,' he said evenly. 'Not yet. Concentrate on the here and now. How do you *feel*? Are you sick, hot, cold? . . .'

She thought about that. 'I'm okay. I guess.' She wiggled her fingers and toes, turned her head this way and that. Everything intact and mobile; nothing aching; not so much as a cricked neck. Her trembling subsided, soothed by a relentless blizzard of detail, of normality. The here and now, yes.

It *was* Reid Malenfant. He was wearing a pale blue coverall, white slip-on shoes. When she glanced down, she found she was wearing the same bland outfit.

He was studying her. 'You were out cold. I thought I'd better leave you be. We don't seem to have any medic equipment here.'

The smell of the fish reached her. 'I'm hungry,' she said, surprised. 'You've been *fishing*?'

'Why not? I mined my old spacesuit. Not for the first time. A thread, a hook made from a zipper. I felt like Tom Sawyer.'

. . . Never mind the fish. This guy is *dead*. 'Malenfant, they buried you. Your burns . . .' But she was starting to remember more. The Neandertals had opened the grave. It was empty.

'Just look at me now.' Emulating her, he clenched his fists, twisted his head. 'I haven't felt so good since the Bad Hair Day twins had a hold of me.'

'Who?'

'Long story. Look, you want some fish or not?' And he loped back to the fire, picked up another twig skewered through a second fish, and held it over his fire of brush wood.

She got to her feet and followed him.

The sky provided a soft light, as bright as a quarter-Moon, perhaps. Even away from that Galactic stripe the stars were crowded. There was a pattern of bright stars near the zenith that looked like a box, or maybe a kite; there was another easy pattern further over, six stars arranged in a rough, squashed ellipse. She recognized no constellations, though.

The grassy plain rolled to the distance, dotted with sparse trees, the vegetation black and silver in the starlight. But where Malenfant's fire cast a stronger light she could see the grass was an authentic green.

Gravity about Earth normal, she noted absently.

She thought she saw movement, a shadow flitting past a stand of trees. She waited for a moment, holding still. There was no sound, not so much as a crackle of undergrowth under a footstep.

She hunkered down beside Malenfant, accepted half a fish and bit into it. It was succulent but tasteless. 'I never much liked fish,' she said.

'Sorry.'

'Where's the stream?'

He nodded, beyond the fire. 'Thataway. I took a walk.'

'During the daylight?'

'No.' He tilted back his head. 'When I woke up it was night, as deep as this.' He glanced up at the sky, picking out a complex of glowing clouds. 'What do you think of the view?'

The larger of the clouds was a rose of pink light. Its heart was speckled by bright splashes of light – stars? – and it was bordered by a band of deeper darkness, velvet blackness, where no stars shone. It was beautiful, strange.

'That is a star birth nebula,' he said. 'It's probably much more extensive. All we can see is a blister, illuminated by a clutch of young stars at the centre – see the way that glow is roughly spherical? – the stars' radiation makes the gases shine, out as far as it can reach, before it gets absorbed. But you can see more stars, younger stars, emerging from the fringes of the blister. That darker area all around the glow, eclipsing the stars behind, is a glimpse of the true nebula, dense clouds of dust and hydrogen, probably containing proto-stars that have yet to shine . . . Madeleine, I did a little amateur astronomy as a kid. I *recognize* that thing; it's visible from Earth. We call it the Lagoon Nebula. And its companion over there is the Trifid. The Lagoon contains stars so young and bright you can see them with the naked eye, from Earth.'

In all her travels around the Saddle Point network, Madeleine had seen nothing like this.

'Ah,' Malenfant said, when she expressed this. 'But we've come far beyond *that*, of course.'

She shivered, suddenly longing for daylight. 'Malenfant, in those trees over there. I thought I saw –'

'There are Neandertals here,' he said quickly. 'You needn't fear them. I think they're from Io. Maybe some of them are from Earth, too. I think they were brought here when they were close to death. I haven't recognized any of them yet. There is one old guy I got to know a little, who died. I called him Esau. He must be here somewhere.'

She tried to follow all that. He didn't seem concerned, confused by the situation. There was, she realized, a lot he needed to tell her.

'We aren't on Io any more, are we?'

'No.' He pointed at the stars with his half-eaten fish. 'That's no sky of Earth. Or even of Io.'

Madeleine felt something inside her crack. '*Malenfant* –'

'Hey.' He was immediately before her, holding her shoulders, tall in the dark. 'Take it easy.'

'I'm sorry. It's just –'

'We're a long way from home. I know.'

'I've got a lot to tell you.' She started to blurt out all that she'd seen since she, Malenfant and Dorothy Chaum had returned to the solar system from the Gaijin's Cannonball homeworld: the interstellar war, the hail of comets into the sun's hearth, the Crackers.

He listened carefully. He showed regret at the damage done to Earth, the end of so many stories. He smiled when she spoke of Nemoto. But after a time, as detail after detail spilled out of her, he held her shoulders again.

'Madeleine.'

She looked up at him; his eyes were wells of shadow in the starlight.

'*None of it matters.* Look around, Madeleine. We're a long way away from all that. There's nothing we can do to affect any of it now . . .'

'How far?'

He said gently, 'Questions later. The first thing *I* did when I woke up was go behind those bushes over there and take a good solid dump.'

Despite herself, that made her laugh out loud.

By the time they'd eaten more fish, and some yam-like fruit Malenfant had found, it was still dark, with no sign of a dawn. So Madeleine pulled together a pallet of leaves and dry grass, and tucked her arms inside her coverall, and quickly fell asleep.

When she woke it was still dark.

Malenfant was hunkered down close to a stand of trees. He seemed to be drawing in the dirt with a stick, peering around at the sky. Beyond him there was a group of figures, shadowy in the starlight. Neandertals?

There really was no sign of dawn, no sign of a moon: not a glimmer of light, other than starlight, on any horizon. And yet something was different, she thought. Were the stars a little brighter? Certainly that Milky Way glow close to the horizon seemed stronger. And, it seemed to her, the stars had shifted a little, in the sky. She looked for the star patterns she had noted last time she was awake – the box overhead, the ellipse. Were they a little distorted, a little more squashed together?

She joined Malenfant. He handed her a piece of fruit, and she sat beside him.

The Neandertals seemed to be a family group, five, six adults, about as many children. They seemed oblivious to Malenfant's scrutiny. They were hairy, squat, naked: cartoon ape men. And two of the children were wrestling, hard, tumbling over and over, as if they were more gorilla than human.

Malenfant asked slowly, avoiding her eyes: 'Why did you come here, Madeleine?'

He seemed stiff; she felt embarrassed, as if she had been foolish, impulsive. 'I volunteered. The Gaijin helped me. I wanted to find you.'

'Why?'

'I got to know you, on the Cannonball, Malenfant. I didn't like the idea of you being alone when –'

'When what?'

She hesitated. 'Do *you* know why you're here?'

'Just remember,' he said coolly, 'I didn't ask you to follow me.' He continued his sketching in the dust, angry.

She shrank back, confused, lost; she felt further from home than ever.

She studied his sketches. They were crude, just scrapings made with the point of his stick. But she recognized the box, the ellipse.

'It's a star map,' she said.

'Yeah. Kind of basic. Just a few score of the brightest stars. But look here, here, here . . .'

Some of the points were double.

'The stars have shifted,' she said.

'Here's where *this* one was yesterday – or before we slept, anyhow. And here's where it is now.' He shrugged. 'The shift is small – hard to be accurate without instruments – but I think it's real.'

'I noted it too,' she said.

'Not just a shift. Other changes. I think there are *more* stars than yesterday. They seem brighter. And they are flowing across the sky –' he swept his arms over his head, towards the bright Milky Way band on the horizon '– thataway.'

'Why that way?'

He looked up at her. 'Because that's where we're headed. Come see.' He stood, took her by the hand and pulled her to her feet, and led her past a stand of trees.

Now she saw the Galactic band exposed to her full view: it was a river of stars, yes, but they were stars that were varied, yellow and blue and orange, and the river was crammed with exotic features, giant dark clouds and brilliant shining nebulae.

'It looks like the Milky Way,' she said. 'But –'

'I know,' he said. 'It's not like this at home . . . I think we're looking at the Sagittarius Spiral Arm.'

She said slowly, 'Which is *not* the arm which contains the sun.'

'Hell, no. *That's* just a shingle, a short arc. *This* mother is the next arm in, towards the centre of the Galaxy.' He swept his arm so his hand spanned the star river. 'Look at those nebulae – see? – the Eagle, the Omega, the Trifid, the Lagoon – a huge region of star-birth, one of the largest in the Galaxy, immense clouds of gas and dust capable of producing millions of stars each. The Sagittarius Arm is one of the Galaxy's two main spiral features, a huge whirl of matter that reaches from the hub of the Galaxy all the way out to the rim, winding around for a full turn. This is what you see if you head inward from the sun, towards the Galaxy centre.'

Under the huge, crowded sky, she felt small, humbled. 'We've come a long way, haven't we, Malenfant?'

'I think we busted out of the edge of the Saddle Point network. We know the network is no more than a couple of thousand light years across, extending just a fraction of the way to the centre of the Galaxy. We must have reached a radius where the Saddle Points aren't working any more. Which is a problem if you want to go further . . . I think this is just the start of the true journey.'

He was speaking steadily, evenly, as if discussing a hiking tour of Yosemite. She felt her self-control waver again. But she didn't want to seem weak in front of Malenfant, this difficult cold man.

'And,' she said, 'where will that *true journey* take us?'

He shrugged. 'Maybe all the way to the centre of the Galaxy.' He studied her, perhaps to see how well she could take this. Then he pointed. 'Look, Madeleine – the Lagoon Nebula, up there, is five thousand light years from Earth.'

And so, therefore, she thought, the year is 8800 AD, or thereabouts. It was a number that meant nothing to her at all. And, even if she turned around now and headed for home, assuming that was possible, it would be another five thousand years before she could get back to Earth.

But the centre of the Galaxy was twenty-five thousand light years from the sun. Even at lightspeed it would take fifty thousand years to get there and back. *Fifty thousand years*. This was no ordinary journey, not even like a history-wrenching Saddle Point hop; the human species itself was only a hundred thousand years old . . .

He was still watching her. 'I've had time to get used to this.'

'I'm fine.'

'Madeleine . . .'

'I mean it,' she snapped. She got up, turned her back and walked away. She found a stream, drank and splashed her face, spent a few minutes alone, eyes closed, breathing deeply.

Perhaps it's just as well we humans can't grasp the immensities we have begun to cross. If we were any smarter, we'd go crazy.

Remember why you came here, Madeleine. For Malenfant. Whether he appreciates it or not, the asshole. Malenfant is strong. But maybe it helps him just to have me here. Somebody he has to look after.

But her grasp of psychology always had been shaky. Anyhow, she was here, whether he needed her or not.

She went back to Malenfant, at his patient vigil.

One of the Neandertal women was working a rock, making tools. She held a core of what looked like obsidian, a glassy volcanic rock. She gave the core one sharp strike, and a flake of it dropped off. A few light strokes along the edge and the flake had become a tear-shaped blade, like an arrow-head. The woman, with a lop-sided grin, gave the knife to one of the males, signing rapidly.

Malenfant murmured, 'She's saying he should be careful of the edge.'

She frowned. 'I don't understand how those guys got here.'

He told her what he'd observed of the Neandertals' burial practices: the mysterious Staff of Kintu.

'So you think the Gaijin were rewarding the dying Neandertal workers for all their labours with this – a soapy Heaven.'

He laughed. 'If they were, they are the first gods in history to deliver on their afterlife promises.'

She paced, feeling the texture of the grass under her feet, the breeze on her face. 'Why is it like *this*? Trees, grass, streams – it feels like Africa. But it isn't Africa, is it?'

'No. But if you ask almost any human, anywhere, what type of landscape they prefer, it's something like *this*. Open grass, a few flat-topped trees. Even Clear Lake, Houston, fits the pattern: grass out front, maybe a tree or two. And you never put your tree in front of your window; you need to be able to look out of your cave, to see the predators coming. After taking us apart for a thousand years, the Gaijin know us well. And our Neandertal cousins. We're a hundred millennia out of Africa, Madeleine, and five thousand light years distant.' He tapped his chest. 'But it's still here, inside us.'

'You're saying they've given us an environment that we're comfortable with. A Neandertal theme park.'

He nodded. 'I think very little of what we see is real.' He pointed at the sky. 'But *that* is real.'

'How so?'

'Because it's changing.'

She slept and woke again.

And the sky, once more, had changed dramatically. She lay on her back alongside Malenfant, gazing up at the evolving sky.

He started talking about how he had travelled here.

'They put me through a whole series of Saddle Point jumps, taking me across the geography of the Galaxy . . . First I headed towards Scorpio. Our sun is in the middle of a bubble in space, hundreds of light years across – did you know that? – a vacuum blown into the Galactic medium by an ancient supernova explosion. But the Saddle Point leaps got longer and longer . . .'

With the sun already invisible, he had been taken out of the local bubble, into a neighbouring void the astronomers called Loop 1.

'I saw Antares through the murk,' he said, 'a glowing red jewel set against a glowing patch of sky, a burst of young stars they call the Rho Opiuchi complex. Hell of a sight. I looked back for the sun. I couldn't find it. But I saw a great sheet of young stars that slices through the Galactic plane, right past Sol. They call that Gould's Belt, and I knew *that* was where home was.

'And when I looked ahead, there was a band of darkness. I was reaching the inner limit of our spiral arm, looking into the rift between the arms, the dense dark clouds there. And then, beyond the rift, I arrived here – in this place, with the Neandertals . . .'

'And the stars.'

'Yes.'

While she had slept, the stars had continued to migrate. Now they had *all* swum their way up towards that Sagittarius Arm horizon, the way Malenfant said they were heading. The opposite horizon looked dark, for all its stars had fled. All the stars in the sky, in fact, had crowded themselves into a disc, centred on a point some way above that brighter horizon – at least she guessed it was a disc; some of it was below her horizon. And the colours had changed; the stars had become green and yellow and blue.

Now, in what situation would you expect to see the stars swimming around the sky like fish?

'This is the aberration of starlight, isn't it, Malenfant? The distortion of the visible universe, which you would see if –'

'If you travel extremely quickly. Yes,' he said softly.

She understood the principle. It was like running in the rain, a rain of starlight. As she ran faster, the rain would hit her harder, in her face, her body. If she ran extremely fast indeed, it would be as if the rain was almost horizontal . . .

'We're on a starship,' she breathed.

'Yeah. We're moving so fast that most of the stars we see up ahead must be red giants, infrared sources, invisible to us in normal times. All the regular stars have been blue-shifted to invisibility. Wherever we're going, we're travelling the old-fashioned way: in a spaceship, pushed up to relativistic speeds. And we're still accelerating.'

She sat up and dug her fingers into the grass. 'But it doesn't *feel* like a starship. Where is the crew? Where are we going? What will happen when we get there?'

'When I found you, I hoped *you* were going to tell *me*.' He got to his feet. 'What do you think we should do now?'

She shrugged. 'Walk. There's nothing to stay for here.'

'Okay. Which way?'

She pointed to the glowing Sagittarius Arm horizon, the place the stars were fleeing, their putative destination.

He smiled. 'And add a couple of kilometres an hour to our eighty per cent of lightspeed? Why not? We're walking animals, we humans.'

Malenfant picked up a sack, which turned out to contain his ancient spacesuit, the wreck she had spent hours fixing up on the Cannonball. Obeying some obscure impulse for tidiness, he scuffed over his dirt-scraped star map. Then they set off.

They passed the Neandertal family, who sat just where they had yesterday.

When Madeleine looked back, the Neandertals were still sitting, unmoving, as the humans receded, and the stars flowed overhead.

The next time she woke, there was only a single source of light in the sky. It was a small disc, brighter than a full Moon, less bright than the sun seen from Earth, tinged distinctly bluish.

Aside from that the cloudless sky was utterly empty.

Malenfant was standing before her, staring at the light. Beyond him she could see Neandertals, a family group of them, standing too, staring into the light, their awkward heads tipped back. Shadows streamed from the light, shadows of people and trees, steady and dark.

She stood beside Malenfant. 'What is it? Stars?'

He shook his head. 'The stars are all blue-shifted to invisibility. All of them.'

'Then what –'

'I think that's the afterglow.' The background heat of the universe, left over from the Big Bang, stretched to a couple of degrees above absolute zero. 'We're going so fast now, just a tad lower than light-speed, that even *that* has been crumpled up by aberration, crushed into a tiny disc. Some spectacle, don't you think? . . .' He held his hand up before him, shading the universe-sun; she saw its shadow on his face. 'You know, I remember the first time I left Earth, en route to the Saddle Point. And I looked back and saw the Earth dwindle to a dot of light smaller than *that*. Everything I'd ever known – five billion years of geology and biology, of sliding continents and oceans and plants and dinosaurs and people – all of it was crammed into a splinter of light, surrounded by nothing. And now the whole damn *universe*, stars and galaxies and squabbling aliens and all, is contained in that little smudge.'

He told her he thought they were riding an antimatter rocket.

'. . . It explains what the Gaijin were doing on Io. Tapping the energy of Jupiter's magnetosphere. Probably turned the whole moon into one big atom-smasher, and picking the antimatter out of the debris.' The antimatter rocket could be a kind called a beam-core engine, he speculated. 'It's simple, in principle. You just have your tanks of atoms and anti-atoms – hydrogen, probably, the anti-stuff contained in a magnetic trap – and you feed it into a nozzle and let it blow itself up. The electrons make gamma rays, and the nuclei make pions, all high energy stuff, and some of the pions are charged, so that's what you throw out the back as your exhaust . . . There are other ways to do it. I don't imagine the Gaijin have a very advanced design.'

'It must have taken the Gaijin a long time, an immense project, to assemble the antimatter they needed.'

'Oh, yeah. Hauling those superconductor cables all the way out from Venus, and everything. Big engineering.'

'But,' Madeleine said deliberately, 'there is no way you could haul all of this –' she indicated the plain, the trees '– a ship the size of a small *moon* up to relativistic speeds, all the way to the Galaxy core. Is there?'

He looked into the sky. 'I saw a study which said you would need a hundred tonnes of antimatter to haul a single ragged-assed astronaut to Proxima Centauri. At the time it would have taken *our* biggest atom-smasher two centuries to produce so much as a milligram. I doubt that whatever the Gaijin built on Io was so terribly advanced over that. So – no, Madeleine. You couldn't haul a small moon.'

She studied her hand, pinched the flesh. The pinch hurt. '*What are we*, Malenfant? You think we're some kind of simulations running inside a giant computer?'

'It's possible.' His voice contained a shrug, as if it didn't matter. 'It only takes a finite number of bits to encode a human being. That's because of uncertainty, the graininess of nature . . . If not for that, the Saddle Point gateways wouldn't be possible at all. On the other hand –' He dug into the ground until he came up with a stone the size of his thumb nail. 'If the universe was the size of this rock, then each star would be the size of a quark. There are orders of magnitude of scale, structure, beneath the level of a human. Maybe we're real, but shrunken down somehow. Plenty of room down there.'

She felt a pulse in her head, a pressure. 'But,' she said, 'if we're just emulations in some toy starship, we're dead. I mean, we're no longer us. Are we? How can we be?'

He eyed her. 'The first time you stepped through a gateway you were no longer you. Every transition is a death, a rebirth. Why do you think it hurts so much?'

She felt weak, her legs numb. Carefully, she lowered herself to the grass, dug her hands into the rich cool texture of the ground.

He knelt beside her, took her hand. 'Listen. I don't mean to be so tough on you. What do I know? – I only have guesses too. I've had more time to get used to this stuff, is all.' He went on with difficulty, 'I know you came here to help me. I remember the way you fixed my suit, on the Cannonball. You were – kind.'

She said nothing.

He said, 'I just don't think you can help.' His face was turning hard again. 'Or *will* help.'

That chilled her, his harsh dismissal. 'Help with *what*, Malenfant? Why did the Gaijin go to all this trouble – to train Neandertals to mine antimatter on Io, build a starship, hurl it across light years?'

He looked troubled at that. 'I think – I have this awful feeling, a suspicion – that the purpose of it all was *me*. A huge alien conspiracy, all designed to give *me* a ride across the Galaxy.' He studied her, face emptied by wonder. 'Or is that paranoid, megalomaniac? Do you think I'm crazy, Madeleine?'

Beyond him, perhaps a half kilometre away, she made out a new shadow: angular, gaunt, crisp and precise before the cosmos light.

It was a Gaijin.

'Maybe we'll soon find out,' she said.

They approached the Gaijin. It just stood there impassively, silent. Madeleine saw how the pencil-thin cones that terminated its legs were stained green by crushed grass, and that a little quasi-African dust had settled on the surfaces of its upper carapace.

Malenfant said he recognized it. It was the individual Gaijin he had come to know as Cassiopeia.

'Oh, really? And how do you know that, Malenfant? The Gaijin are just spidery robots. Don't they all look alike? . . .'

He didn't try to answer.

Madeleine found the Gaijin's calm mechanical silence infuriating. She bent down and picked up a handful of dirt. She threw it at the Gaijin; it pinged off that impassive hide, not making so much as a scratch. 'You. Space robot. You've been playing with us since you showed up in our asteroid belt. I don't care how alien you are. No more fucking *games* . . .'

Malenfant seemed shocked by her swearing. A corner of her found amusement at that. Malenfant really was a man of his time: here they were hurtling away from Earth at a tad less than lightspeed, shrunk to quark-sized copies or else trapped in some alien virtual reality, and *he* was shocked to hear a woman swear. But he just stood and let her rant her heart out. Therapy, for absorbing one shock after another.

She ran out of energy, slumped back to the grass, numbed by tiredness.

The Gaijin stirred, like a tank turret swivelling. Madeleine thought she heard something like hydraulics, perhaps a creak of metal scraping on metal. The Gaijin spoke, its booming voice a good emulation of the human – a woman's voice, in fact, with a tinge of Malenfant's own accent.

She said, NO DOUBT YOU'RE WONDERING WHY I ASKED YOU HERE TODAY.

The silence stretched. Malenfant peered up at the Gaijin doubtfully.

'She made a joke,' Madeleine said slowly. 'This ridiculous alien robot made a joke.'

Malenfant stared at Madeleine. Then he threw his hands in the air, slumped back on the grass, and laughed.

Pretty soon, Madeleine caught the bug. The laugh seemed to start in her belly, and burst out of her throat and mouth, despite her best efforts to contain it.

So they laughed, and kept on laughing, while the Gaijin waited for them.

And, cradling its precious cargo of mind and hope and fear, the ten-centimetres-long starship hurtled onwards towards the core of the Galaxy, and its destiny.

Chapter 33

THE FERMI PARADOX

They drank from a stream, and ate fruit, and lay on the grass, letting the tension drain out. Madeleine thought she slept for a while, curled up against Malenfant in the grass, like two exhausted kids.

And then – when they were awake, sitting before Cassiopeia – the Gaijin waved a spidery metal limb, and the world dissolved. It melted like a defocusing image: grass and mud and trees and streams running together, everything but the three of them, two humans and a Gaijin, and that eerie universe-sun, so that they seemed to be floating, bathed in a deeper darkness than Madeleine had ever known.

She reached out and grabbed Malenfant's hand. It was warm, solid; she could see him, the folds on his jumpsuit picked out by the cosmic glow. She dug the fingers of her other hand into loamy soil beneath her. It was still there, cool and friable, invisible or not. She clung to its texture, to the pull of the fake world sticking her to the ground.

But Malenfant was staring upwards, past the Gaijin's metal shoulder. '*Look* at that. Holy shit.'

She looked up unwillingly, reluctant to face new wonders.

Above them, a ceiling of curdled light spanned the sky. It was a galaxy.

It was a disc of stars, flatter and thinner than she might have expected, in proportion to its width no thicker than a few sheets of paper. She thought she could see strata in that disc, layers of structure, a central sheet of swarming blue stars and dust lanes sandwiched between dimmer, older stars. The core, bulging out of the plane of the disc like an egg yolk, was a compact mass of yellowish light; but it was not spherical, rather markedly elliptical. The spiral arms were fragmented. They were a delicate blue laced with ruby-red nebulae and the blue-white blaze of individual stars – a granularity of light – and with dark lanes traced between each arm. She saw scattered flashes of light, blisters of gas. Perhaps those were supernova explosions, creating bubbles of hot plasma hundreds of light years across.

But the familiar disc – shining core, spiral arms – was actually embedded in a broader, spherical mass of dim red stars. The crimson fireflies were gathered in great clusters, each of which must contain millions of stars.

The Gaijin hovered before the image, silhouetted, like the spidery projector cluster at the centre of a planetarium.

'So, a galaxy,' said Madeleine. '*Our* Galaxy?'

'I think so,' Malenfant said. 'It matches radio maps I've seen.' He pointed, tracing patterns. 'Look. That must be the Sagittarius Arm. The other big structure is called the Outer Arm.' The two major arms, emerging from the elliptical core, defined the Galaxy, each of them wrapping right around the core before dispersing at the rim into a mist of shining stars and glowing nebulae and brooding black clouds. The other 'arms' were really just scraps, she saw – the Galaxy's spiral structure was a lot messier than she had expected – but still, she thought, the sun is lost in one of those scattered 'fragments'.

The Galaxy image began to rotate, slowly.

'A galactic day,' Malenfant breathed. 'Takes two hundred million years to complete a turn . . .'

Madeleine could see the stars swarming, following individual orbits around the Galaxy core, like a school of sparkling fish. And the spiral arms were evolving too, ridges of light sparking with young stars, churning their way through the disc of the Galaxy. But the arms were just waves of compression, like the bunching of traffic jams, with individual stars swimming through the regions of high density.

And now, Madeleine saw, a new kind of evolution was visible in the disc. Like the pulsing bubbles of supernovae, each was a ripple of change that began at an individual star, before spreading across a small fraction of the disc. Within each wavefront the stars went out, or turned red, or even green; or sometimes the stars would pop and flare, fizzing with light.

'Life,' she said. 'Dyson spheres. Star Crackers –'

'Yes,' Malenfant said grimly. 'Colonization bubbles. Just like the one *we* got caught up in.'

The Gaijin said sombrely, THIS IS WHAT WE HAVE LEARNED.

Life – said Cassiopeia – was emergent everywhere. Planets were the crucible. Life curdled, took hold, evolved, in every nook and cranny it could find in the great nursery that was the Galaxy.

Characteristically life took hundreds of millions of years to accrue the complexity it needed to start manipulating its environment on a major scale. On Earth, life had stuck at the single-celled stage for billions of years, most of its history. Still, on world after world, complexity emerged, mind dawned, civilizations arose.

Most of these cultures were self-limiting.

Some were sedentary. Some – for instance, aquatic creatures, like the Flips – lacked access to metals and fire. Some just destroyed themselves, one way or another, through wars, or accidents, or obscure philosophical crises, or just plain incompetence – which last, Madeleine suspected, might have been mankind's ultimate fate, left to its own devices.

Maybe one in a thousand cultures made it through such bottlenecks.

That fortunate few developed self-sustaining colonies off their home worlds, and – forever immune to the eggs-in-one-basket accidents which could afflict a race bound to a single world – they started spreading. Or else they made machines, robots that could change worlds and rebuild themselves, and sent them off into space, and *they* started spreading.

Either way, from one in a thousand habitable worlds, a wave of colonization started to expand.

There were many different strategies. Sometimes generations of colonists diffused slowly from star to star, like a pollutant spreading into a dense liquid. Sometimes the spread was much faster, like a gas into a vacuum. Sometimes there was a kind of percolation, a lacy, fractal structure of exploitation leaving great unspoiled voids within.

It was a brutal business. Lesser species – even just a little behind in the race to evolve complexity and power – would simply be overrun, their worlds and stars consumed. And if a colonizing bubble from another species was encountered, there were often ferocious wars.

Madeleine said sourly, 'It's hard to believe that every damn species in the Galaxy behaves so badly.'

Malenfant grinned. 'Why? This is how *we* are. And remember, the ones who expand across the stars are self-selecting. They grow, they consume, they aren't too good at restraining themselves, because that's the way they *are*. The ones who *aren't* ruthless predatory expansionists stay at home, or get eaten.'

Anyhow, the details of the expansion didn't seem to matter. In every case, after some generations of colonization, conflicts built up. Resource depletion within the settled bubble led to pressure on the colonies at the fringe. Or else the colonizers, their technological edge sharpened by the world-building frontier, would turn inwards on their rich, sedentary cousins. Either way the cutting-edge colonizers were forced outwards, farther and faster.

Before long, the frontier of colonization was spreading out at near lightspeed, and the increasingly depleted region within, its inhabitants having nowhere to go, was riven by wars and economic crisis.

So it would go on, over millennia, perhaps megayears.

And then came the collapse.

It happened over and over. None of the bubbles ever grew very large – no more than a few hundred light years wide – before simply withering away, like a colony of bacteria frying under a sterilizing lamp. And one by one the stars would come out once more, shining cleanly out, as the red and green of technology and life dispersed.

'The Polynesian syndrome,' Madeleine said gloomily.

'But,' Malenfant growled, 'it shouldn't *always* be like this. Sooner or later *one* of those races has got to win the local wars, beat out its own internal demons, and conquer the Galaxy. But we know that not *one* has made it, across the billions of years of the Galaxy's existence. And *that* is the Fermi Paradox.'

YES, said Cassiopeia. BUT THE GALAXY IS NOT ALWAYS SO HOSPITABLE A PLACE.

Now a new image was overlaid on the swivelling Galaxy: a spark that flared, a bloom of lurid blue light that originated close to the crowded core. It illuminated the nearby stars for perhaps an eighth of the galactic disc around it. And then, as the Galaxy slowly turned, there was another spark – and another, then another, and another still. Most of these events originated near the Galaxy core: something to do with the crowding of the stars, then. A few sparks, more rare, came from further out – the disc, or even the dim halo of orbiting stars that surrounded the Galaxy proper.

Each of these sparks caused devastation among any colonization bubbles nearby: a cessation of expansion, a restoring of starlight.

Death, on an interstellar scale.

Their virtual viewpoint changed, suddenly, swooping down into the plane of the Galaxy. As the spiral arms spread out above her, dissolving into individual stars which scattered over her head and out of sight, Madeleine cried out and clung to Malenfant. Now they swept inwards, towards the Galaxy's core, and she glimpsed structure beyond the billowing stars, sculptures of gas and light and energy.

Her attention came to rest, at last, on a pair of stars – small, fierce, angry. These stars were close, separated by no more than a few tens of their diameters. The two stars looped around each other on wild elliptical paths, taking just seconds to complete a revolution – like courting swallows, Madeleine thought – but the orbits changed rapidly, decaying as she watched, evolving into shallower ellipses, neat circles.

A few wisps of gas circled the two stars. Each star seemed to glow blue, but the gas around them was reddish. Further out she saw a lacy veil of colour, filmy gas that billowed against the crowded background star clouds.

'Neutron stars,' said Malenfant. 'A neutron star binary, in fact. That blue glow is synchrotron radiation, Madeleine. Electrons dragged at enormous speeds by the stars' powerful magnetic fields . . .'

The Gaijin said, PERHAPS FIFTY PER CENT OF ALL THE STARS IN THE GALAXY ARE LOCKED IN BINARY SYSTEMS – SYSTEMS CONTAINING TWO STARS, OR PERHAPS MORE. AND SOME OF THESE STARS ARE GIANTS, DOOMED TO A RAPID EVOLUTION.

Malenfant grunted. 'Supernovae.'

MOST SUCH EXPLOSIONS SEPARATE THE RESULTANT REMNANT STARS. ONE IN A HUNDRED PAIRS REMAIN BOUND, EVEN AFTER A SUPERNOVA EXPLOSION. THE PAIRED NEUTRON STARS CIRCLE EACH OTHER RAPIDLY. THEY SHED ENERGY BY GRAVITATIONAL RADIATION – RIPPLES IN SPACETIME.

The two stars were growing closer now, their energy ebbing away. The spinning became more rapid, the stars moving too fast for her to see. When the stars were no more than their own diameter apart, disruption began. Great gouts of shining material were torn from the surface of each star, and thrown out into an immense glowing disc that obscured her view.

At last the stars touched. They imploded in a flash of light.

A shock wave pulsed through the debris disc, churning and scattering the material, a ferocious fount of energy. But the disc collapsed back on the impact site almost immediately, within seconds, save for a few wisps that dispersed slowly, cooling.

'Has to form a black hole,' Malenfant muttered. 'Two neutron stars . . . too massive to form anything less. This is a gamma ray burster. We've been observing them all over the sky since the 1960s. We sent up spacecraft to monitor illegal nuclear weapons tests beyond the atmosphere. Instead, we saw *these*.'

THERE IS INDEED A BURST OF GAMMA RAYS – VERY HIGH ENERGY PHOTONS. THEN COMES A PULSE OF HIGH-ENERGY PARTICLES, COSMIC RAYS, HURLED OUT OF THE DISC OF COLLAPSING MATTER,

FOLLOWING THE GAMMA RAYS AT A LITTLE LESS THAN LIGHTSPEED.

THESE EVENTS ARE HIGHLY DESTRUCTIVE.

A NEARBY PLANET WOULD RECEIVE – IN A FEW SECONDS, MOSTLY IN THE FORM OF GAMMA RAYS – SOME ONE-TENTH ITS ANNUAL ENERGY INPUT FROM ITS SUN. BUT THE GAMMA RAY SHOWER IS ONLY THE PRECURSOR TO THE COSMIC RAY CASCADES, WHICH CAN LAST MONTHS. BATTERING INTO AN ATMOSPHERE, THE RAYS CREATE A SHOWER OF MUONS – HIGH-ENERGY SUBATOMIC PARTICLES. THE MUONS HAVE A GREAT DEAL OF PENETRATING POWER. EVEN HUNDREDS OF METRES OF WATER OR ROCK WOULD NOT BE A SUFFICIENT SHIELD AGAINST THEM.

Malenfant said, 'I *saw* what these things can do, Madeleine. It would be like a nearby supernova going off. The ozone layer would be screwed by the gamma rays. Protein structures would break down. Acid rain. Disruption of the biosphere –'

A COLLAPSE IS OFTEN SUFFICIENT TO STERILIZE A REGION PERHAPS A THOUSAND LIGHT YEARS WIDE. IN OUR OWN GALAXY, WE EXPECT ONE SUCH EVENT EVERY FEW TENS OF THOUSANDS OF YEARS – MOST OF THEM IN THE CROWDED GALAXY CORE.

Madeleine watched as the Galaxy image was restored, and bursts erupted from the crowded core, over and over.

Malenfant glared at the dangerous sky. 'Cassiopeia – are you telling me that these collapses are the big secret – the cause of the Reboot, the galactic extinction?'

Madeleine shook her head. 'How is that possible, if each of them is limited to a thousand light years? The Galaxy is a hundred times as wide as that. It would be no fun to have one of these things go off in your back yard. But –'

BUT, said Cassiopeia, SOME OF THESE EVENTS ARE – EXCEPTIONAL.

They were shown a cascade, image after image, burst after burst.

Some of the collapses involved particularly massive objects. Some of them were rare collisions involving three, four, even five objects simultaneously. Some of the bursts were damaging because of their orientation, with most of their founting, ferocious energy being delivered, by a chance of fate and collision dynamics, into the disc of the Galaxy, where the stars were crowded. And so on.

Some of these events were very damaging indeed.

Cassiopeia said, FROM THE WORST OF THE EVENTS THE EXTINCTION PULSE PROCEEDS AT LIGHTSPEED, SPILLING OVER THE GALAXY AND ALL ITS INHABITANTS, ALL THE WAY TO THE RIM AND EVEN THE HALO

CLUSTERS. NO SHIELDING IS POSSIBLE. NO COMPLEX ORGANISM, NO ORGANIZED DATA STORE, CAN SURVIVE. BIOSPHERES OF ALL KINDS ARE DESTROYED . . .

So it finishes, Madeleine thought, the evolution and the colonizing and the wars and the groping towards understanding: all of it halted, obliterated in a flash, an accident of cosmological billiards. It was all a matter of chance, of bad luck. But there were enough neutron star collisions that every few hundred million years there was an event powerful enough, or well-directed enough, to wipe the whole of the Galaxy clean.

It had happened over and over. And it will happen again, she saw. Again and again, a drumbeat of extinction. That is what the Gaijin have learned.

'And for us,' Malenfant growled, 'it's back to the fucking pond, every damn time . . . So much for Fermi's paradox. Nemoto was right. This *is* the equilibrium state for life and mind: a Galaxy full of new, young species struggling out from their home worlds, consumed by fear and hatred, burning their way across the nearby stars, stamping over the rubble of their forgotten predecessors.'

. . . And this is what the Gaijin tried to show me, Madeleine recalled, on my first Saddle Point jaunt of all, to the burster neutron star: the star lichen, fast-evolving life forms wiped out by a stellar fluke every fourteen seconds. It was a fractal image of *this*, the greater truth.

The Galaxy image abruptly receded, the spiral arms and the core and the surrounding halo imploding on itself like a burst balloon. Madeleine gasped at the sudden illusory motion. The world congealed around her: grass and trees and that black sky, all of it illuminated by fierce blue cosmic light. She was flooded with intense physical relief, as if she could breathe again.

But her mind was racing. 'There must be ways to stop this. All we have to do is evade *one* collapse – and gain the time to put aside the wars and the trashing, and get a little smarter, and learn how to run the Galaxy properly. We don't have to put up with this shit.'

Malenfant smiled. 'Nemoto always did call you a meddler.'

BUT YOU ARE RIGHT, said the Gaijin. SOME OF US ARE TRYING . . .

Ahead of them, she saw a group of Neandertals. They were dancing, signing furiously to each other, jumping up and down in the light of the cosmos. Something was changing in the sky, and the Neandertals were responding.

She looked that way. That cosmic light point seemed to be expanding.

The unwrapping sky was full of stars. It was the centre of the Galaxy.

Malenfant was confronting the Gaijin. 'Cassiopeia,' he said softly, 'what has all this got to do with me?'

The Gaijin said, MALENFANT, YOU ARE OUR BEST HOPE.

And now the Gaijin turned with a scrape of metal, a soft hiss as her feet sank deeper into the loam.

IT IS RISING.

She turned and began to stalk across the meadow, with that stiff, three-legged grace of hers, away from the stand of trees. Madeleine saw the Neandertals were following, a shadowy group of them, their muscles prominent in the starlight.

Malenfant grabbed her hand.

They walked through a meadow. The grass was damp, cool under her feet, and dew sparkled, a shattered mirror of the stars.

They were all immersed in diffuse shadowless light, in this place where every corner of the sky glowed as bright as the surface of the Moon. The light was silvery, the colours bleached out of everything; the grass was a deep green, the leaves on the trees black. Madeleine wondered vaguely if there was enough nourishment in that Galaxy light to fuel photosynthesis, if life could survive on a rogue, sunless planet here, just eating the dense starlight.

They topped a ridge, and looked down over a broad, shallow valley. There were scattered trees and standing water, ribbons and pools of silver-blue, all of it still and a little eerie in the diffuse starlight.

The Gaijin, Cassiopeia, had stopped, here at the crest. The Neandertals had gathered a little way away, along the ridge, and they were looking out over the valley.

But now one of the Neandertals came shambling towards Malenfant, with that clumsy, inefficient gait of theirs. It was a man, stoop-shouldered, the flesh over his ribs soft and sagging, and sweat slicked over his shoulders. That great brow pulled his face forward, so that his chin almost rested on his chest.

Malenfant said, 'Hello, Esau –'

Esau slapped him, and his fingers rattled, his fist thumping his forehead.

Malenfant grinned, and translated. '*Hello, Stupid.*' Malenfant seemed genuinely pleased to see this old Neandertal geezer again.

But now Cassiopeia stirred, and Madeleine grabbed his arm. 'Malenfant. Look. Oh, shit.'

A new star was rising above the valley, over the newly revealed horizon, brighter than the background wash.

It was a neutron star, a brilliant crimson point. Near the star there were multiple lobes of light. They contained structure, veins and streamers, something like the wings of a butterfly around that ferocious, dwarfed body; they glowed pink and an eerie blue, perhaps through the synchrotron radiation of accelerated electrons.

And there was something alongside the star. It looked like netting – scoop-shaped, like a catcher's mitt, facing the star as if endeavouring to grasp it.

Obviously artificial.

Cassiopeia said, OUR JOURNEY IS NOT YET DONE, MALENFANT. WE MUST PENETRATE THE GALACTIC CENTRE ITSELF. THIS IS WHAT WE WILL SEEK.

Malenfant said, 'This is the site of a gamma ray burster. A future Reboot event. I'm right, aren't I, Cassiopeia?'

THE STAR'S COMPANION IS AS YET SOME DISTANCE AWAY – BILLIONS OF KILOMETRES, IN FACT, TOO REMOTE TO SEE. AND YET THE CONVERGENCE HAS BEGUN. THE COLLISION IS INEVITABLE. UNLESS –

'Unless somebody does something about it,' Madeleine whispered.

That strange artefact continued to ride higher in the sky, like a filmy, complex moon. It was a net, cast across the stars. It must have been thousands of kilometres wide.

Madeleine found it impossible to believe it wasn't a few metres above her head, almost close enough she could just reach out and touch. The human mind was just not programmed to see giant planet-spanning artefacts in the sky. Think of an aurora, she told herself, those curtains of light, rippling far above the air you breathe. And now imagine *that*: it would hang there far beyond any aurora, suspended in space, perhaps beyond the Moon . . .

But there was something wrong: the netting was obviously unfinished, and great holes had been rent into its structure.

Malenfant said, 'It's broken.'

YOU WOULD CALL THIS A SHKADOV SAIL . . .

It would be a thing of matter and energy, of lacy rigging and magnetic fields: a screen to reflect the neutron star's radiation and solar wind. But it was bound to the star by invisible ropes of gravity.

'Ah,' Madeleine said. 'You disturb the symmetry of the solar wind. You see, Malenfant? The wind from the star will push at the sail. But the sail isn't going anywhere, relative to the star, because of gravity. So the wind gets turned back . . .'

'It's a stellar rocket,' Malenfant said. 'Using the solar wind to push aside the star.'

THAT IS THE PURPOSE. WHEN COMPLETE IT WILL BE A DISC A HUNDRED THOUSAND KILOMETRES ACROSS, ALL OF IT LACED WITH INTELLIGENCE, A DYNAMIC THING, CAPABLE OF SHAPING THE STAR'S SOLAR WIND, RESPONDING TO ITS COMPLEX CURRENTS.

Malenfant grinned. 'Hot damn. Somebody *is* fighting back.'

Madeleine asked, 'Who is building this thing? You?'

NOT US ALONE. MANY RACES HAVE COME HERE, COOPERATED ON THE SAIL'S CONSTRUCTION. IT APPEARS TO HAVE BEEN A RELIC FROM A PREVIOUS CYCLE, FROM BEFORE A PREVIOUS REBOOT.

'Like the Saddle Point network.'

Madeleine peered doubtfully at the huge, unlikely structure. 'How can a sail like that move a neutron star – an object more massive than the sun?'

THE THRUST IS VERY SMALL, THE ACCELERATION MINUSCULE. BUT OVER LONG ENOUGH PERIODS, SMALL THRUSTS ARE SUFFICIENT TO MOVE WORLDS. EVEN STARS.

'And will that be enough to stop the coalescence of this binary, to stop the Reboot?'

NOT TO STOP IT. TO POSTPONE IT GREATLY, BY ORDERS OF MAGNITUDE. IF WE CAN DELAY THIS STERILIZATION EVENT –

'We might win time,' Malenfant said.

Madeleine challenged the Gaijin. 'Is this *really* the best option? Haven't you come up with anything smarter?'

Malenfant eyed her. 'Like what?'

'Hell, I don't know. You could use antigravity. Einstein's cosmological constant, the force that makes the universe expand. Or you could interfere with the fundamental constants of physics. For example there is a particle called the Higgs boson, which gives matter its mass. If you took it away, switched it off, you could make your neutron stars lighter, and then just push them aside. In fact, take *all* the mass away and they would fly off at the speed of light. Easy. Give me a lever and I will move the world . . .'

WE HAVE NO SUCH POWERS, said Cassiopeia, and Madeleine thought she detected sadness in that synthesized voice. WE HAVE SEARCHED. THERE IS NO CIVILIZATION SIGNIFICANTLY MORE ADVANCED THAN OUR OWN – EVEN BEYOND THE GALAXY.

IT IS LIKE YOUR FERMI PARADOX. IF THEY EXISTED, WE WOULD SEE THEM. IMAGINE A GALAXY WITH ALL THE STARS FARMED, COVERED BY DYSON SPHERES, THEIR PHYSICS ALTERED PERHAPS TO

EXTEND THEIR LIFETIMES. IMAGINE THE GALAXY ITSELF ENCLOSED BY A DYSON STRUCTURE. AND SO ON. EVEN SUCH CLUMSY ENGINEERING, ON SUCH A SCALE, WOULD BE VISIBLE. WE SEE NO SUCH THING, AS FAR OUT AS WE LOOK, AS DEEP INTO SPACE AND TIME.

But it wasn't a surprise, Madeleine thought. How long would it take a galactic civilization to rise – even supposing somebody could survive the wars and assorted despoliation? Because of lightspeed, it would take a hundred thousand years for a message to cross the Galaxy *just once*. How many such exchanges would it take to homogenize the shared culture of a thousand species, born of different stars and biochemistries, creatures of flesh and metal, of rock and gas? A thousand Galaxy crossings, minimum?

But that would take a hundred million years, and by that time the next burster would have blown its top, the next Reboot driven everybody back to pond scum.

So maybe this clumsy net really was the best anybody could do. But still, good intentions weren't enough.

'Tens of millions of years,' she said. 'You'd have to maintain that damn thing for *tens of millions of years*, to make a difference. How can any species remotely like us, or even *you*, maintain a consistency of purpose across megayears? None of us even *existed* in anything like our present forms so long ago.'

. . . BUT, Cassiopeia said slowly, WE MUST TRY.

Malenfant said, '*We*?'

YOU MUST JOIN US, MALENFANT.

Madeleine clutched at Malenfant's hand. But he pushed her away. She looked up at him. His face was pinched, his eyes narrow. He was starting to feel scared, she realized, drawn out, as if pulled into space by the thing in the sky, up towards the zenith.

Because, she realized, this is his destiny.

Malenfant stood before the alien robot, silhouetted against Galaxy core light. He looked helplessly weak, Madeleine thought, a ragamuffin, before this representative of a cool, immeasurably ancient galactic power.

Yet it was Cassiopeia who was supplicating before Malenfant, the human.

'You can't do it,' he said, wondering. 'You can't complete this project. There is something – missing in you.'

Cassiopeia said, THERE IS CONTROVERSY.

Madeleine glared up at that filmy structure. There were holes in the netting you could have passed a small planet through, places where thousand-kilometre threads seemed to have been burned or melted or distorted. *Controversy.*

'Wars have been fought here,' Malenfant said bluntly.

THE RACES OF THE GALAXY ARE VERY DIVERGENT. UNITY DISSOLVES. THERE IS FREQUENT CONFLICT. SOMETIMES A RACE WILL SEEK TO TAKE THIS TECHNOLOGY AND USE IT FOR ITS OWN PURPOSES; THE OTHERS MUST MOUNT A COALITION TO STOP THE ROGUE. SOMETIMES A RACE WILL SIMPLY ATTEMPT TO IMPOSE ITS WILL ON OTHERS. THAT USUALLY ENDS IN CONFLICT, AND THE EXPULSION OR EXTERMINATION OF THE AMBITIOUS.

Malenfant laughed. 'Infighting. Sounds like every construction project I ever worked on.'

THERE ARE DIVERGENCES AMONG US.

Madeleine looked up, startled. 'You mean, even among the Gaijin?'

THERE ARE FACTIONS WHO WOULD ARGUE THAT WE SHOULD ABANDON THE PROJECT TO OTHER RACES, CALCULATING –

Malenfant grunted. 'Calculating that the others will finish the job for you – without you incurring the costs of the work. Gambling on the altruism of others, while acting selfishly. Games theory.'

OTHERS SEEK A TIME SYMMETRY . . .

Malenfant seemed baffled by that, but Madeleine thought she understood. 'Like the Moon flowers, Malenfant. If the Gaijin could train themselves to think *backward in time*, then they needn't face this – terminus – in the future.'

Malenfant laughed at the Gaijin, mocking.

Madeleine felt disturbed at this blatant evidence of discord among the Gaijin. Weren't they supposed to merge into some kind of super-mind, make decisions by consensus, with none of the crude arguing and splits of human beings? Dissension like this, so visible, must represent an agony of indecision in the Gaijin community, faced by the immense challenge of the star sail project. Indecision – or schizophrenia.

Malenfant said, still challenging, 'But your factions are wrong. Aren't they? Completing this project isn't a question of a game, theoretical or not. It is a question of sacrifice.'

Sacrifice? Madeleine wondered. Of what – or who?

MALENFANT, YOU ARE SHORT-LIVED – YOUR LIVES SO BRIEF, IN FACT, THAT YOU CAN OBSERVE NONE OF THE UNIVERSE'S SIGNIFICANT PROCESSES. YOUR RESPONSE TO OUR PRESENCE IN THE SOLAR SYSTEM WAS SPLINTERED, CHAOTIC, FLUID. YOU DO NOT EVEN UNDERSTAND *YOURSELVES*.

AND YET YOU TRANSCEND YOUR BREVITY. AND YET HUMANS, DOOMED TO BRIEF LIVES, CHOOSE DEATH VOLUNTARILY – FOR THE SAKE OF AN IDEA. AND WITH EVERY DEATH, THAT IDEA GROWS STRONGER.

WE HAVE ENCOUNTERED MANY SPECIES ON OUR TRAVELS. RARELY HAVE WE ENCOUNTERED SUCH A CAPACITY FOR FAITH.

Malenfant stalked back and forth on the hill-side, obviously torn. 'What are you talking about, Cassiopeia? Do you expect me to start a religion? You want me to teach faith to the toiling robots and cyborgs and what-not who are building the neutron star sail – something to unite them, to force them to bury their differences, to persist and complete the project across generations . . . Is that it?'

No, Madeleine thought sadly. No, she is asking for something much more fundamental than that.

She wants you, Malenfant. She wants your soul.

And the Gaijin started talking of mind, and identity, and memes, idea viruses.

To Cassiopeia, Malenfant was scarcely sentient at all. From the Gaijin's point of view, Malenfant's mind was no more than a coalition of warring idea-viruses, uneasy, illogically constructed, temporary. The ideas grouped together in complexes that reinforced each other, mutually aiding replication – just as those other replicators, genes, worked together through human bodies to promote their own reproduction.

Yes, Madeleine thought, beginning to understand. And the most fundamental idea complex was the sense of self.

A self was a collection of memories, beliefs, possession, hopes, fears, dreams: all of them ideas, or receptacles for ideas. If an idea accreted to the self – if it became *Malenfant's* idea, to be defended, if necessary, with his life – then its chance of replication was much stronger. His sense of self, of *him*self, was an illusion. Just a web woven by the manipulating idea viruses.

The Gaijin had no such sense of self. But sometimes, that was what you needed.

Malenfant understood. 'Every damn one of the Gaijin has a memory that stretches back to those ugly yellow seas on the Cannonball. But they are – fluid. They break up into their component parts and scatter around and reassemble; or they merge in great ugly swarms and come out shuffled around. Identity for them is a transient thing, a pattern, like the shadow of a passing cloud. Not for us, though. And that's why the Gaijin don't have *this*.' He stabbed a finger at his chest. 'They don't have a sense of *me*.'

And without self, Madeleine saw, there could be no self-sacrifice.

That was why the Gaijin couldn't handle the Reboot prevention project. Only humans, it seemed – slaves of replicating ideas, nurtured and comforted by the illusion of the self – might be strong enough, crazy enough, for that.

Through the dogged sense of his own character, Malenfant must give the fragmented beings toiling here a sense of purpose, of worth beyond their own sentience. A sense of sacrifice, of faith, of self. To help the Gaijin, to save the Galaxy, Malenfant was going to have to become like the Gaijin. He was going to have to lose himself . . . and, in the incomprehensible community that laboured over the strands of the sail, find himself again.

Malenfant, standing before the spidery Gaijin, was trembling. 'And you think this will work?'

No, Madeleine thought. But they are desperate. This is a throw of the dice. What else can they do?

The Gaijin didn't reply.

'. . . I can't do this,' Malenfant whispered at last, folding his hands over and over. 'Don't ask me. Take it away from me.'

Madeleine longed to run to him, to embrace him, offer him simple human comfort, animal warmth. But she knew she must not.

And still the Gaijin would not reply.

Malenfant stalked off over the empty grassland, alone.

Madeleine slept.

When she woke, Malenfant was still gone.

She lay on her back, peering up at a sky crowded with stars and glowing dust clouds. The stars seemed small, uniform, few of them bright and blue and young, as if they were deprived of fuel in this crammed space – as perhaps they were. And the dust clouds were disrupted, torn into ragged sheets and filaments by the immense forces that operated here.

Towards the heart of the Galaxy itself, there was structure, Madeleine saw. Laced over a backdrop of star swarms she made out two loose rings of light, roughly concentric, from her point of view tipped to ellipticity. The rings were complex: she saw gas and dust, stars gathered into small, compact globular clusters, spherical knots of all but-identical pinpoints. In one place the outer ring had erupted into a vast knot of star formation, tens of thousands of hot young blue stars blaring light from the ragged heart of a pink-white cloud. The rings were like expanding ripples, she saw, or billows of gas from some explosion. But if there had been an explosion it must have been immense indeed; that outermost ring was a coherent object a thousand light years across, big enough to have contained almost all the naked-eye stars visible from Earth.

And when Madeleine lifted her head, she saw that the inner ring was actually the base of an even larger formation that rose up and out of the general plane of the Galaxy. It was a ragged arch, traced out by filaments of shining gas, arching high into the less crowded sky above. It reminded her of images of solar flares, curving gusts of gas shaped by the sun's magnetic field – but this, of course, was immeasurably vaster, an arch spanning hundreds of light years. And rising out of the arch she glimpsed more immensity still, a vast jet of gas that thrust out of the Galaxy's plane, glimmering across thousands of light years before dissipating into the dark.

It was a hierarchy of enormity, towering over her, endless expansions of scale up into the dark.

But of the Galaxy centre itself, she could only see a tight, impenetrable cluster of stars – many thousands of them, swarming impossibly close together, closer to each other than the planets of the solar system. Whatever structure lay deeper still was hidden by those crowded acolyte stars.

The Gaijin still stood on the ridge, silhouetted against the pulsar's glow, hatefully silent.

Malenfant still hadn't returned. Madeleine tried to imagine what was going through his head, as he tried to submit himself to an unknown alien horror that would, it seemed, take apart even his humanity.

Madeleine got to her feet and stalked up to the Gaijin, confronting it. She was aware of Neandertals watching her curiously. They signed to each other, obscurely. *Look at crazy flathead.*

Madeleine shouted, 'Why can't you leave us alone? You came to our planet uninvited, you used up our resources, you screwed up our history –'

The Gaijin swivelled with eerie precision. WE MINED ASTEROIDS YOU PROBABLY WOULD NEVER HAVE REACHED. WITHOUT US YOU WOULD HAVE REMAINED UNAWARE OF THE CRACKERS UNTIL THEY REACHED THE HEART OF YOUR SYSTEM. AS TO YOUR HISTORY, THAT IS YOUR RESPONSIBILITY. WE DID NOT INTERVENE. BUT MOST OF YOU WOULD NOT HAVE WISHED THAT ANYHOW.

'You fucking immortal robots, you're so damn *smug*. But for all your powers, you need Malenfant . . . But why *Malenfant*, for God's sake?'

REID MALENFANT IS SELF-SELECTED. MADELEINE MEACHER, RECALL THAT HE MADE HIS WAY, SINGLE-HANDED, TO THE CENTRE OF OUR PROJECTS *TWICE OVER*, FIRST THROUGH THE ALPHA CENTAURI GATEWAY AND THEN THROUGH IO.

'Reid Malenfant is a stubborn, dogged son-of-a-bitch. But he is still just a human being. Must he die?'

The Gaijin hesitated, for long minutes. Then: HE WILL NOT DIE.

No, she thought. He must endure something much more strange than that. As he seemed to know.

The Gaijin raised one spindly leg, as if inspecting it. MADELEINE MEACHER, IF YOU WISH US TO SPARE HIM, WE WILL COMPLY.

She was taken aback. '. . . What has it to do with me?'

YOU ARE HUMAN. YOU ARE MALENFANT'S FRIEND. *YOU* MADE A SACRIFICE OF YOUR OWN, TO FOLLOW HIM HERE. AND SO YOU HAVE RESPONSIBILITY. IF YOU WISH US TO SPARE MALENFANT, THEN SAY SO. WE WILL COMPLY.

'And then what?'

WE HAVE SADDLE POINT GATEWAYS. WE CAN SEND HIM HOME, TO EARTH. BOTH OF YOU. WE CANNOT AVOID THE TIME DISLOCATION. BUT YOU CAN LIVE ON.

'Even if *he* wants to go on?'

IT IS HARD FOR MALENFANT TO MAKE THE RIGHT CHOICE. FOR ANY HUMAN THIS WOULD BE SO. YOUR DECISION OVERRIDES HIS.

'And if you let him go – then what about the project, the sail?'

WE MUST FIND ANOTHER WAY.

'The Reboot would become inevitable.'

WE MUST FIND ANOTHER WAY.

Madeleine sank to the grass. Shit, she thought. She hadn't expected this.

The notion of saving a Galaxy of sentient creatures from arbitrary annihilation was *too big* – too much for her to imagine, too grandiose. But she had lived through the overwhelming destructiveness of the attempted Eetie colonization of the solar system, found evidence of the other wasteful waves of horror of the deep past. She had *seen* it for herself.

And you once built a world, Madeleine. You've been known to show a little hubris yourself.

If this project succeeds, perhaps humans, and species like them, would never have to suffer such an ordeal again. Isn't one man's life worth such a prize?

But who am *I* to make that call?

. . . There was another option, she thought, that neither of them had expressed, neither she nor the Gaijin.

It doesn't have to be Malenfant. Maybe *I* could take his place. Save him, and progress the project anyhow.

She wrapped her arms around herself. Malenfant is full of doubt and fear. Even now he might not be able to make it, make the sacrifice. But he is out there gathering his strength, his purpose. I could never emulate that.

The Gaijin waited with metallic patience.

'Take him,' she whispered, hating herself as she uttered the words. 'Take Malenfant.' *Take him; spare me.*

And, as soon as she made the choice, she remembered Malenfant's inexplicable coldness when she arrived here.

She had ended up betraying him. Just as, she realized now, he had known she would, right from the beginning.

She buried her face in her hands.

After maybe a full day, Malenfant returned. Madeleine was sitting beside a sluggish stream, desultorily watching the evolution of Galaxy-core gas streamers.

Malenfant came running up.

He threw himself to the grass beside her. He was sweating, his bald pate slick, and he was breathing hard. 'Jogging,' he said. 'Clears the head.' He curled to a sitting position, cat-like. 'This is a hell of a thing, isn't it, Madeleine? Who would have thought it? . . . Nemoto should see me now. My mom should see me now.' The change in him was startling. He seemed vigorous, rested, confident, focused. Even cheerful.

But she could see the battered photograph of his dead wife tucked into his sleeve.

She hugged her knees, full of guilt, unable to meet his eyes. 'Have you decided what to do?'

'There's no real choice, is there?'

Tentatively she reached for his hand; he grabbed it, squeezed hard, his calm strength evident. 'Malenfant, aren't you afraid?'

He shrugged. 'I was afraid the first time I climbed aboard a Shuttle orbiter, sitting up there on top of millions of tonnes of high explosive, in a rickety old ship that had been flying thirty years already. I was afraid the first time I looked into a Saddle Point gateway, not knowing what lay beyond. But I still climbed aboard that Shuttle, still went through the gateway.' He glanced at her. 'What about you? After . . .'

'After you're dead?' she snapped impulsively.

He flinched, and she instantly regretted it.

She told him about the Gaijin's offer of a ride home.

'Take it. Go see Earth, Madeleine.'

'But it won't be my Earth.'

He shrugged. 'What else is there?'

She said shyly, 'I've been thinking. What if we – the sentients of the Galaxy, of this generation – *do* manage to come through the next Reboot? What if this time we *don't* have to go back to the ponds? What if we get a chance to keep on building? If I keep on rattling around the Saddle Point gateways, maybe I'll get to see some of that.'

He nodded. 'Beaming between the stars, while the network gets extended. Onward and onward, without limit. I like it.'

'Yeah.' She glanced up. 'Maybe I'll get to see Andromeda, before I die. Or maybe not.'

'There are worse ambitions.'

'. . . Malenfant. Come with me.'

He shook his head. 'Can't do it, Madeleine. I've thought it over. And I bought Cassiopeia's pitch.' He looked up at the sky. 'You know, as a kid I used to lie at night out on the lawn, soaking up dew and looking at the stars, trying to feel the Earth turning under me. It felt wonderful to be alive – hell, to be ten years old, anyhow. But I knew that the Earth was just a ball of rock, on the fringe of a nondescript galaxy. I just couldn't believe, even then, that there was nobody out *there* looking back at me down *here*. But I used to wonder what would be the point of my life, of human existence, if the universe really was empty. What would there be for us to do but survive, doggedly, as long as possible? Which didn't seem too attractive a prospect to me.

'Well, now I know the universe isn't empty, but crowded with life. And, even with the wars and extinctions and all, isn't that better than the alternative – better than *nothing*? And you know, I think I even figured out the purpose of our lives in such a universe – mine, anyhow. To make it better for those who follow us. What else is there to do?' He glanced at her, eyes cloudy. 'Does that make any sense?'

'Yes. But, Malenfant, the cost –'

'Nemoto said it would be like this. Humans can't change history, except *this* way. One of us, alone, going to the edge . . .'

Suddenly it was too much for her; she covered her face with her hands. 'Fuck history, Malenfant. Fuck the destiny of the universe. We're talking about *you*.'

He put an arm around her shoulders; he was warm, his body still hot from his run. 'It's okay,' he said, trying to soothe her. 'It's okay. You know what? I think the Gaijin are jealous. Jealous, of us wretched little pink worms. Because we got something they don't, something more precious than all the Swiss-Army-knife body parts in the universe, something more precious than a billion years of life.'

But now the Gaijin stood before them, suddenly *there*, tall and stark.

Malenfant said, his voice unsteady, 'So soon, Cassiopeia?'

I AM SORRY, MALENFANT.

Malenfant straightened up, withdrew his arm from Madeleine's shoulders. She felt the reluctance in the gesture. She'd provided him comfort after all, she realized; by caring for her, he had been able to put off confronting the reality of it all. But now, in the silent person of the Gaijin, the reality was here, and he had to face it alone.

But here was old Esau, grinning from one side to the other of his flat face, deep eyes full of starlight. He was signing: the fist to the forehead, then left palm flat upright, supporting the right fist, which was making a thumbs-up gesture. *Hey, Stupid. I'll help you.*

Malenfant signed back. *What help me what what?*

Forefinger and middle finger together, on both hands, held out like a knife; a sharp chop downwards, a stark, unmistakable sign. *To die.*

Chapter 34

THE CHILDREN'S CRUSADE

Cassiopeia embraced him.

He was pulled into her body, articulating arms folding about him. He could smell the burning tang of metal that had been exposed to vacuum, to the light of a hundred different suns. And now finer arms, no more than tendrils, began to probe at his body, his skin, his mouth, his eyes.

Through a mist of metal cilia, he could see Madeleine on the hill-side before him, weeping openly. 'Tell them about me, Madeleine. Don't let them forget.'

'I will. I promise.'

Now warm metal probed at his ears, the membranes of his mouth, even his eyes. Probed and pierced, a dozen stabs of sharp pain. Then came an insidious penetration, and he could taste blood. 'It hurts, Madeleine.' He cried out; he couldn't help it. 'Oh, God!'

But now Esau was before him, signing vigorously. *Stupid Stupid. Watch me me.*

Malenfant tried to focus, as the pain deepened.

Esau sat on the hill-side. By the light of Galaxy-centre stars, he held out a core of obsidian.

Malenfant reached forward. His bare arms trailed long shining tendrils, back to the cold body of the Gaijin, within which he was merging. He could move his fingers, he found. But they glinted, metallic.

Esau was still holding out the glassy rock, thrusting it at him.

Malenfant took the rock. He could feel its rough texture, but remotely, as if through a layer of plastic. He turned it over in his hands.

Esau held up a fresh lump of obsidian, hammers of bone and rock. He signed bluntly to Malenfant. *Same as me, Stupid. Do same as me. Copy.*

Obediently, Malenfant set to work, tapping clumsily at the rock, emulating Esau's movements, practising this most ancient of human crafts twenty-five thousand light years from home.

'The Buddhists have a doctrine of *anatta,*' Madeleine murmured. 'It means, *no self*. Or rather, the self is only temporary, like an idea or a story. "Actions do exist, and also their consequences, but the person that acts does not" . . . It won't be so bad, Malenfant. Some people can do this for themselves. Some *choose* it . . .'

She was weeping, he saw, the tears leaking out of closed eyes. Weeping for him. But he must not think about her. He tried to bury himself in the tasks. He focused on the work, the movements of his hands and arms. He would think about Madeleine – and put the thought aside. The differences between his own hands and the Neandertal's struck him, frustrating him with his own clumsiness. But he must put aside that thought too.

For brief periods, he got it. It was as if he saw the stone, the tool he was making, with a kind of stunning clarity: *the thing itself*, not the geologic processes which had produced the raw material, not the mysterious interstellar gateways which had brought him and the stone to this place, not even the tool's ultimate purpose. Just the thing, and the act.

But then the spell would be broken, and plans and analyses and self-consciousness would return to clutter up his head, an awareness of Madeleine and Cassiopeia, and Esau, the trees and grass and the heart of the Galaxy, and the *pain*, that penetrated right to his core.

'You have to let it go, Malenfant,' Madeleine whispered. 'Don't think. Live in the now, the present moment. If ideas come up, reflections, memories, hopes, fears, let them go. Butterflies, flitting out the window. Treat everything equally. Don't filter, don't focus. Watch Esau . . .'

Esau, yes.

Malenfant was like an observer. But Esau *was* the rock he worked in its deep chthonic richness, in a way Malenfant perhaps could never be. It was a smooth, rolling, fleeting form of awareness, without past or future, memory or anticipation. It was like driving a car while holding a conversation. Like being stoned. Or like being five years old, and every moment a delicious Saturday morning.

Madeleine was still talking, but he could make out no words. She was receding, as if dissolving.

Goodbye, goodbye.

He closed his eyes.

. . . No, it wasn't like that:

Eyes that were closed.

There was a blue flash, a moment of searing pain.

He cried, '*Emma!*'

And then –

Limbs that worked. Tactile, graceful. Tasks that were progressed.

The rope: complex, multi-level, a thing of monomolecular filaments, superconducting threads within. The extension of the rope, the repair of breaks, the tasks of the limbs.

Visual receptors, eyes. A repositioning.

Data nets above, below, all around, a great curving wall. At extremes, a flat-infinite plane, in every direction: the sail.

Above, the spitting neutron star, its envelope of gas.

Here, a body, a spider-like form of many limbs, a dodecahedral box at the centre. Multiple tasks for those limbs. The sail that was repaired, extended; the body that was maintained, adjusted, itself extended; records that were kept; a mesh of communications with others that was maintained, extended.

Other workers.

Some near. Some far. Some as this body, a common design. Millions of them. Some not. Tasks that were progressed.

The structure. Vibrations, the shudder of torn threads. Complex modes, wave forms in space and time.

War, in a remote part of the sail.

A position that was adjusted, an anchoring of the body that was improved and secured.

The work that was progressed in one part of the sail, war in other parts.

The anchoring. The self-maintenance. The work.

The universe, of tasks, of things.

No centre.

. . . And he felt as if he was drowning, struggling up from some thick, viscous fluid, towards the light. He wanted to open his mouth, to scream – but he had no mouth – and no *words*. What would he scream?

I.

I am.

I am Malenfant . . .

No. Not just Malenfant. Malenfant / Esau / Cassiopeia.

The pain!

The shuddering of the net. The anchoring. The work that was progressed . . .

No! More than that. *I* feel the shudder. *I* must hold on to the net; *I* must continue the work, in the hope that sanity will prevail, the conflict is resolved, the work is continued, the greater goal achieved.

Thus it must be. Oh, God, the *pain.*

Terror flooded over him. And love. And anger.

He could see the sail.

It was a gauzy sheet draped across the crowded stars of this place. And within the sail, cupped, he could see the neutron star, an angry ball of red laced with eerie synchrotron blue, like a huge toy.

Beautiful. Scary.

And he saw it with eyes beyond the human.

He saw the sleeting rays that flowed beyond the human spectrum: the sail's dazzle of ultraviolet, the sullen infrared glower of the star itself. He saw the sail, its curves, the star, from a dozen angles, as if the whole impossible, unlikely structure was a mote that swam within his own God-like eyeball, visible from all sides *at once*, as if it had been flayed and pinned to a board before him.

And he saw the whole project embedded in time, the sail unfurling, growing, the star's slow, reluctant deflection. He saw its origins – the sail shared design features with the artefact that had been found cupping a black hole in the system of the species called Chaera; perhaps it too was a relic of those vanished builders.

And he even saw it all through the gauzy eyes of mathematics. He could see the brutal equations of gravity and electromagnetism which governed the drag of the star's remote companion, the push of star on sail and sail on star; and he could see, like shining curves extending ahead of and back from this single moment, how those equations would unfold, the evolution of the system through time, out of the past, through the now, and into the future.

Not enough, he saw.

Still the construction of the sail was outpaced by the neutron stars' approach. The project was projected to fail; the stars were mathematically destined to collide before the sail's deflection was done, the great gamma ray burst lethally mocking their efforts. But they must, they would, try harder, the toiling communities here.

. . . And if you see all this, Malenfant, then what are *you*? God knows you're no mathematician.

He looked down at himself.

Tried to.

His gaze swivelled, yes, his vision sparkling with superhuman spectra. But his *head* did not turn.

For he had no head.

A sense of body, briefly. Spread-eagled against the sail's gauzy netting. Clinging by fingers and toes, monkey digits, here at the centre of the Galaxy.

A metaphor, of course, an illusion to comfort his poor human mind. What was he truly? – a partial personality, downloaded into a clumsy robot, clinging to this monstrous structure, bathed by the lethal radiation of a neutron star?

And even now the robot he rode was working, knitting away at the net. This body was working, without having to be told, directed, by *me*, or anybody else.

But that's the way it is, Malenfant. Self is an illusion, remember. You've always been a passenger, riding inside that bony cage of a skull of yours. It's just that now it's a little more – explicit.

Welcome to reality.

But if I'm a robot, why the *pain?*

He looked for Cassiopeia, for any of the Gaijin, reassuring dodecahedral bulks. He saw none, though the unwelcome enhancements of his vision let him zoom and peer through the spaces all around him.

But when he thought of Cassiopeia, anger flooded him. Why?

It had been just minutes since she had embraced him on that grassy simulated plain . . . hadn't it?

How do you *know*, Malenfant? How do you know you haven't been frozen in some deep data store for ten thousand years?

And . . . how do you know this isn't the first time you surfaced like this?

How *could* he know? If his identity assembled, disintegrated again, what trace would it leave on his memory? What *was* his memory? What if he was simply *restarted* each time, wiped clean like a reinitialized computer? How would he *know*?

In renewed terror, lost in space and time – in helpless, desolating loneliness – he tried again to scream. But he could not, of course.

The sail shuddered. Great ripples of disturbance, thousands of kilometres long, wafted through the net. As the waves passed, he saw others shaken loose, equipment hurled free, damaged.

Without his conscious control, he was aware how his body (or bodies? – how do you know you're *even in one place*, Malenfant?) grasped tighter to the fine structure.

He felt a clustering of awareness around him. Other workers here, perhaps. Other parts of himself.

Frightened.

Have faith, he told his companions, his other parts. Or his disciples.

But that was the problem. *They* didn't have faith. Faith was a dangerous idea. The only thing less dangerous, in fact, was the universe itself, this terrible Rebooting accident of celestial mechanics.

All this had happened before. The wars. The destruction. The abandonment of work. The resumption, the patient repairs.

There was a species he thought of as the Fire-eaters. They were related to the Crackers, who had tried to disrupt Earth's sun. But these more ambitious cousins wanted to steal part of the sail and wrap up a hypernova, one of the largest exploding stars in the Galaxy. As best he understood it they would try to capture a fraction of that astonishing energy in order to hurl themselves out of the Galaxy within an ace of lightspeed. And that way, their subjective experience stretched to near-immobility by time dilation, they would outlive this Reboot, and the one after it, and the one after that. He remembered a diversion of resources, a great war, huge damage to the sail, before the Fire-eaters were driven off.

. . . He *remembered*.

Yes. He had surfaced, like this, become Malenfant before, cowering under a sky full of silent, deadly, warring Eeties, in a corner of the sail where the threads buckled and broke.

Surfaced more than once.

Many times.

How long have I been here? And between these intervals of half-remembered awareness, how long have I toiled here, awake but unaware?

Ah, yes, but take a look at where you *are*, Malenfant.

He looked up from the rippling sail, away from the lethal neutron star, and into the complex sky.

He was at the heart of the Galaxy: within the great central cluster of stars, no more than a couple of dozen light years from the very centre. At that centre there was a cavity some twenty light years wide, encased by a great shell of crowded, disrupted stars; the neutron star binary huddled at the inner boundary of this shell.

The emptiness of the 'cavity' was only relative. There was a great double-spiral architecture of stars, like a miniature copy of the Galaxy, trapped here at its heart. The spiralling stars were dragged into their tight orbits around the object at the Galaxy's gravitational core itself:

a black hole with a broad, glowing, spitting accretion disc, a hole itself with the mass of some three million suns. It was the violent winds from the vast accretion disc which had created this relative hollowness.

But still the cavity was crammed with gas and dust, its particles ionized and driven to high speeds by the ferocious gravitational and magnetic forces working here, so that streamers of glowing gas criss-crossed the cavity in a fine tracery. Stars had been born here, notably a cluster of blue-hot young stars just a fraction away from the black hole itself. And here and there rogue stars fell through the cavity – and they dragged streaming trails behind them, glowing brilliantly, like comets a hundred light years long.

Stars like comets.

He exulted. I, Reid Malenfant, got to see *this*, the heart of the Galaxy itself, by God! He wished Cassiopeia were here, his companion during those endless Saddle Point jaunts to one star after another . . .

But again, at the thought of Cassiopeia, his anger flared.

And now, his reassembled mind clearer, he remembered *why*.

He had found out after submitting to Cassiopeia's cold, agonizing embrace, after arriving *here*, an unknown time later.

He had learned that even if all went well here – if the wars ceased, if the supplies of raw materials didn't fail, even if the neutron star sail, this marvellous artefact, was completed and worked as advertised – *even then*, it wouldn't do *him* a blind bit of good.

Because it was already too late. For him. And his people.

This binary, yes: this implosion was far enough in the future to affect, with this low-tech solution, robots and nets and solar wind rockets. But *this* wasn't the next scheduled to blow up.

There was *another* coalescing neutron star binary, buried still deeper in the Galaxy's diseased heart, another Reboot. And it was already too late to stop that one, too late to avert the coming catastrophe.

This unlikely sail would work. But it was too long term. The project would avert *the next Reboot but one*.

We were always doomed. All we could do was make it better for the next cycle, advance the project far enough that *they* – the next to evolve from the pond scum of the Galaxy, the next to stumble on the half-finished sail after another few tens of millions of years – *they* would understand a little better than we had, would know what to do, how to finish it.

The first designers of the sail, sometime before the *last* Reboot, had known it. Cassiopeia had known it.

She hadn't thought to tell him, though, before he – died. Maybe she didn't think it was significant. After all a sacrifice was a sacrifice. Maybe he simply hadn't understood; maybe she'd expected him to be able to think it through himself. After all, she could *see* the mathematics.

He remembered how it felt, to find out. It had been the final betrayal.

And hence, the anger.

But it didn't matter. In fact, it made his work, the role here, still more important.

Humans, Gaijin, Chaera, all of the current 'generation' of galactic sentients – all of those who contributed to the sail's slow building – they were *all* doomed, no matter what happened here.

But this was all they could do: to make things better for the next time.

And, he told himself, thinking of Madeleine, the alternative to all this pain – a lifeless universe doomed to nothing but meaningless expansion – would be much worse.

Have courage, he told himself / themselves. We have a noble goal. Our death doesn't matter. The future, the children . . . even if they are not *our* children. That is what matters. We will prevail.

He must continue. He must reach out to others, working here. Infect them.

Convert them.

This wasn't a project, after all. It was a crusade.

The net shuddered again. That damn war.

He was dissolving, sinking back. He didn't fight it. It was good.

Malenfant sighed, metaphorically. You don't have to be crazy to work here but it helps.

Blue light that gathered around him. Pain that intensified.

. . . *Cassiopeia*, he flared. Why did you betray me?

No centre.

The universe, of tasks, of things.

The anchoring. The self-maintenance. The work.

Always the work.

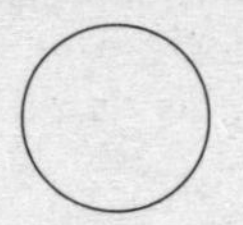

EPILOGUE

The Gaijin colony lay quietly beneath its translucent bubble, the bevelled edges of the buildings making the little city look like a scattering of half-melted toys. Beyond the bubble an airless, desolate plain stretched to a clean horizon. Shadows raked the plain.

Looking up, she traced the quasar's fantastic geometry.

The powerhouse at the quasar's heart, barely two hundred light years away, was a pinpoint of unnatural brightness. Twin sprays of electron flux tore from the poles of the powerhouse, straining to zenith and nadir. And swaddling the waist of the quasar was a torus of glowing rubble. This colony world orbited almost within the torus, so that the debris looked like a pair of celestial arms reaching around the powerhouse to touch the fake clouds nestling under the bubble.

The sky was full of dodecahedral frameworks, triangular faces glimmering, drifting like angular soap bubbles.

It was glorious, astonishing.

She had travelled a billion light years from Earth, across the curve of the universe. She wasn't aware of it. She had been in store, or bouncing from gateway to gateway without downloading, since leaving Malenfant.

I am a billion years from home, she thought. Everything I knew is buried under deep layers of past. Humans must have fled Earth, or become extinct. Earth's biosphere itself could not survive so long as this. Perhaps I am the last human.

Perhaps I am, by now, a construct of alien qualia; perhaps I'm not even human any more myself.

Well, I don't have to face that. Not yet.

She looked to the zenith. A scattering of galaxies glimmered through her bubble.

The galaxies glowed green, every one of them.

Life everywhere. Triumphant. Awe, wonder, love surged in her.

It was proof, of course. Just waking up again, emerging from the

Saddle Point network, had been proof. Humans and their allies – or rivals or successors – had beaten the countdown clock, had bust out of the limits of the Galaxy, and gone on, spreading across the universe, building their Saddle Point links.

And if they had got as far as *this*, they must be everywhere. Hell of a thought.

But –

Where to now, Madeleine?

She wondered if Malenfant could have survived, in one form or another, even over such an immense span of space and time. *She* had, after all. She smiled, thinking of Malenfant, the original grey cyborg.

The quasar dipped to the horizon now; optical filters in the bubble around her softened its shape, turning it red. The electron flux was splayed across the sky like brush marks on velvet. The last traces of quasar light touched the sky like cool smoke.

It was so beautiful it hurt.

She turned away, and went in search of Reid Malenfant.

AFTERWORD

A good recent survey of the state of our thinking on extraterrestrial life is Paul Davies' *Are We Alone?* (Penguin Books, 1995). The passages set on the Moon are based in part on conversations with former astronaut Charles M. Duke, who in 1972 walked on the Moon as Lunar Module Pilot of Apollo 16. There really are naturally occurring nuclear reactors; a reference is 'Fossil Nuclear Reactors' by Michel Maurette, *Annual Review of Nuclear Science* v 26, pp319–350 (1976). I published a technical article on the feasibility of the Moon's deep ocean in the *Journal of the British Interplanetary Society* (v 51, pp 75–80, 1998).

Any errors, omissions or misinterpretations are of course my responsibility.

Stephen Baxter
Great Missenden
February 2000